THE
HICKORY
STAFF

THE HICKORY STAFF

The Eldarn Sequence Book 1

Robert Scott
and Jay Gordon

The right of Robert Scott to be identified as the
author of this work has been asserted by him in accordance
with the Copyright, Designs and Patents Act 1988.

First published in Great Britain in 2005 by
Gollancz
An imprint of the Orion Publishing Group
Orion House, 5 Upper St Martin's Lane,
London WC2H 9EA

This edition published in Great Britain in 2006 by
Gollancz

5 7 9 10 8 6 4

A CIP catalogue record for this book is
available from the British Library

ISBN 9 780 57507 775 1

Typeset by Deltatype Limited,
Birkenhead, Merseyside

Printed and bound in the UK by
CPI Mackays, Chatham ME5 8TD

The Orion Publishing Group's policy is to use papers that
are natural, renewable and recyclable products and made
from wood grown in sustainable forests. The logging and
manufacturing processes are expected to conform to the
environmental regulations of the country of origin.

www.orionbooks.co.uk

The Hickory Staff came into focus over such a long period of time, nearly seven years, we are indebted to many who – along the way – read chapters, made suggestions, praised bits that went well and periodically burned, bagged and carted out chapters that didn't. We are especially grateful to Charlie Nurnberg, to whom we owe everything, and to Jo Fletcher, to whom we owe even more. Thanks to the Idaho Springs Chamber of Commerce and the staff at the Heritage Museum on Miner Street. We have changed a few things about the town, and hope that the good people of Idaho Springs will forgive us a few transgressions. When this process began, we knew nothing at all about mining; any liberties we took that resulted in misrepresentations of the Colorado boom are entirely our fault. Thanks also to the reference staff at the Koelbel Library in Denver for unearthing all manner of resources on ships and shipping, primitive weaponry and Egyptian architecture.

Robert Scott. I would like to thank Burm, Paul, Mom and Dad and everyone in Cherry Creek and Prince William County who encouraged me throughout this endeavour. Thanks to Dan, Christine, Kat Meints and Steve TeSelle for their input, and sincere thanks to Pam Widmann for reading, reading over and reading again. Five years ago, I was sometimes able, with teeth clenched and a borrowed pen, to calculate the gratuity on a dinner check; I owe a debt of gratitude to Uncle G for checking my math and ensuring that one *can* chart time with a pair of orbiting moons. Finally, to Kage and the kids, who were patient with me, I couldn't possibly love you more than I do.

Jay Gordon. Thank you Stacy, Patrick and Karen for taking on so much and for supporting me these past several years. I especially thank Charlie for his friendship and willingness to champion the publication of *The Hickory Staff*. Ultimately, I would like to acknowledge my wife, Susan, who has given more than I can ask for in one lifetime.

CONTENTS

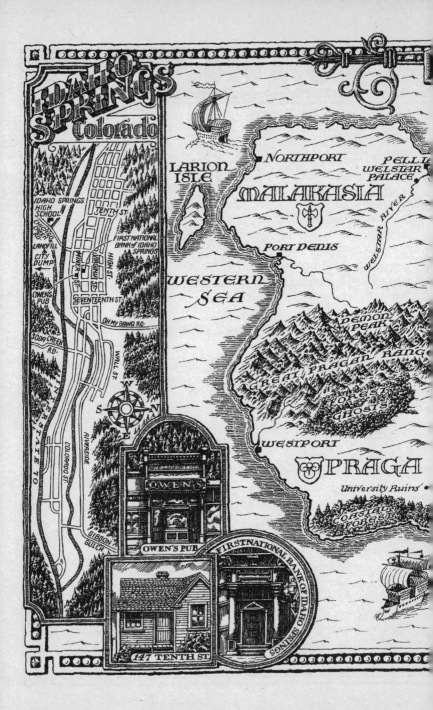

INTRODUCTION

Charleston, South Carolina

FOLLY BEACH

Next winter

The bay waters rolled in gentle swells, almost silent, deep blue colour fading to black. Norman Felson looped a bowline hitch around a small stanchion near the helm of his thirty-six-foot sloop, the *Offshore Maid*, and attached the opposite end to the tiller, fixing the helm to free his hands because a spanker line had come loose aft. He hauled it in, then hustled back to the bridge as soon as he had the errant sheet reset. He was still uncomfortable sailing the sloop on his own, and didn't like to be away from the helm for more than a few seconds. He looked forward to sunrise; he worried less in daylight.

Kay, his wife, was working in their small cabin; he smelled the aroma of fresh coffee mixing with the cool breeze drifting down from the Chesapeake. Save for the distant glow of channel markers and moonlight glimmering in a kaleidoscope of geometric glints flashing from wave to wave, the bay was dark. Felson navigated north and east using his GPS satellite computer, heading towards the Charleston Harbour lighthouse before turning into the Atlantic and setting course for Nags Head. He liked to imagine himself a sailor from a previous age; he'd often try to stay his course using compass and the stars alone – though he was rarely successful. He silently cursed his Coast Guard navigation instructor for encouraging him to rely so heavily on satellite technology.

He checked again to be sure he had programmed the correct coordinates into his navigation computer before calling to Kay, 'Is the coffee ready?'

'Just about,' she replied, 'I'll be up in a minute.'

Felson took a bite from a blueberry jelly doughnut coated with uncooperative powdered sugar and realised he was actually quite happy to live in this age. Certain the doughnut was the finest invention of the last millennium, he found himself imagining with a shudder what Francis Drake might have eaten for breakfast as he prepared to battle the Spanish Armada in 1588: drytack biscuits infested with weevils. Drawing out a dollop of jelly with his finger, he grimaced; the old captain's fare could never have been as exquisitely simple and delicious as the doughnuts Felson bought, still warm, for $2.99 a dozen.

Kay appeared from below. She smiled as she handed him a steaming mug bearing an embossed logo from the *Fairfield Gazette*, the paper that had carried his first story more than forty years earlier. Now he was the editor, and proud of it.

'Thank you,' he said, taking a sip. Kay didn't answer; she stared out into the inky darkness as the undulating waves, unbroken by even the smallest of whitecaps, rocked the *Offshore Maid* in gentle rhythm. Her hair was pulled back with a length of black velvet ribbon; her cardigan was unbuttoned despite the chilly pre-dawn wind.

'Honey?' Felson bent over to recheck their heading on the compass mounted above the helm. 'Kay, are you—?'

He turned to find his wife standing directly behind him and jumped. 'Jesus, you scared me ... what—?' His words were choked off as Kay took him firmly by the throat. With almost inconceivable strength she began to squeeze the life from him. Felson tried to prise her fingers from his neck. He felt his hand, coated with bloody pus, come away from her wrist, and, for a second, he was concerned for her. Why was she bleeding? But confusion was soon supplanted by terror: Kay was not relaxing her grip.

Panic struck. Norman Felson began to struggle furiously, kicking and writhing in his wife's unfeasibly forceful grasp. He felt his nose begin to bleed as capillaries burst and heard himself gagging phlegm against the collapsed walls of his windpipe. As consciousness closed in, Felson watched his wife draw back her free hand. A tiny fist illuminated only by light from the sloop's galley came forward with lightning speed to slam into his chest, tearing sinews and shattering bones.

Kay Felson wiped her bloody hand on the folds of her skirt and tossed her husband's body back against the transom like a load of soiled laundry. A thin trickle of blood ran across the deck and out a scupper into the bay as the elderly woman gripped the helm and brought the *Offshore Maid* about.

With a cry of alarm, arms flailing, Steven Taylor broke the surface of the water. The sting in his eyes and briny taste in his throat confirmed his first suspicion. 'The ocean, Christ, I'm in the ocean,' he shouted, then coughed and began treading water. Thankfully, it was not too cold, and by the dim light of dawn he could see land, a beach, about a quarter-mile to the west. His sodden boots and woollen clothing weighed heavily on him, but he was glad to have them. He set his jaw for the difficult swim to shore.

Kicking towards the beach, Steven's thoughts were churning. Would his credit cards still work? If not, he'd have to steal a wallet. He needed a flight, quickly. He had no idea where he was, or how far it was to Denver; Steven prayed he would come ashore, find an airport and be in Colorado by late afternoon. They would be expecting him between 5.00 and 5.15. After that, at least the immediate pressure would be off, and Steven would have twelve hours more to get home.

Fifteen minutes later, the sun had risen further in the morning sky and Steven recognised that he was on the east coast – he wasn't certain *which* east coast, but he was hoping against hope that it was the United States. He had no passport to ensure safe passage home from a foreign country. He could claim he had lost it, or that it had been stolen, but he did not have the luxury of time to argue with the clerical staff at an American Consular Office in some foreign city. As Steven approached the beach, his concerns were alleviated somewhat by the sight of a dimly lit sign above a closed concession stand: *Bratwurst*.

He laughed to himself. 'Well, unless they put in an ocean off the east coast of Germany, I'm back home ... off course by eighteen hundred miles, but home nevertheless.' If this were Florida, Hilton Head or, even better, New Jersey, there would be an airport close by. Judging from the temperature of the water he guessed he was south of the Chesapeake; although chilly, he hadn't succumbed to hypothermia – at this time of year, northern waters would be much too cold: he would have frozen by now.

As he waded ashore, his feet leaving the only imperfections in the trowel-perfect sand, he noticed someone lying on the beach. It was too early for tourists: this was someone who had been there all night. Shaking water from his clothing, he quickly covered the distance to the sleeping form.

'Hey, wake up.' Steven nudged the stranger lightly by the shoulder. He was a young man, probably in his mid-twenties, dressed in a rumpled suit and ruined tie; he smelled of stale beer and vomit. 'C'mon, wake up,' Steven repeated emphatically.

'What? Christ, what time is it?'

'It's 5.15,' Steven said, though he had no real idea – he had traded his watch for a horse in Rona months ago.

'Are you a cop?' the young man asked, still half asleep.

'No. Listen, I have one quick question. Where are we?'

'What? Leave me alone. Jesus!'

'Tell me where we are.' Steven was slightly amused: this young professional would soon wake to a painful hangover.

'Folly Beach, South Carolina. Now shove off, asshole.' The groggy drunk rolled back onto the sand. As he did, Steven noticed a set of keys lying near a pack of cigarettes, a lighter and nine empty beer bottles.

He waited a minute, counting the man's steady breaths, before he silently stole the keys and the lighter. Running up the gentle slope to the parking lot, he hesitated a moment and turned to look once more at the sunrise. The light had brightened the waterfront, bringing a sense of hope and renewal. The still form of the sleeping drunk seemed out of place, ink spilled on an impressionist landscape.

Steven did not consider the incongruity long. He was home. Now he had twelve hours to get back. 'Charleston Airport,' he said as he hurried towards the lone car parked beside the beach.

BOOK I

The Bank

ESTRAD, RONA

981 Twinmoons Ago

'I am aware they were flying Ronan colours, my dear Detria,'
Markon Grayslip, Prince of Rona, told his irritated cousin calmly.
'I assure you, when they attack my ships, they fly the colours of
Praga or Falkan, or some other territory. It's the ruse they employ
to get closer to our ships. Your captains really should know
better.' As soon as the words were out of his mouth he regretted
it.

Detria Sommerson's face reddened with fury. 'My captains?
Your captains should be out there ridding us of this threat. Your
father wanted sovereignty of that unholy pile of rocks he called
an island, and I was happy to give it to him. I know you didn't ask
for it, but now it's yours and you had better police it.' Beads of
sweat lined the dusty edge of her enormous wig and drew rivulets
of diluted white powder down her forehead. Markon did not wish
to upset her any more.

He tried a different tack. 'How many soldiers did you lose?'

She calmed slightly and admitted, 'As luck would have it, we
didn't lose any. My flagship was able to run off those hideous
ruffians. However, that's not the point—' she made an adjustment to one of the many layers of her dress. 'The point is that
damage was done to one of my ships, and you did not provide an
escort to safely see me and my family across the Ravenian Sea.'

'Hold on for a moment, please, Aunt Detria—' She was always
called Aunt although she was actually his cousin; now Markon
hoped that reminding her of their family connection would
soften her somewhat. 'I offered you an escort, which you turned
down last Twinmoon. How many ships did you bring?'

'As a matter of fact, I brought three.'

9

Markon nearly laughed out loud. 'Three? Great lords, why? Is it not just you, Ravena and Anis? What could you possibly need with three ships?'

'Not that it is any of your concern . . . Nephew.' She may be the family matriarch still, but Markon remained impassive. He did not take orders from her. 'I needed three ships for my carriage, my horses, my palace escort, and—' she paused, reddening slightly, then continued, 'my clothing.'

Fighting to hold back a smile, Prince Markon II of Rona asked, 'And which ship was damaged, my dearest Aunt?'

Detria gave up the fight, bursting out, 'My rutting clothing ship, damn your insolence! And I want everything replaced – today.'

Seizing the opportunity to be gracious, Markon agreed, 'Of course Aunt Detria, please let one of my palace aides know what was lost and I will have the finest tailors in Estrad here this afternoon to re-outfit your entire retinue. And I will also dispatch a force to hunt down these pirates and send word to you when it is accomplished.' Grinning a little devilishly, he added, 'It is lovely to see you again, Aunt Detria. You know you were my father's favourite cousin.'

'Do *not* try to sweet talk me, Nephew. I'm angry. I'm angry at having to drag myself over here to listen to this reunification proposal of yours. I'm angry at the soggy climate in this lowland swamp you call a nation, and I am very sceptical of this representative government you propose.' She tried to stare him down, but Markon would not allow this, not in his own audience chamber. She went on, 'You're going to have to do a great deal of convincing over the next ten days, Markon, a great deal.'

With that parting salvo, Aunt Detria Sommerson, Ruling Princess of all Praga, turned on her heel and stormed out.

Climbing the grand staircase to his royal apartment, Markon found Danae, his wife, waiting for him on the landing.

'Well, she sounds upset,' said Danae, taking his hand.

'You have no idea,' he said. 'I think one of these days she's going to drop dead carrying on like that.' A large stained-glass window above the landing illuminated the staircase and lit his wife's face. She had aged well; he believed her the most beautiful woman in Rona. 'I need her for this to work, though,' he said contemplatively. 'I need all of them, and I have only ten days.'

Markon's cousins, the rulers of Praga, Falkan and Malakasia, had all travelled to Rona to hear his reunification proposal. The nations were independent of each other, and their political and economic relations had been strained for the past three generations. A brutal war between his grandfather, his great-uncle and his great-aunt had ended in an unstable peace agreement many Twinmoons earlier, but border raids, pirates and inflated tariffs were pushing the Eldarni nations close to conflict once again. Secret alliances had been formed, armies quietly levied and outfitted.

Markon was working desperately to stop the downward spiral into armed conflict; his proposal would bring representative government to the known lands and, hopefully, restore a true peace to Eldarn. The visionary prince was frustrated that his cousins had agreed to be his guests for just ten days; that left a great deal of planning and negotiating to complete in a very short time. Still, he was determined.

He squeezed his wife's hand and turned to climb the remaining stairs. 'We begin tonight,' he said quietly. 'Prepared or not, we begin tonight.'

From his apartment Markon looked out across the palace grounds. Normally a haven for quiet contemplation, today there were hundreds of people who had come to witness history, to sell their goods and services, or just to enjoy the fair-like atmosphere of the political summit. Although his royal cousins were housed in various wings of Riverend Palace, their escorts camped on the grounds between the palace and the Estrad River, together with those who had come to sell, to entertain or just to gawp. Markon had offered each a team of squires to act as servants or valets during the summit, but – like Aunt Detria's naval escort – he had been turned down: his cousins mistrusted him. Looking now across the sea of multi-coloured banners, tents and pedlars' carts, he knew he was doing the right thing. Markon imagined the great nation of Eldarn reborn, reconstructed into five equal nation-states, where all citizens could enjoy freedom, equity and an opportunity to build a meaningful life. He just had to talk his cousins into the idea. The Ronan prince believed they shared enough fundamental values to bring this vision to life. No one person should rule absolutely. Markon was certain that absolute power had been the damning variable in his great-grandfather's life: he was killed because he had wielded unchecked power; his scions had been fighting for the shattered vestiges of that power for three generations. It had to stop.

'Danae,' he called over his shoulder, 'would you have someone send for Tenner?'

'Of course, dear,' she said, gesturing to a pageboy down the hallway. She spoke quietly to the boy, who walked quickly off to find Tenner, the prince's personal physician, and closest advisor.

Danae came up behind her husband and ran her hands under his arms and across his chest. He was still in good physical shape for a man nearly four hundred and twenty-five Twinmoons old, his chest and arms kept strong with continued riding and exercise. He had put on some weight above his belt, though, and Danae grabbed him playfully.

'I'm not the man you once married,' he told her quietly. 'What do you suppose happened to him?'

'I'd say he was a bit older, much wiser—' Markon smiled at that, '—and about to bring lasting peace to the known world.' She wrapped her arms more tightly around him, burying her face in his back.

'I hope you're right, my darling,' he said, sighing a little.

'I hope you're right, too, my darling,' a third voice interrupted: Tenner Wynne, the only man in Rona who would dare to enter the royal apartments without announcing himself. 'You've been wrong so many times. I guess I can't blame you, though: your losing streak started when you chose the wrong husband.' Tenner was cousin to Prince Markon, the first-born son of Remond II of Falkan. When his father died, Tenner, a medical student at the time, abdicated the Falkan crown to his sister, Anaria: he believed he would make a below-average politician but a superior doctor.

Now, many Twinmoons later his prophecy was realised as he was responsible for training most of the physicians practising in Rona.

Tenner's friendship with Markon had begun when the two were just boys; it had grown stronger over the Twinmoons that he had lived and taught in the Ronan capital. He was a brilliant surgeon and diagnostician, but he was also respected as the prince's primary advisor.

'Tenner, I'm convinced your parents had you out of wedlock,' Markon grinned. 'And have you, in your decrepitude, forgotten how to knock?'

'I would remind his Highness that I am younger than him, and that the door was already open.' Tenner bowed with false obsequiousness. 'You two really must learn to be more discreet.'

'Ha! You're just jealous.' Markon turned back towards the window. 'Now, tell me where he is.'

'If by "he" you mean your son,' Tenner said, 'I believe "he" is hunting in the southern forest. He'll be back sometime later today.'

'He ought to be here.' Danae was anxious; she feared yet another argument between her husband and her son. At one hundred and seventy-three Twinmoons, the young man had grown independent, and Markon found many of his son's decisions disagreeable.

'Oh, he'll be here,' Tenner said. 'He knows how important this is to you. I believe he wants to make something of an entrance this afternoon – there are, after all, numerous young and attractive women on hand.'

'Yes,' Markon mused. 'I noticed we haven't seen the Larion contingent yet. Any word from our friends in Gorsk?'

'Nothing, but I can dispatch a rider north along the Merchants' Highway to find out why they're late if you want.' Tenner didn't need to say that he was also worried that no one had yet arrived from the northern nation; they had been expected in Rona two days earlier. Detria and the Pragan envoy had been delayed by raiders on the Ravenian Sea; he had no idea what could be delaying the Larion Senate, which was comprised entirely of peaceful scholars who travelled with little or no money. Raiding parties invariably allowed Larion convoys to pass freely, waiting for more lucrative prey.

Markon felt a familiar sense of fatigue: things had not been going according to plan. He was afraid of the news riders might bring back, but he agreed with Tenner: they had to investigate. 'I suppose you'd better. Will we see you later this evening for dinner?'

'Of course – would I miss one of the most important evenings

13

in the past six hundred Twinmoons? Peace in our lifetime, and all that?' Tenner had more confidence in the prince than Markon had in himself. 'I think it's probably rare, your Highness, for anyone to be aware that their finest day lies before them.' Danae smiled, nodding agreement as Tenner continued, 'We spend so much time looking forward or reflecting back; today we get to focus on today and recognise that this is the most important thing any of us will ever do.'

'Trust me; I've thought of little else.' Markon clamped a hand on his friend's shoulder and squeezed it firmly. 'I'm glad you'll be there with Danae and me. Would you send word when our son returns?'

'Of course,' Tenner said as he turned and left the couple alone in their chambers.

The heir to the Ronan throne tethered his horse to a low-hanging tree branch and carefully untied a longbow from his saddle. Danmark Grayslip was tall and powerfully built. He pulled his shoulder-length hair into a ponytail, tied it quickly with a thin leather strap and tucked it down beneath his collar, then surveyed the forest, searching for any signs of game: fresh tracks, broken branches or disturbed leaves. Danmark guessed there would be rabbits, a gansel or maybe even a wild pig near the deep eddy that marked the Estrad River's final turn as it wound its way to the sea.

Stepping carefully towards the edge of a steep slope that ran to the riverbank, he was able to see much of the great bend in the river. A small group of wild hogs were gathered at the base of the slope, rooting for truffles in the mud under a misshapen maple tree. Danmark thought of fresh pork for the reunification feast as he slithered along the ridge on his stomach. He needed to get clear of several small trees to have an open shot down the hill. At this range he thought he could kill two, if they didn't panic and run off right away.

Excited that he had found an easy target so early in the day, the young prince imagined his triumphant ride through Estrad with a boar or two lashed to his saddle. Hundreds of guests, visitors and merchants, had journeyed to the city to hear his father's vision for peace. He would ride slowly, stately, to give them all the opportunity to witness his return from the hunt.

Danmark had his choice of Ronan women; they were all vying for his hand, and not just for his inheritance – the olive-skinned, dark-eyed young man was considered very handsome. Following his impromptu parade, he would select a companion for the evening from the many lovely foreigners visiting Riverend Palace, he thought smugly. Imagining the evening's entertainment aroused him, and the future Prince of Rona had to fight a desire to rush the job.

Danmark froze: one of the hogs had stopped digging and turned to look at him. He watched as the small boar began climbing the slope. Smiling at his luck, he was already rehearsing the story of how he killed the ferocious animal with just his hunting knife. He peered down the hill again; there it was, still staring at him and still climbing. He nocked an arrow and moved onto his knees, into firing position, as the pig came slowly but deliberately towards him. Then something strange happened. The hog stopped its relentless climb, gave the young prince a vacuous look, then collapsed as if rendered completely senseless: a child's stuffed toy discarded in the woods.

Danmark watched it for a moment, shrugged bemusedly, and prepared to fire downhill at one of the larger pigs still digging for truffles.

The ache began as a distant burning sensation in his left wrist. At first the prince ignored it, preparing to fire his bow, but before he could release the first shaft, pain lanced along his forearm. As Danmark dropped his longbow the arrow glanced harmlessly off a nearby tree and fell into the river. Tearing off his left glove, the young man discovered an open wound forming rapidly on the back of his wrist. It was an ugly sore, dripping with strangely coloured pus and dark blood.

'What in all the Eastlands—' He had no time to complete his thought. He was going blind, the forest colours fading from green and gold through blurry grey to black. Covering his eyes, Danmark gave a surprised cry and struggled to regain his feet.

As he stood, he realised he could see nothing and his hearing was fading as well. 'What sort of demon virus is this?' he screamed, but he could barely hear his own cries. He wiped his palms over and over his eyes, as if to massage sight back in.

Now in total darkness, Danmark tried to make his way back to his horse, hoping that the beast might find its own way back to the stables at Riverend Palace, or at least into the village. His head swam, his equilibrium disturbed by the rapid hearing loss. Crying out once again as he lost his footing, he fell backwards down the slope, hitting rocks and trees as he rolled. Danmark was overcome by fear; he tried screaming for help, but could not tell if he made any sound.

His heart raced: he was dying. He could feel it; the burning, the blindness and the deafness had come on too quickly for this to be anything other than death.

Suddenly everything stopped. As Danmark stared into the endless midnight, brightly coloured shapes and forms drifted through his mind, playfully moving about inside his head. For a moment his loss of sight and sound was forgotten; he was distracted by the hauntingly beautiful rainbow of colours. He found he could make them sing or play music; he could hear it resonating behind his eyes. Giggling, he reached out to touch them with his good hand, and discovered that when he commanded, they obeyed. The Ronan prince joyfully organised shapes and shades into a series of moving pictures, a magical parade through his blindness. They called to him, and he answered, in a language he never knew he could understand, but which he could now speak fluently.

On the slope above, Danmark's horse stood idly by as the prince waved one hand back and forth through the air above his head. With one leg resting lazily in the gently flowing waters of the Estrad River, the young man grunted, cried out and laughed in a succession of unintelligible noises, but he made no move to rise from where he had fallen.

'Marek, take a long look at Anis will you?' Helmat Barstag elbowed his cousin in the ribs. 'Lords, but she is put together nicely.' The future prince of Falkan stared unabashedly at Anis Ferlasa's breasts, displayed prominently thanks to the laced and embroidered bodice she had chosen for the evening's state dinner. He reached for his wine goblet.

'She's your cousin,' Marek Whitward commented dryly. 'It's indecent.'

'Distant cousin, my friend, and tell me you wouldn't love a chance at her if you could get one.' Helmat eyed Marek suspiciously. 'You do get involved with women from time to time, don't you?'

'Of course I do, Helmat. It's just that I try to limit my relationships with women who aren't relatives ... however distant.' The young prince of Malakasia lowered his voice when he saw his father scowling at him from across the table. He added, in a whisper, 'I do admit she is beautiful.'

'Beautiful? She's more than beautiful.' Helmat's voice rose. 'She makes me want to forget myself and take her right here on the table.'

'I'm certain your mother would appreciate that,' Marek remarked sarcastically, looking pointedly at Princess Anaria, seated at the head of their table. He liked his cousin; he felt disconcerted and somewhat guilty at how pleased he was Helmat would one day rule Falkan now that Harkan, Helmat's older brother, had been lost at sea seven Twinmoons earlier. Harkan had been distant, serious, and brooding, the very antithesis of the witty and fun-loving Helmat. Marek had dreaded the Twinmoons he and Harkan would have worked together as Eldarni heads of state.

Now that Helmat was the prince-in-waiting to Falkan, Marek looked forward to their collaborations: he would have an ally in the Eastlands when he took his family's ancestral throne in Malakasia.

But Harkan's tragic accident, in a storm off the Falkan coast, had broken Princess Anaria's heart. Now she wore only black, in public mourning for her elder son. In the wake of his brother's death, Helmat was not sure he would be ready to take control when his mother died: his life and education so far had been preparing him to play a secondary role in governing Falkan. Marek was pleased to see his cousin finally warming to the notion that he would eventually oversee the most powerful economy in Eldarn.

The beautiful Anis Ferlasa, the object of Helmat's desire, was seated with Ravena, her mother, and her grandmother, Detria Sommerson, Princess of Praga. Calculating the difference in their ages, Marek guessed Anis was now about one hundred and fifty Twinmoons. The Malakasian prince flushed as he recalled the girl he had known and teased mercilessly as a child: tall, gangly, with pale skin, pin-straight hair and high cheekbones. Stealing a glance at her over Helmat's shoulder, Marek marvelled at how lovely she had grown in the seventy Twinmoons since he had last seen her. He felt his temperature rise, and dabbed at his brow with a brocaded napkin before loosening his collar.

Helmat, not as subtle as his Malakasian cousin, had turned in his chair to gain an unobstructed view of Anis across the grand dining hall.

Noticing their stares, Anis smiled devilishly at the two princes and mouthed the words *meet me later*.

'Did you see that?' Helmat blurted, too loudly. He immediately sat up, ramrod-straight, as Princess Anaria cast him a cold look, her slate-grey eyes staring him down knowingly from the far end of the banquet table. Whispering excitedly, Helmat nudged his cousin. 'Did you see that, Marek? I tell you, my friend, we are set for tonight.' Nearly bursting with anticipation, Helmat quickly downed a third goblet of wine to brace himself for the long dinner ahead.

Riverend's grand dining hall was festooned with fine linen, colourful silk banners and hundreds of freshly cut flowers. A bellamir quintet provided music from an alcove, and dozens of torches brightened the scene with dancing firelight. Warm night air mixed with the faint aroma of woodsmoke to give the chamber a feeling of home, despite the fact that nearly two hundred people filled the long tables: the royal families and honoured kinsmen and courtiers.

Servants hustled to deliver wine and ale around the room; the diners were still awaiting the opening course as Prince Markon II and Princess Danae had not yet joined their guests for the evening's ceremony. Many of the revellers were beginning to get restless in the stifling heat: the fashionable layers of ornately stitched clothing were causing great discomfort. Several of the elder cousins began grumbling their discontent.

Marek took a long draught from his tankard. 'I've heard a rumour that young Danmark hasn't returned from a hunting trip. His father's furious.'

Helmat tore his gaze away from Anis's ample bodice and looked around: the Larion representatives had not arrived either. 'Things don't seem to be going very smoothly for Markon,' he whispered. 'Danmark's missing and no one from Gorsk has bothered to show up.'

18

'I'm not surprised about the Larion brothers,' Helmat answered. 'They can only lose in this proposal. They've been entirely autonomous for thousands of Twinmoons. Now Markon plans to include them in a decision-making body made up of members from across the known world. Their convenient self-appeasement programme is about to get shattered.'

'I thought they were peaceful,' Marek said, surprised.

'They are. There's no question about that.' Helmat reached for a loaf of bread, but another withering glare from Anaria made him think twice. 'But their tendency to be self-righteous will only hurt them when they have to deal with all of us. They won't be able to just sit back, secure in their belief that they know everything, and make decisions for themselves alone any more. They're being thrown into a much larger pot.'

'Why wouldn't they show up for this, though?' the young Malakasian asked.

'That gets me, too,' his cousin answered. 'They aren't powerful enough to ignore Markon if we all decide to adopt his plan. They have no army, no weapons—'

'They have magic, though,' Marek interrupted.

'They do, but you're right, they're peace-loving. They'd be overrun before they finished arguing about whether or not to use it.' Helmat sighed, looking hungrily towards the palace kitchens. 'I'll be rutting drunk if they don't hurry this dinner along, and poor Cousin Anis will find only a shell of my former self at her disposal later this evening.' Helmat nudged his cousin playfully. 'You know, if we—'

Helmat was interrupted as the music modulated from a stately dance in a minor key to a sweeping fanfare. Prince Markon II and Princess Danae of Rona entered the grand dining hall to join their guests. Markon looked calm but determined; his wife was a vision of elegance, striking in a flowing ivory gown brocaded in silver. Before taking his seat, Markon waved the crowd silent. He asked their forgiveness for his tardy arrival, and encouraged them all to enjoy dinner.

Helmat and Marek ate and drank with abandon: fresh venison, pork tenderloin, roasted gansel and enormous beefsteaks streamed in unending supply from the palace kitchens. Finally, when Marek was convinced he could eat nothing more, the tables were cleared and trays of elaborate decorated pastries were presented. Marek's parents, Prince Draven and Princess Mernam, tucked into the delicacies, but he could not manage another morsel.

'Lords, but I am stuffed to bursting,' Marek commented to no one in particular.

'Try one of the pink ones, dear.' His mother wiped puffy cream from the corner of her mouth. 'They're quite light.'

'Maybe later,' he answered, loosening the belt around his tunic.

'I'm having a brief meeting with Prince Markon in his audience chamber,' his father said from across the table. 'I'd like you to join us.'

'Of course,' Marek said, trying to hide his disappointment at missing his evening rendezvous with Anis.

Helmat looked askance. 'You can't seriously tell me you're going to miss Anis for a meeting with Markon about *politics*,' he said through a mouthful of cream-filled pastry.

'Sorry, Helmat, duty calls – but I'll expect full disclosure in the morning.'

'Outstanding,' his cousin replied, all of a sudden re-energised. 'I'll meet you for breakfast.'

The thought of yet more food made Marek wince. He was about to comment on the impending tryst when Markon rose to address his guests.

'Good evening one and all,' he started. 'I am so very pleased you were able to join us here at Riverend, to discuss a proposal of monumental importance to all our people of Eldarn.' He paused, looking around the room, then continued, 'It is wonderful to have you all as our guests: I trust the accommodations and food are to your satisfaction.' At that, a smattering of applause ran through the room, like so many children in hard-soled shoes. 'Danae and I are excited to have our family, the descendants of King Remond Grayslip, here on hand to witness this summit, this recognition of critical common values that will guide us into a new era of peace.'

Markon paused again for effect.

Looking across the Pragan table at her daughter Ravena, Princess Detria frowned. She doubted her Ronan cousin was blessed with the leadership necessary to see his vision realised. Ravena shrugged and turned her gaze back to Markon.

'I have been—' Markon stopped his speech and looked down at the floor in consternation, as if trying to recall a line from a poem memorised too long ago. 'I have been—' Again the prince paused and, flushed from the heat in the dining hall, absentmindedly wiped his brow. 'I have been able to work with—'

Tenner stood and approached the prince nervously. Princess Danae took her husband's hand in a show of support. Reaching Markon's side, Tenner handed his friend a goblet of wine. Markon reached for it, managed a partial smile and raised his head to continue. His face was pale and damp with beads of sweat. He blinked several times in rapid succession as if to clear his vision, and took a long sip from Tenner's wine goblet before clearing his throat.

Marek wasn't sure if he heard Princess Danae scream first, or if he saw Prince Markon collapse to the stone floor. The room erupted with the concerned cries of family and friends. Scores of people rose to aid the fallen prince and Marek's view was blocked until he jostled into position near the head table. He watched as Markon, looking horribly lifeless, was carried from the grand dining hall to his royal apartment, attended by his wife and physician.

Marek's father stood up purposefully. 'Come,' Prince Draven commanded his son, 'let's see if we can help.' He was already moving towards the exit; Marek looked over at Helmat before rising to follow.

Later that evening, Helmat lay beneath Anis. Her exquisite body glistened with perspiration as she breathed heavily down into his face. Her warm breath smelled of stale wine, but Helmat found it the perfect aphrodisiac.

'Lords, my dear cousin, but we must do that again, immediately,' he told her, already beginning to feel his body respond to his desire. They had taken each other furiously, without care or compassion, both fighting a selfish battle for physical pleasure.

'Oh yes, my dear cousin . . .' She leaned into him, her breasts brushing against the sides of his face. 'But first I need a drink.'

Helmat watched as Anis rose and walked to the armoire against the far wall of his suite. She poured two goblets of dark red wine, drank one nearly dry, refilled it and drank again.

Helmat smiled. 'That's my girl. You know that's from my family vineyard.'

'It's good,' she answered, 'much better than the horse-piss we ferment in Praga.'

Helmat stared at her in the flickering candlelight, excited at the thought of taking her all over again. 'You have perhaps the most perfectly formed backside of any woman walking the known lands,' he said softly. 'Do you know that? It's perfect. And trust me, I know; I've examined plenty of backsides in my time.'

Anis said nothing, but turned and slowly approached Helmat's bed. In one hand she carried the wine bottle. 'Oh, that's better,' Helmat said, laughing, 'bring the whole bottle. It cuts down on all those unnecessary trips back and forth. We don't want the sheets getting cold, do we?'

Anis didn't return his smile. It was only then that Helmat noticed the small wound forming on her hand.

'Rutting whores! What *is* that?' he asked, sitting up and reaching for the bedside candle. 'Come here and let me see – it looks like it might be infected.' Suddenly concerned, he sobered somewhat and repeated, 'Come here. Let me look at that for you.'

Moving with unexpected speed, Anis shattered the bottle against the headboard and drove a broken shard of thick Ronan glass deep into Helmat's neck. Blood spurted from the wound as her cousin choked out a guttural plea for mercy. His eyes bulging in terror, Helmat reached for her. In his last moments he ran his fingers over those perfect breasts he had been lusting after all evening. Wine mixed with blood: a sanguine vintage that soaked the bedding as Anis Ferlasa of Praga, naked and spattered in red, stared for a moment at the twitching corpse of her fallen cousin and lover before collapsing to the floor herself.

EMPIRE GULCH, COLORADO

September 1870

Henry Milken, the mine foreman, carried four broken shovels as lightly as an armload of firewood and tossed them into the wagon. A cramped muscle in his back ached momentarily, and his right knee reminded him it was still before dawn on the western slope of Horseshoe Mountain. Milken could see the sun's earliest rays cresting the rocky ridge above Weston Pass and illuminating the mountain's peak with a golden edge. The darkness spilling westward below made the valley look like an artist's unfinished painting. It was his favourite time of day, and he rarely missed an opportunity to watch as the dawn's distant glow heralded the new morning in Empire Gulch.

Milken looked at the flue vents that jutted like silent sentries above the whitewashed plank workroom adjacent to the men's barracks. They had been active in the past several weeks, exhaling great clouds of acrid black smoke. Nothing billowed from them this morning, but Milken could still detect the faint, dank aroma of burning quicksilver. He breathed in the fresh, cold air.

Henry Milken missed sluice-mining. It might not yield all the precious metals and stones he and his men were able to glean from a rich vein deep in the mountain, but the work was cleaner. Water danced through the sluice boxes, dropping irregular bits of gold or silver into small mercury reservoirs: at least there a miner could walk about upright, enjoy a smoke from time to time and feel the sun on his shoulders. He grinned as he remembered working in the valley; he'd been young then. Streams crisscrossed the valley floor like an intricate Roman highway system; Milken had once built himself a sluice box nearly three hundred yards long.

These days Milken was certainly richer, but sometimes he felt as though he went from the stifling closeness of the lode shaft to the foul stench of the refinery stoves without drawing one clean breath.

But now it was Sunday morning. Milken, Lester McGovern and William Higgins had stayed behind when the other mine workers rode into Oro City for their Saturday night off. Whiskey and whores were Saturday night staples, but Milken knew he would see his entire crew this morning at Pastor Merrill's church service. Horace Tabor, who owned the Silver Shadow Mine, expected every one of his employees to be in church on Sunday mornings. Milken grinned to himself at the thought of his men grumbling as they dragged themselves from warm beds and the warm arms of the whores to make it to Mr Tabor's barn by 7.30 – there was no church building in Oro City yet, the barn served Pastor Merrill well for the time being. He arrived a few minutes early each week to construct a quick altar out of two hay bales and a length of old lumber. It did not look like much, but the pastor didn't appear to mind.

The Silver Shadow Mine shut down after supper on Saturday as usual, and within fifteen minutes the men had washed, loaded up in one of the wagons and disappeared down the gulch. Milken, McGovern and Higgins remained behind, ostensibly to pack up and transport certain pieces of equipment that needed repair. In reality, the three men were to act as escort for a large deposit of silver going to Horace Tabor's bank in Oro City. Milken calculated the day's deposits would exceed $17,000, a sum unmatched for a week's work in the mining industry to date. Tabor owned a mine that regularly produced $50,000 a month, but this would establish an all-time record for a week's haul.

Milken had sent word to Harvey Smithson, the bank president, that he would be bringing the silver for assay and deposit at seven o'clock this morning. Tabor owned or managed a number of mines in the Arkansas River Valley and on the eastern slope of the Mosquito Mountain Range; he was well aware that such a large deposit always ran the risk of ambush – bandits, raiders, or even a gang of desperate miners. Milken trusted most of his men, but such a cache of silver coming down the gulch unguarded might motivate even his truest employees to turn.

So none of the men ever knew when Milken was making a deposit at the bank. Sometimes he would leave in the middle of the night, or during lunch break – he never went at the same time or on the same day of the week.

Most of the miners had a small stash of gold or silver hidden away to supplement their salary. Milken overlooked these minor transgressions; by turning a blind eye when they squirrelled a little away now and then, he had never been forced to address a major theft in his five years as foreman of Silver Shadow. He knocked on the wagon superstitiously.

Eight bags of silver were placed carefully under the driver's seat. Milken would drive, with Lester McGovern in the back, his rifle loaded and ready. William Higgins was to ride alongside the wagon on one of Tabor's horses. McGovern and Higgins earned extra each month to accompany the deposit runs. Higgins was deadly with a handgun – few men actually owned one, and even fewer could use firearms accurately. Lester McGovern was along for protection: at nearly seven feet tall, he was the largest – and strongest – man Milken had ever met. He weighed over three hundred and fifty pounds, very little of which was excess fat. The barrel-chested giant had been hardened by his years of mining – Lester McGovern was the region's best mucker, hauling dirt and rocks from the veins so the men could get to the precious metals below. Of all the tasks, mucking was the worst by a furlong; it was a hard, dirty job, but McGovern handled it with ease.

Milken was never worried that McGovern would shoot anyone with the rifle he carried; he feared for the man McGovern struck with the rifle in close combat, for that man would surely be killed instantly.

Sunlight spilled further over the upper ridge of Horseshoe Mountain as the last of the boxes were tied down. The distant peaks across the valley were illuminated in dim pink and muted orange though the valley floor remained dark still. Then Milken saw the rider, a lone horseman approaching up the trail. Squinting in an attempt to improve his vision, Milken thought he could see dark blue trousers. Shit. Another soldier wandering west to seek his fortune in the mines: another beginner who didn't stand a chance working at this altitude or under these conditions, another loner who'd probably lost his family or his mind fighting Americans for America. Winter was fast approaching; he didn't need this. Milken silently cursed the hiring executives at the home office in town. If he had a dollar for every grey-leg and blue-leg beginner they had sent him to train since the end of that cursed war, he wouldn't still be working for Tabor.

'Lester, Billy, get out here.' Milken spat his last mouthful of coffee into the dirt beneath the wagon. 'We got a new digger comin' up the trail. It looks like we'll have comp'ny on our way down.' Higgins emerged from the entrance to the Silver Shadow barracks carrying a pack and a three-quarter-bit axe with a crack in the handle. He loaded both into the wagon.

'Four banjos broken this week?' Higgins asked, examining the shovels Milken had stored in the wagon bed.

'Yup, the damned things can't keep up with McGovern,' Milken replied, laughing.

Looking down the side of Horseshoe Mountain, Higgins motioned towards the lone horseman. 'How do you know he's a greenie?'

'It's a quarter to six on a Sunday morning and he's ridin' *up* the gulch. He's gotta be a greenie. No digger we know would be doin' that.'

'Don't you pick up most of 'em down in town?' Higgins asked.

'Most of the time I find them stinkin' drunk at the saloon. Half of them don't have a pot to piss in, and they know the weeks up here are long, so they blow whatever's left of the scrip they got on 'em before makin' the trip up this hill.' Henry Milken had not taken his eyes off the horseman climbing the trail into the miners' camp.

'Look at that; he's got his own horse,' Higgins observed.

'Yup, and blue pants, another Union boy.'

'He must be from one of them rich Boston families to be all the way out here on his own horse.' Few of the miners owned horses; many couldn't ride and those who could more often used the horses stabled in Oro City for use in and around Tabor's mining operations. William Higgins rode well, but he had not owned a horse since he began mining ten years earlier. When he borrowed a mount, Higgins wore his spurs, spurs he stole when he was honourably discharged from the US Cavalry. He was proud of his

26

part in the bloody campaigns aiming to make the territory safe for pioneers and homesteaders. Wearing his spurs, even for the few hours it took to ride down the gulch and back, helped him remember his glory days.

'He probably come out on the train and bought it in Denver, Idaho Springs, or someplace,' Milken said, almost to himself, and then to Higgins added, 'Well, get McGovern. We gotta move on down there quick this morning. Church in less than two hours, and we still gotta see Mr Smithson.'

Higgins re-entered the mine barracks, calling out, 'Lester, c'mon now, git that giant self of yours out here. We gotta get movin' right quick.'

McGovern's deep bass sounded like an out-of-tune cello: 'I'm comin'.'

The rider came slowly towards the barracks. He looked directly at Henry Milken, but said nothing as the foreman approached, his hand extended.

'Good mornin'. I'm sorry to say you made the trip all the way up here for nothin'. We gotta be in town in two hours. Did they not tell you that Mr Tabor wants us all in church every Sunday?'

The horseman offered no reply, nor did he shake Milken's hand.

Milken tried again. 'I'm Henry Milken. I'm the foreman here at the Silver Shadow. There's a bit of coffee left; it tastes like old socks, but you're welcome to a swig before we head out.' He paused a moment and then, growing irritated, asked, 'What's your name, son?'

Still without a word, the stranger grabbed Milken's outstretched arm and pulled it forward roughly; with his free hand, the horseman delivered a blow that split the foreman's skull and killed him instantly. His body hung limp in the stranger's grasp, twitching, until the horseman threw it carelessly to one side. It lay still in the heavy mountain mud.

Three shots rang out in rapid succession and bullet wounds opened in the horseman's neck and chest. Without flinching, the stranger dismounted and strode slowly to the wagon, where he removed the axe Higgins had stowed moments before. Higgins fired again, this time hitting the stranger in the face and temple. The bullets tore through the horseman's skull, blowing a large

27

piece of his cheekbone and a section of the back of his head away. Oddly, the injuries bled very little.

The stranger came on, unhindered; stunned, Higgins dropped his pistol, knelt down in the mud near the wagon and waited for the horseman to strike him dead with the axe. He felt himself lose control of his bowels and found it odd that he didn't care. He tried desperately to remember the things that had been most important to him – his mother, his wife, the daughter back in St Louis – but he could not organise his thoughts coherently.

Higgins knew he had only a few seconds to live. He made a final plea to God, and waited for the end – but the expected blow didn't come. When Higgins risked a glance up, he saw Lester McGovern's massive arms wrapped around the stranger from behind. McGovern held the man in the air and squeezed the breath from his lungs. The axe, forgotten, lay at their feet.

'Kill him, McGovern! Crush the bastard,' Higgins yelled, feeling hope for a moment, but the huge man's strength did not seem to be affecting the silent stranger. The horseman gripped McGovern's right forearm and began to squeeze. The burly miner screamed and Higgins heard both bones in McGovern's forearm snap.

Desperate to live, McGovern held on with one arm, but the horseman was not slowed. Having freed himself from the giant's powerful grip, the stranger methodically placed his hands on either side of McGovern's head, anchored a foot against the big man's chest and began pulling. Higgins watched in horror, unable to move, as McGovern struggled to scream. One arm hung limp, but he clawed at the horseman's face with the other, pushing one of his huge fingers into the bullet wound in the killer's temple. It had no palpable effect: the stranger was unstoppable.

William Higgins watched the tear begin on the left side of Lester McGovern's neck. The big man's breathing came in short, sickening bursts; he couldn't say a word. The horseman continued to pull and in a fluid motion ripped McGovern's head from his shoulders and tossed it into the back of the wagon. McGovern's enormous body fell forward in a shower of blood and lay still.

The man reached down to retrieve the axe and walked slowly to where William Higgins still knelt in fear. Blood dripped from the killer's hands. Higgins vomited, cried and begged for his life. Again, the expected blow never came.

'You've ruined this,' the horseman said as he probed the bullet wounds in his chest and face with a crimson finger. Higgins coughed twice, tried to catch his breath, and remembered the final bullet in his pistol. With his last measure of reason, Higgins reached for the gun and raised it to his own temple, but he was not quick enough, or strong enough in his resolve. That moment's hesitation as he tried one last time to picture his daughter's face cost him a painless escape. The horseman grabbed Higgins's wrist and forced his shot wide of the mark. His gun was empty, but William Higgins was still alive.

He felt a burning sensation; a perfectly round wound opened on the back of his hand. Then Higgins screamed.

Gabriel O'Reilly opened the front door of the Bank of Idaho Springs just before 7.00 a.m. He lit the oil lamps and stoked the boxy cast-iron stove in the corner, smiling to himself when he saw a few hot coals left over from the evening before. He enjoyed mornings when he did not have to re-light the stove: it gave him a few extra minutes to brew coffee. It also meant the bank had not grown too cold overnight. In early October, days in the canyon remained warm, but the temperature often fell below freezing at night.

This morning his thigh ached: snow would be coming over the pass in the next day or two. His thigh was the best weather forecaster he knew, better than any almanac. O'Reilly had taken a Confederate rifle slug in the thigh at Bull Run; the Rebs called it Manassas. It had been a clean shot, and he'd got to a field hospital in Centerville before it got infected. Many of his fellow soldiers had not been so lucky. He knew he would never have made it to the western frontier if he'd lost his leg; now all he suffered were a slight limp and a mild ache with changes in temperature. He'd been luckier than most.

Bull Run had been early in the war, 1861, and at the age of twenty-two his tenure as a soldier was over. He could have gone back to the fighting, but a chance meeting with Lawrence Chapman during his convalescence had changed his future. Chapman, a wealthy businessman from Virginia, told him about a gold strike in Colorado; when O'Reilly had asked if he planned to open a mining company, Chapman had laughed and told him, 'No, son, a bank. I don't own any clothes suitable for mining.'

O'Reilly had worked in his hometown mercantile before enlisting in the army. Chapman offered him a job on the spot if he were willing to pack up and move west right away.

'Time is wasting, my boy,' Chapman told him. 'All that gold is just lying around waiting for someone to provide a safe place to deposit or perhaps even invest a nugget or two.'

'I appreciate the offer, Mr Chapman,' O'Reilly said, 'but I've another stretch to do for the army.'

'You just rest here young man, and I'll take care of that,' Chapman said.

Two days later, Gabriel O'Reilly had an honourable discharge from the Army of Northeastern Virginia.

Before the war, O'Reilly had thought men who avoided conflict were cowards. After half a day at Bull Run he had seen enough killing to last a lifetime, and he had taken a bullet himself. That had been enough to convince him that getting out as soon as possible was not the bravest, but perhaps the wisest decision he could make. Six months later found him in Idaho Springs, Colorado, building a company and maintaining expense ledgers for Mr Chapman. Although there had been rumblings of both Union and Confederate support here in the mountains, and many men had travelled back east to enlist, for O'Reilly, the war was a distant memory.

That was nine years ago; now the Virginian owned a saloon, a local hotel, a mercantile exchange carrying goods shipped in each week from Denver, and the Bank of Idaho Springs. Two weeks earlier, he had named O'Reilly bank manager and handed over daily operations to him.

Chapman himself now spent much of his time in Denver, where a number of wealthy mining widows helped to keep the bachelor's social schedule full. He had shaken O'Reilly's hand, congratulated him on his years of hard work, and presented him with a gold belt buckle with BIS embossed in raised letters.

This morning O'Reilly absentmindedly polished the buckle as he waited for his coffee to brew. The drawer was unlocked and the scales tared; after he poured himself a cup of coffee he would unlock the safe.

Yesterday's newspaper rested on the counter above his cash

drawer; he looked over the pages as he sipped from the steaming mug and awaited the day's first customer. An ongoing investigation in Oro City had yielded no further evidence in the grisly murder of three men near the Silver Shadow Mine. Henry Milken, Lester McGovern and an unknown man had been found dead two weeks earlier. Though it was not uncommon for quarrels over claims to end in a miner's death, the mysterious and horrible nature of these deaths made it plain that this had not been a run-of-the-mill argument. Milken's skull had been crushed, but no obvious weapon was found at the scene. The unknown man had been shot five times, but his body must have been transported to the murder site because there was so little blood on his clothing or the ground where he lay. The grisliest death was that of Lester McGovern, whose head had been forcibly torn from his body – and was missing.

There was another death report, this time the discovery of a young girl's body less than a mile south of the mine on Weston Pass Road. Her age was estimated at eight or nine years, and her clothing – a light cotton dress – suggested she had come from a warmer climate. She had not been wearing shoes, and apart from an open wound on her wrist, her body showed no signs of foul play.

News of the deaths had quickly travelled throughout the Front Range mining towns; the newspaper reported that miners across the state had seen large, man-like monsters capable of ripping body parts asunder and drinking victims' blood directly from their veins. An artist's rendering of one such creature appeared on page five: a hairy version of a large man with strangely human features, especially around the eyes, which conveyed a sense of homicidal madness.

O'Reilly laughed at the absurdity: superstitious people would latch on to anything outlandish when confronted with a situation they were unable to explain. The real explanation was most likely simple: a robbery, even though Horace Tabor's ownership of those mines was unquestioned and only the most ignorant of claim jumpers would attempt a takeover in that valley. Miners working the Silver Shadow told investigators they had hauled a large quantity of silver that week, but none was found at the site.

O'Reilly's reading was interrupted by the sound of the door

opening; a cool breeze elbowed its way through the lobby. Snow was certainly coming. He peered through the thin vertical bars of the teller window: a man, probably a miner, carrying two bulky, grey canvas bags in each hand.

The bank manager hadn't heard of any large strikes in Empire or Georgetown in the past weeks; such news here in the Springs always reached him within a day. He watched with anticipation as the man hefted his bags onto the thickly varnished pine counter. 'There's more,' he said quietly, and turned back towards the street, returning a moment later with four more bags. These he placed carefully on the floor.

'Looks like y'all had a big strike,' O'Reilly mused aloud. 'I hadn't heard anything around town. Which shaft did you bring this out of?' The miner remained silent, but O'Reilly was not really surprised. There were hundreds of mines between Idaho Springs and Georgetown alone, and most of the men refused to discuss the location of their strikes for fear claim jumpers or bandits would track them back to their camps. O'Reilly didn't press the issue.

'Well, anyway,' he said, looking over at the door, 'where's the rest of your team?'

'I'm alone.'

'Alone? They sent you down here alone? Which company do you work for? Do they have an account here? I mean, I can weigh this, but until it's refined I can't even give you credit unless you're willing to come way down off the New York price per ounce. Your company's probably got credit, though. What's the name on the account?'

'I'm alone. There is no account. I wish to open one today.' The miner indicated the bags and said, 'This is already refined.'

O'Reilly was silent for a moment, then he laughed. 'Millie put you up to this? Or was it Jake? I know I had a few too many in there Thursday, but this is just too much.' The bank manager made his way through the door adjoining the lobby and quickly crossed the floor to where the miner stood silently, surrounded by his eight large bags. They looked filled near to bursting.

He reached for one, then thought twice. 'Do you mind?'

'Go ahead,' the miner replied, removing a glove from his right hand. His left remained sheathed in worn leather.

O'Reilly untied the cord holding one of the bags closed and

felt his heart race. 'Sheezus.' It was silver, an enormous cache of silver. The refined ore still looked dirty, and he could smell the vestiges of burned quicksilver, but he knew that there must be twenty thousand dollars'-worth of the ore right here in his lobby.

His speech took on a more businesslike tone. 'You're alone, and you rode into town with eight bags of refined silver? You wear a holster but no handgun, and no one is with you to make certain you don't run off with their hard-earned strike? And you tell me again you don't work for a mining company? You just want to start up an account.'

The man stared at O'Reilly impassively.

'Are you planning to just stand here while I spend the rest of the day and evening assaying this load?'

The man repeated, 'I'm alone, and I'd like to start an account.'

'Well—' O'Reilly looked again at the bags and nodded. 'Okay. It'll take me a goodly while to get this together, and there are a few forms I need you to fill out. If you can't write, I can talk you through them, and you can make your mark. But either way, we'll get this done. And I swear I'll be straight with you, if you want to deposit this rather than just have an assay, I'll give you a good price against the New York standard. New York was in the paper a couple weeks ago at 132 cents per ounce. With this much silver, I can give you—' O'Reilly furiously calculated how much the bank could make selling this at or near the New York price. 'I can give you 122 cents an ounce. Now that's right fair. You can head on over to Millie's or wherever and ask any of the silver men here in town, and they'll tell you that's fair. It's a bit more than I'm used to moving through here—' which was a lie. It was the largest cache of precious metal O'Reilly had ever seen in one place. 'But I'll get you a good price, and you're going to be a very rich man.'

'I need a safe deposit box as well,' the miner added quietly. He had not moved since placing the last four bags on the lobby floor. He stared, grim-faced, across the counter, waiting for O'Reilly to tell him what to do.

'Well, we got those, too, but they're a bit extra, two dollars a month.'

'Take it out of the account.'

'Yessir, we can do that. It's just another form that allows me to take that money out on the first of each month. You don't ever have to think about it, and I'm sure it'll be the end of my lifetime before a two-dollar charge would drain this deposit to any noticeable degree.' He went to pick up the first four bags, but they were much too heavy.

'Christ! Oh, excuse me, but my, these are heavy,' he gasped as he half-lifted, half-dragged the bags one by one through the door to the rear of the building. He suggested, 'Why don't you run out and get something to eat, and when you get back I'll have the forms together, and I can give you an idea how much you have here. I can't believe you carried these in alone. You must be a strong one. Me, I've never been in a mine. I don't own any clothes suitable for mining.' He chuckled, remembering how Chapman had hooked him with that same phrase.

'I'll complete the papers now, and I need a safe deposit box.'

O'Reilly was getting aggravated with his decidedly odd customer: the man carried hundreds of pounds of silver into the bank as if it weighed nothing, but didn't offer to help carry it to the scales in the back. He was doing his best to be accommodating, but the miner shrugged off all his attempts to be helpful or friendly.

Then the bank manager thought again of the huge quantity of ore and swallowed his ill-humour. 'All right, I'll get the papers for you, and begging your pardon, but can you write, or should we go through them together?'

'Bring me the papers. I'll write them here now,' was the toneless reply.

'Sorry about that, but we have a lot come in here who can't fill out the papers. But of course whoever you work for would send someone who had some schooling down with such a large haul.' He had to work for a company; no one man could mine, refine and haul this much silver from any of the mines in the canyon without a team of at least twenty men.

O'Reilly produced the account and safe deposit box forms and returned to weighing the silver and calculating its net worth. Most miners or mine company representatives insisted on watching the weighing and checking the calculations themselves, but this fellow hadn't asked, so O'Reilly didn't offer. *Let the odd bird catch hell from his foreman tonight*, he thought as he struggled to lift another bag onto the pine table against the back wall of his office. He could skim quite a bit off the top of this weigh-in, and perhaps pocket a large sum for himself, but he would have trouble selling anything he stole. All the buyers who made the trip west from Denver knew he had never been in a mine in his life – and that Chapman paid him in cash. O'Reilly put the thought out of his mind.

It was several hours before he took a break. His fingers were sore from separating and washing the dirt and charred mercury from the silver before weighing it, and his lower back ached from repeated trips to the pump on the corner for more water. It was growing colder outside, and he could see snow flying among the rocky peaks above the canyon. It was snowing hard above ten thousand feet; he figured the storm would be upon them by late afternoon.

He had finished the first four bags and already the lone miner was worth over $10,000, even at 122 cents per ounce. It was nearly pure silver, among the best he had ever seen. O'Reilly would easily bring in 132 cents per ounce, or perhaps more if he could find a buyer willing to speculate on high-grade metals. Pouring another cup of coffee, he went back to the lobby and added a log to the fire; again he felt the pain of the coming storm in his thigh. The skies had turned grey and swirls of dead aspen leaves blew up against the side of the building in small tornadoes that lost their gumption after only a few seconds.

The miner had left without a word, but all the papers had been filled out in the fine-lined script of a well-educated person and left in the teller window on top of the now forgotten newspaper. O'Reilly read through them as he warmed himself near the lobby stove.

The miner's name was William Higgins. There was no next of kin listed as a beneficiary of the account, and the only address given was one in Oro City. O'Reilly stopped. That couldn't be right. Higgins had to come from this side of the pass. Oro City was two passes southwest of Idaho Springs. Neither the stage nor the train travelled that route, and by now the snows would have closed even the horse trails until next April. There was no way one man could have driven a team of horses and a wagon loaded with nearly a thousand pounds of silver across those mountain passes in late September. Claim jumpers and raiders would have killed him several times over had they suspected what he was carrying. Perhaps he lived in Oro City but worked the mines near

Georgetown, Empire or any of the small encampments along Clear Creek Canyon. Nodding contemplatively over his coffee, O'Reilly decided that was the only answer, and went about setting up Mr Higgins's new accounts.

It was after 4.00 p.m. when William Higgins returned to the Bank of Idaho Springs. He stood silently in the lobby; had it not been for the cold breeze that blew in when he opened the door, O'Reilly would not have known he was back. It was snowing hard and the miner had a light dusting of flakes scattered across his hat and shoulders.

'Well, Mr Higgins, you are a wealthy man. I'm about finished and it appears you have—'

'I need the key to the safe deposit box now,' Higgins interrupted. He carried two items: a metal cylinder about fifteen inches long and a small wooden box that looked as though it had been carved from rosewood or mahogany, nothing like the scrub oak, pine or aspen that grew in the area. O'Reilly had seen a rosewood cutlery box in Lawrence Chapman's Alexandria home ten years earlier; he remembered the darkly coloured wood and tight grain pattern.

O'Reilly also noticed, for the first time, that Higgins wore spurs on his boots. He thought again what an odd customer this miner was: wearing spurs to drive a wagon?

'Uh, yessir, well, on that issue we have a small problem. You see the deposit boxes are basically drawers in the top level of our safe. Each has its own key, and we keep one copy here while you take the other copy with you. When I checked after lunch, we only have one drawer left, and I'm sorry to say, there's only one key for that drawer here. I'm not certain what happened to the other copy, but I'd guess the last customer lost it somewhere.'

'That's fine. Bring me the key.'

'Well, that's the thing. I need to keep the last copy of the key here; so you won't actually be able to take a key with you tonight. Do you still want the box?'

'I do.'

O'Reilly opened the door to the lobby, allowing Higgins to enter the area behind the counter near the bank's safe. He indicated a row of drawers inside, each adorned with a slim brass plate, and pointed to the one engraved 17C in short block letters. Handing Higgins the key, he excused himself.

'I'll give you some privacy. If you have trouble with the lock, give a holler and I'll come help you out.' As O'Reilly left the safe, Higgins quickly unlocked the drawer, placed the two items inside and re-locked it with a sense of finality.

The rack of keys from which O'Reilly had taken this one hung on the wall behind the teller's window. The miner stealthily took a key from the hook numbered 12B and secreted the key marked 17C into his vest pocket. 'I'm finished here now,' he called.

O'Reilly came hurriedly out from his office. He quite failed to realise he was returning the wrong key to the rack.

'I'm about through here as well, sir. I have the account established. Here is your account number, and you have a current balance of $17,802. You brought in approximately nine hundred and twelve pounds of refined silver, Mr Higgins.' O'Reilly watched the miner for his reaction: that was an enormous amount of money; when the man failed to respond, he went on cautiously, 'If you don't mind my asking, sir, how did you manage it? How did you get it all here by yourself, across those passes – or do you live in Oro City and work the mines here in the canyon?'

Seconds passed in silence. Setting his jaw, O'Reilly continued with business. 'On the first of each month, we will draw two dollars from the account to cover the rent on your safe deposit drawer. Now, can I get you any cash this evening?'

'No. I'll be back when I need cash,' Higgins said, and his spurs sounded with a rhythmic chime as he turned, left the bank and walked into the coming darkness.

The bank manager sat alone in his rented room above Millie's Tavern. He had money saved, but he was alone. This way he had Millie and Jake Harmon to provide pleasant company in the evening. Women were numerous in Idaho Springs, but most made their living as prostitutes, several right here at Millie's. O'Reilly had not fallen in love with a woman since he moved from out east; unless and until he did, he felt no need to build himself a home.

He generally dined downstairs in the bar, but this evening he had asked Millie to bring a plate to his room so he could finish reading the paper before going to sleep. As he reviewed the news, he came across the linotype of the malevolent beast that was supposedly stalking the mines of Oro City.

Oro City. O'Reilly paused, his hand frozen above a smudged listing of Denver's upcoming social events. There had been *something* about Oro City. Quickly he turned back to the story of the killings in Empire Gulch two weeks earlier. A large cache of silver had disappeared. Could Higgins have made it all the way to Idaho Springs in two weeks? Perhaps he was not alone. He had worn spurs today; O'Reilly had seen them. He must have ridden, and had a partner, or partners, driving the wagon. And he'd been too quiet. He had not talked like most mine workers did when they finally had some time in town – especially those with a large deposit, they always liked to pass the time while he washed and weighed their strike. Jesus, was Higgins that killer? He slowly ran his finger across the raised letters of his new belt buckle. Refined silver. Why keep it in Colorado? Why not head for California, Santa Fe or Kansas City? Why try to sell it here, where it would be under suspicion? And what was in that safe deposit box?

Checking his watch, he saw it was already 10.15 p.m. Late. The silver was locked up and the key to the deposit box was hanging safely on the rack near his office. O'Reilly decided he would contact the sheriff in the morning; tomorrow was time enough to get to the bottom of these strange events. He rubbed his aching thigh and looked out of the window at the falling snow. Tomorrow he could deal with William Higgins.

Just after midnight, Millie Harmon carried whiskey shots to a group of miners squashed around the table. One of them made a joke and she forced herself to laugh, though she did not find the young man particularly funny. He tried to engage her in conversation but she excused herself to get back to the kitchen. As she turned, she saw Gabriel O'Reilly, still in his suit, heading out the front door.

'Gabe,' she called, but he didn't answer. Millie hustled to the door and pushed it open. The snow was coming down hard now; over a foot had fallen in the past three hours, and the gusting wind made the night time seem as though it had a nefarious purpose. Without thinking, she pulled her shawl more closely around her shoulders. O'Reilly was already halfway across the street.

'Gabe,' she called, louder this time, but again he ignored her. Light from the fireplace illuminated snowdrifts through the tavern windows. Millie could see that O'Reilly was wearing gloves, but had no coat or hat. 'You ought to have a coat on, young man,' she yelled after him. 'I'll not be playing nursemaid to one so ignorant as to be out walking out on a night like this.'

Gabriel O'Reilly didn't acknowledge her as he disappeared into the darkness. Funny, Millie thought as she turned back into the smoky heat of the room, but O'Reilly's pronounced limp appeared to have been cured.

RIVEREND PALACE

980 Twinmoons Ago

Tenner Wynne rested his eyes, leaning his head back against the velvet-lined padding of his desk chair. 'Just a short rest,' he promised the empty room. 'I'll get back to work in just a few moments.' It was the middle of the night and he had just come from Prince Danmark's royal apartment on the upper floor of the palace. A barge captain had found the prince wandering along the Estrad River two days after the Grayslip family summit last Twinmoon. Danmark had been struck blind and deaf and driven mad – by what or whom, no one knew. Tenner guessed it had happened on the same day Danmark's father had been felled while addressing his guests in the palace dining hall. Markon's death was believed to have been caused by a virus, although no one, not even the royal physician, had seen its like before. His son's state of health was another matter entirely.

Danmark Grayslip – now Prince Danmark III – had been found stumbling along the river's edge, babbling unintelligibly and waving at invisible demons. He was an unkempt, insane version of his former self, and Tenner could prescribe nothing to bring the young prince relief.

Princess Danae had not left her chambers since her husband's funeral rites. There had been no royal ceremony, no gathering of the Ronan people to bid farewell to their visionary leader. With rumours of imminent war coursing through the Eastlands, Tenner felt a state funeral would be too obvious a target for terrorists hoping to capitalise on any perceived weakness in the royal family.

He had paid the barge captain well to remain silent about Danmark's condition, but the new monarch's failure to surface at any time over the last sixty days hadn't helped. Danae did nothing but sit in her room, her hands folded in her lap, staring out of her window across the palace grounds towards the sea. She was eating barely enough to keep herself alive; at this rate she would soon fall into a coma. Tenner feared she had given up; she might even take her own life. He posted a guard outside her rooms, but Danae had forbidden anyone from entering.

The physician knew he could not remain in Rona much longer. Political stability in Falkan was weakening as well, and he, by default, was now Falkan's prince. Helmat, his nephew, had been found dead with Anis Ferlasa, the Pragan heir, and it was pretty clear to those who found them that Anis had murdered her cousin after an incestuous sexual act and then fallen prey to the same virus that had claimed Markon earlier that evening. The discovery brought additional tension to the already shaky peace between Falkan and Praga. Helmat's mother, Princess Anaria, had committed suicide three days after arriving back in Orindale. She had grieved when Harkan had been killed at sea, but the loss of Helmat as well was too great for Tenner's sister to bear. Now Tenner was left with the Falkan crown, a charge he had never wanted.

He wept silently as he thought of Anaria. If he had gone home with her rather than staying at Riverend to attend to the crisis in Rona she might have found the resilience to hold on, maybe even to take up the reins of government again. Instead he had allowed her to ride north with her dead son in a coffin. She had been a good leader; better, she had been a wonderful mother to his nephews. Tenner realised he had never told her that.

How far had she travelled, alone in her royal coach, before deciding to end her life? Had she crossed the border? Had she seen the Blackstones one last time? Or perhaps she kept the carriage curtains closed for the entire trip. Tenner hoped Anaria had made her decision quickly; he could not bear to think that his sister had spent days contemplating her suicide, days when he could have been with her – when he *should* have been with her. He would never know.

Tenner had not returned to Falkan for Anaria's funeral; his current responsibilities in Rona were far too pressing. He planned to leave within a few days. Then he would make peace with his sister and beg forgiveness from her departed spirit.

*

Some days after the tragic deaths of Princes Markon and Helmat and Princess Anis, Tenner had received word of a massacre at Sandcliff Palace in Gorsk. The details were sketchy, but it appeared there were few – if any – Larion Senators left alive. He had dispatched riders to gather more comprehensive information, but even the swiftest Ronan horsemen would take many days to reach Gorsk. The entire political structure of Praga and the Eastlands was in ruins. The descendants of King Remond I, rulers of four Eldani nations, had been killed off; all that remained of Eldarn's royal family were the Whitwards: Prince Draven, his wife Mernam and their son Marek in Malakasia.

Mistrust was rampant. Border raids had been reported between Rona and Falkan, and several Pragan trade ships had been taken by Falkan battle cruisers on the Ravenian Sea. War was coming, and there were few leaders left to arbitrate in the pending conflict. These circumstances would have been unthinkable a Twinmoon ago; they were why he had elected to stay in Rona until tonight. He had to ensure the continuity of Danmark's family line before the prince succumbed further to his madness.

Tenner needed a commoner so no one would expect her to be carrying Rona's heir. A daughter of one of Rona's wealthy families would never do; her pregnancy would arouse too much suspicion. But he'd been lucky: he had found Regona Carvic, a beautiful sepia-skinned serving girl from Rona's South Coast. He had taken the time to tell her how very important her task was, that she would be the mother of the next Ronan prince, but though obviously intelligent, the young woman was still frightened. He could hardly blame her: there was no way he'd been able to conceal the prince's condition. When he revealed the madness that made it impossible for Danmark III to choose his own wife, the girl began to cry, 'Please, Doctor Tenner, please don't make me do this.'

'I can't make you do it, dear,' he had told her calmly, 'but I need you to help me. We all need you to help us.'

'Is he violent?' she asked, still shaking.

'No. There's no danger. He'll be very gentle,' Tenner assured her, a little unconvinced himself. He repeated, quietly, 'Regona, my dear, this is for the sake of Rona. We need you.'

Regona wiped the tears away and nodded her agreement; she couldn't bring herself to speak.

Tenner had chosen Regona less for her undoubted beauty than for her intelligence. She was remarkably gifted; unlike most of the menial labourers in Estrad, who could neither read nor write, even the common tongue, Regona could do both and, even better, showed an affinity for creative and engaging education. During her infrequent avens away from the kitchens, she told stories, taught writing and made up maths games for the palace children. The offspring of servants and gentry alike regularly begged permission to work with the doe-eyed scullery-maid rather than their classroom teachers. Regona Carvic was special, and Tenner was delighted that she had agreed to participate in his monumental undertaking. He could have ordered her to bear Rona's heir, but Regona's decision not only to conceive, but also to love and care for the infant, would ensure the child's welfare.

As they walked together up the grand staircase to the royal residence, Tenner said, 'I know you would rather not have it happen this way. I know this is a terrible thing to ask of you: it violates one of your most basic freedoms.' She tried to appear brave, forcing a smile at the older man as he continued, 'However, if Danmark dies, Rona's future will be desperately uncertain.' Tenner felt his heart breaking as Regona gave his arm a reassuring squeeze.

'I'll be all right,' she said calmly. She had made her choice and would give herself willingly to the creature – no, the *man*, her prince – waiting upstairs.

Tenner, still guilty, hugged her briefly. 'You are astonishingly brave, Regona, and I am very proud to know you.'

The first time she entered Danmark's chamber, Regona was trembling, her self-assurance draining away. But the prince was not as scary as she had imagined and after their initial coupling, the girl was no longer frightened. He was physically capable of intercourse with her, but apart from a loud, sickening cry with each climax, she did not believe the young monarch knew what was happening.

Every other evening for the next thirty days Tenner led Regona to Danmark's chambers; now, a Moon later, he was confident she carried Danmark's child. He arranged comfortable accommodation for her away from the palace in Estrad. There was too much unrest, too many political machinations and assassination plots, even imminent all-out war; it would not be safe for the child to be born in the palace. Seeing a servant, even one with Regona's talents, being singled out for attention by one of the world's most powerful and influential men would arouse suspicion. No matter how many precautions he took, servants and guards could be bribed. Eventually word would leak out that the South Coast scullery-maid was carrying a Grayslip, King Remond's descendant.

Tenner intended eventually to return from Falkan to share the education of the child. He had remained at Riverend Palace to see his self-appointed task – the continuation of the Ronan line – completed. It might have cost him his sister, but now it was done, and he could go home to attend to the rising unrest in Falkan.

Shaking thoughts of Anaria from his mind, Tenner wrote several lines on a sheet of parchment. Re-reading his notes, he wiped an errant tear from his face and nodded once to himself, grimly determined. He rose, crossed to the fireplace and pulled back and forth on a protruding stone until it came free from the wall. Placing it on the floor near his feet, he folded the parchment into quarters and secreted it in the gap. Groaning a little as he bent down to retrieve the stone, Tenner pushed it back into place until the parchment was completely hidden from view. If you didn't know, it was impossible to see which stone had moved.

A knock on his chamber door woke the doctor from his reverie and he stepped away from the hearth. 'Yes?'

A palace servant entered carrying a tray with a goblet of wine and a small loaf of bread, still warm from the kitchen.

'I thought you might fancy something, sir.' The young man, seeing the physician upset, spoke quickly, shuffling and staring at his feet. 'I mean, I saw you were still awake, sir.'

'Thank you. That was thoughtful of you,' said Tenner, suddenly conscious that he hadn't eaten in a while. 'Would you have some fruit left in the kitchen?'

'Yes, sir. We got some lovely peaches in this morning, sir. Right off the ship and into the scullery,' the man replied. 'I'll get some at once,' he said and hurried from the room.

When he returned, just a short while later, the young servant knocked quietly and, hearing no sound from within, risked opening the door slightly, calling to the doctor as he did, 'I got three of the best for you, sir.' When no answer came, he pushed the door open and stood in the entryway.

The dim glow from two candles and a low fire burning in the fireplace cast a half-light across the doctor's chamber and illuminated Tenner, who had his back to the door. The doctor was on the opposite side of the room, tearing violently at a large tapestry hanging on the wall of his study.

'Can I help you, sir?' the boy asked, stepping forward.

'Get out.' Tenner's voice had changed.

'It just seems like you're struggling with that, sir.' The servant took another step forward.

'Get out, now,' the doctor commanded harshly as the tapestry came loose from the wall and fell across his shoulder. The young servant retreated, failing to notice the doctor igniting the corner of the enormous fabric roll in the fireplace. As flames quickly engulfed the cloth, Tenner threw the burning tapestry towards a shelf of books and watched impassively as they caught fire; he appeared oblivious to the tongues of flame licking their way along one of his sleeves. As he stood in the centre of his room, the fire spread rapidly to the floorboards and ceiling supports. Without uttering a sound, the physician, Falkan's ruling prince, was consumed by fire on the floor of his study.

Outside Riverend Palace a lone rider sat astride a dark horse under the sparse dogwood trees growing along the edge of the palace's neatly manicured grounds. Cloaked in heavy robes, the figure watched as flames spread through the upper floors. Beside him a young couple waited quietly. The man tried to look brave, holding his chin high and his eyes fixed on the fiery devastation. The young woman could not disguise her own nervousness. Wringing a lace kerchief in her hands, she glanced repeatedly over her shoulder into the forest behind them.

Men and women ran from the building, some screaming for help as they worked to extinguish the blaze. The horseman's attention was diverted from those fleeing the palace to an upper-level apartment in which a well-dressed man, coughing and waving violently at the smoke billowing around him threw open the casement of a stained-glass window. One of the windows shattered against the outer wall of the palace and slammed back into place, hitting the man in the forearm and lacerating him deeply. The screaming victim appeared not to notice as he babbled, frightened: the rider could not understand a word. Seeing no rescue in sight, the horseman raised one hand towards the broken window and whispered, 'Rest now, Prince Danmark.'

A sudden change came over the trapped madman. As flames leapt up behind him, Prince Danmark III, monarch of Rona, ran a bloody hand through his hair, pulling the wild, unkempt strands from his pallid face. For just a moment his eyes seemed to focus on the Estrad River in the distance and he appeared to see clearly once again. He took a long, deep breath and stood tall, then he jumped from his window, awkwardly turning in the air until he crashed headlong through the burning roof of the livery below.

Turning to the couple, the horseman said, 'Come. We haven't much time.'

The young woman moved towards him as she pleaded, 'Sir, won't you come with us? I would feel so much—'

'Don't touch me,' the rider commanded, then softened and added, 'You will be fine, but we must go now.'

Prince Draven's body lay in state in the Malakasian capital city of Pellia as thousands of citizens paraded slowly by his ornate, etched-glass coffin in the Whitward family tomb, paying last respects to their ruler.

Draven had collapsed suddenly several days earlier while riding north along the Welstar River. His attendants had rushed the elderly man to the palace doctors, but they had been too late: though the most skilful healers in Malakasia had worked through the night, the prince died at dawn. His body showed no sign of violence or disease, save for a small injury to his left hand. The doctors guessed that Draven had been killed by the same dreadful virus that had taken the Ronan Prince Markon's life.

Draven's body was conveyed in the royal barge from Welstar Palace, then carried from the river in a sombre procession to the city centre. His corpse would lie in state for ten full days, time enough for mourners to make their way to Pellia and bid farewell to the fallen leader.

Many brought gifts, final offerings for their prince: loaves of bread, fruits, tanned hides and wool tunics were left on the casket to ensure Draven's passage into the eternal care of Eldarn's Northern Forest gods.

Marek Whitward, Draven's heir and now Prince Marek, ignored the rumours of unrest and kept silent vigil, standing at his father's side and staring into the distance, day after day. Dressed in black boots, black leggings and a black tunic with the family's golden crest on his breast, Draven's only son looked far too young to take on the challenges he would face in the coming Twinmoons. Sometimes he could not help himself, weeping silently, though it was inappropriate for the Malakasian people to see their new leader shedding tears in public. Across the city, concerned people, commoners, merchants and gentry alike, described what a heart-wrenching experience it had been for them to witness Marek waiting with his father's body, as if he could reanimate the fallen prince by sheer will alone.

On the sixth day, as Marek arrived to continue his lonely watch over the casket, he seemed a little different. Rather than staring straight ahead, as he had previously, Marek watched the parade of mourners filing past the elaborate floral arrangement ringing Prince Draven's coffin. Rumours flew about the village square: the young prince had made sexually inappropriate comments to numerous women in the procession, and had even taken a loaf of bread from the top of his father's coffin and begun eating it. He no longer wore the gold family crest, but he had added black leather gloves to his already dark wardrobe. On the morning of the seventh day, the prince did not appear at his father's side at all.

SUMNER LAKE, COLORADO

July 1979

Michael Wilson checked the flow of air from his regulator and pulled bulky flippers onto his feet. He waited, but Tim Stafford wasn't ready yet. 'C'mon Tim, hurry up,' he said impatiently as he dangled his feet from the dock. It was hot in the mountains today, but the water would be cold in Sumner Lake; it always was. He was glad to have a full wetsuit. Tim wore a wetsuit as well, but unlike Michael, the younger boy did not wear a hood – he said it made his mask flood. Michael always wished he could bear the cold like Tim could, but he couldn't stand the icy temperature against his skin. Although still in middle school, the two boys had been diving since the previous summer when both decided to give up riding the bench week after week at soccer games. Their mothers sat together on the beach near the dock, reading and gossiping.

The lake was one of their favourite dive sites. It was stream-fed and crystal-clear for much of the summer, so a diver could see further than fifty feet, even in the deepest areas, and there were plenty of sites to visit along the bottom. Back in the 1960s a small plane had crashed and had never been recovered from the lake's floor. Michael and Tim didn't know if anyone had been killed, but it was great fun to visit the broken sections of the aircraft. There were several rock outcroppings that were excellent places to find and dislodge lost fishing lures, and periodically they would come across a camera, a pocketknife and other cool items accidentally dropped in the water.

The best part about diving in Sumner Lake was the mining equipment that littered the bottom. The lake, created as a reservoir for Denver-area homes, covered an area mined by gold and silver prospectors more than a hundred years earlier. Michael's teacher had told him there were flooded mine shafts too, but the boys hadn't found any yet – secretly, Michael was glad: he knew fearless Tim would dive headlong into the flooded shafts, while he would be plagued by thoughts of iridescent spirits, ungainly, crippled fish and thick tangles of slippery weeds that would cling to his ankles and hold him prisoner inside the inky darkness for ever.

Scattered across the lake bottom were the remains of miners' shacks and pieces of abandoned equipment, most far too large for the boys ever to haul to the surface. Sometimes they would find a hand tool, a lost boot or some silverware left behind when the mines were flooded. Along with their visits to the aeroplane and their search for lost fishing lures, the boys combed the lake floor in search of mining artefacts. Mr Meyers, the old man who owned the antique store around the corner from Tim's house, paid them a few dollars for anything of value they brought to his shop.

'Just push the clamp down and you're done,' Michael directed impatiently. Tim, who was small and not very strong, struggled with the clamp attaching his scuba tank to the buoyancy compensator. 'Let me help you,' he said finally, pulling his feet from the water and struggling to stand.

'I can do it,' Tim grunted as he pushed hard to close the clamp around the tank. 'See? Let's go.'

'Okay, where should we head?' Tim had virtually memorised the lake floor.

'Forty feet for sixty minutes,' Tim suggested. 'We'll swim over near the big rocks where those guys are fishing and then cover the flats to the plane. We can head back this way when we hit five hundred pounds.'

'That's cool. Maybe we'll find some lures or something.' Michael spat into his mask to mitigate fogging, then, holding the mask and tank, he rolled from the dock into the water. He tucked his face down onto his chest as he felt the icy water rush into his wetsuit between his hood and the back of his jacket. That was always the worst moment, until his body temperature warmed the thin layer of water between his skin and the neoprene; in just a few seconds he felt quite comfortable, despite the cold. He looked up when he heard a splash and watched as Tim leapt feet-first into the lake, then adjusted his facemask and kicked towards the bottom.

Fifty minutes later, Michael motioned to Tim: five minutes before they needed to head back to the dock. Tim was playing outside the fuselage of the aeroplane, pretending to pilot it like a submarine through the depths of Sumner Lake. They had found two fishing lures and seventy-five cents near the rock outcropping about a hundred yards west of the aeroplane; Tim was thrilled with their discovery and Michael could hear him yelling, even through his regulator. Their find had been followed by a long swim to the crash site across the area Tim called 'the flats', a stretch of barren ground with nothing but sand, rocks and a few plants dotting the brown expanse. Tim waved once and headed out across the flats towards the dock. He was the faster swimmer; Michael put his head down and kicked as hard as he could to keep up.

They were halfway across when something caught Michael's eye. It looked like a starfish half-buried in the sand, glinting momentarily in the sun. Michael stopped and waited for the sand to settle before he reached for the small star-shaped object. It resisted his initial tug and Michael realised the buried item was larger than it first looked. As he pulled harder, the strangely shaped metal object came free in a cloud of silt. He raised his find to his facemask: a spur. He shouted for Tim, but his friend was already out of range. As he polished the edge with his thumb, Michael could make out the letters 'US' etched gracefully onto the side near where the spur attached to a boot heel.

This was a great find, the best treasure the two divers had ever pulled from Sumner Lake. The letters carved into the metal meant it must have come from a soldier or a cavalry rider. Michael could barely contain himself as he continued searching the sandy bottom, hoping to uncover more – Mr Meyers would surely give them at least five dollars for the single spur, but if he found its mate they'd be worth much more. He checked his pressure gauge, and saw he had only two hundred PSI left in his tank. Looking around, he made a mental note of the spot: he and Tim would come back the following weekend.

Michael was running his hand through the sand one last time when he saw the key. It didn't look like an ordinary key: it was long and flat, with two differently shaped teeth protruding from both sides of one end. It had the letters BIS etched into one side, the number 17C carved into the other. This would be one for Mr Meyers' key jar, the huge glass jar the old man claimed his great-grandfather had used for making pickles in Austria in the 1800s. Today it held hundreds of keys, many of them fitting antique locks, like those in the cabinets and wooden chests for sale in Mr Meyers' shop. Others were thrown into the jar in exchange for a wish. 'They are the keys to the known world,' Mr Meyers told all who asked. 'If you make a wish when you drop one in, it will always come true.' Michael was too old to believe such fairy stories, but Tim loved to drop keys into the enormous jar.

Michael slipped his latest find inside his wetsuit, gripped the spur like a recovered national treasure and swam hurriedly to the dock.

IDAHO SPRINGS, COLORADO

Last Fall

Steven Taylor walked slowly across Miner Street to the entrance of the First National Bank of Idaho Springs. Steven had few physical characteristics that would make a passer-by take more than a cursory glance in his direction. Slightly shorter than average, he was green-eyed, with a shock of unruly brown hair. He was pale, more from genetics than any aversion to sunlight; rather than tanning he slid gradually from the cold ivory he sported in winter to the alternating blotchy pinks and deep sunburned reds of summer.

His face was a battlefield between worry wrinkles creasing his forehead and laugh lines tugging at the corners of his close-set eyes and surprisingly delicate mouth. He was attractive to the few women who knew him well, more for his wit than his physique, though, as an avid weekend sportsman, he was in good physical condition – and this despite his poor eating habits. Steven's clothes appeared to have been borrowed from two people: one a thickset man with low, slat-sided hips and the other a lean athlete with a penchant for overworking his arms, shoulders and upper body.

It was 7.45 a.m. as Steven fished in his coat pocket for keys to the front door. He'd been holding a pile of files in one hand and a cup of coffee in the other and was forced to put the paper cup in his mouth, gripping the edge firmly with his teeth as he dug through the pockets of his wool blazer. Looking up towards the mountains above Clear Creek Canyon he could see the yellow leaves of the intermittent aspens, now fully changed from their spring green. They dotted the hillsides among the hegemonic green expanse of the Ponderosa pines. Autumn came early to the canyon. The coming winter would be another long one. *I've got to get out of here*, he thought, then laughed at himself: *I think that every morning.*

'Hello, Steven,' Mrs Winter called. She was sweeping the sidewalk in front of her pastry shop next door and stopped to offer a quick wave.

'Good morning,' he answered, his voice muffled by the cup, and burned his upper lip in the attempt. 'Ouch, damnit.' Steven dropped the coffee cup onto the sidewalk, splashing his shoes.

'How's Mark this morning?' Mrs Winter asked, ignoring the coffee accident.

'He's fine, Mrs W,' Steven answered. 'He's teaching the Stamp Act today . . . was up late last night working on some way to make it a bit more palatable for the kids.' Mark Jenkins was Steven's roommate; he taught US and world history at Idaho Springs High School.

'Oh, that's exciting: one of the causes of the Revolutionary War. Tell him I said keep up the good work.' Mrs Winter had known Steven since he was a boy, when his family moved to Idaho Springs. Her pastry shop was one of many local businesses kept afloat by tourists stopping for gas off the interstate. Not many people visited Idaho Springs for more than a few hours; the local LATGO and Sidney mines did not draw many from the masses who rushed by on their way to the ski resorts of Breckenridge, Vail or Aspen.

Steven had started working in the bank after completing his MBA at the University of Denver. He was a bright, successful graduate student, and he'd been headhunted by a number of investment firms from San Francisco, New York and Chicago – but he had procrastinated too long and lost out on several lucrative positions. He put it down to fate and bad luck and climbed back up Clear Creek Canyon to take the assistant bank manager's job for a year; he planned to accept the next decent offer that came his way. That was three years ago. Now he couldn't remember why he had hesitated to accept the jobs when they had been offered. He didn't love the bank business or investment fields, certainly not the way Mark loved teaching. He studied business because he knew it would pay well, but it didn't inspire him to study further, or to explore the nuances of financial theory in action. Actually, he could remember very little that inspired him that much – so he wasn't really surprised when he found himself still here, still home, after three years. Steven never actively sought inspiration; he expected it to come one day, in a great metaphysical epiphany. He would wake one morning and find his calling waiting for him with the morning paper. It hadn't shown up yet, and here he was, as usual, opening the bank at 8.oo a.m., although this time with no coffee and stained shoes.

To make matters worse, today was going to be especially dismal. His boss, the estimable Howard Griffin, had directed him to oversee a complete audit of all open account files – some going back as far as the bank's original customers in the 1860s. Steven had started the job the previous day; he anticipated a great deal of tedious secretarial work with little reward.

'You've got leadership potential, Steven. I want to see you taking on more projects like this in the future,' the bank manager had told him with enthusiasm.

But Steven was finding the assignment was disillusioning him even further, increasing his distaste for a career in finance.

'Who could be inspired by *this?*' he said to himself as he switched on the lights and crossed the lobby floor to the aged pine window and counter top.

Pushing the stack of files through his window, he re-crossed the lobby and switched on the illumination for the display case hanging on the opposite wall. It held grainy photographs showing mine workers, and some hand tools found in the LATGO mines on the northern wall of Clear Creek Canyon, as well as the original ownership papers for the bank, a photo of Lawrence Chapman, the founder, and several pages of accounting ledgers from the original books. Steven rarely considered the items, but he was glad customers had something to look at while they waited in line.

The condition of his shoes this morning made him pause and consider one photo, of Lawrence Chapman and a bank employee. The man wore a uniform with awkward-looking boots, a frilly white shirt, suspenders and a large belt buckle with the letters BIS clearly visible on the front.

'Well, my shoes may be wet and smell of cappuccino, but at least I'm not wearing that get-up,' Steven said, wandering towards his office.

Checking his e-mail, Steven found a message from Jeffrey Simmons, the doctoral student in Denver who shared Steven's only real passion, abstract mathematics concepts.

'You work in a bank, dress like a philosophy professor from the '50s, and you love abstract maths. I'm surprised you don't have to beat the women away with a slide rule,' Mark would tease him.

Even though his roommate couldn't appreciate the beauty of calculus or the genius of a good algorithm, Steven liked Mark immensely; the two had shared an apartment ever since Steven had returned to Idaho Springs. To Steven, Mark Jenkins was the perfect history teacher: he possessed an enormous body of knowledge and had a razor-sharp wit. He thought Mark was the most knowledgeable and quick-thinking person he knew – not that he would ever admit that to Mark.

Jeff Simmons, on the other hand, fully understood the joy of a complex equation: the mathematician often sent Steven problems to consider and solve in an infuriatingly uncomfortable deductive paradigm. This morning's message was no exception. It read: 'You use them both every day but probably have never considered why the numbers on your cellular telephone and your calculator are organised differently.' Steven was about to pull a calculator from his desk drawer when he heard the bell above the lobby door chime as someone entered the bank.

'Stevie?' Howard Griffin, at only 8.10 a.m.? He was early this morning, which meant he hadn't taken time to exercise on his Stairmaster before leaving for work. Steven smiled at the irony of anyone owning a stair machine while living in Idaho Springs: the entire city was constructed on an incline at 7,500 feet above sea level, with mountains on either side of Clear Creek Canyon rising to over 12,000 feet. He liked to think Griffin had lost some sort of bet with the Devil and had to climb his eternal stairway, a corpulent, baby-boom Sisyphus, rather than just go outside for a walk each morning, but he knew better. Griffin had moved to Boulder from New Jersey in the 1960s. When he discovered the decade would not last for ever, he enrolled in the University of Colorado, completed his degree and moved to Idaho Springs to become manager of the small town's bank.

Now, at fifty-five, Griffin was bald and had a burgeoning paunch that he battled every morning as he climbed Colorado's highest peak, the Mount Griffin Stairmaster. His commitment to exercise was admirable, but he had a weakness that regularly bested his determination to regain the thinness of his youth: Howard Griffin loved beer, and most afternoons would find him propping up the bar at Owen's Pub on Miner Street. Steven sometimes accompanied him, and Mark would join them for a few beers or the occasional dinner.

'Stevie?' the bank manager called again, and Steven moved into the lobby to greet his boss.

'Good morning, Howard. How are you?'

'Never mind that. I'm fine, thanks, but never mind that,' Griffin often thought faster than he could speak. 'Myrna called last night and can't be in today. She's sick or something. So I've had to come and cover. How's the audit coming?'

'It's fine. I have all the active accounts pulled. There are thousands of them, by the way. I'll get through many of the oldest today, because most of those haven't had much in the way of transactions since they were opened. They've made enough interest to cover the monthly fees, so the cash just sits there.'

'Great. Stay on it. I'll work the window and we can check in over lunch later. How's Owen's for you?'

'That'll be fine, Howard. I'll appreciate the break.' Steven returned to his office, retrieved the keys to the basement and braced himself for a long, tedious morning.

'Take a look at these.' Steven had brought several pages of notes to lunch. 'We have twenty-nine accounts that haven't had a single transaction in the past twenty-five years. Most of them are forgotten accounts, people who have died. Thankfully, I have information on next of kin from the original applications. But eight of them appear to be accounts for single men killed in the Second World War, and, get this, five accounts date back to the late 1800s – one of which had one deposit and no additional transactions.'

'I'm not surprised,' Griffin said between long draws on an enormous draught beer. 'It was probably some miner who went back to work and got himself killed, got his claim jumped or something. It was a rough time back then. But those assets are among the reasons this bank survived the depression – those and the molybdenum mines.'

'That's not the worst of it, Howard,' Steven interrupted. 'This account had only one deposit, but it was a deposit of more than $17,000. That was *nine hundred pounds* of refined silver. The bank made a bundle on the silver sale alone, because they screwed the guy for over ten cents an ounce off the market price.' Steven paused to take a bite of a thick Reuben sandwich. Continuing with his mouth full, he added, 'This is the part that doesn't make sense. What mining company sends a guy in with nine hundred pounds of silver, lets him take a loss of ten cents an ounce, and then never comes back for the cash? To top it off, he wasn't even from the Springs. This guy was from Oro City. I don't even know where that is.'

'Was, Stevie, was. Oro City was Leadville, but they changed the name in 1877. You're right, though, something's crooked. There were banks in Oro City then, so what was this guy doing over here?' Griffin finished his beer and motioned for Gerry, the bartender, to draw him another. 'You want one more?'

'Jeez, no, Howard. It's only 12.20; I have to go back to work.'

'Well, I often question my own behaviour, but I'm still having one more before we go. Anyway, this account, what's the big deal? Some miner hits it big – huge – drops off most of his haul at the bank, takes a handful of silver with him to the pub, flashes it around, drinks too much hooch and gets himself killed. It happened all the time, I would guess.' Griffin rubbed a French fry around his plate, sopping up hamburger grease.

'The big deal, Howard, is that a $17,000 deposit made in our bank in October of 1870 is now worth more than 6.3 million dollars. It's just sitting there, and the guy didn't list any family or next of kin. So I can't call anyone to say their ship has just come in and docked here in the Rocky Mountain foothills.' He was about to continue when he was distracted for a moment by an attractive young woman who entered the pub and joined a group of friends in a booth near the back. He shook his head wryly and turned back to his boss. 'Anyway, the thing I have to ask you is that this guy, this William Higgins, well, he—'

As Steven lost track of his question, Griffin interrupted, 'Go say something to her. You don't get out enough. She's a pretty girl and you aren't getting any younger. How old are you now, twenty-seven? Twenty-eight? Soon you'll be old and ugly like me, and I'll be fried and eaten before I see you get old and ugly like me.'

'No, maybe another time.' Steven paused. He hadn't been seriously involved with a woman since university. He dated from time to time, but had never found anyone he felt was the right match for him. He grinned at his boss. 'Well, anyway, this guy had a safe deposit box, number 17C, in the old safe. I was thinking, if we looked in his drawer, we might find some clue as to who his family is or was and we could let them know this account exists.'

'No way.'

'Why not? It may be the only way to get this resolved.'

'No. It's bank policy. They put it in there. They pay the rent on the drawer. We leave it alone until they get back.'

'Yeah, I understand, but think about this for a minute. What do you put into a safe deposit box?' Steven asked rhetorically. 'Something you expect to retrieve in your lifetime. You certainly don't put anything in there that you don't plan on your grandchildren or even your great-grandchildren ever having. This guy meant to come back for this stuff, whatever it is. Anything we don't plan on retrieving for a hundred and thirty-five years, we throw in the trash. We don't ensure its safety in a bank.'

'No way. They put it in there in good faith. We take the $12.95 a month from his account. The drawer stays locked in good faith. It's good business practice, Stevie. Our customers have to trust us.'

'Trust us? This guy is deader than disco, and if he has any family they might want to know that they're worth a fortune in accumulated interest.'

'Sorry.' Griffin finished the last of his beer, a light foam moustache outlining his upper lip. 'I don't write the policies,' he said wryly, 'but I will buy lunch.'

Dusk came early to Idaho Springs as the sun disappeared behind the mountain peaks lining the west end of Clear Creek Canyon. It was 5.15 p.m., and already Steven could see its last rays shining in tapered rectangles across the floor. He switched on his desk lamp and took one last look through William Higgins's account ledger. Monthly deductions for rent of the safe deposit box were the only noted transactions since the day Higgins opened the account in October, 1870. Although fees for the deposit box had increased over time, the compounded interest was more than enough to cover the cost. It was a forgotten account, the fees deducted as a matter of course without anyone checking to see if Higgins or his heirs had ever done business with the bank again. Steven looked up from his desk. A doorway led through to Griffin's office and beyond that to the bank lobby. On the far wall, a collection of safe deposit keys, more museum artefacts than tools, hung on a small rack. There were three rows of twenty drawers in the old safe, though only forty-seven keys remained. Thirteen had been lost in the years since Lawrence Chapman brought the Bowles and Michaelson safe from Washington, D.C. in the 1860s, and twelve of those drawers now sat empty.

The safe had come from an English steamship that had piled up on a muddy shoal several miles downriver from Chapman's Alexandria home. Chapman, ever the entrepreneur, had bought salvage rights, stripped the ship to the beam supports and sold much of her rigging to a local shipwright. He hadn't been able to part with the old safe, however, so he arranged to bring it along as he worked his way west to open the first Bank of Idaho Springs.

As Steven stood examining the remaining keys he wondered about William Higgins. Had he met Lawrence Chapman that day in 1870? Had Chapman been the one to convince the miner to deposit his silver rather than taking it to the assay office? And what was in that safe deposit box? Steven, angry at Griffin's intransigence, was certain it held information that would lead to Higgins's family; he was determined to see it opened.

An empty hook hung from the rack under 17C. Steven thought for a moment about picking the lock – it surely couldn't be that difficult – but he would have to do it quickly, because Griffin would see him disappear into the safe on the security screens in his office. He could claim to be cleaning the inside of the safe, dusting or sweeping it out. Yes, that was it; that was his ticket in. He would just have to find time to study the locking device first. He could stay late one night, slip in, open the drawer and be out before Griffin was any wiser. It would work. He just needed a bit of time to—

Steven caught himself. 'My God, Steven, what are you thinking?' He ran a hand across his brow and felt beads of perspiration emerging from above his hairline. 'Let this go. You're going to be the only overqualified, maths-loving MBA ever to get fired from an assistant manager's position at a small town bank.'

He pursed his lips, reached out and turned the hook marked 17C one hundred and eighty degrees and said, 'There, now nothing would hang from it, anyway.' Steven donned his jacket, grabbed his briefcase and left the bank thinking about telephones and calculators. William Higgins's account was safe, and his deposit box would remain locked in good faith.

THE FORBIDDEN FOREST

Last Twinmoon

Garec Haile stalked the deer from downwind. He had tethered his mare, Renna, near a pool in the Estrad River, two hundred paces south of the meadow. Despite the thickness of the underbrush, he made little sound and the deer continued feeding peacefully among the tall grasses growing along the edge of the field. He had already nocked an arrow, but his chances of making a shot from this position were slim. He needed to get closer without spooking the animal: another ten or fifteen paces would be enough. Garec was lean and tall, and had to work to stay low enough, avoiding the sharp brambles. His strong legs and lower back, toughened by Twinmoons of hard riding, helped him hug the ground as he noiselessly approached his unsuspecting target.

The morning sunlight illuminated most of the meadow, but Garec's copse remained dark. A few moments more and he would have a clear shot. He was still some forty paces from the edge of the meadow, but that range meant a certain kill for the skilled bowman. He practised often, far more than Sallax or even Versen: that's how he had earned his nickname, the Bringer of Death – with avens and avens of practice. Few bowmen in Eldarn could match the young archer for speed and accuracy. A breeze blew from behind the deer and he was reminded the southern Twinmoon was coming soon. Far in the distance he imagined he could hear the sound of huge waves crashing into the Ronan coast.

Garec grinned, despite his efforts to remain still. He was in his element: Sallax would eat his words tonight when Garec served up fresh venison tenderloin. Sallax was convinced no hunter could penetrate the forbidden forest south of the river and actually bring out a deer without being captured by Malagon's forces, but Garec had been crossing into the forest for much of his life: he *knew* he could.

He had considered everything as he planned for this morning's hunt, even memorising the patrol schedule along the north bank of the river. He was sure the Malakasian soldiers knew Ronan locals regularly made their way into the forbidden region; periodically they hanged a poacher as an example, but a lot of the occupation officers frequently looked the other way. This morning's problem was not getting into the forest, but getting out with a large deer strapped across Renna's back. Garec reckoned if he could cross below the cliffs at Danae's Eddy, he could be back at the tavern by the midday aven. He stretched out long under a low-hanging branch and for a moment lost sight of the deer. As he rose on the other side, he found his quarry and took aim along the shaft of the arrow. He drew a slow, shallow breath and steadied for the kill. He could not afford to be tracking a wounded deer all over the forbidden forest; this had to be a clean shot.

The attack was sudden, and came from three sides. Grettans! Garec gasped and dropped face-first onto the ground in the thicket. Grettans this far south, that was *impossible*! He fought the urge to turn and run back the way he had come, and silently promised himself he would never again approach any quarry except from downwind. The closest grettan had been crouching in the underbrush just a few paces away: if Garec had approached from the southern side of the field, he would be dead already. Now he had to get back to Renna – he prayed to all the gods of the Northern Forest she was still alive. There was no way he could outrun a grettan, even over the few hundred paces back to his horse.

Garec stole a quick look towards the meadow where several of the beasts were tearing into the deer's corpse. As large as farm horses, grettans had powerful legs, enormous paws spiked with deadly claws and huge mouths with razor-sharp fangs, perfect for gripping their prey while they tore away strips of flesh with their forelegs. Their dense fur was black. Small ears jutted from their large heads, and their broad faces had horse-like nostrils and small black eyes set wide apart. Grettans rippled with thick muscle: they had few predators in the wild.

Garec counted eight of the beasts in and around the meadow, the largest of which was a bull looming over the deer carcase. The unfortunate animal was stripped clean in a matter of moments; bloody, steaming entrails had been cast about the thicket.

How could he possibly have missed grettan tracks – had he been too busy planning his escape from the forest? Forcing the questions from his mind, Garec focused on the problem at hand. He had to remain calm while he made his way, as silently as possible, back to Renna. She was fast: they had a good chance of escape if he could actually get to her.

He painstakingly backed out of the thicket, careful not to break any dry branches or rustle the early autumn leaves already strewn beneath his feet. He was sweating hard despite the cool morning breeze and the stinging sweat irritated his eyes. His legs and lower back tightened, near to cramping, and he was forced to stop for several moments, awkwardly tucked beneath the branches of a wild raspberry bush, while he waited for his muscles to relax. It was fear. He knew it. He took several deep breaths and willed his heart to stop pounding and to fall back into place somewhere beneath his throat. Rutting whores: grettans *here*? What in all demonpissing nightmares were they doing here?

Garec was soon free of the thicket and forced himself to walk, not run, through the forest towards the river. Ahead he could see Renna still tethered near the shallow pool, her nostrils flaring: she sensed the grettans nearby. Impatient with Garec's tediously slow return, she pawed nervously at the ground.

'Easy girl, easy,' Garec soothed. 'We're going to be fine.' He was less than twenty paces from her when Renna let out a sharp whinny. The young hunter felt his blood freeze. A demon scream echoed from the meadow, followed by the sound of the grettan pack crashing through the underbrush.

'Rutting dogs,' he yelled, sprinting the last few paces and leaping into the saddle, 'let's go, Rennie, let's get out of here.'

Danae's Eddy was a short distance east, near a lazy bend in the Estrad River. The cliffs there might provide an escape, if only Renna could outrun the grettan pack for a few moments.

Garec had only seen grettans once before, on a hunting trip to northern Falkan; he'd never tried to outrun one. He knew they were fast: there were stories of the largest grettans easily chasing down horses on the Falkan plains. Renna was galloping flat out now, and it took all Garec's concentration to help guide her along the riverbank. The sun was fully out, but the heavy morning dew had yet to dry from ferns and tree limbs along the trail and Garec's boots and leggings were soaking wet. Looking down at his soggy legs, Garec suddenly had an idea – if they could make it to Danae's Eddy before Renna was hamstrung.

The fastest grettans were close on her heels now; Garec could hear their hungry snarling behind the thud of the mare's hooves. Praying Renna could keep up her pace without his guiding hand, he turned halfway in the saddle and fired an arrow at a large bull that was snapping viciously at her flanks. It struck the beast in the neck, but didn't appear to slow him at all. Garec nocked and fired again, and again pierced the large bull's throat – but even with two arrows in its neck, the enormous creature was still making up ground against the tiring horse.

It was a heroic flight as Renna pounded through the brush, but Garec could feel her slowing beneath him. A smaller grettan came up fast and, leaping, managed to get a paw onto Renna's hindquarter. The horse screamed a desperate whinny but maintained her stride, though blood was flowing from her torn hide. Garec briefly felt rage eclipse his terror. He looked ahead, hoping to spot any low-hanging branches, but, seeing none, he stood in the stirrups, turned nearly all the way around and fired at the smaller grettan. The arrow took the snarling monster in the head just above one eye. Garec spared a moment to thank the gods he had brought his longbow rather than the smaller forest bow, otherwise he'd never have got through the animal's thick skull. The arrow sank deep in the grettan's head and stopped it dead in mid-stride. Four of the slower grettans abruptly gave up the pursuit when they saw one of their own collapse; the coterie of fangs and claws fell upon the still-twitching corpse and began tearing away large pieces of its flesh. Scratching and clawing at one another with blood-soaked paws, the cannibal beasts vied for position over the mangled carcase of their fallen brother.

There were still two grettans continuing the pursuit, and Garec began to despair of reaching the cliffs.

Then he saw them through the trees, perhaps two hundred paces out.

The mossy rocks would still be wet with morning dew, and

there was a razor-thin dirt trail leading across the expansive outcropping that narrowed into thin switchbacks leading down to the deepest part of the river. The huge bull with the arrows in its throat swiped at Renna and managed to tear one of Garec's saddlebags from the mare's back. Two rabbits and a ring-necked pheasant fell to the trail and the last of the smaller grettans stopped to enjoy a less animated meal, but the injured bull continued after the fleeing mare.

When Renna burst from the treeline atop the cliffs, the grettan was running astride her, timing its leap onto the horse's neck. Garec pulled a hunting knife from his belt, hoping to ram it as far into the animal's chest as possible when the inevitable attack came. Seeing the trail at last, he focused his concentration on guiding Renna along it while the grettan paced them on the damp rocks.

It worked. The creature lost its footing for a moment, time enough for Renna to gain those critical few paces on the drooling beast. Stealing another quick look back, Garec saw that the bull had started down the dirt trail leading towards the cliffs. There would be no time to take the precipitously terraced switchbacks down to the river; the turns were too steep.

'We're going to have to jump for it, Rennie,' Garec shouted to the mare, who seemed to understand. She lowered her head and, with her last strength, ran without slowing off the edge of the cliffs. The grettan, close behind, also leaped into the morning air.

Danae's Eddy had been formed by several large rocks below the surface on the north bank of the Estrad. Right at the point where the river made a lazy turn south, the submerged formation forced the water's flow back on itself and carved a deep pool from bank to bank.

In the vivid morning sunlight Garec could see the rocks, a russet blur beneath the surface, and feared for a moment that Renna's momentum would carry them too far and they would land on that inhospitable bed – but as they began to fall, he realised they would barely clear the rocks and trees on the south bank beneath them. He flailed his arms and legs in an effort to get off Renna and as far from the mare as possible before they hit the water; he was still pulling at imaginary lifelines when they did. Although the fall was not great, the impact was powerful enough to force the air from his lungs as he plunged deep beneath the surface.

Gasping for breath, Garec clawed for the north bank. He could see Renna well ahead of him; by the way she was moving it looked as if she had come through the fall unscathed. He was not as certain about himself. His ribs hurt and he could already tell he'd damaged his right knee.

'Relax,' Garec told himself, in an effort to calm down, 'you'll be fine. Just relax.' The hunter allowed the current to carry him a short distance downstream while he caught his breath; when he looked back, he could see the grettan struggling onto the south bank and up the cliff trail, the twin arrows askew in the monster's neck. The bull stopped several times to face the river and scream, an unholy cry that chilled Garec, even though he knew that thanks to the grace of the gods of the Northern Forest, they had made it out of harm's way.

Renna had clambered out of the river and was trotting along the bank, anticipating where he would come ashore; she gave him a knowing toss of her head as she sidled gracefully towards the water. Favouring his ribs and sore knee, Garec began swimming for the distant bank.

The almor waited silently on the south bank of the Estrad River. It had observed the young man's flight through the forest, and the small herd of unshapely black beasts that pursued him; now it watched as the snarling, frothing creatures returned. Several stopped to drink from the shallow pool while others went back to the bloody remains of the fallen deer. The almor's hunger was maddening. It had been summoned early that day by a bold and powerful force, and its mission was clear. The hunt would soon begin, but first it needed to feed, to replenish its energy and to gather knowledge of the surrounding forest.

The largest of the beasts, the great bull that had nearly captured and killed the young man, struggled to the pool for a drink. Two of the man's projectile weapons were lodged in the animal's throat and it would soon fall from loss of blood. Several of the other creatures waited nearby, ready to attack the large male as soon as they were certain death was imminent. The almor did not wait for them. Stepping into the river, it shimmered for a moment, then melted away. An instant later, the bull grettan stiffened sharply, as if struck by a seizure, and then collapsed on the muddy riverbank. While the others prepared to leap on their fallen leader, the grettan's eyes sank back in its skull, its coat turned a light shade of grey and its great mass expanded slightly before shrivelling down to an ashen shell. The grettan was gone, sucked completely dry in a matter moments by the starving almor. Garec's arrows, a skeleton and a wrinkled, leathery putrefying husk were all that remained of the great beast.

THE FIRST NATIONAL BANK
OF IDAHO SPRINGS

'I don't get why it has to be a square unit,' Myrna said as the door closed behind the only customer to visit the bank that morning. 'I mean, wouldn't they have measured the area of a circle in circular units? Isn't a circle a perfect shape?'

'Yes, but it isn't the right shape for area, and the Egyptians knew that,' Steven answered from his office. 'Anyone who dealt with the area of regular and irregularly shaped polygons had to come to the conclusion that area would best be measured in units that could accommodate the angles inherent in their buildings, towns, fields, or whatever.' He outlined the corner of his leather desk blotter with a fingertip. 'So they decided on a square, because circular units don't interlock, nor do they fit into corners. Squares were easy to conceptualise and, having four equal sides, they were easier to use.' He paused for a moment, considering what he had said, and went on, 'At least I *think* that's the way it worked out.'

Steven had received another maths quandary that morning from Jeff Simmons and had shared it with Myrna Kessler, his colleague; it was one way to pass time at work. He had already figured out an answer, but teased Myrna as she struggled to piece hers together. Myrna was a self-proclaimed 'mathsophobe' – she was going to study liberal arts or humanities once she'd saved enough money for college. She'd graduated from Idaho Springs High School three years earlier, but her parents weren't able to help finance a degree.

The bank manager refused to play along with Steven and Myrna unless the problems dealt with compound interest or real estate speculation. 'I had a maths concepts class for a year in high school,' Griffin told them, 'and I still don't know what the hell that class was about. Derivatives – what the hell's a derivative when it's at home?'

'We'll tackle that one tomorrow, Howard,' Steven promised. 'Today we're dealing with the Ancient Egyptians.'

Steven read the e-mailed problem aloud to Myrna: 'Ancient Egyptian architects established the height of the pyramids using the diameter of a circle whose area equalled that of the square footprint at the pyramid's base. How did they calculate the diameter's length?'

'You know, all this maths problem stuff makes you look like a geek,' she said. 'You need to find another hobby.'

'He *is* a geek, and he's found the perfect geek hobby. Leave him alone.' Griffin's voice resounded from somewhere inside his office.

'I am not a geek,' Steven defended himself. 'All right, I might be a bit of a geek, but it's certainly not maths' fault. If I'm a geek, I've done it to myself. At least I'll be a noble geek.'

'And this problem is boring. I like the last one about the phone and the calculator. I haven't been able to figure it out, though.' Myrna went silent as the front door of the bank opened and a customer approached her window.

'Neither have I,' Steven answered to himself. He hadn't thought much about that question in the weeks since its arrival; it was more difficult than it appeared at first. He pushed a few buttons on his telephone keypad, but was interrupted when Griffin poked his head into the office.

'Aren't you heading into Denver tonight?'

'Yeah, I'm hoping to get out of here a bit early this afternoon so I can make it to South Broadway before the antique shops close. Why?'

'Mike Thompson at First American Trust has an extra ticket to the game Sunday. Could you stop on your way down and get it for me?' Griffin was no great football aficionado, but any excuse to drink beer while eating grilled bratwurst would bring out the fan in his boss.

'Yeah, sure. Just call and tell him I'm coming.' Steven grimaced: he never enjoyed the drive into Denver. The opportunity to appreciate the picturesque foothills and long sloping vistas was invariably ruined by interminable traffic. If he left by 2.00 p.m., he would have a couple of hours to shop for his sister Catherine, who had just agreed to marry the man she had been dating for the past two years. The wedding was scheduled for mid-December, and Steven planned to buy her a late-engagement, early-wedding present. As a child, his sister had loved the antique china cabinet their mother had in the family dining room. It was mahogany, with thin glass panes set in an elaborate woodworked pattern on double doors. South Broadway Avenue was lined with antique stores and Steven had seen an advert for a going-out-of-business sale at an old family shop, Meyers Antiques. One way or another, he was sure he would find something just perfect for Catherine.

He missed his sister. They spoke frequently on the telephone and she teased him when he forwarded maths problems to her by e-mail, but he wished they saw each other more often. When they were children he had always been busy with friends, athletics and all those other world-shatteringly vital teenage things he couldn't even remember now. He'd rarely found time for her, despite the fact that she had idolised him. When he reflected on their childhood, fifteen years later, he felt that was his greatest failure, that he had not taken the time to be a good older brother to her. Kenny, the man she was marrying, was a technology specialist and computer programmer. Steven had met him only once, during the Christmas holiday at Catherine's home in Sacramento – Christmas in humid, eighty-five-degree weather, ironic but fun nevertheless. When he'd got back to Idaho Springs, he'd erected a Christmas tree in his living room to enjoy the holiday in a snowy setting, even if it was a week late.

He wanted his gift to show that he *had* paid attention to things that were important to her when they were young, even if it came a score of years too late; he hoped she would realise how much she had always meant to him. So he had to find the perfect cabinet.

Steven collected the papers for a small-business loan application and placed them in a manila folder. He walked to the lobby and handed the folder to Myrna, who quickly put away sketches she had been working on and opened a magazine resting on the counter. 'Were those circles I saw drawn on that sheet of paper?' Steven asked, grinning.

'No. Well, okay, yes, but I'm not working on it any more,' she said, then changed the subject pointedly. 'What's this?'

'This is the Thistle loan application. It's all approved. Would you put it in the computer for me and send out the letter once Howard signs it?' he asked.

'I am *not* your secretary, Steven Taylor,' she answered, trying to sound offended and failing. Steven liked Myrna. He often found himself taking time to tell her the things he wished he'd said to Catherine through the years. She was an attractive twenty-one-year-old with short, raven-black hair, light skin and blue eyes. She had been a member of Mark's world history class three years earlier and Steven knew he would always think of her as one of Mark's former students, even though he often heard her planning evenings out with friends or trips to the resorts for *après ski* parties.

Myrna's father had to give up work after being injured in a car accident, and she'd taken on a number of part-time jobs around town to help her mother make their mortgage payments. Finances had been tight for several years, but last winter her mother had been promoted to assistant manager at the local supermarket, and her father had landed a job helping out in the cafeteria at the hospital. Myrna's dream was to attend college, and Mark had been helping her with scholarship applications; if all went well, she would attend the University of Colorado the following fall.

'I know, I know,' Steven responded, 'I was just hoping you'd help me get out of here early today so I can get my sister a wedding present.'

'Well, in that case, I'll help you. Also, I'm bored. It's been dead out here today.' She cast him a coquettish grin.

'Thanks,' he said as he turned towards Griffin's office, 'okay, I'm off. Howard, I'll drop the ticket by tonight if I'm not too late, or tomorrow morning after breakfast. Myrna, behave yourself tonight. Stay away from the Jägermeister. That stuff will kill you.' He grinned back at her and pulled an arm through one sleeve of his tweed jacket.

'How would you know, Steven? You're never out – when was the last time you had a shot of Jäger – or anything?'

'It may be the only German Schnapps I know, but if you really want to drink like a fat, balding German banker, that stuff is your free pass. Behave yourself anyway.'

Myrna watched through the front window as Steven waited to cross the street. She'd had a crush on him three years ago, but now she looked on him more as a protective older brother than a potential catch. He looked over his shoulder, shook his head in amusement and hopped back up the stairs.

Myrna looked at him expectantly. 'What?'

'It's a square built on eighty-nine per cent of the circle's diameter. The Egyptians had it all worked out long before they ever heard of *pi*. See you Monday.'

GREENTREE TAVERN
AND BOARDING HOUSE

Garec Haile rode hard through the village towards Greentree Tavern. He had taken a few moments near Danae's Eddy to clean the claw wounds on Renna's hindquarter, but the injury needed stitches. Garec thought Sallax had some herbal concoction to help the mare sleep while Brynne stitched her up; for now, the bleeding had slowed enough for Renna to carry him back to Estrad. He hurried to spread the word that there were grettans in the southern forest. Careening into Greentree Square, Garec suddenly reined Renna to a slow walk, a spray of mud about her feet marking the abrupt change in tempo. There were nearly a dozen Malakasian soldiers tethering their mounts to a hitching post in front of the tavern, their black and gold uniforms unmistakable. Some remained outside, encouraging interested passers-by to continue on with their business, while others entered the tavern through the front and rear doors. The platoon would have been no match for an organised group of Estrad villagers, but the Eastlands and Praga had been under Malakasian occupation for so long – several generations now – that few would even think of spontaneously taking up arms against Prince Malagon's forces.

Fighting his fear, Garec rode to the mercantile exchange across the square from the tavern owned by Sallax and Brynne Farro and hitched Renna there, not wanting to lose her to the Malakasians should trouble arise. Lashing his bow and hunting knife to his saddle, he limped across the common and attempted to enter the building. 'Hold there, son,' a burly sergeant called, 'we won't be long.' The soldier was an older man; he looked like he'd been hardened by many Twinmoons' service in Malagon's army. He stood a full head taller than the other soldiers and corded muscle bulged in unlikely places.

'I'm unarmed,' he replied. 'I have friends inside.'

'I said hold here, boy,' the sergeant directed. 'If your friends are smart, they'll have no trouble this morning.' Garec watched as one of the soldiers moved to block the front entrance. These men were more heavily armed than the Malakasian patrols that regularly crisscrossed town and covered the north bank of the river. Something was wrong.

'You don't look like normal patrolmen,' he ventured, 'is something wrong?'

'Mind your business, boy,' the sergeant told him sharply, then softened and admitted, 'Actually, you're right. We're looking for a group of raiders who took a caravan last night along the Merchants' Highway north of here.' He fingered a short dagger in his belt. 'You wouldn't know anything about it, would you, boy?'

'Uh, no sir,' Garec began, 'I haven't—' He was cut short by the sounds of a struggle erupting inside the tavern and started to move towards the door, but before he could enter, he was seized roughly by the guard posted near the entrance and felt a strong blow to his head. Stunned, his vision blurring and his head swimming, Garec fell backwards and managed to sit heavily on the wooden stoop.

'Now, you're lucky, boy,' the sergeant told him calmly. 'I could have you killed for that, but you caught me in a good mood today. You stay smart and stay put, because you come at one of my men again and I'll run you through, armed or not.' Garec did not believe he could stand if he wanted to, never mind fight. Through the ringing in his head, he listened for sounds from the tavern but heard nothing. Soon thereafter, the remaining Malakasian soldiers emerged, mounted their horses and prepared to ride away. Among them was a young lieutenant who gave several sharp orders, then scowled at Garec before waving his platoon northwards out of town.

Garec tried to shake off the queasy feeling and struggled to his feet.

'Have a good morning, young man,' the old sergeant said and cuffed him once, hard, before riding away.

The scene in the tavern was not as bad as Garec had feared; he remembered much worse from any number of Twinmoon celebrations. One well-dressed patron he recognised, Jerond Ohera, lay unconscious near the front windows; others helped to right tables that had been overturned during the search. Sallax and Brynne Farro were behind the bar; thankfully, both appeared unhurt. Versen Bier, a woodsman and Garec's close friend, was kneeling to help Jerond. Garec knew all the remaining customers except one, a travelling merchant from the look of his boots, silk tunic and brocaded wool cloak.

'So what was that about?' Garec asked as he made his way to the bar.

'Lords, what happened to you?' Brynne asked, hurrying around to help him to a seat. She took his face in her hands and began cleaning the blood from his temple with her apron.

Sallax answered Garec's question. 'They said they were looking for three men, part of a group who raided a caravan along the Merchants' Highway last night. Apparently three were killed, but three managed to escape.'

Looking up into Brynne's eyes, Garec could see her concern. He whispered so only she could hear, 'I'm sure it wasn't him.'

A tear began forming at the corner of one eye and she quickly wiped it away on her sleeve.

Garec leaned forward to ask Sallax, 'Why search here? Why this place?'

'They're after something else. This stinks. You saw them. They rode right out of town, no other stops, no other questions. I don't buy it.'

'And why'd they get after Jerond?' Garec asked, motioning towards the unconscious man lying nearby.

'Ah, he'd had a few already this morning,' Sallax answered, 'and some left in him from Mika's Twinmoon celebration night. He ran his mouth off about Malagon's virility and that rutting lieutenant had at him with the flat of his sword.'

Brynne interrupted, 'We need Gilmour back here now.'

Garec nodded in agreement, then turned to the woodsman, who had sat down beside him. 'Verse, you'll not believe this, but I ran into a pack of grettans in the—' He caught himself and glanced at the stranger sitting near the fireplace. He lowered his voice and continued, 'They were in the forest near the river this morning, eight of them.'

'Nonsense, Garec,' the woodsman replied with an amused

chuckle. 'Were you at the beer last night too? They've never been seen south of the Blackstones before, and it was a rutting feat they ever made it that far.'

'Well, they're out there now. Take a look at Rennie's hindquarter if you need proof. We barely made it out with our hides intact.' Garec shuddered and went on, 'I killed one with a miracle shot, and one chased us right into the river. Lords' luck for us they don't swim well.'

'Swim?' Versen teased, 'you had to swim away? Some Bringer of Death you turned out to be, huh?'

'What do they look like?' Brynne asked.

'Like the unholy marriage of a mountain lion, a horse and a bear,' Versen replied. 'And they're big, bigger than most horses. If they're really about, we'll have to let people know to be careful of their livestock, get them in at night and all.'

The well-dressed merchant stood and walked towards the bar. He was handsome, somewhat older than the small group of friends, and Brynne tried to avoid staring at him as he approached. Placing a few coins in front of Sallax, he commented, 'I saw a group of them eat a farm wagon in Falkan once. They were so hungry – or so angry – I think they had it half-finished before they realised it wasn't edible.'

He paused, then added to Brynne, 'Sorry about the mess here this morning. Thanks again for that breakfast. I loved the local beer as well, my dear. Good day all.' Brynne blushed and stole another glance at the good-looking stranger.

'Do come again. We'll try to provide a touch less violence next time,' she said as he walked towards the front door. Before exiting he righted an overturned chair, gave a last smile to Brynne, then left without looking back.

'Who's he?' Garec asked, watching through the window as he crossed Greentree Square.

'I don't know,' Sallax answered, 'he came in late last night. We stabled his horse out back. Big saddlebags. He must be peddling something in the city.'

Few travelling merchants came through Estrad any more. Prince Marek had closed the port and the southern forest five generations earlier and Estrad's shipping activity had trickled away, unlike the other port towns around Rona. The rumour was that the prince had closed ports in Praga and the Eastlands because his navy was not extensive enough to patrol all the shipping lanes around the southeast peninsula – although some believed Marek just wanted to put a stranglehold on Rona because King Remond had chosen the southern nation as his home and established Estrad Village as the seat of the Eldarni monarchy. Marek's Malakasian homeland lay far to the north and west, and shutting down Ronan trade helped shift loyalty to the new Eldarni capital in Pellia.

Today Malakasia was the only nation with a navy; even so, Estrad's port had never been reopened. The lack of seagoing commerce had become a way of life.

Holding a compress to his swollen temple, Garec thought of the occupation army; he had a sense of foreboding. Something terrible was coming, and his anxiety grew as he pictured Gilmour out along the Merchants' Highway. He was the one who had convinced them to build a partisan force, to start raiding caravans and amassing arms: to fight for control of their homeland. He was the one with the knowledge of Malakasian politics and Malagon's armies. He was also the one who would know why the Greentree Tavern had been singled out this morning by a heavily armed platoon of Malakasian soldiers.

Garec looked out the window across Greentree Square: Renna was still tethered safely to the post in front of the mercantile exchange. With a quiet word of goodbye he rose to retrieve her. As he left the tavern, he felt a cool breeze blowing in from the coast. The southern Twinmoon was coming, and with it, strong winds and high tides.

Without thinking, he pulled his vest tight and felt a sudden sharp pain in his ribs. He had told Brynne he was certain Gilmour was not among the highwaymen killed last night. As he stepped out to cross the square, Garec hoped that was true.

North of the village, the Malakasian platoon made camp in a glade near the river. Their horses rested, cropping the grass, while the smell of hickory smoke and frying meat wafted through the camp. Oddly juxtaposed with the idyllic setting were the rigid and broken forms of six dead men, three in the bed of an open wagon, arrows protruding from their bodies, three others hanging from the limbs of a large oak tree on the edge of the glade, their necks neatly broken. The hanging bodies were motionless save for the gentle rocking of the great tree by the wind from the south.

The handsome merchant who had visited Greentree Tavern rode slowly into camp. 'I need to see Lieutenant Bronfio immediately,' he told the sentry.

'And who are you then, my pretty?'

With blinding speed, the merchant reached out, grabbed the sentry's left ear and began turning it violently, as if to tear it from the side of the guard's head. Blood spurted from the wound and ran between the merchant's fingers to the ground. The sentry, shocked by the merchant's unexpected attack, found it impossible to move, or even speak. Slowly the merchant leaned over in his saddle and spoke calmly to his writhing victim. 'I need to see Lieutenant Bronfio now – my pretty. Move it, or I'll gut you like a freshly killed pig.'

Inside Bronfio's field tent, the merchant berated the lieutenant. 'You need to maintain better discipline among these men. I want that sentry punished. These people are on the verge of attacking our outposts. We cannot put down insurrection with behaviour like that.'

'Yes, sir,' the lieutenant answered, 'I'll see to it right away, sir.' Then, frowning, he asked, 'Did you discover anything at the tavern, sir?'

'Yes, I did,' the merchant answered. 'I can confirm that the partisan group is using the abandoned palace as a meeting place and storage facility for their weapons and stolen funds. Thanks to your work this morning, they believe we are searching for three escaped raiders.' He looked out between the tent flaps to where the captured criminals had been hanging since early that morning. 'They will not suspect an attack as long as they believe we are otherwise occupied.'

He paused a moment, then continued, 'Lieutenant, we will attack at sunrise of the Twinmoon. Send a runner to Lieutenant Riskett. Have his men join you here. I'll be back the evening before, or I will contact you in the village with my orders.'

'Yes, sir.' Bronfio hesitated before asking, 'Did you discover any news of the whereabouts of Gilmour, sir?'

'That is none of your concern, Lieutenant,' the merchant answered icily. 'I will deal with Gilmour in my own good time.

You are a promising young officer. Don't ruin your career worrying about things that have nothing to do with you.'

'I'm sorry, sir. It's just that there are rumours floating about that Prince Malagon is using . . . well, "other" means to locate Gilmour, sir,' he said uncomfortably.

'I don't care for one instant what that rutting dog bastard is doing,' the merchant said, his voice quiet but undeniably menacing. 'I will find Gilmour; I will kill Gilmour, and I will eat his heart from a hickory trencher at Malagon's breakfast table. Do I make myself quite clear, Lieutenant?'

Bronfio hastily replied, 'Yes, sir, of course. I will contact Lieutenant Riskett and have both platoons ready for your orders by Twinmoon's Eve, sir.'

The merchant smiled, gave the younger man a friendly pat on the upper arm, and said, 'Excellent, Lieutenant. The men are in your charge until I return or contact you with additional orders.' Without waiting for a response, he left the officer's tent, ignoring the stares of the Malakasian soldiers gathering outside, and rode back towards Estrad.

Malakasian master spy Jacrys Marseth adjusted the cuffs of his silk shirt as he rode back into the village. He had made a mistake referring to the prince in such profane terms with an entire platoon of soldiers listening outside the tent. He knew of many instances in which similar behaviour had been punished by hanging, or much worse . . . the prince did not take criticism from anyone. He would need to rid himself of this platoon fairly soon. He didn't know how many would survive the coming attack on Riverend Palace, but those who did would never make it back to Malakasia. To start with, he would return to the camp this evening and slit the throat of the sentry who had spoken so sarcastically to him. Perhaps that would teach his comrades to see the value in holding their tongues and following orders.

Jacrys enjoyed his time in the field: it was time away from Malagon, and that meant time to enjoy being alive. Those who remained close to the prince risked death far more frequently than he did searching Praga and the Eastlands for rebels like Gilmour and Kantu.

Jacrys Marseth was the best espionage specialist Malakasia had, and he considered it his greatest accomplishment that he had succeeded in remaining away from Welstar Palace for so long. It was safe out here. He was in control. He took lives when he needed to, but otherwise he kept a low profile. Gilmour and Kantu were among the most dangerous men in the world, and he would kill them both. In the interim, however, if Prince Malagon were to pass away, or fall victim to a plot against his life, Jacrys would not mourn him long.

He soon passed Greentree Tavern but continued riding further into Estrad. He hoped to get a closer look at the terrain surrounding the long-abandoned Riverend Palace. He was sure that was where the Ronan resistance had their hideaway, where they stored silver, weapons, perhaps even horses. Any half-wit could memorise Bronfio and Riskett's patrol schedule along the river: the fact that the Ronan resistance crossed into the forbidden forest to meet, stash weapons and plan their terrorist activities did not surprise Jacrys for a moment.

Continuing his reverie, the spy thought again of Malagon. There was something wrong with the prince, just as there had been something wrong with his father, and apparently – as Jacrys had heard from older members of the Malakasian armed forces – with his grandfather as well. Some virus or disease took them, one generation after another. One day they were young, strong and eager to lead, and the next they were paranoid and homicidal. Locals called it the Malakasian curse: the leaders and heirs of Eldarn had been mysteriously killed off in a matter of days those many Twinmoons ago, and Prince Draven's Malakasian family had been left to lead, but only and always in madness.

Jacrys feared it was something worse, something profoundly evil.

Young Lieutenant Bronfio was correct as well. Rumours were flying around the Eastlands that Malagon had developed the ability to summon demonic creatures of unimaginable power to aid in his mission to find and kill his enemies. It did not surprise Jacrys; the spy knew that his services were rapidly becoming obsolete. Were he ordered back to Malakasia now, it would be to his death. He grinned slyly to himself: perhaps, for self-preservation, he would make his way west and kill Malagon himself.

MEYERS ANTIQUES

Meyers Antiques had a floor plan that looked like a Biedermeier salon after a thorough cannonade. A seemingly random collection was strewn about the large front room in a way that would make even the most liberal decorator uneasy. Walnut, oak and mahogany furniture was piled together against one wall while bookcases, china closets and credenzas crowded another. Across the centre were lone chairs and tables, orphans from broken sets. Included in this mix were tables, chairs, sofas and recliners, paired according to Meyers' best guess at what would work together in a customer's living room or kitchen, stepchildren organised by matching wood or colours. Among these were several juxtapositions that caught Steven Taylor's eye: a juke-box from the 1940s with a large cigarette ad pasted across the front panel was draped with cables from three gas lamps that would have provided just enough dim light for Jack the Ripper to gut an unsuspecting East End prostitute. Also odd was the uniform from a Union Army lieutenant adorning a headless mannequin. Across one shoulder the soldier wore his sheathed sabre; across the other he carried four brightly coloured Hula Hoops, artefacts from the future he had fought so bravely to preserve.

Hanging from the ceiling of the enormous showroom was a banner: GOING OUT OF BUSINESS SALE, EVERYTHING MUST GO, in large red letters. In one corner someone had written in black marker **50%+ off all marked prices**.

'This is the place,' Steven thought as he watched several dozen customers working their way through crowded aisles. He could hear Viennese waltzes piped in from above; Strauss, he guessed, played in awkward jangly strums on an autoharp or a zither. It reminded him of a Joseph Cotten film he had seen in college; he couldn't remember the plot, something convoluted about the post-war black market, but he did recall the autoharp, because the annoying refrain had been so prevalent throughout the movie. To him it sounded like the Tyrolean version of a circus calliope.

Steven joined the fray, working his way towards the back of the showroom where a group of china cabinets had been corralled together. As he spotted several mahogany cases that looked in excellent condition, his hopes rose: he was bound to find the perfect gift for his sister here.

'Can I help you find anything?' Steven turned to find a saleswoman smiling at him warmly. She wore glasses on a long cord around her neck and carried a clipboard with a yellow legal pad filled with item numbers and price figures. She was tall, and dressed in a long skirt and tennis shoes with white socks. Greying blonde hair fell about her shoulders and her eyes sparkled. She was strikingly attractive; Steven estimated her to be in her late fifties.

'No thanks, I'm just looking right now,' he answered.

'Take your time; either Hannah or I can help you if you need anything at all.'

'Are you the owner?' Steven asked. 'I mean, are you Ms Meyers?'

'Sorenson. Jennifer Sorenson. Dietrich Meyers was my father. He opened this place when he moved here in the late forties. He died a couple of months ago.'

'Oh, I'm sorry.' Steven could think of nothing else to say.

'Please, don't be. He was ninety and had a very happy life. I'm just sorry I don't have the time to keep this place open. Anyway, let us know if we can help.'

Steven watched as she moved, graceful despite her obvious fatigue, towards the front of the store.

It was nearly 6.00 p.m. and most of the customers had left when Steven finally decided on a Duncan Phyfe cabinet from the turn of the twentieth century; undamaged save for a small crack in the rear panel. He had been in the shop for three hours and was tired, hungry and hot from moving various pieces to get a better look. Steven felt better now he'd found an almost perfect match for his mother's cabinet, and he thought of his sister and her reaction to such a wedding gift. He was glad he had taken the time.

Starting suddenly, he walked around the piece, then laughed. 'Sonofabitch . . . how am I going to get this in my car?' He looked over the large wood and glass case and continued, 'Jesus, how am I going to get this to California?'

'Well, I can help you get it to the car, but getting it to California, you're on your own with that one.' The unexpected voice made Steven jump.

He turned quickly, backing himself against a large bookcase. 'Damnit, you scared me,' he admitted.

'I'm sorry. It's just that we're getting ready to close for the night and I wanted to see if I could help with anything. You've been so hard at work. I apologise, I haven't been able to get back here sooner. We've been busy today.'

Steven only half-heard what she was saying. He was amazed. It was as if Jennifer Sorenson had travelled back in time, thirty years in the past three hours. The young woman standing before him was staggeringly beautiful. She wore her hair in a long ponytail pulled over her left shoulder, a utilitarian hairstyle for working all day in such a hot and crowded setting, but it displayed the perfect line of her thin features. Her light brown skin glistened slightly from the heat and she smelled faintly of lilacs. Her smile brightened her face, and caused three tiny lines to pull at the corners of her brown eyes, a detail that even the world's greatest sculptors would never be able to duplicate. She wore a long skirt, similar to her mother's, and a blouse with the cuffs rolled up her forearms. She had the narrow hips and slight figure of an athlete, a runner or a cyclist. Steven's head swam as he looked at her.

For the second time in one afternoon, Steven Taylor found himself at a loss for words. 'Uh,' he muttered, his breath catching in his throat, 'what's this music?'

The young woman laughed. 'Oh, that was my grandfather's doing. He loved this stuff. It makes me a bit crazy in the mornings, but after a while, I manage to ignore it. Do you like it? I think it's Lawrence Welk after a triple helping of *spätzle*.' She made a quick adjustment to her glasses and looked questioningly at Steven. 'Are you okay?'

'Uh, yeah, I'm fine . . . It's just that it's hot in here and I . . . uh . . . I've been moving all these cases.' Steven wiped several beads of sweat from his forehead as his mind raced for something interesting to say. 'Actually, I really like this cabinet. It's for my sister's wedding. She's marrying some guy I don't know very well and I wanted to get her something special.'

Why was he telling her all this? He couldn't stop himself. 'She moved away several years ago and not having her around has helped me see that I could've been nicer to her when we were younger.' Now he really *was* rambling. 'I'm afraid I don't have room for it in my car. I'll need to come back, maybe tomorrow, to pick it up. Is there any way you can keep from selling it until tomorrow?'

He wished for a massive, exploding aneurysm to haemorrhage and kill him on the spot.

'Well, I do plan to lock the door behind me, and you are the last customer here. So I don't think that will be a problem.'

'Oh, great, thank you. My roommate has a pick-up and I don't have to work most Saturdays, so if that's okay, I'll be back in the morning.'

'I hope so.' She smiled again and Steven's heart pounded in his chest. He was certain she could have seen it moving his shirt from across a stadium parking lot. She went on, 'A lot of people say they'll be back tomorrow, but they don't come back. It's okay if you don't, but I hope you do. My mother and I are hoping to have everything sold off in the next couple of weeks—' she gave a quick glance around the storefront '—it's a lot of stuff, though.'

'No. I really will be back. I have a bit of a drive from up the canyon, so it may be later in the morning before I can get down here.'

'Well, don't worry. I won't sell this piece.' She reached over and gave his forearm an amiable squeeze. 'I'm Hannah.'

Steven watched as she removed her hand from his arm. His breath came in short gasps and he thought how embarrassed he would be if he passed out at her feet. He struggled for composure and introduced himself: 'I'm Steven Taylor.'

'Well, I'll see you tomorrow, Steven Taylor,' Hannah said as she turned and began walking him out.

Meyers Antiques opened at 8.00 a.m. the following morning. Steven was parked out front by 7.15. 'So much for getting here late,' he said to himself as he walked along South Broadway Avenue looking for a place to get coffee. He had thought about

Hannah all night, remembering that moment when she reached out to touch his arm. He was so excited about seeing her again that he had found it impossible to sleep, and was on his way in Mark's truck by 6.20. Was she married? Engaged? He had seen no ring on her finger yesterday. Was she involved with someone? Would it be too soon to ask her to dinner that evening?

Steven was determined to linger over breakfast for at least an hour so he didn't appear too eager to see her. She was so beautiful: he found it hard to think straight when she was there. He was a little afraid he would look like Quasimodo begging for a glimpse of her through the windows if he showed up right on the dot of 8.00 a.m.

Steven walked through the door of Meyers Antiques at 9.15 a.m., inordinately proud of himself for holding off that long. He had eaten pancakes, followed by an omelette with hash browns, two rounds of toast and about six cups of coffee as he waited for 9.00 to roll around on his geologically slow wristwatch. He laughed at himself: if the anxiety failed to kill him in the next hour, the cholesterol certainly would.

The store was already bustling with activity as two dozen customers moved items, tried out chairs, examined first-edition books and pored over china sets for cracks or imperfections. Looking towards the rear of the store, he saw his sister's china cabinet was still there, leaning up against the far wall.

He started when he heard someone calling his name.

'Excuse me, Mr Taylor.' It was Jennifer Sorenson. He saw no sign of Hannah.

'Yes, ma'am,' he answered, navigating through a mismatched bedroom set to where she stood waving.

'I'll help you get the Duncan Phyfe out to your truck. Hannah's making a delivery and stopping off at the post office for me this morning, but she told me to expect you.'

'That's right, ma'am,' Steven answered, furiously thinking of some way to delay his departure until Hannah returned. 'Uh . . . do you know if the keys are available?' The cabinet had two sets of double doors, and both had locks but no keys.

'If they aren't taped inside, you may be out of luck. There's one place you can look if you feel like taking the time.'

'Where is that?' Steven felt his hope rising.

'In the keys to the known world,' the older woman responded, adding nostalgically, 'my father kept a jar of keys. Most of them don't fit anything, but he liked to let children drop keys inside and make a wish. It was a fun way to keep them occupied while their parents browsed around. Sometimes children would come in by themselves just to drop off keys.'

The idea of picking through sixty years of discarded keys did not sound very appealing, but it was a sure-fire way to ensure he'd be around when Hannah returned from her morning errands.

'Terrific,' he said. 'Point me to them and I'll get started.'

The jar was actually an enormous glass container the size of a small barrel. It took him and Jennifer working together to lift it over to where he could sit and try out possible matches in the cabinet's locks. He estimated there were some two or three thousand keys in the container; the task would take hours – but the longer he stayed at Meyers Antiques, the more courage he would summon to ask Hannah to dinner that evening.

By 11.00 a.m. Steven's four-course breakfast was sitting in his stomach like a bag of wet cement, and he was now certain these *were* the keys to the known world. He had seen every imaginable size and style: skeleton keys, house keys, boat keys, even keys to an Edsel – he'd never seen an Edsel outside the movies, yet here he had found the keys for one. He tossed them into a pile at his feet.

He had a rough idea what he was looking for – a type of skeleton key with teeth on one side of a short barrel and a small hole in the end – which at least made searching a little easier.

Steven was both an avid hiker and a mountain cyclist, and he had memorised each turn and switchback of many of the routes in Rocky Mountain National Park. When work at the First National Bank of Idaho Springs began to feel like drudgery, he would drift off in quick, escapist daydreams, remembering fondly every detail of a great climb or a bike trip over the Continental Divide. He sometimes worried this escapist tendency was dangerous, part of his ongoing propensity to avoid living in the moment, but it helped him control stress, and reminded him there was an end to every boring task. Working through the keys, he found himself drifting back to a long climb he and Mark had completed several weeks earlier, along the Grey's Peak trail just below Loveland Pass. He remembered the picturesque vistas and autumn aromas, and the feel of the earth beneath his boots. Before long he was immersed in his memories, absentmindedly checking the keys, but otherwise paying them little attention.

It was then he heard the voice, as if from outside, across the street, somewhere along South Broadway.

'I said, are you having any luck?' It was Hannah. Startled from his reverie, Steven jumped to his feet and in the process kicked a pile of rejects across the faded tile floor.

'Oh, damnit, I'm sorry about that.' He moved awkwardly to his hands and knees and began gathering up the scattered keys. 'I'll have them all together in just a second.'

'Well, let me help you,' she said, laughing, and joined him on the floor. 'I take it you haven't found any that fit the cabinet.'

'No, not yet.' Steven stopped and watched Hannah. In his mind, he heard himself saying over and over again, '*I ring the bells of Notre Dame.*'

She stopped as well and, on all fours between rows of mahogany and walnut china cabinets, said, 'You know, you're well over halfway through the jar. I can help you with the rest after we get these picked up.'

'That would be nice of you.' Steven allowed a long breath to escape his lungs. She was dressed similarly to the evening before, but this morning her hair hung loose about her face and across her shoulders.

'Um—' Now Hannah hesitated. 'Are you free for lunch?'

'Most days, yeah . . . unless of course Howard makes me go to Owen's with him.'

Hannah giggled, then looked embarrassed. 'No, silly, I meant today. Are you free for lunch today?'

Steven was stunned. She had taken him by surprise, and despite his heart bellowing a cacophonous, white-knuckle rhythm through his ears, he almost managed to control his voice when he replied, 'I'd love to.'

As they walked to the Mexican restaurant Hannah had chosen, she did most of the talking, chatting about her grandfather and the store. Steven was happy just to listen. He had managed to put his foot in his mouth so often since meeting her that he welcomed the reprieve. The restaurant was busy with a large

Saturday lunch crowd, but Hannah located a booth near the back where they could enjoy the illusion of privacy. Although Steven was far from hungry – breakfast was still sitting a little heavy – he made certain to order enough to make lunch last as long as possible. He soon discovered Hannah needed little convincing; she appeared in no rush to get back to the shop.

Hannah was a full-time law student at the University of Denver. She had originally studied political science, then took a job with a charitable organisation, but after three years there decided she could better serve those in need as a lawyer. 'I don't expect to make much money at it, but in the long run, I hope to have a greater impact this way,' she explained, stuffing shredded chicken and guacamole into a fajita.

When Steven tried, delicately, to broach the topic of other men, she told him she had recently broken off a long-distance relationship with a boyfriend from college who had moved to Atlanta.

'Was it the distance that created problems for you?' Steven asked, feeling encouraged.

'No, I think it was more his tendency to engage in short-distance relationships while in a long-distance relationship with me.' She took a bite of her fajita, then, with her mouth full, asked a muffled, 'How about you?'

'Me? Oh, God no. I haven't been involved with anyone for the past three years. I finished my MBA, misplaced a couple decent job offers, partly because they were risks and partly because they were . . . well, mostly because they were risks. I'm not much of a risk taker,' he said, folding and unfolding a corner of his napkin.

'I know. I could tell. I mean, how many of those keys were you really going to examine before you talked to me? And your truck was outside the store before I arrived this morning. So I thought I'd take the gamble and help you out.' She looked at Steven, waiting for a response. 'Was that okay?'

'Well, you did interrupt my carefully planned schedule of seven hours' courage-building before twelve seconds of stumbling over myself and two hours of grovelling, but all things being equal, I'm glad you did.' He grinned. 'I'm really glad you did.'

'So am I,' she said as she reached across the table to take his hand. As before, Steven's heart leaped as he felt her fingers wrap around his for a moment. Then, feeling awkward, as if she were moving too fast, Hannah pulled back, waved for their server and ordered a cup of coffee.

Steven changed the subject. 'You know, I'm halfway through that jar. It'd be a shame to have those cabinet keys sitting there near the bottom, never to be reunited.'

'Well, I look forward to helping you in your search,' she told him. Steven watched as she stirred sugar into her coffee mug. She really was one of the most beautiful women he had ever seen, but more than that, she was beautiful without trying. He was always disillusioned by the concept of supermodels and film stars who employed teams of specialists, spackling masons and airbrush artists to achieve that look of perfection. He imagined Hannah rolling out of bed, donning a sweatshirt to read the morning paper and still looking exquisite, her skin flawless and her hair cascading down her back. He wanted desperately to reach over and touch her face, but he was afraid he would scare her off. Surely he was the only man on earth to ever feel this level of insecurity and anxiety when trying to make an impression on a lovely woman. He would have to remember to ask Mark about it later.

Without pausing to think, he blurted out, matter-of-factly, 'I have to see you again.'

Hannah stood, and Steven thought he should stand too, but he wasn't certain that his legs would heed the command.

She smiled. 'Let's go find your keys and we'll figure it out there.'

Walking back from the restaurant, Hannah held his hand as if it were the most natural thing in the world. Steven talked this time, about living in the foothills, working at the bank and his plans to find a more rewarding career – if he could just figure out what that occupation should be. Prefacing his confession with: 'No laughing,' he even revealed his love for abstract maths.

Despite his warning, Hannah did laugh out loud, then asked, more seriously, 'Why not become a mathematician?'

Steven kicked a discarded bottle-cap along the sidewalk. 'Well, because there really is no money in maths, and because I'm not sure I'm very good at it. I love it, but I think – no, I'm certain – I'm quite slow. I have maths problems I've been trying to figure out for months now.'

Jennifer Sorenson did not seem to mind that her daughter had taken such a long lunch; she waved from across the showroom as they walked in.

'I'll go check to see if there's anything she needs me to do,' Hannah said, 'while you get on with key-hunting.'

'I'm going to find something else to buy so she sees it wasn't time wasted,' he called after her, and began searching the room for something outlandish he could buy for Mark or Howard. He soon located a vase that looked as if it had come from a 1920s speakeasy, blown glass moulded into the shape of a nude woman holding a top hat and cane. It was an absurdly ugly piece, perfect for Howard's office.

'I think I'll call her Greta,' Steven said, holding the vase aloft. 'Howard will love her wide hips, and the way he can drink beer right from the top of her head.'

'Please don't feel obligated to buy anything else,' Hannah told him. 'My mother and I aren't expecting to sell everything off during this sale.'

'Are you kidding? Look at her: she's pure kitsch, the perfect gift for a guy who has no taste. I'm not joking; Howard will love her.'

They spent the next hour talking while they went through the key jar, building up a pile of discards so enormous it blocked a whole aisle.

Eventually Hannah sighed and said, 'Okay, that's the end. I'm sorry they weren't in there. That was a lot of work for nothing.' She began returning handfuls of keys to the jar.

'I wouldn't say it was for nothing,' he chided, and turned away, a little embarrassed.

'No. I guess I wouldn't either,' she said, then kissed him quickly on the lips. 'I'll go and write up a receipt for the cabinet. You put the rest of these back in the jar.'

Steven swallowed his astonishment and called, 'Don't forget to add Greta to my bill. She's coming with me.' Then he sat on the floor in front of his sister's china cabinet, still holding Greta. Hannah's kiss had astounded him; he needed a few moments to regain his composure. He closed his eyes and ran two fingers across his lips, exhilarated – until he looked down at the floor and was reminded that a veritable mountain of orphan keys waited to be shovelled up and returned to the jar.

'All right, let's get you all back home. Keys to the known world, sure – I'd have been happy with just the keys to the damned cabinet.'

Then he saw it: a glimpse of a familiar shape with a familiar insignia. BIS. Shifting Greta to his left hand, Steven reached over and picked out the key. He turned it over. 17C. Greta fell from his hand and shattered on the tile floor, the broken pieces of breasts and buttocks strewn about in a confused, connect-the-dots pattern between the china cabinets.

'Holy shit! It's Higgins's key,' he whispered to himself, oblivious to the stares of customers startled by the crash. 'How did it get here?' He gaped down at it and repeated, 'How the hell did it end up here?' After another minute staring like a voyeur, Steven remembered where he was. He slipped the key into the pocket of his jacket, murmuring nervously, 'What *are* you doing, Steven?' Bending at the waist, an animated mannequin, he picked up the pieces of Howard's nude figurine and went across to apologise to Jennifer.

THE ORCHARD

Versen Bier looked around before snapping the reins and driving the wagon into the street. Estrad was quiet this morning; the woodsman listened carefully as he checked for signs of Malakasian patrols. Behind him, Garec huddled in the wagon's bed where he was ensuring the canvas tarpaulin covering their cargo remained in place. Running through a deep rut in the muddy street, the wagon lurched suddenly and one corner of the protective tarp fell away. Garec quickly replaced it, hoping no one had chanced to peer between the wooden slats at that moment. Their load was not farm produce, firewood or baled hay, but hundreds of swords, rapiers, shields, chain-mail vests and longbows. They were heading for the abandoned palace in the forbidden forest, and unless they drove through a nearby orchard, rather too suspicious a move for this time of day, this street was the only way to get such a heavily loaded wagon into the woods near the crumbling castle. Both men prayed silently they would not be stopped for inspection.

The punishment for possession of such a large supply of weapons would be swift, sharp and final. They would be driven to the nearest tree, hanged until dead, and then left there for a full Twinmoon: a vivid example to anyone else contemplating seditious activities. Garec had seen men killed this way; during the rainy season especially corpses decomposed rapidly and few hanged bodies ever lasted a full Twinmoon. Instead, the flesh around the neck and upper shoulders tore away and the body slowly stretched and ripped its way towards the ground.

Garec forced the image from his mind; he would rather die at the end of a Malakasian sword than the end of a rope. Versen felt the same way: they would fight to the death if caught by a passing patrol. Both Garec and Versen were deadly with a bow, but today, to keep from drawing attention to themselves, neither man was armed. Longbows were conspicuous and although they trained with swords and battle-axes, both found them cumbersome weapons; if they had to fight today, it would end badly. Garec closed his eyes, waiting to feel the wagon's wheels leave the muddy street for the relative protection of the forest.

Versen spoke, interrupting his anxious thoughts. 'It's getting too busy out here. I don't have a good feeling about this.' The street was growing steadily more crowded, despite the early aven.

'Let's take a side street and cut through the orchard,' Garec replied. 'At least we'll get some protection behind the buildings that way.'

'I'm worried it's too light out for that. Why would a wagon go through the orchard unless there was something to hide?' Versen's face was grim. 'If anyone sees us go, we're as good as dead.'

'We just have to make it to the corner,' Garec replied nervously. 'We'll check the window above Mika's and then decide.' As they approached a crossroads, Garec stared straight ahead and whispered, 'You do it. We can't look up there at the same time: anyone watching us would find that suspicious.' They didn't know if spies were actively searching for partisan groups in Estrad, but they were determined to take as few chances as possible.

Versen glanced up, casually, and reported, 'One taper, not lit.'

'Get us out of here quick,' Garec said into cupped hands, ostensibly warming them against the morning chill.

Jacrys Marseth watched from the window of a local merchant's stop as the wagon turned slowly down a side street towards an apple orchard that flanked the neighbourhood. When they disappeared from view, he motioned to a Malakasian soldier waiting quietly in an adjacent room and whispered, 'Two streets down. Take them now.'

The soldier hurried out of the back of the shop to join the remainder of his patrol. He leaped into the saddle and led a small group of heavily armed men into the crowded street. Their horses pounded through the morning mud, parallelling the wagon's path, and then turned quickly to cut off the two suspected partisans. Bursting into the orchard, the small patrol briskly surrounded the wagon and forced them to a stop.

'Step down,' a ruddy-faced corporal directed.

'We're unarmed,' Versen answered, slowly raising his hands above his head. Garec did the same and moved quickly from the wagon.

'Kneel down,' the soldier commanded, 'there in front of the horses.' Both men did exactly as they had been ordered. Garec felt his hands shaking uncontrollably and put them firmly on top of his head, tightly gripping two handfuls of hair as an anchor.

'We're farmers,' he said, 'just taking this morning's load to the village market.' He heard his voice crack and decided to remain silent unless absolutely necessary.

'Check it,' the corporal ordered a nearby soldier who dismounted and began unfastening ropes that held down one corner of the large canvas tarp. Finding an unruly knot, the soldier drew a knife from his belt and sliced through the cloth in a long gash that exposed the wagon's cargo. Garec sneaked a glance at Versen, who gave his friend a conspiratorial grin.

'Apples, corporal,' the soldier called. 'It's just apples.'

147 TENTH STREET

'Why do you suppose they call it a trash receptacle?' Mark Jenkins wrestled to fit a large pizza box into their kitchen garbage can. 'I mean, as much rubbish as goes into this thing eventually comes out again, right? So it's not really a receptacle as much as it is a holding centre.' He bent the box in half against his knee as if he were breaking up kindling wood for a fireplace. 'I say we start changing the way people refer to it. We can call it the trash holding centre.' He thought for a moment, then added, 'That really doesn't work, does it?'

Steven Taylor wasn't listening. He sat at one end of the sofa in their living room turning Higgins's safe deposit box key over in his hands.

He had been enjoying one of the most wonderful weeks of his life. He had taken Hannah to dinner on Saturday, Catherine's Duncan Phyfe cabinet lashed securely in the back of Mark's truck while they drove around Denver looking for somewhere to eat. The following day they had gone for a long hike above the canyon. Hannah had joined him for dinner again on Tuesday, when he had, on an impulse, driven into the city after work and told her he couldn't wait until Friday to see her again.

Her reaction had been well worth the headache from using the interstate during rush-hour on a weeknight: as she saw him enter the store she excused herself from her customers and walked towards him, smiling – and she took the last three or four paces at a slight run. He had never had a woman run – even a few steps – to be with him before: it was exhilarating.

He was completely smitten with Hannah Sorenson, and that should have been enough to have him walking on air. But all the while, the question of William Higgins's safe deposit box was festering in the back of his mind.

Mark came in from the kitchen carrying two open beer bottles and handed one to Steven. 'Are you done with the pizza?'

'Yeah, I'm fine.' Steven took a mouthful of cold beer and slipped the key back into his shirt pocket.

'You know, we should start learning how to cook a few things. This Chinese-pizza-peanut butter diet is going to catch up with us someday,' Mark mused. Steven laughed as he looked across the room at his best friend. Mark, at twenty-eight, was in perfect physical shape. A well-built African-American, he swam several miles every morning with student members of the high school swimming team, and was invariably up for running, biking, or the most gruelling climbs Steven could find for them on weekends. Steven was in good physical condition, but Mark was a natural athlete.

'Are you kidding? Look at yourself. You're a specimen; you look like you were constructed by teenage girls during a pyjama party fantasy game.' Steven grimaced, then added, 'But I agree: we ought to start thinking about eating better.'

'After tomorrow night. One last super supreme – with extra everything – tomorrow night. We'll finish the beer and kick off a trial period of healthy nutrition on Friday. Deal?' Mark offered a hand to his roommate.

'Deal. And then on Friday we'll ... I don't know, we'll roast some fish or steam some vegetables or something.' Steven had no idea what was involved in either roasting or steaming.

Apparently, neither did Mark. 'Do we have a steamer?'

'No idea. Maybe we can get a book, or find an idiot's guide to the kitchen website.'

Mark raised his bottle. 'To roast fish and steamed vegetables.'

Steven returned the toast. He thought for a few seconds, then suggested, 'Maybe those things are available as take-out from someplace.'

They both laughed, and Mark headed back to the kitchen: if they were seriously planning to improve their eating habits, it would be best not to leave any leftovers before the start of Nutrition Hell was upon them. As he heaped the remains of the pizza onto two plates, he called, 'You know, you ought to hand that key over to Howard.'

'I know, but I'm curious. I can't even concentrate on work any more.' Steven switched off the television, a boringly one-sided baseball game. 'I'm closing up for Howard tomorrow night. When he leaves, I'll find some reason to go into the safe. I'll grab a quick look and be home in time for our last night of real food: long live fat, sugar and cholesterol.'

Mark walked over and handed him one of the plates. 'Enjoy it: we'll miss it when it's gone. I understand you're curious. But whatever is in there has been in there for a long time. You still ought to give Howard the key. Let him decide whether or not to open it.'

'He'll say no.'

'He's the bank manager. Of course he'll say no.'

'Damnit!' Steven took a frustrated bite. 'One peek and I'll throw the key in Clear Creek. It'll be out of my system for ever.'

Mark shook his head. 'Dead cats. All over town dead cats. I hope it's a hundred-and-thirty-five-year-old tuna sandwich. That'll show you crime doesn't pay.' Changing the subject, he asked, 'So, when do I get to meet the lovely Hannah?'

'We're climbing Decatur this weekend to get some shots of the aspens. The weather's turning; it might be our last run up there without snowshoes. You want to come?'

'Great.' Mark absentmindedly adjusted the dust jacket on a coffee-table book about Picasso, then said, 'You've been seeing her a lot. She must be something.'

Steven brightened suddenly. 'I can't believe it; I'm completely knocked-down-the-road stupid by her. I think about her all the time—' he corrected himself, 'well, except for when I'm dwelling on that miserable safe deposit box.' He added, 'I can't get her out of my head. I've never felt like this before and I'm sure I'm going to blow it – maybe hit her with my car, or catch her hair on fire with a flame-thrower, or something like that.'

Mark chuckled. 'I can't wait to meet her. If you do happen to see a flame-thrower lying around here, remember: flame-throwers don't kill people. *People* kill people.'

Several hours later, Steven was still awake and needing to talk to Hannah. He was worried about waking her, but at last he ventured a call.

'No, I'm still awake,' she told him. 'I've missed you these past twenty hours – this is silly. It's like I'm back in school.'

'Yeah, I don't mind, though.' He took a risk, and added, 'It's been a long time since I've felt like this . . . I don't know, maybe never.'

Hannah's voice dropped slightly. 'Me too . . . I wish I could see you, just for a minute, just to say good night properly.'

'I'll be there in forty minutes,' Steven said.

'We could meet halfway, say, the diner in Golden?' she suggested, not knowing whether Steven was serious.

'I'll be there in twenty minutes,' he said, and hung up.

It was after midnight when Steven crossed the parking lot to her car. Hannah was standing next to it drinking from a Styrofoam cup. The light from inside the diner gave her skin a warm, surreal glow. She was wearing old jeans, running shoes and a navy blue sweatshirt. Her hair hung over one shoulder like it had the day they met.

He hugged her close and bent slightly to catch the lilac aroma that scented her hair, then tilted her chin up and pressed his lips against hers. She fell into the kiss, her tongue teasing his as he probed the deepest recesses of her silken mouth. He ached for her; as he reached to caress the nape of her neck his hand brushed her breast and even beneath her sweatshirt he felt her nipple tauten.

Still kissing him, Hannah took his hand and moved it back to her breast as she stroked down his chest to his thighs. Steven pressed harder into her, backing her up against the car door.

She moaned softly and ground her hips into his. Steven thought he might explode, right then and there in the diner parking lot. When Hannah slid her hand between his legs, he backed away far enough to say, 'You'll need to check the morning paper.'

'What? What are you— Why?' Hannah wasn't paying much attention.

'Tomorrow's paper,' he said again, 'just check it to be sure I make it home all right.'

'Why is that?' She returned to his mouth, licking his lips salaciously before kissing him hard again.

'Because I fully expect to crash my car before getting anywhere near the highway.'

At that, Hannah laughed, an embarrassed, blustery chuckle that filled Steven's heart.

He laughed too, and Hannah released him.

Sliding her hands into the back pockets of his jeans, she pouted, 'All right, if I *have* to stop.'

'I think it's for the best. I'd hate to overhear the paramedics in the ambulance discussing the suspicious wet spot on the front of my jeans – Jesus, what would they tell my mother? "Uh, yes, Mrs Taylor, he was wearing underwear, but they were soiled . . . uh, no ma'am, the other side." Good thing I'd be beyond caring; I'd never live that down!'

Hannah laughed out loud and pushed him away playfully. 'Go on, silly. But this weekend, we'll continue from where we left off, and no excuses.' She growled softly. 'It'll be worth your while, soldier.'

'It will, without doubt, be the greatest eleven seconds of my adult life.' He bent down to take her lips once more.

They laughed together, and Hannah kissed him tenderly a final time. 'Good night,' she whispered, 'dream of me.'

'Believe it.'

Mark walked down Miner Street towards Owen's Pub in the October twilight. It had snowed lightly during the afternoon and the students in his history classes had been impossible to manage: they were convinced a storm was coming and they would wake to a school closure. Mark knew the snowfall was just a dusting, the sight of the buildings coated thinly in white refreshed him: it was as if the entire town had been given a coat of whitewash, a brisk autumn cleansing to rinse away the vestiges of the summer tourist season. His boots left unmistakable prints on the snowy sidewalk.

He was glad the weekend was coming, although it was likely the snow would mean the cancellation of their planned assault on Decatur Peak. Light snow in town could mean several feet above the tree line.

Idaho Springs on a weeknight was an interesting dichotomy: welcoming, colourful tourist shops that were completely devoid of tourists. Mark preferred it that way. Idaho Springs was a tourist stop – just that, a stop, never anyone's destination – but that still meant several important perks for those who lived in town. Mark mentally tallied his favourites: first, a wide variety of news sources. Mark, a New York native, loved being able to pick up the *New York Times* or even the *Boston Globe* to catch up on news from the northeast. The second was great coffee, perhaps the town's most important contribution to the state economy since the mining boom, with outstanding varieties, from Brazilian to Turkish, available every day. Just thinking about it made his mouth water.

He checked his watch and crossed Miner. Steven was slated to close the bank at 5.30, so Howard would have a thirty-minute head start at the bar. The roommates already had plans for their last pizza later that evening, but one never knew how the night would unfold, especially when Howard had a comfortable lead on the pack.

Coming through the front door of the pub, Mark had a moment of self-consciousness about being black. The bar was filled end-to-end with white people and although he knew most of them, it was at times like this he felt out of place. It didn't often happen – he was known and respected by the local community because he taught their children at the high school – but even so, there were not many people of colour in the Springs and from time to time he felt strangely isolated, although he was coming to feel as if the town was his true home.

Those people rushing by on the interstate had no idea how gratifying it could be to live in the foothills. They were all in such a hurry to get to a destination; their stop here rarely merited more than a quick glance while buying an out-of-state paper or stirring sugar into an espresso.

Mark had been drawn to the mountains ever since he was a young boy, when his parents had taken him and his sister on a cross-country trip. The majestic beauty of the Rocky Mountains had made an indelible impression on Mark's father: he had not wanted to leave. Mark's parents had planned and saved for years for this trip; they had hoped to reach the Pacific Ocean and drink expensive wine on Fisherman's Wharf in San Francisco. Instead, their journey was stalled in the Rockies for several days.

It was as though Mark's father could not force himself to drive west over the Continental Divide and on into Utah. Instead, they had gone hiking, taken mining tours, ridden the George-town Loop Railroad and even tried fly-fishing in the national park. While his sister had grown bored, Mark had been happy to remain in the hills. He knew, even then, that he would return.

Grainy 8" × 10" photos enlarged from snapshots of expansive

mountain vistas had adorned the walls of the Jenkins home on Long Island and ten years later Mark's father returned to help his son move into the residence hall at Colorado State University in Fort Collins. It was like coming home for both of them. Mark's father had never forgotten the impact that trip had on him, and the strange way he had made such a powerful connection with the craggy peaks and lush green forests.

Standing in the doorway of Owen's Pub now, Mark thought of his father and decided to call home the following day, then he moved into the crowd and began searching for Howard Griffin. Like any neighbourhood bar at 5.00 p.m., Owen's was noisy, but it was crowd noise, the directionless, rhythmless, flat tones of people carrying on about politics, romance, October baseball and the coming ski season. Mark found weekends at Owen's more enjoyable, when an elderly Italian couple provided music from a small stage in the far corner of the bar. Vincent and Maria Casparelli had been playing together since the fifties and Mark was convinced there was not a song in the entire jazz repertoire they did not know. Enthusiastic patrons would scribble barely legible requests on cocktail napkins and deliver them with a few dollars to the top of Maria's piano. Vincent would glance at the napkins, nod telepathically to Maria and the duo would begin piece after piece without missing a beat. Vincent played saxophone, improvising between verses, but it was Maria who carried the act. Her jazz work verged on perfection; Mark rarely heard her recycle riffs, even though she played hundreds of songs, week after week.

Vincent invariably wore a suit with a Paisley ascot, his pork pie hat hanging on a wooden peg above the piano; Maria was dressed in the uniform of the serious piano matron: a dark skirt with a white blouse and a pink corsage accented with baby's breath pinned over her breast. Buying Vincent a rye on the rocks late in the evening would always bring on a story about summers in the Catskills or playing nightclubs in New York City with Woody Herman's band.

Howard Griffin was not difficult to spot. He was leaning against the bar expounding to a small group of twenty-one-year-olds that included Myrna Kessler, a former student of his. As he headed towards them, Mark overheard Howard's sermon – he had obviously worked his way through several beers already.

'—and anyone who'd ever seen him play would know that even if he did bet on baseball, he would never have bet on his team to lose. The guy had no idea how to lose. Either way, who cares any more? Put him in the Hall of Fame.' Finding little agreement from the crowd of young drinkers, Griffin gave up. 'Ah, you're all too young to know him anyway.' He spotted Mark and called excitedly, 'Hey, Mark, over here.'

It was 5.45 p.m. before Steven arrived, and Mark immediately noticed his roommate looked nervous. Steven greeted the small group, placed his briefcase beneath the barstool and nodded to Gerry, the bartender, who brought him a dark draught beer. Howard, seeing Steven reach for his wallet, insisted Gerry add the beer to his tab.

'Well thanks, Howard,' Steven said, raising his glass to his boss.

'No problem. Did the place get locked up okay?' Howard pulled at a tortilla chip held firmly by a resilient piece of hardened cheese.

'No, I thought I'd leave it open tonight; left the safe door open, too.' Steven forced a smile and avoided eye contact with Mark.

'No one loves a smartass, Stevie,' Howard laughed.

'Steven,' Myrna corrected. Howard ignored her.

The group drank together for another hour as the noise level grew steadily more deafening. Mark watched Steven calm noticeably as he finished his third beer. It was obvious he had investigated the contents of the old miner's safe deposit box and was now feeling guilty, but Mark decided it was not that heinous a crime. He just hoped Steven would manage to avoid getting into trouble for it. He called above the din of the crowd, 'Hey, I'm heading up the hill.'

'Wait; use my phone and we can pick dinner up on the way. I'll just say goodbye.' He turned to Howard, leaned over and shouted above the racket, 'Hannah and I are getting together late tomorrow night. So don't worry about closing up tomorrow afternoon, I'll take care of it again.' He would need a few uninterrupted minutes in the safe the following day; this was the answer.

Howard nodded, ran the back of his hand across his mouth and gave Steven a quick fatherly hug. 'I'm getting out of here myself soon. I already know I'll feel like the Passaic River tomorrow morning so don't expect me on the dot of eight.'

Steven was amused. In the three years he had worked at the First National Bank of Idaho Springs, he had *never* expected Howard Griffin on the dot of eight.

Mark grabbed a book of matches from the large fishbowl on the bar. The bar's phone number was printed on the back so he could call later to check out when the Casparellis were on. He fancied listening to the old Italian duo fire up their amazing rendition of some Art Tatum or Fats Waller tunes over the weekend.

Outside, they loped lazily towards the pizza place. Remembering his list of perks, Mark tallied number three – great pizza – then turned to Steven. 'So, you opened the safe deposit box.'

'Guilty,' Steven answered. 'I did.'

'And?'

'And what?'

'And what was in there? Not my tuna sandwich, I hope,' Mark teased.

'I don't know. I couldn't tell what it was, so I—' Steven paused and glanced behind him quickly, '—I took it with me. It's here in my briefcase.'

Mark laughed hard, nearly doubling over. 'You're a felon,' he said, still laughing until the realisation sank in and he stared at Steven. 'Christ on a plate, you *are* a felon. You just robbed your own bank. I can't believe you robbed your own bank.'

'I didn't rob my own bank,' Steven said defensively. 'I already offered to close up tomorrow night; I'm putting the stuff back. This is more like archaeology than larceny.'

'Sure, Indy. And what do you mean by "stuff"?' Mark was curious now too. 'Were there multiple unidentifiable deposits made into Mr Haggardy's account?'

'Higgins,' Steven corrected, 'and yes, there were two things and I don't know what either of them are. You can help me when we get home.'

'Oh sure, of course, drag me off to prison as well, why don't you? It'll be a great opportunity for me to brush up on my spirituals while I'm bashing rocks on a chain-gang with you.' Mark turned into the pizza restaurant with Steven close behind.

Waiting at the take-out counter, Mark asked, 'How did you deal with the security camera?'

'I made a point of finishing my paperwork before Howard left. That way, I could start mopping and dusting the lobby while he was still there. Tomorrow, his security tapes will show me entering Chapman's old safe with a bucket and a dust rag.' The pizza arrived and as Steven paid for it with his credit card, he told Mark, 'Don't let me forget to write this cheque tonight.'

'What? Your Visa bill?'

'Yeah, I can finally get it to zero. I want to send the cheque first thing tomorrow – no, to be sure I'll put it in the box tonight. I'll sleep better knowing it's already on its way.'

Mark shrugged. 'Congratulations. And I'm thrilled you decided to celebrate by robbing your own bank.'

'Are you going to be able to lay off that any time soon?'

'Probably not, but if I do, I'll let you know.'

Later that evening, the pizza eaten and the kitchen littered with peanut shells and beer cans, Steven and Mark slumped in their living room with Steven's unopened briefcase on the floor between them. Mark yawned and stretched. 'Well, let's open it.'

'All right.' Steven lifted the briefcase to the coffee table near the sofa and opened it. 'Here they are.' He reached into one side of the bag and pulled out a wooden box.

'That's rosewood,' Mark observed, leaning forward in his chair and reaching for the box. 'It certainly isn't native to these hills.'

'No,' Steven answered, 'and I don't suppose this cylinder is either.' He held a long cylindrical container aloft for a moment, then placed it on the table. 'I can't explain it, but this one makes me feel strange, almost like it *wanted* me to open the drawer.' He chose his words carefully as he continued, 'Like it wants me to open *it* now.'

'I think you've had one too many.' Mark came across the room to examine the cylinder. 'Sheez, it's heavy,' he said, surprised, then, looking strangely at Steven, added, 'You know, you may be getting me a little spooked here, too, because it does feel odd. It's like I'm compelled to see what's inside.' He sat on the edge of the sofa and sighed. 'Well, there's no point robbing the bank for nothing. Let's go.'

Steven reached first for the rosewood box. It was a six-inch cube, with twin gold latches holding the top in place. Looking closely at the hinges, Steven feared he would have to pry them apart, but when he pulled on one, it opened smoothly. He felt his heart race and wiped his hands on his jeans before tugging gently on the lid, holding his breath as he did. It also opened easily, as if it had been oiled every month for the last century. Inside was a piece of velvet-like material over padding, protecting what looked like—

A rock. An ordinary piece of rock.

'What is it?' Mark asked.

'My best guess,' Steven said as he reached into the box and removed the stone, 'is that it's a rock.'

Mark laughed and said sarcastically, 'No, officer we left all the cash, but couldn't part with this rock. Oh, sure, we have a whole bunch out in the yard, but look at this one, a dead miner chose this one.'

'Knock it off,' Steven said, irritated. 'What do we know about geology? This might be an enormous hunk of something really valuable.'

'Sure,' Mark answered, 'and it might be a rock. Haven't you heard of mercury poisoning? Some of those miners were flat-out bozo. I think one of them came into your bank to give a permanent resting place to his favourite rock, Betsy.' Despite his sarcasm, Mark could not deny that a curious sensation began to creep along his spine. He looked again at the stone before turning his attention back to his roommate.

'Well, let's open the cylinder. Maybe there's something more exciting in there.'

Steven's hopes were renewed when he picked up the container and began unscrewing the cap. With his first turn, the mood in the room changed. Something was happening. The cylinder hummed with an energy all its own; the air shimmered, almost as if an industrial-sized humidifier were pumping invisible steam into their living room. Mark's expression was impenetrable, a grim mask of determination, while Steven's was guilty, like an eight-year-old who's regretting stealing a few penny candies. 'I'm closing it,' he announced suddenly.

'No. It's okay.' Mark moved a little nearer. Steven changed his mind and continued unscrewing the cap. With each turn, the energy level in the room increased. Mark, uncomfortable, looked for something to do with his hands.

'I'm afraid to touch anything, it's like there's static electricity everywhere.' The room shimmered and Mark was certain he saw various objects, the fireplace tools, a paper plate with a floral print and a bright silver beer can, moving in and out of focus. 'It must be something radioactive. I don't understand it. It's—'

'No,' Steven interrupted, 'it's cloth. It's some sort of strange cloth. Move the coffee table. We'll unroll it on the floor in front of the fireplace.' Mark hastily pushed the coffee table against their sofa, then, a little nervously, backed himself across the room to stand on the hearthstone. In the kitchen the telephone rang, but both men ignored it, transfixed by the strange piece of rolled material. Steven knelt down and began spreading the cloth. 'Look at this, it unfolds lengthwise as well.'

'Go ahead,' Mark encouraged, although he didn't sound completely convinced this was a good idea. His arms were held tightly against his chest, his hands clenched into fists and tucked under his chin. He looked as though he might, at any moment, claw his way up the chimney to safety.

Steven unfolded the long rectangular cloth. It was about ten feet wide.

'Look at that,' Mark said in awe as green and yellow flecks of light danced in the air above the tapestry, like fireflies on a humid summer evening.

'It doesn't hurt to touch it or be near it,' Steven said, bewildered, 'but it must be electric, or maybe radioactive, like you said. It's really changing the atmosphere in here. Is that smell ozone?'

'Uh, yeah.' Now Mark was frightened. 'We need to call someone. This guy must have come across some plutonium or radium in a mine up there. It might even be in that rock. Maybe over time it worked its way into the fabric of this thing.'

'I can't believe how large it is,' Steven mused. 'How the hell did it fit in that small container?' He unfolded the last corner of the tapestry and let it fall from his hand to the hardwood floor. 'What do you suppose these designs are?' he asked, considering the series of strange figures and shapes arranged across the expanse of cloth.

'I have no idea,' Mark answered. 'A lot of Asians helped open the west. Maybe this is some sort of Asian scroll, some art form.'

'I don't know. They don't look like Asian characters to me. Look at that one near your foot.' Steven pointed. 'Is that a tree?'

'Tree? Wait a minute—' Mark cut their analysis short. 'Steven, if that thing is radioactive, we're dying, right now. We need to get out of here.'

Steven paused, his mind racing to come up with some way to avoid getting fired for breaking into the safe deposit box. 'You're right. Let's go. We'll head down to Owen's and call the School of Mines or the police or someone.' He started to back away. 'C'mon, but you'd better not step on it.'

'Right, right, let's go.' Mark started moving around the edge of the tapestry. 'Grab my coat. It's on the back of the chair in the hall.'

Steven went to retrieve Mark's jacket and grab his wallet from the table in the kitchen. When he returned, his roommate was gone.

THE RONAN COAST

Mark's legs failed and he fell to his knees. Struggling to stand, he found he was outside; the ground was soft, wet sand, giving somewhat under his weight.

'What the hell is this?' he heard himself ask, but he found little comfort in the flat sound of his own voice. 'No. This isn't right. This *can't* be right. Where am I? How did I get outside?' Disoriented, he tried to calm down as he slowly turned a full circle, taking in his surroundings. He was surprised at how bright the night was. He was standing ankle-deep in wet sand on the edge of a small stream that emptied into what appeared to be an ocean.

'This can't be.' He took several deep breaths, then told himself, 'Wait. Don't think yet, just look around. This will all make sense when I calm down. Just slow down.'

Feeling the steady motion of cool water against his ankles, soaking down into his boots, Mark began slowly to relax. 'It has to be the pizza. Maybe I had some bad mushrooms or old cheese or something: this is all a hallucination.' Finding solace in that possibility, he continued to talk out loud. 'Wait it out. Just like a bad drunk, just wait it out.'

He stepped from the edge of the stream and wandered out onto the beach. 'It's okay, I guess,' he said, breathing the salty air and feeling a strong breeze blowing in off the water. 'If I have to be stuck in a delusion, at least this isn't too bad.'

His dream beach was much warmer than Idaho Springs. Mark pulled off his sweater, then sat down heavily. He dragged his heels back and forth, digging two parallel ruts in the sand, finding the repetitive motion comforting. He lay back and rested his head on the gritty pillow behind him, closing his eyes. The wind from the incoming tide, a sense of something familiar, helped him to relax, and he breathed deeply, remembering long days at the beach when he was young. His parents would load him and his sister into a behemoth Country Squire station wagon and drive out to Jones Beach. While he dragged an array of plastic toys in a brightly coloured bucket, his mother hauled a lunch basket and what seemed like several dozen towels and blankets across the burning sand. His father, looking taller in a swimsuit, always carried a cooler filled with cold beer in one hand and a large yellow beach umbrella, perhaps ten feet in diameter, slung over his opposite shoulder. Together, they would find a spot among a vast sea of colourful beach umbrellas, run up the yellow giant as if to claim a ten-by-ten foot spot of beachfront for a pastel kingdom and begin settling in as though the beach were nothing more than a guest room at Aunt Jenny's.

Within minutes, every inch of carefully placed blanket or towel would be covered with a light dusting of sand, not enough to merit a complete dismantling of the beach apparatus, but enough to irk his parents, to creep into his sister's diapers and to add a pleasant grit to everything eaten that afternoon. Mark smiled at the memory until reality crept into his reverie. 'No!' he exclaimed, sitting up. 'This isn't real. I'm sick. I ate something. I have to wake up now.' Squeezing handfuls of sand between his fingers, he remembered the large cloth tapestry Steven unrolled on their floor. 'It's got to have something to do with that thing.'

He pulled off his boots and socks and walked towards the water, muttering, 'If that really was radiation, I might be dead already.' He rolled up his jeans and stepped into the surf. 'No, I can't be dead. If I were dead, I wouldn't care if I got wet.' Mark leaned down to taste the ocean water. It was more briny than Long Island Sound. Still feeling the effects of that evening's beer consumption, he wiped a sleeve across his brow. 'Sheez, I hope I'm not dead. I'd hate to be half-hammered for eternity.'

Resigning himself to the fact that time would tell what had happened to him, Mark Jenkins began wandering along the beach, his feet ankle-deep in the frothy shallows.

Rounding a point that jutted out from the forest behind him, he stopped suddenly. Just above the horizon was the answer to why the evening was so bright: two moons hung silently in the night sky, like twin eyes of a vigilant sea god. 'Two moons,' he mused softly, then cried out, 'Steven! What *was* that thing?' His heart began to race and, feeling dizzy, he knelt in the sand and started repeating, over and over, 'It can't be . . . it can't be,' like a mantra.

Then, slowly, as if the truth might dash his hopes for a simple answer, Mark turned his gaze skywards. The constellations were different; he didn't recognise a single star arrangement.

This was no hallucination; he hadn't been poisoned and he wasn't dead.

But no answers presented themselves. He sat down in the sand, his knees pulled up tightly against his chest despite the warm and humid evening.

'Mark?' Steven called down the back hall, 'are you in the bathroom?' There was no response. The bathroom door was open and the light switched off. There was no way his friend could have gone upstairs; he would have passed through the kitchen, where Steven was.

'He must be outside already,' Steven said to himself, hurrying back through the hall and shouting 'Mark!', but the door was locked and the deadbolt securely in place.

'Sheez, didn't you think I was coming with you?' he called, finding it odd his roommate would lock the door from the outside without waiting for him. He had unlocked the door and stepped onto their porch before he heard a light jangle coming from the pocket of Mark's jacket. In his haste to get away from William Higgins's radioactive tapestry Steven had not realised Mark's keys were still in the pocket. He checked the coat to confirm his suspicion, then re-entered the house to continue searching for his friend.

'Mark!' Steven shouted again, 'C'mon, let's get out of here!'

In the kitchen, the telephone rang again; probably Hannah, calling to confirm their date for the following evening. He was tempted to answer it, but right now he needed to find Mark; he'd call her from Owen's later. He listened for footsteps coming from anywhere in the house: nothing. The air in their front room was still shimmering slightly; Steven could make out the small flecks of yellow and green light glowing dimly against the dark background of the old stone fireplace.

Slowly he turned to stare down at the mysterious tapestry, a swirling cauldron of colour unrolled across the floor. It was simple woven fabric – he guessed wool, but now could not remember exactly how it had felt in his hands. It had peculiar designs stitched in light-coloured thread, each meticulously detailed, but completely foreign to him. A dawning realisation brought a wave of nausea.

'Oh, Jesus,' he murmured, 'not in there ... that can't be.' Something deep inside told him no matter how impossible, he was right. Somehow, that cloth had taken his roommate. 'Mark,' he shouted down at the floor, 'Mark, can you hear me?' His voiced echoed off the wood and vibrated the delicate metal chimes in their hall clock. The ringing died away and he heard floorboards creak under his weight as he paced back and forth behind the sofa. No answer.

'Think,' he directed himself, 'think of something, fast.' But though he was desperate, his mind was blank. Maybe he could experiment. He moved to his desk, shoved the rosewood box containing William Higgins's precious rock to one side and searched for a pencil, then turned back to the living room floor.

'I feel okay. It doesn't seem to be doing any physical damage to me – then again, I've never been around anything radioactive before, so I don't really know.' He rolled the pencil between his fingers. 'Either way, it can't have completely vaporised or disintegrated Mark in the fifteen seconds it took me to get back from the kitchen, especially if I'm standing here just fine ten minutes later.' He cursed his inability to think straight in stressful situations. 'So, if he's not here in the house, he must be—' Steven gently lofted the pencil towards the tapestry, '—in there.'

He watched in awe as the pencil arced towards the floor. Tumbling through the air, its bright blue and orange logo flashed twice: Steven had just enough time to recognise the words *Denver Broncos* printed below the pink nub of the eraser. It never landed. As soon as it crossed the plane above the shimmering tapestry, the pencil vanished from sight.

'Holy frothing Christ!' he exclaimed and immediately reached for something else he could throw into the cloth.

Paper clips, a balled-up telephone bill, two empty beer cans and a pizza crust later, Steven was truly terrified. Snatching up Mark's jacket, he ran into the street and down the hill. Sprinting around the corner from Tenth onto Miner Street, he saw Owen's in the distance, the lights and music a latter-day mirage at the far end of an otherwise silent row of city blocks. Despite tearing through Idaho Springs at a dead run, Steven's thoughts caught up with him. He slowed to a jog. His story would sound absurd to the police.

He sat for a moment on a bench, contemplating his boots and trying to come up with a reasonable version, something that wouldn't have them calling the nearest psychiatric unit. He rubbed his fingertips roughly against his temples and burst out angrily, 'There is no reasonable version, you goddamn coward! You have to figure this out. *You* have to find him.'

Feeling alone and guilty, Steven Taylor rose and walked back home.

Two hours later found Steven sitting in a patio chair on the porch of 147 Tenth Street, watching the living room through the front window. He had failed to come up with any viable explanation for what had happened; now he was too frightened to re-enter the house. He kept hoping Mark would suddenly appear, unhurt, and he wouldn't have to come up with some course of action. They would simply turn the tapestry over to someone who would know what to do with it and Steven would prepare himself to receive due punishment when Howard Griffin discovered he had opened Higgins's safe deposit box.

Steven wondered how many other people were like him. His fear dominated him, broke his spirit; in turn, he could think of nothing to do. He was not brave. He was terrified. It must have been something from long ago that started him down this path, maybe something he'd run from as a child, that had grown, layer by layer, over the course of his life until now, when he was literally paralysed with fear.

He and Mark had often laughed that Steven was no risk taker. Everything had its place: he always needed to know what lay on the horizon, what was on the day's agenda, in order to feel comfortable. He began planning vacations twelve months in advance so as to leave nothing to chance. Mark was different, a brave soul who charged willingly into risky situations and always seemed to emerge unscathed.

'Why couldn't I have fallen onto the damned tapestry?' Steven asked of the still autumn night, hoping for some response to alleviate his anxiety. Mark would have known what to do – and if he didn't, he would have leapt onto it anyway, boldly facing whatever it held. Steven couldn't bring himself to stand up, enter his own house and step onto that miserable rug, no matter how thoroughly he beat himself up about it.

'Sonofabitch!' he cried, hating himself and embarrassed by his fear.

Later on he watched as the first light of dawn painted the mountains pink and heralded the advent of the new day. Mark had been gone almost eight hours and still Steven sat on his porch, a coward, suffering every coward's worst nightmare: no escape and no excuse. He could either seek help, or he could go into the house and throw himself onto the mercy of the strange cloth he had stolen from the bank the day before. Neither option was appetising, and both required more fortitude than he had managed to summon up in years.

Watching the mountains slowly change colour in the morning light, he remembered an art history class in college. Impressionist painters believed sunlight on any subject changed slightly every seven minutes. He checked his watch: 5.42 a.m. Staring up at the stony peaks above Clear Creek Canyon, Steven waited. He would see the light change in seven minutes' time; he would watch as the coming day shaded the mountain ridges in slowly evolving hues, and in seven and a half minutes' time he would get up and go in search of Mark Jenkins. 5.45 a.m., and a car passed on Tenth Street: Jennifer Stuckey, heading for the bakery to get the morning's first loaves in the oven. Sunlight inched its way down the sides of the canyon: every minute passed with his full attention. He could not remember the last time he had concentrated so fiercely on any one minute; this morning he would chart the full course of seven minutes. He was more frightened than he had ever been, but this morning was special. He wondered how often Monet or Renoir had waited seven minutes for the light to change on a flower or a small pond. He was seeing so much more than he ever had before: the clarity helped to mitigate his anxiety; it offered a sliver of courage for what was coming next. At 5.49 a.m. he rose to his feet and gave the canyon a long last look. The Impressionists had been right. He *had* seen the change in sunlight. Grasping Mark's coat in one hand, Steven opened the door to his house, crossed the front room and stepped without hesitation into the shimmering haze above the tapestry.

BOOK II

Rona

THE OLD KEEP

Brexan Carderic leaned forward in the saddle, hoping the lower profile would garner more speed from her mount. A strand of wet, matted hair escaped her collar and lashed across her face, momentarily blocking her view. 'Get it cut,' she spat to herself, pushing the uncooperative lock away. Her patrol unit was still far ahead and she had no wish to be riding alone through the Ronan forest. Earlier that morning, Lieutenant Bronfio had sent her into Estrad Village with a coded message. All she had to do was wait in front of a particular inn until a local merchant approached and asked for directions to Greentree Square; she was to hand over a small parcel and return immediately to camp.

Brexan had expected the merchant to arrive shortly after she got to the rendezvous; she was annoyed at being left to wait most of the morning. It was nearly midday when the fashionably dressed young man finally approached.

'Excuse me, but can you tell me how to get to Greentree Square?' the stranger asked.

'Certainly,' she answered, playing along, 'follow this street north until you come to—'

'You don't have to tell me how to get there, you stupid rutting bitch,' the man interrupted in an angry whisper, 'just give me the package.'

Brexan was taken aback at his rudeness. 'Here you are, sir,' she answered, and was immediately upset with herself for showing the man such deference.

The merchant calmed down. 'Thank you, soldier. Nice work.' Reaching into his tunic, he withdrew several sheets of parchment. 'Take these to Lieutenant Bronfio right away.'

Brexan nodded, 'Yes, sir,' and watched the well-dressed man as he wandered off along the street.

By the time she returned to camp, her unit was out on patrol, policing the forbidden forest and the north shore of the Estrad River before joining another unit that evening. Determined to catch up, she rode south, not slowing even when she came to the forest. Standing alone in the centre of the village was relatively safe, but the forest was dangerous to any Malakasian separated from the safety of the unit. Few Ronans would attack an occupation soldier in a town, where an investigation might turn up any number of guilty parties, but the solitude of the southern woods was a different matter.

Brexan reached the beach; she would make up time if she ran along the water's edge on the hard-packed sand. A full Twinmoon was coming the following day and she enjoyed the feel of the strong winds off the water. The southern Twinmoon affected the tides along the Ronan coast; huge waves pounded the beach this morning and Brexan felt the spray splashed up from her horse's hooves. It looked as if the world itself were marking the passage of time.

As she rounded a sandy point, Brexan saw a lone man sitting upright near the water's edge. Reining in quickly, she turned and made for the protective cover of the forest. The pounding surf and near-gale drowned out all sound of her approach. She dismounted quietly, tethered her horse out of sight and slowly picked her way through the underbrush.

Mark Jenkins stared out to sea. He had fallen asleep in the sand and his lower back ached from hours resting on the uneven surface. He had woken just a few minutes before, disappointed for once that he was not in his bed nursing a debilitating hangover. Now, still groggy, he was trying to work out how he came to be at the ocean. Two moons still hung in the sky, although they now looked closer together, as if they might crash into one another in some rare and profound galactic mishap.

Eventually he would have to go in search of food or a telephone ... he wrestled with a sense of foreboding that unfamiliar constellations and a second moon might not be the oddest discoveries he was about to make.

Mark's mind was too logical: he was not ready to accept the fact that he might have been transported to another world, or that he might have died and discovered a two-mooned afterlife.

Beside him were hundreds of small holes where he had pushed his fingertips into the sand in an effort to create a map of visible stars. None of their patterns were familiar. Worse, he had seen no planes, heard no cars, spotted no boats and observed no joggers running along the beach. There were no cigarette butts, no empty soda cans, no gum wrappers and no footprints save those he had left himself the night before. He feared he was alone, but he could not think of an expanse of beach in the world where he would so thoroughly fail to find any trace of humanity.

'Well,' he sighed finally, 'I can't wait here for ever. I'd better get moving.'

He was about to stand when, over the howling of the onshore breeze, he heard someone calling his name. Brushing sand from his clothes, he strained his eyes to see along the beach: someone was running towards him. Squinting, he recognised Steven and shouted out an unintelligible oath. He grabbed his boots and sweater and sprinted towards his roommate, relief flooding through him as he hurried across the sand. Both men were oblivious to the young woman observing from the forest's edge.

Huddled in a thicket, Brexan watched as the dark-skinned stranger rose and began running along the beach. The Malaka-sian soldier marvelled at Mark's outlandish clothing: blue leggings of some sort, a bright red tunic and a white undergar-ment that exposed his bare arms. She had no idea which territory produced such strange clothing, but she knew she had to get word of this intruder to Lieutenant Bronfio and the local officer corps as soon as possible. Feeling in her vest for the pages given her by the merchant in Estrad, she crawled back to her horse as quickly as she dared.

When she came upon her mount, Brexan nearly vomited from the stench. The beast lay dead, rotting at an unnatural rate in the Ronan sun. Dumbfounded, the soldier noticed the tree to which she had tethered the horse only moments earlier was also dead. It was a large coastal cedar, and when she had tied the reins to it, it had been lush with prickly green branches. Now it was grey, dry; it looked as if its life had been drained through the sand, squaring some overdrawn account with nature.

The horse twitched several times and Brexan backed away, fearing the rotten shell of the animal might spring up from the small puddle of blood and bodily fluid gathering beneath it. A moment later, the beast was bone-dry, mummified. The fluids that dripped from the dried flesh were strangely absorbed and the putrid stench faded on the ocean breeze.

Brexan nervously rubbed her palms across the breast of her tunic and wondered what to do next. Her saddle and weapons remained buckled to the corpse. Tentatively she inched towards the remains.

As she began unfastening a short dagger and her forest bow, the almor sprang up before her. Brexan screamed, 'Lords, help me!' and, falling backwards, stumbled over an exposed root. From the sandy forest floor, the soldier looked into the face of the demon creature and watched in horror as the nearly translucent visage peered back at her. Brexan knew the legends of terrifying demons that ravaged the known world thousands of Twinmoons before. She always believed they were tales amplified by the passage of time: monsters grew more powerful, demons more frightening and magic more mysterious as stories were handed down through the generations.

Looking up into the perfectly evil face of her first almor, Brexan realised she had been wrong. The creature's eyes were deeply set, grey, and changing shape as the monster contemplated her. It stood on fluid, shapeless hind legs and its height fluctuated between that of a tall man and a small tree. It appeared to be comprised entirely of a cloudy, milk-white fluid, but if the tales were right, the demon possessed superhuman strength and speed. Fighting back would be pointless. All she could do now was to wait for it to decide whether or not to take her. Brexan tried to close her eyes, preparing to feel her life drain away, but as frightened as she was, she could not keep them shut. She had to look at it.

The almor had experienced ample gratification with the horse and the large cedar tree. Both had given it energy. For a moment it considered taking the young woman cowering on the ground until, reaching towards her, it was reminded of its mission. This was not the one it had been summoned to find. The almor was driven by urges, and with its need for food satisfied, the urge to find its target was renewed. It was being controlled by a distant force, a long-forgotten voice that had commanded it once before. It would not be permitted to return home until it had found and absorbed its target, a sorcerer. Reaching out with one formless arm, it found the root system of a grove of cottonwood trees. Then it was gone.

Brexan lay in the dirt, breathing hard. She rolled onto her side, vomited into a patch of sweet-smelling ferns and promptly passed out.

'I can't believe I found you,' Steven called as the roommates met on the beach. 'I was convinced—'

He was interrupted as Mark hugged him hard. 'I thought I died. I thought this was some sort of afterlife, some crazy hallucination—' Mark stopped and held Steven at arm's length. 'You are really here, aren't you?'

Steven handed him a balled-up piece of paper. Mark unfolded it: their August telephone bill. 'What's this?' he asked curiously. 'Why do you have our old phone bill?'

'We are someplace. We aren't dead and this isn't a dream.' Mark still looked confused, but Steven continued, 'It was the tapestry, the cloth from the safe deposit box. I threw that phone bill into the air above it and watched it disappear.'

'What? So, it's some kind of transportation device, some hole in the universe? What is it? How did we and our phone bill get here?' Mark was frustrated. 'Steven, we live in Colorado, a long, *long* way from the sea: and here we are, at the ocean . . . *an* ocean. I don't even know if there are other people around here.'

'I don't know how it works and I don't know where it's dropped us, but it's sent us *somewhere.*'

'Why?'

'What do you mean, "why"?'

'I mean why would it send us somewhere? What's its purpose? Why would such a thing exist?' Mark's head began to ache again; he rubbed his temples.

'I don't know. Maybe it's some experimental military transportation device they hid in our bank.'

Mark shot him a dubious look. 'A hundred and thirty-five years ago?'

'Maybe not. Maybe they did it six months ago and we didn't know. Either way, I'm certain the answer isn't going to come looking for us here.'

The first arrow struck the ground near Steven's right foot.

Without thinking, he jumped out of the way, then shouted, 'What the hell is that?' Before Mark could answer, a second arrow hit the sand only inches from the first.

'Stand still,' a voice called from the edge of the forest. 'Do not try to run.' Seeing Mark raise his hands in the air, Steven did the same, dropping Mark's jacket to the sand.

'We aren't going to run,' Mark shouted towards the treeline. 'We're lost here and need to borrow a phone. We'll leave just as soon as we can call a cab.'

'Speak Common,' the hidden voice commanded, and accented the order with another arrow at their feet.

Steven looked at Mark. 'I understand what he said. I mean, I can tell what he's saying.'

'So can I.' Mark's face modulated from fear to curiosity. 'It's not German and I recognise enough to know that it isn't Russian. How can that be?'

Instead of responding, Steven turned his gaze towards the forest. Two men appeared from beneath the trees. 'Holy shit, look at them,' he whispered. 'They look like something out of another time. Look at their clothes – and those weapons.'

They were dressed similarly: each wore boots, leggings made from some sort of fabric – cotton or wool, Mark guessed – and heavy cloth tunics belted around the waist. One wore a short dagger and carried what appeared to be a rapier, while the shorter of the two was armed with a longbow. Mark could clearly see it was nocked with an arrow and ready to fire. The three arrows at their feet indicated some skill; Mark suspected any escape attempt would mean certain death.

Garec and Sallax moved warily towards the two strangers. 'I've never seen anything like them before,' Garec whispered, keeping an arrow trained on the lighter-skinned man. 'Look at those costumes they're wearing.'

'They don't look like they're from any tribe or territory I've ever come across,' Sallax answered, 'but I bet the next round they're Malakasian.'

'The dark-skinned one might be from the southern coast, but his clothing is absurd.'

'His tunic is red. Maybe he's royalty.' The big man laughed

ironically. 'Do you think they've been sent here to infiltrate the Resistance?'

'How could they expect to blend in looking like that?' Garec asked. 'Is Malagon that stupid?'

'I've no idea,' Sallax answered, 'but Gilmour will know. Let's get them back to Riverend.'

'How?' Garec began to look worried. 'We're not supposed to be out here ourselves. What if they alert someone?'

'We kill them both and run,' Sallax answered calmly, then added, 'What language were they speaking? Did you recognise it?'

'I don't know. It certainly isn't Malakasian.'

'Lords, do you suppose they've developed some sort of spy tongue? Isn't it enough that they've run our lives and our country for five generations? What do they need with a spy language?' Sallax looked as if he were about to impale the strangers with his rapier.

'Let's wait. Gilmour will know who they are.' Garec looked back along the beach. 'Let's get them out of here quickly, while we're still alone.'

Steven and Mark still had their hands in the air as Sallax and Garec reached them. Sallax glared at Steven. 'On your knees, spy,' he ordered.

'We told you we're unarmed,' Steven replied hesitantly, moving his hands in front of him in a gesture of supplication. 'Just let us explain.'

'We're lost,' Mark interjected, but he stopped as Sallax stabbed the point of his rapier against Steven's chest.

'Speak the common tongue, you rutting animals,' he ordered, 'or I will kill you both, right here.'

Mark looked at Steven, took a deep breath and tried to relax. 'We're lost,' he answered. A look of surprise swept over his face and he nearly smiled at Garec. 'I did it! I— I can talk to you!'

'That's better,' Garec answered, gesturing to Mark to continue.

'I don't know how this happened,' Mark went on, 'but we were home and we found this cloth ... actually he stole it—' and then, thinking twice, he corrected himself, 'well, no, he didn't steal it, that was a joke ... anyway, this cloth sent us here. We don't know how and we don't know why, but we are here, wherever *here* is, and we'd like to get back.'

'You're thieves then?' Sallax asked.

'No, no,' Mark replied quickly. 'I'm a teacher and he's a banker. We're from Colorado. Have you heard of Colorado?'

'No. You're lying,' Garec said. 'There is no such place as Coloredado.'

'Colorado,' Steven corrected, then immediately raised his hands in apology.

'Yes there is,' Mark said. 'It's where we come from. We have no idea how we're talking with you right now. We're afraid we've come to another time, another place, somewhere we never imagined we'd be, and somehow, we can speak with you. We don't mean any harm. We're peaceful. We just want to get back home.'

'Liars, spies, thieves.' Steven flinched as Sallax punctuated each word with short thrusts of his rapier. 'I despise all of them. On your knees.'

Garec drew several leather strips from a pouch at his belt and firmly tied the strangers' hands behind their backs. He picked up Mark's sweater and jacket from the sand as Sallax ordered them up the beach towards the thick foliage of the coastal forest.

'How did you do that?' Steven asked under his breath.

'I don't know. I just relaxed my mind and the words came to me,' Mark whispered back. 'It's not possible, though. I mean, suppose we've come back in time and this is early Europe. I don't speak those languages . . . neither do you.' He took several steps, looked back at their captors and added, 'Listen to me. Back in time, what am I saying?'

'Hey, at this point, all we can do is wait and see. When I saw the phone bill and those beer cans disappear into that tapestry, I knew this was something different from *anything* we could ever have imagined.' Steven closed his eyes and tried to slow down his thoughts. Then it happened; a handful of foreign words took shape in his mind. 'Where are we?'

Mark flashed him a quick grin. 'That's it. That's how I did it.'

'It's none of your rutting concern where we are,' Sallax answered, jabbing Steven in the lower back. 'You just keep moving.'

Steven muttered, 'Sorry I asked, I guess.'

Mark stifled a laugh. Steven felt better knowing they were together. It had taken every ounce of courage he could summon to step onto that tapestry, and when his foot had come down in the shallow inlet, Steven knew they really had uncovered something supernatural, something completely and utterly unexpected. Strangely, he was not as afraid as he'd expected to be – waiting all night on their porch, not *knowing*, had been more frightening; that had paralysed him with fear. Now, even with his life in danger, he was glad he had taken the risk.

'You didn't tell me you brought beer,' Mark continued, softly, 'or were you thoughtless enough to lob empty cans through? Typical – God, but I could use a cold one now.'

Steven surprised himself by managing a laugh, but the moment passed when he felt the tip of Sallax's blade in his back again.

It was early evening by the time they reached their destination: the forest surrounding Riverend Palace. Stopping at the edge of the palace grounds, Sallax pushed his prisoners to their knees, 'We wait here until dark,' he said curtly, leaning against a large maple tree.

Mark looked beyond the trees to the crumbling palace in the distance. 'Why not now?' he asked, more to observe their captors' reaction than expecting an answer.

'Mind your rutting business,' Sallax said.

Garec came to sit near the two prisoners. 'It's several hundred paces of exposed ground between here and the palace. If you're really Malakasian spies, then you'll understand why we wait here. I'm afraid you also understand why we can't allow you to leave with that information.' His tone was almost apologetic.

'We're not spies,' Steven told him, trying to remain calm. 'We already explained—'

'Yes,' Garec interrupted, 'you said a magic cloth transported you to our forest from Coloridio or someplace. Surely you understand our hesitation in believing such a story.'

'But it's true,' Steven tried again. 'We were in our own home last night. Look at our clothes: it's much colder where we live.'

'Yes,' Garec agreed, 'it *is* much colder in Malakasia.'

Steven and Mark looked at each other and shrugged. They mutely agreed to try again after they reached the old castle. It was clear, even from this distance, that Riverend Palace was in ruins, the moat dry and the outer battlements crumbling in numerous places along the wall. Once an architectural monument to Rona's royal family, it was a dismal reminder of a more prosperous time. Mark could see that the roof over several wings of the sprawling stone structure had caved in.

Looking to Garec, he said, 'I love what you've done with the place.'

'Time, weather, nomads, even local masons needing stone have all contributed to its disrepair. Legend has it the palace was once a grand residence. I sometimes enjoy imagining what it must have looked like,' Garec mused, almost to himself.

'Who lives there?' Steven asked.

'Lived,' Garec corrected. 'The Ronan royal family used to live here. Of course, they haven't been around for the past nine hundred and eighty Twinmoons.' Steven and Mark exchanged a curious glance. 'But don't pretend this is all new to you.' Garec was suddenly angry. 'It's your rutting horsecock of a prince who keeps us in this situation. I have to sneak about the forests of my own country. Palace grounds are forbidden, forbidden for Ronans to visit. They should be a monument, a national treasure, but instead they rot out there while we sneak around under the heavy hand of your murdering dog tyrant leader Malagon.' Garec glared at them then rose and walked to the edge of the long meadow separating them from the palace.

Mark pieced the information together and risked a quick exchange with Steven in English. 'So, this is Rona. They're enemies with Mala— Malasomething, wherever that is, and Mala— Malasomethingelse is the prince who rules with, and I'm guessing here, a bit of a heavy hand.' He would have continued, but Sallax hit him hard across the temple with the back of his hand.

'I told you to use Common,' he ordered. 'You wait: if Gilmour says you die, I will be especially pleased to cut your heart out and feed it to a village dog.'

Mark shook the ringing from his head. He'd had enough. He lashed out at Sallax's legs: a wide, sweeping kick caught him behind one knee, knocking him to the ground. In an instant Mark was on him. Although he couldn't free his hands, he did manage a fierce blow to Sallax's nose with his forehead before Garec pulled him away.

Blood ran across Sallax's face as he stood, breathing deeply, and drew his rapier. 'We only need one spy for interrogations,' he growled, seething with rage as he moved deliberately towards Mark. 'Say good night, my friend.'

Mark tried to slither out of his way, but as Sallax raised his blade to strike, Garec stepped between the two men, wrapping his arms firmly around his friend in an attempt to pin the bigger man's rapier to his side.

'No, Sallax. This isn't war; this is murder. We don't kill unarmed prisoners. We are *Ronans*, remember?'

Sallax was too angry to speak; Garec continued, 'Here, wipe your nose. Have a drink.' He drew a wineskin from his pack. Mark crawled back to Steven's side, but he wasn't fast enough to avoid a brutal kick to his ribs.

'This is far from over, spy,' Sallax growled.

'Untie me, you big bastard,' Mark taunted Sallax between laboured breaths. 'Set me free and we'll see how tough you are, shithead. I'll make you swallow that sword, motherfucker.'

'Mark, calm down,' Steven whispered, trying to stop his friend railing at the now-impassive Ronan. 'You'll get us both killed, and I'm pretty sure if we're dead here, we're dead at home too. For God's sake, shut up.'

Finally, Mark gave up cursing and fell back to the ground, coughing violently and fighting to catch his breath.

Brexan woke with a powerful headache. She wasn't sure how long she had been unconscious; just a few moments, she assumed. Sitting up in the sandy dirt, she rested her head in her hands until the pain subsided. She cast a curious glance around the forest, but saw nothing of the almor. 'If it wanted me, I'd be dead,' she said to herself and struggled to her feet. On the ground where she had fallen were the pages the merchant had given her earlier that morning. Retrieving them, she noticed the wax seal was broken. She looked around self-consciously before reading the message scrawled inside. The pages contained a detailed drawing of Riverend Palace and the surrounding forest. Arrows and symbols gave directions for an assault, by two platoons of soldiers, apparently, and outlined the direction from which they were to attack a large building inside the courtyard. It looked like Lieutenant Riskett's platoon would approach from the south across the battlements and through a large window at the east end of the building, while Lieutenant Bronfio's platoon – Brexan's own – would attack from the north, through the portcullis gate, entering the building from the west.

Brexan folded the pages back up: it was obviously important Lieutenant Bronfio get them as quickly as possible. Ignoring her aching head, she began jogging through the southern forest towards the outskirts of Estrad Village. She wondered if the mysterious strangers she had seen on the beach earlier that morning were somehow involved, perhaps even the reason for the impending attack. She cursed her bad luck as she followed a game trail: she *must* reach Lieutenant Bronfio by dawn tomorrow; failing to deliver the message and plans would put her fellow soldiers at risk – and end her career in Prince Malagon's army. As one of only three women in Bronfio's platoon, she already had to work much harder than her male counterparts to earn the respect and admiration of the officers. Losing her horse and failing to deliver critical espionage information would ruin any chance of promotion, even to the rank of corporal, for at least the next ten Twinmoons. She ran on, alone and afraid, hoping desperately to avoid any lurking Ronan partisans who might take her prisoner or, worse, kill her on the spot for being stupid and irresponsible enough to get separated from her unit this far into occupied lands.

The dinner aven had nearly passed when Brexan reached the encampment. Another platoon had arrived; she recognised Lieutenant Riskett pacing outside Bronfio's tent. All around her, people were readying themselves for the coming conflict. She hustled to the lieutenant's quarters to deliver her message.

Brexan explained the delay – leaving out the almor attack; she wasn't sure they'd believe that – to an exasperated Lieutenant Bronfio and waited, sweating, filthy and tired, while he contemplated the pages she had handed over. She'd decided to say nothing of her encounter with the almor: most Malakasians believed the demons to be just a legend, and she was pretty sure her story would be interpreted as nothing more than an elaborate excuse for losing one of Prince Malagon's mounts. Instead, she blamed a riding accident.

Now, standing at rigid attention outside the lieutenant's tent, she ignored stares from Riskett's soldiers while friends from her own platoon grinned at her, some in compassion and others in ridicule: it would be a long time before she would be allowed to forget that she'd lost her horse.

Lieutenant Bronfio appeared through the flaps of his tent, looked Brexan up and down and ordered her to make ready for the assault on Riverend Palace.

'Get a mount from the pack animals. There are a few sturdy enough,' Bronfio told her. 'I commend your determination to get these pages to me, soldier. However, in the future, I would encourage you to be more careful with His Majesty's horses.'

'Yes, sir,' Brexan replied, then, glancing towards her fellow soldiers, added quietly, 'Ah, sir? There were others on the beach, sir. They were—'

'Never mind that now,' Bronfio interrupted, annoyed with the young messenger. 'Just ready yourself for the morrow.' Brexan shut her mouth.

When night finally fell, Garec motioned for the two prisoners to stand. 'We're going in . . . stay low, and don't say anything until we're inside the battlements. One word out of either of you and we'll leave your corpses for the spring flowers.' Steven and Mark nodded assent. Sallax said nothing as he started out into open ground. Covering the distance to the crumbling battlements took less than a minute, but for Steven it felt like an eternity. Remembering the accuracy with which Garec had fired arrows at his feet that morning, he feared there would be other archers, assassins or snipers watching for this Ronan Resistance group.

'I don't even know what they're resisting,' Steven grumbled, staying as low to the ground as possible. Though his head and shoulders were bent, he felt as if his backside were exposed for any passing archer to skewer like a ham.

But when they reached the palace, he thought they might have stepped onto a big-budget film set. Even in its dilapidated state, Riverend towered above them, an imposing stone edifice black against the night sky. It was difficult for him to believe it had all been constructed for one family. The main building alone looked like it could easily accommodate several hundred guests. It stood now, a disintegrating relic from a majestic past Steven could not begin to understand. A small part of him was excited, wanting to get inside and look around.

Steven's thoughts were interrupted when Garec took him by

the arm and guided him to a narrow opening in the battlements. He was glad they didn't have to climb over the walls with their hands tied behind their backs. The stone ramparts reached nearly thirty feet into the sky and although they were crumbling in places, scaling them would be a difficult task, even for experienced climbers like him and Mark. He squeezed through the thin breach in the fortress' defences and found himself in a large courtyard.

Garec and Sallax immediately relaxed and Steven guessed they had reached a safe area. Still afraid to speak, however, he and Mark followed the two partisans towards the main building across the courtyard. There was an enormous stained-glass window in one of the outer walls. Steven had travelled through Europe while in high school; he'd seen many examples of stained-glass, and he was certain this window dwarfed the largest he could remember by several times: he estimated it was nearly a hundred feet high and fifty feet wide. Even in the dark, illuminated only by the light of the twin moons, Steven could see this was a stunning example of both creativity and engineering, even though several of the panes had been shattered – most likely falling victim to children throwing stones before fleeing back across the crumbled ramparts.

He was still appreciating the intricacies of the window by moonlight when Mark nudged him gently in the ribs. His roommate gestured towards the window's lower left corner, from where a soft, eerie glow emanated. Steven understood they were not alone. There were others waiting inside.

SOUTH BROADWAY AVENUE, DENVER

'Have you tried him at the bank?' Jennifer Sorenson hefted an oak rocking chair to Hannah, who was perched in the back of a customer's pick-up truck. 'He must be at work today.'

Hannah wiped her forehead across the shoulder of her T-shirt, leaving a small wet stain. It was cooler in the street than inside the antique shop, and she welcomed the job of loading several purchases for an elderly couple.

'No, I tried there and Mr Griffin said he hadn't seen him all morning. Apparently they were at the pub last night, but Steven left early with Mark. I tried him a few times at home but only got his machine.' She nodded thanks to her mother as Jennifer handed her a length of rope.

She began tying two small end tables together. 'I mean, I can understand if he wanted a night away from me. We've been talking three or four times a day and I do feel a little like I'm back in seventh grade, but why would he miss work today?'

'Maybe they had too much to drink,' her mother suggested. 'They might be home with the phone unplugged, nursing massive hangovers.'

'Not him, he's too responsible for that, and Mark sounds the same. I know they both drink some, but missing work? It doesn't fit.'

'Well, you're supposed to go out tonight, right?' Jennifer asked and, seeing Hannah nod, said, 'Go home. Get ready and see if he calls. If not, try him again, but Hannah, things happen. People sometimes find that—'

'Yes, I understand he could be avoiding me, but I'm telling you it's not like him.' She accented her point by pulling a half-hitch tight against the pick-up's bed. 'We moved very quickly into this relationship and if he's running, it's as much my fault as his. I just want to know nothing happened to him last night, because even if he were dumping me already, he wouldn't be missing work.'

Hannah jumped lightly to the sidewalk, shook hands with the customers and waved as they drove off along Broadway.

Jennifer Sorenson wrapped one arm affectionately around her daughter's shoulders. 'I'm sure he's not dumping you, and if he is, then he's the wrong one anyway.'

'Thanks – but I'll be okay. Maybe I'll drive up there tonight and ask him what's going on. If he really is sick, he might be glad to see me. And if I'm getting dumped, I'd just as soon have him do it before I haul myself to the Decatur Peak trailhead at 4.30 tomorrow morning.' She returned her mother's embrace. 'I could use the extra sleep and you could use the help here on a Saturday.'

'Well, it's after 5.00 already. You go home and get ready. I'll get things cleaned up and close the place down. If you're still home when I get back, I'll take you out tonight.'

'Thanks, Mom.' Hannah gently kissed her mother on the temple.

She unlocked the chain securing her bike to a wrought-iron bench in front of the store and jumped astride for the quick ride across the neighbourhood. Her helmet dangled loosely from the handlebars and Jennifer scolded her from the store entrance. 'The helmet belongs on your head, Hannah.'

Donning the helmet, Hannah shouted back, 'Is that where it goes? I've been wondering where all these damned bumps on my head were coming from. I'm sure I've lost forty, maybe fifty IQ points crashing into things this summer. Oh well, you'll have an unmarried, brain-damaged daughter to look after in your old age.' Shooting her mother a bright smile, she pedalled off.

Jennifer Sorenson allowed the door to close behind her and stood for a moment gathering her thoughts. Twenty-seven years later and she was still amazed at how much love, worry and compassion a parent could feel. It had begun the moment Hannah was first placed in her arms, and had continued unabated, day and night, for the next three decades. As a younger woman, she would never have guessed that raising a child would be the most meaningful and important thing she would do in her life. Feeling inadequate, unable to help Hannah deal with the potential heartbreak of a failed relationship, she quickly opened the door again, stepped outside and called quietly, 'Be careful, Hannah.' Her daughter was already several blocks away; she couldn't hear, but Jennifer, feeling better, returned inside to close up the shop.

Hannah arrived home to find no answer to any of her telephone messages. Showering quickly, she donned jeans, her running shoes and an old wool sweater she had bought in high school. Grabbing car keys and a Gore-tex jacket, she left the house for the drive up Clear Creek Canyon. Hannah disliked handbags, preferring instead to slip a thin leather wallet into her jacket or the back pocket of her jeans. She rarely wore make-up, but for those rare occasions when she needed the extra boost, she had a backpack with an array of beauty products stuffed haphazardly inside. Secretly, she was glad tonight was not an evening that merited that degree of preparation; she left the backpack on a chair.

Traffic was heavy heading west into the mountains. The ski season wasn't yet underway, but October weekends meant changing aspens, and Interstate 70 was jammed with carloads of what the locals called 'leaf peepers'. She didn't want to grow too frustrated with Steven before she knew why he had been avoiding her, so she rolled down the windows and tried to enjoy the crisp autumn evening. She loved the fall and started looking forward to the changing season with the first cool evenings that blew through Denver in late August.

Hannah left the majority of motorists to continue west while she turned off and followed Clear Creek into Idaho Springs. She was surprised to find both Steven's and Mark's vehicles parked in the driveway outside 147 Tenth Street. From the dusting of snow colouring the pavement it was obvious that neither car had been moved. Either the boys had walked to work this morning and been delayed somewhere, or they had never left the house at all.

Lights were on in the front room, hallway and kitchen, but she didn't see anyone moving about inside. She knocked on the side door, but no one answered. As she knocked again, she moved the barbecue grill on their porch and reached under the back wheel for the spare key Steven had used the weekend before. When the door remained unanswered, she took a deep breath and let herself inside.

Almost immediately, Hannah sensed something wrong in the house. She felt a strange sensation; she thought she could feel the air shimmering against her flesh, as if a window had been left cracked open during a hurricane. Reaching the living room, she saw what looked like static electricity, dancing in the air.

'Steven,' she called to the empty house, 'are you here? Mark?' No one answered and she stood riveted by the yellow and green lights flickering dimly above the disintegrating, secondhand sofa the boys seemed to love for reasons she couldn't even begin to fathom. The peculiar nature of the shimmering atmosphere made her uncomfortable and she decided to leave a note for Steven before continuing her search for him in town.

'Maybe they're down at Owen's,' she muttered to herself, looking for a sheet of paper. Against one wall was Steven's desk and she walked towards it, hoping to find something on which to scribble a quick message.

Discovering no pens on the desk, Hannah slid the wooden chair back and pulled open the top drawer – and as she did so, the odd lights and rippling air suddenly went completely still, as if they were operated by a hidden switch someone had just thrown in a different room.

'What the hell?' she asked, looking down at her feet. She hadn't immediately noticed that the coffee table had been pushed back against the couch to accommodate a strange cloth tapestry rolled out on the wooden planks of the living room floor. She crouched down to feel the material between her fingers. It was smooth, but unlike any fabric she had ever seen, and it had been stitched meticulously, decorated with a series of symbols and shapes. Some appeared to be primitive caricatures of trees and mountains, but many were unusually shaped runes she did not recognise from any period in history. The cloth was obviously an antique, but she struggled to date the piece. She could not remember her grandfather ever showing her such an odd ornamentation style.

'Your taste surprises me, Steven,' Hannah announced to the empty room. She decided she would have to learn more about the tapestry once she had found him.

She turned back to the drawer, not noticing that the back legs of the chair she had slid across the floor had caused the cloth to bunch up on itself. Still no pen or pencil, not even a chewed stub. She closed the drawer and looked over at the log mantle above the fireplace. Several pens stood in an old fraternity mug near a photo of Mark Jenkins standing proudly next to a mountain bike atop what Hannah guessed was Trail Ridge Road in the national park.

'Bingo,' she announced, starting across the tapestry. Without thinking, she reached out with one hand and pushed the wooden chair back into place under the desk. The folds of wrinkled material flattened out against the cold floorboards and Hannah Sorenson disappeared from the room.

THE FIREPLACE

'Garec, Sallax.' Versen Bier waved to them from across the ancient hall. 'Where have you been all day?' Gazing into the half-light at the far end of the narrow chamber, Steven saw a group of workers hauling large wooden boxes down stone steps to a room beneath the palace's ground floor. Torchlight brought some hazy visibility to the otherwise dark room, but not enough for Steven to see what was stored in the crates. The woodsman started towards the small group. He was a powerful-looking man with sandy brown hair, boyish features and muscular forearms, and dressed similarly to Garec and Sallax. In his belt he wore a long hunting knife and a small double-bit axe that looked honed to a razor's edge.

'Well, Sallax, look at your nose,' Versen said, smiling. 'What happened to you?'

'He did,' Sallax answered dryly, motioning towards Mark.

'Aha. And who have we here?' the woodsman asked the two foreigners. 'From the look of your bonds, I'd say spies. Unless of course you're making an innovative fashion statement and you expect all of us to be dressed this way in the coming Twinmoons.'

'We're not spies,' Steven told him matter-of-factly.

Noticing Mark's face, Versen asked, 'Oh? And what happened to you?'

Mark forced a grin and nodded towards Sallax. 'He did.'

Steven, Versen and Garec all chuckled, and Sallax turned towards the wall to avoid making eye-contact with any of them. Hearing laughter coming from the group, Brynne moved across the abandoned dining hall to join them.

'Am I the only one who finds it odd you're all laughing together? Especially when two of you are tied up?' she asked. She was sweating openly from hauling boxes, but Mark found her curiously attractive, despite her grimy appearance.

Garec put his arm around Brynne's shoulders and led her to stand before the two strangers. 'This is Mark Jenkins and Steven Taylor. They are from Color— Colorado?' He looked to Steven, who nodded. 'Apparently, they fell through a magic tapestry they stole . . . no, *found*, and were transported to the beach near the point.'

Sallax interjected, 'Or they're spies from Malakasia, here to gather information on the Resistance.'

'Dressed like that?' Brynne asked incredulously.

'That was my point,' Steven ventured. He had been working to loosen the leather thongs that held his wrists behind his back, but he didn't think he was making much progress: the sting from the straps rubbing against his raw flesh burned more painfully with each attempt. Giving up for the moment, he looked through the hall and realised that the palace had at one point been the victim of an enormous fire. The smell of ancient creosote lingered in the air and he could feel the gritty texture of ashes beneath his boots.

He knew the longer he and Mark could keep their captors talking, the more information they would glean, and the greater their chances of escape would be, once they freed themselves – if they freed themselves.

Once again, Steven relaxed his mind and let the foreign words come. 'What's your name?' he asked the girl.

'I'm called Brynne Farro,' she answered, rubbing a thin forearm across her sweat-streaked brow.

'Brynne Farro,' he asked, 'would you have some water, or some food? It's been a long day and we haven't eaten since—'

'You'll eat when I tell you to eat,' Sallax interrupted harshly. 'Brynne, take them upstairs and lock them in one of the apartments on the third level.'

'Why don't you do it?' she asked.

'Because, my dear sister, I am going to take over your duties hauling boxes downstairs.' Sallax handed her his hunting knife. 'If they make any move to escape, cut their throats.' To Mark and Steven he added, 'I would advise you not to test her ability with that knife, my strangely outfitted friends. She is deftly skilled with any number of weapons.'

137

Garec gave Brynne some leather straps and she motioned her two captives towards the huge staircase at the far end of the hall. As they passed the stacks of wooden crates, Steven risked a glimpse into one that had not yet been nailed shut.

'They're weapons,' he whispered in English. 'That box must contain thousands of arrows, just like the ones Garec fired at us this morning.'

'Well, they're obviously mobilising for action against this Malathing character.' Mark hesitated. Above them on the landing, Brynne watched as they carried on their conversation. She held a small torch to illuminate their way upstairs. Mark decided she was quite lovely. Her pale skin contrasted strikingly with her dark brown hair, and although slightly built, he could see that she was wiry and athletic. He imagined she had learned to hold her own in a fight, especially growing up with a brother like Sallax. The way she held his hunting knife, blade forward, ready to slash any would-be attacker, proved his suspicion. Yet she had the porcelain-smooth hands of a woman who, when time allowed, cared for her appearance. At that moment, Mark wanted to be free from his bonds for no other reason than to reach beyond the knife's edge and touch those perfect hands.

Brynne looked at them curiously. 'What is that language you speak?'

'It's the language we use in Colorado, and the region around our home,' Steven answered in Ronan, the words coming more quickly now.

'We're not certain how we learned your language. It must have happened to us when we were brought here,' Mark added. He changed the subject. 'Can you tell us why you are hiding weapons under the floor of this old castle?'

Brynne squinted into the darkness towards her friends, then motioned for Steven and Mark to continue following her upstairs. 'I will tell you as we go,' she whispered. They reached the second floor and Steven could see what might have been a large audience chamber at the end of a short hallway leading from the landing. The remains of a throne stood atop a slightly elevated dais. Charred and blackened in the fire, the ruined chair seemed to be patiently waiting for the return of a flawed king. Steven's view of the chamber faded to black as Brynne continued up the staircase and the light from the torch followed her away.

'If you are spies, then you know why we hoard weapons. If you're not spies— Well, I don't know where you come from.' They had reached the uppermost landing of the grand staircase and were high above the hall where they'd started their climb. She stopped and turned to face them. 'We have been under Malakasian occupation for as long as anyone can remember, four or five generations. Malagon Whitward is an evil and violent man, and the occupation soldiers grow more and more heavy-handed as they *keep the peace* here in Rona.' She brushed a lock of hair away from one eye and then, frustrated, pushed a handful behind her neck. 'We are fighting to win our freedom, the right to govern ourselves, to make our own laws and to live in a free nation, not an occupied one.'

'That sounds reasonable,' Steven said quietly.

'It is,' Mark agreed. 'Those same goals have fuelled revolution after revolution throughout time. I suppose I'm not surprised it's the same here . . . wherever *here* is.'

'But you need to understand,' Steven interjected, 'that none of this has anything to do with us. We are lost. We made a terrible mistake . . . *I* made a terrible mistake, one that brought us here, and we need to find someone who can help us get back.' He strained to look into her face, hoping for some glimmer of compassion. 'Do you know of *anyone* who would believe us – and be able to help us?'

Brynne hesitated for a moment, then said, 'I do. He's supposed to be here, but we're not certain if he's coming back. If anyone would know how to help you, it would be him.' She drew a deep breath and allowed it to escape slowly as she added, 'Ironically, though, he may be the one who orders your death. If you truly *are* lost, and not Malakasians, then I hope he helps you. We've seen so much death here: Malagon just murders us at will.

'I would hate to see the two of you killed if you are innocent . . . especially killed by Ronans. We're supposed to be the good ones.' Brynne used Sallax's knife to gesture down a long stone corridor. Steven understood they were to move along the hall to their cell.

'Why can't you—' Mark started, trying to keep her talking, but she held up a hand to stop him.

'No,' she said firmly, 'no more talking now.' They walked in silence past several doorways until they reached the final chamber off the hall. A large wooden door, charred black and burned almost through, hung awkwardly from one broken hinge. Brynne pushed it aside and motioned for the two men to enter. In the torchlight, Steven and Mark could see the room had been the foyer for a series of rooms. Given the number and size of the chambers, it was evident someone of importance once lived here. A stone fireplace took up most of one wall.

Brynne ordered them to sit on either side of a blackened beam supporting the ceiling in the front room. She threaded several leather straps between the beam and the wall and tied an intricate knot to fasten both men's bonds to the wooden support. Lifting her torch, she took a last look at Mark Jenkins, slipped the knife into her belt and ducked beneath the broken doorframe into the hallway beyond.

Total darkness quickly swept through the room and for several moments, Steven and Mark sat in silence. Finally, Mark said, 'Well, she seemed nice.'

Laughing, an uncontrolled response to fear, Steven replied, 'Sure, maybe she'll take you home to meet her parents, but make sure you have her in by eleven, young man, or her brother will hack you to fishfood with his battle-axe.'

Mark started laughing too. 'Look, I don't even want to think about where we are, or how we got here, or how we are both fluent in a language that doesn't exist. Let's just get untied, get down those stairs and find a way out of this building. Do you have your pocketknife?'

'No,' Steven responded, dejected. 'It's on the kitchen counter.'

'Terrific. You jumped through a magic rug, a *stolen* magic rug, into a new world, perhaps even a new time, and you didn't bring a pocketknife?'

'Hey, I thought I was stepping to certain death,' Steven said. 'You were gone. I figured you'd been vaporised or some damned thing and I was sure I was stepping into oblivion. So excuse me if I didn't figure I'd need a corkscrew in the afterlife.'

'You're right. It was brave, what you did. Stupid, but brave. Me, I just tripped on the hearthstone and fell onto the damned thing.' Mark struggled to loosen the straps holding him to the beam. 'If we work on these all night, I bet we can get free. We have to get out of here before the sun comes up.'

*

Some time later it began to rain, plummeting down as if determined to wash southern Rona out to sea. The strong winds they had felt on the beach earlier that day continued through the evening, blowing sheets of raindrops into the chamber through a broken window to puddle on the stone floor. The din of the torrential downpour coupled with the howling wind made it impossible for them to hear if anyone was approaching from the hallway, so Steven kept a tired eye on the broken door hanging between them and their captors. They persisted in their efforts to loosen or cut through the leather straps: one would rub his end of the leather thongs up and down against the beam a hundred times while the other rested, then they swapped over. Too soon they discovered that although exhausted, sleeping in one-hundred-second intervals was worse than not sleeping at all, so as they took turns wearing through the leather straps they counted out loud. Mark counted in German, in Russian, then backwards in German. He even tried it once in Ronan.

'Ein Hundert,' Mark called out over the roar of the wind and rain. When Steven didn't take up the mantra, Mark nudged his roommate. 'Hey, Steve. It's your turn. Let's try French this time. You took French in college, didn't you?' There was no answer: his friend had fallen into a deep sleep. 'All right, all right, I'll take another turn. You were up all last night, but don't think I'm going past two hundred. I don't know the numbers past two hundred.' He thought for a moment then shook his head. 'Two semesters of German and I can't count past two hundred. Now Ronan, I can count to one hundred million in Ronan and I never had one class. Who would've guessed?'

When Steven failed to answer, Mark continued his own monotonous efforts to break free.

On Ronan number 2,564, he finally felt the straps holding him to the beam break. His wrists were bleeding and his lower back ached from the constant rocking, but he was free. Mark felt a surge of adrenalin rush through him as he stood up straight for the first time in hours. His hands were still tied behind his back, but he figured Steven could untie them, or even bite through those with his teeth if he had to. He looked down at his roommate: Steven had slept through the excitement and still lay slumped forward on the stone floor.

Outside, the rain had slowed. Mark staggered to the window to see the earliest glow of dawn breaking through the thunderclouds.

'Not much time. Steven, wake up,' he said. Steven did not move, and he raised his voice. 'C'mon Steven,' he said urgently, 'we can still make it out of here. Wake up.'

Mark searched hurriedly around the room: a lightning flash illuminated the fireplace and he spotted several jagged bits of masonry. In the darkness he backed up against the stones and felt for a sharp edge, then leaned awkwardly into the fireplace and moved his hands up and down against the stone. He quickly developed a cramp in his shoulder; when he changed position he found a large stone that protruded outward from the masonry at about eye level. Leaning against it with his forehead, he called aloud to the empty room, 'Why does this have to be so goddamned difficult?'

Mark rested his eyes for a moment, waiting for the cramp to subside, then he felt the rock move. Shifting his forehead to the opposite side, he pushed against the stone with his temple. It moved again. Back and forth he pushed it, and with every push he felt it come looser from the fireplace. The cramp in his back gone, he now felt the rough texture of the large granite block rubbing his forehead raw. Back and forth, again and again, he pushed the stone with his forehead until finally it fell to the floor with a resounding crash. 'Shit all over,' he cried and listened for the sound of their captors approaching from the grand staircase.

Hearing nothing, he turned and began furiously rubbing the leather thongs up and down against the sharp edge. This time it worked and within minutes, Mark had severed the straps and freed his hands.

Faint daylight crept into their stone cell. Mark was about to wake Steven when he realised he would need to be able to surprise their captors if someone came to the chamber before Steven was freed and ready to travel. He hefted the large stone block from the floor and was about to push it back into the fireplace wall when he saw several pieces of folded parchment. They had obviously been hidden behind the stone.

'What's this?' He leafed through the pages, but was unable to make out more than a few words of the foreign scrawl – Ronan was apparently easier to speak than read. He held them up to catch the light, but even so, the words were still too difficult to decipher. Mark shrugged to himself. It was probably just some long-ago lady's love letters. He still had the matchbook he had taken from Owen's two nights before: with this, they would be able to make a fire if they managed to escape safely to the forest.

He stashed the parchment in his back pocket, replaced the stone in the fireplace and moved quickly to wake Steven.

Lieutenant Bronfio ordered his soldiers to dismount long before they reached the edge of the clearing surrounding Riverend Palace, even though he was conscious that the increased Ronan opposition to the Malakasian occupation meant that soldiers on foot were vulnerable. Through the early morning light he watched as they unstrapped bows and checked that broadswords and rapiers were loose in their scabbards. Several men were already looking at him expectantly, awaiting his command to march on the seemingly abandoned fortress in the distance.

The horses were tethered to trees in a small clearing. Bronfio raised one arm and gave the silent order to proceed. They would attack from the north, burning the ropes securing the palace portcullis so they could enter speedily. Bronfio's orders were clear: they needed only one or two partisans for questioning. The rest were to be killed on sight, or taken as prisoners for public hangings.

Looking towards the rear of his small company, Bronfio saw three men struggling to carry a barrel to the edge of the clearing. Although small, the barrel obviously weighed a great deal. The lieutenant indicated that Brexan should lend some assistance. Reaching the tree line, Bronfio ordered the platoon to hold their position for a moment while he watched the palace for any indication that partisans were indeed inside. The merchant had given him no idea how much resistance to expect, and the young officer disliked the idea of charging into the palace without knowing how numerous or well-armed their enemy were. The barrel was an equaliser; he intended to employ it before beginning the fight. Riskett had brought one along as well.

Across the clearing, in the palace dining hall, Garec stirred. They had finished stacking the crates of stolen weapons, armour and silver in the old cistern only a short time earlier and now his friends lay about the floor, stealing a few moments' sleep before sunrise. They needed to be away before daylight if they were to avoid being detected by the dawn patrols; Garec planned to sneak up into the hills above the river and sleep the morning away.

He wasn't sure what Sallax had planned for their prisoners, but he shuddered at the idea of assassinating them. He wished Gilmour were around to tell them what to do next. Garec believed in their fight to restore freedom to the occupied lands, and he had killed for that cause – he'd always known that expelling the Malakasian Army from Rona would require extreme sacrifice. Killing unarmed prisoners was a different matter. He wasn't convinced he would be able to do it.

He sat on the floor and watched dawn begin to illuminate the stained-glass window that flanked the grand staircase at the opposite end of the hall. 'We'd better get moving,' he said to himself and began pulling on his boots.

'I don't think you're going anywhere this morning,' a voice answered softly.

Garec whipped around, reaching for the hunting knife he had placed on the floor before falling asleep. 'Who's that?' he asked, peering into the darkness.

A warm glow – burning pipe embers: it lifted the darkness against the wall behind him. Garec detected the faint but familiar odour of Falkan tobacco.

'Gilmour. Lords, you scared me.' Garec lay back on the floor and looked at the glowing pipe bowl. 'How did you get in here?'

'Gilmour?' Versen rolled over and yawned like a swamp grizzly. 'Gilmour. Great rutting dogs, but it is good to see you.' He clambered to his feet as everyone gathered around the elderly man.

Greetings and embraces were exchanged as Gilmour Stow was welcomed back home. He was dressed in a wool tunic over leather leggings and boots, and despite the heat of the Ronan southlands, he always wore a hooded riding cloak. Bearded but balding, Gilmour was shorter even than Brynne, but he had broad strong shoulders and powerful legs. He was old – no one knew how many Twinmoons – but his bright eyes and frequent smile were boyish. His skin was a deep brown, tanned from constant travel, and he carried no weapons except for a short dagger Garec had never seen him draw.

'What do you mean, we're not going anywhere?' Garec asked.

'You are not— *We* are not going anywhere this morning because there are two platoons of Malakasian soldiers forming up in the forest just beyond the edge of the palace grounds,' the old man said as he drew contemplatively on his pipe.

'Pissing demons,' Sallax exclaimed, and quickly moved from window to window in an effort to assess the forces mobilising against them.

Mika grimaced. 'How did they know we were here?' he asked. 'We can't defend this place – or ourselves – against two platoons.'

'Versen, Garec, Mika,' Sallax called, 'get those last two crates back up here and opened. We'll need bows, and lots of arrows.'

The three men leaped into action while Gilmour sat down, back to the wall, watching the frantic activity and enjoying his pipe.

'Brynne,' Garec shouted before disappearing into the cistern, 'you'd better get those two down here. We might be able to use them if we need to negotiate our way out.'

'Or as a shield,' Sallax muttered watching his sister take the stairs two at a time.

'What two?' Gilmour asked, perking up suddenly.

'Just two spies Garec and I found along the beach near the point yesterday. Brynne has them tied up somewhere upstairs.' Sallax tossed the older man a longbow, which Gilmour considered for a moment and then placed gently on the floor at his feet.

The winds had died somewhat, so Steven and Mark heard the girl coming. 'Quick, back on the ground,' Steven ordered as they heard her stop outside their room for a moment.

'Right,' Mark agreed, adding, 'remember what Sallax said about that knife.' When Brynne entered the room, she stopped and stared for a moment at the two strangers she had left tied to the support beam all night. A look of disgust passed over her face, as though she could not believe she was capable of such an act, but as quickly as it came, the look was gone. Brynne pursed her lips, drew her knife and moved towards the prisoners. As she reached to slash through the leather straps holding them against the wall, she gave a startled cry. With surprising speed Mark grabbed her wrist and squeezed with all his strength. He didn't intend breaking her bones, and as soon as her knife dropped to the floor he relaxed his grip.

Brynne tried to scream for help, but Steven clamped a hand firmly over her mouth and nose while Mark retrieved the blade. 'Come with us,' he ordered, speaking Ronan. 'You're our ticket out of here.'

'I still don't see them,' Sallax shouted to Garec, who was busily unpacking swords, longbows and arrows from crates hauled up from the cistern. 'The sun's almost fully up. Why are they waiting?' The Twinmoon winds had abated somewhat from their previous fury, though the trees still rocked and bent in the breezes that accompanied a perfect lunar alignment. Sallax frantically searched the forest for any sign of a coming attack, but it would be impossible to spot the occupation forces until they broke clear of the tree line and started across the palace grounds. He kicked angrily at a charred piece of ancient wood.

Across the room, the old man tapped the ashes from his pipe and refilled its bowl from a leather pouch.

Garec pulled himself out of the cistern and reached back down to take a small box of arrows from Versen. He saw Gilmour stand up and walk towards him, the old man's eyes fixed on the grand staircase.

'Well, good morning, my friends. I have been waiting for you for some time.' Gilmour's tone was one of pleasant surprise.

Garec looked puzzled. 'Gilmour, what are you talking about?' The young Ronan followed Gilmour's gaze, then shouted into the cistern, 'Versen, Mika, get up here now!' He grabbed a rosewood longbow, nocked an arrow and trained it up the broad staircase.

Startled by the sudden commotion, Sallax also turned on his heel. 'Rutting bastards!' he shouted, drawing his rapier and starting for the stairs. 'I swear this time I will kill you both!'

Gilmour broke in calmly, 'It's all right, my friends. Come down.' No one paid the elderly man any attention.

'Not another step,' Mark shouted, stopping Sallax several stairs above the dining hall floor, 'or I will cut her head off by the time you reach me.' Mark had Sallax's hunting knife held fast against Brynne's throat.

'Take him, Garec,' Sallax ordered, 'take the shot. You can

make it.' Versen, armed with a longbow too, hauled himself out of the cistern.

Steven huddled behind Mark, who was using Brynne's body as a living shield. Although she struggled, Mark held one arm around her shoulders and one hand at her neck. With each attempt to break free, the young woman pulled the knife's blade across her own throat; tiny rivulets of blood were running into the bodice of her dress. She cried out, more in fear and surprise than in pain.

'Put the bows down,' Mark called, and to encourage them to act quickly, he placed the point of the knife against Brynne's throat and pushed gently until the tip pierced her skin. The insignificant stab wound was enough: Versen and Garec both dropped their bows to the floor with a noisy clatter.

'What are you doing?' Gilmour asked his friends. 'They aren't spies.'

'What did you say?' Sallax half turned to face him. 'Gilmour, what do you mean?'

He had no chance to respond as a small barrel filled to the brim with burning pitch crashed through the stained-glass window, showering shards of multi-coloured glass across the grey stone floor like myriad refractions from a damaged prism. Acrid black smoke began filling the dining hall almost immediately. Garec, seeing Malakasian soldiers through the gaping hole, retrieved his bow, nocked the arrow he had dropped beside it and fired out towards the soldiers as they retreated across the courtyard to rejoin their platoon. A cry of pain and astonishment confirmed that his arrow had found its mark.

'Back upstairs, now,' Mark said urgently to Brynne and Steven. He pulled at Brynne's elbow, dragging her back to the upper levels of the palace.

'Try not to breathe the smoke,' Sallax called. 'Quick, arm yourselves and get to the windows. Mika, find something to cover this barrel.' Water would not extinguish the burning tar; their only hope was to mitigate the effects of the smoke. His heart sank as a second barrel crashed through a smaller window at the opposite end of the hall.

He shouted to Garec, 'Try to hold them here. If the smoke gets too thick, take up positions along the second-floor landing, and at those windows. There's a lot of room to retreat through this palace, but we don't want to get cornered.'

'Right.' Garec hefted two large quivers and slung them over his shoulder.

Sallax grabbed a battle-axe from the cistern's edge and dashed up the stairs after the fleeing prisoners. 'I'll be right back.'

'Leave them, Sallax. They can't get out either,' Versen called, trying to stop him, but Sallax was already taking the steps three at a time to the upper-level apartments.

Steven rushed along the hallway until he found an intact door. 'In here,' he called to Mark, who dragged the struggling Brynne along and shoved her roughly into the room. He helped Steven to hurriedly set the locking beam and seal the chamber.

Mark slid the knife into his belt and turned towards Brynne. 'Listen, I don't want you to think—' He was cut off as the young woman slugged him hard across the face, knocking him back into the door. Mark's knees buckled beneath him and he sat heavily on the stone floor.

'You cut my neck, you horsecock!' she screamed down at him, raising her fists for another attack.

Steven moved between them and grabbed Brynne. 'Listen, we have bigger problems than that right now. Who are those soldiers? Are they Malakasians?'

'Yes,' she answered, glaring at him. 'Somehow they must have discovered where we've been hiding weapons for the Resistance. *I* don't know how – maybe you two do.' She crossed the chamber floor to the window and looked down into the courtyard where a number of soldiers had taken cover behind the battlements, waiting for the burning pitch to finish its job of choking or blinding the partisan group.

'They're here to kill us – or, worse, to use us to send a very public message.'

Mark joined her at the window. 'What if we give ourselves up? This isn't our fight.'

She wheeled on him, her face just inches away. 'They'll hang you from a tree for an entire Twinmoon as an example to any who might decide to mount a resistance effort.'

Neither Mark nor Steven had any idea how long a Twinmoon

lasted, but however long was too long to be hanging from a tree. They lapsed into silence.

'We'll hide in here then?' Steven asked eventually

'Or we go join the fight,' Brynne said, pointing a bloodstained finger towards the door.

'And wait for your brother to slice our throats? No thank you,' Mark replied adamantly. 'We have to wait it out and hope either your friends turn them away or that they don't find us when they come in. This place is huge. We might be able to find another way out.'

The discussion was interrupted by the sound of Sallax's battle-axe hammering at their door.

'I'm going to kill you both!' he screamed, his axe leaving fresh hack-marks in the blackened wood of the chamber door. Wood chips flew as he continued swinging, his fury unchecked. Inside, Mark looked for anything to brace against the door as Steven stood frozen in place, his face a pallid shade of grey. Brynne backed slowly into an adjoining room. She looked around hurriedly, but there was no other way out. She grimaced. Sallax would have to break through and free her before the Malakasians breached their defences downstairs.

Riverend Palace had a second, unexpected, portcullis inside the battlements. The first, a huge iron and oak gate, blocked the main entrance to the ancient keep. It remained where it had collapsed many Twinmoons earlier as the last of Riverend's occupants fled the raging fire that had claimed the lives of Princess Danae, her son Prince Danmark III, and Prince Tenner of Falkan.

Prince Markon II had installed an additional portcullis to guard the west entrance, which led to the royal chambers. During the brief peace that had preceded his death, the prince had commissioned the largest and most elaborate stained-glass window in the Eastlands; a team of talented artisans had worked for several Twinmoons to design and install the gigantic work of art in the east wall of Riverend's grand hall.

The huge window was a massive weakness in Riverend's defences: any attack on the palace would centre on the east hall as the window would be seen as easy access.

To make up for that, the second portcullis – one no invader

would expect – ensured that a few well-armed soldiers could hold the west wing with little difficulty, even against a far superior enemy force.

Now Bronfio strode towards the portcullis with determination. His confidence had risen as his platoon crossed the exposed circular meadow without incident. Peering intently through the thick latticework of the heavy wooden gate, he could see smoke from the burning pitch accumulating in great clouds throughout the hall.

He waved over his shoulder for a bowman to join him at the palace entryway. Igniting an arrow from a small torch, Bronfio directed the bowman to fire into a length of rope fastened securely on an inner wall. He intended to lift the gate by releasing the ropes holding it fast and hoisting it with a line threaded through a crooked fracture in the palace's western wall. He feared for a moment the weight of the portcullis would bring the entire section of wall crumbling down on them, but the stone lintel held fast as the gate rose and his men were able to secure their lines to a neighbouring wall.

He smiled to himself as he ordered his platoon into the fray. 'Use the smoke as cover,' he told them quietly. 'We don't know how many partisans are inside.' Brexan, like her fellow soldiers, nodded confidently, then slipped under the hanging portcullis, up several stone steps, through a small antechamber and into the palace's dining hall.

Bronfio waited for the last of his force to slip into the building before he drew his sword and started towards the entryway himself. As he ducked beneath the portcullis, he came face to face with Jacrys Marseth, the merchant spy from Estrad.

'I've been waiting for you, Lieutenant,' Jacrys said icily. 'We can't have you sharing my sentiments with His Majesty, now, can we?' Bronfio felt the dagger pass between his ribs. For an instant he was surprised the pain was not much worse. Then a searing heat emanated outwards from the wound, running across his back in a tangled web of white-hot fire and contorting his torso in an involuntary spasm. The young officer felt his legs twitch several times before they buckled, but he didn't fall: Jacrys held him tightly from behind.

Bronfio tried to call out to his platoon before he realised the foppish spy had one hand clamped firmly over his mouth and nose. Unable to breathe, Bronfio gave up. The stinging heat from the dagger wound was so powerful, he could focus on nothing else.

Slowly, the world around him began to dim, as if the great cloud of burning pitch was engulfing him from all sides. He thought of his mother . . . they had played together, kicking a ball around a fountain in the village square. It had rained that day. His mother's soft brown hair had escaped her normal heavy plait and lay loose against her head. He had been young, that day. Then the memory faded into the distant regions of his consciousness and Lieutenant Bronfio fell away into the darkness.

Brexan stayed low to the ground. She found the air there less difficult to breathe; for a moment she considered crawling in to face the enemy. She heard choking from all around her, but she could not be certain which coughs were Malakasian and which were partisan: everyone choked in the same language.

Amongst the hacking and retching, she thought she detected a struggle behind her. Doubling back with her sword drawn, fearing the Resistance forces were attempting a flanking manoeuvre, Brexan found herself back at the portcullis. As her eyes watered and she refocused, she spotted Lieutenant Bronfio's body. He had died before entering the palace, obviously not in a fight with the partisan terrorists. Bronfio had been murdered. This was not right. Things were not supposed to work out this way. The battle plan had been clear. They were not supposed to suffer loses, certainly not like this. Her stomach knotted and she thought she might retch. She swallowed hard, steeling herself against the notion that the morning might be unravelling quickly.

Brexan heard stones tumble from the battlements, and her attention was drawn to the ancient wall across the courtyard. A well-dressed young man was scurrying over the crumbling defences, dislodging a diminutive avalanche of stones in his wake. Brexan immediately recognised the merchant who had passed her the papers outlining their orders for this morning's assault.

It had all been a set-up. The merchant had sent Bronfio in from the north so he could find an opportunity to murder him – but why? No answers emerged as Brexan looked back into the dark cloud of smoke filling the dining hall. Without thinking, she sheathed her sword and started out after the fleeing murderer.

Garec choked on the thick smoke billowing around him, but he cheered up when he noticed most of the foul-smelling cloud was moving in one direction. Their Malakasian attackers had made a mistake when they threw the second barrel of burning pitch into the far end of the grand hall: breaking the second window had allowed strong winds to create a cross-draught through the castle. He and Versen had taken up positions approximately halfway up the first level of the grand staircase. From this vantage point, they could spot any Malakasian attempting to enter through the windows.

Garec thanked the gods of the Northern Forest he and Sallax had taken time to lower the hall's portcullis and secure its ropes when they brought their prisoners in the previous night. The young Ronan still had no idea how Gilmour had managed to enter the building undetected, but there was no time to worry about that now. He knew it would be only a matter of moments before the Malakasians burned through the portcullis ropes and then used horses to haul the huge wood and iron gate up far enough to enter through the courtyard. With limited visibility, there would be no stopping them from taking the hall.

He and his friends would have no choice but to retreat to the upper levels of the palace. What they would do once they were trapped there was another matter.

Mika, Namont and Jerond were not bowmen. Armed with swords or battle-axes, each guarded a window along the walls of the dining hall. They all looked at each other, hoping to garner a collective strength for the coming fight. They were frightened. Above them, Versen and Garec were preparing to rain deadly fire down on the soldiers coming through the stained-glass window. Already many of the lower panes of the enormous glass aperture had been broken out, and two attackers had died with Garec's arrows buried in their chests.

As the moments ticked by, the burning pitch continued to emit thick clouds of choking black smoke and despite the crosswind, the hall was soon filled to the ceiling. 'Versen,' Garec called, 'run up to the first landing and break out the windows. We need to create more breeze in here.' The big woodsman did as

Garec ordered, but it did little to mitigate the dense, caustic smoke.

Garec's eyes watered as he strained to see through the darkness into the dining hall below. He thought he spied a Malakasian soldier crawling through the stained-glass window and fired into the smoke. A cry of shock and pain confirmed that, even blind, Garec was one of the best bowmen in Rona. Time seemed to move in slow motion as he stared into the billowing cloud, hoping to see anything that would give him an update on their situation. He could no longer make out Versen, who had been standing just a few paces away.

'They must be through the portcullis by now,' he whispered into the smoke, hoping the woodsman could hear him.

'You're right,' Versen replied softly. 'We ought to think about getting to higher ground. This smoke is doing exactly what they need it to.' As if confirming his fears, a strangled cry came from the far end of the hall.

'Get up here, get up here!' Garec screamed. 'They're in the hall! Fall back, fall back!' Mika burst into view only a few paces in front of him and Garec nearly loosed an arrow into his friend. Mika was followed closely by Jerond, but they heard nothing from Namont.

'Namont,' Garec called, slowly backing up the stairs towards the first landing, 'Namont, get up here.'

'Namont,' an unfamiliar voice sang up from the floor below, 'Namont, get up here . . . Namont can't join you right now, but don't worry, you'll see him later today.' The stranger laughed cynically.

Though blind, Garec fired into the cloud.

'Rutting dogs,' the suddenly anguished voice cried out in surprise, 'I'll kill every last one of you!'

Versen joined him on the landing, 'It sounds like you hit him.'

'I hope so,' Garec answered. 'I guess they got Namont.'

'We can't worry about it now, Garec. We have to get out of here,' he said, hustling up the stairs to the third level.

The windows Versen had broken pulled some of the smoke outside and the stairway above the first landing was fairly clear. The four men coughed out the vestiges of burning pitch from their lungs as they climbed.

Suddenly, Garec stopped and turned back towards the dining hall. 'Where's Gilmour?'

Mika turned as well. 'I haven't seen him since the first barrel came through the window.'

'I'm going back down.'

'And you'll be dead before you reach the bottom of the steps,' Versen scolded. 'Gilmour can take care of himself. Let's keep moving.'

Garec was unconvinced, but he recognised there was little he could do right then. He followed Versen and as they reached the uppermost landing, they could see, down the long hallway, Sallax hammering away at one of the wooden doors with a battle-axe.

'Sallax,' yelled Garec, 'you'd better get down here. They're in the building – and on their way up after us.'

Sallax stopped hacking at the door and stalked angrily back to his compatriots, rage clearly evident on his face.

'They aren't going to hurt her, Sallax,' Garec assured him. 'They need her to get out of here. Come on, let's go.'

Versen led the small group down a short hall adjoining the upper end of the staircase. 'The spiral stairs will be easiest to defend. We can hold there for some time.'

The narrow spiralling staircase separating the third level of the palace from the royal apartments above was short, but the narrowness of the stone stairwell made it the most defensible position inside the building. Only one soldier at a time would be able to come at the freedom fighters there.

Garec reached the fourth-level landing and ran along the hallway, past a number of closed wooden doors. He stopped at a window facing out onto the palace grounds. He could help most by dispatching as many Malakasians as possible; from here he could pick them off as they approached the palace. He was not a skilled hand-to-hand warrior, so he gladly left defence of the staircase to Sallax and the others.

Looking out over the battlements, he thought he caught a glimpse of the well-dressed merchant he had met at Greentree Tavern. 'What is *he* doing here?' Garec asked himself, but was distracted by the sight of Gilmour far in the distance. The elderly man stood near a clearing cut back into the trees on the south side of the palace. A large number of Malakasian horses were tethered together. Garec watched as Gilmour cupped his hands to his mouth and called into the trees. Garec couldn't hear the words, but he was surprised when Gilmour turned, looked up at the castle and waved to him – as though he knew Garec was watching.

Then, apparently without a care, Gilmour turned and walked back towards the palace: an older man out for a morning stroll. Back along the corridor, Garec heard a shout of surprise.

'Get back here!' Sallax called urgently. Garec hurried to the spiral steps. A Malakasian arrow was deeply embedded in a wooden doorframe across the hall from the stairwell. Without speaking, Sallax pointed to it and gestured down the narrow stairs. Garec immediately understood. A Malakasian bowman had tried – and nearly succeeded – in banking a miracle shot off the curved stone wall, up and around the corner into the small band of Riverend's defenders.

Garec nocked an arrow and estimated a descending angle to the lower level. Drawing quickly, he fired and watched the arrow glance off the wall and disappear out of sight. An enraged howl pierced the stillness. For the third time that day, Garec's blind shot had tallied a Malakasian casualty.

Staring down the stairwell, he beamed with pride, looking at Versen as if to say: 'I *am* the finest bowman in the land.' A moment later, however, Garec came to his senses and dove for the floor, an instant before another Malakasian arrow bounced off the stairwell and buried itself in the wooden doorframe.

Smiling, Sallax helped his friend to his feet. 'Nicely done,' he told him. 'With your trick shots and our battle-axes, we ought to be able to hold this floor all day.'

'What will we do when they send for reinforcements?' Mika asked. 'They know who we are, and we can't hold here for ever.'

'No,' Sallax replied, 'eventually we'll have to find a way we can get down undetected.'

'With them waiting for us right there?' Jerond interjected. 'All they really have to do is wait us out.'

'Yes, but at least this buys us some time to think,' Garec pointed out. He gathered his quivers and was about to retrace his steps to the window when the first tendrils of dark smoke climbed the stairway.

'Oh, no,' was all Garec managed to get out. This time there would be nowhere to escape from the burning pitch.

It didn't take long for the fourth level hallway to fill completely with smoke. Arrows came more frequently up the stairs and soon there were eight protruding from the doorway across the hall. Garec continued to fire back down, but heard nothing that led him to believe he had hit anyone else. Now they were choking with each ragged breath. The partisans knew they couldn't remain at the top of the stairs very long. Taking turns, two stood a painful vigil at the stairwell, coughing and dodging capricious arrows from below, while two stood at the open window breathing clean air and coughing foul smoke from their lungs. It worked until the first Malakasian burst from the stairwell, screaming and swinging his sword wildly through the billowing clouds. Garec ducked the attacker's first blow and heard the man's sword blade impact the stone wall with a metallic clang.

The next sound stayed with Garec for a very long time: a sickening thud, followed by a horrible tearing sound, and then a scream so primal that Garec's blood nearly froze in his veins. He felt a splash of moisture on his face and raised a finger to wipe it off; it was viscous, not water. Even in the smoky darkness he could recognise that he had been splattered by his attacker's blood.

As he dived to the floor to avoid any wild thrusts of the Malakasian's sword, Garec's head came down on what felt like a warm but awkwardly shaped pillow. Feeling for it with his hands, he discovered a human leg, severed just above the knee by a vicious blow from Sallax's battle-axe.

Blinded by the smoke, filled with anger and disgust, Garec crawled back to the top of the staircase and fired arrow after arrow down the stone stairwell into the Malakasian ranks. After several releases, he heard cries of pain.

Garec didn't think he could stomach another frontal attack: he would keep the Malakasians at bay if it took every arrow he carried. Firing blindly, over and over again, into the smoke, Garec did not slow until he felt Sallax's strong arms hugging him from behind.

'It's all right . . . Garec, it's all right. They're going.'

'Going?' he asked, dumbfounded. 'What do you mean, going?'

'Come with me and take a look.' Sallax led him to the window. Gazing out towards the forest, Garec saw ranks of Malakasian soldiers running towards the clearing. Some shouted and waved frantically, while others fired arrows into the tree line. Allowing his gaze to follow one of their shafts, he saw the reason for their hasty retreat. A pack of grettans had attacked their horses: the beasts were tearing wildly at the helpless mounts in a frenzied mêlée, and the horses were screaming in pain and terror. Garec covered his ears to block the disturbing sound.

'Lords,' he whispered in disbelief.

'Yes,' Mika answered excited, 'they left their horses and attacked the palace on foot ... they needed to preserve the element of surprise.' He smiled at Sallax. 'They obviously didn't realise there were grettans in the area: tethering the animals like that was as bad as sounding the dinner chime.'

Sallax slapped a victorious hand on Garec's back and told his fellows, 'Let's get Brynne and get out of here before they come back.' He turned on his heel and moved towards the stairwell.

Silently, they approached the chamber into which Steven and Mark had fled with Brynne. Rage seethed again in Sallax's eyes and Garec noticed he had not bothered to wipe the Malakasian's blood from his battle-axe. As they drew near the door, Garec mouthed redundantly to the others behind him, 'It's open.'

Sallax knew immediately that his sister and their prisoners were gone. 'Rutting foreign bastards,' he yelled, kicking the door open and searching the rooms. 'We don't have time to search the whole rutting castle for them.'

'Let's find Gilmour,' Garec suggested. 'Maybe he can help us.'

'If he's still alive,' Mika said grimly.

'He's still alive.'

The group made their way back to the throne room. In a wall flanking the dais, Mika pushed open a narrow doorway that led to another spiral staircase. This one led down below the grand dining hall into a tunnel that connected the cistern with a palace scullery in an adjacent building. The passageway had been constructed as a convenient exit for the prince.

'Why didn't we use this before?' Jerond asked.

'The palace scullery isn't as easily defended as the upper floors,' Sallax told him. 'Old Prince Markon knew that. Anyway, we had no idea where they were this morning. The scullery could have been crawling with Malakasians.'

'Could have been?' Jerond asked nervously.

When the friends emerged in the palace kitchens, they found Gilmour waiting. 'Where have you been?' Mika asked. 'We thought you were dead.'

'No, I'm very much alive,' Gilmour said, then added sadly, 'I cannot say the same for Namont, however.'

'What happened?' Sallax asked.

'They came upon him in the smoke and cut his throat. I've carried his body into another wing of the palace. We can come back for him later tonight.'

'Right,' Sallax agreed. 'Did you see any sign of Brynne?'

'No,' the old man answered. 'They're still upstairs. She'll be fine, though. Actually, I expect they'll come looking for us in the next day or two.'

'I don't understand.' Garec wiped the blood from his face with a sleeve. 'Why didn't those two join the other soldiers when they left the palace?'

'Because they're not spies,' Gilmour said. 'It will all make sense in time, but for now she's quite safe. Come, we must hurry.' He led them out through the scullery and into a maze of dilapidated palace buildings.

SOUTHPORT, PRAGA

Hannah fell to her knees, toppling slowly until she placed one hand firmly on the grass, arresting her collapse. She was no longer in Steven's living room. Her head swam; her elbow buckled and she dropped to the ground. Her breath caught in her throat and she coughed roughly several times. Peering up through overhanging branches, she watched, dazed, as a light breeze rustled autumn leaves: noisy affirmation that she was indeed somewhere other than 147 Tenth Street, Idaho Springs.

She replayed the last thirty seconds, looking through Steven's desk, seeing the pen on the mantelpiece, sliding the chair across the floor and finding herself here in the forest. It didn't add up. She fought the knowledge that something remarkable had happened to her with all the tenacity she could summon until, growing angry at her inability to reconcile the problem in her mind, she sat up and took in her surroundings. The trees were actually part of a small grove atop a grassy hill overlooking what appeared to be an ocean. Combatting a second wave of nausea, she forced herself to remain open-minded, fighting a growing desire to lose control and run screaming down the hill. Since she found herself outside, she could very well be near an ocean. Hannah was determined to look at one impossible circumstance at a time while she tried to make sense of her situation.

Coming slowly to her feet, Hannah swallowed hard to moisten her throat; she wished she had some water. Taking a long look, she concluded her mind was not toying with her: it was true, an ocean – or at least a sea – lay sprawled across the horizon. For an irrational moment, she hoped she *had* been transported somewhere *other*, because if what lay before her was the Denver metro area, everything she knew – *everyone* she knew – was now submerged.

Scanning the coastline, she caught sight of a bustling town nearby. Built on a long peninsula extending out into the sea, it did not resemble any of the oceanfront cities she knew: Seattle, Boston or San Diego, or the cookie-cutter jumble of resort towns she had visited while in college. The town lay along either side of a narrow ridge that descended sharply from the sparsely wooded heights to the waterfront below, like a gigantic giraffe with its head buried in the harbour. From her vantage point on top of the hill, she could see horses and mules pulling wooden carts along a quay, to and from sloops and frigates, and harbour boats apparently serving several massive galleons moored out in deeper water. She saw none of the telltale signs of a modern working wharf, though: no delivery trucks or industrial cranes, or forklifts hauling crates around warehouses. Also peculiar, she could recognise none of the flags flying from bowsprits or fantails of the vessels docked along the wharf.

With the sunlight fading behind the horizon, Hannah stood totally still, waiting for some answer to emerge from the depths of her consciousness, something that would explain the incongruity of where she found herself now. 'Oh, yes, of course, I understand,' she would say with a sigh of relief.

But clarity did not come. Instead, darkness came, and, looking out at the ocean, her worst fears were confirmed. Two moons rose slowly in the night sky. Hannah sat heavily in the coarse hilltop grass to keep from passing out. She forced her head between her knees and made herself breathe deeply, using her diaphragm to fill her lungs.

The moons drew closer together and with each passing hour, the light breeze that had been so pleasantly rustling the leaves grew in strength until Hannah's hair was blowing wildly about her face. She sat there, staring out to sea, until the moons faded across the southern horizon and the sun prepared to rise once again. Shortly before dawn, exhausted, she fell into a deep sleep.

She guessed it was about midday when she woke. A frigate was putting to sea; even from this distance, she could hear officers calling orders to sailors in the rigging. Rolling to her side, she watched as the fore and main topgallant sails snapped to in the brisk afternoon wind. Despite the fear – of not knowing where she was, or how she managed to arrive wherever she was –

Hannah watched in awe as seamen climbed like lemurs along spars far above plank decks below. She thought perhaps this was a tourist town and the ship departing was filled with bored, overweight businessmen or lawyers buying a week's adventure on the high seas. Then she remembered the moons. She could explain away the ships, even the wagons and mules along the harbour docks. It might be a festival or a weekend fair celebrating eighteenth-century culture. But she could not explain the moons.

Sitting up, Hannah peeled off a leaf that had been clinging to the side of her face. She turned it over several times: it was oddly shaped, nothing she recognised, not aspen, maple, oak or elm. She examined the grove more closely. There were several massive-trunked trees she could not identify, though they reminded her of ancient oaks. She stuffed several of the curious leaves into her jacket pocket.

As if the mundane process of picking through fallen leaves had somehow awakened her sense of survival, Hannah suddenly realised she was ravenous. 'I could eat a horse,' she said out loud – and after almost a full day and night of silence, the sound of her own voice surprised her. It was not comforting. It was a reminder that she was lost, in every sense of the word. And hearing herself express something as commonplace as hunger forced her to look at her current unnatural predicament. Just yesterday she had been living in a place where abject fear had never paralysed her; where she had never been forced to spend a night outside pondering celestial anomalies. Just yesterday she felt as though she were in control of her life, her relationships and her future.

Today, she was uncertain exactly what she did control. She had to accept that enlightenment was not about to seek her out on top of this mountain; she would need to find her way into town, to make enquiries and, hopefully, to find a way back home.

The pain in Hoyt Navarra's shoulder grew irksome. He shifted his weight against the uneven stone, but this new position was still awkward, so he pulled a cloak from his pack, balled it into a makeshift pillow and placed it behind his back as he continued reading. It was nearly midday: he was glad to have been able to read for two full avens without interruption. It was rare these days for him to be able to study without worrying he might be discovered by a Malakasian patrol or a Pragan informant.

Southport City was filled with would-be spies, every one of them willing to sell their own children to Prince Malagon's emissaries for a few pieces of silver, and Hoyt's reputation as a healer marked him especially as a wanted man among the Pragan Resistance.

Wiry and lean, with long hair tied loosely at the back, Hoyt Navarra could pass for a battle-hardened soldier, physically tough and free from excess fat, or a beggar, emaciated, hungry and drawn. Either way, his soft eyes and chiselled features betrayed him as one who fretted over weighty issues to his physical cost. He was uncertain of his own age, but estimated he was somewhere between a hundred and eighty and two hundred Twinmoons old. It wasn't really important to him; he was only half-joking when he said, 'I suppose I'll die when I've lived long enough.'

Here, hidden in a copse outside the city, Hoyt had shelter and a quiet place to catch up on his studies. Malakasian soldiers patrolled the coastal highway only a few paces from his hiding place, but the grove of trees provided just enough cover and he rarely had to do more than duck behind a rock.

Only Churn knew where to find him; Hoyt never spoke of the grove while in town. He planned to exploit his newly found solitude for as long as possible: he had a number of outlawed books, treatises and facsimile reproductions he planned to read, review and re-read before giving up this secluded location. He knew it was only a matter of time before someone followed him, or tracked him from the city, and he would be forced to go in search of another study carrel in another forest.

He was nearly through a chapter detailing the tendons and ligaments of the knee, wishing he could sneak another aven to process all he had learned that morning, but he and Churn had work to do. He closed the book, wrapped it in a waterproofed piece of canvas and replaced it beneath a hollow log, next to a score of others similarly protected from the elements.

Casting his eyes over the impromptu medical library, Hoyt sighed. One day, somehow, he would have his own medical practice.

He had never attended a university – Prince Marek, Prince Malagon's distant ancestor and erstwhile iron-hand dictator of Eldarn, had closed them all. Books were scarce and many citizens illiterate. Hoyt read well, thanks to Alen Jasper, and as he flipped through the pages, he thought once again that he would for ever be in the old man's debt. The idea of a university, buildings filled with students pursuing knowledge and research, was almost too foreign for him to imagine, even after Alen's tales of Eldarn's universities of old. Hoyt dreamed of being there to witness their revival.

The Malakasian royal family believed an uneducated public was less threatening to the government. Hoyt wasn't sure he agreed, because he had never known how threatening an educated populace could be, but the Pragans were a sensible people, and Malagon underestimated their good nature and compassion. They were intelligent enough to know what would be possible if they governed themselves. Recognising the difference between where they were under Malagon and where they might one day be, culturally speaking, did not require a degree in advanced literacy.

Hoyt believed the Pragans would eventually rise up against Malakasia, but as much as he hoped they would succeed in that fight, he planned to be far from the conflict when it erupted. He was torn between his love for the Pragan people and his desire to look out for himself; for him and Churn, Resistance was a lucrative business – and he enjoyed pillaging weapons and silver from wealthy merchants and sea captains.

Deep inside, Hoyt knew he had the potential to give much more: the Pragans were disorganised and desperately needed true leadership. He frowned as he thought of the current array of men and women vying for that status among the Resistance forces. They were passionate and outspoken, and essentially devoid of any leadership skills. Blacksmiths, farmers and sailors, all with their hearts in the right place but their heads in the mist, they were working to raise an army, but any army marching against Malagon would be torn to shreds by his well-trained and merciless occupation forces.

Victory, if it *could* be won, would only be possible if guerrilla strikes on land and sea focused attention away from a small group of highly trained assassins and magicians infiltrating Welstar Palace to kill off the Whitward line for ever. Hoyt was plagued by a conscience he fought to sublimate as often as possible. It wasn't that he felt any compassion for Malagon – quite the contrary: he found it surprising he could so absolutely despise someone he had never met. But a Pragan uprising would mean a great many lives lost, and as much as he wished for a chance at real freedom, he could not bring himself to hoist the flag and join his brothers on the front lines.

So instead of battling for Pragan independence and opening his coveted medical practice, Hoyt remained a thief. It was ironic that in so doing, he perpetuated his own myth and retained his position as one of the most sought-after enemies of the Malakasian state: a healer-thief with a long history of nursing the crown's enemies back to health and robbing its supporters of critical resources and silver.

His reading time in the quiet shelter of his protected copse provided him with an opportunity to wrestle his emotional grettans while perfecting his medical arts. Now he shrugged to himself and, thrusting the ever-present guilt to the back of his mind, began preparing for the trip back to Southport.

Hearing leaves rustle behind him, Hoyt peered up into the trees. No wind. He turned quickly, drawing a short, razor-sharp dagger. One benefit of studying medicine for the past fifty Twinmoons was his advanced knowledge of the human body: Hoyt could disable an attacker in a heartbeat with just a couple of carefully placed slashes. His favourite targets were the tendons in an assailant's wrists. Even the most passionate soldiers ran from battle when denied the use of opposable thumbs. Hoyt never killed anyone, but an ever-increasing number of Malakasian soldiers made the trip home with a clumsy grip on their reins. The dagger held before him, Hoyt dropped into a protective crouch and looked between the trees towards the coastal highway; he sighed in relief when he saw Churn Prellis lumbering in his direction. Churn was his best friend and business partner.

His dagger disappeared as quickly as it had been drawn, and Hoyt smiled a welcome as he watched his companion trudge through the forest. He was the complete antithesis to Hoyt: he looked like a section of granite cliff face that had broken off and walked away. A full head shorter than his friend, with a barrel chest and broad shoulders, rippling with dense muscle: Churn was blessed with enormous strength. Hoyt thought he was probably the most physically imposing man in all the Westlands.

In contrast with his almost inhuman strength, Churn was somewhat simple-minded – not disabled, but rather, slower than average when it came to thinking, solving problems or processing information. He was unable – or unwilling – to speak, Hoyt didn't know which, but he communicated using hand gestures, and over the Twinmoons, their ability to carry on interesting and detailed conversations had grown.

Churn had joined Hoyt after the healer had saved his life. Hoyt had found him lying in a drainage ditch off a field near Churn's family farm, bleeding badly from multiple stab wounds and lashed to several sections of wooden plank Hoyt guessed had been ripped from the walls of his own barn. Churn never discussed what had happened, but Hoyt guessed Malakasian soldiers had most likely tortured and murdered his friend's family. The young doctor nursed the bigger man back to health and from that moment, Churn, in his simple mind, had been motivated by two things: the desire to serve Hoyt, and the overwhelming need to physically tear Malagon's still-beating heart from his chest. Hoyt assumed Churn's silence resulted from being forced to witness his family's torture, and he had been unable to prescribe any remedy for his friend's sense of grievous loss.

He knew Churn wasn't deaf, but he learned the hand gestures anyway. It was something he did initially out of courtesy and friendship, and it became extremely useful in business, providing a silent means of communication when stealth was called for.

Unlike Hoyt, Churn *had* killed. Sometimes the Pragan giant disappeared for several days at a time. Hoyt never asked any questions, but news of Malakasian soldiers missing or murdered always followed in the wake of Churn's absences. His rage was rarely evident, but it simmered there, beneath the calm, friendly mask Churn wore most days. Hoyt supposed murdering Malakasian warriors was cathartic for his muscle-bound companion, a therapeutic act of vengeance that brought a sliver of peace to Churn's simple soul, and who was he to deny peace to a troubled man?

Now Hoyt waved to the lumbering giant and called out, 'Perhaps if you walk a bit heavier you can bring an entire brigade of occupation soldiers in here. Or should I just fetch you a rampart horn and you can announce our hiding place with a fanfare?'

Signing, Churn replied, 'None around. I checked the road.'

Hoyt laughed. 'I know. They went by earlier this morning. I don't expect them back for another half-aven. How are things in town?'

Moving his fingers in a rapid pattern, Churn said, 'Rumours about the new galleon. Silver, silk and tobacco.'

Hoyt sat up, interested. 'Is it heavily guarded?'

'A full platoon, but they look lazy. Maybe too long at sea.'

'Is Branag at the shop?' Hoyt was already planning his assault on the cumbersome Malakasian ship. 'Let's go there right now. We'll need his help if we are to pull this off tonight.' He picked up his pack.

Churn was confused. 'Rob it or sink it?'

Hoyt tossed a few handfuls of leaves over the log sheltering his illegal library. 'Both, Churn. We're going to do both.'

'All right, but I'm not going up in the shrouds.'

'Oh, you great hulking baby,' Hoyt teased. 'Well, the plan will never work then. We'll just have to let them sail off to Pellia free as a bird.'

'I'm not going up there.' Churn was agitated now and sweat beaded his forehead.

'Fine. Fine. All right. You don't have to go up in the rigging. *I* will take care of that.'

'What do you mean, "he didn't call again today"?' Howard was furious and Myrna Kessler was trying to stay out of his way, an impossible task in the small bank office.

'I'm simply telling you, Howard, he didn't call again today.' Myrna glanced past Mrs Winter at the long line of customers waiting for counter service. 'C'mon Howard, we've got quite a queue forming out here.'

Saturdays at the bank were always busy; usually Steven Taylor came in to help Myrna handle the morning rush. Although they closed at noon, Myrna frequently dealt with more customers on a Saturday than she did during business hours all week. Steven had missed work the day before and was out again today.

'I thought he and Mark were climbing Decatur.'

'No, he told me Thursday night they had to cancel because of the snow. He distinctly said he would be able to close yesterday, and be here to help this morning.' Howard slammed a drawer in his desk and poured a third cup of black coffee.

'Where's Stevie?' Mrs Winter asked Myrna.

'Steven,' she said pointedly, 'is not in this morning, Mrs Winter. He'll be back on Monday.' She handed a deposit receipt and twenty dollars in notes through the window. 'Don't spend it all at once, Mrs W. Have a good weekend.'

'Good-bye dear,' the elderly woman answered, and Myrna regretted correcting her. She was only being friendly, after all.

Howard finally appeared at Myrna's side and opened a second teller window. Several customers in the long line across the lobby looked at one another awkwardly for a moment before shifting queues. Myrna's pleasant demeanour was the antithesis of Howard's cold efficiency, but for a bank manager with little time on the teller window, Griffin worked as quickly as Myrna. His tempo this morning was fuelled by anger.

'He should let us know where he is,' Howard whispered while running a receipt through his computer. 'What if I hadn't been available to come in this morning? I really thought he was more responsible than this.' Howard counted out two hundred dollars in twenty-dollar bills as if practising for a Vegas gambling table.

'Give him a break, Howard,' Myrna scolded. 'Maybe he's in the hospital, or in a ditch with his car or something. We'll be closed here in a couple of hours. I'll go up to his house and see what's happening with him.'

'No,' Griffin told her, 'I'll go. You take the afternoon and enjoy yourself. *I'll* figure out what's happening with him.'

Howard had intended to go straight round to 147 Tenth Street, but as he locked the bank door behind him, he smelled the distinct aroma of grilling beef emanating from Owen's Pub down the block.

'My heavens, but is there a better smell on this planet?' he asked out loud, adding, 'maybe just a quick burger to get me through the afternoon.' Walking towards the pub in the bright afternoon sun, he heard a loud cheer go up from the crowd gathered inside. He stopped in his tracks. 'Ah yes, Michigan.' Griffin savoured the words before jogging the last few feet to the entrance while humming the Colorado fight song.

Six draught beers, one bacon cheeseburger, an enormous order of French fries and a forty-two–thirty-one victory later, Howard

Griffin stumbled from the pub and up the street towards the corner of Miner and Tenth. When he reached Steven's house, he was surprised to find the door unlocked and slightly ajar.

'Stevie,' he slurred into the front hallway, 'Stevie, I am pissed at you, my boy, but CU won good this afternoon. So you've caught me in a good mood.' Seeing no one coming out to greet him, Griffin meandered through the house towards the kitchen. Several beer cans stood on the counter near an open pizza box and Howard picked one up, realised it was nearly full and took a long draught from it before spitting the beer back into the sink.

'Christ, it's warm,' he complained, then, shouting to anyone who might be listening, 'what the hell are you doing leaving warm beer out here? Someone might drink it.'

He giggled as he pulled out a cold can from the fridge, then headed towards the living room.

If Howard Griffin noticed the shimmering air and flecks of coloured light dancing above the incongruous tapestry, he didn't show it. Instead, he came awkwardly around the sofa and dropped heavily onto the cushions. Finding no ottoman on which to put his feet, the inebriated bank manager slid the coffee table out into the middle of the room and rested his boots on the finished wood surface. He rubbed one hand across his bulging stomach, and was distracted by the sight of a large expanse of cloth spread out across the floor.

'Sheez, what an ugly rug,' he gurgled, eyeing the tapestry now bunched up against the legs of the coffee table. 'You guys must have stolen that from the bathroom at a bus station. Stevie, I am never going to let you live this one down. I wouldn't even buy that ugly bastard, and I *like* tacky décor.'

Yawning widely, Griffin stood up, stretched and, with a loud groan, started back towards the door. In the kitchen, he found a pen and scribbled a note on the open pizza box: STEVIE: CALL ME AS SOON AS YOU GET IN, YOU DERILECT BUGGER. He was not quite certain how to spell derelict, so he deliberately ran the letters together, but even in his weakened condition he could spell bugger, so he made the letters much larger, as if he were a child practising for a spelling quiz.

Message completed, he moved the box to the edge of the stove near the refrigerator, where Steven would be certain to read it. Then he pulled from behind his ear the cigarette he'd bummed from a drinking buddy earlier that afternoon and, failing to find matches, turned on the gas stove. He placed the cigarette clumsily in his mouth and leaned into the flame until the embers glowed red and the smoke stung his eyes. He had not smoked regularly since his move from Boulder to Idaho Springs, but he allowed himself one cigarette every six months – or when he was under particularly difficult stress. He was not sure which excuse counted today, but he inhaled deeply regardless.

Making certain he had locked the door behind him, Howard Griffin walked into the waning afternoon sunlight. It was much colder outside now, and he took a moment to zip his jacket up tightly before making his way towards home in an ungainly drunken shuffle.

He had no idea the gas stove in Steven and Mark's house continued to burn.

GREENTREE SQUARE

Several hours had passed since the strange beasts had attacked the Malakasian horses, and neither Mark nor Steven had heard any sound coming from the lower floors of the palace, or outside their window. They had fled the first suite of rooms for another on the same hallway, hoping Sallax and the enemy soldiers would be too busy battling one another to find them.

Brynne, exhausted, had fallen asleep several minutes before, despite the afternoon heat. The two friends whispered to one another, trying not to wake her.

'You know what's funny?' Mark looked over at Brynne's silent form, then leaned back against the cool stone of the chamber wall.

'That a teenager who doesn't know the rules governing the use of a semi-colon will have Asian characters tattooed on her ass?' Steven replied, managing a smile.

'No, although that does stagger my imagination,' Mark chuckled. 'Think about it. We're here in another world. With two moons, it *has* to be another world. We can look back as far as the pyramids at Giza, 2,500 BC, long before there was metallurgy or weaponry of this sophistication in Western Europe, and there is nothing that speaks of two moons.' He stopped for a moment to gather his thoughts, then continued, 'And this language we've both apparently learned instantaneously, it's not a Western language and it's not a precursor to any modern European language. But these people appear to live in a culture similar to our early Europe. Their features, this architecture, some of their weapons and even their clothes: they all look like.they fell right out of a history textbook.'

'So, what's your point?' Steven asked. 'You don't think we came back in time. Great. *I* don't believe that's possible. Hell,

I don't believe *any* of this is possible, but it's happened.' He absentmindedly ran one knuckle along a seam between two large stones in the masonry.

'For all the similarities, there are things missing, though,' Mark went on. 'Simple things, critical things we would expect to see in a culture that mirrors early Europe this closely.' Again, Mark glanced over at Brynne, but she still slept deeply. 'For example, every western culture dating back centuries has brewed coffee. Can you think of the Ronan word for coffee?'

Steven smiled. 'In the two days since I fell through an unexplained hole in the universe, located, ironically, in our living room, I have been nearly killed by a bowman sniper, imprisoned, lashed to a stone wall in a crumbling palace and threatened with ancient weapons. I have not, however, at any time during all this excitement, thought about the Ronan word for coffee.'

'Try it now,' Mark encouraged.

Steven closed his eyes and relaxed his mind. Ronan words came almost as easily as English for him now, but, despite his efforts, the word for coffee did not emerge. 'That's strange,' he said. 'I can't get it. I keep coming up with "tecan", but I don't think that's right.'

'I think that's more like some sort of herbal tea: jasmine-sleepytime-fruity-zinger tea or some such nonsense,' Mark replied, 'but I'm only guessing based on the information that magically appeared in my head when I landed on that beach.'

'You know what this means?'

'That our magic tapestry could possibly have brought people from our world to this world long before it brought us,' Mark said. 'I can't think of any other way aspects of this place would so closely resemble our world . . . only a *former* version of our world. Culture is a function of any group's values, traditions, beliefs, myths and behaviours. If cultural values, weapons technology and architecture from early Europe managed to get here, maybe the same way we arrived, those values and innovations might have embedded themselves in the fabric of Ronan life.'

'That's not what I meant,' Steven interrupted.

'What *did* you mean?' Mark's analysis was sidetracked momentarily.

'There's no coffee here. How in all hells are we going to get by without coffee?' He laughed. 'Give this up, Mark. You aren't going to figure it out trapped in this palace room. We'll need to get out of here to get home. Hopefully, the answer lies out there somewhere.'

'I guess you're right,' Mark agreed, 'but there has to be some reason why William Higgins locked that thing in your safe. He must have known about its power, and maybe how to harness it.'

'We'll figure it out,' his friend assured him, then changed the subject. 'Anyway, we can't stay here too long. Imagine a world without coffee; you'll perish. The staff at the café has our morning order memorised: one cappuccino and one just-fill-the-damned-cup-right-now-if-you-want-to-survive-another-minute. If we're here too long, you're a goner.'

'You're right, and we'll both be goners if we don't get out of this ramshackle pile of rocks and find some food. I haven't eaten since our last pizza.'

'I haven't either. Although this whole captive routine is an excellent excuse to avoid steamed vegetables and roasted fish.' Steven grimaced as he remembered their pledge to eat more nutritiously.

Mark stood up to take another look out the window. He peered towards the sun, checked his watch, shook it several times and held it to his ear. 'Let's get out of here, I haven't heard a sound from the palace in four hours.'

'You're right. Unless Sallax is waiting just outside that door, we ought to be able to get away.' Steven moved across the floor towards Brynne. Switching back to Ronan, he nudged her gently and called, 'Brynne, wake up. It's time to go.'

The curtains in the upper room of Mika Farrel's home remained closed as Gilmour Stow and the five partisans hurriedly planned their next course of action.

'We can't go back to the tavern,' Jerond offered. 'They'll have the place surrounded or burned to the ground by now.'

'Yes,' Sallax agreed, 'we have to assume they know who we are, so none of our homes are safe. Mika, Jerond, your parents should lay low for a while as well.' Brynne and Sallax's parents had died many Twinmoons earlier; Garec's family owned a farm half a day's ride from Estrad Village. Versen had moved to the southern forests from his family's home in the Blackstone Mountains:

although he would try to get word to them, he was not worried about their immediate welfare.

'With the level of hatred for Malagon growing in Rona, they wouldn't dare murder four elderly people,' Sallax continued, 'but you ought to have them disappear for the time being just to be safe.'

Jerond and Mika nodded in agreement and Jerond rose to leave. 'I'll meet you in the orchard at dawn,' he told them. 'I can get some silver, and my father has a few weapons hidden in the house.' Jerond was the youngest of the partisans. He hesitated, obviously nervous. 'What are we going to do, Sallax?'

'We're going on a journey, north,' Gilmour interrupted. 'Bring some warm clothing, my boy, and don't worry. Things are moving along as they should, but let your family know they may not see you for the next few Twinmoons.'

Garec shot the older man a worried look, then turned back to Jerond and reminded him, 'The orchard at dawn tomorrow, all right?'

He nodded agreement, then crawled through a window at the back of the building, leaped to the ground below and disappeared along a side street into the village. Mika had been listening from the doorway. He quickly descended the stairs to share Gilmour's news with his parents.

'I worry about Jerond,' Garec told the older man. 'Now, what do you mean by several Twinmoons?'

'I mean exactly that.' Gilmour took a long draw on his pipe. 'We'll most likely be gone through next summer's Twinmoon. We have far to go, and not much time to get organised. Now, how many horses can we get before dawn tomorrow?'

'Plenty,' Garec answered. 'Renna is tethered out behind Madur's farm. He'd sell us a dozen if we can pay.' As if on cue, Gilmour reached into the folds of his riding cloak and withdrew a small leather pouch.

He tossed it to Garec. 'That should be enough. See to the horses, fill your quivers and meet us in the orchard tomorrow. We can't be seen together tonight. It would arouse too much suspicion.' Garec stood, gathered up his longbow and started towards the window as Gilmour added, 'Make sure you get three extra mounts.'

'Why? Madur's horses are strong enough to carry our gear and bedrolls as well as us,' Versen said.

'Brynne and the two foreigners will be joining us for this trip,' Gilmour answered, as if the reason were obvious. Garec snorted in disbelief, then crawled through the window himself.

'I'll need to get back to my cabin and gather a few things,' Versen said as he clapped a huge hand on Gilmour's shoulder. 'See you at dawn.'

Sallax gave the big man a quick wave and watched Versen disappear into the alley.

'What are *we* to do?' Sallax asked Gilmour uncertainly.

'*We* are going to give Namont his rites and then meet your sister,' Gilmour answered, rising from his chair. 'But I am not climbing out of that wretched window.'

Brexan watched the attractive merchant exit through the front door of the small house and move along the street as if he had lived there his entire life. She knew the man was a spy, but she didn't know why he had killed Lieutenant Bronfio. He had arranged for Bronfio's platoon to enter the dilapidated keep through the western portcullis, and he'd been waiting in the shadows for an opportunity to murder the young officer. But why?

Did he not serve Prince Malagon? Bronfio had been a by-the-book officer, Prince Malagon's man to the core. She was quite sure he had awakened every morning asking himself how he could best serve the occupation, and how to be the leader his prince expected him to be.

Bronfio often lectured his platoon on the importance of bringing a forceful but familiar occupation to the Ronan people. 'These citizens need predictability,' he had said again and again. 'That's our job, to be a powerful but steady and predictable occupation army. With that accomplished, we will need to put down fewer insurrections, mark me.'

Killing Bronfio did not make sense. It was essentially an act of war against the occupation forces in Rona. Brexan was determined to discover this traitor's nefarious purpose and bring him to justice – but her goal was easier said than done. If she went back and forth through Estrad Village too frequently, someone would mark her uniform and ask why she was away from her unit. Disguise was the answer – or at least some form of misdirection.

While she waited, she stripped off her Malakasian tabards and markings. The result was not perfect: a black vest over a black tunic, each with regularly-shaped patches of a different colour where the badges had been, but it would give her time to find a change of clothes without interference from her colleagues.

Looking down at the array of torn patches and epaulettes on the ground at her feet, Brexan felt a wave of nausea pass through her, the unsettling feeling of uncertainty that comes in the wake of any drastic measure. 'Am I insane to do this?' Brexan asked herself. She would be hanged without trial simply for stripping her uniform, never mind deserting her unit to pursue an alleged traitor.

Some time after the spy entered the building, Brexan watched a young Ronan man, perhaps one hundred and forty Twinmoons old, go in the same door. She didn't expect to see him alive again.

When the spy exited a few moments later, she knew the Ronan and whomever he had been visiting were dead, victims of the handsome merchant. No one else had gone in or come out. Brexan checked that her sword was loose in its scabbard as she prepared to investigate. She forced herself to count slowly to two hundred before she left the alley, all the while watching the street to ensure the spy had not returned, and that he hadn't left others behind to note any activity around the house.

Then Brexan walked across the street and entered the home, trying to act as if she were a regular visitor. The sight that met her eyes made her shudder, not because of any outward signs of brutality, but because of the cold efficiency of the murders. The merchant had killed Lieutenant Bronfio earlier with a dagger between the ribs. His tactics here were equally simple. An elderly couple – maybe the parents? – sat bound and gagged in two chairs near a fireplace where a stewpot still simmered.

Both had been run through the heart; the Malakasian solider cringed when she thought of one being forced to watch, helpless, as the other was murdered. There were no signs of a struggle, but the old man's fingers appeared to have been broken, Brexan guessed during an impromptu interrogation – maybe about his son's possible espionage activities? There were no bruises betraying harsh beatings and no other broken or severed limbs. The small puncture wounds – made by a rapier, she thought –

and unchecked trickles of blood were the only evidence of death. She almost expected them to call out suddenly and beg her to untie their bonds.

Seeing them sitting so quietly together, in what had probably been their favourite chairs, Brexan imagined the old couple spending thousands of avens chatting together in front of the fireplace, planning their lives, teaching their children, entertaining dear friends. All that was over – and for what?

Then she noticed the young man who had come in while she was watching the doorway. He had obviously been killed without fanfare as well: his short sword was still sheathed. There had been no combat, no questions, no broken fingers and no negotiations for life. The spy had waited for the young man to return home and slashed his throat while the boy gaped at his parents' bodies trussed up like pigs awaiting a butcher. Brexan knew this victim had been taken by surprise, unceremoniously and without a struggle.

She seethed with anger. This was not how an occupation force was supposed to behave, and if this was the method Prince Malagon's spies employed to gather information, she did not want any part of their cause. Her stomach roiling with revulsion, she climbed a short flight of stairs, located the young man's bedroom and stole a change of clothes. She was no longer a member of Prince Malagon's occupation army. Lieutenant Bronfio had believed in their work here in Rona and he was dead, murdered by his own prince's spy.

Brexan had enlisted in the army to bring order to the nations of Eldarn. Periodically, that meant dealing with a handful of insurrectionists. This elderly couple, tied up and cold-bloodedly murdered in their home, did not represent a threat to Prince Malagon's throne, and if for some inexplicable reason they had, the spy who uncovered their plot should have brought them to trial.

Her illusions fading like the twilight, Brexan changed into her new clothes, took what food she could find in the pantry and promised the silent corpses that justice would be done.

She would find this spy, track him and observe his behaviour. If he proved loyal to the crown, she would find some way to report his brutality to the prince's generals in Orindale. If he were not loyal, she would kill him herself.

*

'So what the hell were those monsters that attacked the horses?' Mark asked Brynne as they walked towards Estrad Village. She ignored him, staring silently into the distance.

'C'mon Brynne. I told you we never had any intention of hurting you. We just needed you to get away from the palace.'

Mark reached out for her, but she immediately turned away, 'Don't touch me.'

'Leave her alone, Mark,' Steven suggested in English. 'She's not going to help us. Let's just let her go.'

'I think we ought to hang onto her. She's the only one who's even bothered to try talking to us. Everyone else just starts shooting.'

'There was that old man,' Steven said, switching to Ronan. 'He seemed to know we aren't spies.'

'Gilmour,' Brynne muttered.

'Gilmour,' Steven echoed, as if trying out the name. 'How do you suppose he knew we weren't from Malakasia?'

Brynne appeared more willing to answer Steven. 'He knows many things the rest of us don't understand. We're lucky to have him with us,' she said quietly.

'He's the leader of your group?' Mark tried again. 'He's organising the Resistance?'

'There has been little resistance yet,' she answered, still refusing to look at Mark, 'but there has been too much oppression and murder. One day, hopefully soon, we will fight to rid our land of Malagon's army, and perhaps even succeed in freeing all the lands from his occupation forces.'

'All the lands?' Steven enquired.

'Rona, Praga, Falkan and Gorsk, four of the lands of Eldarn. Malakasia has occupied our homeland since Prince Markon died, nine hundred and eighty Twinmoons ago.' She pulled at a strand of hair that had fallen across her face. 'There was a terrible fire at Riverend Palace . . . you saw the damage it did, even though it was so long ago. And within the space of two Twinmoons, the royal families of Praga, Falkan and Rona had all been wiped out by a strange disease. Even today no one has any idea what caused it.'

'What about Gorsk?' Mark asked.

'Gorsk has never been ruled by a royal family the way the rest of Eldarn is. King Remond controlled all of Eldarn except Gorsk, and his descendants – all taking the title prince or princess – took on the different lands; Markon, King Remond's great-grandson, ruled here in Rona.' She cast a sidelong glance at Mark and continued, 'Gorsk was different: it was ruled by a congress of scholars called the Larion Senate. Legend has it they were all murdered in a grievous massacre a Moon before the fire that took the lives of Prince Markon's wife, son and closest advisor.'

'Why govern Gorsk differently?' Steven pushed down on a sapling branch to clear a path for Brynne. 'Why no prince or princess of Gorsk?'

'The Larions had magic.' Brynne paused, recognising the scepticism in their faces. 'They used magic to bring scholarship, medicine and education to the known world. They were a community of servants, brilliant servants, who brought advanced knowledge and research to our hospitals and universities. Their genocide was the first in a long series of tragedies that destroyed the political and social structure of Eldarn. Nine hundred and eighty Twinmoons later, here we are, an occupied nation surrounded by occupied nations.'

Checking his watch again, Mark said, 'You keep mentioning the Twinmoon. Is that what we saw yesterday, the two moons lining up over the ocean?'

'That's right,' she answered. 'That alignment occurs about every sixty days, one Twinmoon. We use them to chart time, our lives, the seasons. Gilmour sometimes talks of Eras and Ages, but we've got no idea what he means. We have a difficult enough time keeping track of what day it is.'

Looking between his watch and the sun, Mark said, 'Now that you mention it, I don't think a day here is the same as ours, unless my watch is broken.'

'Watch?' Finally she turned to look at him.

'Yeah, my watch.' He held out his wrist. 'It's a simple machine that tells what time of day it is.'

'Why call it a watch? Does it only work when you watch it?'

'No,' he answered as Steven laughed. 'I suppose a more accurate name for it would be timepiece. Look, it now reads four in the afternoon, and here in Rona it's already growing dark. I believe your day has fewer—' He stopped. There was no Ronan word for hour.

'I think you're right,' Steven interjected. 'I noticed this morning it seemed to get light much later than at home.'

Now it was Brynne who was sceptical. 'I don't know if I should believe you. This may be some elaborate ruse to get me to reveal details of the Resistance. It won't work.'

Mark removed his watch and handed it to her. 'Here, take it. It isn't doing me any good anyway.'

Cautiously, Brynne reached out and took the watch. 'How does it attach?' Mark fastened the band and after a rudimentary lesson in telling time, they continued walking.

'Thank you, Mark Jenkins.' Brynne smiled for the first time all day.

'Just Mark is fine, Brynne. Just Mark.'

The trio continued their journey towards the village, bypassing the road for a narrow path through oak, maple, dogwood, walnut and chestnut trees that were interrupted periodically by a particularly prickly and disagreeable type of cedar marked by thin strands of exfoliated bark. There were other trees as well, trees that didn't belong in this sort of forest: white birch, rosewood, beech, and several species Steven couldn't identify.

Steven had many questions for Brynne now that she was willing to talk with them, and the young woman complied as well as she could. So little about this experience made sense; Steven was surprised at how well he and Mark were handling their predicament. Magicians at work, huge ravenous beasts stalking the forest, a battle raging through a crumbling palace and all of it happening around them while he and Mark looked on: Steven felt as though he had fallen headlong into someone else's dream. Now he was trapped. While the story grew ever more peculiar, he was helpless, unable to grasp, let alone solve, the problems that faced them. All he and Mark could do was to continue walking towards town and hope they would find *someone* with the knowledge to get them back through that mysterious tapestry and into their living room.

Rona's southern region felt more like a bayou wetland than a Colorado mountain forest and the two foreigners were sweating openly. Hunger and dehydration were giving Steven tunnel vision. 'I need to eat something,' he said, 'and soon.'

'You're right,' Mark agreed. 'I could eat health food, I'm so hungry.' Turning to Brynne, he asked, 'Is there somewhere we can find something to eat nearby?'

Brynne contemplated her choices for a moment before replying, 'Greentree Tavern. It's not far.' She knew Greentree Square would be packed with Malakasian soldiers, all searching for the band of revolutionaries, but she hoped the confusion that would ensue when she brought the strangers into town would give her an opportunity to escape.

'This tavern,' Mark asked, 'is it safe?'

'It ought to be ... I own it.'

'You own a bar?' Steven was incredulous. Brynne nodded. 'Your own bar?' he repeated. 'Where were you when I went to college?'

'How late is the kitchen open?' Mark said, almost drooling at the thought of hot food and cold beer – even though he had no intention of going anywhere the young woman suggested once they reached the village.

'Late enough,' she said, coyly returning his smile. She resolutely continued her forced march, all the while considering how she might escape from the two foreigners. She hoped against hope that Sallax and her friends had survived the assault on the palace and would be waiting to ambush her captors somewhere between Riverend and Estrad.

Brynne had never known her parents. They had died while she was still an infant; she and Sallax had been brought up in an orphanage in Estrad. The elderly couple who ran the orphanage died fifty Twinmoons later, while Brynne was still a child, so Sallax found a job clearing tables and cleaning trenchers and goblets at Greentree Tavern. It did not pay much, but Sybert Gregoro, the tavern owner, had taken a liking to the siblings and they were given a small room of their own, behind the scullery.

When Brynne was old enough, she began working in the tavern kitchen, preparing food and baking bread for evening meals. She had never been to school and learned to read from an older boy who also worked in the kitchen. His name was Ren and Brynne was smitten with him: the first boy she had ever had a crush on. But Ren had other plans for her.

One night, a wealthy Falkan businessman caught sight of Brynne through the scullery doors. He stayed drinking near the fireplace until the tavern was about to close, then signalled unobtrusively for Ren. When the merchant retired to his room, Ren went back into the kitchen and called Brynne over.

She had no idea what was happening, but Ren grinned at her and gestured that she should follow him up the stairs. Sometimes, when the inn wasn't full, he'd sneak her into one of the guest bedrooms so she could sleep on a luxury pallet. He was her friend and she had no reason to fear him.

When Ren arrived at the door to the merchant's room, he knocked once, softly. Cracking the door slightly, the merchant handed Ren a small leather pouch and the boy promptly pushed Brynne into the room, pulled the door shut and disappeared down the stairs.

Brynne's memory of the night that followed was still clouded by terror. She had spent her life trying to repress the violation; even now, many Twinmoons on, she was confounded by the fact that she had never screamed. Sybert would have heard; she knew he would have come quickly to help. Sallax had been downstairs sleeping in their small room; he might have heard her cry for help.

All she remembered was quietly repeating, 'No, please,' over and over again while the Falkan businessman held her tightly by the throat. 'Let you go? Such a toothsome little morsel, just ripe for the plucking – I think not, my sweet little whore,' he whispered, ignoring her pleas, and took his time abusing her until sunlight broke through the chamber window. Seeing dawn arrive, the merchant dressed, tossed her a silver piece and left the tavern.

Later that morning, Sybert found her. She had not moved from the floor where the man had thrown her after he had finished raping her. She was lying silently, staring up at the ceiling. Her dress had been ripped away from her body, revealing the depths of degradation her attacker had subjected her to: her slim legs were scratched from thigh to ankle, her barely grown breasts were torn and bitten, bloody toothmarks empurpling her pale skin. Tears trickled silently down her still-terrified face, which was as battered as the rest of her frail body.

The publican groaned out loud, then tore the coverlet off the bed and wrapped her gently in it. He summoned a village woman skilled in healing arts, who nursed her back to health over the next few Twinmoons. Sybert himself made sure Brynne was recuperating, refusing to let her take up her duties until he was certain she had healed.

Several days after Brynne's rape, Sallax and Ren were sent across the village to purchase flour, eggs and venison for the evening's meal. Sallax suspected Ren was responsible for taking his sister to the Falkan's chamber, but he had no proof – until that morning, when Ren insisted they stop at the cobbler's to look at a pair of fine leather boots displayed in the window. Sallax laughed at the older boy: the boots cost more than either of them made in three Twinmoons, but Ren brandished a heavy leather pouch and insisted on trying them on. When he was sure they fit well enough, he pulled out a handful of silver coins and paid the shoemaker.

As they left the shop, Sallax turned to Ren. 'If you've got silver, there's something else you should see.' He led him down a side street to a secluded square, empty of onlookers.

Ren looked around. He couldn't see what Sallax meant – then, for the first time, he began to wonder if he had been a little stupid pulling out his money in public. But it wasn't silver Sallax was interested in. Instead, he pushed the older boy up against the wall and, before Ren realised what was happening, Sallax slipped his knife up under Ren's ribs and into his lungs. Blood, deep red, almost black, flowed from the wound and Sallax sat for several moments savouring Ren's laboured breathing as his lungs filled with fluid and he died there on the street.

Working slowly and carefully, Sallax removed the leather purse from Ren's tunic and pulled the boots from the dead boy's feet. He returned them to the cobbler, saying his friend was too embarrassed to ask for a refund, but the silver belonged to their employer. The cobbler was not happy, but he returned the fee, threatening to take the matter up with Sybert himself if either boy ever tried such a thing again.

When Sallax returned with the provisions, he told Sybert he'd last seen Ren disappearing into an alehouse. When he didn't return for the evening meal, the innkeeper shrugged. He too had his suspicions about how the merchant had lured Brynne upstairs.

Seeing the look in her brother's eyes, Brynne knew he was lying about Ren's disappearance. Strangely, it didn't make her feel better; she felt empty inside. The thought of Ren lying dead, somewhere in the village, left her a little remorseful.

Although she recovered physically, Brynne's youthful innocence was gone for good. She never saw her rapist again, but in nightmares she remembered his thick, sweaty jowls, the long half-moon scar across his wrist, and an ugly brown, bulbous mole that grew from one side of his nose. A toughness emerged in her, almost overnight, and it wasn't long before men throughout Estrad knew better than to proposition the lovely but deadly young woman. Twinmoons in the kitchen and scullery had made her quick with a knife, and more than one tavern patron had cause to regret reaching for her bottom as she served drinks. Brynne never maimed them: she just marked them, leaving a half-moon scar across their wrists, a permanent reminder of the man who had so violently destroyed her innocence and broken her spirit.

Thirty-five Twinmoons later, Sybert Gregoro died in his sleep. Brynne sent word to his estranged son, a farmer in northern Falkan, who replied in a careful script that she and Sallax should send along his father's personal effects and savings but should consider the tavern their own. They kept the letter closely guarded in a strongbox under the bar and left Sybert's chambers empty for seven full Twinmoons before they felt comfortable taking over.

It was a longer time before she and Sallax started calling Greentree Tavern their own. For many Twinmoons, Brynne expected Sybert's son to arrive and claim his inheritance, but he never had, and the people of Estrad Village were glad the old man had left his business to the hard-working siblings he had fostered.

It was dark by the time Steven, Mark and Brynne reached the edge of Estrad Village. Steven was glad of the darkness: it would help camouflage their strange-looking clothing.

'If we're going to be around here for any length of time, we ought to get some other clothes,' he observed. 'Your red sweater stands out like a beacon among all this homespun fabric.'

'You're right,' Mark said, appearing to notice his pullover for the first time all day. 'But before that, we have to do something with her. Look for something we can use to tie her up.' Steven pulled the belt from around his waist and, taking his friend's lead, Mark did the same.

'What do you mean?' Brynne implored. 'Are we not going to my tavern? I can get you food, and Sallax has clothing there that will fit both of you.'

'Into the lion's den, my dear?' Mark asked sarcastically. 'Don't be ridiculous. We'll find food and clothing and be back to get you. We need to meet Gilmour, because he's the only other person who seems to understand we're not here to overthrow the damned government, or to infiltrate your resistance efforts, but I certainly don't trust you enough to follow you into town.' Mark felt a pang of sadness as he watched her frown with disappointment. She was lovely. He fought the urge to gently push her hair back off her face.

'I don't want anything to do with you two either,' she spat. 'Why will you not trust me to take you to Gilmour now?'

Steven said, 'Because we don't believe you know where he is. None of you were expecting that attack this morning, so I don't suppose your friends are all snugly tucked in their beds. We'll find food, steal some clothing and be right back for you.' Brynne struggled against the bonds that held her firmly to a handy tree trunk. They were still several hundred paces from the edge of the village and although screaming would do her no good, Steven was taking no chances; he tore a sleeve from his shirt and tied it tightly across her mouth.

'Try to relax,' he whispered as he and Mark turned to make their way stealthily into the village. 'We'll be back in a tick.'

Unable to respond, Brynne's eyes clouded with anger and she lashed out at the foreigners, but her kick sailed wide of its targets.

'You think she was lying?' Steven asked a short while later.

'I'm sure she was lying.'

'That's too bad. I've always wanted to meet a woman who owned her own bar,' Steven mused.

Mark chuckled. 'Yeah, me too, but I was hoping mine would be on 17th Street in Denver.'

'Maybe we can find Gilmour at Greentree Tavern,' Steven guessed. 'Why else would she want to get us there?'

'Sallax,' Mark commented dryly.

'Oh, you're right. He does tend to shoot first and ask questions never, doesn't he.' Steven spoke in hushed tones as they approached a row of single-storey stone buildings with clay-tiled roofs. 'I say we risk it. Maybe he won't try to kill us if he knows we have her tied up somewhere.'

'Let's find clothes first. We certainly can't ask for directions looking like this.' Mark crept alongside one of the buildings and peered through an open window to where a family was sitting around a fireplace, talking and laughing together.

'Not this one,' he whispered. 'Let's keep going.' They moved to the next window, through which Mark could see a family making preparations for their evening meal.

'As great as it smells in there, I say we keep looking,' Mark said.

Steven's mouth watered at the aroma emanating from the warmly lit kitchen, but he nodded in silent agreement.

Crawling on all fours, they discovered the windows in the next house were covered with pine shutters. Through a small crack between the wooden blinds Steven watched a burly, powerful-looking man don a wide-brimmed hat and exit out the opposite side of the house into the muddy street. Steven watched for a full five minutes, in case the man returned quickly, or other family members turned up. From his vantage point at the window he could see clearly through two rooms, but he wasn't sure about the rest of the building.

Mark grew uneasy waiting. 'What do you see?' he whispered at last.

'Nothing,' Steven answered. 'One big guy went out the front, but I haven't seen anyone since.'

'All right, let's go in.' Mark began making his way around the side of the house. The front door was made of wood, with a length of hide hanging from a small hole drilled through the centre board. No locks. Pulling down on the leather strap, Steven felt a latching device inside come free and the door swung open easily on its leather hinges.

The two men made their way rapidly through the house collecting food and clothing. It was sparsely decorated but comfortable, with a small stone fireplace in the bedchamber, a pile of logs and kindling next to it.

Mark spotted the straw mattress and, acting on instinct, lifted a corner of the bedding to find a small pouch and a long narrow sword in a smooth leather scabbard. He emptied the contents of the pouch into one hand: silver coins. Although different sizes, they all bore an image of the same man embossed on one side, with an inscription Mark was unable to read on the other.

'Well, thank God for us some things don't change,' he said. 'People are the same everywhere: the family fortune is stashed under the mattress. I guess they can't trust the banks here in Rona either.'

'Hey, you can trust my bank,' Steven retorted.

'Sure, the bank you robbed.' Mark laughed, then changed the subject. 'I'm taking this sword, too.'

'What are you going to do with a sword?' Steven asked, belting a long tunic around his waist and stuffing what food he could find into a cloth pack.

'Hopefully, protect myself from lunatics like Sallax. You should find some kind of weapon as well, my friend. He doesn't seem terribly fond of you either.'

Mark moved through the back room towards a row of windows facing the forest. On a plain wooden table was a long hunting knife similar to the one he had taken from Brynne. 'Here,' he said and handed the weapon to his roommate. 'Take this one. I'll keep Brynne's.'

Finding nothing more to pillage, Steven and Mark returned to the front door.

'We should leave him something. I feel bad. We've taken everything this guy has,' Steven said guiltily.

'C'mon, let's just go.' Mark gripped Steven's shoulder. 'Of course you feel bad. We're thieves. We just robbed this guy's house. It's not right, but with his help, we might just live through this nightmare.'

Steven moved back through the house, removed two ballpoint pens from his pocket and placed them on the table. 'There, he can make a fortune inventing the disposable writing instrument.'

'Compliments of the First National Bank of Idaho Springs, I assume?'

'Home of the lowest interest small business loans on the Front Range,' Steven said, as if reading a cue card.

'Great, leave him the phone number. Howard will appreciate that.' Mark opened the wooden doorway a few inches and peered into the street beyond. 'We're clear. Let's go.'

'Right.' Steven moved outside. 'Now we have to find Greentree Tavern and, hopefully, Gilmour.'

'If he's still alive.' Mark sounded dubious.

The roommates asked directions of an elderly woman, who spent several minutes explaining how to find Greentree Square. Once he'd grasped the directions, Mark tried to interrupt her, but she continued talking as if the two foreigners were the first people with whom she had spoken in half a lifetime.

Steven was feeling stifled, despite a lingering Twinmoon breeze and the evening's cooler temperatures. He was beginning to regret wearing his tweed jacket under his newly stolen tunic – he'd remove it as soon as they were alone, but for now he had to listen, somewhat impatiently, to the garrulous old woman while sweating through his layers.

Her directions, although lengthy, were easy to follow and they soon reached a busy main street that appeared to run north. Mark suggested they stick to the side streets that parallelled the wide thoroughfare, to avoid Ronan freedom fighters or Malakasian soldiers who might be searching for them. It wasn't long before the road opened into an expansive trade and commercial area, bigger than they might have expected for a village. Even though night had fallen, carts of dried meats, fresh fish, cheeses, tanned hides and wine still lined the small village common: it looked like a tiny grass island in the centre of a divided highway.

Greentree Square.

The evening breeze caused torches illuminating the area to flicker as if the light itself were alive, and shadows cast by those hurrying through town seemed to move in unnatural ways. Greentree Square bustled with activity, much of it caused by Malakasian soldiers moving deliberately through the buildings and back streets, obviously searching for someone, and the Ronans steering clear of occupation forces by taking shelter in any building that would allow them a quick entry through bolted doors. Locals working their carts raised collars, pulled hat brims down or stepped into shadows as Malakasian patrols crisscrossed the streets.

Mark looked out on the bustling activity for several moments before melting back into the shadows where Steven waited. 'We can't go out there,' he whispered, 'they're checking everyone.'

'Let's get Brynne,' Steven said through a mouthful of Ronan bread and cheese he'd pulled from a pocket. The bread was hard, but full of flavour. 'At least the food's edible. We can find someplace to spend the night, eat properly, get some sleep, then come back here tomorrow.'

Mark considered the suggestion briefly. 'You're right. We have food. We just need a safe place to get some rest. I think—'

Steven abruptly reached out to cover his friend's mouth as several villagers hurried along the street away from the common. Mark was relieved to see one of them was black. Apparently he was not the only person with dark skin in the village. From the shadows, the Coloradoans could easily overhear their conversation.

'Well, didn't you see the smoke?' a villager asked. 'It was higher than the tallest spire at the palace, as if the whole place was on fire.'

'I smelled it all the way down at the alehouse. It was burning pitch, I'm certain,' another said confidently. 'I know that smell from that stint I did in the shipyards. It may be Twinmoons ago, but it's not a smell you forget.'

'I hear there were grettans in the forest as well, and *that*'s why the rutting horsecocks abandoned the siege.' The first villager laughed, adding, 'Their horses were tethered in the forest, a right perfect breakfast set out just for them.'

'Grettans, Dakin?' a third voice asked dubiously. 'You've had too much wine again. There are no grettans in Rona and you shouldn't go on spreading such rumours.' The voices faded as the Ronans moved on and Steven motioned that they should begin heading back the way they had come, away from Greentree Square.

They turned a corner into a dark street that ran between two rows of small businesses, all closed for the evening. This small street was much older, an indication of when Estrad Village had first been built: the buildings were similar to the house they'd burgled out near the edge of the forest, stone, with clay-tiled roofing, but here the foundations had sunk unevenly into the ground. In the darkness, they looked like a row of untended gravestones that had shifted haphazardly in a heavy rainstorm; several had sunk forward, as if they were slowly falling on their faces. Steven looked up: their roof peaks nearly met over his head.

Despite the darkness, Mark knew this street faced south because as soon as they turned the corner, he felt a cool breeze blowing in from the ocean. It struck him in the face and brought some small relief from the humid evening.

'Pass me another piece of that bread,' he asked softly.

His roommate complied. 'The food isn't too bad. That cheese is strong, but not so horrible if you eat it with something. Preferably a decent port. I wonder if they even have drinkable wine in this godforsaken pit?' There was a short pause as Steven sniffed a piece of dried meat, trying to determine what it was. 'I've no idea what animal this came from – I'll wait for Brynne to tell us before I try any.'

'Who knows? Maybe it's grettan,' Mark said, echoing the villager who happened by them earlier.

In the distance, two figures entered the side street and turned towards them. One carried a small torch and Steven could see they were shadowed by a large, mangy dog. Even in the dark it looked undernourished. 'Oh, no,' he groaned.

'It should be all right,' Mark assured him. 'We're dressed the part. We can speak the language. We'll wish them a good evening and continue on our way.'

'You're right, I guess.' Steven was afraid. He had the hunting knife, but he already knew he would never be able to stab anyone. Firing a bow from a distance into a group of attackers, perhaps he could manage that, but just straight-out stabbing someone would be a more difficult undertaking. His life would have to be in immediate danger for him to use a knife in his own defence.

As the two Ronans approached, Mark slowed his own stride noticeably.

'What's wrong?' Steven asked.

'I don't know,' Mark answered, staring into the evening wind. 'Something seems strangely familiar.'

'I don't know what you're talking about. There's nothing about this place that's familiar to me at all.'

Mark shrugged. 'Maybe it's the sea breeze. It's been a long time since I've smelled a sea breeze.'

Steven sniffed the air as well, stopped and sniffed again. 'You're right,' he said, 'there is something.'

The strangers were almost upon them when Mark turned suddenly and whispered, 'The old man's tobacco.' He looked anxiously down the street to where the slowly advancing figures had begun to take on a more definite shape. 'Shit, it's Sallax and Gilmour.'

Steven started twitching in fright. For a moment he thought of turning to flee, but Mark gripped his upper arm, holding him fast.

'It's okay, Steven. We needed to find them.'

Sallax and Gilmour were about twenty paces away when Mark cried, 'Wait right there!'

Sallax drew his rapier in a fluid motion and was about to charge when Gilmour put a hand firmly on his chest, holding him back.

'No, Sallax, put that away,' he said calmly. The tall Ronan thought for a moment about defying the old man, then returned the blade to its scabbard.

'We mean you no harm,' Gilmour offered in near-perfect English. 'Actually, as I started to mention this morning, I have been waiting for you for some time now.'

'You speak their language?' Sallax was in shock.

'Of course,' Gilmour answered, 'although it is a difficult language to master: too many odd rules one must break too frequently.' He turned back to the foreigners. 'Please, let us approach,' he asked in English.

'Come on slowly,' Mark called back, 'but remember, we have Brynne.'

'Of course, of course, my friends,' Gilmour said genially, 'I'm certain she's fine. Please, let's find a place where we can talk. I will explain as much as I can for you.'

'Can you get us home?' Steven asked, feeling more confident.

'I can help you get started, but the path back home for you will be long.' As the Ronans drew close, Gilmour reached out one hand.

'I believe this is how you do it,' he said, a little uncertain.

Steven shook his hand. 'That's right . . . I'm Steven Taylor and this is Mark Jenkins.'

'I am so pleased to make your acquaintance.' The old man shook hands with Mark as well. 'I am Gilmour Stow and this is Sallax Farro.' Sallax made no move until Steven reached out to him, then he grudgingly copied Gilmour.

'Where did you learn our language?' Mark asked, 'Not that we're not grateful.'

'I have learned many languages, over many Twinmoons,'

Gilmour said, 'but we are being rude.' He placed a comforting hand on Sallax's shoulder and switched back to Ronan. 'We should speak Common.'

'That's better, Gilmour,' Sallax growled.

The dog following them up the street appeared to be a stray out looking for food. It sniffed at the cloth pack Steven carried and, obligingly, Steven gave the scrawny animal a piece of the unidentified dried meat. The dog devoured the morsel in a second and nudged Steven again with its nose.

'Go on, now,' Steven told him quietly, 'go home.'

'You shouldn't feed him,' Sallax spoke up. 'He will follow you for days.'

'Too late,' Steven replied. 'Well, he can have this meat. We weren't certain whether it was safe to eat, anyway.' Steven offered another piece to the dog, but surprisingly, the hungry beast didn't take it. Steven offered again, pushing the meat towards the dog's nose, but still the animal ignored him. Suddenly Steven detected a foul odour, a sweetish sickly smell emanating from the animal at his heels. He knelt down and found the dog frozen into immobility.

'What the hell is this?' Steven asked, and leapt backwards as the stray began to decompose rapidly, rotting before his eyes.

'It's an almor!' Gilmour cried in alarm. 'Quick, you must run!' He grabbed Sallax by the sleeve and shoved him roughly down the street. Neither Steven nor Mark waited around to discover what an almor was: they took off at a full sprint after the fleeing partisans.

Steven had no idea what had just happened, but he was deeply unnerved. He ran as fast as he was able, and soon overtook both Sallax and Gilmour. Mud from the street splattered up his legs. He heard the old man calling, 'Stay out of the water! It can catch you if you run in the water!'

Steven's mind raced and he muttered to himself, 'Is he kidding? The whole goddamned street is mud. There *is* nowhere to avoid running through water. And what the hell is the "it" he's referring to?' He took a vital second to look back: Sallax and Mark were immediately behind him, but Gilmour, although still running, was lagging badly behind.

'Turn left here!' Sallax yelled and Steven obliged, running into a drier side street. He risked another look but didn't see the elderly man make the turn. He started to slow, until he heard Sallax scold harshly, 'Don't worry about Gilmour. He'll be along.'

Steven was beginning to run badly out of breath when he was drawn up short by a blinding flash of light that illuminated the street around them. The brilliance was accompanied by a deafening explosion, the force of which slammed into him and nearly knocked him headlong into the dirt.

'What the hell was that?' Mark cried, slowing to a jog.

'I don't know,' Steven answered. 'It's as though a bomb went off back there.'

'Hold on, my friends,' Gilmour said as he emerged from the darkness. Steven was surprised at how much ground he had made up. 'We need not run any more, but we ought to get away from this place as soon as possible. The entire Malakasian occupation force will be here shortly and we must be well on our way before they arrive.'

He reached into his tunic and withdrew a pipe. Steven had seen Gilmour drop his pipe before beginning to run – he wondered how many the old man had inside his shirt. It was a little odd that Gilmour did not appear in the least bit winded, while he, Mark and Sallax were breathing heavily and sweating through their clothes.

'What *was* that?' Steven asked through painful breaths.

'That was an ancient creature we call an almor,' the older man told him matter-of-factly. He might have reading a feature in *National Geographic* for all the emotion he showed. 'It is a demon that travels through a fluid medium and feeds by draining the life force from any living thing. Why it is here, I'm not certain. However, I do know it did not arrive of its own volition. It was brought here by a powerful force, an evil force, and it hunts someone in particular.' He took a moment to light the pipe with a taper he drew from his riding cloak. A torch hanging from a wall sconce provided the flame. 'I'm assuming it has been sent here to kill me,' he finished then, thinking twice, he returned to the torch, pulled it from its sconce on the wall and used it to light their way along the street.

'I thought they were legends,' Sallax said. 'Fabled monsters that lurked in dark alleys or forests. I never imagined for a moment that they were real.'

'They are very real, and they are the stuff of legends. There was a time, a dreadful time, long before King Remond's reign, when Eldarn was overrun with almor. It took the combined efforts of numerous forces to rid the world of them.' Gilmour sighed. 'Obviously they weren't all disposed of. An almor will continue to hunt until it finds its target, and nothing will stop it. Time means nothing to it. We will have to beware every moment of every day until we control the force that brought it here.'

'What's that?' Mark asked.

'Nerak,' Gilmour answered, drawing on his pipe.

'What's a Nerak?' Mark was riveted.

'Right now, that's not what's important. I will explain when we have time.'

'Well, what was that explosion then?' Sallax was not willing to let the conversation end there.

Gilmour eyed Steven's cloth pack and, seeing the older man's interest, Steven handed it over. Reaching inside, Gilmour withdrew a wine skin and a loaf of fresh bread. He took a long swallow from the skin and tore a large chunk from the loaf. 'Thank you,' he said, and turned to Sallax.

'I had to throw the almor off our path. The only way to do that was to dry as much of the damp mud behind us as possible. It will not stop it, but it did cause it to lose track of us for the time being.'

'Magic,' Mark whispered to Steven.

'Oh, nonsense,' Gilmour chided. 'Explosions aren't magic. Anyone can learn explosions. Come now, we must collect Brynne. Daylight will soon be upon us.' He gestured for Steven and Mark to lead the way.

Despite her fury at having been lashed to a tree all night, Brynne remained calm while Gilmour explained what had happened.

'Then they were telling the truth?' she asked in disbelief. 'They really are from some distant land?'

'We are,' Mark said, but once again she refused to look at him, as if he were *especially* guilty of angering her.

The small group made their way cautiously through the pre-dawn light towards the orchard and their rendezvous with the other partisans. They took cover in the underbrush from time to time to avoid Malakasian patrols. There appeared to be soldiers everywhere, yet in a certain amount of disarray, still confused by the events of the previous day. The failed siege at Riverend Palace, the searches throughout the village and the devastating blast in the neighbourhood near Greentree Square had platoons running back and forth across the area in disorganised chaos.

As they approached the orchard, with its trees lined up neatly like sentries on picket, Gilmour, despite Steven and Mark's incessant badgering, refused to elaborate further on the almor, his apparent use of magic in creating an explosion, or the sinister force he had called Nerak, promising to explain as well as he could as soon as they were safely out of Estrad.

'You must trust me,' the old man told them. 'I will explain as we go, but right now the most important task we face is getting out of here undetected.'

They found Garec and Versen waiting near a large, crooked tree, with seven horses tethered nearby. Heavy dew coated trees and grass alike and clouds of thick fog blew between the trees like shapeless wraiths hunting for lost souls. Versen waved to the small company while Garec, apparently oblivious to their arrival, aimed carefully into the upper branches. He let an arrow fly and a large red apple tumbled to the ground, pierced cleanly. Garec had retrieved apple and arrow and taken a bite before he realised his friends were on hand.

'Welcome,' he said, hurriedly swallowing his mouthful and eyeing Steven and Mark with curiosity. 'I took the liberty of fetching your horses as well,' he told Sallax and Gilmour. 'Brynne, I chose a particularly fiery mare for you. She's been chasing Renna around Madur's farm for two days.'

'That seems appropriate,' Mark commented under his breath and was rewarded with an angry glare from the Ronan woman.

'I thought so, too.' Garec nodded at the two foreigners before adding, 'This time we meet on better terms, I think.' He showed the Coloradoans to their mounts.

Steven was given a large brown mare with a white patch around one eye and along both forelegs. He patted her affectionately, then picked up a windfall apple and offered it. The mare plucked it nimbly from his outstretched palm; Steven felt they could be friends. He fixed the cloth pack to her saddle, removed his tweed jacket and tied it fast with a leather thong.

Mark stood watching Steven and waiting for someone to tell him what to do next.

'What's the matter?' Steven asked quietly.

'I don't know anything about horses,' Mark answered. 'I've never even been this close to one before – well, unless you count the pony at the Nassau County Fair.'

'I don't,' Steven laughed. 'Look, it's easy. Be nice to him, develop a relationship with him and he'll take great care of you.'

'A relationship? I don't even know how you know he's a him.' Mark looked doubtful, but gingerly patted the horse's neck. 'Okay, I've been nice. Now what?'

'Now you get on him!' Steven grinned. 'It's honestly not as bad as you think. Just put your foot in this thing – it's a stirrup, you've heard of them, right? – and haul yourself up. You've seen enough Westerns; use the reins, use your legs, and make the rest up as you go along.'

He turned to Gilmour and asked, 'Where are we going?'

'North,' the older man replied, and then to everyone added, 'We mustn't travel by the Merchants' Highway; it will be too heavily patrolled.' He looked about on the ground and found an apple, but instead of feeding it to his horse, bit into it himself. 'We'll pass through the Blackstone Mountains into Falkan. From there, it will be up to our new friends which direction we take.'

'Up to us?' Steven asked. 'How will it be up to us?'

Gilmour was suddenly quite serious. 'Do you have Lessek's Key?'

'Key?' Mark asked, fighting to heft himself onto the horse's back. 'What key? What are you talking about? We fell through that cloth rug, landed on the beach and then ran into Garec and Sallax. We don't know anyone named Lessek – do we, Steven?' On his third attempt, Mark managed to heave himself into the saddle. He sat there wondering what would happen when the horse started to move.

'Lessek has been dead for many, many Twinmoons,' Gilmour replied, 'but his key is critical. If we don't retrieve it, we are already partially defeated, perhaps even completely.'

'Defeated in what, Gilmour?' Garec asked. 'You're not making any sense.'

'It *will* make sense, Garec,' Gilmour said sadly. For the first time, he looked and sounded like an old man. 'There is much to discuss along the way, but you will need a history lesson before our current plight and mission will come fully into focus. But that's for later.' He peered furtively around the orchard before giving the order: 'All right, let's go.'

'What about Mika and Jerond?' Versen interjected. 'Shouldn't we wait for them? Although no one had commented on their absence, the partisans were all thinking the same thing: Mika and Jerond were late, and that could mean they had been captured, or even killed.

'We need to get moving,' Gilmour repeated. 'Mika and Jerond will catch up. They know we're going north, and it's many days' ride to Falkan.'

'What are our options once we reach Falkan?' Garec asked, climbing easily onto Renna's back. He scratched the mare affectionately between her ears. 'You said it was up to Mark Jenkins and Steven Taylor. That must mean there are multiple options.'

Steven reached out and tapped Garec's arm. 'It's just Mark and Steven. That's all. Not "Mark Jenkins and Steven Taylor". It looks like we're going to be spending a lot of time together, so let's drop the formality, shall we?'

Garec shrugged, unconcerned, before turning back to Gilmour. 'Without Lessek's Key, we have only one option.'

'What's that?' Brynne was listening intently.

Gilmour tied his riding cloak tightly around his shoulders, as if he felt a sudden chill in the heavy Ronan air. 'Welstar Palace in Malakasia.'

OUTSIDE SOUTHPORT, PRAGA

Hannah's joints ached with the dull, throbbing pain of dehydration. The day was hot and the road beneath her feet dusty: tiny clouds of dirt billowed about her ankles with every step and her trainers were coated with a thin brown film. She had only been walking for half an hour, but having nothing to eat or drink for two days was taking its toll. She felt it first in her knees – it was always her knees; they invariably let her know when she had pushed her body too far – but determined to practise equal opportunity abuse this afternoon, Hannah kept walking.

Soon her ankles, shoulders and neck were crying for mercy as well.

The road flanking the copse where she had slept appeared to wind its way casually into the village along the water. The trip was taking longer than she had anticipated. 'No crows flying along this route unless they have a learning disability,' she groaned. Twisting back into a narrow draw between two hillocks sitting like twin camel humps above the harbour, Hannah could no longer see the city. She assumed the road would follow the valley's curve before dropping down into town. Hoping a stream might flow through the draw at the far end of the gorge, she made her way doggedly into the defile, imagining cool spring water tumbling over smooth rocks and into gentle pools.

'I'll drink a gallon,' she promised herself, ignoring the fact that any number of pernicious bacteria might be lurking, just waiting for her to come along. 'Screw it. I'll take whatever they're serving – Montezuma's worst nightmare, chicken pox, malaria, nitrogen narcosis – I'm beyond caring. As long as it's on the daily special, I'll have an order . . . with fries.' She wiped a sleeve across her forehead and pulled off her jacket.

'Too hot. How did that happen? Not only was I transported

through the floor of Steven's house, but I was transported to the desert, too.' She tried not to think about it. There had to be a rational explanation. Unwilling to accept the fact that she had been the victim of something supernatural, Hannah clung to her no-nonsense, everything-can-and-will-make-sense views with all the determination she could muster. But it was a tiring charge, and only the steady, repetitive pace of her forced march into town provided her with any comfort.

'I'll figure this out when I get to town. I have some money. I have my credit cards. I will call a cab, take a bus, charter a frigging plane; I don't care.' She was chanting to herself, almost a mantra. 'I will get out of this and things will be fine.' Her muscles ached and she was forced to stop for a moment, but as she almost fell to the ground, insecurity began to creep over her.

'I should keep moving . . . keep going, before I start thinking too much about this again. There *were* two moons, no mistake about that. And buses? I don't suppose they'll have buses going quite that far.' A strange feeling snaked along her spine and teased her with the notion that perhaps this *was* real, she had fallen into someplace new, someplace different – possibly even someplace unfriendly.

'Steven might be here, too. Maybe that's why he hadn't called.' She shook her head. Why hadn't that occurred to her earlier? Just the thought of finding Steven energised her and after taking a minute to estimate the distance around the valley's bowl, Hannah got to her feet and started out again.

She rounded a lazy bend and came face to face with three men walking along the dirt road away from town. Hannah was struck by their dress: all three were clad entirely in black and despite the heat, they wore boots, form-fitting leggings, hip-length pullover tunics belted at the waist and thick leather vests adorned with an ornate gold crest. At their belts each wore a short knife and what appeared to be a rapier or a sword; Hannah didn't know the difference. She couldn't imagine how warm they must be in such heavy costumes; she assumed, as she had earlier, that some sort of mock-Renaissance celebration was under way in the town.

'Am I glad to see you guys,' she started – as far as Hannah was concerned, finding anyone at all on the bone-dry roadway was a blessing, even if they were dressed like something out of a TV adaptation of *Ivanhoe*.

'Do you know where I can find a 7-11, or maybe a supermarket? I need a payphone and I want to get some water.' Suddenly afraid of how they might respond, she added hesitantly, 'And can you tell me where we are? I mean ... I know that sounds silly, but what town is that over there?' She gestured towards the harbour.

The three men stared at her, apparently speechless. Hannah, remembering she was alone, endeavoured to keep her distance while remaining polite. She smiled and waited, the smoke-like tendrils of insecurity chilling her bones once again.

The tallest of the three, who towered over his companions by six or seven inches, spoke first. At first, Hannah thought she had misheard him, that his words had been lost on the breeze brushing through the gorge, but then she realised he was speaking a different language, a strange language, one she had never heard before. It was guttural and full of left-footed consonants, a little like Welsh after a few drinks. More curious, though, was the fact that she understood him. She comprehended every word.

A dream, that's what this is, just a dream . . . maybe you hit your head. Just ride it out and you'll wake up eventually. Relaxing somewhat, Hannah searched across the hillside, looking for a purple giraffe, a whale reading a comic book, or the collective faculty of the law school clad entirely in Victoria's Secret underwear.

Her throat closed slightly when the young man spoke again. His words formed phrases in her mind after a two- or three-second delay. '—too far from town, my sweet little morsel,' he said lasciviously. 'No one will hear you out here.'

The men closed on her swiftly. Hannah, stunned by their attack, remained frozen in place. Her limbs filled with concrete and she went down without a struggle. They were tugging at her, fumbling with her clothing and arguing with one another about who would go first when she finally realised what was about to happen.

An alarm clamoured in her head: *Get up! Fight back!* But she was trapped now, their collective weight too heavy for her to move. She overheard snatches of what they were saying – given her panic at what was happening, Hannah was amazed that she could understand the thick, hacking syllables at all . . .

'—strange rutting clothes on her—'

'—look at these hose—'

'—just pull them off her feet, rutting whores' sake, can't you do anything?'

It's happening. Oh Christ, it's happening to me— Hannah had read about rape victims, women who wished they had been trained in self-defence, that they had been carrying mace or pepper spray or a Tomahawk missile, but she had never joined the ranks of those who claimed, 'If that ever happens to me, I'll—'

Instead, she had just prayed it never would happen to her. Now she realised that was not enough. Keys. Someone once told her they were an excellent weapon against a sexual predator. She could scratch a face, open a jagged wound across a cheek, or claw an eye out. She could even use them to rip a hole in his scrotum, gouge out his balls. Where were her keys? Her jacket was tied around her waist, but she knew the keys were not in the pockets. She knew that because she remembered putting them down beside a half-eaten pizza on the counter at 147 Tenth Street.

Finally she screamed, scratching wildly at her assailants – maybe she could jab an eye with her fingernails . . . but Hannah Sorenson didn't have long or especially sharp fingernails; she had never been one for high fashion and her fingernails had been filed down so they didn't get in the way. She was useless.

She tried kicking, and wailing for help, mercy or forgiveness, until one of the men rammed his knee up violently between her legs, sending a sharp pain across her abdomen that paralysed her from the waist down. Another gripped her breasts, squeezing and twisting them violently.

She leaned forward, catching a finger between her teeth. Biting down, trying to gnaw the digit off and spit it back at him, she tasted blood. Heartened by her progress, she continued to grind her teeth through flesh and on into bone.

She heard the rapist scream in agony and her breasts were momentarily forgotten in the interests of retrieving his hand before she did any more damage.

'Rutting whore!' he screamed. The first punch glanced off her temple; compared with the agony in her groin, she barely felt it. Hannah wished it had broken her jaw or crushed her nose, because then the worst would be behind her, but as a harbinger of brutality yet to come, the blow to her temple was about the cruellest thing her attackers could have done.

The breast grabber leaned back, free fist aloft, ready to pummel her into unconsciousness, but she maintained her death-grip on his ruined finger. As his warm blood trickled into her mouth she promised herself she would not let go, no matter how hard or how often they beat her, that finger was never going back.

The punch never landed.

Churn Prellis took the first Malakasian in a full sprinting tackle. The would-be rapist was rearing back to slug Hannah across the face; an easy target. Churn's body blocked the sun for an instant before he carried the soldier – and most of his finger – across the road in a tangled pile of limbs. Horrified, Hannah spat an irregular chunk of flesh into the dirt before lifting her head hesitantly.

The remaining two attackers rolled from her body, stumbled to their feet and hurried to assist their companion. While Hannah self-consciously adjusted her clothing, fastening her jeans and pulling down her shirt, she caught sight of the tangle of flailing arms and legs; although there were three of them, it looked like her assailants were not having an easy time of it.

She wiped the back of her hand across her mouth and came away with a thin smear of blood that ran from her wrist to her fingertips. Suddenly she started shaking. Convulsions began in her bloodstained fingers, moving up her arms to her chest. Wave after wave of rattling shudders wracked her thin form and she started panting breathlessly. Her throat felt raw from screaming.

Ignoring the mêlée going on beside her, Hannah, still hunched in a foetal position, tried to focus her tear-filled eyes on the smooth leather tops of her Nikes. They were dusted in pale beige; she thought she might reach out and scribble a message across each one: 'This is only a dream,' or 'No more spicy Kung Pao, silly.'

Struggling to sit up, she wrapped her shivering arms around her knees. She feared the pain in her groin would force her to lie back down or, worse, to pass out, but she was terrified of what might happen if she retreated into unconsciousness. Her would-be rescuer was one man against three, after all. She bit her tongue until she tasted her own blood, then pushed her palms against the gritty dirt road and wrestled herself to her knees. Pale yellow flashes of light burst and faded before her eyes and she felt tears begin to carve thin streams through the dirt on her cheeks.

Hannah drew several stabilising breaths, then turned to watch her saviour battling her three assailants. She felt sorry she could not help him, but she was both surprised and delighted by what she saw: the big man, the one who had so deftly dragged the breast-grabber from his perch on her stomach, was winning handily. Two of the three would-be rapists were already motionless, their bodies sprawled in awkward, unnatural positions on the far side of the road. The third was hanging on the larger man's back, looking comically like a child getting a piggy-back ride; he held both arms firmly about her saviour's neck, trying with all his might to strangle his muscle-bound opponent.

While Hannah watched, the burly rescuer reached up with one hand and grasped the rapist's forearms, but he made no effort to pull them away; rather, it looked as if he was trying to keep them held firmly about his throat. Perhaps he was ensuring the impromptu acrobat would not decide to let go suddenly and beat a hasty retreat.

Then the bigger man reached around and placed the flat of his free palm against the small of the rider's back, a sort of clumsy, inside-out hug.

Transfixed by the curious struggle, like some ancient ritualistic dance, Hannah nearly forgot the pain in her gut and the swelling in her breasts. At first she couldn't work out what her grim-faced rescuer was planning to do, and she wondered how long he could remain standing with the man in black strangling him so ardently. Then his strategy became clear. Gripping his attacker's arms and back, the giant bent at the knees before leaping as far as he could into the air then, twisting, he brought the full force of his weight down on the smaller man's body. *Whump!* Their impact with the dirt road sounded like gas escaping through a pressure release valve. Hannah felt certain the third rapist was dead; surely no one could have survived a landing like that. She hoped it had *really* hurt.

Hannah was still seated in the middle of the road when her saviour rolled over, checked to be sure none of his opponents were conscious – or maybe alive – and pushed himself to his feet. He strode silently to where she was now kneeling and squatted down on his haunches. Hannah had a flashback to natural history programmes about the lives and habits of the great silverback mountain gorilla. The man, now motionless, stared at her as if waiting for her to try to escape. From the look of his clothes he was from the same Renaissance troupe.

'Oh my God,' she cried aloud, suddenly realising the powerful young man might have beaten the others away so he could have her for himself, 'please, don't hurt me, please.' The tears came again as she begged, 'Please, I didn't do anything to them, I didn't say anything, I just needed to get to a phone.'

Gingerly, she tried to slide backwards, beyond the silent giant's reach, but her legs failed. Shivering, she grasped at the loose sleeves of her coat and made a vain effort to cover the button and fly of her jeans with an improvised Gore-tex chastity belt.

'Not again,' she pleaded, 'not again. I can't take it—'

Churn didn't move. The girl wore no armour and he couldn't see any weapons, so she couldn't be a soldier. And those colours – was she trying to attract attention to herself? She was so small, so helpless; she looked like something he had seen once in a picture, an illegal painting of sea nymphs hidden in a partisan's basement. He had heard stories of sea nymphs too, and their magical powers. They would attract sailors with their beauty and their bright colours, like this woman's bright colours, then they would lure the men out to sea, or into the waiting maw of some ravenous flesh-eating creature.

He reached out with one massive paw to feel the smooth texture of her odd white, blue and yellow shoes. They were the most strange and beautiful shoes he had ever seen; he thought they might shine even brighter if he dusted off some of the dirt that had built up on them. Brushing his fingers gently across their surface, Churn drew back suddenly when the young woman bellowed a terrified scream and kicked him hard across the chin.

Unfazed by the blow, the big Pragan backed away a few paces, hoping that would put the sea nymph more at ease. She continued to cry and carry on in her strange language, so Churn decided it was time to hand any further investigation over to Hoyt. He had beaten the soldiers; Hoyt could worry about communicating with the sea nymph. Churn searched the hillside for his friend; spotting Hoyt sitting complacently on a fallen log near the opposite side of the roadway, he gesticulated in a series of rapid signs.

'No, I don't think she is a sea nymph, Churn,' Hoyt Navarra replied calmly, 'but she's certainly not from around here.' He stood and came forward slowly so as not to alarm the already terrified young woman any further. 'And back away from her will you?' he chided; 'I'd kick at you too if you were hovering over me like the rutting Twinmoon.'

As Churn complied, they could see the strangely clad woman calm noticeably. Stepping near his burly companion, the young healer smiled and asked, 'How badly are you hurt?'

The three-second translation delay was down to about one second now, but Hannah still answered in wavering English, 'I don't think so . . . I don't think so . . . my stomach hurts and my eye is sore, but otherwise, I guess I'm all right.'

Hoyt rubbed his palm thoughtfully across his chin, knelt beside her and offered a wineskin filled with water. 'Here. Have something to drink. We'll try to talk when you're ready.'

'Thank you.' Hannah uncorked the skin and drank every drop. She passed the empty skin back and asked, 'Can you tell me where I am . . . where this is? I haven't been able to figure out—'

'Can you understand me?' Hoyt interrupted loudly, then cursed himself when the strange woman cringed and sidled away another two or three paces. He indicated his chest and said, 'My name is Hoyt Navarra. This—' he clapped a hand on the back of one of Churn's tree-trunk calves, 'this is Churn Prellis.'

'I'm Hannah Sorenson,' she said. She *did* understand them, but was dumbfounded as to how. She was making out the words almost as quickly as they were spoken now.

'Hannah . . .'

'Sorenson.'

'Soren-son.' Hoyt tried it out. 'Hannah Soren-son. Hannah Soren-son, do you understand me? What I'm saying?'

'I do,' Hannah replied, but from the look in the strange man's face, Hoyt's face, she wasn't certain he could understand her. She nodded instead. Maybe, since she could *understand* this weird guttural language, she could speak it if she tried? *God knows how, though*, she thought, *but let's give it a go*. She closed her eyes and took a calming breath, then let the awkward words come on their own.

'Is this better?' she offered in broken Pragan.

Hoyt beamed. 'Excellent! So you speak Pragan. We were

worried . . . well, *I* was worried. Churn here manages to do just fine without any language at all – any language you might read or see scribbled on a piece of parchment, anyway.'

'Where are we?' Hannah climbed painfully to her feet, swaying slightly, but determined to have this conversation standing up so she could break and run if things began to deteriorate.

'Well, we're in a valley near the Pragan city of Southport,' Hoyt said as he reached into a satchel at his belt and withdrew something which turned out to be several pieces of dried fruit. Handing them to her, he went on, 'It's not much of a town, but the harbour remains busy and that keeps interesting goods and people moving through on a regular basis.'

'Pragan?'

'Right. Praga. This is Praga.' Hoyt was confused by her question, but gestured in a semi-circle as if the entire nation was at his fingertips. 'Have you been unconscious for some time? Sick or something? I ask only because Praga is a big place and most people know when they arrive in it.'

One of the Malakasians began to stir, groaning and rolling onto his side. Churn moved quickly across the road and summarily kicked the soldier back into unconsciousness.

Hannah winced, and looked at Churn with a mixture of gratitude and terror. 'Do you know them?'

'What? This crew? No!' Hoyt laughed. "But they're all the same when you get right down to it. So knowing one is knowing them all, rutting dry humpers.' Embarrassed at his off-colour language, he added with a sniff, 'Sorry.'

'But I thought—'

'Thought what?' The young healer looked interested.

'I thought from the way you were dressed that you and they might be part of the same . . . I don't know, troupe?'

'Troupe?' Hoyt cast Hannah a sidelong glance. 'Those are members of the Malakasian Army, the occupation force that patrols the entire nation of Praga – in fact, every land in Eldarn, for that matter – making sure there is no resistance to the royal rule of the great Prince Malagon . . . the horsecock.' His eyes narrowed. 'How can you not know this?'

Hannah's breathing was shallow. It *was* something supernatural. It had been going on too long to be a dream. She had gone somewhere, been dropped somewhere. Steven and Mark were here. That had to be it. Her heart pounded a high-stepping tarantella.

How was she going to get home? Two moons. How was she going to find Steven? The strange mediaeval costumes . . . would there be phones, buses, planes, any of those things she needed?

She shuddered, then squared her aching shoulders and muttered, 'No. I suppose I haven't.'

'Where are you from, then?' asked Hoyt curiously, before realising that he and Churn might have stumbled into a dangerous situation. His dreams of the fat Malakasian galleon and her rich cargo began to fade.

'Denver, Colorado,' said Hannah quietly. 'I'm from the United States of America.'

Hoyt was not surprised the names were unfamiliar to him; Churn obviously had no idea where *Denvercolorado* was either. Shaking his head ruefully, Hoyt realised he would have been more surprised if Hannah had named a city he did know.

'Well, then . . .' He tried to sound reassuring. 'We need to go somewhere safe and talk.'

'Can you help me?'

'For a time, yes, but I think eventually we will need to get you to someone with a bit more clout in situations such as these.' He thought of Alen Jasper, and the curious man's knowledge of many strange and wonderful things.

'Is he far from here?'

'Not really, no, but we have to make a few stops first.' Hoyt looked sadly up the hillside. He would have to find a new hiding place for his library.

'Why?'

'We'll need to change your clothes for a start, and we must have travel supplies.' He turned to Churn. 'Are they dead?'

Churn signed, 'I think one of them is.'

'Demonshit.' Hoyt spat angrily in the dirt near the Malakasian bodies. 'Well, we can't just kill the other two . . . all right, all right, we'll have to hurry, that's all.'

'What's wrong?' Hannah did not like the look on the lanky young man's face: as if he'd just discovered all his carefully laid plans had gone awry. She thought for a moment of bolting, sprinting back the way she had come, to the grove of trees atop the hill. She felt her face flush with fight-or-flight adrenalin.

'Flight, for Christ's sake, go with flight,' Hannah whispered to herself, but she hesitated. There was nothing in that grove, no wardrobe or magic doorway, no curiously stitched tapestry or magic carpet waiting to take her back to Idaho Springs. She had to trust these strangers; they had already saved her life.

Hoyt regained control of his features. 'Nothing's wrong. It's just that one of those fellows might be dead.' Seeing Hannah cringe, he softened. 'Oh, don't worry. It's all right. They were going to kill you eventually. Our problem is that the other two will be awake before too long and that might make for some difficult travel conditions, especially if they give a description of you to the officer in charge. Granted, they probably weren't supposed to be out here, and they most certainly were not supposed to be raping young women, but even so, killing them tends to upset the officer corps. The other two may keep their mouths shut for a while, but they won't be able to cover up their friend's murder – sorry, *untimely death* – for very long.' He tried diligently not to alarm her further. 'So we need to get into town in a hurry. There are a few places we can hide for a few days while we change the way you look, but eventually we'll need to make our way north.'

Hannah had no idea what Hoyt meant by *difficult travel conditions*, but the notion that the Malawhomevers were an occupation army, and that the dead and wounded soldiers – because that's what they were, *soldiers* – on the road were Malawhomevers, was not lost on her. 'So, what will the Mala—' She paused, trying out the unfamiliar word.

'—kasians, Malakasians,' Hoyt filled in the gap.

'So what will the Malakasians do when they discover one of their soldiers has been killed?' She avoided eye contact with Churn.

'Close the roads, shut down the ports, round up anyone accused of separatist activities, tighten their stranglehold on the farmers and merchants who deal in critical goods and services and—' Hoyt chose his words carefully, '—uh, maybe make a public example of a few of us.'

Hannah did not need help understanding the Pragan's sugar-coated explanation. 'So, there will be public hangings, beatings, grim retaliatory measures?'

'Something like that, yes.'

Hannah sighed nervously. 'All right then, let's go.'

'Um, first, I need you to put this on,' he said and handed her what looked like an over-tunic. It was much too large, but it did cover her shirt and jacket. 'And here, tie your hair up with this.' Hoyt drew a section of brown homespun cloth from his belt. 'I promise it's clean . . . well, it was clean recently.'

Despite the tension threatening to close her throat, Hannah had to stifle a laugh as she gathered up her hair and tucked it beneath the makeshift scarf. 'How's that?'

Churn grunted his approval and Hoyt nodded. 'Better . . . certainly a good deal uglier.'

Hannah pouted in mock dismay.

'Oh, no, that's what we want,' he said, reaching out to offer his arm. 'Shall we?'

Together, the unlikely trio began making their way quickly towards Southport.

GAREC'S FARM

The morning ride was hard on the Coloradoans, even though Steven considered himself a bit of a horseman. He was more tired than he remembered being since college and nodded off several times as they rode north through the forests and small towns that lined the Estrad River. The morning sun brought dappled colour to the forest floor and thick ferns shone bright green where sunlight reached them through the dense foliage. Cresting a hill, Steven caught a glimpse of Riverend Palace in the distance, an abandoned and ramshackle monument to Ronan history.

Versen led the group along paths he found easily, as if he had known them his whole life; Gilmour brought up the rear just behind Mark. Garec was riding in front of Steven, and when the path widened slightly, he pulled alongside.

'You haven't had much sleep in several days I'd guess.'

'You're right,' Steven said as he fought off another yawn. 'I'm not certain I'll make a full day on this horse.'

'We won't ride a full day today,' the young Ronan answered. 'We all need rest, and I must warn my parents and sisters, so we'll be stopping at my family's farm. It's not far now.'

'Thank God. Maybe I can get some sleep then.'

'That'll be fine.' Garec reached across and patted Steven's horse gently along the neck. 'What do you think of her?'

'She's wonderful,' Steven said as he ran one hand up the horse's mane and started patting her vigorously. The mare responded with a toss of her head and a pleasant whinny. 'Did you choose her?'

'I did,' Garec answered proudly.

'You've got a great eye for horses.'

'I don't know about that. She did take to you very quickly, though, didn't she?'

'Yes, she did,' Steven said reflectively. He peered at his watch: it was already noon in Idaho Springs, but it had only been daylight here in Rona for four hours.

'What is that thing?' Garec asked, curiously eyeing Steven's wrist.

'It's called a watch,' Steven replied, and briefly explained the instrument and how it worked. 'As far as I can tell, you have about four fewer "hours" in your day than we have in Colorado.' He used the English term, because he still could not think of a Ronan equivalent. Unfastening the watch, he offered it to Garec.

' "Hours"?' He turned the instrument over between his fingers and observed as the second hand made half a revolution.

'Yes, hours. An hour is one of twenty-four equal portions of one Colorado day,' Steven explained, then added, 'and those figures listed around the outer edge represent our number system.'

Garec was fascinated; he endeavoured to find parallels in Ronan time. 'Your hour is similar to our aven then. There are eight in each day, two from dawn to midday, two between midday and sundown, two from sundown to middlenight and two between middlenight and dawn.'

Steven did the calculations in his head. 'So an aven is about two and a half hours, assuming there are twenty hours in a Ronan day.' He showed Garec how to chart one aven on the face of his watch.

'That's very interesting, Steven Taylor.' Garec handed back the timepiece.

'Oh, that's okay.' He waved one hand dismissively at the bowman. 'You keep it.'

Garec grinned like a schoolboy. 'Thank you, Steven Taylor. Thank you very much.' He attached the watch to his wrist before adding, 'You keep the horse.'

Now it was Steven's turn to grin. 'Are you kidding?' He ran his hand gently through the animal's mane. 'Garec, this is too much. I can't take this horse.'

'Well, I can't keep her,' Garec told him, motioning to his own mount. 'Rennie would be jealous.'

'What's this one's name?'

'We'll call her whatever you wish, Steven Taylor,' Garec said, matter-of-factly.

'It's just Steven, Garec.' He thought for a moment before asking, 'Can we call her Howard?'

'Howard it shall be, Steven Taylor. Sorry, "just Steven".' Garec laughed.

Mark, meanwhile, was having a less than easy time with his own mount, a strong-willed animal that would have baulked at commands from an experienced rider. Mark attempted to employ the simple rules Steven had taught him in the orchard, but by midday, when the horse yet again wandered from the path to crop the greenery, he realised the independent-minded beast wasn't going to pay any attention to him no matter what he did. Finally, Sallax rode alongside and, with a withering look, took the reins from Mark and led the animal himself. Mark was left to balance in the horribly uncomfortable saddle, shattered from two nights without sleep, aching from the awkward motion of the horse's unfamiliar gait and desperately embarrassed at his inability to control the wretched animal.

By now the only thing keeping Mark awake was the irregular rhythm of the animal's tread and the throbbing pain in his thighs and lower back. He had tried resting his head on the horse's neck, but whenever he started to drift off to sleep, the horse would jerk about or shake its head and Mark would nearly fall from the saddle. Eventually he decided to sit up straight and welcome the pain as his only distraction from the overwhelming fatigue.

Gilmour trotted forward and touched Mark gently on the forearm. 'Excuse me, my friend,' he whispered, waking Mark from his nearly delusional reverie. 'If you lean forward slightly and use the stirrups to lift your weight just a fraction with each step, you'll find the rhythm begins to make some sense. It will alleviate the strain on your back.' He demonstrated what he meant, then fell back alongside.

'Try it. I promise you it will help.'

Mark felt a fool, but at this stage he had nothing to lose. He was astounded to find Gilmour had not been exaggerating; the relief was almost immediate.

'Thank you,' he said, trying several positions before deciding on one that felt most comfortable, then asked, 'What is Welstar Palace?'

'It is Prince Malagon's home in Malakasia, a particularly

dangerous place for us to travel to. But it's there we'll find Lessek's Key, and a passage for you and Steven to return home.'

'We can get home through Malagon's palace?'

'Well, it isn't really Malagon's palace any more. Malagon Whitward is long dead. What *was* Malagon is being controlled, mind and body, by Nerak, an exceedingly evil force that has been plaguing Eldarn for nearly a thousand Twinmoons.' Gilmour pulled two apples from his saddlebag and handed one to Mark.

'How will we get in without him – it – knowing we're there?' Mark took a bite and waited for Gilmour's reply.

'I'm not certain yet, but I can tell you it will be very dangerous for all of us. Just being that close to Welstar Palace can be deadly.' He sighed deeply. 'Going inside verges on suicide. I hope to enter with you and Steven alone. If all goes well, we will send you home and I will search Malagon's chambers for Lessek's Key.'

'Does Nerak have a tapestry like the one Steven found at the bank?' Mark tossed his apple core into the underbrush and wiped his fingers on the tunic he had stolen in Estrad.

'He does. We call them "far portals". There are only two in existence now. The one Nerak has at Welstar Palace is not as powerful as the one you used to come here. It was actually Nerak who took that one and hid it in Colorado.' Gilmour filled his pipe but left it unlit and dangling from the corner of his mouth.

He sighed again, almost to himself, then continued, 'The Larion Senate in Gorsk used the two far portals for thousands of Twinmoons, travelling back and forth between Eldarn and your homelands, to research medicine, technology and even magic. We used the knowledge we gathered to improve life here in the five nations.' He ran one hand over his balding pate and scratched vigorously at his beard. 'The portal hidden in Colorado can pinpoint a location, the beach where you landed, for example. That is its particular strength. So even if the portal in Nerak's palace is closed, the one you opened will send everyone who comes through to the same place.'

'That's why Steven landed on the same beach,' Mark guessed.

'Exactly. However, once it's closed and re-opened, it finds another place. Anyone else coming through could end up anywhere in Eldarn. The far portal hidden in Welstar Palace can't pinpoint an area unless the one in your home is left open. Otherwise it might drop you anywhere.'

The old man's words took a moment to register. 'You mean if someone closes the portal in our house, we might get dropped back anywhere on the planet – and it might separate us from one another? We might end up half the Earth apart?'

Somehow, while Mark was speaking, Gilmour lit his pipe – although Mark was positive he hadn't struck a match.

'I'm afraid that's right,' Gilmour said. 'All we can do is hope that while you are with us in Eldarn, no one tampers with the far portal on your floor. But if Nerak decides to travel back to your homeland, his portal will drop him right in the middle of your home town.'

'Oh God, no.' Mark had not imagined their situation could get worse, yet here it was. He continued, 'When you were describing the Larion Senate, you said "we" used the far portals. The other tapestry has been locked in Steven's bank for over a hundred and thirty years. How old does that make you?'

Gilmour, caught out by the astute foreigner, winked, then lowered his voice to a whisper. 'My friends here in Rona don't know these things, although I fear I may soon have to let them know who I truly am. Mark Jenkins, I am well over fifteen hundred Twinmoons old. When I reached fifteen hundred, I stopped counting. I, like you and Steven, learned languages and cultures by travelling through the far portals many times while I served the known lands as a Larion Senator.'

Mark, somewhat punch-drunk from shock and fatigue, was surprised to find he *wasn't* surprised by Gilmour's confession. 'So you've been to my homeland?'

'I have never been to Colorado, although I heard much about it on my last trip. No, my last visit to your land ended on 2 July, 1863. It was outside a small town called—'

'Gettysburg,' Mark interrupted. 'Gettysburg, Pennsylvania.'

'That's right.' Gilmour beamed, remembering his younger days. 'And from what I see from your relationship with Steven Taylor, American culture has come a long way since then.' He exhaled a cloud of sweetly fragrant smoke that quickly faded on the morning breeze. 'I am glad to see your society has made such progress.'

'We have done well, but it's been over a long period of time and we still have a long way to go. There are still inexcusable things happening that must be addressed.' Mark paused for a moment. 'Hold on, wait a moment: you were in Pennsylvania in 1863, and you travelled to our world specifically to bring back innovations and progressive technologies?'

'That's right.'

'Where is everything?'

'Everything?'

'We're eating from wooden bowls. Brynne speaks of avens to tell time, but you don't have any timepieces. There were steam engines and blast furnaces in 1863, hospitals, institutions of higher learning and social movements to improve living conditions and ensure basic human rights. Where are they?'

Gilmour suddenly looked sad; Mark was a little sorry he had asked the question.

'That, my dear boy, is the tragic history of Eldarn.' He smoked in silence for a moment, then went on, 'Imagine a dictatorship, five generations long, that didn't value progress, education, research or innovation. Imagine a dictatorship that closed universities, sought out and murdered intellectuals, stripped communities of basic health and human services and then stifled every attempt to revive any of it. Imagine that over time. People forget; progress is stalled.'

'Well, sure, the culture would stagnate somewhat, Gilmour, but surely brilliant people would find a way to—'

The old man interrupted, 'Brilliant people are terrified, and rightly so. There are a few wild revolutionaries operating outlawed printing presses in barns and abandoned warehouses, but too many of them are found out and executed before any real following can pick up the gauntlet and carry on. Eldarni culture has existed for seven Ages, over twenty Eras, literally thousands of Twinmoons, and I can't even tell you what Twinmoon it is right now. A culture does more than stagnate in such a dictatorship, Mark, it dies.'

'So there's no hope?'

'There is now, my friend.'

Deciding not to pursue Gilmour's insinuations right then, Mark diverted their conversation. 'So, you were at Gettysburg.'

'I was, but sadly, I could not stay to see how things turned out.' Gilmour looked up through the low-hanging tree branches and reflected aloud, 'I was with a young man from Maine named Jed Harkness. His division took up their position at the far end of a long stretch of wooded hill called—' He paused. 'I can't remember its name.'

'Little Round Top,' Mark helped him. 'Harkness must have been a member of the Twentieth Maine.' Mark was happy to be discussing something familiar. 'You should have stayed around that day, Gilmour. You missed one of the turning points in the whole war. That group of soldiers from Maine held that flank and, some would argue, saved the Union.'

'Ah, I'm sorry I missed it, but I was summoned back that morning and soon thereafter, there was a terrible tragedy at Sandcliff Palace. I never returned, but I have often thought about Harkness and how he fared that day.' He hesitated before asking, 'Why did they call it a Civil War? It seemed far from civil to me.'

'That's one for the ages, Gilmour,' Mark commented ironically. Then, feeling a numbing wave of fatigue pass through him, he rubbed his eyes with his fingertips and wiped sweat from his forehead. 'I've never been this tired before.'

'We'll be there soon, and you can sleep the rest of the day away.' Gilmour reached into his saddlebag and withdrew a small root that looked to Mark a little like ginger, light brown and strangely shaped. The older man sliced a small portion from one of the root's twisted appendages and handed it to him. 'Until then, chew on this. It will bring you some much-needed clarity and energy.'

The plant was flavourless, but Mark chewed it doggedly and soon felt much better. His vision cleared; his energy level rose and his wits sharpened. Even the pain in his back subsided markedly.

'That's some remedy,' he said brightly. 'What's it called?'

'Fennaroot.' Gilmour handed him the curled stem. 'Some people like to dry it out and smoke it with their tobacco.'

Mark raised an eyebrow. 'Ah, so even here they hit the peace pipe from time to time.' He sniffed at the root and handed it back.

'I wouldn't know about that,' the older man said, 'I do enjoy a bit on my tongue now and again. It does help keep my energy up.'

'You could market that stuff for a hefty profit.'

'I suppose so, but I've never been much for material things,' Gilmour said, then changed the subject. 'How's your horse?'

'I've chosen a name for him,' Mark answered.

'Really? What's that?' He sounded genuinely interested.

'Wretch.'

The riders didn't go straight to Garec's family home; Gilmour insisted they make camp in a far corner of the property, in case Malakasian spies had been sent to report their arrival. The farm consisted of several large fields and Steven and Mark could see a number of people harvesting vegetables; one drove a one-horse cart through the field while a team of pickers pulled ears of corn from tall stalks and tossed them into the back of the wagon. From a distance, it was almost impossible to see the workers walking beneath the stalks and Steven smiled as he watched hundreds of ears of corn flying of their own volition into the harvest wagon, like so many salmon leaping and tumbling their way upstream.

'You two should sleep,' Garec suggested as he dismounted and tethered Renna to a thin dogwood tree. 'We'll stay here tonight and be on our way again before dawn tomorrow.'

'He's right,' Steven agreed. 'You sleep first. I'll stay awake.'

'Why you?'

'I slept while we were tied to the wall. You've been up for almost two full days.' He watched as Garec made his way into the field. The corn stalks masked his movements and the Ronan revolutionary soon disappeared from view.

Brynne hustled forward to the edge of the field. 'Garec,' she called into the corn, 'bring me some wool hose and a pair of your sister's boots, please.'

Garec's disembodied reply came back to them in a sharp whisper: 'All right.'

'You both should sleep.' Gilmour joined the foreigners. 'Nothing will happen to you. Sleep as long as you like. We have much to do tomorrow.'

Mark had no idea whether he would even be able to get down from his horse, let alone protect himself or Steven should an attack come while they slept. Despite Gilmour's equestrian coaching, he was contemplating running alongside the animal rather than ever getting in the saddle again. Feeling a spasm of pain shoot across his lower back, Mark finally gave in.

'Fine,' he said to Steven, 'let's both sleep. If they wanted to kill us, they'd have done it by now.'

'Good point,' Steven dismounted smoothly, 'but I think I'll

take a watch just in case. I want to be able to get you up if that almor thing appears again.' Mark spread his bedroll on the ground under what looked like a large beech tree and in a matter of moments was sleeping soundly. Steven leaned against the trunk, determined to stay awake. He watched the others bustle about camp, organising supplies, gathering firewood and tending the horses. The quiet rhythm of their movements coupled with his extreme fatigue soon lulled him to sleep as well and he sank down until he was lying beside Mark on the soft earth beneath the sheltering branches.

It was dark when Steven opened his eyes. He woke with a start, but found himself so cramped from sleeping on the uneven ground that he made no effort to get up. Instead, he lay back and observed as his new companions continued working in and around their campsite. Light from a small fire threw huge shadows against the forest backdrop; for a while Steven's gaze moved back and forth between the Ronan partisans and their shadows looming above in the tree branches. Brynne stacked logs near the fire while Garec mended a tear in a leather pack. Their familiar movements were magnified tenfold when projected on the forest canopy; the comforting motions of people keeping busy with common tasks became ominous when performed by forty-foot-tall obsidian wraiths.

Fear of the unknown and anxiety about how they would ever return home, welled up in Steven again and he closed his eyes to shut out the surreal theatre playing above his head. Shifting his position beneath the beech tree, he soon fell back into a fitful slumber.

Steven woke to find Mark tugging at his ankle. Rubbing sleep from his eyes, Steven rose hastily to join him. Their small camp was abuzz with activity; Versen, Garec and Brynne surrounded a newcomer, a man Steven thought he'd seen at Riverend Palace. Gilmour sat near the fire, quietly smoking his pipe. Sallax was nowhere to be found.

'What's happening?' he asked Mark.

'Apparently, this is Mika, one of their reb—, er, freedom fighters. Someone named Jerond was supposed to be here as well, but he hasn't shown up.' Mark knelt alongside his blanket and began folding it into a tight bedroll. 'Brynne looks worried. I think they think something rotten has happened to him.'

'Where's Sallax?'

'Standing watch in the forest somewhere.' Mark paused and contemplated Mika's arrival. 'It's a bit odd that he didn't warn us at all when Mika came through the woods.'

'Maybe he fell asleep out there,' Steven said.

'That doesn't seem like him.' Mark was curious now; Steven began to worry that his friend might create more trouble in an already strained relationship with the partisan leader.

When Sallax did return, he immediately wrapped an arm around Mika's shoulder in relief. When he was told of Jerond's delay, he suggested they pack up and begin riding north as soon as possible.

'Great. I have to get back on that reprehensible beast,' Mark groaned. He stood and began stretching his back. Even fatigued and near collapse, Mark still moved with the economic, angular motion of an athlete.

'What's wrong with him?' Steven asked. 'He looks like a fine animal to me.'

'I think he has a thought disorder,' Mark said dryly. 'And his gait is so uneven, one of his legs must be a good fifteen inches shorter than the others.' He began collecting their few possessions, rolling them into his bedroll.

'Come, my friends,' Gilmour ordered, 'it's less than an aven till dawn. We need to get under way.'

Mark caught Brynne staring at him across the fire. She didn't turn away immediately, and Mark struggled to read her facial expression, but it had grown too dark. All he could be sure of was that she was watching him pack his bedroll while the others made hasty preparations to leave Garec's farm.

No one spoke as the company made its way through the darkness. Mark's still-aching back protested from the moment he mounted Wretch, but in the conspicuous silence he elected not to complain out loud. They moved along a narrow trail snaking through the southern forest. Periodically, Mark believed he could hear the muted roar of the Estrad River in the distance. The two moons were now well apart in the pre-dawn sky and both foreigners marvelled at their beauty. One looked smaller, and somehow closer, while the second was a behemoth completing its own stately dance through the heavens, much further away.

Steven noticed Garec's mare was loaded down with blankets, clothing, additional food and a large saddlebag that looked as if it were filled entirely with colourfully fletched arrows. He had made it safely into his parents' farmhouse, warned them of the potential danger coming from Estrad, and collected an array of items he considered essential; seeing Renna so heavily burdened with supplies, Steven realised they were facing a long journey to Welstar Palace.

As the sun broke the horizon's plane, Garec reached into one of the two quivers strapped across his back and withdrew an arrow. He carried a longbow across his lap and appeared ready to fire at any moment. Steven, who now trusted Garec almost as much as he did Gilmour, started to worry: were they being shadowed by Malakasians?

Then Garec drew and fired. A plump rabbit tumbled out of the undergrowth onto the path in front of them.

'Excellent, Garec, breakfast,' Gilmour complimented him. 'I'd love some grouse or perhaps a gansel, a nice chubby male with a soft, tasty breast, if you happen to see one.'

'I'll see what I can do for you,' Garec said cheerfully as he dismounted to retrieve the fallen animal. 'Anyone else like to place an order?'

'A short stack with bacon and a pot of regular coffee,' Mark answered in English, unable to come up with a Ronan word for pancakes.

'I don't know what that means, Mark,' Garec called back, 'but if you see it, point it out and I'll bring it down.'

'God, I wish you could – but thanks for the thought, Garec. I appreciate it.' Mark changed the subject. 'How long will it take us to get to Welstar Palace?'

Gilmour turned in the saddle. 'That's a difficult question. It should take us a Twinmoon or so, but I don't know how long it will be before we can enter the palace.'

'Sixty days?' Mark blurted. 'Well, I suppose the school board might buy my story, especially if I tell them about being attacked by a life-sucking demon in vivid enough detail. They just might let me keep my job, and they might even understand why I missed all of second quarter without calling in or leaving sub plans.'

'I'll get fired, too,' Steven commented to no one. 'And I don't suppose Hannah will think this is very funny, either. That's too bad. I miss her.'

Mark pressed Gilmour for more information. 'Why will it take so long to get into the palace?'

At that, even Sallax turned to listen in. 'Malakasia is patrolled by the largest army in all Eldarn. There are thousands and thousands of soldiers moving throughout the countryside every day. Nerak, in the guise of Prince Malagon, rarely appears to offer any leadership to his people. He rules without advisors and calls his generals and admirals to him only when he has dreamed up another cruelty to enact upon us citizens of the occupied world.

'Few resist him, because he kills without warning or hesitation. When Nerak tires of Malagon's body, he will allow it to die just before he takes possession of the next member of the Whitward family, Malagon's daughter, Bellan. It has happened this way for nearly a thousand Twinmoons. To date, no one has been able to get anywhere near Welstar Palace.'

'Why have you never tried before?' Steven enquired.

'Because, my friend, I have been waiting for someone like you to find the far portal and bring back Lessek's Key.' Gilmour used a boot heel to tap the ash from his pipe. 'With Lessek's Key there would be no need to travel to Welstar Palace. We could simply go to Sandcliff in Gorsk and try to decipher the spell table Lessek used to harness the power of the far portals all those thousands of Twinmoons ago. It was Lessek who discovered a pinprick in the universe, a tiny opening. It is through this the far portals operate. And it was this pinprick that released the evil which eventually claimed the young Larion Senator named Nerak.'

Gilmour paused for a moment, sighed deeply and continued, 'I suppose Nerak had it coming. He coveted power, more power than he could ever control, and one horrible night, his dream finally consumed him – literally.'

'Power over whom?' Steven was intrigued.

'Over what,' Gilmour corrected, 'power over magic, and the knowledge to employ all its forms at will. Nerak's dogged pursuit of ever-more-powerful forms of magic drove him insane ... although the seeds of his insanity must have been there from the beginning, there is no record that anyone had detected such a problem.

'Nerak studied Lessek's writings, and planned what he believed would be an airtight operation by which he would capture the power Lessek released when he opened the path to your world. But Nerak wasn't prepared for the enormous force waiting therein. It was far worse than even Lessek had imagined, perhaps the very essence of evil itself. It sent only one of its minions to deal with Nerak, and that one disciple has been much too powerful for anyone in Eldarn to defeat for the past nine hundred and eighty Twinmoons.'

'A disciple of evil's essence?' Garec sounded dubious. 'How can that be? Evil's not a *thing*, is it?'

'Oh, Garec, that is the most difficult question of all.' The old man organised his thoughts. 'I suppose one way to explain it is to think of any encounter you've had with anything evil, those murderous soldiers at Riverend for example, the ones who killed Namont, rather than taking him prisoner. *Something* made them act evilly. Often it's a combination of variables which work together to form exactly the right pattern. We cannot put our finger on evil any more than we can put our finger on truth. There is no universal, static and observable truth. There is only the perception of reality by those contemplating any collection of attributes, values, experiences, traditions and so on. Evil is the same way. It is collection of thoughts, failed dreams, depressing notions, forgotten friends and myriad other characteristics, all of which, when combined together, bring about a radical change in behaviour.

'We never *see* the evil; we generally experience only a behavioural manifestation of evil's power.'

'Like a soldier swinging a sword,' Garec guessed.

'Or a parent beating a child, or a thief murdering an elderly woman. These are all evil *acts*, but they are not evil itself. No, this is our problem: evil itself *does* exist, and it has been trapped for much of the existence of this world. It has, from time to time, been able to slip one of its minions into our world, or into Steven and Mark's world. And its minions are tiny. They are notions of evil, and they bring unbelievable havoc every time they manage to escape. And in all of our recorded history, no one has been able to successfully trap and exorcise one of evil's minions.

'And it is one of these minions that controls Nerak – and, in turn, Malagon today. Its goal, like every other that has managed to escape, is to open a path for the essence of all things evil to come unencumbered from its prison inside the Fold.'

'What's the Fold?' Brynne asked, slyly checking to see if Mark was as enthralled with Gilmour's story as she was. Versen and Sallax had slowed their horses to a walk so they too would not miss a single word.

'The Fold is the space between everything that is known and unknown. It is the absence of perception, and therefore the absence of reality. Nothing exists there except evil, because the original architects of our universe could not avoid creating it. It was a negative thought, a simple flash of anger or frustration, as insignificant as an ant on a hillside, but it happened. Evil was born and with every negative thought, every angry gesture – most of which were directed at evil's essence by the creators themselves – it grew more powerful.

'Steven and Mark came across the Fold when they fell through the far portal into Rona—' Gilmour broke off for a moment, then clarified, 'actually, they didn't come across the Fold per se. Instead, they navigated through a *window* in the Fold, that pinprick in the fabric of the universe Lessek was able to find and control.

'When Lessek found his pathway, he created an opening, and it was through that Nerak eventually allowed a minion of evil's essence to come to Eldarn. Arriving here, it immediately diversified into the millions of thoughts and ideas people – *we* – construe as evil. It varies wildly: for one person, evil may be murdering another, while someone else may consider lying to a friend is evil.

'So you see, this minion can exist anywhere, inside any living thing that knows what it means to be evil. For some reason, this notion of evil chose the Malakasian royal family. I am not certain why.'

Steven swallowed hard and asked the question everyone feared. 'What would happen if one of these minions managed to open the Fold for the essence of evil . . . this vagrant afterthought of the gods or whatever it is . . . to escape?'

'Nothing would survive,' Gilmour answered calmly. 'Perhaps even matter itself would come apart. It would take only an instant and we would all be gone. Everything horrifying we've ever imagined would become a reality, and then be torn asunder as quickly and irretrievably as we would.'

'How close has it come to succeeding?' Versen asked.

'It knows what Nerak knew – and that is that the collective genius of the Larion Senate exists in Lessek's spell table. Without Lessek's Key, the spell table cannot be accessed, not even by a Larion as powerful as Nerak.'

Gilmour paused to refill his pipe with the aromatic Falkan tobacco before continuing, 'With the key, Nerak might be able to trace Lessek's original strategy and enlarge the opening in the Fold enough to allow his evil master to escape.'

'I thought Malagon – Nerak – already had the key.' Mark was confused. 'Otherwise why would we be going to Welstar Palace to find it?' He glanced across at Brynne who quickly looked away, embarrassed at having been caught staring at him twice in one morning. Mark turned back to Gilmour. 'If Nerak had this key for nine hundred and eighty Twinmoons, why hasn't he gone to Sandcliff Palace and used this spell table thing to release the evil essence on the universe? Can't he do that himself?'

'It's much more difficult than that, Mark,' the older man explained. 'Lessek was enormously powerful, much more powerful than Nerak could ever be, and Nerak knows this. He might begin working with Lessek's spell table and find he accidentally seals the gods' evil creation in the Fold for ever. There's a comprehensive collection of magic and mystical knowledge encoded in that spell table. The Larion Senate was never able to master more than a fraction of its potential. If Nerak taps its power and releases evil on the world, he risks destroying himself in the process. No, I imagine Nerak would keep Lessek's Key as well protected and hidden from mankind as possible. He will want it somewhere it will neither be found, nor be out of his possession.

'Nerak has time on his side. He has nothing *but* time: he can study the magic in the Larion spell table until he has discovered all he needs. When he has learned all that he, Nerak the possessor of souls, rather than he, Nerak the Larion Senator, ever knew, he will take Lessek's Key back to Sandcliff and endeavour to release his new master on all of us.'

'Oh God, no.' Steven barely whispered the words, but Gilmour heard him and looked over expectantly.

'Are you okay, my boy?' he asked. 'I wouldn't worry about these things today. It's been nine hundred and eighty Twin-moons and the rutting horsecock hasn't been able to figure it out yet. We still have some time.'

'Tell me how Lessek's spell table works.' Steven chose his words carefully.

'Well, the table is just that, a table, carved from a granite block quarried deep in the Remondian Mountains of northern Gorsk. Lessek himself is said to have constructed it over several Twinmoons.' Gilmour stopped and checked the position of the sun in the morning sky.

'The key fits in a particular slot carved into the tabletop,' he went on. 'When it's in place the table transfigures from a stone surface to a bottomless pool of knowledge and mysticism. Much of the knowledge is powerful – fiercely independent – and without proper training and practice, it will leap out or, worse, pull you inside. Nerak never understood the intricacies of the table. He was attempting to work with it when the minion escaped and claimed his soul for all time. He had gone too far. He had planned to use the table to overthrow us, but instead his plan backfired and he was taken first.'

Steven and Garec spoke simultaneously; their words had such an impact on the rest of the small company that each rider reined in and turned to stare back at them in stunned silence. Together, in a nearly incoherent marriage of two simple phrases, Garec and Steven changed the course of all their lives.

Garec, in surprise, turned towards Gilmour and cried, 'You said overthrow "us",' while Steven shouted, 'I have Lessek's Key.'

There was a pregnant pause which seemed to last an hour. Then everyone spoke at once.

'What do you mean, you have Lessek's Key?' Sallax asked.

'Gilmour, why did you refer to the Larion Senate as "us"?' Garec repeated. 'How could you have been there?'

The air was buzzing with cries of, 'What did you mean by that?' 'How can that be?' and 'I don't understand.' After several moments of noisy confusion, Gilmour held a hand above his head in an effort to silence the group and restore order to the discussion.

When they had calmed enough for him to be heard, Gilmour

called, 'Please, everyone, please.' They quieted further and he continued, 'I'll answer a couple of important questions, but then I must insist we push on. We have far to go before making camp tonight. Once we're settled we can spend as much time as necessary talking this through, but right now we are in great danger.'

He turned first to Steven, his face alight with anticipation. 'But before we take one more step, we need to hear from you, my boy.' Trying to control the emotion in his voice, Gilmour asked, 'How is it that you suddenly believe you have Lessek's Key?'

Steven inhaled slowly and explained, 'I knew it when you said the evil minion controlling Nerak would put the key in a safe place until it had enough time to master the spell table in Sandcliff Palace.'

'That's right. Why does that make a difference now?' Everyone was hanging on Steven's every word.

'Nerak put it in my bank with the far portal. The key is in a box on my desk in Idaho Springs.' Even though Steven had no idea what Lessek's Key looked like, he was willing to bet William Higgins' stone was the missing piece of the Larion spell table.

'That rock,' Mark added under his breath.

'That's right,' Steven agreed, 'it has to be that rock.'

'It is a small stone,' Gilmour explained, 'about one hand across, and dark, like the land's deepest granite.'

Versen and Sallax exchanged worried glances while Brynne sat transfixed by the conversation between her new friends and her old mentor.

'Damnit,' Mark interjected. 'Now we have to get back there and get that stone before this Malagon-Nerak-minion character manages to figure out your old spell table.' He was growing angry and frustrated.

'You did it too,' Garec pointed accusingly at Mark. 'You called it "his" spell table.' He gestured angrily at Gilmour.

Mark's mistake didn't get by Brynne, either. 'Gilmour, what have you told them that we don't know? How is it you're so familiar with the Larion Senate? You speak about them as if you were there.'

Gilmour looked at Brynne and Garec with all the pride and affection of a grandfather. 'Because I was there. I am one of the two surviving Larion Senators in Eldarn.'

'How can that be?' Versen asked, bewildered. 'That would make you nine hundred and eighty Twinmoons old.'

Gilmour laughed, a bellow that shook his frame. 'I remember nine hundred and eighty Twinmoons, Versen. I remember it fondly. No, I guess I'm about twice that old.' And before any of his incredulous friends could interrupt again, he added, 'Let's keep moving, please. We've learned a lot this morning but nothing that alters our final destination. We have many days' travel in front of us and we won't get anywhere sitting here sharing revelations.'

They rode on in silent disbelief, the southernmost edge of the Ronan piedmont rolling along beneath their mounts. A midday meal was taken in the saddle to avoid another break; everyone – even Mark, who was still bitterly uncomfortable – was content to continue riding through the day. On several occasions, one or more of them tried to make small talk, but those efforts invariably collapsed. Until Gilmour explained more fully, no one would be quite comfortable.

Despite the palpable wariness that hung over the company, Versen set a brisk pace through the forest. Bouncing uncomfortably along, Mark once again started counting the minutes until they would stop for the night. His riding skills had improved since the previous day, but he still pined for a less painful form of travel.

After the midday aven, Versen's horse flushed a pair of grouse that exploded into the air in a startling blur of dark brown feathers. Watching them fly through the trees, Garec saw the birds land in a sun-dappled clearing just off the trail. He and Versen dismounted and stalked the birds through the brush, catching and killing both.

Returning from the underbrush, Garec held one of the limp feathered corpses aloft and called to Gilmour, 'We've filled your dinner order, my exceedingly old friend.'

Brynne chuckled nervously at his attempt at levity.

Gilmour smiled in response to the teasing and happily stuffed the bird into his saddlebag. 'It appears I will have to learn to appreciate old-age jokes now that my secret is out.'

Garec jumped back astride Renna and, glad for the break in the tension, asked, 'So, are the stories of farming in Falkan and working with loggers in Praga all lies to cover up your true identity?'

'Of course not,' Gilmour answered. 'My farm produced one of the finest tobacco crops in Falkan, and I can still strip and ride a log down the river with the best. I've had a long life since the massacre at Sandcliff Palace. Granted, much of what I have chosen to do has been out of necessity to hide from the bounty hunters sent from Welstar Palace to kill me. But I've enjoyed all my occupations over the Twinmoons since I fled Gorsk.'

'Bounty hunters?' Mika asked warily.

'Yes, hideous fellows mostly.' Gilmour brushed an imagined insect away from his face. 'They have been hunting me since Prince Draven of Malakasia died nine hundred and eighty Twinmoons ago. His son, Marek, was the first to send assassins out after me. I can't say for certain, but I believe Marek was the first of the Malakasians to be taken, mind and body, by Nerak. He was just a boy at the time, and a pleasant one too, before all this happened. I imagine Nerak hid Lessek's Key and the far portal in Colorado before returning to ravage the royal families of Eldarn.'

'What happened that night at Sandcliff Palace?' Mika looked frightened, as if the answer might conjure up even more danger for them to deal with.

Gilmour chuckled amiably and tried to put them all at ease. 'I'll make you a deal, Mika. You roast these birds and that rabbit Garec bagged this morning. We'll open a couple of skins of Garec's wine and I'll tell you all about it. There's a clearing on the river about an aven further north of here, a protected cove where we can camp safely for the night.'

Taking his cue, Versen spurred his horse and led the company further north towards the Blackstone Mountains and the Falkan border.

WELSTAR PALACE, MALAKASIA

Torches hanging in sconces dimly lit the stone walls of the narrow passageways in Welstar Palace. Soldiers of the palace garrison lined the halls leading from Prince Malagon's royal apartments to his audience chamber in the north wing. Each warrior was clad in the uniform of the Malakasian Home Guard, with the prince's crest on a thick leather breastplate draped over a chain-mail vest. Black leather boots were laced tightly over dark leggings and flowing hooded cloaks made the platoon look more like students of holy writ than highly trained defenders of the prince. Beneath the folds of each cloak, Malagon's soldiers were armed with broadswords or longbows.

There had not been an assault on Welstar Palace in nearly a thousand Twinmoons, but the Home Guard took their preparation and daily drills seriously. Officers in the garrison demanded nothing less than slavish – and obsequious – obedience from every soldier posted at Welstar Palace. Many had never seen their prince, but each was happy to die in Malagon's defence if necessary. To be stationed at Welstar Palace was deemed a great honour by Malakasian men and women, and most occupation soldiers dreamed of the day they would be ordered home to safeguard Eldarn's supreme monarch. Most did not realise that Prince Malagon rarely left his apartments. His generals and admirals met regularly to discuss the ongoing needs of occupation forces around Eldarn, but the prince rarely joined them.

Instead, he spent days on end meditating in the dark recesses of his chambers. Food was sent up from the palace kitchens, yet his guards spoke in hushed tones of elaborately prepared meals going untouched. Rumours abounded that the prince did not require food for sustenance.

On this night, Malagon had sent word of his intention to meet with his military council: he had a change in policy he planned to implement throughout Eldarn. As his closest advisors waited in his audience chamber, uncomfortable in dress uniform, they chatted nervously about the state of the occupation and the efficiency with which their respective military branches operated. Admiral Kuvar Arenthorn, from the northern coast, appeared to be particularly nervous at meeting the prince: sweat beaded his brow and dampened his armpits as he twittered on anxiously about Malakasia's naval presence in the south. Admiral Arenthorn was the youngest officer present; he had risen quickly through the ranks after several ships were lost in the Northern Archipelago and the prince had ordered a summary execution of the entire naval executive staff. The Malakasian fleet had been pursuing two pirate vessels through the Ravenian Sea when they ran aground on the rocks that dotted the ocean between Malakasia and Gorsk.

Arenthorn drank deeply from a goblet of Falkan wine and quickly refilled the chalice. His under-tunic was soaked through; he feared he would soon discolour his uniform with unsightly sweat stains. A few of his colleagues looked askance at him as they picked at trays of tidbits prepared by Malagon's team of chefs, but Arenthorn didn't care. He gulped the wine, refilled the goblet a third time and moved towards the open window, hoping to find a measure of calm in tobacco.

Back in the shadowy halls of the royal residence, a garrison lieutenant barked an order and his entire platoon snapped to attention. Without fanfare – or even a telltale creak from the ancient oaken doors – Prince Malagon of Malakasia, almost invisible among the folds of a heavy wool cloak, drifted silently from his residence and on towards the palace audience chamber. None of the soldiers dared to look at their prince, but many noted the absence of sound as he passed by. It was as though his feet never touched the floor: he simply floated, more spirit than man, as his cloak billowed around him in the windless inner passageway. It was almost impossible in the half-light to discern where Prince Malagon's robes ended and the ambient darkness began.

Loyal and obedient to a fault, not one of his personal guard would have dreamed of reaching out to test the edges of the infinite blackness that surrounded the prince. All understood their death would be swift and without warning if they so much as twitched. They escorted the prince to his audience chamber, where the door swung open before them, seemingly of its own volition. The guards glanced uneasily at one another as the chamber resealed itself once the shadowy apparition had moved inside. Surrounded by his most trusted advisors, there was no need for the palace garrison to accompany Malagon any further this evening. There were already four guards posted in the chamber.

Hearing the chamber door open, Admiral Arenthorn took a long last draw on his pipe and emptied its bowl into a discarded wine goblet on the windowsill. As Prince Malagon entered the room without a sound, every man dropped immediately to one knee, heads bowed low and eyes on the floor. The prince gazed across the bowed heads of his most deferential and loyal servants for a moment before gliding to the head of a large rectangular table in the centre of the room.

'Join me,' he said quietly, his grim voice echoed in their heads, breaking the strained silence.

Arenthorn looked about the room as the others rose slowly and moved to take their places at the council table. His seat was on the opposite side, near the wall. He crossed behind Malagon to take his place among his colleagues, but as he drew level with the prince, Admiral Arenthorn, his stomach turning and his heart pounding a nearly audible rhythm in his chest, drew his sabre from a jewelled scabbard and struck with all his might at the back of the prince's robes.

Cries of, 'Arenthorn, no!' and 'My prince!' rang out across the room, but it was too late. Arenthorn was grinning at the thought of killing the demon lord who had been oppressing and torturing the people of Eldarn for a generation, and he brought the blade down with all his strength.

The sabre flashed in the torch and candlelight and passed through Malagon's form to embed itself deep in the heavy wood of the council table.

Arenthorn's face blanched and he choked back a cry of alarm as he struggled to free the blade for a second blow. Two palace guards, their own broadswords drawn, were moving towards him, and the nearest general, an elderly man from Pellia, had pushed his way between Arenthorn and the prince.

The young admiral pulled hard on the sabre, determined to try once more before he felt the heavy tearing pain of a broadsword ripping through his body. The blade suddenly came loose from the table and he nearly fell backwards with its unexpected release. He lifted the weapon to strike, but as he did so, he felt something strange. He looked quickly at the grip to ensure it had not come apart, shattered, or bent with the initial blow, but it was no longer a cunning basketweave of gold and iron studded with precious stones; it was a snake, a marsh adder, nearly as long as a tall man, the diamond pattern along its back as bright as the gold and rubies of his sword.

He had little time to admire the deadly beauty of the serpent, for it had already coiled back over its own body and lunged, biting him hard on the wrist, then striking at his face, sinking its venomous fangs into the flesh beneath his right eye.

Arenthorn screamed in terror and collapsed, writhing, to the floor. The snake fell nearby and clattered several times: a metallic clang, a sabre once again. Through blood and tears, Arenthorn saw one of Malagon's guards standing over him, broadsword raised. Then above the cacophony of shouts and curses he heard Malagon's voice boom, as much inside his head as without, 'Stop!'

The soldier held fast, his sword hovering above the would-be assassin cowering on the stone floor. A bloody hand held over his injured eye, Arenthorn wept like a lost child.

Except for the admiral's pitiful cries there was silence. Malagon spoke again. 'Sheath your weapon, soldier.'

The guard immediately complied, but remained standing over Arenthorn.

'Admiral,' Malagon said. Arenthorn was certain he could hear the prince within his own mind; a deep, resonant voice echoed like a god trapped inside a hollow mountain.

'You dared to strike me down.' The prince's cloak was an inky void. 'I commend your bravery and conviction, but you have failed. Now, rise.'

Arenthorn struggled to his feet. His face and wrist were bleeding from the deep puncture wounds. He dropped his arms to his side, knowing death was certain. He choked back a sob and tried to gain control of himself: after all, he had never expected to leave the audience chamber alive. He thought of his father and prepared to die with dignity.

'You are a demon,' he accused as calmly as he could. 'All Eldarn suffers because of you.'

The hollow voice answered, 'Yes, Eldarn suffers, but only because I take pleasure bringing suffering to Eldarn.' He motioned to a guard. 'My coach, now.' The man hustled away and the still-invisible monarch turned his attention back to Arenthorn.

'You come from Port Denis, I believe. We will travel there together, tonight.'

Arenthorn had no wish to discover what the evil lord had in mind for the people of Port Denis; he threw himself at the prince, hoping to be struck dead at that moment, but Malagon waved one hand, almost negligently, and Arenthorn collapsed as a burning sensation flared up inside his mind, pain so strong, so unbearable, he screamed and curled into a foetal position.

'You *will* live through the night, Admiral,' Malagon commanded as Arenthorn fell away into a dark and tortuous nightmare.

The village of Port Denis was many days' ride from Welstar Palace, but the caravan of coaches and riders made the trip in less than an aven. The officers felt the world around them blur into a continuous fabric of darkness; only the ground before their mounts or beneath their coaches was visible in the light of Eldarn's twin moons.

Soon the scent of low tide and the feel of the heavy salt air permeated the night. Malagon's coach slowed to a stop on a bluff above an inlet. Port Denis was built on either side of a narrow stream that ran northwest into the sea, its simple homes and buildings built into the sides of the hill. The members of the prince's military council secretly shuddered. The village below was about to feel the full force of their prince's anger; it might one day be their own homes.

Arenthorn was dragged from the coach and dropped to the ground at the dark prince's feet. Waving one hand over the admiral, Malagon spoke softly, 'You will suffer no longer.' The puncture wounds in Arenthorn's face and wrist healed instantly. The burning pain caused by the snake's venom subsided and the reeling, turning confusion of the agonising nightmare spun slowly to a stop.

Arenthorn climbed to his feet. 'Don't do this, Malagon,' he told the nebulous form standing beside him. 'These people have done nothing except struggle to survive under your thumb.'

'I did not free you from your pain to listen to you giving me orders,' the dark prince said coldly. 'I freed you from your pain so nothing would distract you from witnessing my power.' Malagon pointed towards the village. 'Your wife, children and father live here, do they not?'

'No,' Arenthorn lied. 'I moved them away several Twinmoons ago.'

'Liar!' Malagon screamed. Though Arenthorn covered his ears, nothing could alleviate the force of the evil prince's powerful voice bellowing inside his head. 'They live here still. They probably sit together this very evening, wondering where you are. Would you like to go down and see them one last time, Arenthorn?'

At last the young admiral's façade cracked and he dropped to one knee. He begged forgiveness, and pleaded for the lives of his family. He tried in vain to grab hold of Prince Malagon's robes, but in the darkness their folds escaped his grasp. 'My lord, please,' he pleaded, 'kill me, kill me ten thousand times, but spare the village.'

'I have no intention of killing you, Admiral. You will live for many Twinmoons, enjoying the memories of what happened here tonight: what *you* did tonight.

'Your wife will live as well. She will join us at Welstar Palace. Every morning you will report to my chambers, retrieve her and spend the day nursing her back to health. You will gaze into her vacuous eyes, knowing you murdered her children and killed her spirit. Every day she will beg you to take her life, but you won't. Instead, you will love and care for her, pleading for her forgiveness as you now plead for mine. And every night, I will send a servant to collect her once again. Who knows? Perhaps after a few Twinmoons, I will tire of torturing you and you will be permitted to die.'

Turning to the others, he added, 'This is a lesson to each of you. Never cross me.'

Malagon swept one hand towards the shallow sloping hills flanking the seaside village. Against the already dark night, the landscape seemed to darken even further, as if a blanket had been draped over the hamlet, smothering all light, all hope. The wall of inky nothingness crept slowly along the stream, across the village to the wharf below. Fire and torchlight, a constellation of flickering orange and yellow, died out, leaving the expanse that had been the village of Port Denis as black as pitch. Nothing moved and no one spoke. There were no cries for help and no shrieks for mercy. No survivors fled into the sea.

Then, quietly at first, a lone voice carried through the annihilated village and up the sides of the bluff to where Malagon and his military council stood. A tortured scream, like one damned for ever to hell, carried on the night air.

'Ah,' Malagon said, amused, 'that will be your wife, Admiral.' Motioning to two generals nearby, he added, 'Run and fetch her, will you?'

Admiral Kuvar Arenthorn of Port Denis knelt in the dirt above his village screaming into the night. He began with a plea for forgiveness to the souls of his children, then to the hapless innocents of Port Denis, murdered because of his own stupidity. His screams matched the tortured wailing of his wife, Port Denis's lone survivor.

Marshalling his wits for a moment, he sprang from the bluffs into the darkness, hoping to plummet to death on the rocks below, but Malagon would not permit it. Reaching out, the dark prince caught Arenthorn in a vice-like spell and threw him back violently into the side of his carriage where the admiral finally lay still, whimpering beneath his breath.

'Come, everyone,' the dark prince commanded. 'Let us return. We have a nation to run.'

The heat inside the tavern was stifling and the smell overwhelming: a fug of unwashed bodies and pipesmoke, that heady mixture of Falkan tobacco and fennaroot that was so popular. Brexan longed for a breath of fresh air. She had been sitting for nearly two avens and moisture was running down the small of her back. It was at times like this she missed the chilly evenings of northern Malakasia. Rona was a swamp compared to her homeland and she had no idea how anyone managed to survive in this climate for any length of time. Fighting to keep her mind sharp while she nursed a sixth beer, she laughed along with the jokes and innuendoes as the local lads battled to win her affection. The reprehensible – if handsome – assassin she had followed sat alone, drinking wine and ignoring the other patrons.

She had tracked the killer north from Estrad Village all day, riding with other travellers along the Merchants' Highway when she could so he didn't notice her. He had made several forays into the forest along the river, but invariably returned to the road; she guessed he was tracking someone as well.

As they neared the turn-off for Randel she had joined a group and ridden ahead of him; no one elicited more than a passing glance from the man. It was getting late, so she stabled her horse at the town's largest inn and waited for him to arrive. Unless he planned to sleep alongside the Highway – a potentially dangerous decision for anyone – he would secure lodgings here in Randel and continue his journey the following morning.

Randel was a prosperous town surrounded by family farms that produced much of the beef, pork, milk and cheese, and vegetables, especially green root and pepper weed for Estrad Village and the southern coastal region. Judging from the clientèle, Brexan could see the establishment catered for a wide variety of patrons. Farmhands downed copious quantities of beer alongside landowners sipping fine wines; merchants bargained with farmers while travellers passing through took advantage of the fresh produce to vary otherwise monotonous diets.

Lieutenant Bronfio's killer came into the tavern a while later and took a seat at the end of the bar. He ordered a small meal from the kitchen and a flagon of Falkan wine. Brexan had eaten alone, but soon attracted a group of locals, who were eager to buy her drinks and shower her with compliments. She told them she was travelling north through the Blackstones with her brother, who had been taken ill earlier in the day and was now asleep in their room upstairs.

Although persistent, the boys were harmless; Brexan was glad she didn't have to fend off less-polite suitors. These boys, however awkward, had obviously been raised well and were mindful of their manners, even six or seven drinks into their clumsy seduction. Under different circumstances, she might have enjoyed the attention, but this evening she would have been happy to add several rolls of unsightly flab and sprout a crop of ugly moles on her face so the local pack of sex-crazed youngsters would take their enthusiasm elsewhere.

At last her diligence paid off. A tall man who had been drinking in the corner near the fireplace stood and moved across the bar. He wore a hat pulled low over his eyes; she couldn't make out his features with any clarity through the smoke and bodies. She sat transfixed as the man approached the Malakasian spy. Brexan watched their lips with a faint hope of lip-reading their conversation – but they didn't exchange a single word. Instead, the man reached inside his coat, removed a small piece of parchment and placed it on the bar under his empty tankard. Without a glance in the merchant's direction, he turned and left the tavern.

The barman moved to collect the empty stein and as he did, the spy lashed out with snakelike quickness, gripping the man's wrist. Brexan could not hear what was said, but saw the innkeeper wrench his arm free and motion angrily towards the door. The assassin raised his palms in a gesture of supplication, dropped a handful of coins on the bar and discreetly gathered up the parchment as the tavern owner collected his payment. With a quick look around the tavern, he stood and strode purposefully from the room.

Brexan knew she had to act quickly or risk losing her quarry in the night. She walked up to the bar with her empty trencher and asked the barman casually, 'Do you know him? That man who just left? He looks very familiar to me, but I can't place him.'

Trying not to stare too pointedly at the moisture gathering above her breasts, he said, 'Sure. He's in here from time to time. Says his name is Lafrent, but I've heard others call him Jacrys Marsel, Marseth— something like that.'

'What does he do?'

'He moves about a lot. Does a good bit of trade here in Rona . . . fancy fabrics and textiles.' He cleared several empty goblets from the bar.

'I think my brother must know him from somewhere . . . that must be why he looks familiar.' To the chagrin of her suitors, Brexan waved airily at them and excused herself, claiming she needed to check on her sick sibling. Hurrying upstairs, she moved along the second-floor hall to a window that overlooked the innkeeper's stables. She peered back down the hall to be certain she hadn't been followed, then pushed open the window and leaped out onto a pile of firewood stacked neatly against the wall.

THE ESTRAD RIVER

The cove was a perfect campsite, a small clearing in a grove of evergreen trees, the riverbank almost semi-circular at that spot. Steven felt as though he were back along the Big Thompson in Colorado's highlands. He was still getting used to the way night fell so quickly in Eldarn – he was glad he had given his watch to Garec, as knowing what time it was at home would only confuse his circadian rhythms further. He amused himself by calculating the maths: if a day here was twenty hours long, then the equivalent of one calendar year would have more than four hundred and thirty Eldarn days and seven full Twinmoons. Gilmour had said the massacre at Sandcliff Palace took place nine hundred and eighty Twinmoons ago. According to Steven's figures, that would have been about the same time that William Higgins was depositing the far portal and Lessek's Key in his brand-new safety deposit box at the fledgling Bank of Idaho Springs, late in the year 1870.

Steven's thoughts turned again to the old man. He liked Gilmour, but he still found it difficult to believe the man was more than two hundred and sixty years old. If Gilmour *had* lived more than nineteen hundred Twinmoons, he would be the oldest man in the world – by a century and a half.

'Oldest man in the world,' he whispered to no one. 'He'd be the oldest man on Earth, at least. I guess I can't say whether he's very old by Eldarni standards.' He dismissed the thought as irrelevant right now, but he was a little distressed at the number of thoughts he had been forced to dismiss over the past three days. Nothing made sense anymore. He was afraid that if he endeavoured to deal with everything that had been frustrating, confusing, or terrifying since his arrival in Rona, he would have a complete emotional breakdown. No, if he wanted to keep his head level, he would have to ignore the numerous inexplicable aspects of the life and times of Eldarn.

He strode to the river's edge and peered down at the water. Cupping his hands over his eyes, Steven narrowed his vision so all he could see was the river rushing by, in perfect perpetual rhythm, towards the ocean south of Estrad Village. He took deep, relaxing breaths and imagined himself standing on the banks of Clear Creek as it careened riotously through Idaho Springs. Feeling better, he knelt down and splashed icy water on his face and then rubbed two handfuls on the back of his neck. The cold felt good against his skin and once again he felt his hopes rise, an upswing on the emotional roller-coaster he had ridden since his fateful decision to breach his bank's code of ethics and open William Higgins' deposit box. If there was enough familiarity in Eldarn for him to have a few refreshing moments near a stream, perhaps it was all right to hope he and Mark might find their way home.

Mark joined him on the riverbank. Without speaking, he stripped to his underwear and strode boldly into the water. Steven smiled: that was Mark; finds himself in a foreign world filled with magic, war, demon creatures and no discernable way back home and instead of worrying, strips to boxers and enjoys an evening swim. Looking back over his shoulder, Steven could see the Ronans taking an interest in Mark's antics as well.

Brynne looked at him questioningly, but all Steven could do was to shrug and shake his head.

'Hey,' Mark called, 'c'mon in. It's only cold for a second.'

'I don't believe you,' Steven replied, still smiling. 'How can you just go swimming like that? Like you're at a community pool in the suburbs?'

Mark shook the water from his face and answered, 'Well, I figure either way we have to go into Welstar Palace, and from what everyone says, entering Welstar is just about the most dangerous and life-threatening decision we can make while we're here in Eldarn.' He started backstroking towards the centre of the river.

'What does that have to do with swimming?'

Mark stopped again and trod water. 'I'm swimming because I can,' he said matter-of-factly. 'It helps me to distance myself from this growing certainty that we're never getting out of this place alive.'

Steven contemplated Mark's words for a moment then quickly peeled off his own clothes and jumped into the icy water, shouting as the cold struck his skin with the force of a hard slap. He dived beneath the surface and saw the brown, pebbled river bottom was dotted here and there with larger smooth stones.

The mundane normality of the riverbed, like his first sight of the little cove, brought him a measure of comfort. He was glad Mark had talked him into this pre-dinner swim. He was right: they had to actively control whatever they could, because there were so many things about Eldarn that seemed to flail about wildly out of reach, things they had no control over whatsoever.

Breaking the surface, he gasped for breath, then grinned at his roommate as if to say thank you, but Mark was already moving towards the riverbank. 'Where are you going?' Steven called.

'I've been sweating for three days in this heat. I'm going to wash my clothes.' Mark stepped from the water and collected up his bundle, but just as he was about to throw everything in, he stopped short.

'What's the matter?' Steven climbed up the bank to pick up his own pile of clothing; he tossed it into the shallows along the river's edge.

'I just remembered grabbing a book of matches at Owen's the other night. I don't want them to get wet. Who knows when we might need 'em.' He poked through his pockets until he discovered the matchbook, folded up with several crumpled pieces of parchment.

'Oh, this is the paper I found back at Riverend as well. I'm glad I checked. We might need that too.' He dropped the matches and parchment on the ground before dropping his clothes into the river. The two men sat companionably in the knee-deep shallows, scrubbing their clothing clean, before clambering out to squeeze as much water as possible from each piece and hanging the lot from sundry tree branches around the camp.

When Garec called them for dinner, Mark, still wearing only his damp boxers, moved towards the fire-pit, chivvying up his friend. 'C'mon Steven, there's rabbit to be eaten over here.'

'Grand,' Steven answered sarcastically. 'Let's eat the Easter Bunny, shall we?'

'Hey, don't laugh. It smells pretty tasty.' Mark dragged a fallen log to the edge of the fire and dropped down on it as if he were falling into a comfortable sofa.

'You're right. At this point I'm so hungry I could eat a fried dog,' he said and sat next to Mark.

'I'll check with the chef: I do believe Eldani Fried Dog is on the menu for tomorrow.' They both laughed, but Garec was disgusted that anyone would ever think of eating pets.

'It's really okay, it's just a joke about one of our – er, eating establishments back home ... you know, 20,000 flies can't be wrong,' Mark tried to explain. It wasn't long before the incredulous group were giggling at the thought of breakfast cereal that could be used to spell words, beer that came in metal cans and whole cooked chickens served in colourful paper buckets.

After dinner, Mika cleaned their pots in the river and Versen gathered more firewood to see them through the night. Sallax sipped thoughtfully from a goblet of Garec's family wine and Brynne unrolled her blankets on an area of smooth ground near the fire. Mark felt a tense knot in his stomach loosen when he saw how close to him Brynne had decided to sleep, but he couldn't catch her eye.

He and Steven had borrowed some of Garec's clothes while theirs dried in the warm night air. Gilmour poked at the fire with a branch, then abandoned his apparent fascination with the flames to fill his pipe from a leather pouch tucked inside his riding cloak. There was tension in the air, but no one seemed willing to break the mood by prompting Gilmour to elaborate on his startling morning revelation. Finally, Gilmour himself broke the wary mood as he poured himself a goblet of wine and invited everyone to join him around the fire.

'Come my friends, we have much to discuss,' he said, patting an empty log beside him.

Brynne sat next to Steven. Leaning over to him she whispered, 'This is difficult for all of us. It must be especially maddening for you two.'

Steven ran his palms back and forth along the coarse homespun fabric of his borrowed leggings. 'I'm just glad we met people we could trust. I really am sorry for the way we treated you at Riverend Palace.'

She reached over and took his hand. It was the same gesture Hannah had used when reaching for him over fajitas that afternoon in Denver. Steven smiled inwardly at the memory; that had been a *good* day.

'That's all right,' Brynne said. 'You believed it was your only way out at the time.'

'At least then it felt like we had a way out.' He tried not to allow his anxiety to show in the tone of his voice.

'It will be all right, Steven, I'm confident things will work out in the end.' She patted his hand again, comforting him with her touch.

Versen and Mika joined them around the fire; Sallax stood nearby, keeping watch for potential assailants approaching through the forest.

Gilmour looked at each of them in turn before beginning, 'My friends, I want you to understand from the start that whatever you hear tonight, whatever you may learn, I am still Gilmour, still your friend and your compatriot. You may think I have withheld a great deal from you in the many Twinmoons we have known one another, but do not blame me for that. You are like my children to me, and the greatest joy I have felt in the last fifty Twinmoons has come from knowing each of you.' He looked at Garec as if the young man held a special place in his heart, then turned to Mark and Steven. 'And you two represent the culmination of more than nine hundred Twinmoons' anticipation for someone who has—' he grinned at Steven '—or at least has knowledge of Lessek's Key.'

He waved his pipe around. 'This is the most excited I have been in half my life. I – *we* – may finally have an opportunity to defeat Nerak, to close the Fold for ever and to ensure the clouds of hatred, mistrust, violence and oppression that have been destroying Eldarn for six generations will at last be lifted.

'It's not going to be easy, though. Nerak is the most powerful being in this world, and his mission is to gather enough information to safely release his master. With evil's origin free from its prison inside the Fold, nothing will ever be as it was. No one will survive except perhaps as slaves – and I for one would far rather die in the initial explosion of power and hatred than live to serve such a master.'

Steven interrupted him. 'How can all evil be in one place?' he asked.

'It can't. As I tried to explain earlier, small pieces, the tiniest spores, have broken free from the essence and slipped into our world over thousands of generations. The evil around us is a reality, it is one of the things we learn shortly after birth. There are terrifying and destructive things, hideous, black and frightening things in the world we all avoid, but they are always there.

'The evil we seek to defeat came to Eldarn through the Fold when Nerak attempted to control the magic of Lessek's spell table. Much of it scattered, in myriad directions: angry words, frightening thoughts and violent tendencies. But the minion Nerak freed was larger and more powerful than those tiny spores that have slipped across the Fold throughout time. The spores that make up this minion, perhaps driven by an edict from within the Fold, stayed together rather than scattering: a focused power that claimed Nerak, devoured his soul and gained what knowledge he had of Eldarn. It consumed the members of Eldarn's royal family, hid Lessek's Key and the more powerful portal in your bank, Steven, and then returned across the Fold to begin its reign of terror.'

He tossed a small log on the fire then added, 'It kills for the sheer joy of feeling the fear in its victims' hearts. It knows no reason. It will destroy all that is good and decent around it while it takes as long as necessary to study the magic of Lessek's legacy, the Larion spell table.'

'Wait one moment, Gilmour,' Mark stopped him. 'How did it get back from Idaho Springs if the far portal was closed and locked in Steven's bank? I thought the portal had to be open for it to travel across the Fold.'

'An excellent question,' the old man answered. 'For thousands of Twinmoons, the Larion Senate used far portals to conduct research and exploration in your world, and yes, we ensured both portals were always open. It was the only way we knew we could return home. The portal in your living room will pinpoint a position as long as it remains open. The portal in Malagon's palace will find your world, but unless both portals are open, it will not pinpoint a destination.'

The implications were not lost on Steven. 'So that means we might end up anywhere on Earth when we go back?'

'Only if someone has gone into our house and closed the portal,' Mark clarified. 'If no one closes it, we'll both get dropped right back in the living room, right?'

'Oh, Jesus!' Steven exclaimed. 'With us gone, I'm sure someone will go in there – my parents maybe, or Howard.' Steven's voice dropped to a whisper. 'Or even Hannah,' he said, his voice stricken.

'It's a risk you cannot avoid,' Gilmour interjected, 'but I haven't answered your question, Mark. Yes, Nerak can cross the Fold with only one portal open, but he is at the mercy of the weaker portal, just like the two of you will be. If he enters the portal in Malagon's palace, he will be dropped anywhere in your world. Back when he hid Lessek's Key, he simply entered your world, assessed the area where he arrived and decided on your bank as a reasonable temporary hiding place.'

'So he didn't choose Colorado?' Brynne asked.

'No. He landed there, most likely devoured several souls and used their knowledge to determine the safest hiding place for Lessek's Key.' Gilmour looked around for the wineskin and filled his goblet. 'Coming back, he used what magic he had gleaned from previous trips across the Fold to find the open portal here in Eldarn.'

Steven summed up, as much for himself as anyone else, 'So, if the portal in our house stays open, we can get back home, but Nerak can also get right into the room where Lessek's Key lies unprotected. If the portal in our house is closed, Nerak can still get back to our world, but he will have to make a trip to Idaho Springs and then search for the key when he finds it missing from the bank.'

'That is correct,' Gilmour told him, 'and to be honest with you, I must hope someone closes the portal in your house. If Nerak travels to your world and doesn't find the key in your bank, I'm not certain he will deduce that it lies waiting in your home.'

'What will he do if he doesn't find the key where he hid it back in 1870?' Mark feared the worst and Gilmour confirmed his suspicions.

'He will take any available souls, glean what information he can from them and hopefully track down Lessek's Key from their knowledge of you two.' Somehow Gilmour's pipe became lit and he blew a cloud of sweet-smelling smoke above the fire.

Steven looked at Mark, his eyes filled with terror. 'Howard and Myrna.'

'Oh God, you're right.' Mark was frightened as well. 'But hopefully, they won't have thought anything of a random rock sitting out in our house; maybe that will throw Nerak off our trail.'

'Listen to what you're saying,' Steven implored. 'Even to get to that point means Howard and Myrna will be dead.'

Mark didn't respond immediately, but instead set his jaw with grim determination, an uncertain warrior preparing for an unavoidable battle. 'Then we'll just have to get there first.'

'That is our best option,' Gilmour agreed. 'If we can get back through the far portal in Welstar Palace before Nerak, we will have control of both portals and Lessek's Key.'

'That's it, then,' Garec spoke up. 'That's how we'll do it.'

Sallax was not as encouraged. 'That means we have to get to Malakasia, survive long enough to enter the lion's den, succeed in breaching Malagon's— Nerak's most powerful defences, find and steal the far portal, open it for long enough to get the three of you through, wait around for Gilmour to get back with the stone key and then close off our end for ever. Forgive me, my friends, but that plan does not fill me with confidence.' Looking directly at Gilmour, Sallax asked, 'Can you tell me how you expect us to survive such an assault?'

Garec watched Gilmour; for the second time since they had left Estrad his usually ebullient friend looked old and tired. He stared across the fire at the Ronan Resistance leader. 'I'm not certain we *will* live through it. But I wouldn't even consider this plan were it anything less than essential to the survival of our world . . . both our worlds.' Then, surprising everyone, he added, 'And, as luck would have it, we won't be going in alone.'

'Really?' Garec asked. 'Who's coming with us?'

'Kantu,' Gilmour said.

The entire company looked bemused; the name was unknown to any of them. Garec raised his eyebrows in query.

'Kantu is the only other surviving Larion Senator,' Gilmour elucidated. 'He's in Praga.'

'Only two survivors of that night at Sandcliff Palace?' Mika asked, shocked. 'How did you two live through it?'

'Well, Kantu survived because he was on the opposite side of Eldarn at the time. My survival is another story.'

The river babbled by their small clearing, a watery highway leading through the forest, ignorant of and indifferent to the problems faced by the company of freedom fighters.

Steven was overwhelmed. The idea that the key to save the world from unimaginable evil was lying in a plain rosewood box on his desk was mind-blowing. He feared for Howard and Myrna, but all the same, he hoped against hope that the tapestry was still lying on the floor in their living room, so he, Mark and Gilmour could step through the Fold, retrieve Lessek's Key and send Gilmour back with the rock in a matter of seconds.

If the portal had been closed, they might get transported anywhere on Earth – to the middle of the Pacific Ocean, or to the top of a Himalayan peak maybe. It might take days, or even weeks to reach Colorado from wherever they landed, weeks during which his new friends would have to keep their Eldani portal open. Their only hope would be to steal the portal from Welstar Palace and find a safe place to open it, somewhere they could defend their position until Gilmour returned with Lessek's Key.

Steven was suddenly overcome by a desire to get packed and moving on. Waiting around, guessing at outcomes was nearly unbearable, a stress he couldn't take. He looked around nervously and felt Brynne lay a comforting hand on his back. She rubbed her fingers along his shoulder, hoping to calm him down. Turning towards her, he saw again why Mark found the young woman so attractive. Her skin glowed palely in the warm firelight: she was without artifice and quite beautiful. As he admired Brynne's natural loveliness, Steven's thoughts turned yet again to Hannah. Where was she? Had she called, or driven out to find him? He remembered the telephone ringing several times while he was struggling with the decision to follow Mark through the far portal. It must have been her. He cursed himself for not answering.

Gilmour's revelations, his willingness to disclose everything, had instilled confidence in Mika, the youngest of the partisans; he prompted Gilmour to continue his story.

'Tell us about that night, then,' he said with enthusiastic curiosity. 'How did you survive when so many were killed?'

'Mika, I have never been sure how I survived that night at Sandcliff and except for blind luck, I'm not convinced any other force in the Northern Forest lent a hand to save me. I will admit, though, there have been many times in the past nine hundred and eighty Twinmoons when I wished I had been among those who fell defending Lessek's research and writings. For some reason, I was allowed to escape. I have never been certain why so many had to give their lives while I was permitted to go free. When I face Nerak, and I will one day face him, I might ask him that question.'

Gilmour stood for a moment, stretched his tired back muscles then sat down again near the fire.

'So you believe he let you escape?' Versen asked.

'I am convinced he let me escape,' Gilmour responded. 'He could have killed me very easily. All he had to do was come down a flight of stairs to the scroll library and I would have been at his mercy. He never did.' He broke a wood chip from a log near his feet and tossed it into the fire. 'I can only speculate. Maybe he let me go because he looked forward to the cat-and-mouse games we've been playing since I jumped from the window that night. If evil's disciple read Nerak's thoughts as it devoured his soul, it would have learned that Nerak, Kantu and I were equals, leaders among the Larion Senate. It would also have learned that Kantu was off in Praga, but that I was right there at Sandcliff. Perhaps it let me go because it anticipated an enjoyable time hunting us down and taking our souls.

'The three of us were division leaders of the Larion Senate. Kantu coordinated our efforts in education and public health. I was in charge of research and scholarship and Nerak provided leadership for our ongoing work in magic and medicine. For many Twinmoons, he was one of my best friends; I respected his work both as a scholar and as a magician. But Lessek he was not. Nerak was more acutely aware of that shortcoming than he was of anything positive he and his team brought to Eldarn.'

Gilmour sighed, then continued reflectively, 'It snowed hard that night and I remember watching from the window in my chambers as it coated the palace grounds in a thin white blanket. I loved Sandcliff Palace. It wasn't lavish; far from it, but the Larion Senate was a true community of scholars, and everyone kept an open mind about new ideas and research. The palace was always alive with questions and discourse, true dialogue instead of debate. We Larion Senators honestly believed we were improving life in Eldarn by bringing knowledge, medicine and advanced technologies to the people of the five lands.'

He looked over at Stephen and Mark, who were listening intently. 'We were impressed with the advances your world showed in weaponry and warfare: gunpowder, the cannon and flintlock rifle were tempting prizes. But our culture strictly forbade it. We would never have brought such instruments back to Eldarn. Not even Nerak would have betrayed that belief.'

'What about after he was taken by the minion?' Mark asked, 'why not go back and gather up weapons, bombs, viruses? Our world is filled with weapons.'

'Nerak would not have brought such implements into Eldarn because the Larion Senate would have punished him, limited his access to the far portals and worse, the spell table.' Gilmour looked towards the river; they could hear the gentle rushing over the crackle and hiss of the fire. 'When he was taken, Nerak was controlled by an evil so powerful that I am certain he was convinced such weapons would pale in comparison to the strength of his own magic.'

'Would they?' Steven asked.

'From what I saw that day at Gettysburg, those weapons would have little impact on Nerak.' He went on with the tale. 'Sandcliff wasn't much of a palace, certainly not like Riverend, although the passages were charmed, so they were tricky to navigate if one didn't know the spells. It was just a simple stone-walled keep, the only adornment the colourful Pragan carpets and tapestries we used to keep out the cold; it was our culture that made Sandcliff such a wonderful place to live and work. Our mantras were risk-taking, creativity, service and scholarship, and as I said, Eldarn was a better world for our efforts.

'When Nerak destroyed all that, he opened the door for an era of worldwide mistrust, hatred, selfishness and discord.' He stopped again, this time looking at the Ronans. 'I am truly sorry you have all had to grow up in such a culture.

'As daylight faded on the evening of the slaughter, I knew Nerak would be in Lessek's chamber working to master the spells contained within the great stone table. He was driven to succeed from the start, and more passionate about his work than anyone in the Larion Senate. In the days preceding his fall, he had sequestered himself in Lessek's research chamber, poring over our founder's writings and experimenting with spells he had called from deep within the table's recesses. Nerak was coordinator of magic and medicine, so it was normal for him to keep the stone key in his possession. Although I shared my concern for his safety, there was little I could do to get him to turn it over to me. There were rumours that he was planning to dismantle the senate structure, to banish us all, once he finally mastered the magic that would give him enough power, but there was no proof.'

'When the attack came, I was in my chambers, working. The first thing I heard were great booming sounds coming from several floors below mine. I thought that one of my colleagues was experimenting with a spell to control the weather. Many Larions came from the south, and few appreciated snow. Winters in Gorsk are long and hard; by mid-season every Larion was working on a spell to bring an early spring. Those spells were always terribly noisy.' Steven and Garec exchanged a confused look.

Gilmour continued, 'When Heskar, one of the young scribes, burst into my room unannounced, I knew something had gone terribly wrong. He spoke so fast – the only words I remember were "massacre of apprentices and servants on a lower floor of the palace". My first thought was that Sandcliff had been attacked by pirates or raiders, or maybe even an army from another nation. I would never have guessed just one man could be so great a threat. I raced downstairs to the narrow balcony above the room that served as both audience and dining chamber. I was running along the balcony to get to a stairway at the far corner of the room when I saw Nerak. Even at that distance I could see he had been taken over by something mighty, some vast destructive force.'

He shuddered. 'Although he was still visible, his body was beginning to disintegrate – his flesh looked translucent in the torchlight. At the time I wasn't sure what was happening, but now I know the force that overpowered him along a seam in the Fold had no use for his physical being. It needed only his knowledge – and his soul. It would use others as physical hosts, but Nerak's body was allowed to break apart, to fall away in pieces until only a shadow remained. By the end of the evening, Nerak had taken possession of several Larion Senators, each through a small wound he opened in their wrist or on the back of their hand. With each, evil's minion learned more about Eldarn's people and our weaknesses.

'I saw Nerak holding two Larion Senators by the throat, a woman from Falkan named Callena and a young Pragan man, Janel. Their names are engraved on my memory. They were screaming in abject terror, and both of them were looking at me as if I were their only hope for survival. I stopped then and implored him to set them free. He looked at me from across the balcony, then, without flinching, he snapped their necks. Just a quick turn of his wrists. I heard the bones break. He didn't take his eyes off me as he tossed their bodies over the ledge to the stone floor below.'

Brynne shifted uneasily on the log next to Steven, and Mika absent-mindedly scratched at the back of his wrists. 'Go on,' he said quietly.

'I doubled back and raced upstairs towards the stone tower. All the passageways in the castle were closed by spells to keep intruders from breaking in and stealing potentially devastating magic. As I ran, I shouted the spells out in front of me to clear the way of any enchanted obstacles. At the top of the spiral staircase leading to the tower's uppermost room, I found the door open, the spell already cast. I burst into Lessek's chamber, horribly afraid I would find only the corpses of Nerak's research team. Instead they were all there, poring over Lessek's table, desperately trying to find an antidote to Nerak's possession. Lessek's chamber wasn't used by anyone. The black granite table stood alone in the centre. The room was normally lit by torchlight, but that night the only illumination was the rainbow of colours that flashed and faded inside the spell table. I could see Lessek's Key in its place – at least Nerak hadn't taken it with him when he went downstairs to begin killing off Larion Senators.

'Three members of my own team soon arrived and I ordered them to stand fast at the top of the stairs, ready to hurl every destructive magic they had down upon Nerak if he tried to reach Lessek's chamber. I will never forget their grim faces, the look of fear and determination as the door closed slowly on them. I cast a quick spell to reseal the chamber.

'I was their leader. I should have stood with them on the stairs and fought to the end against Nerak. Instead, I shut them out in the hall, protected only by their pitiful powers and what courage they could draw from one another. They were researchers, teachers, not magicians. I should have known they would be no match for the coming evil.'

'Why did you not stand and fight with them?' Sallax broke the silence, staring hard at Gilmour.

'I feared the worst,' Gilmour responded in flat tones. 'I knew Nerak's team could not interrupt their work to defend the spell table, or even to fetch any necessary scrolls from the library adjacent to the room. They were used to working with the spell table; I was not: but I could fetch spell scrolls, and I would be their last line of defence against the force I knew was coming for us. I called to Nerak's assistant, Pikan Tettarak, a skilled sorcerer herself, that I was available to run back and forth between the spell chamber and the scroll library. She nodded to say she understood and immediately turned back to the wall of blue and red energy that fought to escape the table into the room; instead it found *her* there, channelling its power into a single defensive spell of enormous strength. Harnessing the magic of the table had been a lifelong undertaking for Lessek; it was an ongoing research endeavour for Nerak.

'Pikan looked as if she was being overwhelmed by the power of the table; if she had not been able to call upon the strength of Nerak's other team members, I am certain she would have been pulled into the bottomless morass of knowledge and magic within.

'For what felt like an aven I stood there, helpless. Pikan and her colleagues worked without pause to discover magic that would protect us from Nerak while freeing his soul from whatever entity held it prisoner. Then the crashing began at the chamber door. It started as spell noise in the stairwell, and I hoped that my team members were holding firm. Soon the sounds changed; I could tell these incantations were focused entirely on the outer doorway. I wondered why, if my team were already dead, Nerak didn't simply call out the spell that opened the chamber. I can only guess that in a dying breath, one of my brave martyrs changed the spell and committed suicide, dying before Nerak could take possession of his or her soul and learn the necessary magic.' Gilmour stopped. Steven could see he was trembling as he refilled his goblet and took a long swallow.

'Are you okay to go on?' Steven asked quietly.

'Oh yes,' Gilmour said, visibly pulling himself together. 'I know it happened so long ago, but for me, it will always feel like yesterday. It's not a story I have told very often. Maybe it's time that changed.

'I knew the passageway would soon fall to the demon's power, so I tried to get Pikan's attention, hoping to warn her that Nerak was about to breach our last defence. There was a broadsword leaning against the wall – I don't know whose it was, but I picked it up and prepared to battle whatever burst into the room. I knew magic, of course I did, but nothing nearly as powerful as that hammering away at the chamber door. It shook the stone masonry of the tower itself and for a few moments I feared the palace would collapse and we would all tumble to our deaths.

'Everything seemed to move in slow motion. I realised I was about to die. I was not a brave man. I hoped to perhaps strike out with one fierce blow before my resolve disintegrated and I stood in mute horror awaiting death. No great wellspring of anger or defiance arose from inside my being and I knew the gods were giving me a few extra moments to contemplate how inadequately I had behaved when the end finally came.

'Then, as if from a distance, a lifetime away, I heard my name. I turned to find Pikan calling to me with great enthusiasm. She was such a beautiful woman . . . she actually seemed to smile as I hurried across the room to her side. "I need the third Windscroll," she shouted above the din of so much magic moving in and around the room. "It's in the library near the top shelf behind Lessek's desk." Taking the broadsword, I ran as quickly as I could down the short flight of stairs separating the spell chamber from the scroll library. Lessek's desk stood near the far wall, and shelves upon shelves of parchment scrolls lined every inch of the chamber. Racing to the shelf behind Lessek's desk, I searched for the Windscrolls, powerful ancient spells compiled by Kantu and Nerak on their frequent journeys to Larion Isle, off the coast of Malakasia.

'But I never found them.

'Blue- and red-flecked energy preceded the blast down the stairs into the library and scrolls were blown from their shelves as a shockwave tore through the chamber and knocked me unconscious.

'When I woke, blood had run into my eyes and for several terrifying moments I could see the world only in shades of red.

The only light came from our two moons, shining through the falling snow. I looked out of the window and watched as red snowflakes blanketed Gorsk. I wondered if anyone was left alive in all Eldarn. The silence was dreadful; I called out several times just to hear my voice in the darkness.

'When I felt steady enough, I made my way through the remains of the library, climbing over fallen shelves and through a sea of scattered parchment scrolls to the spell chamber beyond.

'Everyone was dead, their bodies broken. They lay strewn about the room as if deposited there by a Twinmoon hurricane. Only Pikan's body was missing. One of my team members lay on the stone floor near the door: a big young man named Harren Bonn, the son of a Falkan farmer. He had been claimed by Nerak just before the spell that sealed the door was broken. Seeing his limbs twisted at impossible angles, I tried to move him back against the wall, to leave him sitting in a more dignified position, but when I touched him, he was like jelly. I am not certain there was a bone left intact in his entire body.

'I was weeping helplessly now, and I left him there, shaded red in my bloodied vision. It will not matter if I live another thousand Twinmoons; Harren Bonn will always remain blood-red in my memory.' Gilmour's voice shook.

Garec moved to sit beside his mentor and friend. He put a comforting arm around the old man.

Gilmour smiled thanks at him. 'As I came down through the tower, I saw carnage everywhere. I had never really thought about that word before: it was just a word. Made flesh, it's simply indescribable, and I hope and pray you never have to experience it for yourselves. There were bodies of Larion Senators at every turn, many apparently unharmed – except for an open wound on their wrists. I tried to comfort myself by saying over and over again, "They must be sleeping." Those who had put up a fight were torn to pieces. I spent an aven sorting through limbs, fingers and ears: I wanted every Larion to rest for eternity intact. The stone floor was coated in blood. Several times I found little more than a few pieces of a body – someone I had known that morning, a scholar or an educator: a colleague, a person, a *friend*.

'When I reached the balcony above the grand hall, I finally saw Pikan. She was resting her elbows on the ledge, gazing down into the darkness below. She had been hideously injured from the blast; through the half-light I could see part of her face had been torn away, leaving strands of her lovely flaxen hair falling over an open wound that stretched from her ear down to her chin. Her robes had been torn off in the explosion; all she wore now was a pair of short breeches: little enough to stave off the season's chill.

'When she turned to face me, I knew my suspicions had been well-founded. "Well, hello, Fantus," Pikan's body called to me in Nerak's voice. "Do you care to join us in here?" She reached up and began fondling her breasts, squeezing and pressing them together as a man might in the throes of passion. "It's cosy with just us two, but we'll make room for you." The voice was Pikan's now, but I knew she was gone. Nerak must have taken her an instant before she died in the tower. Now he held her by a thread, dangling her a breath away from eternal rest.

'I wiped the blood from my eyes as Pikan made her way slowly towards me. My grip tightened on the broadsword. For a moment I thought I might stand and fight.' Gilmour stared through the firelight into the darkness above the Estrad River for a moment. 'But I didn't. Fear overcame me and I fled like a child. I dropped the sword at Pikan's feet and ran the length of the balcony at a full sprint. As I came to the far end of the room, I screamed a spell to open the windows and when they flew out on their hinges, I dived out into the night without a moment's hesitation. The last thing I heard before I struck the ground was Nerak, laughing like a demon through Pikan's broken body.

'I shattered my shoulder and ankle in the fall, but that was just flesh and bone. My spirit took longer to recover. I have never lifted a weapon again, but I have spent the past nine hundred and eighty Twinmoons studying magic, just like Nerak.

'He must have taken Lessek's Key and the far portal that very night. He made his way south to Rona, killed Prince Markon and a number of other members of King Remond's royal family. Then I'm guessing he travelled to Colorado, where he hid the only weapon that can destroy him in your bank, Steven.

'I have waited half my life for Lessek's Key. Now it is within our grasp, and I will use it to destroy the force that murdered my friends and brought death and terror to Eldarn.' Gilmour took up his pipe after his long narration and smiled at his friends before moving off to his bedroll near the river. No one else said a word. There was too much to take in.

THE RONAN PIEDMONT

Next winter

Steven woke to cramp, and the sound of the river rolling by. He rolled over and, without thinking, checked his watch. It wasn't there. It took a few seconds for him to remember giving it to Garec two days earlier. He could see Mark, already up and kneeling at the water's edge. 'What time is it?' Steven called without moving.

'I don't know.' Mark splashed cool water on his face. 'The time here has my internal clock running like a drunk Pamplona tourist. The sun is up, so I guess it must be daytime.'

'Insightful of you,' Steven grunted as he sat up and rubbed his eyes. He looked around: Brynne was dousing the vestiges of the evening's fire with a pan of river water. Everyone else was missing. He pulled a clean tunic over his head and asked, 'Where did they go?'

'Good morning, Steven.' Brynne waved, moving towards him. 'They've gone to check traffic along the Merchants' Highway. It's not far from here; they're concerned there may be soldiers moving north to search for us.'

'Terrific. I was hoping we'd have another day of fleeing for our lives. I'm just beginning to get skilled at it.' He crawled to his feet and went to join Mark by the river.

'Oh, by the way,' Brynne called after him, 'it's still about two avens before midday.'

'Did you hear that?' he asked Mark. 'It's about seven o'clock.'

'First period is just about to start.' Mark stood up and used his T-shirt to dry his face. 'I bet my substitute is making a mess of the Industrial Revolution right now.'

'Don't feel bad about it,' Steven teased. 'With any luck we'll

254

have you home in time to teach your students about the Yalta Conference.'

'Grand.' Mark looked back towards the campsite. 'What's for breakfast?'

'I don't know,' Steven shook the excess water from his hands and stood beside his friend, 'but I can leave the two of you alone if you want to make your peace with Brynne.'

'I'm not sure she wants to,' Mark said, his face solemn. 'I think she's still angry that I tied her to a tree.'

'Wouldn't you be?'

'Good point,' he said as he slipped into his tunic and belted it around his waist. 'All right, here goes nothing.'

Steven watched as Mark wandered back to where Brynne was busying herself rolling blankets and packing supplies, then turned to the river. He reflected on Gilmour's fantastical tale of evil demons and homicidal magicians possessing Malakasian royalty. He didn't even *like* fantasy literature: he liked logic, things that made sense, not the utterly impossible. And this *was* impossible: here he was, standing by a river in a grove of trees so similar to dozens of rivers and groves he had visited over his lifetime, and yet he was in danger – the sort of danger he could not even have imagined a week ago.

He was facing a journey he might not survive: that fact was beginning to sink in, to become less an external reality rearing up periodically to frighten him and more an inherent part of who he was. *This* river was different. *This* river was haunted by the terror awaiting them in Malakasia.

Like the evening before, Steven began to feel a need to pack up and rush to Welstar Palace, to get there as quickly as he could. Kneeling once again, he took a long drink and splashed cold water over his head. 'We might not make it,' he repeated several times as the water ran across his down-turned face and dripped onto the smooth rocks below. Slowly, Steven began to get used to the idea.

Mark moved around Brynne's horse to help tie down her bedroll and saddlebags. 'I'm sorry I didn't trust you,' he said without warning, 'it's just that we weren't certain what was happening. We still aren't certain what's happening, but I know you want to help us.' He looked down at his feet before adding, 'I was afraid and I thought you might lead us into town to—'

'It's all right,' she interrupted, 'I was taking you to Greentree Tavern because I knew there would be soldiers around. I was hoping to lose you in the confusion.'

Mark laughed. 'So I was right.'

She smiled. ''Fraid so. I was planning an escape – but I was glad Sallax didn't kill you at Riverend. I still am.'

'So am I. It would've really put a damper on our relationship if your brother had shot me full of arrows or run me through with his rapier. I'm not certain I would ever have been able to build up the courage to ask you out after that.'

'Out?'

'Yes, out, on a date,' he tried to clarify.

'A date, like today or yesterday?' She seemed confused.

'No, not that kind of date!' He searched for the right words in Ronan.

'Mark, I would very much like to help you, but I don't understand what you're saying,' she said.

Finally, he caught a glimpse of her smile. 'You're toying with me, aren't you? You know exactly what I mean.'

'I might be, but it's always fun to watch you stumble over yourself,' she said and reached across the saddle to give him a playful shove.

Grabbing her hand, he said sarcastically, 'Oh, sure, mock the foreigner, why don't you.'

'Well, you did tie me to a tree.'

'And your brother tried to kill me with an axe. I'd say that makes us even, wouldn't you?' He held her hand for as long as he dared, then released it to secure an errant leather strap to her saddle.

'Even?'

'Oh, don't start that again.' Mark moved to collect his bedroll while Brynne stored the last hickory trenchers in her saddlebag. With his back turned, the young teacher did not see her watching him from the fire-pit. Kneeling near the log Mark had dragged from the forest as an impromptu sofa, Brynne played with his watchband, turning it slowly around her wrist. Then, smirking, she started preparing the remaining horses for the day's journey.

*

When the Ronans returned from the forest, it was obvious Gilmour and Sallax were engaged in an argument.

'I understand why you want to raid them, Sallax,' Gilmour said calmly, 'but we cannot afford to bring attention to ourselves. Who knows how many Malakasians are already tracking us north?'

'That's exactly my point.' Sallax was determined. 'We have no choice but to flee. Why not hit that caravan before they reach port? You know it's nothing more than yet another group of merchants and landowners buying peace from Malagon's generals.'

'That's true,' Gilmour conceded, 'but our mission now is clear. The days of raiding caravans are behind us.'

'Forgive me if I'm not as confident in your mystical solution to this very real problem. Raiding has worked for us for many Twinmoons, Gilmour, and a fat cat is lumbering by out there just waiting for us to play with it.'

'Now that's not exactly accurate, Sallax,' Gilmour countered. 'They are very well protected. We might lose people, or be slowed by injuries. It is too risky.'

'One strike,' Sallax mused aloud. 'What if we hit them with one quick strike, bows from above and a slash-and-burn attack at a full gallop? Who knows what damage we might do?'

'That might work, Gilmour,' Garec said. 'Versen and I can inflict a good deal of damage from the heights above the road.'

Versen agreed. 'That's true. We could certainly open a hole in their defenders' ranks.'

Mark leaned towards Brynne and whispered, 'What are they talking about?'

Leaning back into him, ostensibly to keep her voice low, she answered, 'For Twinmoons now, we have been raiding Ronan merchant caravans riding north to the Falkan border to meet with Malagon's occupation generals. They push their workers near death, pay them next to nothing in wages and hoard enormous sums of money.'

'They buy the right to be rich in a dictatorship,' Mark said. 'It's nice to see nothing's really different here.'

Brynne put one hand on Mark's shoulder and spoke directly into his ear. 'So, we hit the caravans. We take silver and weapons to help fund the Resistance.'

'That's what you were hiding at Riverend Palace.' Mark turned towards her, their faces only inches apart. 'But with Riverend's fall—'

'Everything we worked for is lost, and worse, the Malakasians now know Estrad Village was the centre of the Resistance.' She looked worried and Mark's heart broke for her. 'Who knows what horrors they'll commit while combing the village for us? They'll use it as an excuse – not that they need one – and I don't like thinking about it.'

Gilmour dismounted and ran one hand across his balding pate. 'You want to hit them?'

Garec, Sallax and Versen nodded, while Mika, less confidently, added, 'Yes.'

'All right, we'll hit them.' He walked to the edge of the river where Steven was standing listening to the earnest debate. 'You should stand behind me, Steven,' Gilmour said. Cupping his hands over his mouth, the old Larion Senator emitted a shrill cry into the forest on the opposite shore. It was pitched very high, almost beyond the range of their hearing, and Steven was glad he had moved back. As Gilmour's call sounded, Brynne immediately covered her ears and Garec let out a cry of pain and pushed his hands firmly against his temples. Mark's equilibrium was thrown off balance and he sat heavily to avoid falling down.

Sallax shook the dizziness from his head and asked, 'What in a thousand Twinmoons of pestilence was that?'

The old man smiled and reached into his tunic for a pipe. He filled the small bowl and gripped it firmly between his teeth before answering, 'You said you wanted to hit them. We just made arrangements to hit them.'

Versen was confused. 'How? What did you do?'

'I called the grettans.' Gilmour exhaled a cloud of blue smoke that loitered around his head before dissipating. 'We ought to move along right away. Once they get here, I'm not certain I will be able to control them.' He pursed his lips and prepared to remount his horse.

Versen looked shocked. Mika wiped several beads of sweat from his forehead.

'Riverend,' Garec pointed accusingly. 'I saw you from the palace. You called those grettans in to attack the Malakasian horses.'

'Of course I did,' he answered, as if it had been obvious all along. 'I couldn't have you all taken prisoner or killed. We have a great deal of work to do and I need you.'

Garec pursued the issue further. 'Did you call them all the way down from Gorsk? What are they doing this far south? The rutting bastards almost had my hide for breakfast in the forbidden forest.'

'I think that was Malagon, or I suppose I should say Nerak. I would guess he sent those grettans down here to kill me—' he paused for a moment before adding, '—or perhaps each of you.'

Versen swallowed awkwardly. Mika looked as though he might fall from the saddle. Gilmour patted the youngest Ronan gently on the knee. 'Malagon doesn't realise I can communicate with these grettans as well.'

'Communicate?' Brynne asked.

'Yes, I can call them around, or suggest they move off somewhere else – they can understand that much. But I can't keep them from attacking us if they arrive while we're still here jabbering on about them.' He motioned for Mark and Steven to mount up.

Garec stared at Gilmour with mixed admiration and amazement. 'So, it's true.'

'What's true?' The older man was impatient to get the group moving again.

'You really are a magician.' Garec searched for the words. 'It was all true, everything you said last night.'

'Of course it's true. Did you think I was making it up?' he answered with feigned indignity. 'Come now, we must hurry.' Before riding into the forest, Gilmour turned to Sallax and added, 'The grettans will hit the caravan. I imagine they'll hit it hard, rout the wagons and ensure that silver never reaches port.'

Sallax nodded grimly in response.

They rode through the day, always north, and Steven soon noticed a change in the landscape. Hardwoods gave way to evergreens and the rustle of leaves under foot quieted into a soft carpet of fallen pine needles. The climb in elevation was gradual, nearly undetectable, but by the end of the day they had reached the southern slope of what appeared to be a range of more substantial foothills that spread far into the distance as misty indigo swells along the horizon. From time to time the group came within sight of the Estrad River; the once-deep current had narrowed to a fast-moving stream.

Versen led the way, accompanied by Mika, who was eager to learn everything the more experienced woodsman could teach him. Steven could understand why Mika was so impressed with Versen: his knowledge of the forest seemed second to none.

Steven rode between Garec and Gilmour and the trio spent much of their time talking. Garec, always alert with his bow, felled several rabbits and a pheasant along the way; the small band would eat well again this evening.

As the new friends exchanged questions and answers about their different lands, Gilmour would periodically chime in with an explanation of Pragan, Falkan, or even Malakasian culture. Garec was astounded at the level of technology in Steven's world; the young banker's description of air travel, medicine and warfare had him transfixed. Steven was equally impressed by the complacency about magic that permeated the Eldarni populace. Garec talked about magical incidents, places and historic events as if they were as common as a spring thundershower.

Gilmour's questions related to the history of various nations on Earth; Steven had to keep reminding himself that the venerable Larion Senator had been there to see much of it unfold. He was most interested in the American Civil War, and spoke in fascinating detail about troop movements and political decisions Steven had never known about. He rattled on at great length about the carnage at Sharpsburg, the accuracy of artillery fire on Henry Hill at Bull Run and the esoteric eating habits of General Lee.

'I do wish I could have stayed on to observe the end of the war and the reconstruction that followed, but regrettably, my knowledge and leadership were sorely needed in Eldarn,' Gilmour confided wistfully.

When he heard that President Lincoln had been killed before the Confederate surrender, his mood turned dark. He told Steven he was certain John Wilkes Booth had no sense of fairness and ran one hand thoughtfully through his whiskers before adding, 'If they were going to kill him, they ought to have waited until after the war.'

Steven had taken a Civil War course as an undergraduate and

promised to retrieve all his textbooks from a cardboard box in his basement if Gilmour could spare a few moments while in Idaho Springs. He thought the old man was going to actually kiss him, but Gilmour contented himself with slapping Steven hard across the back and shouting, 'Outstanding! It's a nine-hundred-Twin-moon-old novel I will finally get to finish.'

While Steven was trawling his memory for any Civil War trivia that might amuse his companions, Mark and Brynne were getting to know each other too. They rode together all day; occasionally Sallax would cast them a disapproving look. The Ronan partisan was slow to trust anyone, and he was still uncertain about Steven and Mark: were they truly refugees from another world? He had forced himself to believe Gilmour, so for the moment he decided to keep his doubts to himself.

Brynne had obviously put aside her fury at being carted round as a hostage and tied to a tree. The friendly banter she and Mark were exchanging had Brynne blushing and Mark grinning like an adolescent about to steal his first kiss. Sallax cringed each time his sister reached across to touch Mark's hand or to give his arm an amiable punch, even though he thought he respected the foreigner: at least he had shown a willingness to fight, a tough resilience in the face of danger. He appeared to be extremely bright, and skilled at solving problems under pressure. Sallax supposed Mark *might* be his choice for Brynne – *if* he knew the two strangers could be trusted. Until that moment, though, he would look with caution on his sister's new suitor.

They made camp that evening in the Blackstone foothills. Versen said the bulk of the great range was several days' ride north and west; they would turn west in the morning, leaving the river and the Merchants' Highway behind. Although there were a number of passes between the tallest peaks in the Blackstone range, the most commonly accessed trails would be patrolled, perhaps even guarded, by Malakasian sentries. If word of their flight had reached the northern border patrols, no passage through the mountains would be unwatched by occupation forces.

Versen was confident that their only safe route lay to the west, over uncharted peaks and through unmapped passes. Both Garec and Sallax were loud in their dismay at the prospect of navigating a new trail north this late in the season. The potential for bone-chilling cold and deep snow grew with each passing day, and none of the travellers knew enough about the northern slopes to speculate what lay beyond the westernmost peaks.

Gilmour tried to reassure them, telling them their turn to the west was necessary for another reason. 'We must get to Seer's Peak,' he said that evening as they sat around the fire-pit. 'I must try to contact Lessek before we set sail for Malakasia.'

'Lessek, the founder of the Larion Senate?' Garec asked.

'That's right. He sometimes visits me when I pass within the shadow of Seer's Peak.' Gilmour sucked the last bits of meat from a pheasant leg and tossed the bone casually into the fire. 'Although this will be the first time I have ever tried to contact him. Usually he comes to me without warning.'

'Can you do it?' Mika asked, amazed that anyone could be able to summon a spirit.

'I don't know, Mika,' Gilmour said honestly, 'but I have to try.' And, in an offhanded way that surprised everyone around the fire, he added, 'So must Garec and Steven as well.'

Steven sat bolt upright. 'Why?' He looked around the fire hoping for an ally. 'What could he possibly tell me? I'm not Eldarni.'

'No, but you have brought Lessek's Key back to Eldarn,' Gilmour explained. 'Your role in this endeavour may be more important than you think.'

'I didn't, though. I mean, it's still there on my desk. I didn't bring it anywhere.' Steven tried to talk his way out of meeting with the long-dead ghost of the world's most powerful magician. 'I just stole it from— well, found it, really, at the bank.'

'Without you, Steven, it would not now be within our reach.' Gilmour glanced at Mark before continuing, 'Lessek may expect more from you than you can imagine, perhaps from Mark as well.'

'And why me?' Garec asked quietly.

'That will become clear in time, my friend,' Gilmour answered. 'But I know Lessek will wish to speak with you.'

Versen was sharpening a small axe against a whetstone. Slowing the rhythmic pattern, he commented, 'You make it sound as though Lessek can control what will happen to us. Is that true?'

'No,' Gilmour answered. 'I don't believe he can have an impact on anything directly, at least, he hasn't in a long time, which is why we must go to him and hope he communicates with us.' The old man leaned forward and warmed his hands near the flames. The firelight danced off his bald forehead; it looked as though a small, flesh-coloured moon had risen over their camp. 'Lessek has an important vantage point from which to observe the goings-on here in Eldarn, a view from the balcony, if you will. He has access to histories and ideas we cannot understand, and his insights are critical to our success. He may disclose much, or he may not come to us at all, but we must endeavour to tap that resource before making plans for our assault on Welstar Palace.'

'Welstar Palace,' Steven said, 'Nerak's stronghold.'

'Malagon's,' Garec corrected.

'What *do* we call him, Gilmour – or should he be *it*?' Mark was looking a little confused.

'Nerak and Malagon: right now, they're essentially interchangeable,' Gilmour said.

'Great,' Mark grinned, 'so we'll agree on *shithead*, shall we?'

'Works for me,' Steven agreed.

'I'm not sure what a *shithead* is,' Brynne pronounced the English word awkwardly, 'but there are more important things to worry about right now.' She turned to Versen. 'How far is it to Seer's Peak?'

'I don't know,' the tall woodsman answered. 'I've never been there myself. We have about three days of rolling foothills to traverse before we come in view of the Blackstones.'

'That's correct,' Gilmour confirmed, 'and making good time, we will clear the range and be on the down slope into Falkan before winter hits with all her fury. But now my friends, let's get to bed. We have far to travel tomorrow.' He dropped several small logs on the fire before announcing, 'I will take the first watch tonight. Mika, I will wake you in an aven.'

Late that night, Steven stirred in his sleep. He rolled over and pulled his blanket tight around his shoulders, trapping a loose corner between his knees. Still half-asleep, he hoped being bound as tightly as possible, with nothing exposed to the night air, would help warm the relatively small spaces between the contours of his body and the unruly wool blanket. Adjusting his position on the uneven ground, Steven knocked his jacket off the stone he had been using for a pillow. The cold rock against his face slapped him fully awake.

The night was silent, and except for a dull glow from the last embers in the fire-pit, he could see nothing. Nearby, Mark's even breathing lent a stately rhythm to the darkness. Slowly Steven's eyes grew accustomed to the night. Versen stood watch near the fire, sitting up with his back propped against a large stone, but Steven could see the woodsman's head had fallen forward on his chest. He slept soundly.

Footsteps . . . coming through the forest behind him, Steven could tell that whoever approached was trying to come unnoticed. He thought about crying out, but he was afraid an arrow hurtling unseen through the Ronan darkness would silence him for ever. His stomach tightened in fear and, almost without thinking, he curled his legs up under him, preparing to leap to safety. He reached for the hunting knife still secure in his belt but it was awkward in his hand; he knew he would be ineffective against any would-be attacker. Without breathing, he craned his neck to peer across their camp.

The footsteps were closer now, just beyond the rock where Versen slept. Straining his eyes, Steven saw a bulky form emerge from the darkness, stow something in a saddlebag, pull back the blanket of an abandoned bedroll and lie down in the fire's dying light. It was Sallax.

Steven breathed easier, assuming the big man had sneaked away to relieve himself outside the periphery of their camp. Half-awake, he didn't think to wonder what Sallax had placed in his saddlebag. Soon sleep reclaimed Steven for the night.

For the next three days, the company made their way further into the Blackstone foothills. Scrub oak and evergreen trees grew in abundance; Steven noticed that with the ever-increasing altitude, the hardwoods that had been common in Rona's southern region were scarce. The scrub oaks were clumsy trees, growing close to the ground in a confusion of twisted branches and oddly placed leaves.

The temperature had dropped significantly as well and for the first time since their arrival, Steven was glad he had worn a tweed jacket to the bank that Thursday. The coat fit tightly over his Ronan tunic, giving him an ungainly appearance, but he didn't care about Mark's ribbing that he looked like a university professor visiting a Renaissance festival: it kept him warm.

Though chilly, the weather was clear, and periodically there was a break in the trees that allowed them to see far into the distance. It was late on their third day in the foothills when Versen pointed towards the horizon and, squinting into the slowly setting sun, they could finally make out the distant peaks of the Blackstone Mountains. *Ominous, even from this distance*, Steven thought. He felt a sinking feeling in his stomach.

The Blackstones were much taller than the Rocky Mountains surrounding his home, and their jagged ridges and deep valleys promised a hard, treacherous journey ahead. Steven loved looking up at the Rockies from the Colorado prairie: you could see the Front Range stretching from north to south in a picturesque combination of green foothills, red stone cliffs and snowy granite peaks. For anyone driving west, the Rockies were a welcome sight, a majestic end to a long journey across the endless flat fields of wheat and corn. Steven cherished that view; he could never tire of looking at the mountains back home.

But the Blackstones were different. Nothing about them made Steven feel welcome. They rose from the foothills at a steep angle, as if the gods themselves had thrown up a sheer granite wall to keep travellers out of Falkan.

'Have you ever been through this way?' Mark asked Versen, who was still peering into the distance.

'No,' he answered, 'I've crossed over the eastern peaks, but never this far west. These mountains are very different to those out near the Merchants' Highway.' He looked at Gilmour as he added, 'This isn't going to be easy.'

'Which one is Seer's Peak?' Steven asked, still shielding his eyes against the setting sun.

Versen shrugged. All eyes turned to Gilmour who pointed towards the tallest mountain in the range. 'You see that tall peak there in the middle?'

'Is that it?' Mark asked, 'the big one with glacier snow on top?'

'No,' he said, 'instead, look immediately east of there. It's difficult to see, because it's not a very tall peak, but if you look really hard you can spot it. It's a much shorter mountain, with a long narrow ridge opening out onto a nearly flat surface at its west end.'

'I see it,' Brynne exclaimed. 'It doesn't look like much, Gilmour.'

'I suppose it doesn't,' he answered, 'but there is something powerful about it, something that makes it possible for Lessek to visit us in that place.'

Sallax, as ever, was all business. 'Well, let's get there. We still have a good half-aven of light left. We might be able to clear the next hill if we push on now.'

Without answering, Versen spurred his horse forward and led them down the north slope of the hill, picking his way through the trees, careful in the fading daylight.

Near the bottom of the shallow valley, the woodsman noticed what looked like a game trail winding around the base of the next foothill. Turning in the saddle, he called to Sallax, 'We ought to follow this. It may lead to fresh water.'

'I don't like the idea of being on trails,' Sallax said tersely.

'There are no signs that any riders have been through here in a long time,' Versen countered. 'I think we'll be fine.'

'All right, let's keep moving,' Sallax agreed grudgingly, adding, 'Garec, stay alert through here, we might find something for dinner.'

As the sun's last rays gleamed through the evergreen boughs high above, Garec imagined the forest atop the hill in flames. For a moment he felt unaccountably glad that Versen had elected to seek refuge here on the sheltered valley floor. Turning his eyes from the luminous orange rays he allowed them to readjust in the semi-darkness, then began scanning the forest for wildlife: rabbits, game birds, there might even be deer. The quiet rhythm of the horses' hooves on the pine needle carpet was the only sound he could hear. Hunting in a pine glade was more challenging; with no telltale autumn leaves on the ground his quarry were able to move about in near-silence. He tuned his ears to the forest.

Then he heard it: a faint rustle. Craning his neck to pinpoint its direction, he heard it again: scratching, like the sound of a boot crushing a few shards of broken glass. Garec didn't recognise the sound; he thought it strange any animal would make such a noise, calling attention to itself and then moving again before freezing to scan for predators.

Garec suddenly realised what he'd heard, just an instant later, but it was already too late. Before he could cry out, a group of Malakasian soldiers attacked from the underbrush, coming all at once in a howling blur from all sides. They were taken entirely by surprise.

Strangely, the attackers did not strike at them with weapons; instead, they pulled the riders from their mounts and grappled furiously with them on the ground.

Having a heartbeat's warning gave Garec time enough to draw and fire at point-blank range into a charging soldier's chest. The man had no shield and Garec's arrow killed him almost instantly. Not slowing for a moment, the bowman nocked another shaft and felled a second warrior who had Mika pinned beneath his horse. He was beating Mika's face with his fists, and the arrow took him in the neck, showering the youngest partisan in blood.

These were not normal soldiers; there was something different about them, something dark, almost apelike. Garec wished in vain for more light as he released a third shaft into the ribs of yet another of the curious assailants; in spite of the rapidly increasing gloom of twilight, the arrow found its mark. The Ronan bowman was reaching into his quiver again when strong leathery hands finally pulled him to the ground.

As the attack started, Steven watched dumbstruck as Garec felled several enemy soldiers with lightning-fast bow-fire. A moment later, two of the warriors burst from the underbrush and wrestled the Ronan from his horse. Garec blindly fought to ward them off as they clawed at his face. In the distance Mark struggled to pull one of the attackers away from Brynne as Versen and Sallax hacked at their assailants with battle-axes. Mika lay still beneath his horse. The scene was surreal.

Through his fear, Steven felt time begin to slow. He and Gilmour were the only members of their party not yet fighting; it looked to him as if they had been spared, maybe because they had been riding at the end of the line. He remembered the feel of cool water cascading across the back of his neck and his own words, repeated over and over: 'We might not make it.'

In slow motion he dismounted, stooped for a moment to pick up a length of hickory from beside the trail. *We might not make it.* A Malakasian soldier emerged from a thicket to his right and with effortless grace, Steven turned, bringing the staff around violently in a deadly arc that crushed the unsuspecting soldier's skull. The man's face was animal-like; he had a wild look, almost brutal.

Steven paid him no more heed and moved instead to where Garec lay, still fighting to free himself from the two soldiers ripping at his flesh with clawed fingers. *We might not make it.* Steven released his anger in a crushing blow that took one soldier under the chin and broke his neck cleanly. Thrown backwards into the brush along the trail, the Malakasian's body continued to twitch reflexively as Garec's second attacker turned his attention to Steven. Seeing the now-bloody hickory shaft, he tried to tear it from Steven's hands.

'We might not make it,' Steven heard himself cry, and then laughed inanely as he punched the Malakasian hard across the face. The soldier lost his footing and Steven brought the wooden staff down across the outside of his knee, shattering it beneath him. The warrior screamed, it sounded like an ancient, primaeval curse, and flailed wildly as he fell to the ground.

Steven ignored him and moved to help Mark and Brynne. Mark was fighting to escape from the iron grip of a brutal soldier pounding away at him with sledge-like fists and granite elbows. Moving with mercurial quickness, Brynne ducked and closed in on the enemy soldier. Her short blade in one hand, she spun, took a glancing blow on the side of her face and rammed her knife to the hilt in the big soldier's chest. She gave a guttural shout of satisfaction when the blade broke through the sinewy muscles above the Malakasian's breastbone.

Steven made his way around the injured soldier and took aim. Swinging like a lumberjack felling an ancient redwood, he splintered the hickory staff against the small of the enemy's back, breaking his spine. The man collapsed like a pricked balloon.

Brynne helped Mark to his feet and the couple scurried away from the now disabled but still vicious Malakasian. 'Steven, get back!' Mark shouted when he saw his roommate standing over their fallen attacker.

'We might not make it,' Steven cried in a voice that sent chills along Mark's spine. And he watched in terror as his best friend raised a short, jagged piece of hickory and drove it deep into the soldier's neck, killing him.

Steven, sprayed with the explosion of blood from the soldier's carotid artery, fell to his knees and began to sob. The world caught up with him: now time moved at breakneck speed. He felt alone, terrified, and certain he would die in this strange land.

Mark wrapped an arm around his friend's shoulder and led him away from the bloody aftermath of the fight.

'We might not make it,' Steven cried against Mark's chest.

Versen and Sallax had dispatched their assailants in a flurry of deadly axe blows; now they moved towards Gilmour, who was sitting in the mud beneath Mika's horse, cradling the young man's head in his lap. Mika was dead. His head had struck a rock when the Malakasian wrenched him from the saddle. He died as the soldier battered his already fractured skull. Over the din of Steven's sobs, and the raging screams of the injured soldier dragging his ruined knee through the forest underbrush, Sallax heard Gilmour say quietly, 'He was just a boy.'

When she saw Mika's broken form lying still in Gilmour's lap, Brynne began to cry. Versen, white, brushed a hand over his eyes, trying not to give way to emotion, and Garec too fought back tears as he held a patch of cloth against a large gash across his forehead.

Then Gilmour's face changed. Shock and sadness were wiped clean, to be replaced with cold, calculating rage. Gently he rested Mika's head on the ground, where it lolled awkwardly to one side. He rose to face the last surviving soldier, still doggedly dragging himself to freedom despite his shattered knee. The Malakasian grunted malevolently and spat at Gilmour as the Larion Senator glared back at him.

'Our time draws near, Nerak,' he said almost to himself as he raised one hand above his head. 'I am coming.'

With inhuman speed, Gilmour brought his arm forward in a crooked, throwing motion, releasing the full force of his anger in a focused magical stroke. As he did so, the Malakasian was lifted from the ground and thrown several paces back into the underbrush. It looked as if he had been hit in the chest with an invisible boulder, a shattering blow that audibly broke bones and punctured organs. There was no need for anyone to confirm that the last of the attack party was dead.

Without speaking, Gilmour moved to the soldier Steven had killed with the broken branch and withdrew the short length of splintered hickory from the dead man's neck. More blood ran from the wound; Mark wondered briefly how that could be possible since the man's heart had stopped beating. He was distracted by Gilmour stepping over the body to retrieve the shattered pieces of the rough staff Steven had used to fight off the Malakasians. Turning to face the forest, the old man fit the shaft together piece by piece until each section was back in its original place. His hands glowed a warm red in the dim light of early evening as he ran them along the length of wood, magically reshaping the hickory staff.

When he had finished, the Larion sorcerer recited a barely audible spell. The glow from his palms grew bright for an instant, then faded to match the surrounding darkness.

Steven had calmed down somewhat; like the others, he was watching the old man with great curiosity. Gilmour handed the remade hickory bough to him and said, 'Take this. You wield it well.'

Steven felt his breath catch in his throat. 'I killed people today. I don't know if I can—'

'You must.' Gilmour's look was one of warmth and genuine compassion. 'We would have lost Garec, Mark and Brynne as well as Mika if you hadn't intervened.' Again, he pushed the staff to the younger man. 'Take it.'

Steven found himself accepting the weapon. It felt strange in his hands: just a bulky length of wood. He hoped he would never have to use it again. Near the top, where Gilmour had magically melded the shattered pieces together, the grain was stained with blood from the soldier he had killed.

Not killed, Steven mentally corrected himself, *murdered. You murdered an incapacitated soldier.* He stared hard at the bloodstains left by the dying man. The dark rivers of colour had soaked into the grain pattern like a work of abstract art. Steven was afraid to touch it. He feared it might sear an indelible brand on his soul, mark him as a murderer for all time. He knew he would carry this burden with him back to Idaho Springs, and even there, home, surrounded by everyone he loved, he would for ever be a murderer.

Garec broke the silence. 'What were they?' He hooked the toe of his boot under one dead body and rolled it over. 'They look human, but they're not. They fought like animals, scratching and biting.'

'They *are* human, or I should say, they *used* to be human,'

Gilmour said grimly. 'They are called Seron. I have not seen one in more than five hundred Twinmoons.'

'Where do they come from?' Brynne asked as she helped Mark dress Garec's head wound.

'They are the product of a sickening process Nerak employs. He tears the souls from the bravest soldiers, those most skilled in combat, and replaces them with the souls of rabid, furious animals – wild dogs, or even grettans. He breeds them for several generations, all the while torturing them to foster intense hatred for mankind. He trains them to become fearless assassins, his personal pack of ravening wolves.'

Gilmour started to gather up fallen pine boughs and stacked them neatly in a small clearing near the trail. 'He can command large numbers of Seron from afar,' he went on. 'They always fight to the death, but they rarely use weapons. Like animals, they use surprise and ferocity to overwhelm their opponents. They'll often eat the remains of their enemies – whether they're dead or not.

'I think Nerak is sensing our coming conflict, because he hasn't dispatched Seron warriors in hundreds of Twinmoons.'

Steven, feeling a growing pain in the pit of his stomach, asked, 'Why were we not attacked?'

'Who?' Mark asked.

'Gilmour and me,' he said, 'we weren't attacked. At least, I wasn't attacked until I made a move to help Garec. I wonder why.'

'Because they need you, Steven.' Gilmour had filled his pipe and was now smoking contentedly. 'You arrived in Eldarn via the far portal Nerak hid in your bank. I imagine he thinks you have Lessek's Key.'

'But you said he would just go there and find out where the key is hidden by taking over the minds of my family and friends,' Steven said bitterly.

'That's true, he can, but if he has you, Nerak doesn't need anyone else. You or Mark can tell him everything he needs to retrieve the key to the spell table.'

Versen chimed in, 'So why weren't you attacked, Gilmour?'

'I think someone else out there wants to kill me himself.'

'Nerak?' Brynne asked, suddenly fearful.

'No, I would sense Nerak coming,' Gilmour assured her, handing a bandage strip to Sallax who was dressing an injury on his forearm. 'This is someone else, a cunning someone who has been tracking us since we left Estrad Village. The Seron who came for us tonight were created and sent here by Nerak, but tonight they were obeying that someone's orders.'

'Should we push ahead then?' Versen asked, hoping they could move beyond their vulnerable position in the ravine.

'Yes,' Sallax suggested quietly.

'I don't think so,' Gilmour interrupted. 'We must give Mika his rites, and we should burn these Seron bodies as well.'

He glanced about the clearing again, almost sniffing the air to detect threat. Sensing nothing, he returned to his work collecting pine boughs for Mika's funeral pyre. 'We'll see no more trouble tonight.'

Jacrys Marseth murmured a string of curses into his fist as he watched Gilmour destroy the last of his Seron warriors. Although he was certain the old man's magic was focused entirely on killing the injured soldier, the spy felt a curious energy ripple through the forest and up the hillside where he lay hidden. The attack had failed miserably: only one of the pathetic 'freedom fighters' lay dead. Communicating with the filthy and unpredictable Seron was an unappetising task, and watching them fail to dispatch the Ronans threw him into a brooding rage.

He had planned to kill Gilmour himself, to take the old man while he grieved for his fallen comrades, but now that pleasure would have to wait. His teeth clenched tightly together, Jacrys fought the urge to charge down the wooded slope and run the old man through with his rapier.

A throbbing pain began in his temples, spread across his forehead and lanced down the back of his neck. He had been tracking Gilmour since the attack on Riverend Palace and the constant vigilance and pursuit had left him on edge. He was hungry and tired, and furious that his carefully orchestrated ambush had gone so awry.

Jacrys breathed deeply and rubbed his temples vigorously in an effort to calm himself down. Meticulous planning, a level head and a ruthless nature had always been his most effective weapons. He could not afford to fly into an uncontrolled rage this close to such a dangerous target.

He fastidiously pulled evergreen needles from his tunic as he watched Gilmour gather boughs for the dead man's funeral rites. Malagon would sense the magician's continued presence in the Blackstones; he would know Jacrys had been unsuccessful in this assassination attempt. His life would be worthless if he did not see the job finished before Gilmour arrived at Welstar Palace. Malagon would certainly send more Seron, and perhaps another herd of grettans. The almor continued their hunt, but he had no idea where the closest demons were now.

He bit off an obscenity. Swearing wouldn't help now. If he failed to get ahead of the travellers once again, he might be forced to make his way into their camp and kill the old Larion Senator in a more traditional fashion.

Jacrys turned his attention back to the band of partisans. From this distance they looked battered and bleeding, ragged and worn threadbare, like a handful of third-generation dolls. Only the pale stranger had a sense of strength about him. It was difficult to see, because the foreigner knelt weeping near the trail. But he had fought bravely, an unexpectedly deadly foe, especially as he was armed only with a length of wood he had picked up off the ground.

Jacrys was rarely surprised by the actions of his enemies. This one surprised him. For some reason, Malagon wanted him and the South Coaster alive, transported to Welstar for torture and interrogation. Jacrys had no idea why they were so important, but he silently promised he would discover more about the foreigners before he brought them to Malakasia.

Wiping his palms dry on the front of his tunic, he moved slowly up the hillside and out of sight.

Later that night, Brexan struggled to locate a trail in the darkness. Straining her eyes in an effort to pick out overturned or disturbed ground, she considered giving up until dawn. A light breeze blew down from the north. She took a moment's respite, turned her face into the fresh air and inhaled deeply. Flesh. Somewhere beyond the next ridge, someone was incinerating bodies. Resolutely, Brexan turned her horse towards the sickeningly sweet aroma. Certain Jacrys was somehow responsible for the lingering smell of death above the foothills, she spurred her mount into a brisk canter.

BRANAG OTHARO'S
LEATHER GOODS AND
SADDLERY EMPORIUM

In the days since her arrival in Praga, Hannah Sorenson had seen nothing of Southport; except for a few nervous glances around as Hoyt and Churn led her hastily to Branag Otharo's Leather Goods and Saddlery Emporium, she had no idea what Southport was like. She had seen the harbour from the hilltop where she spent her first night, but since then she had been sequestered in the storage area at Branag's. Her deadly dull routine was occasionally enlivened by having to duck inside a hidden antechamber tucked artfully between the saddler's workshop and the cold room adjacent to the Seaweed Inn, a tavern catering for the more reprehensible of Southport's wharf rats, sailors and dockside whores. Those were the worst moments: Hannah nearly gagged every time Branag or Hoyt adjusted the replaceable planks to create a space for them to crawl inside. Hannah was becoming increasingly certain nothing but rancid meat and spoiled beer were ever served at the Seaweed, and that every single patron in the dilapidated waterfront structure chain-smoked something Hoyt called fennaroot; in an effort not to breath in the foul stench she kept her face pressed against the ancient boards forming the back wall of Branag's storage room. From that position, she could at least imagine the tangy aroma of tanned leather and heavy polish breaking through the miasma.

The drill was always the same. A riotous clamour would begin at the far end of Branag's narrow street whenever a Malakasian patrol was conducting a house-to-house search for the fugitives who had allegedly murdered five – or perhaps even seven – soldiers in a surprise attack outside the city. With each search the brutality worsened as the number of supposed Malakasian casualties grew. On their first night in Southport, a squad of black-clad soldiers burst through the entrance of Branag's store looking for the murderers who *might* have killed one soldier somewhere along the coastal highway east of town. They were especially interested in finding a young woman dressed in odd, brightly coloured clothing, wearing white cloth slippers and heavy breeches.

Several days later, the number of Malakasian dead had increased, as had the fugitive band of killers, now a veritable brigade of well-armed, half-crazed homicidal monsters who at any moment might turn against the peaceful citizens of Southport.

The din was a reaction, people crying out, shouting for family members, children, even pets to come inside, but in actuality, the noise was nothing more than a warning that the patrol was coming. Anyone who needed to be hidden had better get hidden quickly, to ensure the Malakasian scrutiny passed harmlessly over the otherwise quiet street.

Branag's response was always the same as well. Hustling back into the storage area, he whistled a quick warning to Hoyt, who in turn scurried behind the rows of tanned cowhides dangling loosely from the ceiling like macabre curtains to pry open two planks leading to the hidden chamber. Once inside, the trio would sit absolutely still, saying nothing, avoiding positions that forced them to shift their legs or arms, and counting the moments until the platoon moved on to the next block. Hannah would bury her face in her hands and listen to the shuffle and scuff of heavy Malakasian boots as they made their way through Branag's building. She would try to slide deeper into the shadows, shrinking and folding her thoughts down into the darkest parts of her mind, sitting stone-like, somehow closer to death every time those boots stopped shuffling about. Had they seen something? Did they notice a plank askew? Had one of them finally seen that this building was slightly narrower inside than out? There would be no escape; they were trapped in a closet.

But the soldiers never came. They never noticed. With their departure each time, Hannah would slowly raise her head and bright fireworks of yellow and white light would dance about where she had pressed her eyes too tightly against the hard surface of her knees.

The first night in Southport, Hoyt insisted they remain in the foetid chamber as random searches continued until dawn. Teams of soldiers burst in and tossed saddles, leather harnesses, belts, half-finished boots and even untreated hides aside in hopes of turning up evidence that the saddler was harbouring criminals. That night had been the worst of Hannah's life. After a while Hoyt, sensing her burgeoning anxiety, lit a thin paraffin taper to bring the tiniest, muted half-light to the foul closet. In the candlelight, Hannah saw weapons, hundreds of primitive axes, swords, daggers and bows, hanging from hooks and wires along the narrow interior of the hidden chamber. Behind her were five bloated hemp bags; one, slightly open, revealed thousands of silver coins.

At that moment Hannah realised she had been rescued by two members of some kind of organised militia. If she were found in this place, with this cache of weapons and money, she would most likely be interrogated, tortured and killed. Wrapping her arms tightly about herself, she tried not to think about how they might try to extract information – information she didn't have and couldn't give them. 'Steven,' she whispered, too low even for Hoyt to hear, 'where are you, Steven?'

When not huddled together and holding their collective breath in Branag's secret hidey-hole, Hannah, Hoyt and Churn were confined to the storage room. While the two men planned their trip to a town called Middle Fork, they passed the time working on some of Branag's leather creations. Hannah, bored, discovered she was quite skilled at polishing and buffing saddles to a mirror shine; she beamed when the saddler complimented her work. Branag managed to spirit them food and beer in wooden crates draped with untreated hides or leather goods in need of repair. He was renowned locally for his titanic appetite, and did not think occupation soldiers were scrutinising his behaviour so closely that he would be questioned for having an abundance of food on the premises – but he had learned never to take risks. Preserving his anonymity while protecting the weapons and silver stashed behind his store was of paramount importance, so all their food tasted faintly of leather.

In spite of that, Hannah found the food acceptable. Some of it was delicious, though she elected to pass on a few items: some were unidentifiable, others frankly so disgusting she couldn't manage, even for politeness, to force herself to eat the gristly morsels. Her jacket and sweater were traded for a wool tunic with a leather belt and, despite her pleas, Hoyt demanded she give up her trainers and blue jeans for sturdy homespun leggings and a pair of newly sewn boots – at least they were Branag's finest.

Churn cut her hair. Motioning for her to turn around and sit on a short stool, he used a pair of Branag's sharpest shears to slice off the flaxen tresses. After six or seven deft snips, any evidence that Hannah's hair had ever reached below her shoulders rested now in a clump at Churn's feet. He whistled for Branag, who must have known Hannah's impromptu shearing was on the agenda because he came into the storage room stirring a palm-sized ceramic bowl with a fine horsehair brush. A heavy-bodied dog, a wolfhound, Hannah guessed, padded along beside him.

'This won't be permanent,' Branag told his apprehensive customer. 'It's a mixture of berries, tree bark and thin sap, all boiled down with fish oil to make it smooth.'

'Lovely.' Hannah looked around the room for the most appropriate corner in which to wretch. 'Uh . . . what colour are you— Well, not to be picky, but what colour—'

'Light blue.' Branag's face was stone, the dog at his side, silent. Hannah blanched. 'How about if we look into a hat or something?'

The big Pragan's icy countenance broke and his bright smile warmed the room. 'Brown, Hannah Sorenson. I thought we would dye it a darker shade of brown.'

Hannah sighed with relief. 'Oh, well, brown shouldn't be—' She craned her neck to get a view inside the bowl; for a moment she'd worried that Churn might forcibly hold her down while Branag painted the top of her head the colour of a cloudless summer sky. The leather craftsman tilted the mixture towards her and Hannah calmed noticeably when she saw the grim-smelling amalgamation. It smelled like a fisherman's socks, but at least the colour would pass.

When they were through, Hannah's face wrinkled into a grimace she feared she might wear for the rest of her life. 'How long will it smell like this?' Even Branag's wolfhound had moved to the other side of the room, his nose buried beneath two enormous paws.

'Not long,' Hoyt assured her, 'eight or nine days at the most.'

She laughed and slugged him hard in the shoulder. 'Well, I won't need to worry about them finding me in that closet. They'll get within two or three steps of the door and decide something hideous must have died in there.'

Periodically, Hoyt and Churn ventured out separately to check on the disposition of the Southport citizens. Branag had told them several young men had been accused and hanged for the soldier's murder and Hoyt had to fight the urge to summarily strangle every occupation soldier who happened by. Neither he nor Churn had ever had an innocent bystander punished for their efforts before, and he didn't like it.

'We will make them pay for this,' he promised under his breath. Hannah detected a different side of the otherwise cheerful young man, a sinister side normally veiled from view by his carefree demeanour. She made note of it, and vowed to be out of the Pragan healer's reach if he got angry again.

During the next couple of days Hannah marvelled at how Hoyt could change his appearance without apparently trying. A sunken chest, a dropped shoulder, or a protruding stomach: Hannah was startled at the difference such simple changes made. He would leave the store a different person altogether.

When Hoyt returned, he and Branag would speak in hushed tones while signing for Churn. She was sure they were planning something, some retaliation for the innocent lives lost; she was almost glad the trio was keeping her out of the discussion. But as much as Hannah worried their plans might bring her into harm's way, she did not want to flee and turn herself over to the Malakasians. The only occupation soldiers she had met had been determined to gang-rape her; the Malakasians she was now experiencing – albeit second-hand – were responsible for murdering innocent civilians and trashing Branag's store at regular intervals for no reason.

Though she tried not to eavesdrop, she could not control herself and strained to make out anything that might give her more information on her whereabouts, on Eldarn, and especially on how she might find Steven and get home.

One morning, Hoyt dared a limp, a dangerous endeavour, he explained, because limps had to be consistent. 'I'll never get away with the now-you-see-it-now-you-don't kind of limp popular on stage. All of those actors are trying to appear as if they have a limp. That's their mistake. People with a limp are always trying to look as if they don't have a limp. That's my secret.'

'I'm sorry, Hoyt, but that doesn't sound like much of a strategy to me.' Hannah was dubious. 'You're going out as a man with no limp pretending to be someone with a limp who doesn't want people to know he has a limp?'

'Churn!' the young man bellowed excitedly, 'we have a virtuoso among us.' He grinned. 'That's exactly it. Well, that and rhythm.'

'Rhythm?'

'Yes. I have to ensure I have the rhythm down. People can live with almost anything if it eventually has a predictability ... I mean look at Eldarn. No one really gets riled up about revolution until Malagon starts ordering his emissaries to play too rough and people start dying. Predictability breeds a sense of consistency and security. As long as my limp has a steady rhythm, a steady beat, let's say drag-toe-step-drag-toe-step-drag-toe-step, I'll look like I have been struggling with it for fifty Twinmoons.'

'Amazing,' Hannah said, surprised herself at how impressed she was with the young man's resourcefulness, 'but why not just change your hair or wear a hat – or maybe grow a beard?'

'Amateurs.' Hoyt draped an irregularly shaped length of tanned cowhide over one shoulder, tousled his hair until it fell in ragged unkempt strands across his face and shuffled awkwardly out front, the rhythm of his limp perfected already.

When Hoyt returned that evening, he came back in a rush. His hands were dirty, stained almost black by what appeared to be a mixture of soot and blood. He was breathing heavily and sweating, and his face was covered with a thin coating of dark grey dust.

'We need to be ready to move into the back,' he said, signing simultaneously to Churn, 'there may be searches again tonight.'

Churn was sitting against one of Branag's trestles while Hannah rested against the far wall. Two tall candles illuminated the room. She fought the desire to ask Hoyt what had happened, deciding he would tell her if it were something she needed to know. She was quietly impressed that even in the wake of whatever blow he had struck for the Pragan Resistance, Hoyt's adopted limp was still there, drag-toe-step-drag-toe-step. She watched him move towards his bedroll in the back corner and wondered if the sinister side of the healer, the invisible spirit that haunted Hoyt from time to time, had been permitted to emerge and stretch its gossamer legs that evening.

Branag Otharo was a different matter. From what Hannah had gathered during his periodic visits to the storage room, he was an honest businessman who hated the Malakasian occupation force and their leader, someone called Malagon, a prince of some sort. His long days at the shop were fuelled by venison stew, fresh bread and cold beer at the corner tavern, which led her to believe he was not married, or attached, or whatever they called it here in Eldarn. Flanked constantly by the dog Hannah never heard him refer to as anything but 'dog', Branag didn't appear to have any other companions besides the customers who stopped by periodically, and the itinerant rebels hiding in his back room.

He was a powerful man, with a barrel chest and thick forearms, dressed in a long-sleeved cotton tunic tucked into wool breeches with high boots, regardless of the heat. But what made the greatest impression on Hannah was Branag's kindness. Despite his size, he appeared to be a gentle soul; he didn't strike her as the kind of person who would hold anyone, even an occupation force, in such contempt. Like Hoyt though, there was something beneath the surface of the artisan's jovial demeanour, something unspoken that was motivating him. Hannah could not bring herself to ask what Branag's grim secret was.

One evening, after a particularly difficult stint in the foul-smelling secret chamber, Branag made a special trip to the tavern to find Hannah some tecan. He brought back a flagon-full, and bottles of beer for Hoyt and Churn.

As she sipped it gratefully, he asked if she had any children.

'No,' Hannah replied, 'at least not yet.' The question was unexpected; no one had shown much interest in her background so far. She tried to read him, but his face was impassive, not brooding or sullen, but rather devoid of any emotion at all. 'I do hope to have children one day . . . perhaps even one day soon,' she added optimistically.

'I see,' he said as he poured her another cup, then he patted the big dog affectionately behind his ears and wished them all good night. Turning to leave, he paused momentarily in the short hallway separating the storage area from the shop's main showroom. Backlit by a rank of thick candles casting a hazy yellow glow across the burnished saddles and leather goods, he whispered, 'I believe children are as close as we are allowed to come to feeling as though we have, for just a moment, been singled out by the gods. It is their way of touching us, even briefly, as we make our way to the Northern Forest.'

Hannah could not see his face, but the emotion in his voice answered all her questions. They were gone, and of course he would fight. She felt her chest tighten; she hoped she could reply before he heard her choke back a sympathetic sob. She didn't feel she had earned the right to cry for the older man.

Casting him a bright smile, Hannah replied, 'When I have children, Branag, I will remember that, I promise.'

'A good journey to you, Hannah Sorenson,' he said, then turned to the Pragans. 'Hoyt, Churn, good luck.'

Before dawn the following morning, Hannah Sorenson made her way silently out of Branag's saddlery shop, crouching low behind Hoyt as she moved into the dark street beyond.

Steven Taylor was up and in the saddle, awaiting his companions, before dawn. He felt no hunger or thirst, just an urgent desire to move away from this place. Maybe time and distance between himself and his violence would mitigate the anguish he felt every time he pictured the Seron, dying with a broken length of hickory jutting clumsily from his neck.

He had not been able to participate in Mika's funeral rites. He had no right to be there. The stench of burning flesh when Sallax ignited the pine boughs beneath the body made him vomit. But he did feel a sense of closure, if not happiness, when Versen and Garec tossed the Seron dead onto their own fire. Even from a distance, Mika's funeral had been touching. The young Ronan looked as if he were sleeping soundly on a bed of soft, scented pine needles; disposing of the Seron was its antithesis, a makeshift common grave for the animal-like warriors. Soulless and perhaps godless, they burned away in an anonymous pile of broken and dismembered bodies. Garec and Versen tossed the dead into the flames of the pyre, then paid them no further attention.

Now Steven sat astride his mount and waited for the coming

dawn. In his hands he held the hickory staff he had used to save his friends' lives. He absentmindedly ran his thumb over the bloodstain that discoloured the wood: how could Gilmour have reconstructed it so perfectly? Steven could detect no scars where the fragments had broken apart. This morning, as it rested across his lap, he began to grow more comfortable with it there, if no less terrified of what he had done with it.

Steven thought of the magic that had glowed between Gilmour's fingers; he hoped the old man had enough sorcery left to reconstruct *him*, to help him forget his experiences in Eldarn and return to Idaho Springs as the timid, scholarly, assistant bank manager he had been only two weeks earlier. He had lived his life as a coward and a pacifist. Although he had discovered bravery in recent days, bravery he had never imagined finding inside himself, he could not accept that he had become violent too. He was deeply uncomfortable with the fact that he had killed two Seron warriors in hand-to-hand combat, even though it had undoubtedly been necessary to save his friends' lives, but it was the third man who would haunt him for ever.

He had won the fight, disabled the enemy, and then shown no mercy.

Ignoring the sharp chill that sent cramps rippling through his legs, Steven realised he had never known how important mercy was to him. He had often been shocked and horrified at newspaper or television reports of the brutal behaviour of terrorists, or soldiers battling for a cause. His mental tally included kidnappers who killed victims even after collecting ransom money and gunmen who fired on bystanders even though their escape routes lay open. He had hated those people, he abhorred anyone who chose to be merciless: they were the cruellest and most deplorable examples of humankind.

He had become one of them.

He and Gilmour had murdered Seron in blind rage even though, ironically, they were the only members of the Ronan company who had not been attacked when the assault began.

Steven looked down at the hickory staff. It would never happen again. He would never again forget to show mercy. There was no cause worth fighting for if victory meant he was devoid of compassion. He ran his hands along the smooth wooden grain and raised the stained end to sniff at the vestiges of dried blood that clung to the shaft. He had learned bravery and violence in the last weeks. He was strong and athletic, with a sharp mind; Steven was afraid he had only begun to uncover the potential he had for warfare. Death would surround him on this journey; to live through it, he had to remember his true values. He had been a coward and pacifist, and his life had been empty. He could not afford to be a coward or a pacifist here in Eldarn. Somehow he had to tread the thin line between being a killer and killing to preserve love, compassion and peace for the people of Eldarn.

'Ah, you're lying to yourself to soften the blow,' he chided. 'That's a bullshit excuse, and you know it.' He wanted it to be true, though. He wanted to be the one who would fight for something good, something meaningful for those around him. His grandparents talked of the Second World War, and a common unity in the resolve to prevail against evil. He and Mark faced evil now. Why then could he not achieve that righteous vision, a vision his grandparents had realised in the 1940s?

Perhaps, Steven thought, *it's because we have the illusion of happiness. Perhaps we all live with fear or regret, and that is a tragic reality we face but never discuss.* He glanced at the remains of Mika's funeral pyre. *Perhaps my inability to differentiate between killing and killing for a cause is the reality that will crack the foundation of my illusion of contentment.*

With resolve and time, maybe his conscience would settle. For today, he would use Garec's dry Ronan wine to soften his guilt.

'Again the coward,' he said, and forced a laugh.

'What's that?' Mark approached carrying two brass goblets filled with the hot tecan Garec had brewed over their small campfire. He handed one up to Steven. 'Good morning to you too. How long have you been sitting up there?'

Steven pulled a tunic sleeve down far enough to protect his fingers and took the cup gratefully. 'I don't know, a couple hours, an aven, a lifetime.'

Mark drank as well. 'I think I have this tecan figured. When Garec strains it twice and adds an extra pinch of the darkest leaves, it tastes almost like a French roast.'

'You're right,' Steven agreed, 'it is good.'

'Now if we could only get some decent coffee cups . . .' He grinned, before turning serious. 'How are you doing this morning?'

'I've stopped shaking, if that's what you mean.' He inhaled the aroma, then gestured at Mark's scratched face and bandaged shoulder. 'You?'

'I'm alive, thanks to you.' He patted Steven's horse gently on the neck. 'I know you're sitting up there analysing yourself to a standstill, but that Seron would have killed us. You saved my life, and Brynne's too: we couldn't handle him on our own. You didn't start this.'

'How is she this morning?'

'I haven't talked with her, but I'm sure she's fine,' Mark replied. 'She's tough, tougher than any woman I've ever known. She didn't hesitate to pull her knife. Sallax was right; she *is* skilled with that thing. I can't believe how she moved in on that big bastard, stabbed him right in the chest, and it barely slowed the motherhumper down.'

'I hope she's okay,' Steven moved to dismount, 'and I'll be all right, too. I just never imagined I would kill anyone, never mind three people in fifteen seconds.' He handed the hickory staff and goblet down to Mark. 'Hang onto these for a second.'

Mark ran his hand along the smooth wooden staff. 'It's remarkable. I can't see where it was broken.'

'I can't either, and it seems stronger than it was last night, almost as though Gilmour's magic has imbued it with some impenetrable strength.' He laughed at himself. 'Listen to me: I sound like I believe all this voodoo magic shit.' He shuddered slightly, then added, 'I wonder why he insisted on repairing it anyway. It's just a piece of hickory.'

'I've been thinking about that too,' Mark said.

'And?'

'Do you see any hickory trees in this ravine?' Mark gestured towards the hillside. It was true. There were no hardwoods in sight save the twisted scrub oaks growing beneath the evergreens. 'The more I think about it, the more I'm convinced it was no accident you picked up this piece of wood.'

By midday, Steven had finished most of a wineskin by himself. He was drunk, not falling-from-the-saddle-drunk, but numbingly, pleasantly drunk. It was a skill he had learned after graduating from college: how to drink just enough to maintain a happy and painless stupor. College had taught him nothing about alcohol except that drinking as much as he could stand inevitably resulted in poor sexual performance, sickening bed spins and powerful all-day hangovers. It took years to learn to slow or stop drinking when he achieved the perfect inebriated state, somewhere between sober and falling down.

His thoughts began to drift back to Colorado, and the many trails, each turn and switchback memorised, that crisscrossed foothills similar to these. Loosely gripping the reins, he imagined himself wandering through Three Sisters Park or along the Mt Evans trail above Evergreen. He could feel glacier snow beneath his boots and smell clouds of pine pollen as spring breezes cascaded along the Front Range. He saw himself break through the tree line above Leadville as he approached Mt Elbert's peak, and remembered the lush ferns growing near a stream that flowed past the Decatur Peak trailhead.

Decatur Peak. He and Mark had planned to climb it one last time before winter set in. Hannah had wanted to come with them.

He thought of Hannah Sorenson, and the lilac aroma that lingered in the space between her neck and hair. It was like an alcove, a tiny cave where he could hide away, inhale her essence, and close his mind to the frightening and terrible things he had seen and done since his arrival in Eldarn.

He wondered where she was, and if she was worried about him. He imagined her brow furrowed as she leaned patiently on the staff sergeant's desk at the Idaho Springs police station. Would the officer find that wrinkled brow endearing, or would he simply push a sheaf of papers across the desk at her? 'Fill these out, ma'am,' he would say, unconcerned that she might be losing hope, or worse, losing interest. Steven worked to keep his thoughts focused, frightened of the pain that lay just beyond the edge of his consciousness. If he allowed his mind to run its course, he would convince himself that Hannah had become distracted by more important things in her life. She would forget him and move on. Did she not know how he cared for her? If their roles were reversed, he would never stop looking for her.

Then it was too late. He crossed the line and his musings were out of control. He was a murderer, lost and alone in this curious world of terror and hatred, and he had just convinced himself that his girlfriend was already forgetting him. Reaching for the wineskin again, he decided a comfortable, relaxed stupor was not enough to get him through the afternoon. He needed the whole package, the falling-down, blubbering, sobbing, blacking-out inebriation he remembered from his youth. If Sallax and Versen were disappointed in him and his weakness, so be it. They could tie him to the saddle if they were so damned set on getting to Welstar Palace.

'Good night,' he called aloud to anyone listening, and was about to take a long swallow from the wineskin when Gilmour interrupted his tailspin.

'They weren't human, you know.' The old man took the wineskin from him and swallowed a mouthful.

'What's that?'

'The Seron aren't really human.' Gilmour re-corked the wineskin. 'You didn't kill human beings last night, Steven. It was more akin to killing a pack of wild dogs that attacked you in the forest.'

'No it wasn't, Gilmour. It was exactly like killing people, because at the time I killed them, I believed they were people.'

'You make a good point. However, if it's any comfort, those Seron were denied the opportunity to enjoy a full human life many Twinmoons ago. Look at it as bringing peace to unthinkably tortured creatures.' He gave Steven a compassionate look before adding, 'We may face much worse before we reach Welstar Palace.'

'And even worse when we arrive there?'

'Yes.'

'I'm not sure I can do it, Gilmour.' Steven tightened his grip on the hickory staff.

'You rose to the occasion last night.'

'I was in a blind rage last night. I didn't know what I was doing.'

Smiling his boyish grin, Gilmour reach over and gripped Steven's shoulder in a show of empathy. 'Yes, you did. It's just that you never realised what it feels like. All rage is blind rage, Steven. Learning to tap it to save yourself or your friends will see you through this ordeal.'

'I don't want to learn to tap it; it's not a tap I can turn on and off.' He searched for the right words. 'I'm afraid that if I master that skill, I will lose myself. I will never again be Steven Taylor, the person I was before I unfolded that bloody tapestry, or before I picked up this miserable stick.'

'I can tell you already, my friend, losing Steven Taylor, the bank employee from Colorado, was done the moment you withdrew Lessek's Key from the safe.'

'I'm not ready to accept that, Gilmour,' Steven said, even now knowing, deep inside, that the old magician was right.

'You need to get ready. I can't guess what Lessek will tell you, but I do know we must try to summon him tomorrow night.'

A narrow canyon, invisible from a distance, cut a snakelike path through the precipitous slopes of the Blackstone Mountain range. Brynne squinted against the dwindling sunlight, trying to pick out the pathway Gilmour assured her was there, but she couldn't see it against the shadowy grey of the cold granite wall before them. Her back was sore from days of hard riding, and she longed to make camp for the night, eat a hot meal, and pass out in her bedroll. The brief but unexpected skirmish with Malagon's Seron warriors had left her shaken, but she worked to divert her attention to more productive thoughts. Their journey was important to the people of Eldarn, and she knew much more would be expected from her in the coming Twinmoons.

Reflecting on the battle, Brynne found it curious that she had feared more for Mark Jenkins than herself; she'd been deeply relieved when he emerged from the struggle unscathed. Her anxiety grew as she imagined the coming conflict, especially now that she knew she would put herself in harm's way to protect the charismatic stranger. It was an awkward time to discover she had feelings for him and ironic that her most ardent feelings rarely emerged at a convenient time.

The day passed quietly. Steven Taylor was drunk but rode well enough to keep up with the rest of the group. An air of nervous tension lay over the sober members of the party, and though no one mentioned it, they were all contemplating Gilmour's disclosure that they had been tracked from Estrad by an unseen enemy. Anticipating another attack at any moment, Garec kept an arrow nocked on the longbow across his lap. Versen held a short battle-axe in one hand, and even Mark had his sword loose in its scabbard.

Despite their exhaustion, Sallax pushed them ever forward,

encouraging Versen to find a navigable trail over the last wooded foothill that lay between them and Seer's Peak. When they finally reached the mountain's base, just before twilight, Brynne nearly fell from the saddle. Mark had to reach up to help her dismount. He was shattered and there was no affection in his touch; rather, it was a courtesy offered from one spent traveller to another. Steven half-climbed and half-rolled from the saddle, clumsily untied his bedroll and collapsed. Within moments, he was asleep.

Mark felt badly for Steven, but didn't envy his friend the hangover he would have in the morning. Taking in their surroundings, he noticed the valley they were in was lush with shrubs, ferns, evergreens and the ubiquitous scrub oak. Gilmour told them they would camp here for two nights while he, Garec and Steven climbed Seer's Peak and attempted to summon Lessek's spirit. Breathing deeply, Mark smelled the cool mountain air and wished he were in a valley along a stream near home. He found a comfortable place in which to unroll his blankets and was about let sleep take him for the night when Sallax approached across the clearing.

'You're first watch tonight,' the indefatigable Ronan partisan said sharply. Brynne tried to pretend she wasn't eavesdropping on the exchange.

'You trust me, Sallax?'

'I saw you fight that Seron. You were trying to protect Brynne.'

'Of course. I would have fought to protect any of us—' He stood and looked Sallax in the eye. 'Even you.'

Surprising Mark, Sallax laughed out loud, a sound like a muffled gunshot. 'Yes, perhaps even me. Let's hope we never have to find out.' Reaching into his belt, he withdrew a deadly-looking axe and handed it to Mark. 'Here, use this. That rapier doesn't suit you.'

Accepting the menacing little weapon, Mark thanked Sallax before asking, 'Why is this better for me?'

'The rapier takes many Twinmoons to master, and even then it leaves too many holes in one's defence.' Using his hand as a makeshift axe, he demonstrated. 'The battle-axe is much easier to wield. Just remember to make snap blows with your wrists and forearms, retracting as quickly as you strike. Don't try to hack off limbs. It will slow you down and leave your upper body open to counterattacks.'

'Very good,' said Mark, swallowing hard, 'I won't try to hack off any limbs.'

'Excellent!' Sallax hugged Mark in an uncharacteristic show of camaraderie and commanded, 'Wake Garec in an aven.'

Dawn found Gilmour awake and already brewing a large pot of tecan. He knew Steven and Mark missed their daily coffee; this was the best compromise he could come up with. Though he had racked his brain, he could not recall coffee's flavour. He had finished his last cup on Little Round Top above Gettysburg, Pennsylvania just before Confederate artillery began shelling those heights from far below. The Larion Senator promised himself that if they succeeded in ending Nerak's reign of terror, he would return to Pennsylvania and perhaps brew another pot there in the trees above Devil's Den. That was for the future. Today, he would climb Seer's Peak and, hopefully, contact Lessek. While his friends slept around him, he questioned whether his determination and magic were enough to defeat Nerak. He lacked confidence, and although he would never do so in front of the others, he wondered seriously whether they could really win against evil itself. Could it work? He knew of no force in the universe strong enough to defeat evil. The best they could hope for was to equalise it, to evenly match it with powerful magic, not to destroy it. He believed there was as much good in the universe as evil, and far more good in Eldarn than the evil Nerak represented. But Nerak was evil itself, an intact minion of evil's essence held together by a supreme mandate from beyond the plane of the universe, the Fold.

If this were to be done, he would need Lessek's help. Gilmour yearned for the founder of the Larion Senate to offer encouragement and to give him a strategy to save Eldarn. 'And ourselves,' he added quietly in a hopeful whisper, 'to save ourselves as well.'

He needed to be more careful. He had put himself in harm's way so frequently in the Twinmoons since the fall of the Larion Senate he never considered the potential consequences. With him dead, Nerak would come down on Mark and Steven like a firestorm. It would take only a moment, and the location of Lessek's Key would no longer be a secret. Gilmour represented their only protection. He would use his own magic to safeguard Steven and Mark from the dark prince's possession. He *had* to stay alive.

'Nerak believes we have the key with us,' the old sorcerer mused aloud. 'That's why he's trying so diligently to kill us.' He warmed his hands over the fire and stirred the tecan. 'As long as he thinks we have the key and as long as I'm alive, we'll have an advantage.'

Branag Otharo perched the tankard of beer precariously on his upturned wrist, placed a small loaf of bread atop a mountain of steaming venison stew in a wooden bowl and freed one hand to tug down on the leather strap threaded through the door to his saddlery emporium. He felt the latch inside come free, retrieved the mug and nudged the door open with his toe. The day had been warm, but with sunset, a cool wind had moved in with the rising tide.

Branag paused in the doorway and searched the street. 'Dog!' he shouted, then peered along the road in the opposite direction. 'Dog! Come on now!' The big wolfhound had been at his side all day, even as he walked to the tavern to pick up his dinner. 'Dog!' Branag cried again and waited several moments before adding, 'All right then, but you'll be out all night.' He paused, hoping to detect the familiar sound of the great hound's loping run along the muddy thoroughfare. Hearing nothing but the distant jangle of a ship's bell, Branag entered the shop and allowed the door to close behind him.

BOOK III

The Blackstone Mountains

SEER'S PEAK

Seer's Peak, flanked by towering, jagged mountains, looked like an unfinished building in a city of skyscrapers. Short, nearly flat on top, the crest looked as if it had been hacked off, truncated by some vindictive god with a scythe. The initial slope was steep, but Gilmour's camouflaged trail, although precipitous and narrow, was easily navigable.

Steven, well used to mountain trekking, passed his sturdy length of hickory to Gilmour to use as a support.

'Thank you, my boy,' the old man said, leaning on the staff and breathing heavily. 'I expect this climb will be quite easy for someone with your experience.'

'I don't know, Gilmour,' Steven replied, perspiring. 'I'm already wishing I'd had less wine yesterday.'

Garec laughed before chiming in, 'Not to worry, Steven. It's happened to the best of us.'

Steven's head still felt as though it was about to crack open and spill out onto the ground, even though he had finished a full skin of water to help the pain subside.

The trio climbed in silence, accustoming themselves to the thinner air as they ascended. The game trail ran along the southern slope of the hillside and disappeared into the narrow canyon that separated Seer's Peak from the closest of the titanic neighbours. Once within the canyon, Steven could see their trail snaking back and forth along the western hillside in a series of switchbacks until it disappeared out of sight near the end of a razor-thin ridge running westwards along the mountain's crest.

Pausing momentarily, he voiced his thoughts aloud: 'I fear it's going to be a long day.'

'I hope we'll be there by midday,' Gilmour said. 'That ridge can be dangerous in the dark.' He wiped a hand across his brow. 'If the weather holds, we should have no trouble reaching the landing by evening.'

Garec turned from where he had been looking up the trail. 'The landing?'

'There's a flat expanse of rock almost directly above us now, where we'll camp tonight. I hope we'll be in communication with Lessek before dawn tomorrow.' Neither Steven nor Garec were looking forward to their first meeting with the founder of the Larion Senate; Gilmour, noticing their discomfort, changed the subject. 'Anyway, if I'm going to drag these old bones all the way up there, we had better keep moving.'

They climbed most of the morning, admiring the majestic peaks in the distance and chatting aimlessly to keep their minds off the coming evening. Garec was impressed with Steven's hiking boots: he had never seen anything like them before and was curious to try them out, especially after Steven showed him how tightening the laces gave more support going downhill.

As they climbed higher, Steven noted several new species of hardwood growing along the slopes. In the crisp autumn morning, the hues of the changing foliage looked like an artist's palette against the stark grey and black of the rocky cliffs beyond.

Lunch – bread, cheese and dried fruits – was taken during a brief halt; Steven flinched when Gilmour drew a wineskin from his pack, helped himself to a hefty swig, then passed it to Garec. The bowman took a satisfying drink and motioned for Steven to join him.

Steven felt his stomach tighten. 'Sorry, I'm not quite ready. Perhaps in a month or two I'll join you again.'

The English word confused Garec. 'Month?' he asked, 'what's a month?'

Steven, who had been thinking about Eldarni time himself, replied, 'A measure of time, about a half Twinmoon, I suppose. We have twelve months in one year, the measure we use to chart the length of our lives.'

'So, how many *year* are you?' Garec asked.

'I am twenty-eight years old now,' Steven replied, stressing the plural. 'I'll be twenty-nine years old next spring.'

Calculating furiously, Garec said, 'We have a Twinmoon about every sixty days. That means there would be six Twinmoons for every one of your years. That makes you about one hundred and seventy Twinmoons, close to my age.'

'Yes, but your days are only about five-sixths the length of our days. So, I would need to add another sixth of one hundred and seventy to find my true Eldarni age.' Steven basked in the mathematics and the joy of having a simple multi-step linear algebra problem to solve. 'So I must be just over one hundred and ninety-eight Twinmoons.'

'Excellent!' Garec almost shouted, 'we will plan a great two-hundred Twinmoon celebration for you. It is an important milestone for us.'

'That should just be about enough time,' Steven replied, grinning, 'I might be ready for alcohol again in a hundred and twenty days.'

Shortly after lunch, they reached the eastern edge of the narrow ridge that led up to the landing. Now there was only a gradual incline, but the footing on the ridge trail was precarious as it climbed over boulders and up sharp rock faces. There were dangerous drops on either side. They had not realised the north and south faces of Seer's Peak were nearly sheer when they had looked up from below; a wrong step or loose rock might mean a gruesome fall to the forest floor.

They had no rope and Steven cursed his shortsightedness every time Garec or Gilmour slipped, however slightly: he was an experienced climber and should have known better. Steven sympathised with Garec as he periodically peered over the edge in terror.

'We were always told to avoid looking down.' He tried to sound reassuring. 'But I find it helpful sometimes to take a good long look.'

'Helpful?' Garec looked doubtful. 'How could it possibly be helpful?'

'Well, it does keep you focused on the task at hand. I mean, there's nothing like fear as a motivator.'

'Then I have quite enough motivation, thanks.' Garec forced a tight-lipped smile. 'If it's all right with you, I'll work on staring straight ahead.'

Steven made his way to a large flat rock that jutted out over the precipice where he lay flat on his stomach and peered over the edge, following the path of the river to their previous night's campsite. Versen, Sallax, Brynne and Mark looked like ants from here as they hauled water and firewood. Steven rested for a moment while watching them, feeling sunlight on his back and the familiar texture of rock against his face and hands.

We might not make it. The haunting mantra started once again, but he quickly forced the memory from his thoughts. Another bout with despair would do him no good up here. To distract himself, he thought of how much Mark and Hannah would love navigating this ridge: the challenges, the danger, the stunning vistas; this climb was almost a microcosm of his experiences in Eldarn. Down there, he was the weakest, the least capable, unable to find sources of strength, determination and support. Why could Mark so easily make the transition? He appeared to be completely at ease, acting as though he had grown up in Rona. He had even begun a relationship with a Ronan woman.

Steven lay there in the afternoon sun, pondering his shortcomings, until Garec and Gilmour caught up with him.

The Larion Senator interrupted his thoughts. 'You look quite at ease up here, Steven.'

'I am.' Steven jumped nimbly to his feet. 'I've lived most of my life in a mountain range similar to this. It's the closest I've felt to home since we arrived in Eldarn.'

'I am glad you're enjoying the day,' Gilmour said. 'I hope tonight we'll discover it was not a wasted effort.'

Once Steven had toured an aircraft carrier. He remembered the feeling of awe at the size of the thing, particularly the breadth of the main deck. The flat expanse of rock that marked the western end of the Seer's Peak crest reminded him of that gargantuan vessel. The landing was a geological anomaly. The stone was nearly flat for hundreds of paces and it looked flawless – no cracks, mineral intrusions or crevasses. Steven picked up a small stone and threw it as far as he could and it bounced to a stop less than a quarter of the way across the open area. A skilled pilot could land a plane here with room to spare.

Equally amazed, Garec asked, 'How can this be? The mountain couldn't have formed this way naturally.'

Having reached their destination, Gilmour was already smoking his pipe. The chill afternoon breeze carried his residual smoke eastwards along the ridge trail. Clenching the pipe firmly between his teeth, he answered, 'It seems impossible this is a natural formation, I agree. However, if this area were the result of some mystical force, it occurred long before I was born and long before the Larion Senate began practising magic.'

'Where – or how will Lessek find us?' Steven wasn't sure which question was more appropriate.

'We can camp anywhere you like, Steven,' Gilmour responded, 'but I suggest we stay close to this end because it will be cold tonight and the closest firewood is back down the ridge a few hundred paces.'

'Good point,' Garec agreed. 'You two get dinner started. I'll go back and get some now.' He dropped his pack and headed towards the trailhead.

Steven followed. 'I'll come too – we'll need as much as we can carry.'

When darkness fell, Steven felt as though they had built a campfire in the middle of the world's most expansive desert. Wind swept across the top of Seer's Peak, carrying much of the fire's heat with it, but Steven was too nervous to be cold; he was dreading the coming conversation with Lessek. He huddled deeper in his blankets, hoping, like a child, they might protect him from evil. He could see nothing except black stone and blacker sky.

Soon emotional and physical exhaustion caught up with him and Steven Taylor fell into a deep sleep.

He dreamed of the bank in Idaho Springs and the playful banter he'd exchanged with Myrna Kessler as she tried to solve his weekly mathematics problems. He had caught her trying to deduce the Egyptians' formula for the area of a circle, just before he had visited Meyers Antiques for the first time. He had walked to the lobby and asked Myrna if she would process some loan papers so he could get to Denver before the store closed. Peeking over her shoulder, he saw her sheet of paper was filled with squares and circles and notes about circumference and diameter. She had been tracing the base of her coffee cup when he emerged and surprised her.

Embarrassed, she had quickly put her notes aside and said something charming about not being his secretary. What else had she said that day? Her image moved in and out of focus, reminding him he was dreaming. She had teased him about having a geek's hobby. Howard had agreed. Steven had warned her not to drink too much that night, then left for his drive into the city.

As winds buffeted Seer's Peak, Steven Taylor, sleeping soundly, pulled his blankets close and rolled over towards the fire.

Garec tossed the last pieces of firewood onto the smouldering coals before curling up inside his blankets. He wanted to stay awake until Lessek arrived, if only so he did not awaken to find the spirit hovering over him. He was quite sure he would expire from shock if that happened.

Seated across from him, Gilmour smoked contemplatively, saying nothing as he stared into the flames.

Garec thought about his family and the farm. He prayed that the Malakasians had not connected his partisan activities with them.

He would miss the late-autumn festival that celebrated the crops successfully harvested and sold, preserves canned, meats dried and smoked, grapes pressed and barrelled and firewood stacked for winter. The festival was five days of celebration: hearty food and plenty of local wine. For the past ten seasons he had provided a deer; the farmers working the land north of Estrad Village would expect him to arrive with fresh venison as usual. He wondered if they would miss him, or just the meat.

He would dance late into the night with the farmers' daughters, stealing an occasional kiss, but more often simply revelling in the company of vibrant, beautiful young women. He had grown up a farmer and a hunter. Becoming a resistance fighter – a *patriot* – was something he had stumbled into. Now, awaiting a visit from the ghost of the most powerful man in Eldarni history, Garec realised it would likely be many seasons before he saw another harvest festival.

Looking over at Gilmour, Garec could see his lips moving slightly, but he could not hear the words. Garec guessed the old magician was chanting a spell to let Lessek know they had arrived. Now he was nervous, and fully awake. He checked to be sure his bow and quivers were at hand – he didn't imagine for a moment that he would fire on Lessek's ghost, but knowing his weapons were ready reassured him. He had known Gilmour for nearly fifty Twinmoons, but now he had to get used to the idea that one of his closest friends was one of the most powerful sorcerers in Eldarn.

As Gilmour continued the incantation, his lips hypnotically marking time through the avens, Garec soon grew tired and, like Steven, drifted off to sleep.

His dreams came: desultory images, confusing and scattered. He watched as the Estrad River dried up, as crops shrivelled and villagers across Rona starved to death. He saw the land his family tilled, its rich soil dried to hardpan and cracked like the skin of a dying man's face. He observed ghostly wraiths moving silently through the forbidden forest south of Estrad Village, too many to count, an army of disembodied ghouls searching for something lost.

Then he saw Riverend Palace, the way he always imagined it had looked before it was abandoned and left to crumble: a proud and majestic edifice, with the Ronan colours flying above her battlements. Strong Twinmoon breezes blew in from the sea. Prince Markon strode around, supervising installation of the largest stained-glass window Eldarn had ever seen.

His perspective changed again: a young South Coast woman, stripped naked, stood on the cold floor of a palace apartment. He gazed on her features and became aroused at the idea she might be longing for him – until he realised the look in her face was not one of lust, but of fear and foreboding. An intricately woven rug lay nearby, but she was too afraid even to move her bare feet to the relative warmth of the heavy wool carpet.

Soon Garec discovered why. A beast of a man lay on the rug, also stripped bare. The naked monster appeared aroused, but then Garec saw the maniacal creature was not looking at the girl; instead, he was crying out, shouting unintelligibly at the ceiling. He grabbed his genitals and writhed about on the floor. Riveted, Garec watched as palace guards held the man down while the beautiful, almond-eyed woman moved to straddle the drooling, wretched creature. Behind them, Riverend was in flames. Ceiling supports crumbled, tapestries flared. Servants rushed for the safety of the palace grounds.

All the while, the woman ignored the fire and coupled furiously with her terrifying partner.

Chanting in a soft murmur, Gilmour felt his spirit move outside his body. Standing beside his seated form, he gazed into the darkness beyond the firelight and waited for Lessek. Although he knew the winds above Seer's Peak were strong, he felt nothing as they passed through him and continued into the night. Steven and Garec slept on peacefully near the fire, which slowly burned down to a pile of dimly glowing coals.

He waited nearly an aven before he detected Lessek's spirit approaching.

'Here, Fantus,' Lessek called from inside his consciousness. Gilmour hadn't heard his given name in a hundred Twinmoons. His spirit self turned to face that of the long-dead sorcerer. Lessek looked as he had when a young man: tall and confident, with a trim beard and a piercing gaze, wearing the style of robes long ago adopted as standard uniform for all Larion Senators. For a moment Gilmour felt as though he were back at Sandcliff Palace.

'Welcome, my lord,' he said softly.

'You look weary,' the spirit observed, his voice echoing inside Gilmour's mind.

'This struggle has gone on for so many Twinmoons, Lessek. I am tired these days.'

'You are wondering if you can manipulate the spell table?'

'I am,' he said. 'I have studied for nearly a thousand Twinmoons and yet I am still not certain I'm up to the task.'

'You have found the key?' Lessek's ghost scratched absent-mindedly at his beard and Gilmour was momentarily surprised a spirit could feel an itch.

He motioned towards Steven. 'This one, Steven Taylor, discovered where Nerak had hidden the far portal as well as your key.' He paused before asking, 'Will it be enough, Lessek?'

'There is enough magic, sufficient power, yes. But you will need more courage than even you can imagine if you are to defeat the evil that controls Nerak.'

'It *can* be destroyed, then?'

'Defeated, not destroyed.'

'I must banish it back to the Fold?'

'Not all answers lie in the spell table, Fantus. Evil might be defeated there, but Nerak's weakness lies elsewhere.' He raised one hand in a show of encouragement and brotherhood and said, 'Rest now, Fantus and farewell for the moment.'

Gilmour felt his spirit fall back into his body as dawn was breaking over the horizon. He wrapped himself in his riding cloak and allowed sleep to carry him away. Although the old magician required only a fraction of the rest most people needed, he welcomed the respite from his responsibilities, a moment's grace from the arduous tasks that lay before him.

He rarely dreamed, but this morning a brief vision came to him, a glimpse of Kantu and Nerak. They had travelled together to Larion Isle, off the coast of Malakasia, to practise their spells, to harness heretofore-unknown power and to synthesise knowledge of magic and sorcery for the Larion Senate. It was during this trip they had penned the Windscrolls. Gilmour remembered that particular journey; when he saw Kantu limping beside Nerak, supporting himself with a staff and wearing a makeshift cast on his foot, Gilmour had teased the great scholar that he was brilliant enough to wield Eldarn's most powerful magic but too clumsy to step from a boat without twisting his ankle.

Gilmour woke with a start. The Windscrolls. Pikan Tettarak had sent him to Lessek's library to find one as she prepared the spell that eventually took her life at Sandcliff Palace. That was what Lessek meant by Nerak's weakness being elsewhere. He had to get to Sandcliff and find the Windscrolls; he would need to use their wisdom in concert with Lessek's spell table if he were to succeed in defeating Nerak and sending evil's minion back into the Fold.

Rejuvenated, Gilmour sprang to his feet and called, 'Wake up, my boys. We have much to do.'

The sun was well above the horizon now and their campsite was draped in the bright yellow of morning. The winds had died in the night and Gilmour could feel the temperature rising already. To the north, the Blackstones glowed so intensely it looked as if they had caught fire. The clear morning possessed a sense of renewal that sent Gilmour's heart racing. Moments such as this, moments of clarity of purpose, were rare. He knew *where* he would find the power to emerge victorious; now he wanted to get there. He had spent half his life waiting for Lessek's Key to come back to Eldarn without realising that the key alone would not have been enough: thanks to Lessek, they all had been saved from a potentially deadly mistake.

Steven rolled over with a groan. 'Is it dawn already?' His legs were sore from yesterday's climb and his back ached from sleeping on rock. Although riding all day was steady exercise, he had not enjoyed a good cardiovascular workout in weeks. He promised himself as soon as he found some decent shoes, he would run halfway across Rona and back. Stretching, he sat up and squinted through the morning sunlight at Garec. 'Are we in a hurry?'

Yawning, Garec twisted awkwardly several times to loosen his back muscles. 'It appears we are,' he said and then to Gilmour, 'I assume you received instructions last night.'

The old man was hurriedly packing his bedroll. 'No, but I did speak with Lessek and I do now have some notion of how we will defeat Nerak.' He reached into his pack and withdrew the last of their bread, fruit and cheese. Pulling a short dagger from his belt, he cut several pieces for himself before passing the remainder to the younger men.

'Here, let's eat quickly so we can get down as—' He stopped suddenly. 'Did he speak with either of you?'

Steven and Garec exchanged a worried glance before answering in unison, 'No.'

'Rutting dogs.' Gilmour kicked an imagined pebble towards the precipitous southern cliffs. 'I was certain he would have some insight for both of you.' Shaking his head, he added, 'I don't understand it.'

Steven began rolling his blankets. 'I'm sorry, Gilmour. I slept soundly all night.'

'As did I,' Garec said. 'I tried to stay awake. Perhaps if we had been awake, he would have spoken with us as well.' He pulled on one boot, then remembered their conversation of the previous day and motioned for Steven to trade footwear with him.

'I did have some strange dreams, though,' he added.

Gilmour grabbed his wrist, interrupting Garec's clumsy attempts to lace Steven's Timberlands. 'Tell me. Every detail.'

'I dreamed as well,' Steven chimed in.

'You too, then.' Gilmour stopped rushing and sat down beside them. 'Tell me everything you remember. Take your time.'

The old man had Steven and Garec relay their dreams to him, over and over again, asking probing questions about people or places his companions had seen. He was trying to get a comprehensive picture of exactly what they had experienced in their sleep.

Garec's dream did appear to be a message from Lessek, although aspects left the trio confused and guessing. Images of the land dying, of ghosts haunting Rona's forbidden forest and of the Estrad River running dry were disheartening, but neither Gilmour nor Garec had any idea what they really represented. Garec's vision of Riverend Palace in flames was real; Gilmour speculated that the bowman's vision of two people coupling during the blaze was Lessek's confirmation that a final effort had been made to continue the royal bloodline.

'What do you mean?' Steven asked. It was nearly midday and he was not convinced they could learn anything more from the evening's alleged message dreams.

'Prince Danmark was struck blind, deaf and insane by the same force that killed his father.'

'Nerak,' Steven confirmed.

'Nerak. Correct. The young prince was not killed right away,' Gilmour said. 'He lived another full Twinmoon, not dying until the night of the fire that destroyed Riverend Palace.'

Garec put the pieces together. 'Someone could have been impregnated by Danmark during that Twinmoon.' His voice rose slightly as he pieced together his dream. 'So that bloodline may still be intact today. Prince Danmark could have a living heir somewhere in Rona.'

'That's right. And that heir is – or I should say, *would be* – the rightful king or queen of Eldarn.'

Steven interrupted, 'How can that be? I thought Brynne said the nations of Eldarn were all ruled by cousins, descendants of some long-dead King Reginald or something.'

'Remond,' Gilmour corrected. 'True, but legend has it that Prince Draven of Malakasia was not the father of his only son, Marek.'

Steven thought about this for a moment, then understood. 'So, the wife, Princess—'

'Mernam,' Garec chimed in.

'Princess Mernam had an affair, managed to get herself pregnant, spent a long weekend in the sack with Prince Draven to make it all look legitimate and gave birth to a bastard—'

'Prince Marek,' Gilmour accented the interruption by slapping his hand against the stone landing. 'He was the first Malakasian to claim the Eldarni throne and his family has been in power ever since.'

'But controlled by Nerak,' Steven said and Gilmour nodded in affirmation. Steven was suddenly interested in the twists and turns of Eldarn history. 'What about the other families? Were there no surviving heirs?'

'None who produced any additional children,' Garec said, then speculated, 'I'd guess Nerak killed off everyone young enough to carry on King Remond's bloodline, then laid claim to Prince Marek the bastard, who was still capable of having children.'

'I wonder why he would care,' Steven mused aloud.

'What do you mean?' Garec asked.

'If he was being controlled by an evil force from outside the observable universe, why would he care that Remond's line die off? What threat could they possibly be?'

Garec guessed again, 'Perhaps he needed some semblance of order here in Eldarn while he studied the spell table and learned the magic necessary to free his master from the Fold.'

'Maybe,' Steven agreed, 'or maybe Remond's family holds some secret that would interfere with his plan to tap the power of the spell table.'

Running a hand through his whiskers, Gilmour said, 'This is all very interesting, but we can't interrupt our journey to begin looking for some mythical Ronan heir. That might take another hundred Twinmoons. Our current goals are more important, at least for now.' He stood and stretched, then, with an audible sigh, added, 'I'm afraid Lessek can be very confusing. Now, Steven, back to your bank.'

'All right, all right,' Steven answered, 'but I need a break first. I'm beginning to get a headache.' He rose and began walking about the plateau, hoping to clear his mind. It was obvious Lessek had spoken to Garec, but Steven did not believe his own dream had any cryptic messages. It was just another day at the bank as he, Howard and Myrna enjoyed each other's company and tackled a maths problem together. He hadn't been to Meyers Antiques yet, so he knew nothing of William Higgins's deposit-box key. It was just a dream, just a run-of-the-mill night-time recollection of one day at work. He certainly hoped so, because if Lessek had overlooked him last night, that might mean he and Mark would be able to find the far portal, return home to Colorado and be finished with Eldarn for ever.

Leaving this mountain without a supernaturally imposed to-do list had become an important short-term goal for Steven and he didn't wish to dwell on the scene long enough for Gilmour to start inferring something outlandish from what was just a simple dream.

With Mark on his mind, Steven wandered across to the edge of the landing and lay down on his stomach, looking towards their base camp. Nothing moved. No one was there. Second-guessing himself, he found the river and followed it to the grove of trees where he had fallen asleep two nights earlier. They were gone.

Anxiety welled up in him and his hands started shaking. Leaping to his feet, he sprinted across to where Gilmour and Garec remained deep in conversation.

'Something's wrong,' Steven shouted, 'they're gone from camp!' He quickly hefted his pack. 'Everyone, even the horses, they've all disappeared.'

Versen snapped a branch in two across his knee and tossed both bits onto the burgeoning pile of firewood. Brynne tended the horses, brushing their coats and leading them to the river for water. Fearing another Seron attack, Sallax told her to leave them saddled in case they were forced to leave in a hurry. Sallax himself had gone to scout a trail through the narrow canyon adjacent to Seer's Peak.

Mark was trying inexpertly to catch fish from the river using Versen's bow and arrows. Spotting what looked like a small trout shading itself beneath a rock outcropping, Mark took careful aim and let fly, far-fetched hopes of skewering dinner running through his mind. When he missed, which was always, he would leap into the river to retrieve his arrow before the current carried it away, in the process effectively frightening off any fish for several hundred paces along the river. He found himself waiting ever-longer intervals for his quarry to return.

Brynne teased him from the grove. 'You'll never hit one, Mark. Give it up.'

'I'm sure I will, if I can just get the angle correct. I'm going too high,' he motioned with one arm; 'I need to aim lower.'

'Perhaps it doesn't have anything to do with the angle,' Versen said, joining their conversation. 'Perhaps you just don't have any skill.'

Feigning indignation, Mark retorted, 'I resent that. I've come quite close several times.'

'How many times have you tried?' Brynne asked.

'Um. That one makes thirty-two.'

They all laughed and Versen joined him at the water's edge and retrieved his bow. Shading his eyes, he squinted into the shadows along the far bank. 'Watch this,' he said, drawing three arrows from the quiver, jamming two in the ground at his feet and nocking one on his bowstring. 'It's really very simple.' He took aim and fired three shots in rapid succession at different targets under water. Three large trout bobbed to the surface, each pierced cleanly.

Handing the longbow back to Mark, Versen said, 'Keep practising.'

Dumbstruck, Mark accepted the weapon and stared out at the fish as they disappeared around a lazy bend, the arrows sticking up like little masts on toy boats. Versen clapped a hand on his shoulder and added in a sympathetic tone, 'Our dinner is floating away. You might want to hurry along after it.'

Sallax returned before nightfall; he licked his lips at the smell of fresh fish grilling over their campfire. 'Who caught these?' he asked, accepting a wineskin from Versen.

'I pulled these from the river myself,' Mark told him proudly.

Brynne chuckled and Sallax understood. 'Versen?'

'Of course, Mark did fetch them from the water before they floated all the way to the Ravenian Sea,' Brynne clarified. Sallax gave a rare grin and joined them around the fire.

Shrugging, Mark admitted grudgingly, 'I'll grant you my skills with a longbow aren't quite honed to perfection. I think the person who coined the phrase "shooting fish in a barrel" must have been using a machine-gun.'

Sallax tossed him the wineskin. 'You stick with the battle-axe and you'll be fine.'

'So will the fish, I'm sure,' Versen commented dryly and everyone laughed again at Mark's expense.

Like Garec, Steven and Gilmour far above them in the night, the Ronan freedom fighters ate bread, dried fruit and cheese as they huddled close to the fire. Passing the wineskin around frequently, they avoided discussing Welstar Palace, Nerak and the journey ahead, talking instead of their families and homes. Mark was saddened to hear that Sallax and Brynne's parents had died so long ago, even though Brynne said she had been too young to remember them, but Sallax looked so grim that Mark did not pursue it further.

Versen reflected on growing up in a large family of hunters and woodsmen; he smiled proudly as he talked of learning to shoot better than his older brothers. 'I still can't shoot as well as Garec, though ... but never tell him I said that out loud!'

Brynne changed the subject again. 'How far did you get through the canyon today, Sallax?'

Motioning towards the narrow breach in the rock, her brother replied, 'I managed to get about halfway up the slope of that big mountain behind Seer's Peak. There's a pass between it and that crooked fellow to the east, I think, but I couldn't see beyond those two.' He broke off a piece of dry bread and scooped up the last piece of trout. 'I found the Seer's Peak trailhead as well. It's about two hundred paces into the canyon, but it's well hidden behind a stand of pines.'

Versen said, more as an affirmation than a question, 'So the horses stay here.'

'There are some high meadows with plenty of grass for cropping, but I can't imagine we'll get much further than this pass with the horses.'

Brynne inhaled sharply. 'Garec will be crushed if he has to leave Renna behind.'

Versen nodded. 'He'll want to leave her down here where he knows she can get to water.'

'I'm quite sure we'll come home this way to look for her if he has anything to say about it,' Sallax muttered.

Mark felt for Garec as well. He had only known his own horse, Wretch, for a few days and despite all the pain and agony, he wasn't happy about leaving the beast to survive on its own in the wilderness. 'Is there anything else we can do?' He half-hoped the would come up with some creative means to bring the animals along.

Versen shook his head. 'Not without doubling back to the nearest farm and paying to stable them there.'

'But that puts us at risk of more Seron interference,' Brynne added.

'Or worse,' Sallax confirmed. 'They'll be all right here. There is shelter in the canyon and plenty of water.'

Versen stood. 'I'll bury our saddles beneath that birch tree near the water.' Motioning to Mark, he said, 'C'mon, help me with this.'

The horses were tethered in a stand of trees just upstream from their campsite. Mark, enjoying the friendly conversation, hadn't noticed the sunlight fading behind the Blackstone peaks in the west. He absentmindedly checked for his watch: the sudden onset of darkness was a striking contrast to the relative daylight near the fire. He wished, absurdly, that he knew what time it was in Colorado.

Unbuckling Renna's saddle, he let it fall to the ground, pulled the soft wool blanket from the mare's back and gave the horse a slap on the hindquarter. 'Good luck, Renna. Garec will be down to say good-bye in the morning.'

Moving to Wretch, he grimaced. 'You, on the other hand – I have half a mind to leave you tied to this tree.' He glanced over at Versen before adding, 'No, I'm just kidding. Maybe your next owner will be a true equestrian.' Wretch gave him a dispassionate look, then bent to continue cropping the undergrowth.

Mark was still stroking the ungrateful animal when he noticed a strange tree across the grove, a large pine; he had not seen it there before. It captured his attention now because it looked dead, as if it had been ravaged by an extremely selective wildfire. He froze. Moving his hand as slowly as possible from Wretch's neck, he tried frantically to get Versen's attention without shouting or moving. He was not certain how an almor detected its prey.

The burly woodsman saw Mark waving over at him and called, 'What's the matter with you? Get that saddle off and let's get busy. We have a hole to dig.'

It was too late to warn him. The demon exploded from the ground between them and Mark heard Versen scream as he fell backwards into the underbrush. For what felt like a lifetime, Mark watched as the almor reached out with one shapeless, glowing white arm to grab Brynne's horse bodily from the ground. The animal gave a terrified scream, shrill, like a tortured child, before choking to a sickening silence as the creature sucked its life force dry. It took just seconds, Mark realised dully. The almor tossed the husk of skin and bones to the side; it glanced off a tree before shattering into pieces on the soft needle carpet.

Mark sprinted back through camp. 'Run!' he screamed. 'The

almor!' For two or three heartbeats, Brynne looked confused, until she saw Sallax grab his saddlebag and begin running towards the canyon. She reached for Mark's outstretched hand and sprinted off behind her brother. Mark did not look back. He leaped over their campfire, half-dragging Brynne along behind.

Sallax paused once to check they were following. He couldn't see Versen, or hear him either, but there wasn't time to search. 'Hurry!' he called. 'It can move very fast – and get away from the river!' Then he was gone, disappearing up the narrow path towards the Seer's Peak trailhead. Mark and Brynne followed on his heels. Mark didn't want to run faster than Brynne for fear the beast might suddenly appear and take her, but she speeded up markedly when the demon gave an unholy cry from the canyon entrance behind them. It echoed about the rock walls of the narrow crevasse, sounding like the collective pain and suffering of generations of oppressed souls screaming at once.

'Lords, what is that thing?' Brynne called between shallow breaths.

They hurried after Sallax as he burst through a thickly overgrown stand of trees and began climbing the lowest slopes of Seer's Peak. The mountain was dotted with trees and shrubs nearly all the way to its broad, flat apex and Mark realised the almor could easily find some fluid pathway to cut them off.

There was no way they would be able to maintain this pace until they reached the safety of the granite expanse above the tree line. Already he was slowing, his diaphragm cramping stiffly and his lungs feeling as if they were about to burst. Remembering the tremendous blast Gilmour had produced in Estrad to divert the almor, Mark wished he had thought to ask the old sorcerer what he had meant by *explosions aren't magic*.

Mark searched the trail above in the fading sunlight. They needed to reach a safe place soon; having to flee from the almor in the dark would be disastrous. 'Someplace dry,' he panted, 'where can we find someplace dry?'

They were still running at full speed when they rounded the trail's first switchback. With darkness nearly upon them, Mark saw it, stretched out above like a titanic grey blanket thrown up against the side of the mountain: a rockslide. He shouted ahead, 'Sallax, stop.'

'Stop?' he heard Brynne cry, 'no! We have to keep going – that thing could be right behind us!'

Sallax slowed to a jog, then turned to face them. A look of disappointment flashed across his face, as if he had to accept that something might best him, that this demon, a nightmare creation of the most twisted god, might beat Sallax of Estrad. As quickly as it appeared, however, the look was gone.

'What?' he asked. 'What do you suggest we do?'

Without slowing, Mark moved past him off the trail and up into the rockslide. 'Come up here, now,' he commanded. 'It's a more difficult path, but there are no plants or trees.' Surveying the rocky field, he explained, 'The almor: it travels through water, doesn't it? So it might not be able to reach us out here.'

Sallax understood what Mark was planning before he finished speaking; he climbed onto the rockslide behind the nimble foreigner.

Brynne joined them, but said sceptically, 'We can't possibly climb this at night, Mark. It's worse than scaling a building – we'll be dead in half an aven.'

'We'll be dead in less than that out there,' Sallax told her and pulled her up to balance beside him.

Mark, suddenly feeling more at home, caught his breath and explained some basic climbing rules. 'This isn't any more difficult in the dark than it would be at midday. Climbing a slope this steep means you have to get a feel for the mountain. Climb in a steady rhythm and you'll grow less tired. Be sure to check every hand and foothold before you put all your weight on it. Most important, don't panic. For every loose purchase that fails below you, there are up to three holding you fast. Keep your weight into the slope but not against it. Climb the mountain; don't try to slither up it.'

He forced a smile back at Brynne, then went on, 'I'll find the easiest pathway. Stay behind me and use the light from the moons to see where I put my hands and feet. Don't forget: if it supports your weight when you grab it, chances are it will support your weight when you step on it,' and then, in a less confident tone, added, 'but not always.'

Sallax seemed almost excited by the potentially deadly challenge. 'Lead on, Mark Jenkins,' he called, 'we'll be right behind you.' He positively exuded enthusiasm where, just moments earlier, he had been convinced they were lost, that the almor would suck them dry like the stray dog he had watched disintegrate to a leathery shell. Mark had renewed Sallax's confidence; now he was almost willing to fight the demon beast hand-to-hand.

There were plenty of solid handholds at the base of the steep, rocky slope and their initial ascent went smoothly. Brynne found the rhythmic pace of Mark's climb hypnotic and she moved almost without thinking. It didn't take long for the trio to get several hundred paces up the side of the mountain.

'You are skilled at this, Mark,' she called softly.

'Would you believe Steven and I do this for fun as often as possible?' he asked. 'We're actually disappointed weekends we can't risk life and limb. Of course, we try to limit our climbing to daylight avens.'

'What is a *weekend?*' Sallax interrupted.

Mark chuckled. 'A weekend is a glorious concept I will introduce to all Eldarn if we manage to live until morning.' His right hand slipped and several stones dropped on the others below. 'Sorry,' he called, 'we're coming into a difficult section here, lots of small, loose stones. Be careful.'

Neither Brynne nor Sallax answered; they were struggling to make out the cliff face, trying desperately to get some sort of visual confirmation that their handholds were solid.

Their progress slowed as Mark clawed his way up towards the switchback trail above. The next hundred feet would be arduous and he knew his friends needed a break. Through the dark, he could see neither trees nor shrubs; no complex root systems growing along the path, but even if there had been water flowing there in abundance, the trio would have to stop, risking attack, just to gain a momentary respite from the difficult ascent. *He* was an experienced climber and *his* shoulders and thighs ached: he was impressed with the fortitude Brynne and Sallax were showing as novices on a difficult hill in the dark.

When the demon creature burst from the trail above, Mark's heart sank. Towering over the rocky hillside, a glowing, formless wall of undulating fluid, the almor screamed down at them. Mark thought he could see into its eyes, vacant pools of suffering and death.

'Wait!' Sallax cried. 'Stop here.'

Laughing – a response to abject terror – Mark replied, 'I hadn't planned on going much further, Sallax.'

'No, I mean it can't reach us here.'

'How do you know that?' Brynne asked, her voice trembling.

Mark realised what Sallax meant. 'Because it would have already,' he told her quietly. 'We need to stay put, to hang on here as long as possible.'

'And hope it doesn't rain,' Sallax added under his breath.

For the first time since he fell through the far portal in Idaho Springs, Mark was glad days in Eldarn were four hours shorter. Clinging to the side of Seer's Peak, his arms and legs numb, he could do little more than pray, and trust that by remaining completely still he would not fall to his death – or, worse, drag the Ronan siblings with him. He guessed it had been three hours since they had last seen the almor. He called to Brynne to find out what time his watch read.

'I don't know, Mark.' She sounded desperate. He ached to be able to whisk her to safety.

'Well, now Brynne, I'm disappointed,' he teased, hoping to lighten the mood. 'After all those lessons, you can't tell me what time it is.'

'I can describe it,' she said. 'Will that help? The long arm is straight up and the small arm is just next to it.'

'To the right or the left?'

'Left. On the rune you called ... um ... levelen.'

'Eleven,' he corrected. 'Great, the news is on. I wonder what the headlines are tonight.' Straining his eyes to see below her, he called to Sallax, 'How are you doing down there?'

'I will be all right.' He did not sound convinced. 'But I'm not sure how much longer we can hang on this slope.'

'I know,' Mark answered, 'but try this, both of you: put your weight on your feet and shake your arms, one at a time. It'll loosen the muscles and alleviate some of the pain.'

'I can't do it, Mark,' Brynne told him plaintively. 'I'll fall.'

'Yes, you can,' he encouraged, 'that's the easy part. The hard part is the next bit: hanging on with your arms and shaking out your legs.'

'No,' she cried again, 'I just can't.'

Mark considered his options, swallowing a curse as he called back to Sallax, 'Don't let her fall, Sallax. I'll be right back.'

'Very well,' the big Ronan answered. Though he sounded defeated, Mark knew Sallax would fight on to the last ounce of his strength.

'Brynne, I'll be back before the long arm reaches the three.'

'I don't remember the three.' She sounded anxious.

'It's the one that looks like breasts on a sleeping woman.'

Sallax grunted in ironic amusement. 'I must learn this system of runes, Mark.'

'Just hang on until the arm reaches the three and I'll be back.' He shook the stiffness from his arms and legs and then, worried he might lose his grip and fall backwards down the slope himself, began hurrying, as fast as he dared, towards the path in the distance. After five minutes of hard climbing, he discovered there was about fifty feet of difficult loose rock before the terrain became more manageable and he could ascend again with some certainty.

By the time he reached the trail, he had worked out how he could rescue the others. Ignoring the potential threat of the almor, he jogged back along the slope until he reached a thin evergreen tree growing along the path. Its growth was stunted by strong winds that raked the sides of Seer's Peak. Although it had shallow roots, there were sturdy branches along its trunk. He wasn't positive it would be long enough to reach Brynne across the expanse of loose stones, but if he wasted too much time questioning his strategy, both she and Sallax would fall. He set about trying to push the tree over.

Mark's watch read 11.22 by the time he reached the upper end of the loose gravel slope. He found two solid rocks on which to brace his feet and shouted to Brynne, 'I'm going to lower a tree down to you. Grab on with all your strength and don't let go. I'll pull you up.'

There was no answer.

'Brynne,' he called into the night, his heart racing, 'Brynne, take hold of the tree. All you need to do is walk up the slope. It's much easier climbing up here.'

'I'll try,' he heard her answer weakly, 'but you are well past the three.'

'I'm sorry, but I am here now, and I'm going to get you to

safety. This tree was tougher than I expected.' He braced himself, then yelled down again, 'Sallax, you hang on. I'll send this back in just a moment.'

'I can wait,' Sallax shouted back.

Mark lowered the tree trunk-first, fearing Brynne's hands might slip on the fragile green boughs near the top; he removed his tunic and wrapped it round the top to ensure his own grip held fast.

He still couldn't feel Brynne's weight and was about to call when she shouted up the slope, 'Mark, it doesn't reach.'

'Son of a pregnant, mother-humping bitch!' he cried into the crevasse, then, thinking quickly, pulled the tree back up the hillside. 'Hang on, I'll send it right back.' Resting the tree beside him, Mark removed his boots and stripped off his jeans. Pulling his sweater off as well, he tied the sweater sleeves to the legs of his jeans and secured the jeans to the tree with his belt. 'I hope to God this holds,' he prayed in a whisper, then added, 'and I hope that godforsaken monster doesn't kill me here in my boxers.'

This time his makeshift rescue line reached and he soon found himself hauling Brynne up the slope, heaving with all his might. When he pulled her up beside him, she threw her arms around his neck and kissed him long and hard on the lips. He breathed a heavy sigh of relief and ran his hands through her thick hair and across the supple skin of her face: he had wanted to touch her for days now.

They might have taken things further had Sallax not interrupted from below. 'Hello? I'm still down here,' he called crossly. Mark wasn't sure if he had seen them kissing, no matter how fiercely he burned for Brynne, this wasn't the time.

'Jesus, Sallax,' Mark exclaimed and lowered the tree once again. The big man was much heavier than his sister and Mark slipped twice, almost pitching headlong into the ravine. Once Sallax was safe, Mark retrieved his clothes and let the tree fall down the slope. They watched as it disappeared from sight, then heard it strike the trail far below. No one said anything, though all three wore a look of great relief.

As he pulled on his jeans, Mark caught Brynne watching him by the pale light of the Eldarni moons. He flushed, and fastened his belt before pulling on his sweater. The stolen tunic, now ripped to shreds, was tossed into the darkness.

'Follow me up this slope,' he told the others. 'It isn't far and there are solid rock footholds all the way to the trail.'

When they finally reached the safety of the path, they collapsed on the ground, breathing heavily. Sallax reached over and clapped a strong hand on Mark's forearm. 'That was well done, very brave. You saved us all.'

'Don't mention it,' Mark replied. As an afterthought, he added, 'We were there a long time. Did either of you hear anything of Versen passing us along the trail? I didn't.'

Brynne's breath caught in her throat. She hadn't thought of the woodsman since fleeing the campsite. 'Lords, do you think we lost him?'

'I guess we'll find out tomorrow, when we get off this mountain. That almor leaves behind the barest remains of its victims, but if it took Versen, there should be enough left for us to identify him,' Sallax said, putting into words what they knew, but were hesitant to say out loud. 'Anyway,' he went on, 'right now we have to worry about ourselves, and the others up there—' he pointed up at the wide, flat area atop the mountain. 'They have no idea that thing is coming.'

'Mark, can you get us up there by dawn?' Brynne was worried. 'I mean, we can't go up the hillside again.'

'I can get us there,' he answered, 'but we'll never make it by dawn. We have to risk the trail.'

'So be it.' Sallax punctuated his decision by standing and tossing his saddlebags over one shoulder. He reached down to help Mark to his feet. 'Like breasts on a sleeping woman?'

Mark grinned. 'That's right – but if you've never seen any, I'd be happy to explain the concept to you.'

Steven hurried along the trail as quickly as he could without leaving Garec and Gilmour behind. Perhaps he was worried for no reason: maybe his friends had moved their camp to a safer location, inside the canyon and out of the open. But scrambling over rocks along the treacherous pathway, he was certain something dreadful had befallen them; he had a gut feeling he couldn't ignore. If only he had looked over the cliff sooner; they could have been halfway down the mountain by now. Instead, he'd wasted half the day trying to work out the confusing dreams and visions sent to them by Lessek's spirit. He still thought his dream was just that: a memory of three friends together at work, nothing more.

Steven actually remembered that day well; that afternoon he had met Hannah for the first time. Myrna was planning to go out with her friends and Howard had sent him to pick up tickets to a football game that Sunday. There had been nothing mystical, magical, or even questionable about that day at work. Steven played it over in his mind, but every time he came to the same conclusion: Lessek had nothing to say to him, and he was happy with things that way.

Reaching the floor of a shallow gully, he paused to allow Garec and Gilmour to catch up. Seeing Garec in his boots, Steven was sorry he had agreed to trade for the day. Garec's own footwear was made of soft tanned deer hide, but it didn't compare with his own top-of-the-range boots. It was obvious Garec agreed; Steven could only hope he'd get them back one day.

Gilmour was quiet, almost brooding. Although he hustled along at Steven's urging, his thoughts were elsewhere, deep within Riverend Palace or buried among the Windscrolls at Sandcliff. He made Steven promise to reflect on his dream in an effort to uncover anything out of the ordinary; Steven agreed he would investigate every single detail, if only they could just hurry back down Seer's Peak. He needed to know the others were safe – after that, he would be happy to spend *days* talking about his recollections of Howard and Myrna.

Cresting a short rise in the path, Steven could see eastwards towards the sunlit end of the ridge trail. To his surprise, he saw Mark, Brynne and Sallax climbing towards him. Turning back to Garec and Gilmour, he shouted, 'They're here!'

Gilmour looked up. 'Who is here?'

'Everyone, I think – well, everyone except Versen. I can't see him yet.'

The old magician hurried up, using Steven's bloodstained hickory stick for support. Squinting at their companions rushing along the dangerous ridge, he calmly warned, 'Get ready. Something's wrong.'

Gilmour handed Steven the staff and dashed along the path with the speed and agility of a mountain goat. Steven could barely keep pace; Garec, still nursing his sore knee, was left well behind.

Working to keep his footing, Steven cursed Gilmour as they trotted over rocks, loose soil and rotting deadwood. Razor-thin bottlenecks had sheer drops to the forest floor on either side.

'He's like a damned Sherpa,' Steven muttered to himself, angry for believing, even for a moment, that there was anything Gilmour could not do. He lost sight of the old man around an enormous boulder that lay directly on the trail, then, hurrying past it, he nearly ran headlong into him: Gilmour had stopped suddenly on the opposite side and was now standing motionless. About twenty paces away, Mark, Brynne and Sallax, mirroring Gilmour, were standing absolutely still as well, their eyes fixed on one another. No one moved or spoke.

'What's happening?' Steven asked of anyone listening.

'Quiet,' Gilmour commanded. 'It's the almor. It has found us.'

Embarrassed that he had been unable to keep up with the older man, Steven swallowed hard and endeavoured to catch his breath quietly.

'Where is it?' he whispered. 'Is it hunting us?'

'It is hunting *me*,' Gilmour replied.

Garec had climbed up onto a small pile of rocks some fifty paces behind them; he had his bow at the ready, an arrow nocked and two full quivers at his feet. But even though Steven had never known a bow could be fired with the accuracy and precision Garec showed with every shot, he wasn't filled with confidence; he didn't believe traditional weapons would have any effect on the soul-sucking demon.

Still no one moved. It was the world's largest game of Russian Roulette and no one knew when the gun would fire.

He glanced around at his friends, looking from face to face. Everyone was anticipating the inevitable. When would the gun go off? Whom would the almor choose?

Mark, Brynne and Sallax looked as though they had already been in a war; they were ready to collapse from fatigue. He guessed they had run up the trail overnight to warn him. Versen's absence must mean the Ronan woodsman had been the demon's first victim. What had it been like? Would he have felt the almor grab him from beneath the surface of the ground? Or perhaps his consciousness simply faded to black, like Steven's had when he had his appendix removed.

Versen knew. It had killed Versen and now it was here for

Gilmour, and doubtless anyone else who stood between it and the old man. Steven felt fear begin to well up inside him once again, but he forced it back down.

'No! My dream didn't mean anything,' he said to himself. 'Lessek did not speak to me because I'm done here; I did my job. I showed a surviving Larion Senate member where to find Lessek's Key. That was my role. I can go home now and God can shit on this place. I can go home and be a coward for ever. I can be a coward who murdered a Seron. That's goddamned perfect. I'll be a murdering coward, assistant manager in a small town bank, overqualified and uninspired. That will be my lot. Great.'

Steven had never given much thought to the possibility that his life had evolved the way he allowed it to. He knew only that he was unhappy and disappointed with choices he had made. Choices. That was the crux of his problem. He never *made* any choices. A fatalist and a coward, he left things to the winds and accepted consequences, jeopardising and abandoning whatever values he may have had to keep his life heading roughly in the right direction.

Versen had not been that kind of person. *Versen* made decisions in the best interests of his friends and family. He worked to free Rona from the chokehold of Malakasian occupation. *Versen* was a better person, a stronger person. Steven realised in an instant that he would never be that brave, that compassionate, or that willing to cling to his beliefs no matter what the consequences were.

At that moment, Steven's fear was overshadowed by rage, not the blind rage he had felt whilst battling the Seron, but a seething, controlled rage spiralling up from twenty-eight years of cowardice.

Without thinking, he strode to the centre of the path, separating Gilmour from Mark, Brynne and Sallax. They all cried out, almost in unison, for him to stand still, but he ignored them. It was clear what he had to do.

Steven began banging the staff against the earth, as if he were summoning the devil from its core.

'Come out, you demon bastard!' he shouted. 'Come out here and fight me!' He cried out at the top of his lungs, as if anything less would mitigate the moment, 'Show yourself, you chickenshit tapioca nightmare. I'll kick the shit out of you – if you're not afraid to come out here and take me!'

Mark, watching from a distance, was dumbfounded. 'What the fuck are you doing?' he screamed. 'It will kill you, Steven!'

He started down the path towards his roommate, but Sallax tackled him from behind, pinning him to the ground. 'You go and it will kill you both,' he whispered urgently in Mark's ear. 'This way Gilmour will know where the almor lies waiting and perhaps be able to save your friend's life.'

'No!' Mark shouted, but his plea was muffled by the explosion of earth and rock that enveloped Steven as the almor burst once again from the depths of Seer's Peak.

Blinded momentarily by the eruption of debris around him, Steven held his breath and tried to maintain his footing. The demon had not yet taken him. It towered above him, all around him. His vision was blurred, his hearing dulled by the cloudy fluid of the almor's mass.

Then Steven realised why he was still alive as the ghastly abomination spoke. 'We will battle now and you will learn what it means to feel fear.' The hollow voice rang in his head like the reverberations of an out-of-tune pipe organ.

'Then you can teach me nothing,' Steven shouted as he raised the hickory staff. He figured he had one shot before the beast dragged his soul into hell.

'I will savour your energy for a thousand lifetimes,' it roared back, but Steven was not listening; he was preparing for his last act of defiance: a mighty swing of the hickory staff he had found in the forest south of the Blackstone Mountains. That swing held all his trepidation and insecurity, all his tendencies to please others at his own expense, all his cowering in the shadows waiting for safe opportunities to be or become Steven Taylor. He held nothing back. He had one strike only and even that would be useless: a whittled section of tree branch had no chance against an ancient, otherworldly demon. He was about to die.

As he unleashed his blow, Steven began to feel his own life force draining into the almor. It was all right. He did not mind, just as long as he had just this one chance to do something for himself, of his own volition.

Against all the odds, it worked. He felt the shaft tear through the milky fluid of the almor, rending it open and spilling its malodorous blood into the dirt of the Seer's Peak ridge trail. The agonising cry rang in his head like an artillery volley and he nearly passed out at the shock wave.

Falling back, he watched as Garec fired into the creature as quickly as he could draw and release; shaft after shaft passed through the almor's frame. And as he fell outside the demon's grasp, Steven felt the blast of Gilmour's magic slam into the monster, opening the wound further and casting the creature off the cliff and down to the forest below. It screamed inside Steven's head as it fell, the terrified roar of a god's fall, an immortal seeing the ash-grey face of mortality.

The force of the almor's savage grasp tearing itself from Steven's mind caused him to roll over and vomit repeatedly into the dirt. He felt the creature slam into the rocks below. It was a surprisingly soft thud. Then it was gone.

Steven's head swam as he fell in and out of consciousness. He had done it. He had challenged and bested the demon. Dazed, he managed a smile – and realised Mark was supporting his head and shoulders. 'Do *not* try that at home, boys and girls,' he mumbled.

Mark laughed, a nervous chuckle to mask his fear and exhaustion. His voice cracked as he asked, 'You reckless bastard, do you need some water? What can we get for you? Anything?'

He tried to give his roommate a drink from Garec's wineskin, but Steven shook his head. 'Need?' he rambled on, delirious, in English. 'Need? I *need* to go home. I *need* a howitzer, the defensive squad of the New York Giants and a tactical nuclear weapon. We'll show that Nerak a thing or two.'

Garec leaned down to offer the young foreigner his hand. 'Can you stand?'

'Sure, I can stand,' Steven looked up into the faces of his newfound companions. The relief in their eyes was in such contrast to the stark fear he had seen there only moments earlier, he decided *that* alone was worth the risk he had taken in summoning the almor to the surface.

'I can stand,' he repeated shakily, then passed out on the dusty, rock-strewn trail.

When Steven woke again, it was dark. He rolled over to find Gilmour sitting near a small campfire. Around him, the others slept, breathing the steady rhythm of those who were troubled by nothing. As he sat up, he found they were once again camped on the flat surface of the landing. Gilmour waved him over nearer the fire.

'We're back up here,' Steven observed, stretching.

'It was the safest place for all of us,' Gilmour replied. 'Brynne, Sallax and Mark had a long night reaching the ridge-trail. You slept most of the day.'

'Versen?' Steven asked, fearing the worst.

'They're not sure what happened. No one saw him taken by the almor, but then again, no one saw him along the trail either.' Gilmour filled his pipe bowl with tobacco. 'We will return to camp tomorrow morning to see if we can find his remains.'

Steven nodded, then changed the subject. 'You know that staff is magic.'

'I do,' the old man confirmed, 'but I have no idea where it comes from. It is not familiar to me. It's not mentioned in any of the scrolls or spells I have studied for the past nine hundred and eighty Twinmoons. It is either very, very old, or essentially brand-new.'

'Seems strange.'

'If there's anything I've learned, Steven, it's that if it seems strange, it's probably strange.'

'You should wield it,' Steven said. 'Think of how powerful it would be in your hands. You're the sorcerer, after all.'

'It would do nothing in my hands, Steven. It chose you.'

'Chose me?'

'Of course. We both know there were no hickory trees in that valley. That staff found you, a half instant before you desperately needed it.' He tossed a big chunk of bark onto the fire. 'It found you for some reason, Steven, but I don't know what it is.'

'Why did it shatter that night but remain intact today?'

'The power of the magic you wield.'

'I don't wield any magic,' Steven said.

'Sure you do. We all do.' He thought for a moment, then asked, 'Tell me, what did you feel the night you killed the Seron?'

'Hatred,' Steven said, remembering the experience with pain. 'Hatred, and maybe fear that I might not make it home alive.'

'And what did you feel today?'

He thought back to the moments before he challenged the almor to confront him one-on-one. 'I suppose I felt fear and embarrassment, frustration and a lack of control.' He hesitated a moment. 'And cowardice. Mostly that. I felt acutely aware of twenty-eight years of cowardice.'

'But that's not all you felt,' Gilmour said, guiding his thoughts. 'At whom were these emotions directed today?'

'At no one. It wasn't like the Seron warriors. They were easy to hate. Today was different. Today, I was angry that we were all standing there waiting for one of us to die so the others would be able to pinpoint the threat.' He reached for a wineskin, but it was empty, so he tossed it back to the ground. 'I felt as though I needed to be the one killed so you all might live.'

'Compassion?'

'No. More like inadequacy. I looked around myself and thought, "Whose is the most expendable soul?" and I answered the same way.'

'Yours.'

'Yes, mine.'

'So, compassion.'

'I suppose so,' Steven agreed. 'That got me started, anyway. From there, all those other emotions took over and my course of action was inevitable.'

'That, Steven Taylor, is the secret of your magic,' Gilmour grinned, firelight dancing in his eyes. 'You killed the Seron warriors out of fear for your own life. I heard you shouting, "We might not make it", again and again. Today, you fought for others. Granted, your emotions were still very powerful, but today, you fought the way the staff wants you to fight, with compassion.'

'It's strange you describe it that way, Gilmour, because after killing the Seron, I promised myself I would never be so merciless again.' Steven peered off into the distant Blackstones as something began to form in his mind. 'I was angry with myself, because anyone incapable of mercy is the most evil enemy we can face. That night, I became that person.'

'And your magic weapon shattered with the effort.'

Steven nodded before going on, 'But today, it remained intact. It allowed me to funnel all that emotion into one furious strike at the almor.'

'Because you were acting out of compassion. Today, you were not afraid for your life. There was nothing selfish in your actions.'

'I suppose I was hoping to trade my life for yours.' He peered around the campsite at the bodies thrown into sharp relief by the flickering campfire. 'And theirs.'

'Well, my boy, that is your first lesson in the use and appreciation of magic.' Gilmour reached for a saddlebag. 'Come, sit down here. You must be hungry.'

Back along the ridge trail, Jacrys kneeled down in the dirt where the battle had taken place. He dabbed his fingers in the thick, foul-smelling gore, the almor's vital fluids. The young stranger was braver and more powerful than the spy had imagined. And although he was glad to see another of Malagon's disgusting pets destroyed, Jacrys felt a momentary lapse in his confidence. The old sorcerer was surrounded by a skilled group of killers, which would make Jacrys's task much more complicated. They had defeated the Seron beasts; now they had killed an almor. He had never heard of *anyone* killing an almor. Historically, the creatures could only be banished by the combined resources of powerful magicians and mystics – never by ordinary people, let alone one man or woman. That was impossible. Jacrys considered the dilemma another moment, then hurried along the ridge into the night.

Later, the dream came again; Steven watched it unfold on the broad canvas of his mind. It was the same Friday afternoon, and once again he was joking with Howard and Myrna about his own passion for maths and her passion for *Jägermeister*. He watched himself come out of his office and catch her trying to fit diameter lengths around a circle. She was organising it incorrectly, but he didn't tell her; it was fun to watch her struggle with knowledge she had learned in high school but assumed she would never apply. The circle itself was no help: she needed to use the shape to construct a rectangle. He demonstrated it once when Howard ordered pizza for lunch. 'Like giant teeth,' he explained. 'Organise the pizza slices across from one another. What do they form? A makeshift parallelogram. Now, imagine ten million tiny pizza slices organised in the same area. What do they form?'

'It's a rectangle,' she cried.

'Almost a rectangle,' he told her, 'but close enough for Egyptian architects to figure out the area of a circle is basically—'

'Length times width!' Myrna nearly came out of her chair, especially when she realised the problem was still confounding Howard Griffin.

'Exactly,' Steven confirmed. 'You see? There's no reason to make it more difficult than it needs to be.'

Howard reached for a slice of pizza, interrupting the quasi-edge of Steven's impromptu quadrilateral. 'There,' he said, 'figure that one out; I call it subtraction.'

THE RIVER CAMP

Brexan kneeled over the woodsman. He was alive, but he had not yet moved from where he had fallen after the demon's attack. The Malakasian soldier removed her cloak, folded it into a lumpy pillow and placed it carefully under the big man's head. Blood was coagulating around an open wound just above his neck: he had hit his head hard; he would be unconscious for some time. She counted his breaths, marking time as his broad chest moved up and down. She struggled to make out his features clearly in the half-light of evening, but she could tell he was handsome, although not necessarily in the traditional sense. This was a woodsman, a man to whom physical appearance meant little, but the unkempt, sandy hair, the wrinkled clothes and the short, scraggly beard did not detract from his striking countenance. His powerful hands rested on the ground and, acting on an impulse, Brexan folded them across his abdomen. From his belt she removed a battle-axe and a long dagger, afraid he might roll over on them and wake too soon.

Hearing a noise, she looked up as several horses wandered back into the remains of the Ronan camp. They had been frightened away by the almor, but had obviously not run far; now they sensed it was safe to return. Brexan took some comfort in that. Despite her confidence that the monster had pursued the others into the canyon, she couldn't help but worry that it might come back at any moment. She was still surprised it hadn't killed her on the beach that day after it had taken her old horse – maybe the almor was saving her for some later date.

She rose and walked as softly as she could, so as not to draw any undue attention to herself. Coaxing gently, Brexan corralled four of the animals, tethering them to nearby trees. She took particular care with one fiery mare, a strong animal who appeared to be looking askance at her as she looped the reins over a branch. Brexan stoked their small campfire into a blaze and rummaged through one of the abandoned saddlebags for something to eat. Finding a stash of apples, she removed two, bit into one herself and sliced the other into quarters for her horse. The beast whinnied once and took the fruit greedily from her outstretched palm.

She returned to the woodsman; he hadn't moved, so she made herself comfortable on the ground beside him. A light breeze blew through the grove as she leaned back against a crooked scrub oak. Gnawing contentedly on the apple, Brexan took stock of her current situation. She was absent without leave from the Malakasian Army. Her stomach tightened, remembering the moment when she had stripped her uniform of its patches and epaulettes. She hadn't wanted to be seen as deserting her platoon, but she wouldn't live long travelling alone, in uniform, through Rona. Perhaps she would return to Estrad one day and explain everything to whomever had replaced Lieutenant Bronfio – maybe Lieutenant Riskett. He had always been more reasonable: he was willing to listen to the soldiers and actually responded to their concerns or suggestions, unlike Bronfio. Considering this option a moment longer, she laughed and shook her head.

'Don't be silly,' she said out loud, biting the apple as if to punctuate her thoughts. 'You know you can't go back there.' Brexan could only hope Lieutenant Riskett had listed her as lost in the skirmish at Riverend Palace, although without a body to identify her, that was unlikely.

No, if she returned to Estrad, it would be in shackles, and she would be imprisoned, tortured, and hanged at the next Twinmoon as an example to all soldiers of Prince Malagon's army.

She inhaled deeply. It was cooler here than in Estrad; she was happy to sit quietly and enjoy the evening. The road north had been challenging: Jacrys was difficult to track. She had lost his trail entirely several times, but he kept turning up and now she had no doubts that he was trailing this band of partisans on their flight north. Though she had not seen the enemy they had faced that morning at Riverend Palace, she knew this group had been involved. She was still struggling to make sense of it all: Jacrys had ordered the platoons to take Riverend Palace because partisans had been using it for meetings, as well as storing weapons and silver. That was fine. But in the process, Jacrys had murdered Lieutenant Bronfio and the family of at least one partisan, before taking off after the fugitives. Why Bronfio? And why this particular band of freedom fighters?

Still she had no answers, nothing to explain why Jacrys had followed them into the mountains and ambushed them with a platoon of filthy Seron warriors, nor how he had managed to bring an almor along with him. He did not appear to have a sorcerer's skills – yet the almor had appeared twice while Jacrys was near of this group of Ronans. Was he controlling it? She bit off another mouthful of apple and, finding it bruised, spat it into the underbrush. He might have some magic at his disposal, but magic enough to control a demon would have to come from elsewhere, from the north. Prince Malagon.

A strand of hair fell over her shoulder and she played with it absentmindedly. It was long, too long. She had meant to have it cut before the last Twinmoon, but hadn't found time. She looked about the camp for something with which to tie it up. Among the putrefied remains of a dead horse, lying where the almor had tossed the husk of skin and bones after its attack, was an old saddle. Drawing a knife from her belt, she sliced off a thin leather thong tying up a tightly rolled wool blanket. As she cut it free, the blanket fell to the ground and partially unrolled across the leaves and dirt.

'That's better,' she said as she tied her hair back. Night had fallen and Brexan was growing somewhat impatient. She kneeled next to the partisan and shook him gently by the shoulders.

'Hey,' she whispered, 'wake up. You're safe; wake up.'

The man groaned in response and Brexan spilled a few drops of water across his lips from a wineskin she had found.

'Try again,' she encouraged, 'wake up.'

Versen opened his eyes and, grimacing, tried to sit up. 'Rutting dogs, it's you,' he exclaimed as he looked at Brexan.

Brexan, taken aback, said simply, 'Yes, it's me,' though she had no idea how he could know who she was.

Versen reached out and took her firmly by the shoulders. 'I never told you . . . I should have told you. I love you.' He pulled her to him and kissed her awkwardly on the lips before falling back onto her cloak and drifting back into unconsciousness.

'Of course you do, of course you love me.' Brexan leaned back against the twisted oak once again. 'What else would you say, really? "Hello", maybe. "Who are you?" perhaps. But no, not you, my brain-damaged Ronan buffoon, you open with "I love you". Fairly direct of you, and I must give you credit for bravery.'

She drank from the wineskin and added sarcastically, 'And I know it might be sudden of me, but I love you, too.' Sleeping soundly, Versen did not respond.

Brexan pulled herself to her feet. As she collected logs for the fire she looked about nervously for any sign of the almor, but the energetic mare was still cropping grass complacently nearby, so she assumed all was well for the moment. She began spreading out her own blankets for the night.

'Sleep well,' she called towards the grove. 'If you still love me in the morning, I might even brew you some tecan.' The Malakasian soldier lay still in the firelight, watching the stars and feeling the ominous presence of the Blackstone Mountains behind her in the dark, ponderous, black as pitch. Brexan was not looking forward to the next leg of her journey: the Blackstones were renowned for their treacherous cliffs, razor-thin trails and uncertain footholds. 'I'm not sure I have any choice, though,' she whispered to herself. 'I certainly can't turn around now.'

The breeze along the river had grown into a gusting wind. She shook her head, then sat up, pulled on her boots and walked back into the grove where Versen lay asleep. Finding the blanket she had cut free earlier that evening, she cast it over his still form and started walking back towards her own blankets.

She stopped and set her jaw in frustration. 'Motherless, inbred, whoring . . .' she muttered and turned back towards the trees. When she finally lay back down to sleep, Versen's boots had been removed and now stood side-by-side on the ground next to him; a blanket Brexan took from Brynne's abandoned saddle had been carefully tucked beneath his back, legs and shoulders to keep it from blowing away in the chilly evening breeze.

Brexan woke in the grey pre-dawn light to a gentle nudging at her ribs. She kicked the blanket aside as she sprang to her feet, hoping to confuse her attacker and grab a moment's edge in the coming fight. She had a dagger in one hand and her short sword in the other before reaching her feet then, blinking several times to clear the sleepy fog from her mind, she recognised Versen standing beside her, his hands raised.

'Whoa, hold on there,' he cried. 'I'm unarmed and I think you had something to do with that.' He lowered his hands slowly to his sides and added, 'Calm down, please.'

'What are you doing, coming up on me like that while I'm sleeping, you ox?' Brexan felt dizzy: the effect of leaping up so suddenly. 'I could have killed you.'

'True and you could have passed out.' He motioned for her to sit down and reached for a wineskin. 'Don't you know the moment you wake is the most stressful of the day? Going from deep sleep to *anything* is a chore; you jumped up like a rutting chainball champion.' He passed her the skin. 'Here, have a drink.'

Sheathing the dagger, Brexan accepted the wineskin and took a long draw.

'My name is Versen. I'm from Rona.'

'Brexan, and I know.'

'Did you cover me and take off my boots last night?'

'Yes.'

'Thank you.'

'It was cold.'

'Yes, it was and again, thank you.' Versen ran one hand across his empty belt. 'Did you happen to take my weapons?'

Brexan nodded towards the packs and saddlebags stacked near the fire. 'They're over there on the ground. I wasn't disarming you. I just didn't want—' She paused. 'I didn't want you to roll over and slice yourself open.'

'Well, again, I must say thank you, Brexan.'

'You do a lot of that.'

'You're right; I do seem to.' Versen took a seat near the remains of the campfire and proceeded to stir the flames gently until they crackled anew. 'Do you know what happened to the others?'

'The almor pursued them that way, into the canyon, but only the woman's horse was killed.'

Rubbing the back of his head, Versen pulled several bits of dried blood from his hair. 'I wasn't much use, was I?'

'Don't blame yourself.' Brexan finally sheathed her sword and sat down beside him. 'The almor is a magical creature, ancient and powerful. The fact that you aren't dead is good fortune enough.'

'Well, when it's fully light we have to go after them.' Versen caught himself, looked across at her and corrected himself. 'I should say, *I* have to go after them.' He hesitated another moment, then asked, 'Who are you, anyway? And what are you doing out here alone?'

Inexplicably, Brexan found herself telling Versen of her role in the battle at Riverend Palace, of Bronfio's murder and of her decision to pursue Jacrys until she either understood his motives or brought him to justice. Halfway through her tale she wondered if it was wise to tell this stranger so much – after all, he was a partisan, a freedom fighter sworn to rid Rona of the Malakasian occupation forces. But there was something about him that helped her feel at ease; although she did not know why, she believed he could be trusted.

As she finished, the sun broke the horizon.

'Did you not think they would kill you if they caught you?' Versen was incredulous. 'Why leave your unit, make yourself a fugitive from your own army in a land where travelling alone is almost certain to get you killed by partisans who hate you?'

'I admit I didn't put a great deal of thought into my decision at the time,' she said as she took a couple of apples from a saddlebag and tossed him one. 'I was furious. Killing innocent people is not why I became a soldier.' She paused to chew and swallow a mouthful before adding, 'I don't know; I guess I didn't think it through.'

'Well, it looks like you're on the run now.'

'No,' she answered matter-of-factly, 'I'm going to discover what Jacrys is up to. He murdered a Malakasian officer. That makes him a traitor.'

'Are all things really so black and white to you?'

'Many, yes.' Her directness surprised him. 'Too many people make things too rutting confusing. Sure, it might be fun sometimes to consider all those other variables. Maybe Bronfio was a spy. Maybe Jacrys was acting under orders. Maybe the lieutenant was sleeping with his wife. Who knows? But eventually, so many things end up making sense just the way you expected from the start. So start there. Jacrys is bad news.' She began rolling her blankets into a tight bedroll. 'How is your head?'

'Cracked clean through, I think.' He kicked dirt onto the fire. 'None of my hats will fit any more.' The flames died a smoky death, billowing dark clouds into the morning air. 'We ought to fetch me a new one at some point this morning.'

'Hat? Are you kidding?'

'Head, and yes I was.' He moved to the pile of satchels and began consolidating their contents, repacking them into a pair of large saddlebags. 'You are an intense woman, Brexan.'

'Soldier,' she corrected him.

'You don't look much like a soldier.' He smiled and replaced the dagger and battle-axe in his belt.

'Circumstances forced me to change out of my uniform. I might no longer be a member of the Malakasian occupation force, but I *am* a soldier and I *am* good at it.' She drew herself to her full height and endeavoured to look Versen in the eye. Realising she only reached the upper part of his chest, she looked away quickly. 'So,' her voice dropped, 'I would be grateful if you would try to remember that.'

Versen wanted to come up with something witty to somehow crack her angry exterior, but his head hurt and nothing came to mind. He changed the subject. 'Where are you heading today?'

Brexan pointed towards the canyon. 'In there.' She turned to face him. 'I lost his trail two days ago, but found yours instead. If the old man took the others up this hill—' She paused to gaze towards the top of Seer's Peak; Versen watched as the wind played with the strands of her hair that had come lose from the leather thong. Brexan grimaced and continued, 'That's where Jacrys will be going.'

She already knew Versen would follow his friends in the hope of finding them alive. 'You must remember the almor can only travel through a fluid medium, plant roots, underground water-ways and the like.'

'I know.'

'So if your horse senses it, or if you see evidence that it is nearby, you must get to somewhere it can't reach you, someplace bone-dry – no plants – a rock outcropping, or up a dead tree,' Brexan flushed, her face warm despite the cold morning. She did not want the big Ronan to believe she cared at all for his wellbeing.

She turned and caught him staring at her hair. Flushing again, she gathered it in one hand and pulled it self-consciously over her shoulder. Certain it was abysmally dirty, she wished she had a hat, even one of Versen's that no longer fit his crooked, broken head. She breathed deeply, then set about organising her pack. Irritated with herself, the Malakasian woman had not noticed Versen was now standing absolutely still in the centre of their camp. Shoving a short knife, a length of twine and her tecan pot deep into the satchel, she allowed herself to get lost momentarily in her packing. She wanted to be angry with this man. He was the enemy, a partisan, a criminal, traitor to the Malakasian throne. She ought to kill him right here and leave his body in the grove where she found him.

And how dare he disparage what she did? Look at him, out here, days' travel from anywhere. Did he really expect his revolution was going to begin here at the base of the Blackstones? She nearly laughed out loud – then she heard the mare whinny; she turned to see the horse pulling nervously on the reins that tethered her fast to a pine at the edge of the clearing. Brexan froze, her breath catching in her throat. Now she could see Versen standing motionless, staring into the trees. His battle-axe and dagger were drawn; his face had changed: no longer the handsome, charming woodsman, now he looked like every inch the revolutionary. For an instant Brexan hoped she would never have to face him in battle.

Rutters, she thought. *The almor.* Gingerly she let her pack fall to the ground, then cursed silently when it landed harder than she expected. 'Lords, why not just stomp your feet?' she whispered, but Versen paid no attention to her. Renna whinnied again; now the other horses began to show signs of anxiety as well, stamping nervously and pulling at their reins. Brexan considered the possibility of getting to them and slicing their leather harnesses to set them free. She didn't rate her chances of being quicker than the almor.

Then she heard it: a twig snapping, some leaves rustling . . . a momentary silence – before the woods around them came alive with a cacophony of footsteps, breaking branches, heavy movement through the underbrush and a series of unintelligible grunts that came from everywhere at once. Brexan began backing away, an involuntary response to the wall of sound bearing down on them.

'Don't move,' Versen commanded in a harsh whisper. 'Stand fast, here, next to me.'

She hurried to his side. Despite the nearly paralysing fear, her senses were alive and finely honed; she caught his scent, wild herbs mixed with a distant aroma of woodsmoke. She surprised herself by inhaling deeply, in hopes of breathing him in again before the attack came from all sides.

'What is it?' she asked softly.

'Seron.' Versen's reply was confident, and Brexan found that comforting, as if he somehow knew they would emerge unscathed.

He tucked the dagger under his arm and reached over to take her hand. 'It's all right,' he said, squeezing her fingers tightly in encouragement. 'They want us alive.'

'How do you know?' Her voice shook and she cursed herself for betraying her fear.

'Because this is not how Seron attack.' He dropped her hand; Brexan could feel the warmth of his grip fade with her resolve.

The first Seron came into view, emerging from the trees like a misplaced herd of cattle. The warriors hooted and grunted excitedly when they saw they had their quarry surrounded. Brexan estimated there were twenty of them; she understood immediately there would be no battle. The circle about them closed as the half-human warriors came forward. They were unimpressed by Versen's show of force: one man, one dagger, one battle-axe. Brexan was relieved she had left her Malakasian uniform in Estrad. Had these Seron realised she was absent without leave, she would be dead already, torn to pieces by the band of foul-smelling creatures.

There were no escape routes. The circle tightened, then the Seron stopped. Many grunted aloud, spat on the ground at their feet or pounded hairy hands against leather and chainmail breastplates. Brexan reminded herself to breathe. She dared not draw her weapons, even though she knew gripping a sword would help steady her shaking fingers.

Take my hand again. She cast her thoughts at Versen and was surprised she did not feel more embarrassment at wanting to feel the big man's touch. She was shorter than the Seron and could no longer see the forest behind them. In every direction, she could see only the black and brown leather of the Seron uniform. It was as though all Eldarn was folding up inside this clearing; she struggled even to hear the river rushing by. Convinced things would be all right if she could just capture the sound of the water in her mind, the ceaseless stream cascading over perfectly smooth rocks on its endless journey to the Ravenian Sea, she concentrated, but it wasn't there. It had stopped.

'Take my hand again.' She said it aloud this time and without hesitating, Versen dropped his dagger and gripped her hand so tightly she thought he would snap her fingers like so many brittle twigs. *Fine. So be it. Just don't let go.*

A huge warrior, a full head taller than Versen, strode forward and stood before them. Pounding a closed fist against his chest, he barked, 'Lahp.'

Versen dropped the battle-axe rather than letting go of Brexan's hand. He touched one finger to his chest and replied, 'Versen.' He nodded towards her and added, 'Brexan.'

'Glimr?' it grunted back at them. Brexan guessed it was a question, because the creature's voice rose slightly with the word.

'I don't understand,' Versen said calmly. 'What is Glimr?'

'Glimr,' the creature tried more forcefully this time. 'Glimr.'

'Gilmour?' Versen asked. Brexan felt his grip tighten. The heat from his touch grew in intensity. 'You are looking for Gilmour?'

Brexan could not remember the last time she had taken a breath. She watched in horror as the hideous Seron ran its tongue over a cracked and bulbous lower lip. Was it about to take a bite out of her?

Instead, it responded to Versen with a nod. 'Glimr,' it repeated.

Versen's hand began to shake, but his face remained calm, still the grim look of a revolutionary willing to fight to the death. The fact that she could feel his fear, and she knew he felt hers, brought them closer together. All at once, Brexan felt she understood the partisans.

Taking another moment in an effort to flatten the conspicuous tremor in his voice, Versen looked the Seron, Lahp, in the eye and replied, 'In a thousand Twinmoons, I would never tell you where to find Gilmour, you rancid, open-sored horsecock.'

Lahp struck with unexpected speed, his fist coming forward like a cudgel to land just under Versen's chin. The thud was audible. Brexan felt the woodsman's hand go limp an instant later as he fell. Without thinking, she reached for her sword. Gripping the hilt, its leather handle familiar against her palm, Brexan tried to draw the weapon from its scabbard, but she was too slow. Lahp's fist took her just below the eye in a cruel blow that cracked her cheek and sent her reeling unconscious to the ground.

The first thing Brexan noticed was the breeze. It had picked up. From her vantage point in the dirt, she thought she could see dark clouds massing far to the west. Although the sun still shone, it would rain soon. Her cheek throbbed, a dull ache that resonated through her head with the flat *clank* of a broken bell. Powerful hands held her down, one gripping the narrow edge of her hip while the other pressed flat against her breastbone. Waiting as the blurry edges of her vision came back into focus, she watched Versen's face take shape before her eyes.

'What? Think you're getting lucky, Ox?' she managed, almost blacking out again with the effort.

'Stay down,' he commanded gently. 'You took quite a shot.'

'I'm all right,' she lied, feeling a spasm of pain rush across her face, a searing sensation that brought tears to her eyes.

'No, you're not,' Versen replied and gave her a reassuring squeeze. 'But you will be in time.'

Deciding not to fight, Brexan lay back and closed her eyes. Tears began to well up behind her lids, but she fought them off. Inhaling sharply, she asked, 'Are they going to kill us?'

'I don't think so, not yet.'

Swallowing hard, she ran two fingers over her swollen face. 'How can you be sure?'

Versen pulled her hand away and touched her cheek, not the gentle touch of a friend, but the diagnostic touch of a healer. 'It's not too bad. I tried to set the bone while you slept, but it wouldn't move and you kept screaming when I pushed on it.'

'Well, thanks. Remind me to run you through the heart when I get my sword back.'

'Better than doing it now while you're awake. Good news is if it didn't move, it's probably just a fracture, a hairline crack.'

'Grand.'

'We need to get you to the river. The cold water will help with the swelling.'

Brexan lifted her head far enough to see they were still in the camp near the grove. She could hear the sound of the river and felt better, despite the pain. Their saddlebags and packs had been pillaged and lay about where the Seron warriors had tossed them. It looked as if the last of their food had been eaten; their weapons were now in the hands of the Seron. Resting her head once again in Versen's lap, she asked, 'You didn't answer my question. How do you know they won't kill us?'

'They're looking for something and they haven't found it; until they do, they have to keep us alive.'

'Find what?'

'A key.' Versen paused, searching for the best way to explain. 'A key to operate a magic chamber that will give Prince Malagon enough power to destroy the world, and all the other worlds as well, I suppose.'

'Other worlds.'

'Yes. Steven and Mark, the two strangers you watched on the beach. They're from another world, a world they call Color-ado, or something like that.'

Brexan agreed for the moment to give him the benefit of the doubt, no matter how crazy his explanation. They were still alive, after all and there had to be a reason for that. 'So, they're looking for Gilmour, because they believe he has this key?'

'That's right, but he doesn't.'

'Who does?'

'At the moment, no one.' Brexan looked confused, so Versen tried again. 'Right now, it is in Color-ado, where Steven left it. You see, he mistook it for a rock.'

'A rock? The key to enough magic to destroy Eldarn—'

'And other worlds as well—'

'And other worlds as well ... The key to more magic than anyone in their right mind can imagine was left somewhere, because some foreigner thought it was a rock.'

'That's right, at least as far as I can gather.'

'So that's why you're travelling north. To find this key.' Brexan was fascinated.

'In a matter of speaking, yes. We have to get to Welstar Palace to reach a portal that will take Gilmour, Steven and Mark back to Colorado where Gilmour can retrieve the key.' Versen realised he had been speaking too loudly and lowered his voice. 'Then Gilmour can use the key to destroy Prince Malagon— well, Nerak, really.'

'Nerak?'

'Never mind now; I'll explain later. You should rest if you can. We don't know what these monsters have in mind for us today. We should save our strength.'

Brexan suddenly noticed the bruise along Versen's jaw. 'He clobbered you pretty well, didn't he?'

'This?' Versen grinned broadly down at her. 'Oh no, I've been hit much harder than this!'

She tried to return his smile, but her cheek reminded her it would be some time before that would be possible again. Instead, she asked teasingly. 'Oh yes? By whom?'

'Women in taverns mostly,' he replied, deadpan, which made her laugh.

'Don't,' she begged, 'don't make me laugh, Ox. My face hurts.' Brexan closed her eyes, caught the distinctive aroma of wild herbs and woodsmoke on the brisk wind and managed a crooked smile despite the painful swelling in her cheek.

The midday aven had just begun when Lahp appeared, hulking across the clearing to where Versen and Brexan were still sitting together. Worried the Seron might strike her again, Brexan moved closer to Versen and pressed her cheek softly against his chest. *Please don't*, she thought, clenching her teeth in anticipation of another bone-rattling blow.

It never came. Instead, Lahp stood before them and gestured firmly with one hand for them to stand, grunting, 'Up, up!' as he did so.

As Versen helped Brexan to her feet, Lahp roughly shoved them in the direction of the horses and motioned towards the saddles that were lying nearby.

'Saddle the horses?' Brexan guessed. Her face twisted with pain and a thin trickle of spittle ran down her chin.

'Ah, ah,' Lahp grunted and shoved them both again before returning to directing the Seron preparations for travel.

Versen picked up Renna's saddle, watching as Lahp gave orders

337

to his platoon. Teams of leather-clad warriors scurried about, preparing weapons, distributing food and wineskins and scratching rudimentary maps in the dirt.

'We don't seem to be too well guarded,' Versen whispered. 'What's to keep us from saddling up and riding away?'

Brexan considered his question for a moment, then said, 'I don't know exactly, but I think I'm afraid to risk it.'

'Look at them, though,' he pressed, trying to convince her. 'It looks as if they've mostly forgotten we're here. They knocked us out, searched our bags – and then ignored us the rest of the day. It doesn't make sense.'

'Versen, no. We don't have any weapons. If they ran us down, they'd kill us for sure.'

'Yes, but we have Renna.' He draped Garec's saddle over the mare's back and patted the horse affectionately. 'She's fast, Brexan, faster than any horse I've ever known. She outran a pack of grettans once. She'd have no problem with this lot of crippled plough-horses.' Renna tossed her mane, as if anticipating the coming chase with enthusiasm. Even after the smooth hair along the horse's neck came to rest, the wind lifted it once more in a momentary illusion of speed and strength.

'All right,' Brexan whispered. 'Let's do it – but I am *not* going to get hit again. If we get caught, I want to go down fighting. I don't ever want to be that frightened again.'

She was preparing the second horse when she caught sight of Lahp coming towards them, this time with three tough-looking Seron in tow.

As if reading her mind, Versen said quietly, 'Hold fast. Let's see what this is about.'

Without speaking, Lahp pushed Versen towards Renna and he climbed into the saddle. Grabbing Brexan by the upper arm, the Seron leader shoved her towards the mare as well. Versen reached down to help her up behind him.

Resting one enormous paw on Renna's pommel, Lahp handed Versen and Brexan two blankets and a wineskin filled with river water. Uncertain if she was allowed to drink from the skin, Brexan held it firmly against her swollen cheek.

Lahp laughed, an ugly, wet and raspy sound. It reminded Brexan of the cry of a beaten dog.

Then the Seron leader grunted a series of orders and the three warriors with him donned packs and climbed onto three of the remaining horses.

One turned to them, balled up his fist and slapped it against his chest. 'Karn,' he said malevolently, as if the name meant famine, or death, or some other equally unpleasant thing.

Not wanting to anger their escort, Versen in turn pointed to himself and then to Brexan and said their names clearly: 'Versen. Brexan. Happy to meet you.'

Brexan nearly cried out in horror when she realised one Seron, the smallest of the group, was a woman – or at least *had been* a woman, before Prince Malagon purloined her soul and turned her into a monster.

'Brexan,' she said quietly, pointing a finger at her broken cheek.

'Rala,' the Seron woman replied gruffly.

Brexan glanced at the third member of their escort. He did not speak, but glared back at her in silence. She noticed a long scar that ran across his face like the map of a great river. It had obviously been a deep wound, slicing through his cheek and severing part of his nose.

'Brexan,' she tried again, but he stared straight ahead, ignoring her and Versen entirely. With a shiver, Brexan wrapped her arms around Versen's chest and buried her face in the folds of his cloak.

The leader, Karn, spurred his mount toward a break in the trees. Rala followed, nodding to the scarred creature and grunting, 'Haden.'

The Seron with the ruined face turned to stare at the prisoners. 'Ah,' he growled, pointing towards Rala's mount.

Versen nodded and nickered Renna into line. They rode off southwest with Haden bringing up the rear.

After breakfasting on the last of their provisions, the travellers made their way down Seer's Peak and back into their former base camp. It was an aven past midday by the time they reached the forest floor. Steven purposely averted his eyes from the area where the almor's remains were scattered. He found it odd a demon would be comprised of flesh, albeit rank and putrid flesh, and he had no wish to see what was left of it.

Instead, he kept his gaze fixed on the Blackstones while

contemplating the next dilemma facing them: getting safely to Falkan before winter set in. He and Mark were the only experienced climbers in the group; although Gilmour had shown uncanny agility, it would be up to them to get the band of freedom fighters safely over the passes and into Orindale.

Steven gripped the hickory staff and breathed deeply. He felt reborn. The air smelled fresh and clean; the earth felt familiar under his feet and the evergreens were starkly outlined against a flawless blue sky. He wasn't certain if he felt better because he could summon a mysterious and powerful magic, or because he had faced his fears and emerged unscathed. Either way, he had to admit to being almost excited about their journey to Welstar Palace – and the inevitable confrontation with Prince Malagon.

During the descent from Seer's Peak, Steven allowed his mind to wander, not along memorised trails in the impossibly distant Rocky Mountains this time, but along the path he imagined his life taking in the future. Looking back was safe but humiliating. Looking forward was terrifying but exhilarating and he was determined not to make his old mistakes again, not here in Eldarn, or back home in Idaho Springs.

He had been both victim and coward for too long; now he could see with more clarity; he could feel with more compassion and genuine concern. His only regret was that Hannah was not there with him.

The remains of the camp punctured Steven's mood. Seron and grettan tracks crisscrossed the area in a confusing jumble. Splatters of blood disappeared south and west and numerous footprints ran into the canyon and along the western edge of Seer's Peak.

Sallax went immediately to the grove where the almor had first attacked. Garec could hear him moving about in the fallen leaves. Everyone held their breath in anticipation of the grisly report, but their immediate fears were unfounded.

'No sign of Versen,' he started, pausing as a collective sigh ran through the group. 'Except for the remains of Brynne's horse, the other mounts are gone – saddles too.'

Garec snapped into action. 'Then one of these blood trails might be Versen's. Mark and Steven, you follow the blood south. Brynne, you and Gilmour follow to the west.'

They all nodded as Garec warned them, 'Remember, a

wounded animal is always dangerous and a wounded grettan is worse: it will be an angry nightmare. If Versen is injured, it was most likely by the Seron, not the grettans, but that doesn't matter right now: the loss of blood might mean he doesn't have much time left.'

They drew weapons and, crouching close to the ground, followed the tracks into the forest.

Garec was already wishing Versen were there to help him decipher the clues hidden in the footprints. They had, between them, managed to work out that a large group of Seron had stormed into camp, probably expecting to take the Ronans by surprise. Finding the camp deserted, it looked as if the Seron had pillaged the abandoned packs and saddlebags, drinking – and spilling – the wine and eating the last of the food. They had taken time to re-saddle the horses before setting off again, although Garec could see from the hoofprints that several mounts were missing. His stomach turned: he feared he would never see Renna again.

The grettans had come from the west, so not the pack Gilmour had summoned to the Merchants' Highway to raid the caravan. Thin telltale ruts running through the clearing showed where the ravening beasts had dragged their hapless victims; Garec wasn't sure if he hoped that Versen were still alive at that point. He even felt a little sorry for the Seron.

Most of the grettan tracks then left the camp together and headed east, though a couple disappeared into the canyon, most likely in pursuit of fleeing Seron warriors.

Steven and Mark's prompt return confirmed Garec's suspicion.

'It looks like a grettan dragged one of those Seron soldiers off about a hundred paces,' Mark told him, 'and ate it. We couldn't find any blood beyond the large stain where it tore the body apart.'

'Are you certain it wasn't Versen?'

'Yes,' Steven said, grimacing. 'It left the boots there.'

'And any tracks?' Sallax asked.

'They moved off east,' Mark confirmed.

Gilmour and Brynne had found a similar scene, but the grettan they had tracked headed south into the foothills after feeding on an injured Seron. Brynne carried what was left of a thick hairy forearm. She dropped it into the ashes of their forgotten campfire where it settled, a mutilated stump half dusted in black and grey.

'We ought to make camp in the canyon tonight,' Sallax suggested. 'If we can get to higher ground that would be even better. We only have about a half aven before it'll get dark so we had better get moving.'

'I wasn't able to find Versen's boot prints,' Garec explained, 'so we should assume he is alive and that he rode out of here on one of the horses.'

Gilmour chimed in, 'Hopefully, he has ridden into the canyon and has a head start on us.'

'He knew we couldn't get far up the first pass with the horses, so if we don't find him in the next two days, there's a good chance he rode south or west,' Mark added.

Sallax interrupted, saying, 'It doesn't matter. We have to clear out of here and get as far up that hill as possible before it gets too dark.'

'I'll get us some fish for dinner,' Garec said as he drew several arrows from his quiver and hurried off towards the river.

'And I'll fill the skins,' Brynne said. 'We don't know how far into the mountains we'll go before we find a stream.'

'Good,' Sallax agreed, then turned to Steven. 'See what you can salvage from the packs and saddlebags strewn about here on the ground.'

The evening grew cold as the group navigated the twists and turns of the narrow canyon. Passing the Seer's Peak trailhead, Gilmour became lost in thought once again. Garec guessed what troubled his friend. The almor, the Seron and the grettans had found them at the base of Seer's Peak shortly after their arrival. They were being watched, tracked. Malagon knew where they were every step of the way.

Garec was not sure why the Seron would be battling grettans when they had both been sent to kill the Ronan partisans; perhaps Nerak simply didn't care if they killed one another. Perhaps the use of all three killers was designed to bring as much deadly force down upon the band of travellers as possible. It appeared to be a pretty safe bet that as long as Gilmour and the others were killed, Nerak was indifferent to his servants getting killed themselves in the process.

Snaking through the canyon, Garec thought again of his dream, watching as the land died, turning into an arid wasteland as the Estrad River slowed to a trickle. He hoped Lessek's vision was not one of an unavoidable future. He remembered ghostly wraiths moving between trees in the forbidden forest, a thousand eerily silent souls floating effortlessly above the ground. Garec had no idea who – or what – the spirits sought. And he pondered the significance of the strange pair coupling furiously on the woollen carpet of a Riverend Palace apartment. Garec did not understand why such an exquisite woman would be willing to engage with such a partner.

If it had been a final effort to carry on the Grayslip family line, maybe there was an heir to the Eldarni throne somewhere in Rona. Garec was still confounded by the fact that Lessek had shared such a vision with him. Was he destined to seek out and serve Eldarn's next king or queen, to remain in Rona while his friends continued north? It might take hundreds of Twinmoons to locate the great-great-great grandchild of an unknown woman who had been impregnated by a dying prince so long ago.

And if it were true that Prince Draven of Malakasia was not Prince Marek's father, then the Malakasian line was ruling Eldarn illegally. Perhaps that was his mission: to restore to Eldarn its true king.

Garec realised suddenly that he, like Gilmour, had fallen into deep thought. Looking around at his companions, he guessed they were all sorting out difficult questions for themselves as they slogged dejectedly north.

The canyon ended in a slight draw running between two imposing peaks, the beginning of a pass over which the travellers would climb the following day. It was nearly dark now and Sallax suggested they make camp and eat the meagre supplies they had been able to salvage. Garec immediately backtracked down the canyon to a rock outcropping that provided an aerial view of the narrows in both directions. Maybe there was light enough for him spot and shoot any unwary animal in search of a safe place to bed down for the night.

A half-aven later he could no longer see far enough for an accurate shot. He returned to camp empty-handed, tired and hungry.

*

Versen stretched his stiffening muscles in an attempt to alleviate cramp: they had been riding without a break all day and he was feeling the strain. Their Seron escort had paid them scant attention, other than to ensure they kept moving. Karn led the way southwest along a narrow path through the foothills which would eventually reach the Ravenian Sea. Renna was between Karn and Rala and the scarred Seron, Haden, brought up the rear. Although Karn and Rala conversed in grunts and odd phrases, Haden did not communicate with anyone.

The company ate an unappetising midday meal on horseback: day-old fish, stale bread, and a few pieces of welcome tempine fruit. Later, Versen tried to recall its sweet orange flavour. Behind him, Brexan appeared unaffected by the long ride and poor food. The Malakasian soldier was obviously very fit, for she rode all day without complaint. Versen marvelled at her stamina.

'Aren't you tired?' he asked, shaking his hands to get some feeling back in them.

Brexan smiled. 'Thirty-five Twinmoons of dance lessons, Ox. I have better posture than you.'

'So you're aching a bit too?'

'I think my bottom fell off an aven ago,' she responded, grinning wryly.

Versen laughed aloud for a moment, quieting quickly when Karn glared at him. Leaning back, he whispered, 'I'm sure you have some part of it left down there.'

Brexan whispered back, 'Thank you for not peeking, Ox. I meant it about the posture, though.'

The Ronan woodsman sat upright in the saddle, straightening his back and holding his head high. 'There, how's that?'

'You'll make a fine dancer.'

Versen scoffed. 'Dance lessons? Only in Malakasia. Ronan kids have to learn those things in secret, dancing in basements or barn lofts, thanks to your occupation.'

'Oh lay off, Ox. I never had dance lessons.' Brexan scowled. 'I'm a better rider than you, that's all.' The scowl vanished as she added, 'And I didn't grow up planning to occupy Rona; I just wanted to be a soldier. My division was sent to Rona. I wasn't happy about it and I left without permission because I realised how unfair our occupation had become. I'm a criminal in my own country now. I'll be executed the moment they find me. So you should be more pleasant to me.'

Versen slouched forward and muttered, 'I'll give you the better posture, but you are *not* a better rider than I am.'

Refusing to back down, Brexan retorted, 'One day, we shall see.'

Smirking, the big Ronan teased her, 'Well, I can certainly sing better than you.'

'Love arias? Songs about the many intelligent and engaging women you meet in taverns?'

'Maybe a little of both.'

'Well, I can't wait to hear your "Ode to Capella of Capehill".'

Versen feigned surprise. 'Do you know her?'

'Stop it, Ox,' she said as she poked him in the ribs.

'*She* never minded my peeking.'

At that Brexan laughed and rested her head between his shoulder blades. Her cheek still ached; she longed for the healing power of querlis leaf. Periodically Versen asked how she was and periodically she answered, 'I'm fine.'

She had been too embarrassed at her obvious fear of the Seron to discuss the incident with Versen earlier, but now that he had seen her as low as she could possibly get, she brought it out in the open. Drawing away from the comfort of his broad back, Brexan said quietly, 'I am sorry about this morning.'

'Why?' Versen said. 'It wasn't your fault. We were surrounded.'

'No—' She hesitated. 'I'm sorry I wasn't more—'

'Brave?'

'Well . . . yes.'

'Don't worry about it. You were brave enough.'

'I was terrified.'

'So was I.'

'I thought they were going to kill us.'

'Had we been more brave, they probably would have.'

'I wanted you to think I was a good soldier.'

'I am quite certain you are a good soldier and I am also quite certain all good soldiers are afraid when under attack.' He turned slightly to look into her swollen face. 'You deserted your platoon to pursue a spy and murderer. You followed him halfway to Falkan, alone. You risked everything to bring justice to a dead lieutenant you didn't particularly like.'

Versen reached down and squeezed her knee gently. 'You're one of the bravest people I have ever known.'

Brexan inhaled sharply and held her breath. She did not want him to see her cry. It was somehow important to keep her emotions under control.

Versen sensed her discomfort and changed the subject. 'How's your face now?'

Brexan's voice caught in her throat. 'It hurts. It really hurts.' This time she couldn't stop the tears.

'Don't worry,' Versen said, trying – and failing – to think of anything comforting. 'I'll look at it when we stop.'

'I don't want them to hit me again,' she said, crying openly now.

'I won't let them hit you. I promise. Why don't you try to get some rest? I won't let you fall.'

Brexan muttered a thank-you and rested her face against his shoulder again. Talking with him helped.

Versen, trying to take Brexan's mind off the pain, said, 'The first caravan we raided along the Merchants' Highway, I was young, maybe one hundred and ten Twinmoons. It was heavily guarded, but we went in anyway.'

'What happened?'

'I never drew an arrow or lifted a sword. I just stood there until an escort soldier, a Ronan mercenary hired to protect the shipment, came at me with an axe. I pissed myself, right there in the road.'

'How did you get away?'

'My friend Garec killed him – a miracle shot, right through the neck, dropped him in mid-stride.' Versen's voice fell to a whisper. 'Garec was even younger than me, maybe eighty-five Twinmoons. He was already the best shot I'd ever seen, and I've still not met a better. He killed six people that morning, saving my life and others . . . it was the day Sallax started calling him "Bringer of Death".'

'You were so young.' Brexan lifted her head. 'You shouldn't have been there.'

'That may be true, but my point is that I learned early how to hide my fear.'

'I'll work on that for next time.'

'Up to you, but not necessary.' Versen took her hand. 'I'll never judge you – or anyone – for being afraid during a battle.'

'What happened to your friend?' Brexan asked.

'He's even more deadly these days, a real virtuoso with a longbow. It bothers him to do it, though.'

'To kill?'

'Right. He hates it. He may be better at it than anyone in Eldarn, but he hates it. Every arrow he fires saps the strength from his soul.'

'Perhaps he should stop.'

'Perhaps he should.'

With that, Brexan snaked her arms around the Ronan's torso and once again buried her injured face in the folds of his cloak until she fell asleep. Something had changed between them in the last half-aven; each felt easy with the other's touch.

Versen revelled in the knowledge that the young woman felt comfortable enough with him to sleep soundly against his back, but, no longer distracted by their conversation, he realised just how much he still ached.

'Dance lessons,' he laughed to himself, 'well, it can't hurt to try.' Moving carefully so he didn't awaken Brexan, he adjusted his posture, sitting up straighter and lifting his head. Rutters. She was right. It helped.

A half-aven later Karn motioned for them to rein in and dismount. Unsure what to do next, the captives remained standing next to Renna. Brexan, whispering meaningless phrases, ran her hands along the mare's neck. She wished she had an apple or some oats to offer the tired beast.

Rala pushed them both out of the way and led the mare off the trail to a small clearing. She looped the reins over a low-hanging branch, leaving the horse free to graze.

Karn motioned for Versen and Brexan to join him. He tossed them each a blanket, then gestured for Versen to gather wood for a fire.

Versen, mindful of his promise and unwilling to leave Brexan alone with the Seron, demanded, 'She comes with me.'

Karn lumbered over to him and the Ronan winced in anticipation of another painful blow. Instead, the Seron surprised him by smiling, flashing him a mouth filled with discoloured, crooked teeth.

'Na, na,' the foul soldier insisted and indicated that the young woman should retrieve his saddlebags.

'It looks like they want you to cook,' Versen said, relieved. 'I think you'll be all right.'

Brexan forced a lopsided smile, her cheek bulging. One eye had swelled nearly shut. 'Well, when they discover I can't even brew tecan without a recipe, they'll put me on wood collection next time.'

Dinner consisted of pale mush, a mixture of crushed oats, wheat, nuts and some herbs, Brexan guessed. Her job had been to find and boil water, stir in a small bag of the grain concoction and stand by as it began to congeal. She watched as their Seron escort ate heartily; beside her, Versen did the same. He paused to look at her quizzically when he noticed her staring.

'What?' he asked between mouthfuls.

'How can you eat that stuff?'

'This?' Versen gestured into his trencher. 'This delicate soufflé of finest quails' eggs, over which you laboured for avens?'

'Ox—'

'I am famished,' he told her, 'and you must be. It may be bland, but it's perfectly edible. At least it's not some rotting animal. You should eat. You know better than to go hungry when you don't have to.'

Brexan scooped up a finger full of the gloop, ate it and scowled. 'It tastes like yesterday's laundry.'

'Eat it anyway.'

Pouting like a schoolgirl, Brexan finished her portion, but nearly retched when Versen reached into the pot and ladled another helping into her trencher. She soon recognised that he was as much interested in seeing the Seron's response to him acting without permission as he was in feeding her up.

Surprisingly, Karn grunted his approval and motioned for Brexan to eat as much as she desired.

Opposite the prisoners, Rala and Karn began arguing. Versen couldn't make out the topic of their disagreement, other than Rala was disagreeing with her leader about something. Though Karn was in charge, he didn't appear to be as dangerous or violent as Lahp. At least Karn was willing to listen to Rala –Versen imagined Lahp would have run Rala through simply for daring to question his orders. Versen hoped their less rigid approach might provide him and Brexan an opportunity to escape . . . but Haden was always lurking on the periphery. He said nothing.

After an animated exchange, Rala cursed angrily and wandered off to unpack her bedroll. Karn looked upset as well. He moved the horses to another area of the clearing, where sedge and grass grew in abundance. Neither Seron spoke, and neither seemed concerned with their prisoners. Without looking at Brexan, Versen whispered, 'If they continue like this, I'm sure we'll be able to get away.'

'They aren't paying much attention to us at all,' Brexan agreed.

'No and I'm not sure why.'

'Maybe they don't care if we escape. We obviously don't have that key you were talking about.' She pulled her knees in tightly against her chest and rested her chin on them.

'That's why they have to keep us with them, though,' Versen said. 'If they capture Gilmour, they'll find out that none of us have it.'

'What will happen then?'

'They will most likely kill Gilmour and torture the others.'

'And us?'

Versen didn't mince words. 'This one with the scar . . . he will kill us.'

As night fell, Haden placed the last of their firewood on the dimly glowing coals and rolled into his blankets to sleep. Rala dozed against a nearby tree trunk; Brexan watched as her head slumped forward onto her chest. Karn remained awake for another aven, whittling at an oak branch with his dagger and humming an out-of-tune melody to himself. Finally he nodded towards his captives and shuffled off to his own bedroll.

Despite her fatigue, Brexan was completely awake, but she feigned sleep, breathing in a slow, measured rhythm, until she was confident all the Seron were asleep.

'What are they doing?' she asked quietly. 'They must know we'll run.' The thought was so loud and vivid in her mind that she was sure the Seron could hear it.

'I don't know.' Versen was sceptical as well. 'But we have to risk it. You get Renna. I'll get Karn's saddlebags.'

'No,' Brexan said, too loudly. She lowered her voice and continued, 'You'll wake them. Let's just go. We'll find food tomorrow.'

Versen furrowed his brow, then agreed. They crept to where Renna was tethered and Brexan gingerly disentangled the mare's leather reins from the oak tree while Versen saddled her, trying to avoid the stirrups clanging together.

Brexan stroked the horse's neck and whispered, 'We need you to be quiet, Rennie, very quiet. We're going to find Garec.'

Versen reached down and helped the Malakasian up behind him. His hand lingered in hers a moment. 'That's what Garec calls her, too.'

'Rennie?'

Kicking the horse softly in the ribs, the woodsman added, 'It appears you've made another friend this trip, Brexan.'

The young woman responded by wrapping her arms more tightly around Versen's waist.

As silently as they could, they rode towards the trail. Renna appeared to have understood their need for haste and stealth; she stepped lightly despite carrying two riders.

As they turned east along the forest path, Versen thought for a moment they had made it. His heart leaped as he peered back at camp. None of the Seron had moved. The remaining horses would be no match for Renna in a race. Still, running a full sprint carrying two riders was dangerous and would tire the mare more quickly, so Versen determined to put as much distance as they could between themselves and the Seron. With every step their chances improved.

But some fifty paces outside the firelight, Versen realised something was wrong. He heard a faint rustle coming from a twisted scrub oak along the trail. He reined Renna to a stop.

'What's the matter?' Brexan whispered. 'We have to keep moving.'

'Quiet just a moment,' Versen whispered, then asked, 'Do you hear that?'

'It's just the wind.'

'There is no wind.'

He could feel the young woman tense behind him. 'Again, the soldier,' he whispered to himself. 'She's freed her arms, ready to fight.' He grinned, despite the tension. 'And she thinks she's a coward.'

Versen squinted into the darkness, struggling to see what was making the tiny oak shrub quake before them.

'Maybe it's just a bird,' Brexan suggested, but as she spoke the faint moonlight broke through the confounding tangle of pine branches overhead and lit the tree, which appeared to shrink. It grew smaller, then withered.

'Rutters,' Versen spat. 'They have an almor. No wonder they didn't care if we wandered about.'

'I thought it went after the others.' Brexan trembled; watching the scrub oak wither to a husk, she thought better of their plans to escape.

'Maybe there's more than one,' Versen speculated. 'Who knows what demons Malagon can summon?'

'Should we run for it, run the other way?'

'We'd never make it. They're too fast. It would have Renna in an instant and then we'd be left on foot.'

As if reading their minds, the almor extended one fluid appendage above the ground. Glowing palely white, starkly contrasted against the darkness of the forest, it was a ghostly warning: 'Turn back.'

Bringing Renna about, they covered the short distance back into camp, tethered the mare to the same oak branch and returned to their bedrolls. Karn and Rala still slept soundly, Rala snoring loudly through her nose while Karn lay on his back, his arms thrown above his head in a gesture of mock surrender.

Brexan adjusted her cloak, folding it into an uneven pillow. She was about to close her eyes against the night, against their captivity and against her fear when she saw Haden peering at her through the firelight. He grinned, hideously.

Brexan did not sleep until exhaustion overtook her an aven before dawn.

THE SOUTHERN SLOPES

Morning in the Blackstones brought rain, a cold drizzle that soaked through cloaks and tunics, leaving everyone chilled to the bone. Garec's knee was seizing up in the damp; although the injury was healing despite his refusal to rest, much of this sort of weather might damage it permanently. He remembered twisting his knee falling from a cliff above Danae's Eddy into the Estrad River, escaping from the largest gretdan he could ever have imagined. It felt so long ago.

Garec blinked: he had just realised that day had been the beginning of this whole ordeal. He'd got home to find soldiers interrogating everyone. They had beaten Jerond that morning. Now the young partisan was missing; Garec feared he was dead. Namont and Mika were dead and Versen was gone; they had found no sign of him.

Garec wanted to believe that Versen had escaped on Renna and maybe ridden west to find another route through the Blackstones, but he thought it was a bit of a vain hope.

Now searching for a passable route through the southernmost peaks, the small group fought their way up the muddy slope. Despite its gradual incline, the narrow draw was a natural runoff and the travellers found themselves ankle-deep in freezing water and covered with heavy, wet filth.

Garec, the last in line, struggled to make his injured leg move. To take his mind off the pain he replayed images from his dream, trying to work out what Lessek might be communicating to him. Gilmour kept saying Lessek's message would become clear in time, but Garec was afraid he was letting his companions down by his lack of insight.

Climbing, slipping, cursing, sliding, pointlessly scraping mud from his clothes, pushing on . . . the Ronan bowman missed his family's farm. He missed nights sitting around the fire after stuffing himself with roasted meat, mounds of potatoes and succulent fresh vegetables. His father baked bread above the hearth, its aroma permeating the house, maybe even the entire countryside. It was the near-perfect scent of 'everyone is welcome here'.

He and his sisters would drink red wine and cool ale from casks stored in the family cellar and chat and laugh together for avens on end. Was there any better place in Eldarn? Were there ever better times than those? Garec was clinging to the side of the mountain, yet another mountain, pushing ever forward to battle an unbeatable foe and every part of him wanted nothing more than to turn back, to go home and to fall into the comfort of predictable, familiar, *safe* routines of life on the farm.

Then they were upon him again, the visions of a beautiful young woman, naked, her body exposed: he was embarrassed to look at her; did she know he was there watching, peering at her longingly in his mind? Her insane partner was there as well, screaming and cajoling unseen demons that scudded across the ceiling, visible to no one but him.

Had they succeeded in creating Eldarn's king or queen?

If the Estrad River ran dry, if the land cracked and burned, he would never again enjoy a day at the farm. If Rona itself died, there would be no family feasts, no all-day preparation capped by long nights eating, drinking and dancing together.

That was why he continued north. *That* was why he was cold and wet and miserable. He was looking for answers. Would he be forced to kill Malagon to save Rona? Would he have to die himself?

Garec did not discuss his feelings as easily as the two foreigners did, but like Steven, he was uncomfortable killing. He was skilled; his arrows almost always found their mark. But too often he imagined the pain his enemies experienced, the intense and terrible fire burning from inside out. Garec reflected upon and regretted every arrow, while at the same time knowing he had to sublimate his regrets if he were to survive himself.

'Just until this is over,' he promised, 'just until Eldarn is free.' With the battle won, he vowed he would find some way to reconcile his actions. Garec imagined how disappointed his sisters would be if they knew their baby brother had become such a finely honed instrument of death. Steven had found great courage and killed with efficiency, but the foreigner killed with a discovered magic, a powerful talisman. Garec had no mystical excuse. He faced his enemies on equal footing and still emerged without a scratch. He was perhaps the most dangerous weapon the Ronans had, because he represented what anyone could become when oppressed or tortured long enough. He was just such a man; he hated killing, yet he killed more often than anyone he knew.

Perhaps, Garec thought, that was why he found himself haunted by visions of ghostly wraiths. Perhaps the souls of those he killed would stay with him for ever, taking up residence in his woods, crowding him out of his most beloved hunting grounds. He saw them again, drifting through his mind's eye, flitting from tree to tree, their faces hidden from him.

He hoped time would bring him answers; now he struggled to force the images from his mind as he clawed his way uphill.

One particularly resilient ghost remained. Garec closed his eyes and shook his head from side to side before peering into the trees just off the pathway. It was still there, a disembodied spirit, hovering inside a stand of young evergreens. Garec stopped.

From up ahead, Brynne noticed and called over the din of the rainfall, 'What is it?' The others, curious, stopped to watch him.

Garec pointed towards the wraith and whispered, 'It's one of the spirit creatures I saw in my dream.'

'Great rutting Pragans! So it is,' Gilmour exclaimed and started towards the trees. 'You there,' he ordered the spirit onlooker. 'Stay where you are.'

Steven and Mark exchanged a surprised glance and Steven moved quickly to accompany the older man.

'What is it, Gilmour?' Steven asked, nervously turning the hickory staff in his hands.

'I don't know. But it is watching everything we do.'

'Can you talk with it?'

'I plan to try.' Searching between the young evergreens, Gilmour added irritably, 'If we can get it to stand still for half a moment.'

'Do you suppose it was sent here by Malagon? Like the Seron or the grettans?'

'I don't know.' Gilmour moved rapidly into the trees in an

effort to flush the spirit out into the open. 'It doesn't seem to mean us any harm ... yet.'

The trees, just tall enough to block his view, would have made perfect Christmas trees for the average Colorado home, but as a grove, Steven thought, they were a confusing maze of identical clones, all conspiring to keep him at least one half step behind Gilmour as the old man hustled about. Steven rounded a corner and suddenly came upon the wraith; Gilmour was nowhere in sight.

'Christ,' Steven yelled and raised the staff to ward off any ghostly attack.

None came. The spirit simply hovered above the ground, its head, shoulders, upper arms and torso now clearly visible. Its extremities seemed to have been forgotten, as if hands and feet were useless in the afterlife; Steven marvelled at how its fringes appeared to dissipate like a cloud of pipe smoke on an undetected breeze. Gilmour came up behind him and Steven jumped. 'How did you get back there?'

'Never mind,' the old man said as he studied the wraith with a practised eye. Steven was convinced this was not the first spirit Gilmour had ever chased through the woods.

Drawing confidence from the magician's presence, Steven turned to study the creature more closely. One strange feature moved in and out of focus; Steven suddenly realised what he was looking at.

'It's a belt buckle, B-I-S! ' Steven said excitedly, 'I recognise it! It came from my bank, many years ago. And I know who he is – his photograph hangs in our lobby. He was one of the first tellers at the Bank of Idaho Springs.'

Barely had Steven finished speaking when the wraith vanished, breaking apart with a sense of solemnity and floating off through the rain.

They made camp in the lee of a rock formation: mean shelter, but the best they could find. All were exhausted, but with wet blankets wrapped around wet clothing, no one anticipated sleeping well. Garec was unable to get a fire started so the companions dined on cold rations.

Gilmour's pipe still burned, though and Mark speculated on the magician's other means of keeping his tobacco fresh and dry.

Steven forced a smile as his roommate motioned towards Gilmour's pipe; he shrugged as Mark indicated the dripping stack of tinder and sticks Garec had tried unsuccessfully to ignite.

Gilmour caught Mark's pantomime and smiled wryly. 'Even if I lit the tinder, the rain's too heavy to allow any fire to keep going,' he explained.

Emotionally and physically exhausted, no one felt like talking. In spite of the cold and wet, after nearly two avens, Garec, the last of the company still awake, finally drifted into uneasy sleep.

Steven woke with a start shortly before dawn. The rain had stopped at last and the mountain was deathly quiet. Blanketed with a heavy, humid coverlet, the dank hillside felt like the foetid interior of a freshly breached tomb. Nothing moved; Steven lay there silently staring up at unfamiliar constellations before rising slowly to a sitting position. There at the edge of their small encampment, hovered the pale, ghostly remains of Lawrence Chapman's first employee.

Steven couldn't remember the man's name, but he had often gazed at the photograph in the lobby case, admiring his outlandish attire, particularly the enormous belt buckle embossed with the letters BIS. And here they were once again, this time staring at him from across the hillside.

Steven stealthily reached for the hickory staff, bracing himself for yet another battle with a monster from a netherworld that should never even have existed – but the wraith did not charge. Instead, the creature's diffuse facial features came sharply into focus. Steven watched it; he thought it might be trying to communicate. The wraith's lips moved silently; Steven struggled to understand.

'Mark, wake up,' Steven urged quietly, but Mark did not stir. 'Garec,' he said, poking the Ronan with the staff, but Garec slept soundly as well. 'What's happening?' Steven asked, then understood. 'You've done this to them.'

The wraith nodded.

Steven grew angry. 'Leave them alone.' He stood and drew the hickory staff up with him. 'Leave them alone, or you'll have to deal with me.' Secretly, he hoped his threat would work. He had no idea whether the staff's magic would respond to his summons again.

Ignoring him, the wraith continued its ardent effort to communicate.

Steven looked askance at the ghostly apparition. 'Okay, I guess you're not harming them. What are you saying? Is it Nerak?'

The nearly translucent bank teller nodded again. Then, strangely, its face blurred, as if it were looking off into the distance behind Steven. It mouthed some urgent, unknown message – and disappeared into the night.

As Steven watched the wraith fade, he heard footsteps behind him. Turning on his heels, he brought the staff up in a protective stance as he strained to see into the darkness. It was Sallax. Steven exhaled a long sigh, the pounding in his chest making it difficult to speak.

'Sonofabitch, Sallax,' he whispered in English, 'you scared me.'

'Steven?' Sallax was surprised anyone had heard him approach. 'Go back to sleep.' Mark and Garec stirred sleepily, the wraith's spell now broken; Steven assumed the spirit would not return that night. He was wide awake now, so he peeled off his wet blanket and set about trying to start a fire. Searching under the rocky shelter for anything even remotely dry to use as kindling, he wondered where Sallax had been. He summoned his courage and turned to ask, but the big Ronan had already fallen asleep.

At dawn, Garec woke and immediately started up the trail ahead of the group. 'With this rain, any game below the tree line will have taken cover,' he said as he adjusted his twin quivers. 'I'll see if I can flush something out.' He moved off quickly before Sallax or Gilmour could stop him.

Just a few hundred paces above their camp Garec heard the sound of an animal, probably a deer, bounding through the underbrush. Sliding along the ground Garec felt like a wraith himself: invisible and deadly. His senses were strangely acute this morning – he credited hunger and fatigue. Garec kept his face down, almost in the dirt and held his breath. He didn't want anything catching sight of his pale skin in the early light. Even a squirrel might cry out a warning and cause the deer to change direction. He and his friends needed this meat. Garec thought he could smell the animal approaching.

Exhaling slowly, he timed his leap with practised precision. As his arrow bedded itself deep into the animal's chest he was certain he saw a look of horror pass over its face. The deer didn't have a chance; it stumbled once, then crashed headlong into a dense thicket. It barked loudly, a death rattle, and then fell silent.

Garec felt the usual bitter mixture of exhilaration and regret. The Bringer of Death had struck again. He stood up, brushed mud and leaves from his tunic and moved towards the thicket.

The deer moved. Without thinking, Garec dropped to one knee, nocking an arrow as he did so in the fluid motion perfected when he was still a boy. He did not fire blindly into the underbrush, but waited, watching for the deer to burst from the thicket. It was impossible the animal was still alive. He had hit it squarely in the chest, driving the arrow deep into its lungs; perhaps even through its heart. Yet he could hear it blundering about.

Garec waited. His companions would be coming along the trail pretty soon and the prospect of fresh venison would surely motivate them to help him flush out the animal and kill it. The beast was quite likely to attack in a final rush of defensive adrenalin and he had no wish to face the deer's antlers by himself.

Garec sighed. Maybe the deer would die before the others got there. The Bringer of Death, the deadly bowman, an archer so skilled that a Larion Senator has ordered him to Malakasia to rain death upon enemies foolish enough to wander within striking distance: here he was, this fearsome warrior, waiting for a defenceless deer to bleed to death or drown in its own blood. He had killed any amount of game in his lifetime, but he could not remember ever sitting idly by and waiting for an injured, suffering creature to expire. A dull throbbing pain began thumping at his temples; he resisted the urge to drop the bow and massage his head.

The waiting was exacerbating Garec's headache, so he decided to brave the brush and finish the deer off himself. If it charged and gored him with its antlers, so be it.

The forest shone, intensely bright, where the sunlight refracted through the raindrops. Garec imagined this was what the realm of the gods must be like; he drew a strange confidence from this as he crept closer to the edge of the thicket. With his bow fully drawn, he crouched down at the spot where the deer had dived for cover beneath the underbrush and peered through the tangled branches.

The deer was there, lying motionless, quite dead. Garec watched it for some time before relaxing his bowstring and returning the arrow to its quiver. 'I hope your suffering was brief, my friend,' he called and began peeling off his cloak before crawling through the dense, thorny foliage.

'Garec!' someone shouted from the trail.

'I'm here,' he called back, squinting against the morning sun as he watched his friends approach, 'and I've organised breakfast.'

'Outstanding!' he heard Gilmour cry. He smiled and turned back to the task at hand. Stripping the quivers from his back, he placed them beside his longbow and drew a short hunting knife from his belt. He would need to clear a path into the thicket to be able to pull the animal out.

Something moved. The faint rustle was too large to be a bird or a squirrel.

'Bleeding whores,' he exclaimed and rolled back on his heels. Kneeling in the mud, he could see the deer had not moved. It was still dead. Something else lay hidden inside the thicket. He reclaimed his bow, quickly nocked an arrow and stabbed three into the ground, fletching skywards, for easy access should he find himself in need. Painstakingly, Garec moved along the periphery of the thicket, squinting through leaves and branches to spot what he assumed was a carefully camouflaged foe.

Then it was there: an unnatural-looking hump protruded from the ground in a lazy curve too smooth to be a rock. It was covered with autumn leaves, but Garec's well-trained eye caught sight of man-made items half-buried there as well – a boot sole, a patch of fabric, two fingers from a leather glove – they, and the telltale stains of blood, told him his instincts had been correct.

He climbed to his feet and motioned for his friends to stay back. Sallax ignored him and came on, his battle-axe drawn and ready.

'What is it?' He knelt down where Garec had been and tried to see through the undergrowth.

'An injured man, but I can tell it isn't Versen.'

'How badly is he hurt?'

'I'm not sure, but I can see dried blood. It's maybe two or three days old . . . old enough not to have run in that rain yesterday,' Garec kept his bow trained on the stranger.

Sallax stood up and called into the thicket, 'You in there! Either come out on your own, or I'll have my friend here fire a few arrows into your broken hide to motivate you.'

The leaves covering the injured stranger moved and Garec heard a distinct snarling, like that of a cornered mountain lion.

'Horsecocks! It's a Seron,' he cried and double-checked his aim.

Sallax contemplated the mound a moment, looked around for Gilmour and ordered, 'Go ahead, Garec, kill it.'

'No,' Steven interrupted, pushing his way to the front of the group. Mark looked over at him questioningly, but Steven repeated, 'Don't kill it. If it dies, fine, but we should not kill it.'

He joined Garec and called to the injured creature, 'Seron. Do you understand me? We do not wish to kill you, but we will do so if you make any move to attack. Do you understand?' There was a low growl in response. Steven searched the brilliant hues of the forest morning for an answer, then grimaced. He looked apologetically at Mark and announced, 'I'm coming in. Do not touch me or my friends will kill you. Do you understand?'

'Steven, don't be a bloody idiot,' Mark began, but Steven cut him off.

'I know what I'm doing,' he said as he groped in his pocket for his hunting knife. 'It'll be fine,' he continued, trying to convince everyone, himself included. He turned to Gilmour and added, 'You said they were human once. Just because Malagon has turned them into animals doesn't mean they can't respond to human compassion.'

Even Gilmour raised an eyebrow at this proclamation, but Steven was determined.

'At least take the staff,' Mark implored, 'or let me come with you.'

'The staff won't work on this one. That's how I broke it last time. Come if you like, but I'm going now.' Steven dropped the staff, brandished his hunting knife and pushed his way clumsily inside the thicket. Mark followed.

The Seron had scrambled back against a tree trunk and was emitting a low growl as Steven made his way to the deer carcase.

'Just keep an eye on the Seron, will you?' he asked Mark and crouched by the deer, using the knife to hack off one hindquarter. It was a hard, bloody task and he was soon covered in the still-warm bodily fluids.

'I'd give up hopes of retraining as a coroner if I were you,' Mark joked, but he couldn't hide the fear in his voice. 'Can't we just drag the deer out and let Sallax do the butchery?' He was convinced that he and Steven would have been breakfast for the Seron if the creature hadn't been so badly wounded; as it was, he still felt uneasy.

While Steven struggled to free the deer leg, Mark got a close-up view of the misshapen hulk Malagon used to assassinate his enemies in Rona. The Seron looked like an exceedingly large man with huge muscular arms, very hairy: but only in his mid-twenties, Mark guessed. The forehead sloped backwards at an exaggerated angle; the bearded chin protruded out. Mark thought the most striking difference was in the Seron's oval eyes, which were black and lifeless, devoid of all colour. They looked as if they had been inked out by a frustrated creator. Mark wondered if all Seron had such dead eyes. He imagined the torture it must have endured to end up like this and suddenly felt sorry for the beasts. He was glad Steven had decided to give the warrior a chance at survival.

As the Seron cowered in a corner, Mark noticed it was favouring one leg. Nudging Steven, he motioned towards the injured limb and Steven nodded. 'Don't shoot, Garec,' he called out in low soothing tones. 'Everything is fine in here.'

'I can take him at any time,' Garec replied. 'Just give me the word.' Behind him, Sallax and Brynne watched in silence. Gilmour cleaned his pipe.

With great effort, Steven finally managed to separate the deer leg from the corpse and, wiping blood from his face, turned to look at the Seron. 'Food,' he said, just above a whisper, and tossed the deer leg carefully towards the Seron.

The Seron gave an inhuman snarl and moved awkwardly behind the tree trunk. Neither Steven nor Mark moved as they waited to see what it would do next. After what felt like an eternity, the soldier reached out with one hairy arm and gripped the deer leg with curled grey fingertips.

Steven tried again. 'Your leg is injured.' The Seron cast the two friends a menacing glare, but Steven was not to be dissuaded.

He pulled a waterskin from his shoulder, drew the cork and poured a thin stream of liquid onto the ground.

'Water,' he said quietly. 'You need water.' Instead of throwing the wineskin, Steven, maintaining eye contact with the Seron, crossed over and placed the skin at its feet. Again he was rewarded with a low growl and an angry snarl. Steven quickly backed away to deter the soldier from pouncing on him despite its injuries.

He began to fear the creature didn't understand. A little crestfallen, he looked at Mark and motioned him to back out of the thicket when the Seron finally spoke.

'Grekac,' it said, a hoarse whisper like late autumn corn stalks crunching underfoot.

Steven's heart pounded as he searched his mental lexicon of Ronan terminology. *Grekac* did not emerge. 'I don't understand,' he replied, 'What is *grekac?*'

The beast motioned with one hand towards his leg. 'Grekac.'

Mark understood. 'Grettan,' he said, fighting to contain his sudden enthusiasm. 'It's trying to say grettans did this.'

'Ah, ah,' the Seron barked, more adamantly this time.

'Grettans?' Steven asked, 'Malagon's grettans?'

The Seron howled, a furious cry towards the heavens, and pounded the ground with its fists. It was obviously not happy with the idea that its master had sent grettans to Seer's Peak. Its mind, however twisted and warped by Malagon's torture, obviously recognised that it and its fellow Seron were expendable commodities. Malagon had taken no steps to protect his warriors from his grettans, even though they were both on the same mission: to hunt down Gilmour and the Ronan partisans.

Steven wiped a hand across his eyes, trying to clear the sweat that ran in thin streams through the mud and bloodstains splattering his face. 'May I look at your leg?' he asked the Seron. 'I might be able to help you if you let me look.'

'Grekac ahat Lahp.'

'The grettans hurt your foot. Yes, I understand,' Steven said, venturing closer. 'May I have a look at your foot? I want to help you.'

'Na, na,' the Seron said, pounding on its chest, 'Lahp, Lahp, Lahp.'

Steven got it. 'Of course, Lahp,' he said, smiling without baring his teeth. 'You are Lahp and the grettan hurt your leg.' He reached out and began clearing the leaves stuck to the matted blood on the Seron's injured leg. Working slowly and carefully so as not to startle the creature, he pulled apart the shredded remains of its leggings and exposed several deep, badly infected wounds that ran down its calf and across its ankle.

'Shit,' he whispered to Mark, 'it needs antibiotics right away. It looks like the grettan bit him badly – it slashed right through his boot.'

'Sorry, I can't help you.' Mark's breath came in short, rigidly controlled gasps. 'The last pharmacy I saw was next to frozen foods in the supermarket on Riverside.'

Steven tore a length of cloth from his tunic, soaked it with water from the skin and washed the Seron's wounds, then bound the leg as tightly as he dared. When he finished, he held out the skin bottle and waited for the creature to take it from him. He knew the beast was battling an urge to kill him, an urge implanted by a twisted, evil master, but he was determined not leave the thicket until he was certain the Seron understood Steven was merciful and compassionate.

He couldn't explain to anyone, not even himself, why he so badly needed this twisted abomination to recognise his redeeming features; maybe he needed to prove to himself that he could exercise some control over the Steven Taylor who had emerged in this strange new world, that Steven Taylor who knew terror and violence firsthand; who had inflicted death himself. He wouldn't leave the thicket until he and the Seron had displayed mutual trust.

'Take it, my friend,' he said, moving the wineskin closer. 'I know he is pushing you from inside, but I need you to take this from me.' Steven looked the Seron in its lifeless eyes. 'Show me you understand.'

'Lahp ahat Glimr.'

Steven thought for a moment, then realised what he was saying. 'No, Lahp,' he reassured the Seron, 'you are free. You do *not* have to kill Gilmour.' Again he urged the soldier to take the offered water. 'Take this. Drink it. You've lost a great deal of blood. This will help you.'

Slowly, as if he had to fight instinct to make every move, Lahp accepted Steven's wineskin. It drew the cork, drank the skin nearly dry, then spoke again in a hoarse growl. 'Lahp tak—'

'Steven,' Steven said, thumping himself on the chest, 'my name is Steven.'

'Lahp tak Sten.'

'Steven.'

'Sten.'

'Fine, Sten it is.'

As he turned to leave the thicket, Steven placed a hand gently on the Seron's injured leg. 'Good luck, Lahp.' Before he could remove it, the warrior reached down and gripped his wrist with surprising strength. The soldier's enormous hand, although leathery and covered in thick coarse hair, was still surprisingly human.

The skin on Steven's forearm tightened into gooseflesh. He felt something move with mercurial quickness beneath his skin: a dancing current sparked.

Lahp's eyes widened in surprise; he watched Steven, seemed confused for a moment, then nodded. 'Lahp tak Sten,' he said finally and released Steven's arm.

'You're welcome, Lahp.' Something had passed between them; Steven didn't know what it was, but this wasn't the time to examine the feeling. He grasped Garec's deer by the antlers and together he and Mark dragged it out into the clearing.

Once they had relinquished the carcase into Garec's capable hands, reaction set in. Mark took Steven by the shoulders and shook him soundly.

'Are you completely mad?' he shouted in a whisper. 'That thing could have *killed* us – maybe Garec could have killed it back, but not before he'd taken at least one of us out. What the fuck were you thinking?'

Steven was shaking. He held Mark at arm's-length and said, 'If it's any help, I apologise—' he looked around at their companions, 'I apologise to all of you. It was just something I had to do – I'm not sure I even know why.' He turned back to Mark. 'Thanks for coming with me. That was an incredibly brave thing for you to do. Stupid, but brave.'

Mark pounded him on the shoulder. 'Stupid I definitely agree with. Next time you intend playing the damnfool hero, perhaps you'd give me a bit of warning.'

While Garec set to dressing the deer, warily keeping one eye on the thicket in case the injured Seron should decide to rush the company in a suicidal charge, Sallax stalked angrily over to Steven and spat, 'That was foolish. Let's hope it will be dead by nightfall, because we are going to have to keep a watch going in case it gets better enough to attack us.'

'He,' Steven said, 'it's a "he" and yes, *he* might be dead by nightfall, but *we* will not have killed him. It makes a difference, Sallax. And I think we're quite safe from him now.'

Steven looked at Gilmour. 'He was sent for you.'

'Yes, I'm sure it – sorry, *he* – was.' The old man stared down the hillside through the trees standing like monuments to the passage of time. Gilmour was already an old man when these trees were seedlings. 'Nerak has been trying to kill me for Twinmoons. It looks like he has stepped up his efforts.'

'Because he's afraid you have grown too powerful?' Brynne asked.

'Perhaps, but more likely because Kantu and I represent the only real threat to his dominion. With us out of the way, he could take a hundred thousand Twinmoons to master the magic necessary to release his evil master from the Fold.'

'So having you around forces him to rush his studies and perhaps make a mistake.' Mark ran a hand over the battle-axe in his belt. 'And he has no idea how much you have learned already.'

Gilmour nodded.

'It's an interesting dilemma,' Mark went on. 'He knows you're coming to confront him so he unleashes all the demons and slathering homicidal misbegotten creatures he can conjure. He has that luxury, because he couldn't care less what level of destruction his minions do on their way to find and kill you—' Mark nodded in the direction of the thicket, '—even if they kill each other.'

'And he cannot rush his studies too much for fear that the spell table will take him.' Gilmour nudged a group of yellow aspen leaves aside with the toe of his boot. 'The pressure is on him. He has the greater task ahead.'

'Opening a rip in the universe?'

'Exactly.' Gilmour's voice brightened. 'That is an amazingly dangerous endeavour that will probably cost him – it – its very existence.'

Mark frowned. 'That may be true, but in the meantime, you can't use magic to send your own devils out to hunt him down, because—'

'Because he would immediately know both where I was and how powerful I have grown.' Gilmour smiled at each of his companions in turn, then gestured towards the underbrush.

'So you're right. He has every terrifying and insidious resource at his disposal and I have—'

'Us,' Steven chimed in dejectedly.

'Grand,' Mark echoed with an equal lack of enthusiasm.

'And,' Gilmour interrupted their emotional tailspin, 'we have a certain degree of surprise on our side as well.'

'How is that?' Garec looked up from skinning the deer; he'd been following the conversation with interest.

'Nerak believes we are on our way to Sandcliff. Though he may suspect you two came here without Lessek's Key, he cannot be certain.'

'That's right,' Mark brought the issue full circle, 'because with it, we would head right for the spell table.'

'Exactly. So the fact you ignored the most powerful talisman in Eldarni history as a worthless piece of stone may help us before this is finished.'

'It didn't look like much at the time,' Mark said. Garec grinned up at him.

'So, how do we mask our approach to Welstar Palace?' Brynne changed the subject.

'We avoid using certain forms of magic,' Gilmour settled into lecture mode. 'Common tricks and spells should be fine, because lots of people employ them, but I will try to avoid using any incantations Nerak would recognise from Sandcliff.'

'He can hear it?' Even Sallax was interested now. He had moved slightly closer while still watching the thicket, his battle-axe in one hand.

'He can sense it. Magic has a rippling effect on energy planes in the immediate vicinity. The greater the spell's impact, the greater the ripple. Those with some training or knowledge of sorcery can sometimes feel the change in energy level. Nerak can detect these changes from quite a distance.'

'So that puts us at an additional disadvantage,' Sallax mused. 'We have to enter Malakasia and make our way to Welstar Palace without benefit of your skills.'

'That's true to some extent,' Gilmour confirmed. 'But it's not all bad news. I have yet to detect even the faintest disturbance when Steven summons the power of the hickory staff – even when I've been standing next to him.'

Mark put a hand on his roommate's shoulder. 'So Steven will have the full force of the staff at his disposal.'

'I believe so, yes.'

Steven blanched. 'But wait. I don't know what this thing can do and I certainly don't know how to summon its magic at will.'

Gilmour beamed. 'Well, that adds some complexity to our predicament, doesn't it? Now, how's breakfast coming along, Garec? I for one could eat a deer.'

The company broke through the tree line just after midday. Brynne felt the abrupt change in temperature through her riding cloak. The Blackstone peaks, although picturesque – in a menacing way – stretched on for ever and Brynne could not yet see much north beyond the slope they ascended. A nervous tension that began in the pit of her stomach had burgeoned into cramp as she made her way up the trail; she had no idea how she would be able to summon the fortitude to continue if the view north mirrored the vast expanse of craggy and inhospitable-looking mountains to the east and west.

By sunset they were only a few hundred paces below a ridge that appeared to mark the upper rim of the pass. With daylight fading quickly, Garec pointed at a narrow depression in the rock: cramped but adequate shelter for the night. Everyone had carried or dragged as much wood as they could manage from the tree line; now Sallax set about building a fire. With darkness clawing its way up the slope behind them, the high altitude air had grown frigid. Sallax silently hoped they would be spared rain or snow overnight.

Brynne dropped the tree limb she had dragged along for most of the day and scrambled hand over foot up the steep final slope: a fanatical pilgrim finally reaching a holy place on the far edge of a vast desert. The anticipation of seeing out above the peaks to the north had nearly driven her mad; she had spent much of the day engaged in an animated conversation with Mark and Steven just to avoid thinking about what awaited them beyond the pass. Now, with the end in sight, she moved as quickly as she could manage in the thin mountain air. Try as she might to control her anxiety, she felt her breath coming in ever-shorter gulps. Her vision tunnelled and her legs buckled weakly as she reached for the rocky ridge.

Mark saw her go and sighed. Having lived in the mountains, he knew what she would discover. He smiled sadly to himself and hustled after her.

He was halfway there when Brynne reached the summit. Her body became rigid for a moment, as if she had been met by an unexpected cold wind and then she slumped, her shoulders collapsed and her knees gave way. She appeared to age fifty years in one breath. Worried she might fall, Mark hurried the last few paces to catch her. When he reached her side, he was breathing heavily from the effort. He estimated they had climbed to an altitude of nearly thirteen thousand feet – the peaks on either side of the pass were far higher than the tallest mountains he and Steven had ever tackled back home.

He took the last few steps slowly, uncertain how Brynne would respond to him, but when she looked back and saw him there, she opened her cloak, inviting him inside its thick woollen folds.

She laid an arm over his shoulder and Mark reached one around her waist. Together they stood, taking comfort in the shared warmth. Brynne rested her head on his shoulder and stared into the distance. 'We'll never make it before the snows come.' The panic attack had passed as quickly as it had arrived. The tough, knife-wielding tavern owner was back.

'You're right.' Mark gazed out across the endless range of forbidding peaks and high-altitude passes. In the waning sunlight, the Blackstone Mountains were utterly beautiful. They would be unmerciful. Loose shale, glacier ice and sheer rock faces would force the travellers to double back, wasting valuable time. Mark would not have wanted to traverse this range in the best conditions. Moving into the sea of valleys, peaks and passes with winter only days away verged on the suicidal. Resting his cheek against Brynne's soft tresses, Mark realised he was looking on the place he would most likely die.

Turning, he felt her body press against his beneath the cloak. Constant travel with little food or rest had hardened them all. Mark felt her lean body as Brynne pulled him closer; her scent aroused him unbearably. Burying his face in the fold of her neck, he ran his hands across her back and pulled her tightly against him. She kissed him with such urgency Mark wanted to carry her away someplace safe, someplace where they would be uninterrupted.

'We can't go back south,' she said quietly. 'They'll be looking for us all the way to Estrad.'

'Steven and I have no choice. We must push on if we're ever going to get home.' He ran one hand through her hair, letting it glide between his fingers. 'We'll just have to hope the weather holds.'

He tried to chart a course north in the fading light. Each morning he and Steven would map each visible peak, noting the shallowest passes and picking out secondary and even tertiary routes, in case the way was blocked or impassable. For tonight, however, there was the promise of fresh venison and the solace of Brynne's woollen cloak.

'Hey, come and eat,' Steven shouted, 'dinner is about ready.'

'On our way,' Mark replied.

Brynne took his hand and led him back down the rocky slope.

At first light, Mark rose carefully, trying to avoid waking Brynne. Covering her with his blanket, he joined Steven and Garec as they stared out over the Blackstones from the ridge above.

Garec had saved enough wood to heat water for tecan. He handed Mark a steaming mug.

'Thanks,' Mark said.

'I wish I hadn't left those pens in Estrad,' Steven said. 'We could really use one to sketch out these passes.'

'Pens?' Garec asked curiously.

'Writing instruments,' Steven clarified. 'I felt guilty robbing someone's home and I left him two pens from my bank. I thought he might find them fascinating.'

'Of course, he was probably illiterate,' Mark added dryly. 'So right now he's probably using them to pick his teeth, or perhaps to scratch his backside.'

'Great,' Steven said dejectedly. 'Although they wouldn't do us much good without any paper.'

Mark perked up. 'I have some paper.' He reached into his jacket, then checked his jeans. Finding nothing, he groaned. 'I must have lost it. I found it at Riverend, tucked behind a rock in the fireplace. Remember?'

'I do. You had it at the river when you washed your clothes.'

'I guess I left it there. Sorry.'

'Well, we still don't have a pen. I suppose we'll just have to commit as much to memory as possible.' Steven sipped the tecan, exhaled loudly and added, 'I don't like the idea of going through there without a map. It could take all winter.'

'I have a leather saddlebag,' Garec suggested. 'We could scratch a map on it with a stone.'

'Better than nothing, I suppose,' Steven agreed and turned to follow him back to camp.

STRANDSON

Brexan lost count of the days they had been riding. Always south and west, towards the sea. Karn did not drive them hard and they rarely pushed their horses faster than a gentle canter, but save for a short break during the midday meal, the Seron escort did not allow the prisoners to dismount. From time to time Versen toyed with the idea of spurring Renna into a full gallop and taking their chances with the almor . . . but without knowing where it was, he was afraid he would just drive Garec's beloved mare straight into the demon's waiting maw. Periodically, he or Brexan would catch a glimpse of a nearby tree or bush withering to dust; the knowledge that such a terrifying adversary flanked them day and night made them both feel sick to the stomach.

On they rode. Sometimes Brexan sat behind him and other times she rode in front. The Seron paid them little heed, so at least they were able to talk freely during the interminable avens in the saddle. They were fatigued to the point of imminent collapse and their bodies ached cruelly, until the steady rhythm of Renna's stride numbed feeling. It wasn't long before emotional exhaustion exacerbated their physical pain and began to sap their strength and, worse, their hope.

Versen no longer looked forward to their evening break. Gathering firewood took too long; often he could carry only a branch or two at a time for fear the pain in his back would overwhelm him. He was in constant fear of being struck down on the spot. Brexan, on water duty, struggled to fill a pot and several wineskins, then she would open a bag of the crushed oat and herb mix they had eaten every night since their capture, mix it with hot water and serve it in wooden trenchers.

After dinner, the two prisoners would collapse onto their blankets, no longer even bothering to remove their boots and cloaks, but exhausted though they were, cramping in their backs and thighs combined with hard, uneven ground robbed them of sleep.

And the following day the nightmare began all over again.

Late one day, as the shadows lengthened in front of them like folds in a landscape painting, Brexan dozed against Versen's back. He in turn allowed his head to slump forward on his chest, shifting slightly every twenty paces to break up the monotony and alleviate the pain. They had moved south of the Blackstones and back into the Ronan lowlands. Despite the coming winter both captives found the heat and humidity oppressive. Versen sweat openly beneath his cloak; he thought he might never be dry again, and the rivulets of perspiration that soaked him attracted no end of biting insects. He spent much of the day fruitlessly swatting at tiny stinging invaders.

Brexan didn't appear to be bothered by Versen's flailing, but she did chide him about his aroma. Without lifting her head from its place between his shoulder blades, she said 'You smell like grettan flatulence.'

'You have such a special way of putting things,' he replied. 'You really must have to beat the men away with a stick.'

'This isn't about me, Ox. You smell bad.' She winced as Renna stepped over a fallen log. Maybe a bit of playful banter would lift Versen's spirits.

'Well, okay, I suppose I have no excuse – but look at it this way, you've definitely seen me at my worst. Imagine how attractive I'll be after a day-long bath.' As if to emphasise his point, Versen crushed a gargantuan fly, leaving a trail of blood and insect gore down his cheek. 'Yuck.'

Brexan licked the fleshy part of her thumb and scraped the carnage from his face. 'Make it two days and you have a deal.'

But Versen was not listening. Instead, he sat sharply upright, forcing Brexan's head back and sending sharp bolts of pain down her already stiff neck.

Angry at first, she scolded, 'Hey, that hurt!' Then, worried her jesting might have injured his feelings, she added, 'You know I was just kidding before.'

'Do you smell that?' Versen craned his neck forward.

'What? Karn?' Brexan laughed. 'Oh yeah, he smells much worse than you. Good point. I take it all back.'

'No, no.' Versen was serious. 'The breeze. Can you smell that breeze?'

Brexan inhaled deeply – then distant but clearly evident through the scents of trees and pounded mud, she caught it: the ocean.

Adrenalin coursed through Versen's body as he sniffed the air: an onshore breeze, there was no mistaking it. Now his ears were attuned, he could hear, faintly, seabirds cawing boisterously to one another. He imagined them diving along a town wharf, battling for scraps as the fishermen cleaned and filleted their day's catch.

'We must be near the end of the line,' he announced quietly.

'That could be good or bad news; I suppose.' Brexan, her pain momentarily forgotten, sat tall in the saddle. She looked nervously about for Haden.

'It may be an opportunity for us,' Versen pointed out. 'If they wanted us dead, they would have killed us long ago. If we get near a town, we might be able to lose the almor, confuse it in a crowd—' although even as he said it, Versen doubted it could be done. The almor would not be shaken off like a half-drunk pickpocket. Their only hope would be to escape to someplace dry, a rooftop or a tall building maybe.

Strandson had thrived since the Malakasian Navy closed down most commerce in the southern and eastern cities five generations earlier. The northernmost port on the Ravenian Sea, Strandson was the closest Ronan trade centre to Eldarn's central markets and commercial emporia in Orindale. Although Prince Malagon's navy kept a tight customs blockade outside the harbour, vessels carrying all manner of consumables – textiles, lumber, grain, Falkan wines and even livestock – were granted passage to the docks, where the army controlled the waterfront traffic.

There were strict rules for vessels hoping to use Strandson Harbour: blockade-ship captains ensured safe passage for legitimate trading fleets, but were quick to prevent illegal or smuggled goods docking. Smugglers' transports were burned to the waterline; the flames could be seen as far away as the heights above the city.

This public display of Prince Malagon's control in the

Eastlands was intended to quell Ronan traders' complaints at the consistently heavy tariffs on imported goods. Citizens of Strandson were well aware that they were better off than most other Ronan, Pragan and Falkan ports. Limited paperwork, easily bribed customs officials and well-policed roads leading east through the Ronan countryside made for prosperous businesses. Trade had expanded over the Twinmoons and merchants were used to the unwritten rules that kept the city turning like a well-oiled wheel. Agreements had been established between Strandson and Malakasia and many of the port's businessmen had grown wealthy thanks to their symbiotic relationship with the occupation force.

Strandson folk were never alarmed when Malakasian soldiers appeared in the city, even though most patrols covered the surrounding forests and roads. From time to time soldiers policed the harbour as a reminder of Malakasian strength, but they rarely made arrests and, unlike parts of southern Rona, murders in Strandson were the exception rather than the rule.

Despite the city's familiarity with occasional Malakasian interference along the waterfront, Seron warriors had not been seen in northwest Rona in five hundred Twinmoons; and the arrival of Karn's party created an uneasy stir among Strandson's citizens.

They had already caused a bit of excitement as the Seron marched their captives through a Malakasian checkpoint leading into the port. Two occupation soldiers appeared, swords drawn, and demanded identification. Karn barked at the confused sentries, showed his Malakasian tabards and motioned them aside. When they hesitated, Haden rode up from his position at the rear, dismounted and began striding towards the soldiers. He did not draw his weapons, but growled, low and menacing. The soldiers looked at each other, then decided discretion was the better part of valour and backed into the trees. As Karn led the party onwards, one soldier made a feeble attempt to recover some of his dignity, squeaking a broken, 'Proceed!' as they passed.

Once inside the port limits, the riders drew a crowd of curious and frightened onlookers. Although few challenged them directly, Versen heard several people shouting obscenities from behind; he wondered how brave they would be if the Seron turned back to answer them. Children were hustled indoors, pedestrians scurried out of the way and some less brave merchants drew their blinds and closed up business for the day. None of the Ronans had ever seen a Seron warrior before; most had no idea what the sinister-looking creatures dressed as Malakasian soldiers could possibly want in their peaceable city.

By the time the company reached the main green, the crowd gathering about them had tripled and several burly farmers dared to confront the Seron. Forming a human barrier across the muddy road, they attempted to force the strangers to stop.

Karn, remaining calm, reined in and gestured for the others to halt as well, but neither he nor Rala made any motion to dismount, or to draw their weapons. Looking backwards, Versen could see Haden was prepared to do battle; he swallowed thickly as he pictured the Seron tearing the citizens apart and eating the flesh of the wounded.

As the throng closed in Versen heard people calling out, 'Are you prisoners?' and 'Have they kidnapped you?', interspersed between sundry rescue offers and shouts of encouragement. 'Those two must be partisans,' and 'Free the prisoners,' rang above the din as a rallying cry.

Brexan released her arms from Versen's waist and looked nervously at the ever-tightening circle of angry citizens. Certain the crowd was too thick for them to escape with Renna, Brexan searched for an alley or a side road, or even an open building into which they might disappear. The thick mud caked about the mare's hooves made Brexan think their progress on foot would be slow. Then her stomach sank.

Raising her arms to the crowd, the former occupation soldier screamed a warning, but as she shouted, 'Get out of the mud! Get back! Off the street, hurry!', it was already too late.

Some hesitated, looking to Brexan questioningly as the almor struck. Its first target was an obese woman shaking her fist angrily in Karn's face, but unlike its attack on the scrub oak, the demon did not absorb this victim slowly. Instead, she imploded: her flabby arms, flour-sack breasts and wobbling stomach collapsed inwards. Brexan, anguished, saw the woman's eyes widen in horror before the eyeballs, devoid of anything resembling a life force, collapsed backwards into her now-vacant skull. Within moments nothing remained of the woman except a leathery skin bag and a collection of brittle bones.

This was only the beginning.

The angry throng still hadn't quite grasped what was happening when the second victim was taken. The opaque figure, glowing with the energy of its first kill, burst from the mud like a rogue ocean wave and enveloped a man who had been encouraging Versen to escape. The almor rained over the unsuspecting merchant like a cloudburst, each droplet of the demon leaching the vitality from the hapless businessman. His rubicund face turned as pale as the demon itself; the blood drained visibly from his limbs and he collapsed like a puppet with its strings cut. The almor was reabsorbed by the dense Ronan mud; the merchant was gone.

The mood had changed in a heartbeat as anger gave way to curiosity and, an instant later, to terror.

Versen and Brexan were still shouting, 'It's an almor!' and 'Get off the street!' but the ancient demon took two more victims before the onlookers managed to push their way back to the relative safety of the wooden plank sidewalks lining the road.

Calmly, Haden spurred his mount forward until it stood abreast of Renna. Though the almor appeared to have gone, Versen turned to shout another warning to the fleeing townsfolk. As he did so the Seron cuffed him hard across the mouth. The backhand swipe knocked the Ronan from his saddle and into the mud with an audible splash.

Brexan, terrified, reached for him frantically, crying, 'Get up. Get out of the mud!'

Versen slowly regained his feet. Never removing his eyes from the Seron, he ran a hand across his mouth and wiped a stream of blood onto his cloak, then reached for the mare's reins and began leading Renna towards the green. He stroked Brexan's thigh reassuringly and said, 'It's gone. It won't hurt me. I'm fine down here.'

The young woman turned on Haden, set her jaw and used Renna's stirrups to spring between the horses into the soldier's lap. Surprised by the sudden attack, the Seron did not get his hands up in time to ward off her blows. Cursing wildly, Brexan was able to land several solid punches to the Seron's already marred face before he managed to grasp her by the tunic belt and heave her into the mud. Brexan landed solidly on her back. She didn't notice Karn and Rala, who had turned in the saddle and were laughing out loud.

Despite his rage, Versen was too tired and in too much pain to join in the fray. Instead, he moved to Brexan's side and half-helped her to her feet, while half restraining her from another attack.

She screamed angrily up at Haden, 'It is not over between us, you ugly, motherless horsecock.'

The scarred one spat a mouthful of blood at her feet and Brexan tried to charge him anew. Versen held her tightly, but she continued to berate the soldier, screaming at him like a fishwife.

Versen was surprised once again at the fiery, resilient soldier masquerading as a small, pretty woman. Even in her furious state he found her alluring.

'I'd go into battle with you anytime,' he said as he gave her a playful squeeze, then brushed several large clumps of mud from her back.

'I am going to kill that one,' she seethed as her injured eye wept a steady stream down her lacerated, still swollen cheek. 'That one,' she pointed again, 'and the soulless horsecock who broke my face. By the lords, Versen, I am going to gut those two and eat their hearts.'

She paused to catch her breath then added, 'And I want you there with me when I do it.'

Versen smiled and picked some dried mud from her hair. 'Well, that may just be the nicest thing you've ever said to me.'

Brexan laughed, wincing at the pain in her cheek, then reached for Renna's bridle. The mare whinnied once in approval before following Brexan through the mud towards the wharf beyond the green.

Versen hesitated for a moment to take in their surroundings properly. There was not a person in sight on Strandson's main thoroughfare except for the gruesome remains of the almor's four victims, lying haphazardly like pockmarks in the earth. Versen shuddered. Each of the mummified husks was like an open sore on the land, sores that might never close or scab over. He was careful to avoid stepping near any of the demon's victims for fear that the world might open and swallow him and Brexan into a glowing, pearly-white Eldarni hell.

*

377

Beyond the green lay Strandson Harbour. Normally a hive of activity, the docks now were silent. Word of the almor attack had spread throughout the small port and save for a pair of drunks sleeping soundly beside an empty wooden crate, Versen was unable to find a stevedore, sailor or merchant, or even a prostitute, out among the abandoned cargoes and shipments. It felt as if they were riding through the inside of a sea god's tomb, complete with ships, channel markers, trawlers and mooring buoys. Versen and Brexan whispered together, loath to break the silence that blanketed the city. A squabble of seagulls padded contentedly along the wooden docks, searching for food and Brexan shuddered at the thought that even these most clamorous of seabirds remained silent in the wake of the almor's carnage.

Strandson had five docks stretching out into the harbour. The longest of these, an improbable structure balanced precariously on oak pylons and reaching out into the deeper water, accommodated a twin-masted topsail schooner. Drafting deep in the water, the ship was stocked and ready to sail with the morning tide.

Despite her size, the *Falkan Dancer* was a sleek vessel with a narrow beam and fluid lines; to Versen it looked like she was already in motion, even though he could clearly see she was tied securely to enormous stanchions. Squinting in an effort to improve his vision, he detected motion on the schooner's decks. He had a horrible thought that he and Brexan were bound for the open sea.

Almost in answer to Versen's silent query, Karn and Rala shepherded their charges across the wide plank boardwalk, between stacks of wooden crates bound for unknown Eldarni ports and onto the dock where the *Falkan Dancer* was moored. Versen caught sight of the Malakasian colours, hanging limply from the stern rail. There wasn't enough wind to lift it into life, but he didn't think many needed the flag to know this was a vessel of Prince Malagon's Imperial Navy.

Turning slightly, he whispered, 'What do you know about ships?'

Brexan leaned against the woodsman's back, her arms wrapped about his torso: a position she found most comforting. 'Well, that appears to be a ship over there.' Every word made her face hurt and she would have given ten Twinmoons off her life for a handful of querlis. 'Why? Don't you know anything about ships?'

'I'm a woodsman,' he said, a touch of sarcasm colouring his quiet voice. 'That's wood: as in trees. This is the closest I have ever been to a ship. I don't particularly want to get closer.'

Brexan squeezed him more tightly. 'I can't say I blame you. I *do* know that if we board that one, we're probably bound for Malakasia.'

Versen grimaced. 'I was afraid you might say that.'

As they approached the end of the wharf, Versen could see the schooner's crew was made up entirely of Malakasian soldiers and sailors dressed in a motley collection of rags. Surprised, he said, 'It's not a naval vessel. Those are merchant seamen.'

Brexan watched as the horde of sailors and stevedores busied themselves about the ship and up aloft in the rigging. Despite her concern for their future, she was almost excited at the prospect of a journey across the Ravenian Sea. 'From the looks of those crates they're loading, we might be a late addition to this cargo,' she said. 'Judging by the response we got back there, I don't believe too many people were expecting us.'

As if on cue, a squat, pig-faced merchant, puffy about the eyes, balding and sweating profusely, approached the gangplank. The man dragged a sodden handkerchief over his shining pate again and again, as if polishing it. He wore a highly unsuitable silk suit over a delicate, frilly tunic; Brexan guessed that he was the *Falkan Dancer*'s owner as he looked absurdly out of place; he was too well-dressed to be a captain. When he turned to look directly at her, Brexan was hard-put not to react to the sight of a large, misshapen mole growing from the side of his nose.

The merchant struggled for several moments to communicate with Karn, then glanced over at the two prisoners with disappointment. His voice rattled, as if his larynx were coated with phlegm. 'This will be easier on both of you if you tell me where I can find the talisman.'

'We don't have it,' Versen answered.

'Where is it, then?'

'It was left at home.' Versen glared down at the merchant in disgust. 'What are you doing working with this bunch? Where's your honour? Your sense of decency?'

'I have no decency. I am a businessman and this is business.

The prince is interested in—' The fleshy merchant hesitated a moment, as if confounded by the idea that Malagon would be searching for so dishevelled and disagreeable a quarry, then continued, 'The prince is interested in you two and I am here to deliver you – for a handsome fee.' Rolls of flab wobbled about his abdomen as he chortled. Brexan shuddered with distaste.

'If you tell me where I can find the stone, I will see to it that you are well cared for: good food, comfortable accommodation, a change of clothes and perhaps—' he glanced at Brexan as if imagining her after a hot bath '—perhaps even some querlis for that face, young lady.' He was suddenly serious. 'Now tell me where it is.'

Unimpressed, Versen glared down at the merchant, which sent the man retreating slightly across the pier. 'Not ever, and you, especially you, should pray to the gods of the Northern Forest I do not get my hands on you.'

The merchant laughed at Versen from a safe distance. 'Not to worry, my malodorous friend, I have special quarters arranged for you for our journey to Orindale.'

Orindale. Versen forced himself to remain calm. Smiling contemptuously on the sweaty merchant, he drew a long, slow breath and said, 'Well then, let's get to sea.'

Hannah Sorenson slogged through ankle-deep mud. For the first time since her unexpected arrival in Eldarn she was happier to be wearing boots than her running shoes. Their progress along the road to Middle Fork had speeded up since they had moved north of what she guessed was the greater Southport area. Although the local Malakasians had identified and hanged a number of Pragans, ostensibly for murdering the soldier who attacked Hannah along the coastal highway, everyone knew those hanged were not the guilty parties. Searches continued for the killers, as well as for that small group – or perhaps even one exceedingly brave (or exceedingly addle-pated) member – of the Resistance who had burned a Malakasian cargo ship to the waterline. No one died in the fire, but an enormous supply of weapons, silver, food and clothing was destroyed by the blaze. The only clues to the arsonist's identity came from one witness, who claimed to have seen a man fleeing the quay. The man must have been injured because his limp was clearly visible, even from a distance, as he hurried into the night.

As they moved north Hannah, Hoyt and Churn were stopped several times a day and questioned about their destination and their business. They stuck to the same story: they were migrant workers who had finished the autumn tempine harvest outside Southport; now they were heading to Middle Fork to find scullery work for the winter season. Hoyt always gestured towards Churn and added, 'Except for him, of course. We're just hoping he'll bring a few copper Mareks for hauling some firewood or shovelling snow.' Frequently the Malakasian platoon sergeant would cast him and Hannah an understanding nod after taking in Churn's vacuous expression.

So far the trio had been permitted to proceed without additional delay. They were obviously law-abiding, hard-working Pragans, already burdened with caring for the simple-minded giant, hardly the sort to be out there killing armed soldiers with their fists, or burning Malagon's galleons in late-night raids.

Hannah remained silent during the interrogations, allowing Hoyt to work his special magic and gain them safe passage for the next leg of their journey. Every time they were stopped, she was conscious that she could get them captured, or even killed almost instantly: her underwear and her socks were a dead giveaway that she was not a local peasant. Hannah had initially made the decision to keep her bra, her panties and her socks because she had no idea what women in Eldarn wore beneath their clothing. She couldn't face making a trip on foot without socks, and there was no way she was going to hike for untold miles in scratchy homespun wool without underwear. She decided that as long as she never disrobed where anyone could see her, there would be no problem.

Now she was regretting choosing comfort over caution. Every time they were stopped her heart missed a beat: what if they were searched? What if some randy soldier decided to have a tug at her tunic? Whilst her underwear was not especially racy or provocative, it was certainly not from Eldarn. There would be no hiding it – especially not if it rained; Hannah was terrified that her breasts would give them away more than any verbal slip she might make as a wet tunic plastered against her body would display the unnatural ability of her breasts to defy gravity. They might not be especially large or cumbersome, especially not by American standards, but they did benefit from the support of her bra.

Hannah, guessing Malakasian men were no different in that regard to any man in her world, began to hunch over and tug at the front of her tunic every time soldiers approached and as they moved through the checkpoints.

'What in all the rutting world is wrong with you?' Hoyt asked in a harsh whisper as a mounted platoon trotted slowly southwards. 'Appearing to have one intellectually challenged individual is enough for us. We don't need you playing at loopy as well.'

'It's my—' Hannah struggled for the word as her boots made strangled sucking noises. 'It's my – my figure.'

Trying not to laugh as the soldiers cantered by, Hoyt asked, 'What's wrong with your figure?'

'What do you mean, what's wrong with my figure?' Hannah hadn't intended to sound quite so indignant.

'*Nothing*'s wrong with your figure; that's not what I meant. Bleeding whores! Do you see those soldiers? Are we having this conversation now?' There was a slightly frantic tone in Hoyt's voice. 'I didn't mean there was anything wrong with your figure. Your figure is fine . . . nice even . . . Demonpiss! What's it got to do with you acting like a halfwit?' He turned as the platoon lieutenant rode past and said, 'Morning sir.'

'It's coming up now because, if you haven't noticed, my figure has a way of *presenting* itself, especially in the rain, for any man's enjoyment. Any *soldier*'s enjoyment. For God's sake, Hoyt, look at my breasts!'

Hoyt chuckled. 'I didn't want to say anything, but that is something of a neat trick. I know a few women in Southport I'd like you to teach it to.' The last of the horsemen passed, their mounts churning the roadway into mud. 'What is it, some kind of corset or something?'

'Or something, yes, but it appears to work . . . better. I don't know how, but it supports more completely than whatever Pragan women wear.' Hannah was hideously embarrassed, fighting the flush rising in her cheeks.

Churn grunted his amusement at the absurd way his friends were carrying on.

Hannah made another self-conscious adjustment before going on, 'So, until it stops raining or until I get to a town where I can acquire something more appropriate and throw mine away, I have to resort to rolling my shoulders and tugging a bit at the front of this deplorably hot and itchy tunic you provided me to stop it clinging in such a revealing fashion. So, if that means you have to spin a tale about travelling with two palseated lunatics instead of one, then I suggest you get creative, my friend.'

At that Churn bellowed, a curious belly-laugh that sounded both joyous and somehow tragic, a fanfare blown through a broken tuba.

'Fine,' Hoyt gave up and started laughing himself. 'You deal with your— er, "figure", and I will come up with a convincing story as to why I'm travelling with a woman whose "figure" is so very pointed in the rain!'

Hannah finally chuckled too, despite her fear that something as stupid and embarrassing as her underwear might get them caught. Then she changed the subject and asked, 'Tell me more about Alen Jasper.'

Hoyt was happy to comply; he too was blushing by now and the pair of them looked like twin victims of mild heatstroke. 'Alen. He's an interesting man. I've known him since I was young; I guess I know him as well as anyone. He taught me to read when I was a boy – that might not sound like much, but I was never very good at getting myself to school and without him, I probably would be illiterate; I certainly wouldn't know anything about healing and medicine.'

'Is he a doctor as well?'

'No.' Hoyt searched for an explanation. 'When Prince Marek came to power, what, almost a thousand Twinmoons ago—' He stopped as Hannah looked confused and started again. 'When Marek took over, let's say five or six generations ago, he closed all the universities, and over time, the idea of studying to be a doctor was lost. These days our healers all learn through oral tradition. We don't officially call ourselves doctors, because we still have a sense of what doctors used to be. I've learned more than many, but even I don't have nearly the education they did before the Grayslip family collapsed.'

'That's a tragedy. How can a ruler have let his land get so debased?'

'I have no idea, but there isn't much I can do about it now. Even if we *could* get the universities open again, we don't have any practising doctors, *proper* doctors, to re-create the teaching programmes.' He kicked a thick wad of mud off the toe of one boot. 'There isn't anyone left alive who knows what we need to learn.'

'How did *you* learn?'

'Alen helped.' Hoyt gestured for Churn to turn around, then reached into the bigger man's pack and withdrew a wineskin. 'He taught me a great deal himself, but more importantly, he gave me books and told me where to find more.'

'Are books that scarce?'

'Apart from those we study in school, they're very rare. I would probably be hanged for a full Twinmoon if anyone found the books I have stashed outside Southport.'

Hannah's head swam. It was all too much to believe – what kind of place was this? What kind of person was Prince Marek – how could *anyone* condone such a brutally narrow-minded policy? 'How did Mr Jasper get so many medical books if he isn't a doctor?' she asked.

'Alen,' Hoyt corrected her. 'That's a great question, because the books he gave me are old. They're jammed full of medical knowledge and procedures, and they're eight hundred, maybe nine hundred Twinmoons old. None of them came off any underground or outlaw presses operating in Praga today.' Hoyt took a drink and passed the skin to Hannah. 'My guess is that he somehow found a way into an old university library and stole the books.'

'That doesn't sound so outrageous.'

'Well, it is when you think that all our university libraries were razed to the ground when Marek came to power.'

'They must have missed one.'

'That doesn't sound like Marek to me.' Hoyt was doubtful. 'But anyway, after Alen gave me the initial collection, he told me where to find more, all over Praga, hidden in dilapidated buildings, forest cottages, cabins along the seashore, all kinds of places. And can you guess what I discovered?'

'They were all old?'

'Right.' Hoyt retrieved the skin and passed it back to Churn, who drank nearly half of what was left before corking it and stuffing it back in his pack. 'They were all old texts, not illegally printed books or manuscripts from the Pragan underground, but rather, all vintage stuff. Medical journals and leather-bound treatises.'

Hannah was looking forward to meeting Alen with growing anticipation. 'Sounds intriguing. Did you ever ask him where they came from?'

'I did and he told me he once worked in education and public health. I don't know if that explains anything, but that was all he'd tell me.'

'All right, regardless, go back to Mr— to Alen. Tell me about him. Why do you think he will know how to get me home?' Hannah had already realised the strange tapestry rolled out on Steven's floor at 147 Tenth Street must have been responsible for her improbable arrival on the hilltop outside Praga. *Why* was a different matter entirely.

'On that you have to trust me,' Hoyt said matter-of-factly. 'If there is anyone in Praga who can get you back to Denvercolorado, it's Alen Jasper. The breadth of his knowledge is colossal. I have yet to find something he doesn't know or can't speak to first hand – it's as if he's somehow lived everywhere and experienced everything. He will deny it, but I have seen him work actual magic. Only mild spells, mind you, playful tricks he learned as a child.'

Hannah had heard and challenged the notion of magic so many times since the trio began travelling together that she didn't even bother to argue with Hoyt this time. He spoke of impossibilities with such nonchalance that Hannah thought perhaps the word meant something slightly different in Eldarn – although given the uncommon way she had arrived in Southport, by way of Steven's living room, the strength of her initial disbelief was beginning to wane. 'When is the last time you saw him?' she asked.

'It must be fifteen, maybe seventeen Twinmoons ago. Churn and I haven't been this far north in a while. Things along the south coast were good for us for a long time and we decided to stay on there.'

'Does Alen not travel to Southport?'

'I have never known him to be anywhere but Middle Fork.' Hoyt stopped suddenly and turned to face Churn. 'I've never thought of it before, but it's true. I have never known Alen to leave Middle Fork. I wonder why.'

'Is it much further now?'

'No,' he said, signing briefly to Churn, who nodded and answered with a turn of his wrist. 'Maybe two or three days. It depends on the weather.'

Hannah had seen nothing in Praga so far that made her feel confident *anyone* here had the means, mystical or otherwise, to send her back to Colorado. The land, people and culture were so archaic, almost mediaeval; it would almost have to be something supernatural to get her back to a reality she recognised, something able to manipulate the gears, locks and switches of this impossible place and all its impossible characteristics.

What had happened still staggered her, still made her shake her head in disbelief and pinch herself and cry out, 'Wake up, silly. This isn't real.' Yet here she was, slogging through thick mud, undoubtedly alive, undoubtedly awake, undoubtedly lucid, travelling through a fantasy land that shouldn't exist but *did*, in search of the one man who might be able to offer both an explanation and help.

The road wound its way over gently rolling hills, always heading north and Hannah imagined herself taking in her surroundings as the first settlers might have as they rolled into Virginia or Massachusetts. The landscape was green, the torrid green she had seen in films of rain forests or jungles. The grasses and rushes of the meadows, cloaked in a humid mist, gave way to the foliage of the forest underbrush, dense in spite of the interwoven canopy of leaves and vines. Shafts of sunlight intermittently broke through and lit the brush beneath the towering trees.

It was beautiful, and pristine. The endless green was dotted with patches of the grey-white fog. Stuffed far too full to rain, the clouds came to rest for a moment on the soft meadow grass, where Hannah imagined they dissipated into ten thousand miles of dew. And everywhere she looked, the land itself cried out that this place was alive and this place was dangerous.

Hannah wiped rain and tears from her cheeks and stared north along the muddy path, wishing she could find something familiar, anything, that might help her feel it was wise to maintain hope. Although her eyes rested for a moment on the mud-splattered mangy dog trotting past them, the sight of a stray wolfhound wandering along the road did not register as curious with the anxious young foreigner.

THE NORTHERN SLOPES

Eight days after sketching their rudimentary map inside Garec's saddlebags, the company faced their first snowstorm, which began as a light dusting. The delicate snowfall reminded Steven of winter mornings waiting at the bus stop or playing with friends in the schoolyard. He welcomed the first flakes as a momentary trip home; as it coloured his hair and newly grown whiskers white, he mentally tallied how long he and Mark had been gone and the number of shopping days left to Christmas. He imagined his family would be struggling to maintain any semblance of normality or holiday spirit; he had no idea if they would be able to celebrate despite his unexplained absence. His mother would worry most, but she would also be the one making the greatest effort to help the others relax and enjoy the season. He saw her in his mind's eye, apron-clad and scurrying from the kitchen to the living room, her face modulating between despair and encouragement as she carried tray after tray of home-baked cookies and pastries back and forth. 'Remember that time when—' she would call above the din each time she crossed the threshold, hoping to start up another two-minute conversation to keep everyone's mind off where Steven had gone, or if he were even still alive. That's how she would handle it. She would pass the holidays in two-minute increments as the oven roared on at 375 degrees for three weeks without pause, its insulated aluminium maw the one-way entrance to her own personal hell. He wished he could get some word to her that he was fine – well, granted, he was fleeing an occupation army and an array of homicidal demons, heading for the most dangerous place in Eldarn, but right now, here in the falling snow, he was fine. He wiped the flakes and tears from his eyelashes, gripped the hickory staff and continued trudging towards the tree line.

They had spent days working their way north, using the mountains' physical characteristics in place of a compass, assigning nicknames for easy memory. Over the first two days they had moved between *Flat Nose* and *Kneecap* while always keeping the southern face of *Turtleneck* directly in front of them. Passing through a valley the friends called *Broad Belly*, they had climbed *Dog Tooth* to the tree line before turning east towards *Chubby Rump*.

Each night they had camped within the tree line. Winter was fast approaching, so each day without snow was a bonus. Sallax was a wellspring of determination, pushing them onwards. No one knew when the first storms would blow down from Falkan, and a sense of urgency permeated each day.

Their first night in the mountains had taught them a valuable lesson; exposure to the altitude and elements had already sapped their strength and left them dangerously vulnerable. Now Sallax and Gilmour demanded they move into the relative protection of the forest each night before darkness made the footing uncertain.

Mark taught them how to cross a glacier, and how to remain vigilant for crevasses and areas of thin ice unsupported from below. Their progress had been slow but steady: in eight days they had navigated three high-altitude passes and two long valleys.

Reaching the highest point of their fourth mountain pass, Steven peered south. He felt encouraged by the distance they had covered, until he looked ahead. Even making adjustments to their map he was beginning to feel certain the Blackstone range would stretch ahead for ever.

'Eight days to get this far,' he muttered as he closed his coat against the wind. 'We have at least another twenty – and that's just what I can see from up here.'

'We need a string of days in which we don't climb,' Mark agreed. 'We're pushing the limits of what we can handle already and it's getting colder all the time.'

Steven pointed northeast towards an open tract of still-green valley. It looked as though the gods who assembled the Blackstones had forgotten a thin patch, or maybe they wanted a flat stretch for a foothold among the jagged peaks. 'Look there, beyond those meadows. If we clear that pass tomorrow, we might be able to drop behind that range and run northwest along the valley for seven or eight days. It might be a hundred miles through there.'

'That's true,' Mark said. 'I'm sure there'll be some exposed areas along that valley floor, but at least we won't be at altitude, or risking getting stuck out here overnight.'

'And in a valley that long, we're certain to find water.'

'All right.' He turned to the others. 'My friends, it appears we can get away without climbing for a few days.'

'Thank all the gods of the Northern Forest,' Garec said, tightening the bandage supporting his swollen knee.

'But we do have to cross this next valley tomorrow and clear that pass the following day,' Steven said as he pointed towards the range of cruel peaks awaiting them in the distance. 'With that done, the going should get easier.'

They reached the tree line by early evening, and Gilmour suggested they continue moving down into the hollow vale before the snow accumulated. 'We'll have better footing now,' he explained. 'We should push on until it is too dark to see.'

'Let's keep moving then,' Steven encouraged.

'Wait here a few moments,' Garec said, 'then follow me down. I'll see if I can find us some dinner.' He slid the rosewood longbow from his shoulder, drew an arrow and sidled quietly into the trees.

An aven later, Garec stoked the fire and rotated a large chunk of meat one-half turn above the flames. He had killed a large boar with one shot through the neck; he could have felled another, but didn't believe he and his friends would be able to carry so much meat over the pass. They were having problems enough with what possessions they had. And if tonight were any indication, he expected to find rich hunting grounds and ample game in the valley just beyond the next ridge.

As the snow continued to fall the travellers found shelter in a grove of evergreen trees. The aroma of pine and cooking meat mixed in the fresh mountain air, nearly making Steven swoon. The idyllic setting made him grin despite his exhaustion.

'Garec, that smells so good, I might need to you to go out and kill another just for me,' he said as he inhaled deeply, savouring the scents.

'I'm sorry we're out of wine,' Garec answered, adding redundantly, 'It would taste much better with a skin or two.'

While Garec cooked, the others made camp. Sallax hung their cloaks and blankets near the fire, hoping to dry as much as possible. Keeping dry was as important as eating well; Sallax was determined to make it through the remaining mountain pass in as much comfort as possible. He motioned for Garec to unwrap his damaged knee and hung the makeshift bandage near the flames. He was worried about his friend and vowed that he would carry Garec over the next rise if necessary.

Sallax turned to listen as Gilmour and Mark pored over the map sketched inside Garec's saddlebag. Their breath clouded, then dissipated in the frigid air; Sallax imagined two ancient dragons facing one another, their nostrils a smoky warning of incipient firestorm. Then Gilmour exhaled and the cloud hung in the air, a diaphanous mist floating between the two men. Strangely, it did not fade, or disappear on the breeze. When Mark's breath joined it, the cloud began to take shape: buttons first, then a shirt, a leather belt. Startled, Sallax drew his rapier and shouted, 'Rutting lords, it's the wraith!'

Mark stood, looking about anxiously, and demanded, 'Where is it?'

'Right there, right in front of you.' Sallax approached, holding his rapier like a lecturer's pointer.

Seeing the misty apparition take shape before him, Mark fell backwards into the snow. Gilmour stood slowly and, inches from the mysterious intruder, reached out one hand and felt his fingers pass through the old banker's gossamer torso. 'Sallax, stay there,' he ordered, firm but calm. 'It's all right. He's not here to harm us.'

Steven rose to join the others. 'Can you feel it, Gilmour?'

The old sorcerer waved his hand back and forth through the wraith, but if his violation irked the ghostly visitor, it showed no sign. 'It's cold,' he told them. 'Much colder than the air.'

'What does it want?' Brynne asked. She put down the bundle of firewood she had been collecting and edged closer to Mark.

'It's taking news of our position back to Malagon,' Sallax answered. 'You said we were being followed. This thing has been in contact with Malagon since we left Estrad. That's why Lessek warned Garec about them. That's why Malagon has been able to send the almor, the Seron and the grettans out for us. Steven Taylor, use that staff, kill it like you killed the almor.'

Steven looked at Gilmour, but before the old man could respond, the wraith lifted one translucent arm and pointed at Sallax.

'What?' the angry Ronan asked defiantly. 'What is it? I'm right, aren't I? You're here spying on us, you horsecock.'

They stood, almost frozen, waiting to see how the wraith would respond to Sallax's anger. Gilmour realised his hand was still extended inside the spirit visitor and quickly retracted it. Around them the forest was deathly quiet, save for the falling snow and the crackling fire. Slowly, the former bank teller lowered its arm and floated across the camp to face Steven. Its features came slowly into focus and Steven clearly recognised the man from the lobby display case. As before, the wraith tried to communicate, moving its lips exaggeratedly, but before it could complete its first words, Sallax was moving.

He grabbed the hickory staff and raised it to strike at the ghostly visitor. 'I'll do it myself.'

'No!' Gilmour shouted, reaching for the weapon, but before Sallax could swing, the wraith disappeared, moving with fluid ease inside Steven's body. A look of rueful consternation passed across Steven's face. Then his head lolled forward to rest limply on his chest.

Stunned, Sallax froze. Gilmour hastened to Steven's side and, gripping him by the shoulders, spoke several words in an unknown language. Whatever Gilmour had said, it worked. Mark breathed a sigh of relief as the wraith oozed out of Steven and hovered in the air again. Steven himself sat down hard in the snow and rubbed his temples for a moment before telling Gilmour, 'It's all right. He's here to help.'

Sallax, still unconvinced, moved back into position, but before he could lash out, the apparition moved with mercurial speed, this time entering the big Ronan. Sallax's eyes rolled back in his head and he choked off a cry. It was gone; as quickly as it had entered it was gliding from Sallax's body and turning back to Steven. In a final show of good faith, it appeared to smile, then it faded into the forest, invisible against the slate-grey sky between the pines.

'Sallax!' Brynne screamed as she dashed over to her brother.

Kneeling in the snow, she cradled his head in her lap and waited frantically for his breath to cloud the air. Mark climbed to his feet and hurried to assist Brynne. When Sallax finally exhaled, his sister nearly burst into tears. 'Mark, Garec,' she begged, 'help me move him near the fire.'

They wrapped him in several blankets. Then, after opening his eyes once, looking up through the intertwining pine branches at the falling snow, Sallax drifted off to sleep. Gilmour touched him gently on the forehead, stared down at the back of his hand as if a diagnosis lay hidden among its wrinkles, and smiled reassuringly at the rest of his companions. 'He's sleeping now. We should let him rest.' He reached out and turned Garec's roast a half-revolution above the fire.

Brynne looked to Steven. 'What did it do to you?'

'Nothing.' Steven searched for an accurate description. 'It felt as though a cold breeze blew through my clothes and pressed against my skin, but then, rather than simply chilling the surface, it pushed on and blew right through me.'

Garec tucked the ends of his blanket beneath Sallax's heels before asking, 'What did you mean when you said it was here to help?'

'He spoke to me. He said his name was Gabriel O'Reilly and that Nerak knew where we were. He tried to tell me more, but something Gilmour said forced him out. He was only able to tell me he wanted to help.'

'Why did he harm Sallax?' Garec asked. 'Especially if he wants to help us.'

'I'm not sure. Perhaps he felt threatened by the staff. Maybe it can destroy him; it certainly made short work of the almor.' Steven looked to Gilmour. 'What do you think?'

'I think if Nerak knows where we are it is because we have been followed. I have not used enough magic for him to trace me.' The old man made an awkward motion that Steven found unsettling. 'If he already knows where we are tonight, we might as well enjoy a few creature comforts. There is no more use trying to hide.' Gilmour waved one hand over the small campfire and the flames leaped to twice their height. Heat from the blaze warmed their campsite and Steven removed the hunk of boar from its wooden spit.

'Garec,' Gilmour directed, kneeling beside the blaze, 'come and sit here near the fire.'

As the bowman complied, Gilmour rubbed his palms together contemplatively until they glowed the same red hue they had the night he restored Steven's splintered wooden staff. 'Bend your knee,' the Larion Senator commanded, and again Garec did as he had been told. As the old man rubbed his hands gently on both sides of the injured leg, Garec could feel a warmth course through his torn cartilage and strained ligaments. The therapeutic spell lasted only a few moments, but the young Ronan was certain, even before he stood to test the leg's strength, that Gilmour had healed him completely. In fact, he felt better than he had in Twinmoons.

'Now for the snow,' the old man said to himself, rising from the ground. He closed his eyes, concentrated for a moment and gestured with both hands above his head, as if drawing the outline of an invisible dome. A brilliant light shone through the pine boughs, illuminating the forest around them and blinding everyone momentarily.

Steven rubbed the flash from his eyes in time to see Gilmour pull a piece of meat from the roast. 'There,' the old magician said, chewing thoughtfully. 'Now there's no doubt that Nerak knows where we are.'

Steven could feel the intense heat of their now-roaring fire warm the forest around him. He gazed through the trees and saw snow continuing to drape the pine grove in soft winter white, but no more snow fell in the area immediately surrounding their campsite, as if some kind of mystical canopy sheltered them from the storm. Impressed, he moved near the fire and asked, 'How would the ghost – or whatever it was – of a dead bank teller in Idaho Springs get here to Eldarn if the far portal on our side was locked away in a safe deposit box?'

'Nerak must have brought him back through,' Mark said. He gestured to Gilmour. 'You said he can cross over with only one portal open. Can he make the trip while in possession of an unwilling soul?'

'Certainly. And although I believe he, like all of us, is subject to the desultory whim of the weaker portal—'

'That's the one that drops you anywhere, right?' Mark interrupted.

'Yes, exactly,' Gilmour continued, 'even though he would be transported almost anywhere in your world going through, coming back, he has the power to pinpoint the open portal at Welstar Palace.'

'Can you do that as well?' Steven asked hopefully.

'No,' Gilmour answered almost apologetically. 'My role with the Larion Senate was to oversee research and scholarship. I learned a few useful spells, but I never had access to the portals like Nerak or Pikan or their team.'

'But you've been researching for so long,' Garec suggested. 'Just like Nerak.'

'That's true, and I might surprise myself and detect the open portal, but I haven't made a trip across the Fold in half my lifetime. I wouldn't want to risk it on my first attempt.'

'So the ghost of Gabriel O'Reilly haunts the Blackstone Mountains,' Steven said. 'Why?'

'I think he escaped,' Garec suggested softly.

'What's that?'

'I think he escaped. I think he managed to get away from Nerak.' He drew his hunting knife and began slicing thick portions of meat. 'When I dreamed of Rona that night on Seer's Peak, I saw hundreds, perhaps thousands of those wraiths moving through the forbidden forest near Estrad. I thought they were the souls of people I've killed coming back to haunt me, but I've not killed nearly that many. Seeing Gabriel O'Reilly again, I think he might be an unwilling member of a terrifying army of spirits, each one the disembodied soul of another of Nerak's victims. I am not sure why Lessek showed them moving through southern Rona, but I don't like to think about those implications.'

'Holy Christ,' Mark whispered under his breath.

'So, what's he doing here?' Brynne asked.

'He's obviously trying to tell us something,' Garec answered. 'He must be aware of who he is, or who he *was*, and he's defying Nerak by making a trip across Eldarn to warn us about another assassin, or some pending challenge.'

'Like facing an army of those things?' Mark asked.

'Perhaps,' Garec shivered, 'although I really hope not.'

Noting Sallax still asleep near the fire, Mark began to grow anxious. O'Reilly's ghost, a benevolent wraith with good intentions, had sidelined the company's toughest and most dedicated warrior in a matter of seconds. How could they fight an army of wraiths, especially an army bent on killing them? They would be overrun in a heartbeat. 'We can't fight them,' he said cautiously, hoping the others would agree.

'That's right,' Gilmour agreed. 'We could manage a few, but if Nerak controls the souls of every victim he's ever possessed, we would be defeated very quickly.'

'So what *do* we do?' Brynne asked. 'What if Garec's vision comes to pass and we find ourselves facing thousands of those things?'

Gilmour reached for a second helping of roast boar. 'We'll just have to move through them undetected.'

Mark looked down at the slab of cooked meat resting in the bottom of the wooden trencher he had been using since the company of travellers rode north from the orchard outside Estrad. Trench mouth. As a student he'd misheard the term and thought it was the result of eating from wooden bowls, trenchers that had begun to rot. Disgusting. Although he later found out the only thing close was some equally unpleasant disease of the mouth and throat, named for Vincent Price, Vincent van Gogh, Vincent-his-sister's-dry-cleaner— who knew? Vincent someone, anyway, but whoever it was, he'd never liked using porous crockery. Just to be on the safe side, he had fastidiously cleaned and dried his trencher after each meal. Now his determination to avoid bacteria seemed pretty trivial. Fight an army of ghosts? Move through them undetected? It made trench mouth sound little worse than a cold.

He and Steven had learned to trust Gilmour, but he wasn't convinced the old man could make them all invisible enough to get past a homicidal ghost army. Shaking his head, Mark turned to watch Steven. He looked very different these days: unwashed, sporting a short beard, and he ate heartily, wiping the grease from his mouth with handfuls of snow from the forest floor. The hickory staff lay across his lap and he seemed more confident than he had ever been. Mark could not remember when Steven had changed from the man terrified of the staff's power to the man who went nowhere without it.

For a moment Mark wished he had a mirror in which to check the progress of his own transformation. Eldarn was changing him as well; he could feel it. He knew he was losing weight, and that his face was drawn and tired. But what of the wraith hidden within his soul, whatever would be left if Nerak won? Steven said the ghost that haunted them along this trail was the same man whose picture hung in the bank lobby, a grainy black-and-white photograph that radiated seriousness and superiority as only a nineteenth-century professional man could. The wraith version of Gabriel O'Reilly's soul still looked like the man in the photograph. Mark wondered whether his own spirit would look like an unshaven, emaciated black man lost in a foreign world. Ignoring any bacteria festering in his trencher, he picked up the roughly hewn chunk of meat and began to eat.

Garec woke Steven, shaking him gently and murmuring, 'It's your watch. There's some meat left on the stone near the fire if you're hungry.'

'Thanks, Garec.' Steven stood, stretched and faced the blaze. It roared on, although no one had added wood to it since before dinner; Brynne's abandoned pile was unneeded. Steven, pleasantly warm for the first time in days, loosened his tunic, hefted the hickory staff and took several long swallows of water from Brynne's wineskin. Around him he could hear the sounds of the forest and the steadily falling snow. He walked towards the periphery of their camp and saw the snow had piled up to nearly twelve inches – he was standing in less than an inch, all that had fallen before Gilmour cast his protective spell.

'At least we'll be able to pack up with relative ease,' he said to himself. Steven was dreading the coming journey. The sun would most likely not appear all day and he and Mark would have a struggle to keep the group moving in the right direction.

From the top of a mountain pass it wasn't too hard to select a destination and estimate travel time through the next valley, but from the valley floor, they had been used to relying on the sun for guidance. It was easy to get turned around: a crooked trail through thick underbrush or around a dense grove of trees could often send even the most experienced travellers back over their own tracks. He and Mark would be forced to use the slope of the hillside, as well as their best guess, to ensure the company reached the opposite tree line by sundown.

Standing on essentially dry ground and looking out a few paces to where the snow was piling up in the forest, Steven marvelled at Gilmour's power. He wondered if the old man might be able to illuminate a path across the valley and up the opposite slope so that he and Mark might use landmarks below to chart their course towards the summit. They'd barely glanced at this valley before descending into the trees; for a moment Steven considered climbing back up to reconnoitre the final pass before the long green vale and the Falkan border.

Then something moved.

Outside camp, the snow was an ethereal white curtain that impeded Steven's view of the surroundings woods. Staring at the place where he thought he had seen something, Steven felt the staff warm slightly in his grasp, as if it sensed potential danger and was ready for a fight. He felt rather than heard footsteps, a distant vibration. Something approached from the tree line above, making its way down the hillside. He thought it was something large, perhaps a rider. As the minutes ticked by, he began to feel the presence all around him.

He wondered whether he should wake the others, but if he were imagining it he'd feel pretty stupid. Just as he'd made up his mind he *was* imagining things, Steven caught sight of eyes, glowing eyes, like those of a deer reflecting car headlights. But save for the soft radiance from Gilmour's fire, there was no light for these eyes to reflect. Instead, they were shining amber, like a glint of sunshine on a muddy puddle. He adjusted his grip on the staff, bent his knees in readiness and moved to the edge of Gilmour's protection to await whatever creature possessed these eerily incandescent orbs.

Slowly, as if disgorged by a retreating bank of fog, the intruder began to take shape in the firelight: dark as pitch, and broad across the shoulders. It came in on all fours, and Steven gasped when he realised he was facing an enormous grettan, much larger than those that had routed the Malakasian platoons at Riverend Palace. Curiously, the beast did not charge. Instead, it came forward to the edge of the camp and sat on its haunches in the deep snow, only five or six paces away. Steven studied the monster towering over him. His staff, now radiant, was at the ready. He could see enormous teeth spiking the creature's powerful jaws. Its front legs were thick with muscle and its paws were ringed with hooked claws. Saliva dripped from its maw and it ran a large pink tongue once over its mouth. Though the height of a Clydesdale, the grettan shared more physical features with a jungle cat than a horse. Steven thought his arms would just be able to span the beast's massive chest.

Unlike Versen's description of grettans encountered in the northern territories, this one was alone, not with a pack, nor did it have it the lifeless black eyes the Ronan had described in such detail.

The creature kept its glowing amber gaze fixed on Steven, then startled him by speaking. It made no audible sound, but Steven was able to hear it inside his mind, a carefully contained roar that echoed from the walls of his consciousness.

'Steven Taylor, it is my distinct pleasure to meet you.'

Behind him, Gilmour's eyes opened. The magician sat bolt upright. Nerak was here. He looked frantically throughout the camp, but he could not see Steven anywhere. 'Stop! Steven,' he shouted into the darkness as he climbed to his feet.

Steven, only a few paces from Gilmour, had no idea he had faded into the night, that he had been swallowed by the dark prince's spell. He had become a shadow, invisible to his compatriots. Nerak wanted a few moments alone with the surprisingly powerful foreigner.

'Prince Malagon. Or should I call you Nerak?' Steven thought he would collapse. He had never felt so frightened, nor so absolutely helpless. 'You've come for Lessek's Key.' Under the circumstances, it was perhaps the smartest thing he could say. Howard and Myrna's lives were all but lost if the evil minion had any notion the key was lying unprotected in Idaho Springs. It was certain now that Nerak was under the assumption Steven had the key in his possession, or the dark prince would not have bothered to come here searching for it.

'Lessek's Key will be mine in time,' the voice growled in his mind, and Steven felt his stomach drop. 'This evening, I come to share some interesting news with you – just you.'

Despite the cold mountain air, Steven began to perspire; he prayed Nerak could not detect his insecurity. He did his best to compose himself, then responded, 'You have nothing that I am at all interested in hearing, unless you plan to send out more Seron warriors – or perhaps another almor. I assure you, the last one was delicious.' He forced himself to grin despite the dryness in his mouth; for a moment his lips were stuck fast to his gums freezing his face in a virulent, toothy glare.

'Ah, yes, the staff you wield. How nice of Gilmour to make you that little toy. A nightlight to hold me at bay, is it? Let me assure you, the Larion weakling has no idea how powerful I have grown. I was stronger than him at Sandcliff, and I am even stronger now. Fantus will think he has come up against a god when we battle, and I will bask in his terror.' The grettan seemed to smile back at him as it shifted slightly in the snow and Steven tightened his grip on the wooden staff, hoping desperately the magic would rise to the occasion once again.

'Even now,' the grettan went on, 'though you stand only a few paces away, Fantus has no idea where you are.'

Steven dared not risk a glance over his shoulder to confirm the grettan's claim. He knew the beast would leap on him as soon as his attention shifted. But then he paused: why had it not torn him to pieces already? Why was it having a conversation with him instead of just breaking into the camp to retrieve Lessek's Key?

Suddenly, it made sense. Nerak was too far away to break Gilmour's canopy spell. Nerak – the grettan – could not enter. Emboldened, Steven spoke up. 'So what's this news you have for me, you evil piece of shit? Speak up. If you're hoping to trick me, it won't work. I know you can't enter this circle; and if you can, just bloody get on with it.' The staff grew warmer in his hands, apparently in response to his growing anger. 'I'll take my chances against you with Gilmour's toy.'

Unfazed, Nerak went on, 'The woman Hannah Sorenson.'

Steven's heart stopped. The gears keeping it beating stripped their cogs and ground together in a nearly audible breakdown. His mouth fell open, his eyes glazed with unshed tears. The staff, now ruby-red and throbbing with latent power, shook in his suddenly weakened hand. His knees felt like jelly and he had to force himself to stay standing.

'I assume from your struggle to find a witty retort the woman means something.' Once again, the grettan ran its long tongue over the dripping spikes lining its jaws. 'Well, Steven Taylor, I thought you might be interested to know that as we speak she is making her way through Praga to meet with Kantu, my other dear Larion colleague. Trust me, Kantu is as much use as Fantus;

I could shit more destructive magic than those two simpering fops could ever hope to wield against me.

'But I lose my thread. Hannah Sorenson—' The grettan licked his lips in a positively lascivious manner; Steven wanted to retch. 'Hannah Sorenson.' The voice was sibilant now, as Nerak relished the sound of her name. 'Hannah, young Hannah. Such a pretty name. Such a pretty woman. And I will strip that prettiness from her like flaying a deer. The tortures Hannah Sorensen will suffer at my hands will be endless and nameless. She will suffer for aeons, and I assume it is *your* name she will scream, over and over again, as I tear her mind apart from the inside out. I will leave her her tongue for a while, so I can listen to her agonies.'

Watching Steven for a reaction, the grettan continued, 'Of course, her suffering will only truly begin *after* I have destroyed her body.'

Anger and hatred exploded through Steven like the shock-wave of a subterranean volcano. It welled up inside him and any vague memories of Gilmour's lecture on the appropriate use of magic vanished in the heat of his fury. Wild with rage, the staff in his hands responded, now exuding a searing heat. It seemed to be willing him to strike out at the creature: *Be the aggressor! Kill the motherless bastard!* He could feel it through his hands and wrists, and the muscles of his forearms rippled as Steven gave in.

'No!' he screamed and brought the staff around in a killing stroke. Steven expected to feel the magic tear through the grettan's flesh as it had torn through the almor; he was shocked when he felt the force of his blow ripping through Gilmour's canopy like a flaming razor through tissue paper. An instant later, he realised his mistake. He had opened a rift in the protective spell and allowed Nerak to enter their camp unchecked.

'Thank you, my boy,' the grettan roared, leaping over him towards his unsuspecting companions.

Steven was dumbstruck: he had been fooled, and he cursed his stupidity as he rushed towards the grettan, hoping at least to wound it so his friends could escape into the forest. But there was Gilmour, already on his feet. Somehow, the old sorcerer had detected Nerak and was waiting for the break in the canopy as his lifelong enemy attacked. The grettan was still in the air, stark and black against the firelight, when Gilmour released the force of his own magic in a bone-shattering blow. Struck in the centre of its massive chest, the beast gave a cry and flipped backwards on itself to land heavily in a confused pile of broken limbs and bloodied fur.

This time Steven did not hesitate. He brought his staff around again and, glowing bright red in the night, it held fast and slashed through flesh and bone, sending the grettan's left forelimb spinning into the fire.

Almost immediately, the creature's glowing amber eyes dimmed to black. The grettan, screeching in agony, retreated stumbling into the trees. Garec, who had managed to come to his knees, fired several shots after the fleeing animal. Steven could see arrows protruding from its hindquarter as the grettan disappeared up the slope, leaving a heavy blood trail and deep footprints in the otherwise undisturbed snow.

In a secluded apartment in Welstar Palace, Prince Malagon roared in pain and, rising angrily from the floor, cast a frustrated spell of such magnitude that a heavy stone wall in his chamber cracked and fell to rubble, leaving a new entry to the hallway beyond.

'Fantus, I will eat your heart!' he screamed. The guards who had rushed to investigate the crash were struck dead instantly by the waves of magic still coursing through the corridor. The dark prince bellowed again, his fury uncontrolled. It was not that weakling Gilmour's blow that had driven him from the grettan: the power to dispel him from the Ronan camp had come from Steven Taylor and that pathetic wooden stick.

How powerful had Gilmour become if he could create such a weapon for an untrained and untested sorcerer? And where was Jacrys, his so-called *master* spy? Why had the man not made his way into their camp and stolen the cursed key? He had failed in every attempt to kill the wizard and his band; now Malagon had gown impatient waiting for Gilmour to reach Sandcliff before him.

He would send a wraith to Jacrys with a message: *Succeed immediately, or die immediately.*

But no, he needed to take more drastic measures. Jacrys was unreliable and Fantus had grown too resourceful. He would send a platoon of wraiths – an army – to wrench the sanity from their minds, to leave them lost and babbling, to join his invincible army of spirits – and to bring Lessek's Key home to him.

He should have done that in the beginning.

'I'm sorry; I'm sorry,' Steven repeated again and again, 'I let him into camp. I broke through your spell for him. I'm sorry.' The news that Hannah was in Eldarn had set his mind racing; he paced back and forth, desperate for some plan, some course of action to emerge.

'He knew Hannah's name. He said she was going to meet Kantu. She's in Praga. I mean, she must be. Right? How would he have known her name? Or anything about her at all if she weren't here? Can he read my thoughts? Did he simply pull her out of my mind while I was sleeping?' Steven raged on despite Mark and Brynne's efforts to calm him; he could not regain his composure.

Finally Gilmour took him firmly by the upper arm and forced him to slow his urgent pacing. 'It's all right, Steven,' the old sorcerer said calmly. 'He tricked you, that's all. He couldn't get into camp and needed you to create a tear in the canopy. It's fine. The blow you struck with that staff dispelled Nerak and broke his hold on the grettan. He's back in Welstar Palace right now, probably nursing a massive headache.'

Steven would not be calmed. 'What of Hannah? Is she here? Can you tell if she's here? How could he know?'

Instead of responding, Gilmour ran one hand slowly over Steven's sweaty brow. 'Rest, Steven. I need you to rest.' Before the elderly man could remove his hand, Steven slumped in his grasp, sleeping soundly.

Like a father bidding good night to a sleeping son, Gilmour carefully laid Steven's comatose body near the fire and covered him with two heavy blankets.

In the sudden silence Mark asked, 'Is it true that Hannah's here?'

'I'm afraid it might be,' Gilmour answered. 'I can't think of any other way Nerak would know Hannah's name would get such a strong response from Steven. He's too far away to read our minds, unless we're focusing our thoughts towards him directly. So I am very afraid that we must assume the worst.'

'The worst?'

'That Hannah is here, and the far portal in your home remains open.'

Mark mused over their last days in Colorado. 'I don't think Steven spoke with Hannah the night we opened the contents of the safe deposit box ... unless he called her before he left the bank.'

'Why would that make a difference?' Brynne asked.

'Because she would have no idea Lessek's Key was at all important ... you know— In case Nerak gets to her ... takes her—' Mark was a little surprised at how pragmatic he sounded when discussing Hannah's possible death. He kicked a blood-stained log onto the fire. 'We must assume the key is still sitting there on Steven's desk.'

Gilmour brightened. 'And we must also assume Nerak remains unaware of that fact.'

'Right,' Garec joined the conversation. 'Or else why would he come here, or at least project himself here, to threaten and attack us?'

'But Gilmour,' Mark interrupted, 'if he knows where we are all the time, won't he be tipped off when we make for Welstar Palace instead of Sandcliff?'

'Yes, he will,' Gilmour nodded. 'And there will be nothing to keep him from stepping across the Fold, finding Lessek's Key and sending his collected forces against us while he studies the spell table at his leisure.'

Brynne pushed an errant lock of hair behind one ear. 'Do you believe that wraith is the one following us?'

'Not from what Steven said,' Gilmour answered, and Garec nodded in agreement. 'It must be someone else, someone resourceful, with the fortitude and skill to make his way through these hills alone.'

'Could Malagon be watching us?'

'No, it's too far. He would be forced to focus his will for long periods of time.' Gilmour tore a piece of cold meat from the uneaten chunk of boar still lying near the fire. 'This is someone crafty, with enough magic to camouflage his or her presence when I cast about searching for them. When we were in the foothills or out near the river, I detected many others about, travellers mostly. However, now that we're in an uncharted section of the Blackstones, I am confident that when I find someone, it will be our Malakasian shadow.'

Garec completed Gilmour's thought. 'So we need to be certain we find this spy before we make a definitive move towards Welstar Palace.'

'Right.' Looking towards the stars, Gilmour added, 'Dawn is approaching. Let's get things packed for the day. Sallax and Steven may sleep a bit longer, but then we must continue on.'

By midmorning, Garec realised the group dynamic had changed dramatically. Sallax, their confident and indefatigable leader, had grown sullen and quiet. He trudged through knee-deep snow, brooding, not talking. He had awakened with a start, crying out and springing to his feet as Garec was repacking their saddlebags. Brynne had rushed to her brother's side, but he refused to discuss the wraith's attack, even with her. He assured her he felt fine, and then refused to elaborate. Garec watched him now as he pushed his way downhill through the drifts while his cloak dragged behind him; it looked like an exceedingly long cape draped over a man half his height. Garec felt a pang of doubt ripple through his stomach. No one had appointed Sallax their leader, but he was a source of strength; he helped the others feel as though they would never be defeated as long as he was there to push them onwards. Though Sallax looked physically sound, Garec was worried Gabriel O'Reilly's ghost had done something to break his friend's spirit, to weaken him emotionally, maybe even killed his desire to win back Rona's freedom. The mysterious wraith had told Steven it wanted to help, but that had been the extent of its communication. Who knew what it had done to Sallax?

Steven was different too, desperate in his determination to move on, and he shouted back at them, encouraging everyone to move as quickly as possible down the slope and across the narrow valley to the next incline. Progress was slow and Garec doubted they'd make it to the pass before nightfall. He thought deep drifts might have collected at the base of the mountain, forcing them to make camp among the pines and put off pushing for the tree line until the following morning.

Unable to make his way through the snow and remain vigilant for passing game at the same time, Garec wore his longbow slung across his shoulders and used both hands to maintain his balance as he hurried along behind Steven.

However worried about their progress he was, Garec did spare a thought for Steven's anguish: he was obviously tortured by the thought that his love was alone in Praga. They could hear the guilt in Steven's voice, and he gripped his hickory staff as if he expected Malagon to rise up bodily from the earth. Steven was convinced this woman – Hannah – would be safe at home if he had never opened the far portal. Garec felt for him.

Like Sallax, Steven looked as if he had been cut off at the knees and propped up in the drifts. 'Please, everyone,' he called, sounding harried, 'we *must* hurry. We're facing a really difficult climb and we need to reach the base of this slope as soon as possible.'

Mark shot Steven a glance; Garec could see the two friends disagreed on how far the group would progress that morning.

Steven too noticed Mark's doubt and he stopped for a moment, crestfallen, as if he had only just realised they would not be able to walk all the way to Welstar Palace without rest. He set his jaw, brushed a clump of snow from his cloak and entreated his friends again, 'We *must* try. I'll break the trail. Stay in my tracks and you'll find the going easier.'

Behind him, Garec detected the aroma of Gilmour's pipe. The old sorcerer had said nothing all morning.

From time to time Garec peered through the highest pine branches towards the sky, but the sun was invisible behind the unbroken cloud. Garec recognised that Steven was doing a heroic job maintaining a direct line to the base of the mountain; it had taken an aven or two watching him, but Garec had finally worked out that Steven was checking and adjusting their progress when, periodically, he would hold the hickory staff aloft and sight along it towards two peaks visible in the distance. Garec promised himself he would learn this navigation strategy.

Steven's breath came in laboured gasps as he forced himself to continue breaking the trail. Garec almost wished Steven would just keep staring into the distance rather than turning around to speak with them at all, for his desperation was written all over his face. Despite the biting cold, he was sweating profusely and his skin shone palely white, nearly matching the snowy hillside around them. Had it not been for the bright red flush across his cheeks and the billowy clouds marking time with his breath, Garec would have rushed down the slope to see if Steven was still alive.

The insecure banker who had arrived in Eldarn such a short time ago had given way to the angry, frustrated and guilt-ridden warrior who stood before him now; Garec was beginning to think that without Sallax's leadership, the future of the Ronan Resistance might rest in the hands of Steven Taylor. He couldn't work out why Gilmour had remained silent all morning, nor why the old man was allowing Steven to push them so hard. They were wet and cold, and uncertain they could make the climb over the next pass. Mark knew it. Brynne knew it, and he knew it. If Steven continued at this pace, none of them would have the strength to go on. They would never make it at this pace; they would not succeed. Sallax, Gilmour, even Mark: one of them needed to take control. Steven needed to understand that his guilt at Hannah's plight was not reason enough to put them all at risk. Garec longed for Versen to appear and take charge.

He looked back at Gilmour, who gave him a warm, ironic smile through a cloud of pipe smoke. Then, surprised at the sound of his own voice, Garec cried out, 'Stop!'

Everyone turned to look. Steven, irritated at the interruption to his forced march, called back, 'No, Garec, we must continue moving. We've nearly reached the base of this valley. It won't be long before we're climbing that slope.' He gestured towards the ominous rise awaiting them in the distance.

'I'm sorry, Steven,' Garec called back, 'but we have to take a break. Sallax is ill and we're all wet and cold. If we push ourselves to exhaustion today, none of us will clear that pass tomorrow.' Garec was worried the others might disapprove, but if he didn't try, they would probably all die in the snow.

Steven ran a sleeve across his forehead and, panting loudly, tried to convince them to move on. 'Do you all know what is happening up there?' He pointed towards the hillside before them. 'It's snowing up there and every hour – every *aven* – we spend dawdling down here, the deeper it gets and the more difficult our passage becomes.'

'Garec's right, Steven,' Mark said, but Steven interrupted angrily.

'How the hell can you suggest we stop?' Steven was incredulous. You know what's waiting for us up there.'

'That's exactly why we ought to camp on the valley floor tonight,' Mark said. 'Sallax needs more rest. Hell, we all do.'

'Sallax is fine. He's the only one keeping pace without complaining.'

Sallax said nothing, and his very indifference concerned everyone but Steven.

'Fine.' Steven's voice rose. 'Camp down here. Camp here until spring. I'm going over that pass tomorrow morning.'

'Steven.' Gilmour finally spoke. 'Your passion is commendable, and I'm certain Hannah would appreciate it. But the only way for you to help her now is to stick to our plan.'

'Don't you see, Gilmour?' He looked from side to side through the trees, as if someone who understood him might appear and take up his cause. 'Finally, something about this mystical, enchanted nightmare of a world you call home makes sense. She's here and she needs me. I'm going to her now.'

Gilmour remained calm. 'She needs you, and you can help, but not by killing yourself and us. Nerak cannot detect the magic of your staff. It leaves no ripple as our own magic does. We will not make it into Welstar Palace on my power alone.' The old man's words fell, solid as bricks. All eyes turned back to Steven.

'Come with me now to Praga,' he begged, 'please. I *must* save Hannah.'

'No,' Garec answered, 'our mission is clear. We must win back the key. If we fail to do that, Hannah will be only one of millions upon millions of deaths at Nerak's hands. Our world, yours – and who knows how many more—'

Steven looked as though he might expire. He rubbed one hand across his face and wiped away the tears, then turned to Mark. 'You know where you're going.'

'Steven, no.'

'You know where you're going. Keep moving north. If there's a river into Orindale, you're bound to run right into it.' He looked up at Gilmour. 'Wait for me at Orindale. I'll find her and be back.'

'You must stay with us.' Garec was beginning to lose his temper. 'You know where Lessek's Key is.'

'So does Mark.'

'And if Mark dies between here and Welstar Palace, what then?' The Ronan bowman took a few steps forward. 'Stay with us, Steven. Defeat Nerak and Hannah has nothing to fear.'

Steven felt confused and cornered and lashed out at Garec. 'Stay back,' he called, raising the staff as if to strike. In an instant Garec had his bow drawn and an arrow trained at Steven's chest.

'Don't make a mistake, Steven,' he warned in steady, even tones, 'I am impressed with your newly acquired magic, but I will drop you in your tracks before you can think to summon it against us.'

White fire burst from the spaces between Steven's fingers and, crying out in pain, he dropped the staff.

Thinking Steven had cast a spell, Garec grimaced and released his arrow. It never left the bow. Instead, the shaft remained nocked, frozen in place with the bowstring drawn full. Garec stared in disbelief at his weapon and then turned to see Gilmour, his eyes closed and his palms extended before him.

The old Larion Senator spoke. 'We will not fight among ourselves.' Slowly, Garec's bow relaxed in his grip and the arrow fell to the ground.

Gilmour said. 'Steven, we cannot defeat Nerak without you. When we find shelter, I will endeavour to contact Kantu in Praga. It will take me a day, and I must channel all my energy to that task; I cannot risk it here in the forest. I will tell him that Hannah is looking for him and he should bring her to Welstar Palace.' His tone was firm but understanding, a worried parent struggling to communicate with an angry teenager. 'He will see her safely north to join you and Mark before your return home.'

Steven knew Gilmour was right. Despite his near inhuman need to find Hannah, he knew the best course of action would be to recapture Lessek's Key and give the sorcerer the tools he needed to ensure victory. Still his emotions ran through him like a flood tide and the thought of camping overnight in the valley made him furious. Torn between his desire to find Hannah and his reborn determination to help his friends, Steven felt his head begin to spin. The sweat on his face and neck grew suddenly cold; his vision tunnelled and he fought to remain lucid.

He lifted the hickory staff from the snow and delivered a mighty blow to the trunk of the nearest lodge pine. Swinging with all his strength, he bellowed into the forest, crying even as the staff tore through the trunk and the enormous pine came crashing down in a blurred cloud of snow and green boughs. Once again surprised the staff had not shattered in his hands, Steven turned and ran towards the mountain slope in the distance.

Diving involuntarily away from the massive tumbling pine, Mark could have sworn he saw colour, bright neon colour, and text. COLD BEER illuminated for a fraction of a second in the wake of Steven's swipe at the tree. Dispelling the idea as a momentary hallucination, or perhaps a trail of thin fire clinging to the shaft, Mark propped himself up on one elbow, brushed the snow from his face and cried after his friend, 'Steven, wait!'

'It's all right,' Garec said calmly, 'he'll come to his senses. He can't keep up that pace very long.'

Angry, Mark turned on the bowman. 'Where's your head? You were going to shoot him.'

'I was not going to shoot him,' Garec assured them. 'I thought he was going to turn on us with that unholy stick.'

Sallax stared blankly at the others. Brynne, getting increasingly worried about her brother's wellbeing, pleaded, 'Let's rest here. Maybe Steven will come back when he tires. We have to give Sallax a chance to recover.'

Steven struggled to catch his breath as he raced blindly down the slope. The forest around him was a jumble of greens and browns cast randomly on a backdrop of ghostly white. His thoughts overwhelmed him, an involuntary mosaic of ideas and images, and he fell hard twice, rolling through hillside drifts. Coming to his feet, he fought for control and pushed on again, running with knees high, forcing himself to lift his feet clear of the snow with each step. Finally, his adrenalin waning, Steven felt himself calming and the athlete in him took over. *Find a rhythm,* he started repeating as a mantra. *Run with your legs, not your lungs.*

Stopping for a moment, he wiped his face clean with a handful of snow and dried his eyes on a corner of his cloak. Drawing several deep breaths, he felt his heart rate drop and his thoughts clear. Deliberately, Steven removed the cloak, folded it neatly and fastened it to his pack with a thin length of rawhide. Hefting the pack under one arm like a bulbous football, he carried the staff in his opposite hand.

Steven was disappointed none of the others had followed. Turning to the unbroken snow ahead, he began jogging towards the distant mountain pass. With his first few steps, he felt a pang of guilt at leaving his friends, but soon he forced it from his mind. They would be fine. Gilmour would ensure their safety and he would rejoin them after he had found Hannah. He had no idea how he would get to Orindale – even where Orindale really was – and was even less certain how he would cross the Ravenian Sea, so he ran, until his breathing, heart rate and pace all met in a steady aerobic plateau. He could do this for hours, skimming through the snow, his feet leaving postholes behind him like tiny air shafts to subterranean chambers. Soon he had crossed the valley floor and began making his way up the mountain slope towards the tree line. He would find her.

Years of running had taught Steven that as long as he did not overwork his lungs, he could maintain a steady, loping gait for great distances. He adjusted his stride to be certain plenty of oxygenated blood coursed to his leg muscles. He sustained his pace; if he broke his stride, he wouldn't be able to continue – he'd taken part in dozens of road races where he felt as strong as a lion through ten or even twenty miles, then nearly collapsed when crossing the finish line. Sucking on handfuls of snow as he ran to hydrate himself, he allowed the rhythm of his stride to lull him into a state of subdued awareness. Only the steady pounding of his feet and the quick but gentle repetition of his breathing made any sound.

He was pleased to discover the snow at lower elevations had not accumulated much above his ankles. Feeling stronger as endorphins rushed through his bloodstream in a natural narcotic fix, he leaped over a small stream babbling east, flushed a covey of what looked like Eldarn's version of quail from beneath a juniper bush and spooked a large deer from a thicket. The forest was beautiful, undisturbed by the myriad nefarious horrors that haunted the rest of Eldarn. Steven could smell fresh pine, a sweet aroma that lingered on the furthest edge of the morning air. He inhaled as deeply as possible to wallow in the delicate scent; despite a painful chill in his nose, the rewards justified the effort. Lodge pines similar to the one he had so viciously truncated that morning grew to impossible heights all around him, determined contestants in an interminably slow competition to reach the heavens. He found it comforting they could never move; anything more than the gentle sway in the mountain breeze might mitigate their flawlessness. Steven was certain he would never encounter anything as simple and beautiful as a tree. If he were to remain trapped in Eldarn, he would come back to this secluded valley and live in isolation, protected by the forest from the dark magic of Malakasia and Welstar Palace.

Dicot, a five-letter word for pre-paper. That clue was clever, but not one Steven could remember solving. Instead, he kept trying to fit the word *trees* into the allotted spaces even though he knew 'd' was correct, because he had solved *Daniel*, a six-letter word for lion tamer, and then 'n', in *nectar*, a six-letter word for Dionysus's lunch. There was a woman who could solve the *New York Times* crossword puzzle, every day, in ink, some sequestered and genetically anomalous freak of nature from Parsippany, New Jersey. Steven periodically measured himself against that same benchmark. Every morning, his routine was the same. Turn left from Tenth Street onto Miner, walk two blocks to the café, buy a cappuccino and choose a newspaper for the day. Some mornings he did choose the *Times*: Idaho Springs had an abundant selection of out-of-state newspapers. But most days he would look at its small fonts and its crowded front page, shake his head and dejectedly purchase the *Clear Creek County Gazette*, a local rag with gripping headlines, regional news and a much easier crossword.

The *Gazette*'s puzzle was nothing like the *Times*'. Rather than frustrating prompts, the *Gazette* contained large, obvious clues that broke the puzzle's back early so working the crossword quickly became nothing more than filling in the blanks. Enormous, mid-line clues such as a 14-letter word for bilateral Christmas treat, *gingerbreadman*, or a 17-letter word for Georgia raptors, *theatlantafalcons*, made the victory inherent in inking the last box both shallow and fleeting. Steven could only guess at what would cause a person to choose the *Gazette* over the *Times*. Perhaps it was the comprehensive local sports scores and statistics from high school basketball games. Maybe it was the full column account of the roast beef supper at the United Methodist Church the previous Sunday. Or possibly it was the fact that any barely literate child could struggle through the *Clear Creek County Gazette*'s crossword puzzle, oftentimes in ink, while it took a more resilient and soundly tempered individual to navigate the *Times'* cryptic spaces.

'Ah, bullshit ... Give me the *Gazette* any day,' he said in a soul-cleansing confession. 'If I can't tell the truth out here, I'll never be able to.'

Slipping on an icy branch, Steven woke from his reverie. He tapered his pace to a slow jog and peered up through the trees in search of the peaks he had been using to triangulate his position. Slowing to a walk, he felt dizzy for a moment and quickly swallowed two handfuls of snow. Dropping his pack, he held the hickory staff aloft and sighted along its edge towards a naked granite mountaintop in the northeast. He was out of position. Looking northwest, he repeated the motion and failed to find the second peak. 'Well, damn it all to hell and back,' he spat, and sat down dejectedly in a nearby drift to catch his breath. His daydreaming had put him far off course to the east. Now he would have to backtrack, realign his position between the mountains and make up for lost time. Drawing a cold piece of boar from his tunic, he took several hearty bites before it occurred to him that he would need to ration what little meat he had until he found another food source. With snow on the ground, he had plenty of water, although he would need to start melting it over a fire before long; he couldn't continue to eat snow by the handful without risking a change in his body temperature. That would be a deadly mistake out here.

He would also need food soon, and without a bow, or even a rudimentary spear, Steven realised he was looking at going hungry for the next day or two. He wrapped the slab of meat and replaced it securely in his pocket.

'Okay, time to move. I'll get nowhere sitting here.' Steven cursed as he pulled himself to his feet. His thighs and chest ached. He was finished running for the day.

Moving west along the lower slopes of the mountain, he craned his neck in an effort to catch a glimpse of the peak he had been using as a fixed navigational point. Realising he could not look around the mountain, no matter how far he stretched, Steven suddenly felt awkward. He peered about the forest just to make sure no one was watching him. The stillness of the valley struck him as unnatural and he listened for a moment before shrugging and continuing through the snow.

He estimated he had come about half a mile too far along the valley floor. If he climbed at an angle, splitting the difference between a direct assault on the peak and a full trip around its base, he should eventually cross his original path to the top of the mountain. But climbing at such a curious angle soon made the soles of Garec's boots roll beneath his feet, and with each uncomfortable step he pined for his own hiking boots. He cursed himself for not retrieving them when he had the chance. The day that Garec had borrowed his boots to descend the rocky slopes of Seer's Peak seemed a lifetime ago.

Remembering that brought the memory of Garec aiming an arrow at his chest. Steven forced the image from his mind, reassuring himself that his friend would never really have fired to hit him. Secretly, he was glad Gilmour had intervened. Steven swallowed hard as he imagined the shaft piercing his rib cage. It would have come fast, too fast to avoid, but not so fast that it would be invisible. He would have seen the arrow coming . . . he cringed, and tried hard to think of something else.

When the blow did come, it was different. A blur of mercurial darkness from above and slightly behind him, its force took Steven in the ribs. It wasn't the precision targeting of a Ronan arrow; instead of piercing his flesh, the impact sent him reeling backwards down the hillside. The blow was rough and clumsy: he felt like he'd been struck by a truck. The air exploded from his lungs as he landed hard on his back, then rolled over several times before he finally came to rest against the trunk of a thick pine. Several clumps of snow fell from its branches, landing on his face and shoulders, and he rubbed his eyes clear as he struggled to fight off the disorientation and see what had hit him.

Still dizzy from the fall, it took a moment for his eyes to focus, but as his vision sharpened he flinched in terror as the hulking form of a huge grettan took shape before him. It was missing a forelimb and Steven could see a mass of congealed blood matting its fur. It was obviously the same animal that had attacked their camp the night before, but now it was just a grettan, a gigantic, wounded and most likely ravenous grettan. Its eyes shone black in the dim winter light; Steven's first thought was relief that at least Malagon was not controlling the beast today.

Now the creature lay in the snow only a few paces away, obviously exhausted from the effort of attacking Steven. Slowly it lifted its enormous head and turned on him, its jowls dripping with the effort. Its initial leap had drained it; now it needed to muster the strength to come at him again. Steven fought to regain his feet. He cried out as a sharp pain lanced beneath his arm. At least one of his ribs was broken. As he fell back against the tree he looked around frantically for the hickory staff: it was lying some ten paces away and there was no way he was going to get to it before the grettan pounced. The animal growled and Steven, bracing himself for the inevitable, closed his eyes tightly against the pain in his side and sprang to his feet.

Two, three, then four steps. Behind him, the grettan was on its feet now.

Five, six steps. An unholy cry: the beast howled in pain. Steven's heart soared; he might just make it.

Seven steps. Foes, both injured, fighting with the last measure of their strength.

Eight steps. Steven was unable to bring his right foot forward. He looked down to see his boot, Garec's boot, disappear into the grettan's jaws. Eight steps. He hadn't made it. *We might not make it*. Throwing his body forward, a sprinter finishing a dead heat, he reached for the staff, but as he fell face first into the snow, he knew it was beyond his grasp.

The grettan clamped its jaws down on Steven's calf and he felt the razor-sharp teeth pierce his flesh to the bone. He screamed, forgetting the staff, forgetting everything. His thoughts focused on nothing. Nothing. Not Hannah, nor his mother. Not the mountains of Colorado or the vast, surf-tipped surface of the ocean. Not his myriad embarrassments or failures. Nothing. No bright light, no symbolic tunnel, no benevolent deity and no cinematic review of his life.

At the moment of his death, nothing passed through Steven's mind except: *We might not make it*.

We might not make it.

These were the last in a string of moments he had naïvely believed would go on for ever.

Steven felt the bones of his lower leg snap just before he heard it, like twigs breaking under his boots, Garec's boots. Uncertain whether his leg had been torn from his body, Steven Taylor fell away into darkness.

THE SANCTUARY

Garec was snapping branches into kindling when he saw Gilmour stand suddenly and stare out into the forest. 'What's wrong?' he asked, tossing two ends of a damp twig onto their struggling fire.

'Steven is in trouble.'

At that moment, they heard the distant cry of a grettan emanating up from the valley. It reminded him of the scream he had heard when he and Renna swam to safety across Danae's Eddy. Unconsciously he ran one hand over the knee that Gilmour had healed.

'Let's go.' Mark was already on his feet, pulling on his cloak.

'You and I can move quickly down the hill,' Gilmour said. 'Garec, stay with Brynne and Sallax. Follow our trail when you can. We'll wait for you wherever we find Steven.'

'Right.' Garec felt helpless, but the plan was sound: although Sallax appeared to be improving, he was still in no condition to run anywhere, let alone through knee-deep snow in the freezing cold.

As Mark and Gilmour moved to depart, Brynne caught Mark by the arm. 'Wait,' she cried, pulling Mark to her. She brought his face close, looked deep into his eyes and whispered, 'Be careful.'

'We will,' he promised, and kissed her quickly on the lips. 'Don't worry, we'll be fine. I'll see you later tonight.' He hugged her hard against him, feeling a sudden rush of emotion, and kissed her again, more deeply this time, before reluctantly letting her go.

'We'll see you soon. Take your time, and don't rush Sallax. We'll be there. *I* will be there, waiting.'

Steven's trail was easy to follow. As Gilmour set a rapid pace through the snow they heard another wail from the valley floor, a thin and insubstantial shriek. Mark could not tell whether it was a cry of anguish or rage, but the ensuing silence implied that one of the distant combatants had emerged victorious.

Every now and then Gilmour stopped without warning and closed his eyes in concentration. Mark assumed he was casting about the valley floor for some sign that Steven was still alive. When Mark suggested he search for the staff instead of trying to trace Steven, the magician reminded him the magic in the hickory stick left no detectable ripple in its wake, even when it was being used.

'It has enough power to kill a grettan, though,' Mark said, grasping for reassurance. 'Look what it did to that one last night.'

'That's true,' Gilmour answered, 'but grettans travel in packs, and are quite intelligent enough to plan surprise attacks when hunting, even when they're not housing evil sorcerers.' He smiled grimly.

'So if Steven didn't see them coming—'

'Right,' he confirmed quietly, and continued down the hillside.

Mark, desperately worried, started cursing Steven for running off alone. 'Hang in there, Stevie,' he muttered under his breath, 'I need you healthy so I can beat the holy shit out of you. You ever do this again and I'll kill you, I swear to God I will.' Gilmour pretended not to hear.

It was late in the day when they finally crossed the valley floor. Mark slowed to look towards the peak Steven had dubbed *Toilet Brush* because of the oddly shaped glacier adorning its craggy ridge. Gilmour watched as Mark's gaze moved back and forth between Steven's trail and the distant mountain.

'He's moved off course?'

Mark nodded. 'But I'm not sure why.' He motioned ahead along their current path. 'The going here is easy. It's not like Steven to get turned around – he's one of the best climbers I know. He's got a really keen sense of direction.'

'Then we must assume his thoughts were elsewhere,' Gilmour said quietly. 'He was angry and frightened when he left. Perhaps he forgot to check his progress against the mountains.'

'I'm afraid you're right. We'll just have to pray he's not gone too far east.' He drew his hunting knife and cut a length of red wool from his sweater. Tying it to a nearby tree, he went on, 'We'll have to come back here. It's the most direct route to the pass above. Hopefully, Garec will see this marker, see the change in our path and realise they need to make camp here.'

'Perhaps this will help as well.' Gilmour gestured with one hand above Steven's footprints and flame burst from his fingers. The heat was so searing that Mark was forced to turn away as Gilmour burned a long black line through the snow and into the frozen earth below. Smoke rose from the deep wound that delineated their change in direction.

'Yeah,' he commented dryly. 'That ought to work. You'll have to teach me that one someday, Gilmour.'

It wasn't much later when Mark came to a stop and pointed towards a set of footprints moving at an angle up the hill.

'There,' he told Gilmour, 'that's where he realised his mistake. Looks like he was trying to cut the corner to make up time. Let's keep moving before it gets too dark to see.'

Gilmour wiped his forehead. Mark guessed the sorcerer was mentally tallying a list of spells, searching for something that would ensure Steven was alive and unhurt. How ironic: here was one of the most powerful people in Eldarn, and yet he was unable to cast a spell to get them through this predicament. Mark gripped him by the shoulder and squeezed. 'I'm sure he'll be fine.'

As a light breeze began to blow Mark found himself increasingly irritated at the incessant whisper of the pine tree branches. He bent low over the snow, struggling to follow Steven's tracks in the dim light. His back ached and he realised for the first time that day that he was hungry, as well as emotionally exhausted. He was ready to collapse.

'We need light,' he groaned as he clambered to his feet. 'Can you make a torch or something for us?'

Borrowing Mark's battle-axe, Gilmour moved to the nearest tree and hacked off a bough thick with green needles that were quickly fading to black in the waning daylight. No sooner had the branch come away in his hand that it ignited, seemingly of its own volition, with a pleasant yellow flame. Gilmour handed the branch to Mark. 'Will this do?'

'Thanks,' Mark answered wryly, 'I didn't mind spending the last hour stooped over looking for disappearing footprints!'

'It was not an hour.'

'You don't remember how long an hour is. Gettysburg was one hundred and forty years ago,' Mark reminded him. 'I'm surprised you remember—' Mark stopped in mid-sentence and stared at the scene before him now illuminated by the burning branch. It looked like the aftermath of a violent battle, and there was a circular patch of ground that seemed as if Eldarn itself had been wounded: an open sore left infected and festering in the Blackstone Mountains.

'Good God,' Mark whispered. 'What on earth happened here?'

The snow had been dyed a deep crimson and the trees around were splattered with gore. Mark looked around and swallowed, hard. All his previous optimism vanished in an instant. There was no hope of finding Steven alive.

Pieces of something – maybe a grettan, or perhaps a pack of grettans – lay strewn about: a random collection of limbs, entrails and patches of fur. It looked as if the beasts had exploded with enormous force. Squinting through the thin yellow light thrown out by his makeshift torch, he saw the hillside was dotted with bloody fragments. They looked oddly out of place, red splashed on the otherwise unbroken blanket of snow.

Gilmour tore a second branch from a nearby pine and created a torch for himself. He moved rapidly, searching for any sign of Steven, but he could see nothing amidst the carnage.

'What could have done this?' Mark asked, his voice hushed.

'Steven,' Gilmour said.

'But I though he couldn't use the magic to destroy at will.' Mark sounded confused.

'It looks like that is no problem when he is protecting us, or the integrity of our eventual goal.'

'But what about that tree this morning? Why did the staff respond then? That tree was no threat.'

'That was strange, wasn't it? I wondered if anyone else had found it odd that he was able to summon the magic by the sheer force of his will.' Gilmour scratched at his beard. 'He certainly is an interesting young man.' He bent over to pick up a section of what appeared to be a grettan forelimb. Turning it over in his hands, he sniffed it, then added 'This wound had begun to clot and heal. This is the same beast that came for us last night.'

'Malagon?'

'I don't think so.' Gilmour paused, and closed his eyes for a moment. 'No, I didn't detect Nerak's presence earlier and I don't now. I think this animal was injured, perhaps dying, and it attacked Steven out of fury, hunger and pain.'

'So where is he?'

Gilmour moved around the periphery of the carnage, still looking for evidence that Steven had walked away from the devastation. He hadn't found Steven's pack or the staff, so he still had some hope that the young man was alive.

Finally, they came upon footprints, moving east through the forest. 'There,' Gilmour said, pointing into the distance, 'that way. Let's go.'

'But why would he go east?' Mark knelt beside the footprints and dabbed his fingers in the congealed blood trail that dotted the snow.

'He wouldn't,' Gilmour stated, as if his conclusions were obvious. 'He was carried.'

A look of fear passed over Mark's face and he felt for the battle-axe as he considered their options. 'I'm going after him,' he said finally.

'Mark, look at these strides,' he said quietly. 'They're long, much too long for the average man moving through snow, especially while carrying someone.'

'What does that mean? Who carried him off?'

'I'm not certain, but I *do* know you will never catch up with them in the dark.'

'What should we do?' Mark was trying hard not to break down. His best friend was injured, maybe dying, and had been carried off into the night by an unknown someone – or some*thing*.

Gilmour put an arm across his shoulder. 'We should collect the others, wait until dawn and then follow along this path as quickly as we can.'

'Then I'm going ahead now,' Mark said, resolute. 'I'll move slowly enough to give you a chance to catch up, but quickly enough to reach Steven if they stop for the night. If this is his blood, they won't be able to get far without stopping to bind up his injuries.'

It was obvious Mark would not be swayed, but Gilmour made one last plea. 'Mark, it really isn't wise to break up the group even more. Especially not in this weather.'

'I won't leave this path,' Mark promised, 'and if the trail splits, I'll follow the blood.'

Gilmour nodded. 'Fair enough. We will be along as soon as possible. Do not take any unnecessary chances.'

'Okay,' Mark said as he hefted his pack. Holding the pine torch aloft, he asked, 'Any chance you can keep this thing burning for me?'

Gilmour waved once; Mark could see his lips moving slightly. 'Done,' he called, and waved again as Mark disappeared into the night.

'Which one is he?' Hannah squinted. The tavern was dark and a cloud of tobacco smoke billowed out when Churn pulled open the unwieldy wooden door.

Hoyt joined her at the top of a short flight of stairs that provided a slightly elevated vantage point from which to view the entire great room of the Middle Fork Tavern. Alen apparently frequented this bar during the dinner aven. A great fire roared in the massive stone fireplace at one end of the room and a veritable maze of small tables dotted the landscape between it and the actual bar against the opposite wall. Behind racks of casks, ceramic jars and blown-glass bottles, two windows looked out on a broad thoroughfare running east to west through the village.

The windows, though large, were made of many tiny panes and let little natural light into the room. Hoyt thought the Middle Fork Tavern was as close to drinking in a cave as one could hope to achieve without actually climbing into the mountains.

'I don't see him,' he replied, 'but the light's dreadful. Let's take a walk; I'm sure he's here somewhere.'

Churn gripped Hoyt's shoulder and began signing.

'Right,' Hoyt agreed, 'if we don't find him, I'll talk with the bartender. He's sure to know where Alen has gone.'

The room was oddly shaped, much longer than wide, and canopied with an arched stone ceiling. It looked as if some entrepreneurial investor had walled up an unused section of sewer and dropped a staircase down from the street. Great beams framed the walls and outlined the arched canopy in a corps of flying buttresses holding nothing aloft. Hannah shuddered: she felt as if the ancient stone and mortar ceiling might drop on them at any moment.

'Tell me again what he looks like,' she said, 'then we can split up.'

'Older than me, maybe four hundred and fifty Twinmoons.' Hoyt did the maths for Hannah and went on, 'I think you would say about sixty or sixty-five years.' He pronounced the strange word like *ears*, and Hannah stifled a giggle.

'He had short hair last time I saw him, greying – it's probably all white by now. Not imposing, slightly shorter than me, and a bit heavy around the midsection. If he's eating, his plate will most likely have a gansel leg, two potatoes with the skins on and half a loaf of bread dipped in gravy.'

'You know him well, then,' Hannah laughed. 'Good. You check the bar; I'll go towards the fireplace.' She reached out for Churn and asked, 'Would you come with me? I don't like the look of this place. It makes me feel like it's about to come crushing down on us.'

Churn nodded and followed her through the crowd as Hoyt wandered over to the bar, smiling at several patrons and nodding to the bartender. He didn't want to draw attention by asking for Alen by name, but if their search turned up nothing he knew he'd have to. Most people were drinking beer, but there were a few wine drinkers; Hoyt admired the heavy ceramic goblets they were using.

From an antechamber off the room came the aroma of gansel stew, venison steaks and roasting potatoes. Hoyt's stomach groaned a *sotto voce* complaint; he decided they would eat here, whether they found Alen or not. He completed a circuit of the bar, but there was no sign of his old friend. He paused momentarily to watch three venison steaks being laid in a pan; the cook poured a generous quantity of red wine over each and Hoyt's stomach growled again.

His mouth watering, he looked around for Churn and Hannah. When he spotted them they were near the other end of the room, moving between tables searching for the old man with the soft paunch and the white hair. Hoyt was heading towards them when he spied an empty space on one of the benches; he hustled to claim it before anyone else got there. As he sat down, more patrons rose to leave.

He caught Churn's attention and signed, 'Come over here; let's eat.' The giant took Hannah gently by the upper arm and began steering her towards the benches while Hoyt moved to the bar and called above the din of the tavern, 'Bartender!'

A gangly young man with an unsightly skin condition scurried over and asked in a gruff basso, 'What do you want?' Hoyt was taken aback at the incongruity of such a booming, resonant voice from such a spindly body. For a moment he was speechless.

'Come on, speak up. I haven't got all day to stand around here waiting for you,' the barman muttered.

Hoyt shook himself. 'Three beers, three steaks, three bowls of gansel stew, one loaf of bread, the hottest you can find above the hearth, and one dancing girl, preferably younger than two hundred Twinmoons.'

The barman scowled. For a moment Hoyt wondered if the pox marks across the boy's forehead could be connected to outline a map of the Pragan south coast. 'For women, you need to see Regon,' he boy said, gesturing towards a well-dressed patron sitting behind a corner table and speaking with two scantily clad young women. Hoyt estimated their age at just over one hundred and ten Twinmoons, far too young for that sort of work.

'No thanks, I was just kidding,' he said. 'Just the food, thanks.' He tried to manoeuvre himself onto the bench without kicking anyone: he needed to find Alen and he needed a hot meal – the last thing he wanted to do was get into a bar fight. He cast the bartender a friendly smile and adjusted his position on the bench. Shifting, his foot came down on something soft, a bag of laundry, maybe.

He bent down and peered beneath the seat. The bag of clothes was actually a man, passed out, dead drunk – or maybe even just dead. He looked as if he'd been down there for several avens. He was soaking wet, stinking of beer, with shards of gansel bones caught in his matted hair. He appeared to have fallen asleep in a puddle of vomit.

Hoyt's stomach churned at the image of this foul-smelling old grettan first crawling under the bench for some rest, then throwing up, and finally passing out. 'I do not envy you, my friend,' he said to the inert heap, 'you are going to feel like you've been pissed on by a demon when you wake.

'But now, be a good fellow, will you? Bend your knees so I can sit down here without stepping on you all day.' The man did not comply and for a moment, Hoyt thought perhaps the inebriated stranger really was dead.

'Come on,' he tried again. 'Just a little now ... bend your knees.' This time the drunk obliged, rolling slightly to one side, and Hoyt gently nudged the legs out of his way. The corpse-like figure opened his eyes for a moment, peered out at a spot at the far end of the universe and then closed them again with a delicate flutter.

Hoyt shuddered. He looked long and hard into the man's ghostly features and grimaced. He had found Alen Jasper of Middle Fork.

His heart sank. 'Alen, oh rutting dogs, she is going to be furious.' Churn and Hannah were making their way across the crowded room, eager for a hot meal.

'Think, Hoyt, think,' he commanded himself, then called for the bartender's help.

'What now?' the boy said sullenly.

Hoyt tossed him a thin silver coin and watched as the homely splotched face split into a narrow grin. 'Keep the change, and—' he pointed under the bench, 'and keep him here.'

Surprised anyone would be interested in the drunk, the bartender shrugged. 'He's not going anywhere. He hasn't for quite some time.'

'What do you mean?'

'He's been in here every day—'

'How long?' Hoyt interrupted. Churn and Hannah were nearly there; if the foreign woman were not to lose all hope he had to act quickly.

'Oh, I'd say about ten or eleven Twinmoons now. I'm surprised he's not dead yet.'

Bleeding whores. Hoyt turned and unobtrusively signed to Churn, 'We need to leave, *now*.'

'Why?' Churn recognised the need for stealth and Hannah did not notice the two men communicating.

'Later. Just go.'

Hannah smiled and took one of Hoyt's hands, as if touching him would make it easier to hear above the tavern's din. 'This place isn't so bad once you get used to it,' she said, agreeably. 'It's a bit smoky, but we can wait a while if you think he'll be along later. Should we eat? It actually smells quite good.'

'No,' Hoyt said quickly, 'no, I know a better place down the street.' That was an out-and-out lie, and Hoyt started praying to the gods of the Northern Forest that there was a reputable inn with hearty food within a short distance. Surely the gods owed him something.

'I let the bartender know we needed to find Alen and he'll keep an eye out for us.' Gripping her hand, he turned Hannah back towards the stairs. 'Let's take a walk, find a room for the night and then eat someplace a bit less smoky.'

Hannah, still none the wiser, smiled. 'That sounds great. Let's go.' Mounting the stairs, she added, 'You know, I'm beginning to feel more confident about my chances of getting home. I hope we find him tonight. I don't think I could sleep knowing he's somewhere close by.'

Hoyt gave a half-nod, half-shake of his head and muttered under his breath, 'If you only knew!'

Steven woke screaming as the bones in his lower leg were set. The morning sun was blinding and he could barely make out the blurry features of the dark Samaritan lashing his leg between two heavy pine branches. He lashed out involuntarily, but only one arm responded; pain exploded from his shoulder as he struck his anonymous nurse a solid blow. His lungs ablaze with the fire of a smouldering Eldarni hell, Steven screamed again before passing out from the pain.

Later, he was bathed entirely in white. No discernable line marked the delineation between earth and sky. Steven was moving slowly through a perfect ivory world. It was neither cold nor warm, and there was no scent, no fresh air, no colours. Squinting against the iridescent brilliance, he felt dizzy, and vomited across his chest. Sickened by the sudden foul stench corrupting this pure world, he attempted to move his head to one side, but discovered he was immobile, trapped in a chalky white dream. Unable to escape his own wretchedness, he vomited again, choking out a barely audible cry.

The blurry stranger appeared, more a dark intrusion among his bleached surroundings than an actual person. The silent care-giver wiped Steven's tunic clean with a length of cloth and forced a wineskin filled with cold water into his mouth. Steven managed a swallow before the stranger spun away into the distance and the dark edges of unconsciousness swallowed him once more.

He was running through deep sand on a beach. It was summer and his thighs ached with the effort. A sea breeze blew in off the bay and he felt it pushing against his chest, holding him fast. *I have to get down closer to the water; the sand will be firm there.* He heard music, someone playing Bach on a pipe organ. The notes were clean, and each fell into place amongst the fabric of contrapuntal tones that bounced about his head like so many colourful balls. There were wonderful flavours, hearty sauces and grilled meats. Was there more in the kitchen, or should he take less and allow their guests to eat as much as they wanted? *Be certain not to inconvenience anyone, Steven.*

He ran his tongue over his lips, expecting to capture the vestiges of a delicious meal, but instead he felt them cracked, dried and scabbed over with clotted blood. When had he been hurt? Did he fall? *Keep playing that music; it's a nice way to pass the time, much better than pondering safe deposit boxes, Egyptian geometrics, or cell phones and calculators.*

And then the stranger was with him again. Together, they were back in the seamless, bleached-white realm and Steven tried to smile, for no other reason than to let the stranger know he was happy here. He felt his lip tear open and tasted blood trickling into his mouth, no sauces or meats this time. And what was that behind him? Two tracks, long imperfections scratched in the ivory blanket thrown over everything in sight. Following their path, he realised they had been made by his own heels, dragging two thin lines into the distance.

Pick up your feet, Steven. You're ruining the carpet. What would Lessek say? Lessek would say something confusing or incoherent, something to make him believe his role in Eldarn was complete when he knew he had more to do. Lessek would mock him from beyond the grave, sharing otherwise pointless images from Steven's life, staying up late to watch the '86 series or breaking his elbow one summer in Maine. Or he would show him a slow-motion film of the afternoon he met Hannah. Joking with Howard and Myrna, and why? To confirm that Hannah is really here, here in this foul Eldarni prison? The answers lie elsewhere, Steven. Was that it? No. Nerak's *weakness* lies elsewhere. That was it. Terrific. The answers lie elsewhere; so our time climbing

Seer's Peak, risking our lives against the almor and possibly losing Versen was time wasted?

Screw you, Lessek. Save your own fucking world. It was the first time Steven realised he had been moving backwards. He started to cry.

Fever. What did Dr Wilson say? Fever was the body's natural response to unwanted intruders. Anything that can live at body temperature will struggle to survive when the environment gets warmer. There was a song about fever, a line from that rolling Beethoven song. But this was Bach, one of the fugues. Steven could not name it; he could never keep them straight. His sister had a fever once; he had watched from the hallway as she writhed about on her bed. It had been strangely erotic, and at the same time, terrifying. He had worried she might die. She had been submerged in a cool bath before being rushed to hospital. Had she died?

He was sweating now. It stung his eyes and ran in cold rivers behind his ears and across his neck. He fought to wipe his face, but could not. He begged for someone – anyone – to mop his brow, but no one came. His ivory surroundings had disappeared. Or had he lost his ability to see?

No, she had not died. She was marrying Ken or Karl or someone and he had to get her china cabinet to California. It had been cold in her room that night. His teeth rattled together and he felt himself begin to shiver uncontrollably. The white world was gone, but a spiralling, colourful array of bright dancing rainbows had replaced it. Sweating. *I wonder how much weight I've lost. Maybe I'll wrestle next season. It's a long time to stay this thin, though.* How did it not make them crazy? Wrestlers. It was too cold to wrestle now. The referees would have to wear knit gloves. *I wonder if I might scratch imperfections in these colours as well. Bring back the white blanket. I won't ruin it.*

I'll pick up my feet if someone will just wipe my eyes. It's give and take. I can avoid becoming a burden for all of you if someone will just clear this stinging, sodding, salty sweat from my eyes.

Crying out, Steven shivered, hyperventilating, as the faceless nursemaid wiped his face and neck. Then the stranger was gone and Steven was moving backwards once again.

Gilmour had been right. Whoever carried Steven away from the massacre had far more strength and stamina than Mark. He had been following the trail for several hours and the distance between footprints had not diminished at all. Steven's captor was either enormously tall or running at full speed while carrying his injured companion; he would shatter all international marathon records back home. Mark knew there was no way he would catch up unless Steven's injuries forced the stranger to stop.

Mark thought about making camp and waiting for the others to join him: it was obviously going to take more than a battle-axe to free Steven from whomever – or whatever – was carrying him. Having Gilmour's magic available would help. Mark shook his head and continued trudging alongside the footprints. Steven might not survive the night. It was up to Mark. He might have the chance to kill his friend's captor or to spirit Steven away if the opportunity presented itself. For either of those, he had to be there.

Shortly before dawn, the footprints turned northwards up the slope of a mountain still invisible in the darkness. Mark estimated he had run some fifteen miles east along the trail and his legs and back were aching from the uneven ground. He used snow to keep himself hydrated and finished the last of the boar meat for energy. He was pining for a glass of orange juice, or maybe a steaming cup of coffee. His body burned a dangerous number of calories every time he swallowed a handful of unmelted snow, but he didn't have the luxury of time to thaw enough to fill his wineskin.

Mark was more concerned about food; none of them had eaten much other than meat since they started climbing. They would all need proper nutrition soon: Mark laughed to himself at the thought that he was actually craving vegetables. It was just a few days since he and Steven had promised to turn over a new leaf in the culinary department, but it felt like a lifetime ago.

The slope made him slow to a quick walk; he was staggered that the stranger's pace didn't change or falter, not even when the trail turned uphill. Gilmour's makeshift torch continued to burn brightly and despite the freezing temperature, Mark had to mop his brow repeatedly with a corner of his riding cloak. 'They're heading over the mountain,' he concluded out loud.

He hoped their path had not taken them so far east that they would miss the valley he and Steven had spotted several days earlier. Mark was certain that valley was their passage to Orindale. It ran northwest for as far as they could see; neither thought to estimate how far southeast it stretched as well. They never imagined they would need to know. Mark felt a pang of insecurity as he tried to picture the vista in his mind. He couldn't recollect the far end of the valley clearly enough. Even though his plan of travelling north one pass and then heading west until they reached the valley sounded simple enough, the Rocky Mountains had taught him that apparently obvious orienteering decisions often left one lost or stranded.

Seeing his entire boot print disappear into one left by Steven's captor, Mark's thoughts shifted to how he might rescue his friend. Gilmour had said that they were being tracked by someone; might this be the *someone* he had sensed? And if so, how powerful a foe was he chasing? He wasn't a confident enough swordsman to be much of a threat to anyone more skilled than the average twelve-year-old; he was even more uncomfortable at the thought of fighting with a battle-axe. Sallax's words echoed in his mind: *Don't try to hack off any limbs*.

Great Christ-on-a-stick, was he about to engage in a conflict where that would be a viable option? He wasn't much of a fighter. He had been in a scrap with Paul Kempron when he was fourteen, and he'd walked away with a split lip and chipped tooth as he tried to avoid a burgeoning mêlée between hundreds of drunken Bostonians at a football game. That was the sum total of his fighting experience so far.

He tried to imagine what he was going up against: taller, stronger, certainly faster and more skilled . . . Mark wasted little time convincing himself that he was not about to get badly beaten, perhaps even killed. And if it was a creature with magical powers, like the almor, or the wraith that had so *changed* Sallax, then he had *no* resources to tap.

Instead, he forced himself to concentrate on how he might fool his quarry into leaving Steven unattended long enough for them to disappear into the underbrush. He had never felt less brave in his life.

Jacrys approached from above the tree line. He had worked his way around their camp and moved out onto the exposed slopes of the hillside before descending silently, a predator in the night.

He knew the old man rarely slept, but even a Larion Senator would need *some* rest after the pace they had been maintaining, especially with the tricky slope awaiting them the next morning. He used a cloaking spell which made him virtually invisible, even to Gilmour, and was so close he could smell meat roasting above the campfire. They were discussing the foreigners' disappearance; they had been tracking one all day, and were about to follow his path over an uncharted peak to the north. The woman, Brynne, was concerned their detour had taken them too far east, that they would have to retrace their steps to find passage to Orindale.

Jacrys was tired. He was tired of climbing peak after peak, tired of finding no real opportunity to complete his mission. He was tired of focusing solely on one kill. He was not a murderer by nature; he thrived on espionage, on the analysis and evaluation of situations and information, the political, economic, emotional and religious factors that influenced human behaviour. Travelling for days at a time with just one goal – and that simply murder – was boring, and exhausting. He might be about to kill the most powerful man in the occupied lands, but he would rather have been in a smoky tavern exchanging silver for news, or eavesdropping on a rogue Malakasian officer as he shared state secrets with a whore. Jacrys was adept at violence when necessary, and certainly not squeamish, but this was different. There was a point of no return for the nations of Eldarn, and he was about to push the entire world beyond it. With Gilmour dead, only the seldom-seen Kantu would have the knowledge and power to rival the dark prince, but it would not be enough. Malagon would rule unchecked until the end of his days.

Jacrys closed his eyes briefly and ground his teeth together until his jaw ached. Malagon's family had ruled for nearly a thousand Twinmoons. Would it really matter if Gilmour died now?

Peering through icy brambles, Jacrys watched as the Ronan partisans prepared to turn in for the night. This was it: he would finally do away with Gilmour and win his freedom from Malagon's continuous scrutiny – that was an uncomfortable place to be. Too many otherwise talented soldiers, spies, magicians and political figures had died without warning just because they *had* been under his watchful eye. Steven Taylor, the one with the key Malagon wanted so badly, was gone, disappeared after the rogue bull grettan attacked their camp. At least he had taken the deadly staff along with him. That was one less potentially life-threatening variable to contend with. The other was the bow-man; he wouldn't be able to flee quickly enough to avoid the young man's lightning-fast bowfire, so he needed to disarm the young killer first.

Garec was posted to the first watch. He propped himself up against a tree trunk near the old man. Perfect. It wasn't long before the bowman's eyelids started to flutter, evidence of his losing battle to remain vigilant. When Garec's chin slumped onto his chest, Jacrys drew two knives and moved slowly through the thicket towards his prey, thanking the gods of the Northern Forest for the blanket of snow muting his approach.

As he reached Gilmour's side, the Malakasian spy hesitated for a moment. Prince Malagon was a cold, cruel and dangerous man, devoid of compassion or empathy. He killed without warning, and appeared to care little for the wellbeing of his Malakasian citizens, let along those of the conquered lands. Gilmour was a legend, the protector of the ideal that all people should be permitted to live in peace, free from fear and want. Could he actually kill this man? He was under no illusion of what would happen if he did not: he would be summoned to Welstar Palace and tortured for a Twinmoon or two, and then – if he were *very* lucky – he might be allowed to die.

The waning firelight illuminated Gilmour's silent profile in a warm yellow glow. What would come of killing this man? Poverty? Civil unrest? The collapse of the Resistance movement in Rona? Most likely.

But Jacrys would escape, he would find a niche somewhere. Glancing at Brynne's form, shapely, even beneath her blanket, he imagined he might even find happiness. He was resourceful, enormously so, and he would make his way as far from the coming conflict as possible.

As long as he did his duty, and emerged unscathed, he would survive. He wiped his forehead with his tunic sleeve, then raised his dagger to strike.

Jacrys slammed his arm down with all the force he could summon. The blade's tip caught for the briefest moment in the thick cartilage over the breastbone, then plunged hilt-deep into the old man's chest. There was a thin snap; it sounded like a pine knot exploding in the dying embers of the fire. The old man's eyes flew open, a look of absolute terror. He drew breath to scream, but all he could manage was a gurgled, shuddering groan.

Jacrys felt his hand slide down the knife's grip and come to rest on Gilmour's chest. He was suddenly overcome by surprise. A look of genuine perplexity passed over his face: Gilmour, the legendary leader of the Larion Senate in the Twinmoon of its collapse, the most powerful man in Rona, was nothing stronger than flesh and bone. He was human. There was no great release of deadly magical force, no explosion of mystical ancient power. No brilliant burst of colourful flame radiated from the site of the old man's now-mortal wound.

Rather, Jacrys's knife slid smoothly into the old man's heart and stopped it a breath or two later. Gilmour Stow was dead.

Lucid again after his unexpected moment of empathy, Jacrys did not pause to enjoy the fruits of his labour but turned and lashed out with the second blade towards Garec. The groggy bowman woke with a start, but he was too slow. Reflexively he tried to use the tree trunk to deflect the knife. Its edge reflected firelight and glinted in the air as it whistled past Garec's throat and up over his shoulder.

But Jacrys was not intent on killing Garec; as his blade found its target the Ronan's bowstring gave a sharp, punctuated cry and Jacrys quickly sprinted into the woods, disappearing before anyone could gain their feet.

Garec began running almost immediately, but the attacker was too far ahead to track down in the dark. Surprise had served the man well. Garec cursed loudly into the night as he gave up the chase and turned back towards camp.

As he approached through the trees, he saw a shapeless lump, rimmed by firelight, rocking slightly back and forth on the ground. Finally he recognised Brynne, and ran the last few paces into camp to join her. She was cradling Gilmour's head in her lap, sobbing in anguish against his chest, her thin body wracked periodically as she drew short, raspy breaths. Sallax, his lips pressed flatly together, stood nearby, staring at his sister. He showed no emotion. Garec dropped to his knees, but he did not need to find Jacrys's knife protruding from Gilmour's breastbone to know the old man was dead.

*

'Good night, Hannah – and please don't worry. I know we'll find him tomorrow.' Hoyt waited for the door to close before he turned to Churn. 'I saw him. I saw the mule-rutter there at the tavern.'

Churn gestured, 'Why did we leave?'

'He was flat-nosed, ass-over-hill dog-pissed.'

Churn waved one hand irritably in front of the smaller man's face.

'Yes, I know I can sign those things, but sometimes, Churn, we need to express ourselves a bit more eloquently.' Hoyt's fingers moved in a rhythm that somehow matched the timbre of his voice. 'He was drunk ... crushed ... ruined as a whore at Twinmoon Festival.'

'So? I'm sure she's seen drunks before.'

'Not drunk, Churn, absolutely demonpissing comatose. I should have checked him for a pulse.' They made their way down a flight of stairs into the great room of the more reputable inn they had found.

'I'm still not entirely convinced he's alive down there.'

'Are we going back?'

'Yes. I didn't want Hannah to see him. It's better if she sleeps now, anyway. She's been so nervous. I think she would faint if she saw him in this condition.' Hoyt paused a moment, trying to remember something the pox-scarred bartender had said. 'I think Alen's been at this for a long time.'

'Why?'

'I don't know—' Hoyt broke off and announced, 'Let's go find him. We'll bring him back to our room, let him sober up and make introductions in the morning.'

The Middle Fork Tavern was three muddy streets away. It wasn't long before the Pragans were back in the dark room with the exposed beams and fiery maw blazing at the base of the far wall. They found Alen exactly where Hoyt had left him two avens earlier. The healer politely asked the men sitting around him to clear an area so he could extricate the drunk.

'Shove off,' a gruff, elderly man barked at Hoyt. 'These seats are taken.'

'Oh, no, sir, you misunderstand: I don't want your seat, I just want to dislodge my friend—'

'Do you have a hearing problem, son?' The grizzled patron

turned round with some difficulty. Hoyt's charm obviously wasn't working too well.

He tried a different tack. 'Ah, no,' he said, gesturing with an outstretched thumb towards Churn, 'but he does.'

Churn stepped forward, gripped the bench with both hands and lifted. The heavy wooden seat, along with the four drinkers astride it, began to rise, slowly, from the floor. The old man's quickness belied his age: in a heartbeat he was brandishing a thin dirk and lurching towards Churn's exposed ribs. Hoyt was faster. Without a flourish he drew a small steel blade, honed to a surgeon's edge. Two quick slashes, one to the old man's wrist, just behind the thumb, and another across the fleshy part of the forearm: the dirk fell to the floor.

The old man, his hand now useless and hanging limp, slid off the bench to his knees. 'You bleeding horsecock!' he screamed, more in fury than pain. 'You crippled me, you bastard.' He started to choke back embarrassing sobs. 'How am I going to work now?' He looked around the room, hoping for sympathy, but everyone looked away, gazing thoughtfully into goblets and tankards.

'Any local healer can stitch that,' Hoyt told him calmly. 'Go soon, and for the forest gods' sake, keep it immobile until you get there. If you don't, you'll rip those tendons – and then you really *won't* be happy. Go on, be quick about it. Get moving.'

Hoyt didn't wait to see if the old man did as he was told but turned his attention to the filthy plank floor. There was Alen, still in a crumpled heap, sleeping – or perhaps even dead. He didn't appear to have moved since Hoyt had nudged his feet out of the way earlier that day. Churn bent down to peer under the table himself. He raised an eyebrow at Hoyt and when the healer nodded, hauled the stinking figure out as if he weighed less than the sack of dirty laundry he so resembled.

Back at their own far more salubrious lodgings, they discussed what to do. Hoyt was nervous that Hannah might have been looking for them; perhaps, unable to sleep, she'd come downstairs to sit near the fire and sip tecan or try a goblet of the local wine.

'We have to be quick and silent,' he gestured in twists and flicks of his hands. 'Up to our room. We'll decide what to do with—' he cast a sidelong glance at Alen's cadaverous face, '—with *him* once we get there.' He peered through a crack in the front door: they were safe, the room was empty. Throwing the door open, he and Churn carried their foetid bundle across the great room and up the stairs along the back wall. Hoyt could feel his heart rate slowing once they'd tiptoed past Hannah's door. They were going to make it. Only a few steps further along the hall, then they would have all night to clean him up.

Creak!

Churn stepped heavily on a loose floorboard and Hoyt froze, holding his breath. He waited for what felt like a Twinmoon, then moved to their own door. He grasped the leather thong that threaded through a small hole to the latch inside the door and pulled.

Creak!

The ancient wood groaned as the door swung open slowly. Again Hoyt waited, motionless, his gaze fixed on Hannah's door across the hall. The planks were pretty warped, he noticed. Nothing moved.

Shaking his head, he relaxed and indicated that Churn should go ahead into the narrow chamber. He closed the door as quietly as the moan of leather against wood and protesting hinges would allow and was several steps into the room before he noticed the candle.

'Did we leave that—?'

'No. I lit it.' Hannah smiled enigmatically. 'Hello boys,' she said.

Hoyt was rooted to the floor as she stood up and stretched, then moved closer to get a better look at the grim carcase Churn had slung over one shoulder like the evening's kill. 'And who is this? A friend you met at a bar, or another body we need to dispose of before morning?' Hannah was enjoying herself. 'Oh, relax, you two! I don't care if you went out for a drink. I just couldn't get to sleep. So I started thinking about ways to find Alen and—' She paused. They still hadn't moved.

'Are you all right?' Hannah took a step towards them. 'And who *is* this? Oh God, is he dead? Not another one. I was *joking*! What happened? Please tell me; don't just stand there like frightened children. Who is he? Did he try to kill you? Is he a spy?'

Something broke and finally Hoyt was able to move. 'Hannah,'

435

he began tentatively, 'this is my dear friend, Alen Jasper of Middle Fork.'

Steven woke in the night; though it was cold, he could feel the warmth of a fire somewhere nearby. Struggling to lift his arms, he realised he was tied down, lashed to pine boughs and covered with thin wool blankets. He swallowed; his parched throat felt like sandpaper. Above him he could see an interlocking mass of branches, a near-impenetrable canopy.

He abandoned the struggle to loosen the straps when the tangle of irregular green branches started spinning before his eyes and he nearly lost consciousness. Slowly he realised he was not alone.

'Who's there?' he croaked, shocked at how weak his voice sounded.

No one answered. He tried to lift his head far enough to see across the campsite, but this time pain shot from his ribcage across his back. He remembered the grettan attack and his breath quickened as he recalled the image of his leg disappearing into the beast's canine-studded jaws. Wincing, he hesitantly tried to move his feet. His left leg, although tied firmly, moved with little pain, but his right did not respond at all. Steven remembered the sickening snap of his calf bones as the grettan slammed its jaws closed above his boot. Now he could feel nothing from the knee down. Despite the cold, he started to perspire as he imagined the mutilated stump the animal might have left him. Sharp, jagged canines. Those pierce and tear flesh. It must be gone.

His ribs were broken, his shoulder was dislocated, his leg was ripped off below the knee: Steven was surprised he was not more terrified. He must be in shock. He was aware of himself and his surroundings, but his mind was protecting him from the thought that he was gravely, perhaps mortally injured. Except for the searing pain in his ribs and the dull throb in his leg, he felt little pain. His shoulder ached with every motion, but since he could still move his fingers, his arm was clearly intact.

'How am I supposed to treat a shock victim?' he wondered aloud, but nothing came to mind. He couldn't remember how he'd done with first-aid training, but he was pretty sure he had not excelled. Mark would have scolded him and accused him of not paying attention. For a moment Steven stopped thinking about his own condition.

'Mark, Garec?' he called out over the campfire, 'Gilmour?' Nothing. Panic began to set in: had they been attacked as well? Were they all dead? If that were the case, how had he escaped – and more to the point, *who* had tied him up like this – was it for his safety, or to confine him?

All of a sudden Steven's mind was beset with questions: where was he? With whom? Why? Using his good arm he examined the bonds that held him: several wool blankets were wrapped around him, thick leather straps and coarse hemp kept his legs, hips and torso straight. His head was held in place by a padded leather thong tied between the two pine branches that made up the skeletal frame of what he thought might be a makeshift stretcher. He couldn't have been left to die because his – captor? saviour? – had left a fire burning.

'Why won't you answer me?' he called in as calm a voice as he could muster. 'I know you're there; I can feel you.'

Straining to bend his neck, Steven watched smoke from the fire leaving a ghostly white trail. The ethereal tendrils danced slowly in the soft evening breeze. Steven watched, transfixed, as several pieces of lighter-than-air ash drifted upwards from the crackling fire. Then the smoke trail began to take on a more definite shape.

'Gabriel O'Reilly,' Steven said softly when he realised what was happening, 'Gabriel, please come down here.'

The dead bank teller floated slowly down from the treetops to join Steven near the fire. He thought he could see genuine concern and compassion in the spirit's features as he gazed on his broken form.

'Is it that bad?' he asked.

The spirit shook his head, as if to say, 'I have seen much worse.'

'Are both my legs intact?'

Again the wraith paused a few seconds, but this time he nodded.

'Thank Christ,' Steven sighed. His lower leg must be broken and numb, perhaps from the cold, or maybe because of a more serious infection.

'Did you rescue me from the grettan?'

The spirit shook his head.

'Who did?' Steven felt anxiety begin to well up in him once again. This method of communication was so *slow*.

The wraith pointed towards the forest. Maybe he – or they – were off gathering food, water or firewood.

'Are my friends nearby? Can you bring them to me? Can you find them?'

Gabriel O'Reilly's spirit shook his head again, then extended a translucent finger into the air.

'One of them is searching for me? Who?'

The wraith rubbed the back of one smoky white hand across his cheek.

'The one with the dark skin, Mark? Yes! Will you guide him, Gabriel? I know you don't owe me anything, but please, will you bring Mark here?'

The spirit stared down at Steven for several seconds before nodding slightly.

Then, hesitantly, as if his abandonment of his friends and his failure to defeat the grettan somehow made him unworthy to wield it, Steven asked, 'Is my wooden staff here?'

Gabriel nodded again.

Steven asked, 'Do you know from where it gets its power?' When the wraith shrugged, he went on, 'But Malagon fears it?'

The spirit shrugged again and Steven said quickly, 'Right. How would you know? Sorry.' He felt out of sorts, awkward and vulnerable without the staff. Now that he was alone and incapacitated here in the forest, he was deeply embarrassed at his behaviour. He hoped his friends would forgive his impulsive – *stupid* – decision to rush off in search of Hannah. As if one man, even with a magic stick, could face down Nerak . . . Steven's face flushed as he imagined himself admitting that he had been attacked and nearly killed by a grettan less than a day later.

Steven turned his attention back to the wraith: he needed more information. 'There is a woman; she is special to me . . . Lessek sent a dream, a vision, to me – at least, I think he did. Anyway, I think the dream may be his way of telling me she is here.' Steven was waffling; he started again, 'I need to know if she is really here, in Eldarn.'

Again, Gabriel O'Reilly shrugged.

'That's all right. I had to try. I am just so – so *stuck* here, so

438

lost.' Exhausted now, his voice trailed off. His head began to swim and he felt his vision fading. He tried to steel himself for more questions, but he lacked the strength. He made a final effort, croaking, 'Please, Gabriel, bring Mark Jenkins here.'

This time the wraith nodded emphatically. He brought his facial features into focus, as he had on previous visits, and Steven realised O'Reilly was trying again to tell him something important.

'There is one—' He mouthed the words, but Steven did not understand.

'What?' Steven was drifting in and out of consciousness. 'Say it again.'

'There is one—' O'Reilly tried a second time, but Steven's eyes glazed over as his breathing steadied. Gabriel O'Reilly extended a nebulous hand, rested it on Steven's forehead for a moment, then slid through the trees towards the mountain pass behind them.

Garec stood up and backed slowly away from the body. 'He's dead,' he murmured to Brynne. 'I can't believe he's dead.' He filled his hands with snow and tried to wash off Gilmour's blood.

'He's not dead,' Brynne sobbed, 'he's going to be fine. He just needs some time.' Supporting Gilmour's head in her lap, Brynne looked as though she had been dipped in blood. Her face was streaked with tears and she coughed violently as she tried to regain her breath. She rolled up her sleeves and bared her forearms, then awkwardly pushed Gilmour's flesh around the knife, hoping to stem the flow of blood from the wound. Though her arms were stained red to the elbows, it appeared her efforts had been successful, because no additional blood was seeping out.

But Garec knew otherwise.

'He's dead, Brynne,' he said, reaching for her. 'That's why the bleeding has stopped. His heart isn't beating.'

Brynne's gaze dropped and she looked at the old man's drawn, grey visage. In a sudden burst of revulsion, she pushed the Larion Senator's body away and scrambled a backwards retreat across their camp to where her brother was still standing his silent vigil. Gilmour's ancient body looked smaller, thinner than it had earlier that day. Garec reached down to close an errant flap of tunic that had torn away to reveal ashen skin.

Now sobbing uncontrollably, Brynne collapsed at Sallax's feet.

He reached down and placed one hand gently on his sister's shoulder, the first show of emotion since his encounter with Gabriel O'Reilly's spirit.

Garec looked around at the stoic lodge pines, tall and stately, ignoring the pitiful human drama being played out at their feet. This clearing, here in the Blackstone Mountains, was as close to a Larion Senate sanctuary as they would ever find outside Sandcliff Palace.

'We have to give him his rites,' he said softly. 'We have to burn his body.'

Dawn was breaking when Garec finished amassing enough tinder for Gilmour's pyre. Brynne had insisted on an enormous pile of prickly, dry tinder, to be certain their friend's body would burn entirely away, even in that cold, snowy wilderness. Sallax helped, and despite his sadness, Garec was heartened at his improvement.

Garec hacked away at the exposed limbs of several fallen trees, then trimmed off the lowest hanging branches from a circle of lodge pines ringing the clearing. He felt a wave of fear and loneliness pass over him, turning his stomach and causing a moment of dizziness. The clearing seemed to brighten as his pupils dilated and his head swam. Angrily, he fought off the urge to cry. They were too far from home, in too much danger from freezing to death, being killed by grettans, Seron, an almor, let alone whatever other monstrosities Malagon was saving up for them. He had to keep himself under control.

Sallax methodically gathered branches; save for the gentle touch he offered his sister, he showed no other emotion, and said nothing. Brynne knelt near Gilmour, her bloodstained hands wrapping the body tightly into his cloak and brushing hair away from his cold forehead. Garec knew he would have to keep them moving, to keep them busy, or they would lose hope. Perhaps even he would lose hope.

A thick branch, still green, snapped back and struck Garec in the face. The stinging sensation across his already cold cheek was painful and he felt tears welling up behind his eyes. He choked back an almost inaudible, 'No,' and began chopping furiously. His vision blurred, but he continued hacking with all his might, cutting and chipping away at the majestic pine as if it had murdered Gilmour. The branch fell away, but Garec continued to chop at the tree trunk. *He* was guilty. *He* had fallen asleep, drifting off while standing watch. He had been awake a moment later, but it was a moment too late. Visions of the killer's knife sticking out of Gilmour's chest flashed through Garec's mind and his rage grew.

Brynne and Sallax turned when they heard his scream, but neither made a move to comfort him. They watched, nearly motionless, as the young man's anger played itself out. Then his arms, weak from effort, slowed, and his determination to bring down the entire Blackstone forest was thwarted before even one of the proud, disinterested trees fell.

Despite the thick wool cloak, Gilmour's body looked tiny on the pyre of freshly cut branches. Brynne thought perhaps the magic of the Larion Senate had kept him robust despite his age. Now, with his magic gone, only a hollow shell of the great leader remained, like Riverend Palace: a broken monument to a fallen era of strength and prosperity.

Brynne watched as Garec drew a burning branch from the fire. She felt the urge to say something. There they were, the three of them, responsible for the funeral rites of one of the most powerful, the most influential heroes in Eldarn. It would be wrong just to set fire to his body without offering a eulogy or prayer of some sort.

'We ought to say a few words.'

Garec hesitated, then returned the branch to the fire, kneeled in the snow and told her, 'Absolutely. You're right. Say what you think . . .' Behind him the sun crested above the distant peaks; to the north a storm was brewing.

Brynne looked at the billowy, slate-grey clouds, searching for the words, but nothing came. A feeling of abject despair crept up on her once again, and she muttered, 'Someone else should be doing this. Someone eloquent. Someone powerful. We were just his friends. For most of our lives we never even knew who he really was.'

'Maybe that's enough.' Sallax spoke for the first time in days. Garec looked up in surprise.

Seemingly unaware of her brother's comment, Brynne steeled herself and went on, 'His goal was to save Eldarn, to bring peace and hope back to the people of the world.' She paused, thinking of the hopelessness of their situation. They probably wouldn't make it to Orindale alive, never mind find a way to retrieve Lessek's Key and return Steven and Mark to Colorado.

'What can we do now, Gilmour?' she asked rhetorically, her voice dropping to a whisper as she turned and nodded at Garec.

The flames began as a flicker at the base of the entangled branches and Garec thought he would have to ignite the tinder a second time to make sure it took. Just as he was reaching to light another branch from their little fire, a great cloud of smoke blew through the camp and the pyre burst into flame with an audible roar. Thousands of pine needles crackled and caught and fire danced around Gilmour, an ancient *volta* of spiralling scarlet and orange and vermilion and yellow . . .

Garec's secret hope, that the old man might wake suddenly and spring to safety before his flesh burned away, disappeared with the pine boughs. The Larion Senator lay impossibly still as his cloak and then his hair caught fire. Garec turned towards the trees, unable to watch any longer.

'Come on,' he said as he hefted his and then Gilmour's pack. 'We have a long way to go today if we're going to catch up with Mark and Steven.'

Brynne was clinging to Sallax's arm, looking as if she might collapse if she let go, but she wiped a sleeve across her eyes and bent to retrieve her own pack. Sallax watched the flames a moment longer, then turned to join his sister.

They left the clearing and started moving north. The storm they had seen on the horizon was much closer now and Garec knew it would be upon them long before they reached whatever meagre shelter they could find inside the far tree line.

They were several hundred paces out in an exposed snowfield before any of them realised the fire had spread to the surrounding forest. Branches that had been difficult to ignite now burned readily in the chilly dawn breeze. Garec smelled the aroma of wood smoke and spun round to view his handiwork. Several towering lodge pines were burning brightly in the morning sun and he watched impassively as the fire spread like spilled quicksilver along the hillside. Somehow it seemed fitting that Gilmour's funeral would be more than just another pyre of sweet-smelling pine and burning flesh. It was appropriate that the forest would burn with the Larion Senator's body, the sanctuary itself collapsing onto its once-powerful leader.

442

Brynne had struggled to find something to say as they stood over the old man's broken form. This was better. Garec wiped tears from his cheek and gripped his longbow as he watched the flames reach into the sky like prayers falling on a god's deaf ear.

The Bringer of Death had destroyed the sanctuary. He had burned down the walls of the very place he had hoped Gilmour's spirit would call home for all time. He pulled his cloak close and silently hoped he would be strong when the day came to reckon for his transgressions.

Huge clouds of black and grey smoke climbed above them and they could feel the heat of the flames as they tore through the forest like the last act of a rogue demon.

'Actually,' Brynne said, 'it is quite beautiful.'

'Yes,' Garec agreed, 'and it may serve to let Mark – and Steven – know where we are.' He adjusted the hunting knife at his belt, shifted the crisscrossed straps of his dual quivers, turned back north and led the others through the snow.

'It does end an era,' Sallax said, but neither Brynne nor Garec heard him over the roaring flames and northerly winds. 'Or maybe it begins an era.' He cleared his throat, spat back towards the blaze and turned to follow Brynne over the pass.

THE STORM

Private Kaylo Partifan, a soldier in Prince Malagon's Home Guard, tried unobtrusively to scratch at an irritating itch beneath his tunic. He stood at sentry outside the prince's royal apartments; his watch was nearly over. His chainmail vest was weighing heavily on his shoulders and the wool tunic beneath was nearly driving him mad. He was not permitted to move whilst on sentry duty, so he bit down hard on his tongue to distract himself from the agony. It didn't work.

Quickly peering up and down the darkened corridor, he brought one arm up, worked two fingers beneath the chainmail and began scratching furiously at his shoulder.

Across from him, Lieutenant Devar Wentra, his platoon leader and friend, smiled knowingly at the younger man. Kaylo himself would never dare speak while on duty, but Devar whispered softly, 'You had better hope the prince doesn't see you doing that.'

Kaylo smiled back and considered chancing a brief response when an ear-splitting roar exploded from Prince Malagon's chambers.

Visibly shaken, Devar said out loud, 'Lords, now you've done it, Kaylo.'

The private snapped to attention, his itch forgotten as he felt the prince's approach through the wall.

The door to the royal apartments was nearly torn from its hinges as Prince Malagon burst into the hallway. Kaylo felt his heart pound. He was sure the prince could see it.

Malagon's voice reverberated in the sentries' heads, nearly knocking them senseless. 'Lieutenant Wentra! Do you smell that?'

Devar could not remember the dark prince ever looking at one

444

of his Home Guard, never mind addressing any of them face-to-face. Terrified, he fell to one knee and asked meekly, 'Smell what, sire?'

Malagon's shriek was a mixture of ecstasy and frustration. The lieutenant slumped face-first to the floor. Private Partifan stared straight ahead, his eyes fixed on a crooked seam between two stones. He was quite certain he could stare at that small patch of grey mortar for the rest of his life if necessary.

'Kaylo Partifan,' Prince Malagon called, gesturing towards him with a robed arm from which protruded a cadaverous white hand.

Kaylo dropped to his knees as if he had been struck in the back of the legs with a broadsword. 'Yes, sire.'

'Do you smell that?'

'I am sorry, sire. I do not, sire.' He hoped that was the right answer.

'It is woodsmoke,' Malagon roared, making Kaylo jump. 'Woodsmoke, a Twinmoon's journey away. Woodsmoke, Private Partifan.'

'Yes, sire.'

'They're burning his body, his dead, broken, frail, *dead* little body.'

'Yes, sire,' Kaylo said. That response seemed to be keeping him alive.

'Fantus, you old, *dead*, peace-loving milksop,' Malagon chuckled. It was the sound of an insane executioner after a lifetime at the block.

'Yes, sire.'

'Now, my soulless hunters, bring me the key,' the dark prince cried towards the ceiling, and coupled his order with a little jump of excitement. It was so inappropriate and unusual that Kaylo shuddered.

'And while you're at it, feel free to finish off the rest of his little band of patriots,' Malagon continued. 'Do you not agree, Private Partifan?'

'I do, sire.' He had no idea what the prince was talking about, but he certainly wasn't going to disagree with anything his master said.

Suddenly reserved once again, Malagon turned and made his way, almost floating, back to his chambers.

'Private Partifan,' he turned back, almost as an afterthought.

445

'Sire?'

'Order the *Prince Marek* readied. We leave on the dawn tide two days hence.'

Kaylo was terrified. If he asked where the prince planned to travel, he would be struck dead there in the corridor, his body sprawled alongside Devar's. But the prince's advisors and generals would surely hang him themselves if he arrived at the docks with an order and no destination.

Malagon was feeling generous. 'Orindale, Private Partifan. Tell them we sail for Orindale.'

'Yes, sire.' The soldier did not wait for Prince Malagon's chamber door to slam closed once again before he was up and hurrying along the corridor.

Mark Jenkins was freezing to death. The pace he had maintained had taken its toll. As his vision tunnelled and bright pinpricks of yellow light danced before his eyes, he knew he was about to fail. He had eaten a great quantity of snow trying to stay hydrated and his body temperature was falling. He had finished the last of his rations the previous day and hunger pangs were roiling through his stomach. Dehydration made his joints ache and he began falling to his knees more frequently. The first few tumbles he had rationalised by telling himself he was weary from running through deep snow, but he knew his legs were failing beneath him. If he did not get warm and dry he would most likely pass out . . . and if that happened, he would never wake again.

How had he managed to get himself into this state? He was alone, and lost in a foreign mountain range, in a foreign world – not just a foreign world, but an impossible world, a fantasy world: a land that by rights shouldn't even exist. And who was this person who was dragging Steven so effortlessly over such massive mountain passes?

Mark struggled to lift one leg, and then repeated the motion with the other. Again and again. *Lift and step*; *lift and step*. Completely exhausted, his thoughts came in short bursts, brief snapshots like old black and white photographs, followed by long, silent periods of nothing: no images, no ideas, or no reflections. Those were the better times. Those were times when he covered a great deal of ground, when all he could think was *lift and step* and all he could see was white and green. He continued his battle not because he believed he could summon the strength to defeat Steven's captors or even because he believed he could carry his friend off through the forest. He resigned himself to the fact that neither of those outcomes was realistic. Rather, he continued trudging across the Blackstone Mountain range, because he could generate no other options, no creative ways to save his own life. Keep moving or die. It was a simple but motivating mantra and Mark mumbled it to himself during times when his thoughts came too rapidly to sort. Keep moving or die.

So he kept moving.

Mark spent the night dug into a snowdrift with his back pressed against a fallen pine tree, but the night was long. Some time before dawn the torch burned out, snuffed suddenly, as if the force keeping it lit had somehow lost track of Mark's position. He was so thirsty he had eaten nearly twenty handfuls of snow, even though he knew his body would cool quickly and expend much-needed energy. But he was *so* thirsty. He decided he would risk death to begin the next day well hydrated.

Mark lay there beneath the unfamiliar constellations he had mapped so carefully one warm night back in Rona. He and Brynne had named them as they huddled together under the blankets. There was the one Brynne called *the fisherman*, because it resembled a man casting a net across half the galaxy. Another lit up the sky to the north; Mark had affectionately dubbed it *Tarzan*, because it looked like a man swinging towards heaven on a celestial vine. As he looked at the stars, he thought of Brynne, the feeling of her body pressed tightly against his, the smell of her hair, the touch of her lips, her gentle, clever fingers . . . lost in the sweet memories, for a moment the omnipresent cold and fear faded.

Mark's half-dream was rudely interrupted as, from the north, a squall-line of grim-looking storms approached fast. An alarm rang in the back of his mind, but he could do nothing about it. He did not have the strength to build a fire, nor dry the wood even if he could summon the energy. He would be buried alive if he tunnelled beneath the snow for shelter. The coming storm would cover the trail he had been following; if they deviated from their northward course, Mark would never find Steven in the Blackstone wilderness.

He looked at the hillside below, then at his boots, buried beneath him in the snow. How many miles had he travelled? How many places had he seen? It would end here. The whole of the world, *his* world – Eldarn – it didn't matter, because the whole of the world ended here, with his feet buried in the snow, here in this place.

'That's it, then,' Mark murmured and began searching around for a suitable place to await the end. He was alone. *That* thought was stronger than the fear, or the cold, or the worry about Steven and Brynne. Mark recalled a preacher at his mother's church, who regularly entreated congregation members to foster healthy relationships in the Lord's name, so when death came, no one would feel alone. Now, dragging himself through knee-deep snow, Mark wondered whether, if he had been better about going to church, he would still feel so alone at this moment.

He feared it was true, but it was too late. He was about to die by himself on the side of an Eldarni mountain.

Finding something that looked like a stalwart old ponderosa growing near a rock outcropping, Mark removed his pack, sat heavily on the cold stone and leaned against the tree to watch as the storm blew in overhead. It was then he smelled woodsmoke, faint at first, then growing stronger. Mark craned his neck to look back towards the mountain pass, now a long way behind him. A curious cloud of dark smoke blew across the peak where a downdraught captured it and brought it racing to where he sat awaiting the coming blizzard. 'Sonofabitch! Garec? Brynne,' he mumbled with the last of his strength, 'did you set the whole goddamn mountain on fire?' Clenching his frozen fingers into stiff, painful fists, he added in a barely audible whisper, 'You're going to have to find Steven, guys. I'm done here.'

The view from his perch was beautiful. There was not a peak, a tree or boulder out of place, and Mark wished he could stay awake longer to appreciate the natural perfection of the valley they had fought so hard to reach. He tried to focus his thoughts on Brynne, but it wasn't long before his eyes closed of their own accord and he drifted away.

'Jacrys.'

The Malakasian spy woke with a start. Rolling over quickly, he reached out to brace himself and realised he had planted his hand firmly in the burned-down coals of his campfire. 'Blast and rutting dogs!' he cried, driving his scorched palm into the snow beside his bedroll.

'Who's there?' He reached stealthily for the knife he kept tucked inside his blankets.

'Jacrys,' the voice repeated, and the spy watched carefully as a small deer emerged slowly from a nearby thicket. Its eyes burned amber: Prince Malagon was in residence.

Moving quickly to one knee, he replied, 'My lord.'

'You have done well, Jacrys.' The deer's mouth did not move; Jacrys was hearing the dark prince in his mind. 'You took your time, but in the end, I am pleased with your efforts.'

'Thank you, sire. Gilmour was a powerful man, difficult to trap.'

'I would expect nothing less of him.' The deer shot him a disinterested look. 'Meet me in Orindale.'

Jacrys's mind raced. Orindale. Why? What would Malagon be doing in Falkan? And why would he want to see his most effective field agent outside the confines of his palace? If anyone saw them together, Jacrys's cover would be jeopardised for ever. He stopped. That was it then; Malagon was calling him in.

He tried to calm his racing thoughts; who knew how much Malagon could read at this distance? 'Yes, sire. Will you require me to bring the foreigner to you? I am certain now that he is the one who bears the stone.'

'I will take care of him. You get to Orindale.' Malagon's voice echoed in his head.

What did Malagon mean, *he* would take care of Steven Taylor? And retrieving Lessek's Key had been *his* charge. How exactly did Malagon plan to see this through from so far away? Even from Orindale, Steven Taylor was too well protected to be an easy target for one of the prince's black spells. Was he sending another almor? More Seron warriors? Too many unanswered questions, and Malagon brooked neither curiosity nor delay, so Jacrys replied only, 'Yes, my lord.'

'For your own safety, move west for three days. Then turn north to the valley and follow the river into Orindale.' The deer paused for a moment, as if ruminating, then added, 'I will meet you there.'

So Malagon was sending more of his pets. Grand. More

bloodthirsty demons wandering about Eldarn killing without warning, hesitation or remorse. Now, more than ever, Jacrys knew he had to find a way to escape to some place where he could live out his days free from the threat of the dark prince's minions. And why was Malagon bothering with the Ronan partisans now? Gilmour was dead; the rest were scattered throughout the mountain range with virtually no chance of survival. What did they have that Malagon feared enough to dispatch another killer . . . and, more importantly, why not him? He was right there on the scene already – surely he could find the young man, retrieve whatever it was the prince desired so ardently and be on his way to Orindale without losing more than a day or two.

Jacrys grimaced. It was obvious: Malagon was using his pets for this task because he no longer trusted his field agent. Jacrys was being summoned back to his execution.

He started suddenly: while he had been kneeling here trying to understand the inner workings of his prince's decidedly unusual mind, Malagon himself, in the person of the deer, was standing there watching him. He hurriedly looked up. Was it too late?

'Yes, sire,' he said. 'Your word is my command.'

'Of course.'

Jacrys didn't think a deer could look sardonic, but this one made a good try.

'Here is sustenance enough to reach Orindale.'

The deer collapsed dead at his feet.

Jacrys tried not to flinch as the voice in his mind continued a moment longer, 'Remember, Jacrys, three days west before turning north into the valley.'

Whatever Malagon was using to dispatch the remaining Ronan travellers, he was sending it soon. And unlike the Seron, or even the grettan packs, this threat was dangerous enough for Jacrys to be removed from the area. Now he was scared.

Not wanting to waste another moment, Jacrys rubbed another handful of snow across his blistered palm and began gutting the deer.

By sunrise, he knew he needed more time. He needed to work out why the foreigners and the stone talisman so threatened Prince Malagon, and the only way to do that was to mask his arrival in Orindale. At least he was just the man for the job. He would wait, observe, and then do whatever was necessary to retrieve that stone, even if it meant killing Steven and rifling through his clothing on a busy Falkan thoroughfare.

Steven was cold. He had fallen into a deep sleep after his encounter with the spirit Gabriel and had been awakened by the periodic jolts as his pine-bough gurney bumped its way over fallen trees and rocks only half-submerged by the snow. The sharp pain that burned across his shoulder and ribcage had subsided; Steven wondered how long he had been drifting in and out of consciousness. The piercing agony in his lower leg had eased too. It had been replaced by a rhythmic throb, and for a moment Steven thought he might be able to escape under his own power if he could get free.

He tested his theory by wiggling his toes, but in the end he couldn't be sure he felt them rubbing back and forth inside Garec's boots, or if he was imagining their movement because he so desperately wanted them to be all right. He was still at the mercy of whomever was dragging him backwards through the forest.

There was no sign of Mark. Steven wondered whether the mysterious wraith had failed to locate him, or if they had fallen upon some misfortune of their own. It was a bit dumb of him to assume his friends were following along behind, warm and dry and happily chatting back and forth about Falkan cuisine. They'd be facing their own share of hardship and delays as well.

The warmth of last night's roaring fire was a dim memory now as Steven, unable to move his limbs and increase blood flow to his extremities, was struggling to stay warm. He was beginning to wonder if he were freezing to death; was this how it felt?

Their path had levelled out sometime earlier in the day, and Steven could hear the sound of a river nearby: they had finally reached the valley floor. Although he still had no idea who held him captive, or how one person could drag him along so effortlessly, he was a little consoled by the thought that they were traversing the same route he and Mark had mapped out. Maybe their paths would cross and his companions would be able to spirit him away from his anonymous guard.

His heart sank when, between breaks in the trees, he caught sight of heavy clouds presaging more severe weather. He had to do *something*. As loud as his still-sore throat could manage, he shouted, 'Hey, you big bastard—' he wasn't sure if that was derogatory in Ronan, but what the hell, '—you bastard! Show yourself, you jackass!' That word definitely didn't have a Ronan translation so Steven used English and hoped his tone would make his point. He struggled to free his hands once again, and as before he felt pain blaze across his shoulder and ribcage. This time he ignored it and twisted violently, but found that not only were his arms and legs secured, but his head was lashed firmly in place as well. He had overlooked the thick leather strap across his forehead.

'Shit,' he cried in a frustrated rage. 'Shit, Mark, where *are* you? Goddamnit! How the hell can I have been so stupid? I've seen enough sodding movies—'

The gurney stopped.

Steven's heels rested quietly in the snow and he tried to anticipate what would happen next. Terrifying images flashed through his brain: he would be thrown, still lashed in place, into the freezing river, or run through with a sword, or ripped, limb from limb, and fed to a pack of ravening grettans . . .

The stretcher was lowered to the ground.

As he strained to see, Steven felt cramp building at the base of his neck and was forced to relax and try to will the pain away. In the seconds that followed he heard the sound of something being tossed to the ground nearby, then unhurried footsteps. He started shaking, cold and fear combining to rob his limbs of strength; if he were not so dehydrated, he knew he would have lost control of his bladder. He was helpless.

Steven gritted his teeth and awaited his captor, but at the sight of him, the shock was too much for Steven to bear. He burst into unexpected tears.

'Lahp.'

The Seron warrior grinned a crooked smile, gave a grunt of genuine concern and patted Steven gently on the chest.

'Lahp hep Sten.'

'Lahp, oh Lahp.' He was so overwhelmed he could scarcely speak. 'Oh yes, Lahp help Steven. You *have* helped me, you have saved my life.' Overcome with emotion, pain and fatigue, Steven laughed out loud, a disconcertingly maniacal chuckle.

'Thank you, Lahp. Thank you, thank you, thank you—'

'Lahp hep Sten.'

'Yes,' he said again, gaining a little control, suppressing his tears, 'yes, Lahp hep Sten.'

The Seron had been huddled in the underbrush when they had first met, and Steven had no idea how large and powerful his new friend really was until now. Looking up at him, Steven estimated that Lahp would stand a full head and shoulders taller than Mark: he was perhaps a shade over seven feet tall, barrel-chested, with enormously powerful arms and thighs. Steven suppressed a grin: next to Lahp, he was a puny dwarf. No wonder the Seron had been dragging him up and down the steepest slopes of the Blackstones so effortlessly, even with his injured leg.

Lahp drew a wineskin from a large leather pouch at his belt and offered Steven some water. For the first time since he had awakened, Steven realised how thirsty he was. He drank deeply as the Seron held the skin carefully for him.

'Thanks, Lahp,' Steven said, smiling, 'Lahp, can you untie me? I have to move. I'm too cold here.'

The giant considered Steven's request for a moment, peering into the distance as if the correct response would babble by in the river. He turned back and answered, 'Na, na, na,' shaking his head furiously to help make his point. 'Grekac ahat Sten.' He placed one hand gently on Steven's injured leg.

Steven felt nothing. 'Yes, Lahp. I understand; the grettan hurt my leg, but I must move about. I am cold here.' He pantomimed shivering, aware that it wouldn't be too long before his teeth would be chattering for real. 'It's too cold. I cannot feel my hands or my feet.'

'Na.'

'Lahp, I promise I will not run away. I will not move far. I just have to get some blood flowing through my feet.'

'Lahp a Sten Orindale,' the Seron countered, pointing northeast along the river.

Steven smiled again. Mark had been right. The river did flow through the mountains to Orindale.

Falling snow was collecting in his eyebrows and lashes and he blinked them away before trying again to convince the Seron to untie his bonds. 'Lahp, I know you are taking me to Orindale and I thank you for saving my life, but I will not make it to Orindale unless I get warm. So, please untie me. Let's make a fire and both

453

warm up, and we can continue later today or tomorrow morning.'
Using his eyes to gesture towards his leg, he added, 'And I must
have a look at my leg as well, Lahp. Please.'

Begrudgingly, the Seron drew a hunting knife, gave a long sigh
to show he was giving in against his better judgement, and sliced
through the leather thongs holding Steven's injured body in
place.

Steven slowly brought his hands to his face and felt his cheeks
and mouth. He ran his fingers through his hair: his beard was
thicker now, and his hair had grown quickly. He longed for a
steaming hot shower, and then a long, long soak in scalding-hot
bath ... shampoo, and soap, and bubbles, a razor ... and a
comfortable bed near a blazing fireplace.

His shoulder ached fiercely, but despite the pain, he planted
his palms on the ground beside the gurney and lifted himself to a
sitting position. Lahp, worried, tried to support Steven's lower
back with one of his enormous hands. Steven was absurdly
grateful for the help.

With Lahp's aid he levered himself so he was sitting upright
and took stock of his condition. His ribs hurt, but less than they
had. They were bound tightly with a length of cloth that looked
as if it had been torn from a blanket. His shoulder was stiff and
cramped, but when he raised his elbow he could feel the
dislocated joint had been expertly replaced.

Turning his attention to his legs, Steven flinched as he
brought his healthy foot up under his body. He made no effort to
stand but spent some time rubbing feeling back into his thigh and
calf. Wiggling his toes, he felt the familiar sting of wintry cold,
but he was heartened to see that the limb responded so well
despite having been immobilised for several days in the freezing
cold.

He blew several warm breaths into his hands, steeling himself,
then reached down to unwrap the blanket around his injured leg.
Methodically, like an archaeologist unravelling an Egyptian
mummy, he removed the blanket bandages that wrapped his leg
from ankle to thigh. He felt strangely detached, as if he were
viewing the scene from behind glass, but even so, he gasped as
the full damage was revealed. All of a sudden he was back in the
real world, swallowing hard to keep from throwing up. It was far,

far worse than he could have imagined, even in his worst nightmares.

His leg was a putrid mess of brown, rotting flesh, moist and dripping. In shock, he touched the horribly discoloured skin and nearly passed out when it stuck to his hand and a fistful of noisome tissue came away.

He fell backwards in the snow, screaming, and Lahp quickly pushed one hand down on Steven's chest and grabbed his left wrist with the other.

'Querlis, querlis,' the Seron warrior said, 'querlis! Lahp *hep* Sten.'

Fighting to regain his composure, Steven cried, 'What's happened to my leg?'

Releasing his grip, Lahp pulled several pieces of the rotting flesh from Steven's hand and repeated, 'Querlis.'

'Querlis?' Steven echoed, still shaking, 'what is— What are you talking about?' Now he examined the contents of his fist more closely, and found that instead of a handful of rotting flesh, he was actually holding dark-brown leaves.

'Leaves,' Steven said, nearly weeping with relief. He could have kissed the Seron. '*Leaves*. They're just leaves.'

'Querlis.'

'Querlis,' he agreed, then asked, 'So what is querlis? Why is it all over my leg?'

He painfully hauled himself up so he could see Lahp had entirely encased his lower leg in the damp brown leaves. As he peeled the layers away to examine the wound he asked, 'Is it some kind of medicine? Is it healing me?' Lahp nodded, but Steven didn't notice. His exposed injury had answered the question.

Though the leg was pale, and thinner than the other, that was the worst of it: the limb was intact. The bones that had been snapped like twigs by the angry beast appeared to be set. Where Steven had expected to find irreparably damaged, badly infected flesh, he saw only long thin scars running the length of his calf, as if the grettan had run its claws from knee to ankle. Each wound was meticulously sewn up with crisscrossing stitches. Steven ran his hands along the limb gently, as if to reassure himself that the relatively healthy-looking appendage really did belong to him.

'Lahp.' He looked up at the Seron warrior. 'Did you do this?'

'Lahp hep Sten,' he repeated like a mantra.

'You did, Lahp.' Steven shuddered as the full implication of his situation sank in. 'You saved my leg.'

The big man laid a huge hand on Steven's shoulder. 'Lahp hep Sten.' Then he pointed excitedly along the river and said, 'Lahp a Sten Orindale.'

'Right, Orindale – but first, we need a fire.'

Steven rested against a pine trunk while Lahp quickly built a gigantic campfire; the heat was intense, but Steven welcomed it. The Seron ran back and forth to the river to fetch several skins of water as Steven finally sated his thirst, then he wrapped the injured leg back up in a fresh layer of querlis leaves. This time Steven thought he could detect a slight tingling sensation as they began their work, a warmth that penetrated his skin and soothed his muscles.

Feeling drowsy, he wondered if the leaves contained a mild opiate; though he endeavoured to stay awake, to watch out for his friends and to learn more about his new companion, it wasn't long before he was fast asleep.

Lahp patted him on the shoulder and drew the cloak back over the sleeping man.

Steven awoke to the mouthwatering smell of roasting meat and the crackle of hot fat spitting in the flames. Lahp had positioned two thick steaks on a rock at the edge of the fire; all of a sudden Steven felt ravenously hungry. He couldn't remember when he had last eaten.

Lahp gave Steven a crooked grin. 'Grekac,' he said, pointing at the slabs of meat.

'Grettan?' Steven was taken aback. 'You eat grettan?'

'Sten a Lahp grekac,' he said, and made a show of gesturing at both of them as if proud of the fact they would finally share a meal: travellers and friends.

'I don't know if I can eat grettan, Lahp.' Steven felt his stomach tighten; he *was* starving, so maybe he could eat grettan. 'I guess the last one did make quite a production out of eating me!'

'Na grekac,' Lahp grinned again and tapped Steven's leg gently with the end of one stubby finger. 'Sten grekac.'

'This is *my* grettan? The grettan that attacked me?'

Lahp's smile grew even wider.

'How did you kill it?'

'Lahp na.' He shook his head emphatically before pointing at Steven. 'Sten.'

'Not me, Lahp. I didn't kill the grettan,' Steven said wryly, 'I passed out. It was still very much alive then.' The fire burned bright, crackling away comfortingly.

Lahp stood up and walked over to the stretcher and picked up Steven's hickory staff. 'Sten ahat grekac.'

Steven hadn't even thought about the staff; he found himself pleased to see it again. It looked like that length of wood really had saved his life.

They were still many days' travel from Orindale, but Lahp planned to build a raft to take them down the river once they had passed through the northwest end of the valley that Steven, in a moment of sentimentality, had dubbed Meyers' Vale. He was quite sure old Dietrich Meyers had hiked through many a similar valley in the Tyrol as a young man. The keys to the known world. Was that where all this had started? Ghosts of dead bank tellers, gigantic ravenous beasts, life-sucking demon creatures and the threat of evil's ascendancy in Eldarn . . .

And where was Hannah? Malagon had told him she was lost and alone in Praga. If that were true, was that what he was supposed to work out from Lessek's dream?

If Hannah was in Eldarn, he hoped she had discovered a way to blend in, to bide her time while searching for a way back to her own home. He was little good to her now; embarrassingly, he envisioned *her* waiting for *him* when he arrived in Orindale. She would have mastered the cultural differences, charmed a small army of Pragans into assisting her, chartered a ship and sailed the Ravenian Sea to Falkan to rescue him. Her arms folded across those exquisite breasts, she would shake her head at him as his raft floated aimlessly into the city. That would be a sight.

Steven smiled as he remembered the faint aroma of lilac that drifted about her, the delicate line of her neck that, already perfect when she looked directly at him, grew nearly impossible in its beauty when she turned away.

'Lahp.' He was afraid to ask the question. 'Lahp, do you know where my friends are?'

'Na.' He chewed a piece of grettan, then gestured up the

mountain behind them. 'Lahp fol Sten Blackstone. Sten hep Lahp. Lahp fol Sten.'

Steven had helped Lahp – probably saved his life – so the Seron had followed him through the Blackstones, shadowing him until the grettan attack. When Steven left his friends in the forest to search for Hannah, Lahp had moved ahead as well.

'I want to wait here,' Steven said, more a request than a command. 'I believe they are coming this way.' There was no response, so he tried again. 'Maybe just for a day or two.'

He expected Lahp to argue with him and was surprised when the Seron merely nodded in agreement.

Warm, well-fed – the grettan was surprisingly tasty once he'd overcome his initial reluctance – and comfortable, Steven let his head fall back against the tree trunk and closed his eyes. Slowly, he tried to bend his leg, to lift it from where Lahp had it wrapped so thickly in the coarse blankets. After a few moments, he felt it respond. It would not be long before he was walking again.

Always do a little less than you know you can and in the end you will go much further. Steven planned on sticking to the runner's rule; tomorrow he would bend the leg all the way, maybe even try to stand, but tonight, he would bundle up near the fire, tuck his embarrassed tail between his legs and hope for an opportunity to beg forgiveness from his friends.

He saw the hickory staff, leaning against a tree. He had no idea how he had managed to kill the grettan. 'Maybe I'll pick that up again tomorrow as well,' he said. 'Hold on, Hannah, we're coming.'

The patch of grey moved back and forth across the darkness, a thin film superimposed over an obsidian night. Curious: for no light existed here, only cold and darkness.

And then cold began to give way, little by little. His legs were empty vessels, his torso a shell, his arms hollow, and all cold, cold as ice, cold as the breath of the Fimbulwinter, cold as Death . . . but his arms were growing warm and his chest moved in a ragged breath. Still cold, though . . . he could not see, except for the grey patch that moved across his field of vision, but where there is no light, there is no sight.

No grey should exist here, but there it was again, and there should be no warmth in this bitter chill, but the impossible warmth intensified as the cold dissipated. He was growing warmer, from the inside out. His empty legs filled, flesh and bone encroaching on the empty space, stinging as the frigid cold was pushed out from bone and sinew and flesh.

His torso next, as air filled the shell, and arms close behind as his body took shape and substance.

He was warm, warmer than he could ever remember being, and still the grey patch floated just out of reach, out along the edge of his vision.

Mark Jenkins woke with a cry. Night had fallen. He closed his eyes again, expecting to open them to inky darkness, but there was the dim grey patch. Not hallucination, but real, almost tangible, a shade lighter than the night, it floated there. Mark felt around himself. He still wore his pack and was sitting against the pine tree he had chosen. This was supposed to have been the perfect place to die, but he appeared to be alive. He needed to take stock.

He was buried almost to the chest in freshly fallen snow. Wrapping an arm around the tree, he hefted himself to his feet and brushed snow from his clothes.

But there was something amiss.

'I should be dead,' he said, staring into the night. 'I might have *been* dead. Might still be dead. Oh God!' He thought he heard someone approaching and snapped to silent attention, but after several seconds he decided he was alone. All he could hear was the softly falling snow, the creak of weighted branches and his own frantic breathing.

'How did I get so warm?' he asked aloud, then added, 'This can't be right. It must be something—' He turned in a circle, his eyes straining to search the forest as he called, 'Gilmour, are you out there?' He brushed the snow from his pack and mused, 'It must be him. He must have found me and cast some kind of spell down here . . . unless—' He thought for a moment, then slowly, as if afraid of what he might see, Mark closed his eyes. There it was, a light grey patch of colour, brighter with his eyes closed than open. What was it? Should he keep his eyes closed – or open his mind? That was it!

'Open your mind, Mark,' he commanded. 'This will make sense if you open your mind.' He remembered falling asleep once at the wheel; as his car drifted he had heard a voice crying to him as if from across a summer hayfield. It had saved his life that night. Now Mark was strangely convinced that if he relaxed and listened carefully, he would be able to hear Gilmour, for it had to be Gilmour who sent the life-saving warmth that had awakened him from what would otherwise have been eternal sleep.

He sat back down on the rock awkwardly. His clothes, frozen solid, made a cracking sound as he bent over, but still he felt warm and comfortable, not cold at all. 'Open your mind, Mark,' he said again. 'Close your eyes and open your mind.' He shut his eyes tightly and watched the grey patch move slowly across his field of view.

'What is this?' he asked of no one, then allowed the question to linger in his consciousness. *What is this?* he thought. *Who is doing this to me? Gilmour?*

There had been an awareness, that night on the Long Island Expressway, something in his mind that understood, regardless of the fact that he was asleep, that he was making a mistake. That was the voice that had called to him from so far away; Mark searched for that voice again now. He knew it was there; he trusted it – the difficulty was being able to give away control of his thoughts.

The grey patch held the answers. Focus on the grey patch. It ought not to be here when I close my eyes, yet it remains.

Then he heard it, faint, like the breathing of a sleeping child, whispering, 'Mark Jenkins, you must hurry along.'

'Gilmour? Where are you?' Mark imagined himself on a journey inside his own mind, searching for this voice.

It came again. 'Not Gilmour. I used to be called Gabriel. I am called nothing now.'

'O'Reilly?' Mark focused his attention on the voice. 'Gabriel O'Reilly? Where are you? How are you doing this?'

'I am here. Inside you. I am warming you. You were nearly dead.'

'Right.' Mark was dumbfounded. The wraith had somehow worked its way inside his body. He remembered their encounter in the forest, when it had spoken to Steven and battled briefly with Sallax. It had entered both their bodies in a matter of seconds; now it was dwelling inside his frame?

How are you keeping me so warm? he thought to himself, wondering if the wraith could still hear him.

'I am a creature of energy now. It is not difficult for me to provide you with this, maybe much more. Nerak took my soul many years ago. I have been tortured without mercy for an eternity. But now I have escaped, and I offer my meagre powers in your struggle against the dark prince.'

'How did you . . . get away?'

'You freed me, Mark Jenkins, when you fell through the far portal. I had drifted, blind and mindless, for uncounted ages. Perhaps I drifted near the seam through which you fell; perhaps it was that same seam that carried my body, my stolen body, through the Fold with Nerak in tow those many years ago. I was lucky. Thousands like me are still trapped there in the Fold. They wait as slaves for Nerak to command them.'

Mark listened intently as the wraith continued, 'It was many days before I regained control of my own thoughts, but once I did, I came looking for you and Steven Taylor.'

Mark suddenly remembered his friend; he wondered how he could have forgotten him. 'Where is Steven?'

'He is far below, in the valley.'

'Is he still alive?'

'Yes,' O'Reilly replied, 'he is badly injured, but the Seron is nursing him back to health.'

'Seron?' Mark instinctively felt at his belt for the battle-axe. 'How many are there? The tracks I followed were made by just one person.'

'That is correct. Only one Seron cares for your friend.'

'But that doesn't make sense. I thought they hunted in packs, killing wildly and eating the bodies of their enemies—' Mark ran a hand across his forehead and thought for a moment. 'No, there was that one we helped back on the southern slopes near Seer's Peak. Is that the one? He named himself—' Again Mark broke off as he tried to recall the conversation.

'Steven saved it – *him*. Maybe that's why . . . Yes, that must be it. Thank you, Gabriel, for saving my life. Now I have to go.' He bent down to reclaim his pack.

'I will accompany you,' said the ghost. 'You will need me.'

Drawing a deep, cleansing breath, Mark asked, 'Out there or . . . in here?'

'I must remain in here, Mark Jenkins. Your newfound strength is only because of me. Were I to depart now, you would collapse.'

Mark was uncomfortable with the idea of a dead man's soul inhabiting his body. The few moments it took to revive him was one thing – although he was deeply grateful to the wraith for saving his life, he wasn't sure he wanted to prolong the relationship. His mind wandered for a second, picturing a multitude of embarrassing memories and experiences he wouldn't necessarily want to share.

'Do not be afraid.' The spirit's hollow voice rang in his mind. 'I have already seen everything you have ever seen and I know everything you have ever known.'

'Well, shit,' Mark muttered, then reminded himself that what was important right now was finding Steven. He resigned himself to Gabriel's continued presence.

'Okay, then,' he said, thinking he needed to formally agree. 'I suppose you ought to stick around in there. I can use the company, anyway.' He started back on the trail that led down through the pines blanketing the mountain's north face.

Now that was settled, he allowed his thoughts to turn to the rest of the group, and Brynne in particular.

'Do you know where my other companions are right now?' he asked out loud.

'I do not. But one of them is a traitor to your cause.'

Mark, shocked, had to fight the immediate urge to stop and interrogate the ghost further. Instead, he would have to learn as much as possible from the former manager of the Bank of Idaho Springs while making his way rapidly towards the valley floor. And first, he had to get more comfortable with the idea of carrying a dead man around inside himself. He had always considered himself an agnostic, although more out of a fundamental lack of interest than any real question of faith. Communicating with a man who had been dead for more than a hundred and thirty years called everything he believed into question.

The spirit had detected Mark's religious dilemma. 'I agree. It makes us doubt our faith. I was a dutiful Catholic, a Union soldier, a hard-working businessman.' Gabriel's hollow voice was unnerving; though it lacked human resonance, it still sounded like the fatigued reflections of anyone grappling with a misplaced faith. 'My only goal was to ascend to a Christian Heaven, as I assumed so many of my fellow soldiers did after Bull Run.' There was a brief pause; Mark thought he should offer some condolence to the spirit, but then O'Reilly continued, 'I will fight Nerak to his destruction, or be enslaved by him and his evil master for all time.'

Mark was suddenly angry. He wasn't sure if it were *his* anger, or Gabriel's, but it was welling up inside him and at that moment he ignored the fact that he was no fighter; he was ready to battle the dark prince hand-to-hand if necessary.

'You're right, Gabriel,' he said as he clenched his teeth together. He felt his shoulders tense with the desire to go to war, to vanquish the enemy and return safely home. 'And I don't know if you can, but I want you to come back with us . . . back to Idaho Springs. Maybe there you can find the peace you deserve.'

'I will try, Mark Jenkins.'

'But first, we have to kill Prince Malagon.'

'You will find no dissent in my mind, Mark Jenkins.'

The threatened storm arrived mid-morning, careening between the sullen peaks like a frozen tidal wave. There was no place to hide on the exposed mountainside. Neither Garec nor Brynne spoke as the winds howled about them; there was nothing to say. Like Mark, they knew they had to continue moving or they would die.

Sallax spoke periodically, but not about the storm, or their route over the pass. He sounded unconcerned as he chatted aimlessly about friends and old times back home in Estrad. Brynne could not hear much of what her brother was saying, but she was getting increasingly concerned at his apparent complacency about their situation. Did he not realise how serious this was?

Even though she bowed her head forward into the wind, she felt the sting of thousands of fast-moving snowflakes pelting her forehead and cheeks. Like tiny needles, the flakes ravaged her flesh until the cold took over and a forgiving numbness set in.

All the while, Sallax prattled on as if his will to live, lost for days, had returned in a rush, like the very storm through which he sauntered so gaily. Brynne heard his voice through the wind, a resonant bass line beneath the screaming soprano bearing down on her from the north. Periodically, she could make out fragments of what he said.

'Capina, remember her?' The storm interrupted him for a

while, but he didn't appear to stop. '—had a backside on her that must have been created by a god.'

Brynne, trying to catch up with Garec, slipped on the ice. No one appeared to notice. 'Garec,' she called, despairing, 'Garec, something's wrong with him.' She heard no response; Garec, almost shapeless under his cloak, continued trudging ever upwards towards the narrow break just below the mountain's peak.

Brynne squinted into the blinding snow, but she could see nothing beyond Garec. The rocky peak above had disappeared long ago and the ground beneath her feet extended to blend with the ice-white sky in an endless expanse of nothingness.

'We will be here for ever,' she whispered to herself. 'There can be no path through this.'

Sallax's voice came again from behind, '—always did favour Garec . . . remember her, Garec? Drank too much beer, though, thought you'd marry her . . . for no other reason than to be around that backside every day . . . glorious backside—'

Brynne felt her resolve begin to wane. She found solid footing for a moment, on what she guessed was a snow-covered boulder, and she wondered if she should stay there. Even her thoughts were interrupted by desultory static, she mused, difficult to decipher over the noisy winter around her.

Sure footing, a place to sit down later. Ahead there is nothing, an endless white void and behind there is Sallax, my brother, and his madness. Please, gods, let it be a passing illness. Who would know of a cure? Sallax would. We would turn to him were it anyone else.

Suddenly Sallax was there with her, lifting her up by her armpits. When had she sat down?

'Come on Brynne,' he shouted, 'I'm sure there are safer places for you to sit out this storm.' His eyes stared down at her, through her, and his mouth hung open slightly, the inane visage of a bewildered halfwit.

'Right, okay, I'm fine,' she answered with a groan and climbed to her feet.

'Do you remember the name of that wine we had at Mika's last Twinmoon?'

She reached out and touched her brother's face. He was grinning at her, his eyes alight with enthusiasm. 'Sallax, what's wrong with you?' she asked.

'It was grand. Don't you recall?' He looked into the distance. 'Gods, but that was a good one. Of course, Mika is dead now. But we had it with those venison steaks Garec brought from home . . . where is Garec?'

'He's just up ahead,' Brynne said in a comforting tone as she rested her head against Sallax's chest. She felt her breath catch in her throat; she didn't want to cry again today. She had no idea what had happened to her brother, nor what to do to help him. And as Sallax carried on about wine and women, she kept getting flashes of memory: Gilmour's lifeless body catching fire among the pine boughs in his funeral pyre. Brynne's world shrank to a point. A little rip in Sallax's cloak caught her eye and she studied it, learning its imperfections, watching as the frayed strands of wool blew back and forth together in the cold wind. Her breath cascaded over Sallax's chest and she blew gently on the fabric wound to watch the threads fight back against the storm.

Then Garec was with them, bearing a coil of rope he'd unearthed from his pack.

'Garec,' Sallax called jovially, 'd'you remember Capina?'

Garec blinked, but replied, 'Of course – how could I forget her?'

'She was built like a brick alehouse, though, wasn't she?'

Garec gripped his old friend by the shoulder and grinned. 'You should have seen her naked, Sallax. Break your heart to see that girl naked.'

'I knew it, you dog rutter!' Sallax, apparently thrilled with Garec's confession, laughed out loud. He appeared to be completely unaware that the Blackstone Mountains were trying once again to kill them.

All the while Garec was indulging Sallax's madness, he worked with the rope, one end of which he tied to Sallax's belt. He ran out a length of some three feet and looped a hitch around Brynne's belt, then did the same for himself.

'This way none of us will get lost in the blizzard,' he shouted to Brynne. 'We need to keep moving, to keep together. We're near the top of the pass now. We'll deal with Sallax once we're safe, but for now, we need to get out of here.'

As Brynne smiled waveringly, he came back and hugged her. 'It will be okay, Brynne. You're the strongest, bravest woman I have ever met.' He rubbed his hands briskly up and down along her back. 'This storm will kill me ten times before it even begins to dent you.'

'I'm afraid, Garec.'

'So am I,' he said as he pushed her hair back and pulled the hood of her cloak firmly over her head. 'I don't know what will happen when we find the others, and I don't know how we'll get to Malakasia, but I do know that we're not going to die on this gods-forsaken mountain, not today.'

'I've seen you get angry, Brynne. It's your strongest survival skill.' He looked down at her feet, invisible in the snow. 'It's all right if you get angry today. Get mean with this storm and you'll be fine.'

'I'll try,' she muttered, still fighting back tears.

'You'll do it.' He smiled at her again. 'And you'll be toasting my memory a hundred Twinmoons after I'm gone.'

She took his hands in hers and squeezed as tightly as she could. 'We can make it together.'

'Just one step at a time, and don't be afraid to hang on to the rope. Let's go,' he shouted as he turned back into the wind, 'Sallax, we're off!'

Lahp constructed a hasty but durable lean-to from several fallen trees, then gingerly moved Steven into its shelter, trying hard not to jostle the injured man. 'Firood,' he said, and when Steven nodded to show he'd understood, the Seron bounded off nimbly towards the river.

Steven rested in relative comfort, listening to the sound of the river rushing by and feeling the delicate tingling sensation of the querlis interacting with the muscle and bone tissues of his lower leg. Adjusting his position, he focused his attention along the trail and up the slope behind their camp. Several minutes passed and he began to grow impatient.

'C'mon Mark,' he called, as if it might speed him along. The moments ticked by at an agonisingly slow pace while he tried to remain vigilant. A clump of snow, falling from an overburdened branch, made him crane his neck, hoping to spot his friends appearing suddenly from the underbrush. Soon his legs fell asleep and his lower back began to ache from sitting up straight. He realised he was getting hungry.

Finally, admitting to himself that his companions were not

about to arrive right away, Steven allowed his thoughts to wander back to Lahp, and his immense good fortune at having been rescued by the Seron. Lahp was nothing like Gilmour had described: although the soul of a man may have been torn from the Seron's body long ago, Lahp was as caring and compassionate as anyone Steven had ever met. He could not imagine Howard Griffin, for example, going out of his way to build a stretcher and then drag him for mile after mile across the Rocky Mountains.

He thanked God that he'd not just walked away and left Sallax to murder the injured Malakasian warrior. Lahp had repaid that moment of compassion in full. He wondered if other Seron might behave differently if they, like Lahp, could escape the iron grip of Prince Malagon. Though the Seron attack had become a little hazy in his memory, he knew they had been fierce, eager fighters. He had a sudden pang of guilt when he remembered how easily he – well, the staff, really – had dispatched the other Seron. Mark and Garec had tried to convince him that he had not killed people; it was more akin to putting an injured animal out of its misery, but perhaps they too could have become friends if Gilmour had been able to help them free themselves from Malagon.

He had made a promise to himself the morning after the Seron attack. Sitting astride his horse, there in the foothills, he had smelled burning flesh from the twin funeral pyres. One represented last rites for a friend; the other was little more than basic sanitation, but the aroma was the same.

He *knew*, intellectually, that he had had no choice; if he had not killed the Seron, then he and his friends would likely all be long dead by now. But emotionally, he could not justify the killing, and the promise he made that morning was this: he would be compassionate and merciful. Regardless of what happened, he would show kindness, because kindness itself was a powerful weapon.

Now he had proved it: Lahp was an ally, one who knew the roads and trailheads that would provide him, Mark and the Ronan freedom fighters a safer passage to Welstar Palace. Steven let his chin fall forward onto his chest. He pulled a blanket around his shoulders, stared at the snow and waited for Lahp to return. Before long, Steven fell back asleep.

*

When he awakened, it was to the sound of Lahp moving about under the lean-to, searching inside his pack for something. Darkness had fallen and two grettan steaks grilled near the fire. Steven felt warm, dry and quite comfortable cocooned in blankets. He wiggled his toes, hesitantly at first, but there was little pain, so he tried moving his injured leg. This time, when he bent his leg at the knee, it moved with greater ease and far less agony.

'It feels better, Lahp,' Steven called, patting his knee firmly. 'I think I might be able to walk some once the others get here.' He looked about the lean-to and added almost to himself, 'Although it might be tough in this snow, so I will probably need to use my staff for support.' Hearing no response, Steven looked over at the Seron, who continued to root around inside his pack. 'Lahp, what's wrong?'

Lahp turned, and once again Steven was awed by the soldier's massive arms and shoulders. 'A one comes,' he said, pointing back along the trail.

Steven immediately reached for the hickory staff, and listened carefully, but he heard nothing. Twisting the staff in his hands, he asked, 'How do you know, Lahp? I can't hear anything.'

'Na, na.' Lahp shook his head then inhaled deeply, sniffing the air. He pointed again, along the river. 'A one comes.'

'You smell them coming?' Steven was incredulous. 'I can't smell anything except the smoke and those steaks.'

'A one comes.'

'If you say so, Lahp.' He tried to see outside the circle of firelight. Beside him, Lahp gave a grunt of satisfaction and pulled a long hunting knife from his pack. He drew a second from a sheath at his belt, and as he turned back to face the river, Steven gave a jolt. Lahp's face had changed: the gentle giant who had saved his life and nursed him back to health was no more; in his place was a Seron warrior, a deadly efficient soldier. At that moment Steven realised his companion was a killer.

Crouched near the ground, his lower jaw set firm and slightly forward, Lahp looked as if he could fight an entire platoon of soldiers without breaking into a sweat. Steven was almost afraid to ask what was happening.

'Lahp, what should I do?' Steven whispered, struggling to

stand. He leaned heavily on the wooden staff; he was not going to be much help in a fight.

'Na. Sten stay,' Lahp commanded quietly, and motioned for Steven to sit back down beneath the lean-to.

'How far away is he?'

There was no answer. Lahp crouched lower, his enormous legs like those of a pouncing jaguar, motionless except for the movement of his eyes as he strained to see into the darkness and the flaring of his nostrils as he sniffed the breeze.

Steven backed up but planted the hickory staff firmly in the ground and clung to it rather than retaking his seat beneath the lean-to. Lahp's concentration was unnerving and Steven too began to share the Seron's concern that whoever was approaching was not a friend.

Still unable to detect movement outside the camp's periphery, Lahp closed his eyes and listened. Steven was about to whisper another question when a low humming broke the silence an instant before an arrow ripped through their camp and embedded itself in a tree just over Lahp's right shoulder.

Before Steven could move, the Seron had taken cover behind a narrow pine trunk and was gesturing furiously for him to get out of the line of fire while ordering, 'Sten, dahn, dahn!'

The only way to move quickly was to fall. As he did, a second arrow, its thin shaft illuminated by the firelight, hurtled through the night and found its mark scant inches from the first, deep in the bark of the nearby pine. They were warning shots, carefully placed warning shots.

A weak voice, raspy with weariness, called from the forest in as threatening a tone as it could muster, 'Get away from him, you monster, or the next one will find your throat.'

It was Garec.

Steven wrestled his body from the icy ground and managed to reach his knees. He was not going to stand by and witness the inevitable outcome of a duel between the seemingly indestructible Seron warrior and the exhausted bowman.

'Garec,' he shouted, 'don't shoot! I'm fine! He's a friend!' Lahp looked at him questioningly, his broad forehead furrowed in consternation. 'It's all right, Lahp,' he said more quietly. 'It's Garec, my friend.'

Lahp went from battle-readiness to calm right away. He tossed the second dagger down and helped Steven regain his feet, tapping at his leg questioningly.

'No, Lahp. I am fine,' Steven said, 'no more damage – but thank you.'

Nodding, Lahp busied himself building up their campfire, apparently completely uninterested in Garec's approach. Steven scratched his beard and considered how extraordinary it was to have earned Lahp's confidence. *He trusts me*, Steven mused. *He could not care less who comes down that path right now.*

With that thought, Steven heard footsteps crunching through the snow and he began hobbling out to meet his companion, the pain in his leg forgotten momentarily.

Garec looked gaunt and completely worn-out, but he hugged Steven fiercely. 'We thought you dead, Steven Taylor,' he said as he removed two packs and placed his bow on the ground between them. He glanced over at Lahp and added, 'I see you have a tale to tell us. I am very glad you are all right—' He looked at Steven's carefully bound lower leg. '*Are* you all right?'

But Steven had not heard him; he was staring at the satchel on the ground beside the longbow. He swallowed hard before raising his eyes to meet Garec's. 'Why are you carrying Gilmour's pack?'

Lahp had scrutinised Garec carefully when he followed Steven into the lean-to. He examined the longbow, tugged several times at the bowstring and even sniffed at the fletching of the arrows in the twin quivers.

Curiosity satisfied, he drew another grettan steak from what looked to be a bottomless pack and placed it carefully next to the two already cooking.

Garec ate hungrily; he told his companions he had never realised how lean and tender grettan meat would be. 'I'm too tired even to remember what fresh bread tastes like,' he joked. 'There's bound to be fish in the river, even in this cold. I'll get some for breakfast; we must, after all, have a varied diet.'

Grunting his culinary approval, Lahp bid them both a good night and retired to his own pile of blankets next to the fire, leaving space beneath the lean-to for Garec. When the Ronan tried to protest, the Seron just pushed him back.

'Na, na,' he said. 'Lahp na cahld. Lahp good.'

Wrapped up in a white-coated huddle, Steven thought the

Seron looked rather like a pitcher's mound after a spring snowstorm.

Later, huddled together under the entwined branches of their shelter, the two men caught up on each other's news. Garec said he had moved ahead of Brynne and Sallax once they reached the valley floor. He had been looking for game to shoot when he smelled the smoke from Lahp's fire. Brynne and Sallax would be along sometime soon; as for Mark; they had split up some days before. Steven, deeply concerned at this news, kicked angrily at a wayward ember that popped from a burning log and landed near his feet.

'I'm sure he's fine,' Garec said, a little unconvincingly. 'He is at home in the mountains, far more than the rest of us, certainly.'

'That's true,' Steven answered, feeling horribly responsible for his friend's wellbeing. 'He's tough, much tougher than me.' He reached behind Garec for more wood. 'We need to keep the fire going until the others get here.' He leaned forward and gently placed the logs into the blaze. 'Until all of them get here.'

Finally, he asked about Gilmour. When Garec hadn't answered earlier, Steven knew the news was bad. He did not cry; he didn't believe he still could. Instead, he felt his stomach tighten, as if he had eaten something rancid and was about to retch.

The feeling lingered and intensified: without the Larion Senator, he and Mark might never get home. Selfish, but true. And Nerak would use Lessek's spell table to tear open the Fold and free his evil master. If they were to cross the Ravenian Sea and make their way to Welstar Palace without Gilmour, he might be called upon to wield the hickory staff in defence of his friends. Steven nearly choked. He leaned forward, wrapping his arms around his knees in an effort to ease the pain across his stomach. It was hard to breathe, as if the air had thinned suddenly, and he reached for the staff, pulling it close under the lean-to, a magical comfort in a wild and desperate land. Garec patted him gently on the shoulder and Steven realised that he had to do it. He would risk everything to save them. He would go to Malakasia, and face Nerak, even without being able to say goodbye to Hannah, or, more importantly, to say sorry.

He would lose, that was a given: it was as clear to him as anything he had ever known – but he was not as afraid as he had expected to be. Rather, he was sorry. He was sorry he would never see Hannah again. She was here; she was so close that he could almost feel her, smell the aroma of lilac that surrounded her . . . and he would not see her again in this lifetime. It was sad, but not tragic.

'She must know I love her,' he whispered, and Garec squeezed his shoulder more tightly.

'I am certain she does.'

'I'll have to face Nerak.'

'Yes.' Garec stared into the fire and again saw his sisters, the farm and his family back in Rona. 'But I'll be there with you.'

'You?'

'Of course.' He forced a smile. 'I never imagined it would be the thing I do best.'

'What's that?'

'Kill.' Garec stared down at their boots, side by side in the snow. He could not remember when they had traded. 'I wanted to be a woodsman, a hunter, like Versen, but circumstances forced me to become a killer. I fire arrows that find their target. It's not magic; it's just my willingness to do so. Its simplicity is beautiful. I am the best bowman I have ever known, and I say that not as a boast but as a matter of fact. I never hesitate, but afterward, I have frightening regrets; I often wish I had not fired at all. But if I can help you at Welstar Palace, Steven, I will.'

'Your arrows will have no effect on Nerak.'

'True enough, but I imagine there'll be hundreds of guards on hand, and servants too, every one willing to give their life to save his.'

Steven remembered Garec standing atop Seer's Peak, his bow at the ready. When the almor attacked, he had fired shaft after shaft with almost inhuman speed. Garec was right; he would be a powerful ally when it came time for their assault on Nerak's keep.

'Well, don't we make a pair,' he said. 'Two hesitant killers out to battle evil, hopelessness, tragedy and suffering.' Steven paused a moment before elbowing Garec gently in the ribs. 'I think we're going to get our asses kicked.'

The Ronan archer needed a translation, but when he had deciphered the colloquialism, he burst into laughter, a jovial belly-laugh that woke Lahp from his slumber and brought a moment's grace to the frozen valley floor.

*

Steven had fallen asleep when Brynne and Sallax entered the clearing, but he awakened when Garec leaped up to help them. Lahp, seeing their drawn faces and emaciated bodies, was rummaging for more grettan meat before they'd even sat down. Hugging Steven tightly, Brynne whispered, 'Have you seen him?'

'No,' Steven answered, 'but I'm sure he's all right. He's very strong.' He released her, dried a tear from her cheek with a corner of his cloak and said quietly, 'I am so very sorry about Gilmour.'

Brynne's brow furrowed and her mouth turned down slightly at the edges, a tiny gesture that spoke volumes. Her eyes glistened and she shook her head sternly from side to side. 'No,' she said firmly, 'I will not—' She paused to drag a sleeve under her nose, a starkly unladylike gesture that made Steven grin with genuine affection. 'I will not lose them both.' She looked at him as if her will alone would bring Mark Jenkins jogging contentedly along the trail. 'I will not.'

'I know,' Steven responded reassuringly. 'He'll be along. He has to. Who's going to save my life the next time I go wandering off on a fool's errand?'

'Steven,' Sallax said loudly, and slapped him hard across the back, 'it's good to see you doing so well.'

'And you, too, Sallax,' Steven returned. 'The last time I saw you I was quite worried.'

'That has passed,' the big Ronan grinned. 'That demon wraith hit me hard, but I've recovered. We shall have to be on the lookout for that horsecock, and I hope you'll have a chance at him with that staff of yours.'

Steven risked a glance back at Brynne. Something was wrong. This wasn't the same Sallax who had led them from Estrad. Garec had mentioned that Sallax was still sick, despite his seeming improvement, but this was a very curious condition. The man standing before him had a wild look in his eye, as if an untamed beast lay just beneath the surface of his jolly exterior.

It was as if Sallax were carrying something wicked that was chiselling away at him from within, leaving him half-sane, just a few fragmented and disjointed pieces of Sallax that had been rearranged, twisted about and whitewashed over with a boyish grin and a hearty laugh.

Deciding to wait until he could find a suitable time to discuss her brother's condition with Brynne, Steven redirected the conversation. 'Come, let's get you something to eat,' he said. 'I know you'll enjoy grettan steaks; I'm quite a convert.'

Sallax grinned.

By dawn it had stopped snowing and the air felt a little warmer than of late. Steven discovered a bit of a thaw had left very little in their small but now crowded camp dry; he intended stoking up the fire to dry clothes and blankets before they got underway. Garec and Lahp were already gone, but Sallax and Brynne were still deeply asleep.

Asleep, Sallax looked the same as he had back at Riverend Palace, a bit thinner, perhaps, but his face looked calmer, much more the confident partisan Steven remembered.

In the distance, he saw Garec making good on his promise to provide fish for breakfast. Crossing the Blackstones had toughened Garec; he didn't appear to be having as much fun as he had in the orchard outside Estrad, when he'd brought the highest apple to the ground with one shaft. He had been young then, filled with excitement at the promise of a journey north. Mark and Steven were strangers to him, still enemies at the time, and Garec had paid them little heed as he entertained himself there among the apple trees.

Now Steven knew that despite Garec's intense focus on the riverbed, he was also acutely aware of their surroundings. Nothing would threaten their camp this morning without first experiencing Garec's skill with a longbow. Gathering fish to stay alive was not fun. Steven grimaced as he watched the archer loose another shaft into a shallow pool. It *ought* to be fun; given time and extraordinary luck, perhaps he would live to see Garec firing arrows through apples again.

Breathing the crisp morning deep into his lungs, Steven rose slowly, tested his leg and found it stronger. The querlis was working well; he was healing quickly now. He draped his blankets over the edge of the lean-to to dry and made his way, slowly and carefully, down to the river to watch Garec.

For the next three days, the company made their way northwest alongside the river towards Falkan and Orindale. Steven, still unable to walk very far, reluctantly allowed Lahp to drag him in the pine gurney. Lahp seemed to mind far less than he did, and he didn't appear to tire. Although nights were still cold, the days were bright with sunshine and warm enough for them to remove their cloaks and walk along in tunics and wool hose or leather breeches.

Brynne walked with Sallax. The two spoke for avens about what was happening, where they were going and how they might successfully navigate their way to Welstar Palace without Gilmour. Brynne worked to keep her brother focused, emotionally and intellectually. Without her incessant reminders and redirections, his mind would wander, latching on to silly ideas or amusing memories, going off on a tangent or forgetting where they were and why they were heading for Malakasia. No one found his behaviour threatening, but they were all hoping he would make a quick recovery once they arrived in Orindale.

Periodically Sallax would show some improvement: his speech slowed to a normal rate, his excitability waned and his eyes managed to focus on the people and places around him – but this never lasted long; Brynne was conscious that she needed to get him to a healer as soon as possible.

On the morning of the third day they reached a cabin, set back in the trees from the south bank of the river. Garec guessed the cabin, a pretty basic structure, was used by trappers who worked the river and surrounding mountains for pelts. To them it represented sanctuary, a safe haven to rest, heal and plan.

Inside, they found a cache of food stockpiled for winter: dried fruits, smoked meat, a stack of bottles of Falkan wine and even a block of Ronan cheese, all neatly stored in a dry closet near the fireplace. Garec assumed the trapper who owned the cabin must be nearby, because the cheese was not too mouldy and the wine had been bottled recently.

Lahp helped Steven to a chair near a dusty table in the centre of the front room. A short hallway ran to bedrooms in the back. A neat stack of wood was arranged carefully beside the fireplace and as soon as he was certain Steven was comfortable, Lahp set about building a fire. Brynne looked haggard; she was worried for Sallax and anxious for news of Mark. To take her mind off things, she busied herself searching for candles, wiping the table and hanging their wet blankets and clothes to dry above the fireplace. Occasionally she looked over her shoulder at Sallax, who sat on the floor changing Steven's dressing. Lahp's supply of querlis was dwindling, but he indicated that he would find more of the miracle leaves in the valley.

Steven assured him his leg was much better. 'A few days by this fire and I'll be ready for the four-hundred-metre hurdles,' he said, using English where he could not find an appropriate Ronan translation. He was sad to see Sallax didn't react: either he did not notice or, more likely, did not care to understand what was said.

Garec emerged from the hallway drinking from a bottle of red wine. 'There are two rooms in the back with thatch mattresses that don't appear to have bugs or lice. Whoever sleeps back there ought to sleep on a blanket, though, just to be safe.'

'I'm just glad not to have to sleep on the bare ground tonight,' Steven said. 'Someone else can have the rooms. I don't mind.'

Brynne came to kneel beside her brother. She took Steven's lower leg in her hands and examined his wounds closely. 'They look much better,' she said, 'but you're still not cured. Take one of the beds. You need rest.'

Garec grinned at them. 'Fight all you like over the rooms. I'm sleeping out here, as close as I can get to the fire without burning, and then maybe just a little closer. I don't think I remember what it's like to be warm.'

Brynne looked up from her work. 'What if the trapper comes back?'

'I checked outside and there aren't any recent tracks. The cheese is still fairly fresh though, so he can't be more than a few days away.'

Steven chimed in, 'Can we leave him money? Mark and I found some silver back in Estrad.'

'Found?' Garec took another swallow.

'Okay, stole, but I'm happy to leave it here. This place may have saved our lives.'

'Fine,' Garec agreed. 'We'll pay handsomely for his hospitality.' He passed the bottle to Steven, who took a long swallow and suddenly remembered how much he liked Falkan wine – in fact, *any* wine.

'Garec, if we live through this, I want you to take me to a Falkan vineyard for a full Twinmoon. My treat.' Again Steven used an English colloquialism.

'Treat?' Garec asked, trying the word out on his tongue.

476

'I'll pay.'

'Ha,' Sallax laughed, 'if Steven is paying, count me in too.'

Brynne smiled as the friends engaged in friendly banter – the first time they'd felt secure enough for a long time. Her relief that Sallax would have a safe place to rest for a few days was mitigated only by her continued worry for Mark. Looking up at Steven, her smile faded.

Steven squeezed her hand tightly and passed her the wine bottle. 'Don't worry,' he whispered. 'He'll be along any time now, probably on skis, or with a posse of St Bernards in tow.' Despite the levity in his voice, Brynne was not comforted.

Later that day Steven dozed in a chair near the fireplace as the querlis worked its healing magic, dancing along the injured tissues and through his ever-strengthening bones. Garec had pulled a string of large trout from the river and they were all looking forward to a hot meal of fresh fish and dried fruit – they had found apricots, apples, tempine and pears, and an assortment of nuts and berries. Steven opened one eye long enough to pop a piece of dried apple into his mouth. Bliss!

When he woke again, the sun was low in the western sky. Lahp was stoking the fire while Garec prepared the trout. Sallax stared out of the window, watching the sun sink behind the mountains. By the time Brynne announced dinner it was dark. The flames crackled cheerfully as they gathered around the table; Steven realised it felt like home, and these people were family. It would be so wrong of him to return safely to Colorado leaving them to suffer. He would encourage Mark to go home, but he would stay. They had rescued him, cared for him and treated him as one of their own. There were no excuses for him to flee, to find safety a universe away in the First National Bank of Idaho Springs. Mark would fight him on it, but he would stay and he would wield the hickory staff in their defence until this business was done.

A short while later, Mark Jenkins knocked softly on the door.

477

THE TRAPPER'S CABIN

Santel Preskam cleared her throat, a raspy inhalation, and spat a mouthful of mucus into the underbrush. She stooped to make sure she was right; it was green. 'Rutting demonshit,' she cursed. She didn't have time to be sick.

'Rutting demonpiss river,' she muttered, 'if I wasn't soaked to the bone every rutting day, I wouldn't catch every rutting disease that floats by.'

Two days. It would be two days before she could get back to the cabin, but once there she promised herself she would crawl into bed and remain under the covers until the Twinmoon. But for now she trudged back up the riverbank, two empty traps in tow and tossed them over her horse's saddle. She had not pulled anything from that run all season; it was time to move the traps further upstream in hopes of snaring a beaver, a weksel, or perhaps a muskrat.

She withdrew a plain green bottle from her saddlebag, pulled the cork and took a long draught of the dry Falkan wine – she might be an ill-educated trapper, but she did know her wines. Before moving south into the mountains, she'd worked in the scullery on a vineyard in the Central Falkan Plain. It was there she had vowed that even if she lived another two hundred Twinmoons, her life would be over too soon to ever drink anything but good vintages. It cost her a great deal in pelts, but she justified the expense as a trade-off for all the clothing and accessories she would need if she lived in a city. 'I need good wine more than I need clean clothes out here,' Santel told her horse before enjoying another mouthful. 'Could do with a decent crystal goblet though,' she said with a croaky laugh.

As the wine warmed her, she felt a little more confident she would make it back to the cabin despite the infection and fever.

She stashed the bottle safely in her saddlebag and peered up through the woods.

Something moved.

Pulling a short forest bow from her shoulder, Santel nocked an arrow and stepped gingerly around her horse, hoping not to draw the attention of whatever it was that had passed between the trees up above. She squinted into the forest, then, seeing nothing, closed her eyes and listened. Nothing again. Exhaling in frustration, Santel whispered to her horse, 'Whoring rutters! Now I'm seeing things.'

She was about to replace the bow when she felt something cross the path behind her. 'Lords and gods!' she exclaimed, pulling the bowstring taut against her cheek.

It moved again, this time to her right, and then again on the hill to her left. Santel held her breath. They were all around her. She was being hunted.

Desperate for a clean shot, she tried shouting, 'C'mon out here, let's settle this like adults!'

She detected movement again, behind the horse, and then on the hillside. Straining to catch a glimpse of whatever it was, Santel suddenly felt the hairs on the back of her neck rise.

'Behind me!' The words echoed in her mind, an instant too late. She felt that horrible, familiar sensation, the hollow certainty that had followed close on the heels of every careless, *costly* mistake she had ever made. She whirled about to face her attacker, screaming as she fired directly into its face. They were close about her now.

As the sun glinted through the window, Mark woke and lifted his head from the pillow with a start. Where was he? Nervous insecurity gripped him and he searched the unfamiliar room for the opaque grey patch, until his anxiety relaxed its hold on his memory and the events of the past Twinmoon returned in a flood. The Blackstone Mountains, his brush with death, Gabriel O'Reilly, and finally, finding Steven: the scenes replayed themselves in his head.

But here, safe, lying next to Brynne, it was easy to forget the hardships he and his friends had suffered. He was glad his memory, as if working independently, had softened the images for him this morning.

Gently, so as not to wake her, Mark settled back down and contemplated Brynne's sleeping form. She lay on her side, her back to him. The edge of her right shoulder and upper arm blocked the sun's first rays; her flesh was rimmed with a brilliant gold border. Her beauty left him breathless.

He reached out to pull her towards him; as she rolled over, the sunlight shone across her chest and stomach and momentarily blinded him. He ran his palm across the taut firmness of her abdomen, stroking her like a cat. Still asleep, she moved lazily under his hand; as he brushed away several adventuresome strands of hair that had journeyed boldly across her shoulders and now obscured her breasts she sighed softly and, eyes still closed, reached out for him. His arousal was almost instantaneous; as her gentle, clever fingers teased him harder than he had ever thought possible, he bent and kissed the indentation at the base of her neck, running his tongue across her soft skin.

Brynne opened her eyes a slit and smiled up at him. 'Waiting for permission?' she whispered, tracing the hard curves of his buttocks. 'It's a little late for that, I think.' She pulled him down and kissed him tenderly. Mark lost himself in her softness and moistness and an almost lazy coming together that exploded into hard, fast emotion that overwhelmed him.

That same emotion had been almost as much a surprise as their passion the previous night. He blinked in an effort to adjust to the sudden brightness as the sun poured into the room. Brynne, smiling like a well-satisfied cat, rolled onto her stomach, pulled the wool blanket over them both and drifted back into slumber.

Last night their passion had been unchecked, their embrace powerful, ardent, fierce in its urgency. Shrouded in darkness, skin on skin, legs lost among legs and fingers entwined as if they would never again be free, they had clung and clawed and come together, a tumultuous wellspring of feelings in the knowledge that they had nearly died among the Blackstone peaks, relief that they had found each other, and fear for the morning, when they would once again have to face the evil that was threatening both their worlds.

Mark had not believed they would ever feel as much again as they had last night, but in the sunlit sensuality of morning, he found that he had underestimated both of them. Last night was not just frantic sex to forget the days and weeks of fear, or to celebrate their survival: it was far more than that.

Now he smiled to himself, because he knew he was falling in love with this woman – *had* fallen, already. He smiled, because he had held her tightly, had made love with her furiously, here in this bed, had fallen asleep by her side and awakened to find her still there.

Brynne's reaction to Mark's sudden appearance had been suitably dramatic: she had leaped up from the floor where she had been sharpening her hunting knife against a whetstone. She pushed the others aside and flew into his arms, alternatively crying against his neck and gazing deeply into his eyes, as if to ensure it really *was* him, and to ward against the possibility that he might vanish from the room and leave her alone again. In her enthusiasm, Brynne had forgotten to drop the knife; Mark had briefly worried that she might cut off one of his ears, or even accidentally stab him in the back. Now, watching her lush brown tresses fall across her cheek, Mark whispered, 'That's my girlfriend, my beautiful, sexy, knife-wielding revolutionary girl-friend.'

He closed his eyes and revelled as long as he could in the moment before the reality of their predicament crept into bed with him. With Steven injured and Sallax in his peculiar state, how were they going to get the small company to Orindale?

They had talked long into the night, discussing options. Mark agreed that Lahp's plan to build a raft and float the rest of the way was the most viable suggestion so far. There was no way Steven could walk; he couldn't yet manage more than a few paces at a time – and the rest of them were not much healthier. A few days' rest here was what they needed first off. It would do them all good, and it would give him and Lahp a chance to construct a decent-sized raft.

Thinking back on what he'd been though, Mark found himself remembering Idaho Springs. This morning he was especially missing the steaming-hot coffee served up by the Springs Café. Coffee. It was high time someone introduced the coffee bean to Eldarn.

Moving softly, trying not to wake Brynne, he slid out of bed and padded over to the washbasin near the window. The clear river water was freezing; as he splashed his face he tried not to cry out. At least he was now fully awake.

Mark hadn't mentioned Gabriel O'Reilly's warning last night, that one of them was a traitor. Sallax. It had to be, although it didn't seem feasible. His condition had improved since Mark last saw him: Sallax was beginning to act more like the determined partisan he and Steven had first met back in Estrad. He once again spoke in confident tones, certain of their eventual victory over Prince Malagon. But there was undoubtedly something missing; he had changed – though Mark couldn't pinpoint what had altered. When talking with the others, Sallax exhibited his old familiar strength, but when he sat by himself, his countenance changed. Mark noticed the difference as Sallax sat near the fire: his face was that of one who had lost hope.

The wraith said he had temporarily weakened the Ronan's convictions, but Mark didn't know quite what the spirit meant. Now he cast about inside his mind for the banker's ghost. Looking back at Brynne, lying naked beneath the blankets, he *really* hoped Gabriel was elsewhere this morning. After a moment's concentration, he was convinced the spirit had not returned – Mark hadn't felt him since the previous evening. Just moments after entering the cabin, he felt the ghost break their connection, calling out in a hoarse whisper before disappearing, 'I have failed.'

Failed at what? Mark thought back, but Gabriel O'Reilly was already gone and his friends were pulling him into the welcome warmth. There was a lot of news to exchange, including Gilmour's death. Mark could see Garec felt responsible; his eyes had filled with tears when he talked of organising Gilmour's funeral pyre. Mark finally understood the smoke over the mountains.

Now, watching the sun creep slowly across Brynne's blanket-wrapped body, Mark pulled his filthy red sweater over his bare torso and felt it hang on him like a dead sail on a wooden spar. He had lost weight. They all had. Steven looked worst of all. They had talked about Steven's battle with the grettan – *there* was something impossible. Although Mark was getting used to believing in a dozen impossible things before breakfast, this was a bit harder: how the hell could Steven have killed the beast *after* losing consciousness? Lahp insisted that he had not come upon the scene until *after* Steven had torn the grettan apart. A powerful force must have intervened on his friend's behalf – maybe the curious wooden staff, working of its own volition to save his life? *That* possibility was unfathomable too. Mark laced up his boots and left the bedroom.

Except for Lahp, who was already gone, no one else was awake. Mark poured a full skin of water into a cast-iron pot. If he couldn't have a triple espresso, heavily sugared, he would drink an entire pot of Eldarni tecan by himself. Using some of the dry kindling near the fireplace he coaxed a small flame, added a log or two and began heating the water.

'The whole pot, mind you,' he whispered to the room. 'Don't test the mettle of my conviction.'

Conviction. There it was again, swimming just beyond his grasp. What did Gabriel mean? *He attacked Sallax's convictions, temporarily weakening them.* Sallax's convictions about what? He was a partisan. He hated Malagon and fought for Ronan freedom, for Eldarni freedom. Why attack his convictions? The mysterious wraith had said, 'One of them is a traitor to your cause.' A traitor to our cause. That's not Sallax; he gave birth to this cause. What other cause could there be? Killing Malagon? Keeping evil at bay and imprisoned inside the Fold? Stirring the simmering tecan with a section of kindling, Mark, frustrated, wished Gilmour were there to help him work through these questions.

· *Gilmour.*

'Oh, no,' Mark said, and swallowed hard. 'Gilmour?' He turned slowly to gaze at Sallax, asleep near the fireplace and asked himself more than the Ronan leader, 'Did you kill Gilmour? Why would you do that? What convictions do you hold that need weakening?'

Brynne had told him Sallax began to improve almost immediately after Gilmour's death. Could it be that whatever magic the ghost had used to weaken Sallax had worn off after Gilmour died? 'No,' Mark muttered, 'not worn off, rather, became obsolete. Sallax's convictions were no longer an issue, so the wraith's power no longer had a target.' Mark's heart began to quicken. He needed to discuss this with someone – but not Brynne, not yet.

Steven was in the second bedroom. He had retired much earlier than the rest of the group, a fresh poultice of querlis making him drowsy. Now Mark tiptoed to the door, stepping gingerly to avoid noisy floorboards. Once inside, he pushed it closed on its leather hinges before attempting to wake his roommate.

'What?' Steven groaned, rolling over. 'What is it?'

Mark was struck by how thin and weak Steven looked, but he grinned broadly, hoping to raise his friend's spirits. 'Hey, it's me,' he whispered. 'How're you feeling?'

'My shoulder hurts, my ribs ache and my leg was nearly bitten off by a prehistoric creature with a bad temper and a glandular disorder. I feel like I want to sleep for another twelve hours or avens or whatever the hell they call time here, but you, my *former* friend, are waking me up at the crack of whatever time it is.' He paused for breath, then asked, 'What the hell time *is* it?'

'I don't know,' Mark laughed. 'I haven't known in weeks – do they even have weeks here?'

'Never mind,' Steven sat up. 'I smell tecan.' He rubbed the back of one hand across his eyes. 'Well, if I can't think of a better reason, good strong tecan is enough for me to be glad to have you back.'

'Sorry, this morning I can't help. I promised myself I'd drink the whole pot.'

'Really? No sharing? That's not like you, Mister Public School Teacher.'

'Nope, not a drop. It was cold where I was. I'm still warming up.'

Steven grunted, 'Okay, I'll join you for a second pot after I sleep until noon or whatever they call the time a whole lot later than right now.'

'Sorry, you can't do that either.' Mark was suddenly serious. 'We may have a big problem.' Steven raised one eyebrow and Mark continued, 'No, another big problem: Gabriel O'Reilly told me that Sallax is a traitor.'

'Oh, shit.' Steven was instantly awake and lucid. 'Why? What reason did he give?'

'He didn't.' Mark gestured in the air above Steven's bed. 'He's a bit—'

'Dead?'

'Cryptic. But I believe him. He says he crippled Sallax's confidence – no, his *convictions* – that night in the forest when

Malagon attacked you. And last night, when I finally got here, he fled my mind right after telling me he had failed.'

'Failed to do what?'

'I don't know. Maybe he failed to save Gilmour.'

'But Sallax didn't kill Gilmour.'

'Right, but maybe he was working with the killer. Remember Gilmour told us someone had been tracking us all the way from Estrad? That's probably who killed him.'

Steven nodded. 'And twice I woke up before dawn to find Sallax creeping back into camp. I thought he had just gone off for a pee or something.'

'Sonofabitch.' The word lingered in the room. 'What do we do?'

'We should confront him.'

'Yes, by all means, confront me.'

Sallax was standing in the doorway, his rapier drawn. Mark cast his eyes about the sparsely furnished chamber for a weapon. An old wooden chair stood below the window and he rested one hand on it as he asked, 'Why?' His grip tightened. 'You're their leader; you're a revolutionary.'

Steven rolled from the bed and managed to stand, but he dared not pick up the hickory staff for fear of driving Sallax to attack.

Tears began to form in Sallax's eyes as he closed the door behind him. The rapier's tip was just a few feet from Steven's chest.

Steven started, 'All of Rona needs you, Sallax. There are so few who bring—'

'I am *not* Ronan,' Sallax nearly shouted, then lowered his voice. 'I am from Praga. Brynne and I are Pragan.'

Mark made an attempt to downplay this revelation. 'I don't care if you're from Ontario. Isn't Praga under Malagon's rule as well? Are Pragans not suffering?' He watched Steven sidle slowly towards the staff, but not pick it up. *Smart, Steven*, he thought. *Don't piss him off any more than he already is.*

'My parents were kind people.' Sallax's voice broke and he fought to control the tremor. 'They owned a rigging shop on the wharf in Southport. Hawsers, line, cleats, brass quarterdeck bells my father let me polish.' His gaze drifted to the window and a thin smile graced his lips as he recalled a happier time. 'They caught the early sun off the water and turned the whole storefront to gold, rippling fluid gold. My mother mended sails; her fingers were calloused from Twinmoons pushing and pulling huge needles through tears in the sheets. She always had pots of tecan brewing on the woodstove, but I can't remember anyone ever paying for a cup. "The first cup of tecan every day should be free," she would always say, but I never remember anyone paying for tecan at any time of day. They didn't make much, mind you, but we were always happy and the shop was always filled with people.'

Neither Mark nor Steven had ever heard him say this much, and Mark was about to entreat the big man to put down his rapier when Sallax went on, 'Brynne played in her crib or on the floor near the woodstove. She could barely stand when they died, and I stole milk for Twinmoons until she was old enough to eat solid food.'

Crying now, he ran a tunic sleeve across his face and it came away slick with mucus and tears. 'Malagon had just come to power, his father dead only a few Twinmoons, when we began to feel Malakasia's grip tighten. My parents didn't mind because all ships – Pragan, Malakasian, even the occasional craft from Rona – they all needed rigging after fighting through the Twinmoon storms on the Ravenian Sea. Business for them was good. I learned a lot, and I was happy. I thought things would be perfect for ever. I was perhaps fifty Twinmoons at the time.'

'What happened?' Steven whispered, his eyes still locked on the tip of Sallax's rapier.

'People were starving. There were raids, civil unrest, bread lines that became full-scale riots, day after day. You would be surprised what otherwise decent people will do to feed their families.' His eyes seemed to glaze over and his face paled as he continued in a soft monotone, 'A raiding fleet came into Southport, probably out of Markon Isle, three of them, heavy ships, several hundred men each. My father had seen them when they were hull-up on the horizon. They flew Pragan colours. He was excited; that meant work for him and my mother that night.'

'They were Malakasians?' Steven asked. 'Flying Pragan colours to allay any suspicion?'

'No,' he shook his head slightly, 'they were Ronan. Searching for food and silver, and girls to work the whorehouses on the Isle. They came in like a pestilence, under full sail. My father knew something was wrong when they didn't strike their mains but maintained flank speed much too far into shallow water. Most ships would come into port under topgallants alone. These three came on as if they planned to crash through the wharf and dock somewhere on the opposite side of the city.' Mark leaned on the chair and Sallax, mistaking his movement for something more aggressive, broke from his reverie and barked, 'Sit down! Both of you!' His fist closed tightly around the rapier hilt. Although tears fell freely, his voice no longer trembled. Instead, his tone was flat, deadly.

Steven sat near the end of the bed, as far from the rapier as possible, and within an arm's length of the staff. His left hand almost burned with the desire to reach out: it was the staff's power calling to him, trying to protect him from Sallax. Suddenly, he thought he understood how the grettan had been killed.

He turned back to Sallax as the partisan continued his story.

'When they finally struck their mains and topsails, my father sighed. I remember that sigh, because he was relieved, you see. When he saw those sails come down, his thoughts went from worry to amusement. In his mind, those ships went from a threat to a comedy and I will never forget him smiling at me, gripping me by the shoulder and saying, "They just don't know how to sail, Salboy." We watched them together, waiting for them to come about and drop anchor. The sun was setting behind them and we had to strain our eyes to see. I squinted directly into the sun to catch a glimpse of one captain. He was backlit by fire, and I could see him giving orders to men in the rigging, and then, in an instant, I remember the sun going out.'

'Was it magic?' Mark glanced over at Steven, who nodded slightly. They needed to keep him talking.

'No.' Sallax looked between the two roommates without blinking. 'It was the mainsail snapping back into the wind. It blocked the sun for a moment, but in that instant, I knew we were dead.'

'They reset the sails,' Steven said softly. 'It was all a trick to get in close to the shoreline.'

'That's right.' Sallax said. 'And then it began.' He ran a thumb along the edge of the battle-axe in his belt and Steven saw a trickle of blood cross his palm.

'Was there no Malakasian occupation force in the port?' Steven asked.

'Oh yes, a huge frigate, with a crew of hundreds. That was their first target. One came from the north, the other from the south. They attacked at flank speed right there in the harbour. Those captains must have been madmen, absolutely insane, or they knew the harbour bed better than anyone in Eldarn. The two ships closed on the frigate, but before they grappled and boarded, they strafed the wharf with thousands of flaming arrows, pitch and tar arrows set alight. Within moments every building was in flames. They wanted to create as much mayhem as possible onshore, to scatter shop owners and merchants, and their plan was executed perfectly. The fires kept the townspeople busy, and many believed the arrows were a diversion to draw attention away from the naval frigate. Somehow, I knew better. I knew they were coming ashore just as soon as they finished destroying that ship.

'My parents' shop was one of the first hit and my father turned to hustle me inside. I imagine to this day, he planned to collect Brynne and my mother and spirit us all out the back to safety.'

'But he was hit,' Mark predicted under his breath.

'Right again, Mark,' Sallax confirmed. 'We were two, maybe three paces from safety when a burning Ronan shaft took him right between the shoulder blades. I heard my mother wail, an inhuman cry of despair. You see, the pitch on the arrows sprayed out when they struck something hard, which spread the flames to the surrounding area. So while my mother screamed and Brynne cried in her crib, I stood and watched as my father's body burned to a cinder, right there on the front step.'

Sallax paused a moment and Steven ventured to ask, 'But why kill Gilmour? This was a raid, a pirate band.'

Sallax ignored the question. 'They burned the frigate to the waterline. Archers set the rigging aflame; so the captain couldn't order the sails set to make way. They never even hoisted the anchor. It was like watching sharks on a sleeping whale. They killed the crew and hanged the Malakasian captain from the stern rail. His legs dangled beneath the surface and I imagine he tried to find some solid purchase among the waters of Southport Harbour as his life ebbed away. There were a few Malakasian soldiers in town, but in typical Malakasian fashion, they were out of practice.'

'What do you mean?' Mark asked. He could smell his tecan burning; the water hissed as it boiled over. Jesus, but Garec could sleep through anything . . . or maybe he was already dead—

'They hadn't been drilling. They had grown fat and lazy. There was no army or navy to oppose them, no resistance movement in Praga at the time, so they all attacked the wharf. Two or three platoons massed out on the edge of the dock firing arrows into the pirate ships and calling curses and promises of a swift death to anyone bold enough to come ashore. Stupid horsecocks.' He almost smiled and Steven realised Sallax truly had no love for Malakasia. At least that much was genuine. 'They forgot the third ship, or if they didn't forget it, they didn't consider it a threat. Well, it was. Nearly two hundred armed mercenaries, tough bastards, came ashore from the third ship, strolled along the wharf as if they were courting some Pragan merchant's chubby virgin daughter. They proceeded to hack and slash those platoons to ribbons, drove them right off the town docks and into the sea. Then, with a whooping holler, they came for us.'

The burn in Steven's hand intensified: the staff was warning him Sallax was about to come at them, there would be no subduing him. This would be quick, bloody and to the death.

Sallax went on in matter-of-fact tones, 'My mother was taken. They dragged her right over my father's burning body and I watched as the hem of her dress caught fire on his back, a small flame that connected them one last time. It soon went out. I held Brynne tightly to my chest and waited to die, but they ignored us. They took what valuables they could find, including the brass bells I had polished so lovingly, and left the shop to burn. I carried Brynne outside, not out back but out front, out past my father and onto the cold cobblestones of the street. Behind us, the waterfront was in flames, but I couldn't put Brynne down on the chilly stones because she might catch a cold. So we stood there and waited. That's when I saw him up close for the first time.'

'Prince Malagon?' Steven was confused.

'No, Gilmour.'

'Gilmour was there?' Mark interjected.

'Gilmour was the captain I had seen giving orders to reset the main and top sails. He then ordered his archers to set fire to the town. When his ship slammed into the naval frigate, he ordered his men to fix grappling hooks and board her, to kill every Malakasian aboard and to burn her to the waterline. With that done, he ordered a launch to carry him ashore where he strode along the waterfront surveying the damage as his men pillaged and raped their way through town. Any who resisted him were murdered. It was simple, beautiful in its efficiency.'

'I can't believe it, not *Gilmour*.' Steven realised he had made a mistake as soon as he opened his mouth, but he couldn't stop the words.

Nor could he stop Sallax from reacting: the man took a step towards him and screamed, 'It was Gilmour, you rutting foreigner! No one rutting asked you into this!'

Then the staff was there, in his hand, and he felt its power course through him. Compassion. He heard himself say it and looked at Mark to see if he had said it aloud. *Compassion*.

'Sallax, don't do this. I don't want to kill you.'

'Kill *me*, you whoring dog?' His rapier was inches from Steven's throat. 'I'll run you clean through before you draw another breath. So sit there and shut up! I am not yet finished!'

'Right. Yes. Okay.' Steven felt it grow stronger. *Compassion*. This was a sick man, not a murderer. Sallax did not want to kill them. He was suffering, and Steven had to find a way to help him. He dropped the staff to his side and apologised.

'Sorry, I interrupted,' he said quietly.

Sallax glared, but continued, 'I carried Brynne for days, begging for milk and buying what I could with the few coins my mother had kept inside an iron pot near the fireplace. Brynne cried so much, I thought she would die, but I kept her clean and managed to feed her, stealing when I had to.'

'How did you get to Estrad?' Mark asked.

'We heard a rumour that Malagon was sending a brigade of soldiers down to reclaim the town. The pirates were long gone and no one wanted to be around when a vengeful army showed up with no one to fight. So, many of us piled into anything that would float and made for Rona. We found a husband and wife travelling together who made certain we had food and water during the journey. I have tried for two hundred Twinmoons to find them, but I can't even remember their names. They saved our lives.'

'And she doesn't know any of this?' Mark asked, trying to keep him talking. He doubted he could get the chair around in time to defend himself against Sallax's rapier.

'She believes our parents died in Rona.'

'But still,' Steven entreated calmly, 'how could you fight for Ronan freedom while planning to betray Gilmour?'

Sallax had the look of one already lost, a tragic hero with no escape from the reality of his own weakness. 'I did not betray Gilmour and I did not betray Rona. I avenged my parents. I never told Jacrys that Lessek's Key was waiting for Nerak on your writing table, Steven Taylor, and I never passed along secrets of the Ronan Resistance. I avenged my parents; that's all.'

'But you have known Gilmour for—'

'For fifty Twinmoons, yes, but it wasn't until about twenty-five Twinmoons ago that I realised he was the same man who had ordered the attack on Southport.'

'How is that possible?' Mark needed clarification.

'I had a vision – call it a dream, or a message from my parents. I saw him there, as clearly as if I were standing there, and in that moment, I knew it was he who had led the raiding fleet against my home. The memory of his face had been lost to me for so long; getting it back was like being reborn. I planned Gilmour's death while fighting alongside him in raids on the Merchants' Highway. I planned his death while drinking with him at Greentree Tavern. I planned his death while watching him walk with my sister, his arm around her shoulder like the father she never knew.' Sallax's voice rose as he spoke and he stood tall, towering over Steven and Mark.

This is it, Mark thought and prepared to dive at Sallax, hoping to distract the man long enough for Steven to call forth the staff's magic.

He was tensing for his leap when Steven interrupted. 'So, you succeeded,' he said quietly. 'You avenged your parents. Any of us would have done the same thing, but now you are conflicted. You are wrestling with demons over this decision, Sallax. Why? Will you tell us? We're here, at your mercy. We can't get the jump on you, you've got us at sword-point. Why are you struggling now?'

Sallax exhaled, a long sigh. 'Gabriel O'Reilly, the wraith.'

'What did he do?' Steven asked.

Sallax's tears came again. He broke down and buried his face in his hands. Mark looked over at Steven, thinking hard, *Now! Let's go now!* – but before he could spring forward, Sallax lifted his head and pointed his rapier at Mark's chest. 'The spirit, O'Reilly, showed me the captain's face. My vision, my memory of Gilmour as the captain of that dreadful ship was not real. It was planted in my mind by Prince Malagon. I worked for Malagon for twenty-five Twinmoons planning Gilmour's death.

'I killed him, my mentor, my leader. He was my friend and I prepared his death. The captain was not Gilmour.'

'Why didn't you say something? If you'd told us the killer was coming, we could have saved him.' Steven was frustrated.

'I couldn't,' Sallax admitted. 'I wanted him dead. It sounds stupid, but I couldn't let go of my desire. It was as though the truth wasn't strong enough to clear Malagon's false image from my mind.

'So I ruined our chances for survival, for Eldarn's freedom. We are going to die at Nerak's hand, and it is *my* fault. I didn't have the courage to kill myself – I was afraid of what I would find in death. Instead, I watched Gilmour die. I watched his body burn away, my second father, burning like a shadowy image of my first, and all I could think to do was to take care of Brynne again, to get her safely off that mountain. It was Brynne's heartbreak that pulled me from O'Reilly's spell. I couldn't let her fail, because it was the only good thing I had ever done. I saved her life then and I had to save it now.'

'But it didn't work,' Steven said.

Sallax chuckled ironically. 'No, it didn't. Instead, it became more difficult to control my thoughts. I hallucinated as guilt warred with magic. I have been lost.'

'You sound pretty lucid now,' Mark observed. 'What's different?'

Sallax broke down again and Mark took advantage of the opportunity to stand up slowly.

'Now, this morning, I am lucid. Call it a moment's respite from myself, but I know why.' Sallax sliced the rapier's point through the air with a thin whoosh. 'Because now it is time for me to die. Steven? Will you do the honours?'

'No, Sallax,' Steven replied firmly. 'I will not kill you.'

'Then, my friend, you will watch as Mark dies.' With that, Sallax lunged towards Mark.

'No!' Mark cried; there was no time to move, other than to draw his arms in against the sides of his body, his elbows firmly tucked against his ribs. But the fiery pain never came; though it was just a couple of feet, Sallax didn't land the simple thrust that would have ended Mark's life in an instant.

As Sallax lunged, Steven opened his mind to the power of the staff and, like the night he killed the Seron warriors, time slowed down for him. He had ample time to reach for the staff, to deflect Sallax's thrust and to bring the shaft about and take him solidly across the chest. Steven felt the staff's power: it would kill Sallax as readily as it had killed the Seron, as brutally as it had dismembered the grettan.

But he did not want Sallax dead; he wanted to help. *Compassion.* He reached out to take control of the magic. 'I will *not* kill you, Sallax,' he heard himself shout. As the staff hit him in the ribs, Sallax was lifted from his feet and thrown with a resounding crash through the door and into the front room.

Garec finally awakened with a start. 'Rutters!' he cried, 'what's happening?'

Sallax was lying absolutely still and Steven thought for sure he was dead. 'Oh shit,' he said as he tossed the staff on the bed, 'I killed him. Goddamn it all to hell in a handbasket.' Ignoring his injured leg, he limped towards the front room. Before he made it, Sallax rolled onto one side and began vomiting out the contents of his stomach.

'Thank Christ,' Steven exclaimed, 'he's alive.'

Mark was still checking his abdomen for the puncture he was certain he would find there, the blood seeping into the red wool of his sweater as Brynne burst through, a look of terror on her face. 'Sallax!' she cried, rushing to her brother. 'What happened to you, to your face?'

No one answered, but Sallax pulled himself to his feet and turned to glare wild-eyed at Steven. 'You're cheating me,' he shouted.

'You're right, Sallax. I will not kill you, not ever.'

'Don't make promises,' he said and lifted his rapier towards Steven. 'You have no idea what I might do.'

Brynne gripped his upper arm. 'Sallax, tell me what's wrong.'

Turning on Steven, she scolded, 'Steven, you know he's ill. What have you done?'

'Tell her,' Steven said, turning to look at Sallax. 'Tell your sister what you told us. She needs to know – and you need to tell her. It's what Gilmour would ask.' Steven took a step forward. 'You know he has already forgiven you.'

'Forgiven him what?' Brynne demanded, but Sallax screamed and pushed her to the floor, then turned and ran through the front door and out into the forest.

He nearly ran into Lahp, who was hauling a load of firewood that would have crippled any of them. The Seron shot him a crooked grin and greeted him warmly, 'Ha, Sallax.'

His face changed when Sallax barked, 'Out of my way, you half-human beast,' and stabbed the point of his rapier deep into the Seron's thigh. Lahp bellowed and fell to the ground, his massive paws gripping the puncture wound closed. The moment he realised it wasn't life-threatening, he picked up a piece of firewood, lumbered to his feet and, furious, hurled it at Sallax's back. It struck with a sickening thud, followed immediately by an audible snap, and Sallax pitched forward headlong into the dirt. His shoulder was broken.

Lahp chuckled, a deep arrhythmic bass. Sallax would live, but he would be in considerable pain for a while. Oblivious to the cacophony erupting from the cabin behind him, the Seron rechecked the wound in his leg, tied it tightly closed with a length of cloth he tore from his tunic and began picking up the firewood he had dropped along the trail.

Having recovered from his own initial shock, Mark grabbed Brynne before she could pursue her brother. 'Don't follow him, Brynne,' he implored, holding her tightly, 'not yet. He's not thinking right. He might hurt you – kill you, even.'

'Let go of me.' Brynne's voice was desperate and she fought to escape Mark's embrace. 'I have to catch him. He's sick.'

'Yes, and he's dangerous,' Mark pleaded. 'He tried to stab me.'

Brynne ignored him and broke free. She pushed her way roughly past Lahp, who filled the doorway with his gargantuan frame. The Seron, his breeches stained with blood, looked after her with confusion, took several steps back into the forest and then stopped to wait for Steven to tell him what to do. Brynne disappeared along the trail.

Inside the cabin, no one spoke. The silence was unnerving. Mark watched Brynne sprint off through the trees and then looked questioningly at Steven.

'Go,' he said. Mark stooped to pick up Sallax's own battle-axe before rushing through the door behind her.

It was two avens before Mark and Brynne returned. He held her tightly around the shoulder and their feet fell in perfect sync, stride for stride. Garec watched them, smiling at the comforting rhythm of their step and glad that they remained connected despite the morning's events. Sallax wasn't with them; Garec could see Brynne was upset and feared the worst.

Although it was only midday, the young woman looked exhausted, about to collapse. Mark escorted her into their bedroom and several moments later emerged alone. He threw himself into one of the chairs and reported, 'We tracked him along the river a way, then he turned up into the foothills, then back into the valley.'

'Did you catch him?' Steven asked. 'Isn't he running with a broken arm?'

'I don't know, but he's fast and he's strong. I've no idea how he's managing to keep it up – adrenalin, maybe. To be honest, I'm glad we didn't catch him.'

'Why?' Garec asked.

'What would we have done with him?' Mark took a long swallow from an open wine bottle and looked around the room for something to eat. 'He might have killed us both. I'm no match for him, even if he has got one useless arm.'

'Where do you think he'll go?' Steven asked.

Garec said, 'I've no idea how far it is to Orindale, but he'll need to have those bones set sometime soon. I suppose he'll stick to the river until he comes to anything that looks like a town, maybe somewhere on the outskirts of the city.'

'But we don't know where we, are or how long it'll take us to get downriver,' Mark added.

'Unless he scales the mountains again, he doesn't have many options.'

Steven said grimly, 'Neither do we.'

'I still think we ought to stay here a few more days,' Garec said, surprising them. 'Your leg needs to heal. Brynne needs rest. We all could use a break to deal with Gilmour's loss and— and, well, Sallax's disappearance.'

'That makes sense,' Mark agreed. 'We don't know what comes next. We can't just march into Malakasia and demand the far portal. We need a plan.'

Steven and Garec shared an anxious glance. Without Gilmour, no one could operate the spell table. Even if they made it into Welstar Palace and managed to find the far portal, they had no idea how to use Lessek's Key. All they knew was that it had to be kept from Nerak. Who else could tap its power for good? Gilmour had mentioned a colleague, Kantu, another Larion Senator, but he was in Praga and no one knew what he looked like, or where to begin searching for him. They were alone, lost in the northern Blackstones, and they had no idea how to proceed. A few days' rest might give them a chance to come up with some options.

'Yes,' Steven finally agreed. 'We ought to stay here a while.'

The day passed slowly. Brynne slept, and Mark looked in on her occasionally, watching her chest rise and fall steadily in the waning twilight. Steven and Garec busied themselves with simple tasks, stacking firewood, organising rations and fletching arrows. Steven's leg felt stronger, and he diligently replaced the querlis with new leaves Lahp had found somewhere along the riverbank. The three men talked idly of their families, their work, and finally, sports, while Lahp listened, resting in one corner of the room with his leg straight out in front of him, his own wound bound and treated with querlis. Steven had no idea what, if anything, he understood, but it was comforting to talk of home. Garec was fascinated at the notion of golf and Mark promised to teach him to play if they could somehow fashion appropriate clubs. Garec reciprocated with an offer to teach the foreigners chainball as soon as they reached a flat stretch of land. They avoided discussing Gilmour, Sallax, Welstar Palace, or Lessek's Key, and each was happy to bask in the illusion of normalcy for a day.

Just before dark, Garec took his bow and quivers out to the river. Mark watched as Steven redressed his leg, wrapping strips of cloth over the therapeutic leaves on his calf. For the second time that day, Mark took stock of how much his friend had changed. His hair was too long, tucked under his collar, and his trim beard made him look older. Rather than his sometimes lackadaisical attitude of old, now Steven's motions were deliberate, with little wasted effort; he moved with the purposeful conviction of a warrior preparing for battle. Perhaps that was it, the crux of his transformation: Steven had become a warrior. Although still untested in real battle – he had fought only to protect himself and his companions – it looked as if he had developed a willingness to risk his life for a cause he had embraced wholeheartedly.

Steven's spirit had changed as well. He was no longer the bored assistant manager who would never complain or inconvenience anyone; now he was a powerful foe who would somehow find a way to confront Nerak, even without Gilmour along to lead them home. Mark had watched him in a Denver restaurant one night, eating roast chicken with red potatoes, asparagus and corn bread. Steven ate the entire meal, commenting on the flavour and the artful presentation – and Mark teased him for weeks afterwards, because Steven had ordered a salad. He had eaten someone else's meal, because he didn't want to inconvenience anyone by complaining or sending food back to the kitchen.

Mark wondered how Steven would manage when they did finally return to Idaho Springs. Watching as his friend ran his hands thoughtfully along the wooden staff, inspecting every grain pattern and bloodstain, Mark was glad Steven had been forced to fight, to toughen his spirit. It might prove to be the one thing that ensured their eventual survival.

What was most ironic was that Steven didn't see the change in himself; he was still convinced that if he showed compassion, everything would be all right in the end – but would it? Mark doubted Nerak could be defeated with *compassion*; as a historian, he believed there were times when destroying the enemy utterly and completely was the only real option. Nerak needed to be destroyed, annihilated. Did Steven's compassion give him real strength? Mark could only guess. Garec was different. His strength was formidable: he fired arrows and killed foes. Real strength, real results and an unquestioning will to win.

That's what Steven needed. He might be developing the spirit of a warrior, but unless he also had the tools of a warrior, the magic of a Larion Senator and the willingness to destroy Nerak, Mark worried their cause might be in jeopardy.

Feeling a little guilty for doubting Steven, Mark went to inspect his roommate's medicinal handiwork. 'How's the leg?'

'Much better, thanks.'

'Maybe we'll get you out for a walk tomorrow. If the weather holds, it will be nice along the river.'

Steven looked puzzled. 'What's on your mind, Mark?'

'Nothing much, just the fact that you're our only hope.' He pointed at the staff in Steven's lap. 'Do you think you can get us into Welstar Palace and through the portal without Gilmour?'

'I don't think so,' Steven admitted, 'but we've still got to try. I was hoping Gabriel would help us to find a way to get in.'

'I hadn't thought of him. That's actually not a bad plan.'

'To be honest, I have my doubts that we should be making this attempt at all.'

'Do we have any choice? It's our only way home.'

Steven stared into the fire. 'We could stay and fight.'

Mark almost laughed, and then he realised his friend was serious. 'What? Here? For ever?'

'No, just until Nerak is defeated. Going into Welstar Palace before I really know how to use this thing is suicide.' He adjusted the hickory shaft across his lap. 'We ought at least to find someplace safe to research the staff, to practise with it. I can feel its power. It calls to me when trouble is coming. I do nothing; *it* controls everything.'

'And it killed that grettan.'

'Yes,' Steven finally looked up. 'After I passed out. At least I think it did; I can't remember.'

'Do you have enough power to beat him, though?'

'I can't say. Gilmour wasn't much help; he had no idea how powerful the staff might be. I may be ten times stronger than Nerak, or a hundred times weaker.'

'Then this is crazy. We'll get in there and be dead in minutes.'

Steven remembered his mantra, and how it calmed him. He repeated it now, to explain. 'We might not make it. You're right, but somehow I'm certain the strength of the staff lies in my willingness to wield it.'

'So wield it then. Crush him, if you're convinced it's strong enough.'

'No.' Steven shook his head to emphasise the point. 'It doesn't work that way. You saw it shatter on that Seron. It broke like a piece of kindling. I have to show compassion.'

Mark moved towards the fireplace and tossed a misshapen log into the flames. 'I don't know that Nerak is the kind of enemy who deserves compassion. Maybe the staff will recognise how insidious he is.'

Steven stood and hobbled awkwardly across the room to stand beside Mark. 'We have to find the far portal. Nerak controls it. He doesn't seem to be able to detect the staff's magic, nor can he locate Lessek's Key from afar. If he could, he would know we don't have it, and God love Sallax for not sharing that information with Malagon's spy. So, there are five things we know, and there are about seven hundred things we don't.

'I think we need to buy ourselves some time, work with the staff, decipher its purpose and its power and then make a decision about how to get home.'

There was something Steven hadn't said, so Mark added it for him. 'And we may find news of Hannah.'

'*If* Hannah arrived here,' Steven interrupted hopefully.

'It just doesn't feel like a lot to go on.'

'To me it does.'

Mark pushed his palms against the mantel and leaned there, enjoying the warmth of the fire. Garec pushed his way into the room, brandishing dinner: five large trout, each neatly skewered through the gills. 'Fish, anyone?'

Steven grinned. 'Fry 'em up, Garec!'

'I'll get Brynne,' Mark said. As he made his way through to the bedroom, he thought about Steven's desire to study the staff's power and use its magic to help the Eldarni people win back their freedom. He obviously had no intention of going back to Idaho Springs before the evil controlling Nerak was banished into the Fold.

Stopping before the door to their bedroom, Mark's thoughts moved to Brynne. Could he leave her here alone with an unholy fight looming before her? No, of course not. She could return to Colorado with him – they all could. But now *he* sounded like the coward, a sensible coward, but a coward just the same. Despite his friend's confidence, Mark believed Nerak would kill them all.

Steeling himself against the wellspring of emotion he felt

whenever he saw Brynne, Mark entered the room quietly, hoping not to disturb her right away. They would remain in Eldarn until this business was finished.

Garec pulled hard until the resistant plug popped from the bottle with a satisfying report. 'Whoever this trapper is, he has great taste in wine,' he said as he poured for each of the friends, topping his own glass to the brim before handing the unfinished portion to Lahp, who proceeded to drink directly from the flask. The bottle looked like a toy in the Seron's hand and Garec laughed as Lahp finished the contents in one enormous swallow.

'Remind me not to get into a drinking contest with you,' he said, crossing to the fireplace to removing his trout fillets. 'Sorry it's fish again tonight,' he told the company, 'but tomorrow I'll see if I can't get a deer or something.'

'This is fine, Garec,' Brynne replied. She looked much better for having slept most of the day. 'Without you we'd be reduced to roots and berries.'

'She's right,' Mark agreed, sipping noisily. 'You missed my archery display at Seer's Peak: thirty-two shots and not one fish.'

They all laughed at Mark's admission except for Brynne, who continued to watch the front window anxiously. She was cross that she'd slept the day away and promised herself that dawn would find her scouting the riverbank to find some sign that Sallax was all right.

Mark gripped her hand beneath the table. 'I'll come with you tomorrow,' he whispered.

At that moment she loved him, for knowing what she had been thinking, and for saying what she needed him to say.

Garec finished the last of his dinner, examined the bottom of his wooden trencher and chucked it into the fire. 'These bowls are too old,' he observed. 'We'll have sores in our mouths if we keep eating from these.' He watched as the wood burst into flames. Rising from his seat, he crossed the room to retrieve the worn canvas pack. 'I think Gilmour had a few fresh trenchers in here,' he said, unfastening twin leather straps.

No one spoke as Garec started absentmindedly pulling out items, placing things on the wooden table like exhibits at a trial: a hat, one glove, a pair of wool socks, some tobacco in a leather pouch, a small book written in Pragan. Then Garec's hand came to rest on a carved wooden pipe and he stopped short, appalled.

'Sorry,' he whispered, almost crying, 'I'm really sorry.' He began returning the old man's possessions to the bag. Brynne crossed and took him in her arms.

'It's all right, Garec,' she said. 'You're doing the right thing. There's no sense in you carrying two packs. Combine what you need in your bag and leave the rest here.'

Garec hesitated, as if waiting for something to happen. His forehead began perspiring and he released the pipe, now moist from his grip, to fall into the bottom of the satchel.

'Garec,' Steven said, 'his memory doesn't live in those things.'

Garec nodded, without looking at anyone, and, unable to reopen the pack, handed it to Steven. The young bowman picked up his quivers and started mending fletching.

Steven looked quickly at Brynne before reopening Gilmour's bag. Garec was right. The old sorcerer did have three fresh trenchers, and Steven stacked them neatly in the centre of the table. Not knowing whether to continue, Steven reached gingerly back into the pack and withdrew three pipes, two more packs of tobacco, a short knife, some lengths of twine, several articles of clothing and a small bar of clean-smelling soap. Mark grabbed one of the trenchers and began turning it over in his hands, ostensibly inspecting the wood for worms, termites or rot. The vestiges of Gilmour's life looked like a pile of junk: his socks had holes in them, his knife was bent and its leather sheath was torn and useless. These were not the final possessions of a powerful educator and magician; they were more like second-hand items distributed at the reading of a homeless person's will. Mark drank deeply from his goblet and hoped the unnerving ritual would end soon.

Steven broke the silence. 'That's it.' He fumbled about inside the pack for another moment before adding, 'Except for these.' He tossed a book of matches to his roommate. Mark caught it in one hand, flipped it over and read the advertisement printed on the back: *Owen's Pub, Miner Street, Idaho Springs*. 'And this,' Steven removed several pages of old parchment, folded over and ragged along the edges. He placed it on the table near the trenchers and dropped Gilmour's empty pack to the floor.

'Sonofabitch!' Mark exclaimed and Brynne looked at him

curiously. 'My paper and my matches, that old dog. He must have picked these up that night we went swimming in the river.'

'*Machess?*' Brynne asked, fumbling with the foreign word.

'Matches.' Mark tore one from the book and struck it into flame. Both Brynne and Garec gasped when the small torch ignited and Garec reached over to test the flame with a fingertip, as if somehow it might be an illusion. 'It's magic,' he said in awe.

'Nonsense,' Mark replied. 'It's chemistry, exceedingly simple chemistry.' He handed the burning match to Brynne who watched as the flame crept closer and closer to her fingertips before burning out on its own. 'I'm surprised the Larion Senate didn't bring these back from one of their trips.' He considered this a moment, then said, 'Actually, they probably did. I bet they just ran out of them, or didn't write down the formula to make more . . . who knows? Maybe some smoker there at Sandcliff used them up.' No one laughed; so, Mark proceeded to unfold the parchment. 'Damn, but I could have used this up there.' He gestured towards the southeast and the Blackstone peaks.

'Where did you find it?' Garec asked, examining the burned match stump.

'At Riverend, in the room where Steven and I were tied up. These pages were hidden behind one of the stones above the fireplace mantel.'

'What's written on them?' Brynne leaned over to look.

'It's probably an ad for a Gore-tex parka and some snowshoes,' Steven teased.

'No,' she went on, 'it looks like a letter, a note to someone.'

'Who wrote it?' Garec asked, only half listening as he worked on his arrows.

Mark handed Brynne the pages and she flipped through them quickly in search of a signature. She froze when she reached the final sheet. 'Garec?'

'What?' he mumbled without looking up from his fletching.

'It's from Tenner Wynne.'

Garec returned the arrows to his quiver and reached for a wine goblet. 'Tenner Wynne? *The* Tenner Wynne?'

'Mark found these in a third-storey chamber at Riverend. How many Tenner Wynnes lived there before the fire?' She continued scanning through the parchment for additional evidence that the letter she held was authentic.

'Who's Tenner Wynne when he's at home then?' Steven asked, nibbling on what he guessed was a dried apricot.

'*Was*,' Brynne corrected, 'Tenner was a prince of Falkan, a descendant of King Remond.'

Garec said, 'But he abdicated the Falkan throne to his sister—' He groped for her name.

'Anaria,' Brynne supplied. 'Princess Anaria. She was a Barstag by marriage.'

'Right,' Garec said, adding sheepishly, 'Brynne paid attention in school better than I did.'

'Too bad you missed me on the Stamp Act,' Mark told him, 'you'd have been sound asleep before the end of first period.' Garec grinned and raised his goblet. Mark responded in kind and said, 'To the Stamp Act.'

'The Stamp Act, whatever that might be.' He emptied his glass and reached for another bottle. Lahp, who had been listening in silence, shrugged before crossing the room to stoke the fire again.

Steven refocused the conversation. 'So Tenner was at Riverend the night of the fire?'

'He lived there,' Brynne explained. 'He was a famous doctor, probably the most famous healer in Eldarn, but he was known throughout the world as Prince Markon's best friend and closest advisor.'

Uncorking the new bottle, Garec said, 'Tenner organised the medical programme at the university in Estrad and students came from all over to study.' He poured for everyone and gestured to Lahp, who shook his massive head and began rolling out blankets on the floor. 'He was a great leader, but he's remembered more as an advisor and protector of the king.'

'King?' Mark was confused. 'I thought Remond was already dead.'

'He was,' Brynne continued, 'but Remond ruled Eldarn from Rona, from Riverend actually, right there in the forbidden forest. Prince Markon was the eldest son of Waslow Grayslip and rightful heir to Eldarn's throne.'

Garec chimed in again, 'He actually died while hosting his cousins, the royal families of Falkan, Malakasia and Praga. They were all at Riverend when the virus killed Markon and several guests. I think it was Anaria, the Falkan princess, Tenner's sister, who killed herself when her son died, and Prince Draven of Malakasia died of the same virus in the next Twinmoon.'

'The virus we now suspect was Nerak?' Steven queried.

'In one Twinmoon the descendants of King Remond and the ruling families of Eldarn were toppled.' Brynne leaned towards Mark; he wrapped an arm around her waist.

'But not Marek,' Steven said hoping he was beginning to get the family genealogy organised in his mind.

'Correct,' Garec confirmed. 'Marek Whitward was the first Malakasian dictator to rule Eldarn from Welstar Palace.'

'But his legitimacy was questioned.' Steven remembered their conversation atop Seer's Peak.

'Right again,' Brynne said. 'Marek was believed to be the bastard child of Princess Mernam and a member of Prince Draven's court.'

'So any Malakasian claim to the Eldarni throne is illegitimate,' Mark said thoughtfully.

'Some believe so.' Garec sipped from his goblet. 'Although it's been nine hundred and eighty Twinmoons and no one really thinks about it any longer.'

'Sallax does,' Brynne said quietly.

Mark continued trying to understand. 'Tenner gave up the Falkan throne to be in Rona. He built a career there as a doctor, but he was really there to protect King Markon?'

'Not King Markon,' Garec corrected. 'Markon never wanted to be a king. He wanted the five lands to unite, to share resources in education, commerce and medicine. He was happy to rule Rona, but he wanted to see Eldarn reunited under the collective governance of King Remond's descendants.'

'Parliamentary government,' Mark reflected. 'Good for him.'

'But he was killed before it could be established,' Brynne snuggled in close to Mark, who tightened his grip around her slim form. 'Tenner was one of the most powerful people in Eldarn at the time. If he hid these pages in the fireplace, they must mean something.'

'Brynne, read it out, will you?' Steven asked. He leaned forward, resting his elbows on the table, as Brynne looked over the brittle pages.

To whomever finds these notes:

I will not stand on ceremony; there is no time. If these documents are discovered after my death, they should be considered my last testament. Their contents do not supercede or nullify anything I have written in an official context or in my personal papers. Those can be found in the Falkan archives at my family home in Orindale. These notes are my last testament, because they contain information critical to the continuation of the Ronan and Falkan family lines. The royal houses of Rona and Praga lie in ruins. With my sweet sister's death, I alone am left to carry on the Falkan line and to date I do not have a living heir. Word has reached us here in Estrad that the Larion Senate has been destroyed and only the Larion Senator Kantu remains, but his whereabouts are unknown. He no doubt waits, gathering information to combat this virus that hunts us all down. But in my capacity as Professor of Medicine, I state here that the deaths of Prince Markon and Princess Anis were not caused by a virus. There is no virus that is so selective as to limit its impact to members of one family. Their deaths are the direct result of something sinister, something evil, something that seeks to supplant Eldarn's leadership with terror, chaos and fear.

Thus far, it has proven effective. Over the last Twinmoon, the arable lands of my beloved Falkan have been razed and farmers murdered, unfairly suspected of growing the grain or harvesting the fruit that killed Prince Markon or that drove Princess Anis to murder. I say now, though it is too late for them, that they are not the guilty parties. There have been riots at the markets. Flocks of sheep and herds of cattle have been slaughtered and left to rot in the Ronan sun and the harbours at Southport, Estrad, Strandson and Orindale have become battle zones as ships carrying wine, fleeces and foodstuffs have been summarily boarded and sunk, or burned to the waterline by terrified citizens.

Princess Danae waits quietly in her chambers to die. She will never rule this country now. Prince Danmark remains confined to his chambers, a mad shadow of his former self. He too will never recover from his encounter with this virus. The Ronan people have demanded an audience with their new ruler and I do not know how much longer I will be able to convince them that he is alive and well, but remains in private, mourning for his father. My ruse will certainly not last through the next Twinmoon.

By the gods of the Northern Forest, I am tired.

Princess Detria struggles to maintain order in Praga, but her people know she and Ravena are too old to produce new heirs. Anis was Ravena's last child, and Ravena, in her grief, confines herself to her country home. Detria is strong, but she is old and I worry that the uncertain future of Praga will kill her if the virus does not.

I must return to Falkan to salvage what is left of my sister's court and bring peace to my people, but I will not leave until I have assured the future of the Ronan line. It is of this I need now to write. Regona Carvic, a servant of no noble birth, has lain with Prince Danmark for this last Moon in an effort to produce an heir to the Eldarni throne. It has been an ugly business and I know I will one day be held accountable for my actions over these past days. Regona ranks among the most strong-willed and loyal people I have ever known; it is my misfortune that our acquaintance came so late.

At long last, this very evening, I am confident she carries a child and I have asked my valet to escort her north, where she will give birth in hiding as an adopted family member to the merchant Weslox Thurvan of Randel. When the current turmoil surrounding the royal family subsides, I will return to Estrad and stand by the child as he or she assumes leadership of the Ronan court and the Ronan people.

I have given my support and duty to the Ronan prince for my entire adult life because he was the rightful King of Eldarn. His vision to see Eldarn reunited in a representative government shall not die while I live.

Finally, I recognise that I too am a target for the virus that has killed my friends and relatives. If it has sought to kill the heirs of Eldarn, as I believe, I am certainly at risk and might be taken at any moment. Therefore, in the wake of Markon's death last Twinmoon, I took Etrina Lippman of Capehill to wife. Although we have done this in secret, it is a lawful union. She is a Falkan noblewoman of good family and I can think of no one better able to carry on our work to bring peace and prosperity to Eldarn. She does not love me, but these times demand sacrifice, and her bravery and commitment are a model for us all. One day we may have the luxury of time and love may follow, but for now we are content that Etrina and I have succeeded in conceiving an heir to the Falkan throne. Should I perish, a victim of this demon plague, Etrina will go immediately into hiding and ensure our child will grow up safely, that he or she may eventually take on the mantle of rulership of my beloved Falkan.

I wait now only to hear of Regona's safe arrival in Randel. A court doctor has been ordered to force-feed Danae while I am away, and I will pray daily that she comes through her grief to find something for which to live before I return.

I have put these things in motion. My own efforts, and those of my two brave, patriotic, loyal women, Regona Carvic and Etrina Lippman, may be the only way to ensure Eldarn's future. Prince Draven survives in Malakasia and young Marek stands to inherit the throne should his father pass on as well. Marek is a good-hearted, well-read young man. I have sent word for Draven and Marek to meet me in Orindale next Twinmoon. Perhaps, together with Detria and Kantu, we can rebuild what has so quickly fallen into ruin.

May Prince Markon's vision for Eldarn become reality.

In my own hand, by me,

Tenner Wynne of Orindale, Prince of Falkan

For several moments, no one spoke; only the crackling fire and Lahp's resonant breathing could be heard. Then Brynne paged back through the document, in case she'd missed something. Finding nothing new, she carefully folded the pages and passed them across the table to Steven. 'We need to keep that,' she said, embarrassed she had broken the silence with something obvious.

Placing the parchment in his inside jacket pocket, Steven asked, 'Did Tenner die before he knew about Marek?'

'He did,' Garec replied. 'Riverend Palace burned before Draven died so Nerak must have gone from Estrad to Malakasia.'

Mark asked, 'Did Tenner ever meet those people? Kantu, Marek and the rest? He wrote about inviting them to a meeting the following Twinmoon. Did it ever happen?'

'No,' Brynne said, 'I don't believe so.'

'Why?' Steven asked. 'Maybe if we can find Kantu, he'll have some news from their meeting that might be helpful. If he was there, maybe he knows something Gilmour doesn't.' Mark shot him a withering look.

'Sorry,' Steven amended, flushing, '*did* not.' He looked apologetically about the table, but no one appeared upset with him for mis-speaking.

'I don't believe they ever met, because we know some of what happened in the wake of Prince Markon's death.' Brynne laughed wryly. 'Sallax knew a lot about it, which meant I had to learn a lot about it. Anyway, there was a flurry of political posturing and activity throughout the Eastlands and Praga, as anyone with forged papers and decent clothing had a go at claiming the thrones of Rona and Falkan. I remember Gilmour telling us there was even one family that claimed to be rightful heirs to Gorsk – that was the land ruled by the Larion Senate for thousands of Twinmoons.'

When Steven and Mark didn't respond, Garec laughed through his nose. 'It was funnier when Gilmour told it, but no matter.'

Brynne thumbed her teeth at him and continued, 'Detria Sommerson and Ravena Ferlasa worked furiously to draft a policy ensuring Praga would be governed by a Grayslip family member, even if it meant some obscure second cousin of questionable pedigree.'

'A bastard,' Garec said.

Brynne nodded. 'Princess Danae died in the fire with her son, and not long afterwards a Ronan admiral established a temporary government enforced by a military council.'

'A dictatorship,' Mark said.

'Exactly,' Brynne went on, 'and several wealthy merchants battled in what was left of the court system – and in the streets of Orindale – as they sought to claim the Falkan throne. Without Tenner or Anaria to bring any leadership to the Falkan people, anyone with money could hire a band of thugs, call it a peace-keeping force and use brutality and terror to quiet the masses and hold areas of the country hostage.'

Steven anticipated the next event in Brynne's tale. 'And then Prince Marek arrived.'

'Like a plague over the land,' Garec murmured, 'his armies

came down from Malakasia, killing every false king, insurrection-
ist, partisan, military leader – in fact, just about anyone who even
dreamed of his or her own gain.'

'So he was seen as a hero,' Mark surmised.

As Brynne leaned up against him, he shifted in his chair and
brought his knee to rest against hers beneath the table. He felt
like he was sixteen all over again. Brynne hid a smile and went
on with her lecture. 'At first, yes, but it wasn't long before
everyone in Eldarn knew Prince Marek had changed. He set up
military outposts throughout the Eastlands, choked trade along
the Ravenian Sea, closed universities in Rona, Praga and Falkan
and forbade unauthorised travel in or out of Gorsk.'

Garec ran one finger around the rim of his glass. 'That was the
beginning of the dark period – and we're still living in it now.'

'What I don't understand is why the heirs never surfaced.'
Steven pulled pieces of lint from his sleeve. 'Regona Carvie or
the woman from Capehill, what was her name?'

'Etrina Lippman.'

'Etrina.' He hesitated a moment, pulling his thoughts together.
'Why would they never come forth with a legitimate claim? Sure,
Danmark's child would be a bastard, but he was in no shape to
marry anyone anyway, was he? And Tenner wrote that he
married Etrina. I'm surprised *she* never emerged.'

Mark responded, 'He also wrote that Etrina knew what to do
and where to hide. Maybe she never came forward because she
knew she wouldn't have a hope in hell against Marek.'

'So the child may never have known he or she was rightful
heir to the throne.'

'Exactly. Oh my rutting gods of the Northern Forest!' Garec
leaped to his feet. 'My dream! I *saw* it! That was Regona and
Danmark! How can I have been so stupid? Demonpiss, but I'm
blind!'

He recounted the dream he'd had on Seer's Peak. Now,
remembering the girl – Regona Carvic – cold and frightened in
the moments before one of her encounters with Danmark, it all
made sense. *That* was what Lessek wanted him to know. He
sighed, suddenly deflated. 'But their efforts to impregnate these
women were for nothing.'

Steven agreed. 'What good is an heir if she or he never
emerges to rally the people in revolution?'

'Any enthusiastic leader can organise a revolution, Steven,' Brynne said. 'I bet the heirs remained hidden to protect their bloodlines. Perhaps that was Tenner's directive: wait for a revolutionary force to assemble; *then* reclaim the throne.'

Garec said, 'Or they remained hidden when Tenner never came looking for them. He wrote that he planned to come back and stand beside the Ronan heir. He probably told Regona to remain hidden in Randel until he returned. He died and she melted into the background to save the child.'

'And herself,' Brynne agreed. 'Etrina probably did the same thing.'

Steven said, still curious, 'I wonder if they ever told the children?'

'Why would they?' Mark said. 'The kids would have been crushed by Nerak. Why put notions in their minds that would get them killed for no reason?'

'But a generation later, no one knows the heirs are alive.'

'They do now,' Garec said. 'And Lessek knew, because he showed me.'

'So the fate of the world rests in the serendipitous discovery of a few wrinkled sheets of parchment?'

Brynne smiled. 'It sounds almost as silly as betting the future of all humankind on the propensity of a bank manager to grow curious and steal a tapestry and an innocent-looking rock.'

Steven feigned offence. '*Assistant* manager – you overestimate my skills – and I did *not* steal them.'

Mark rose and started towards the trapper's pantry. 'Anyone want more of this dried fruit? I like these orange ones particularly. What are they, Garec?'

'Tempine.'

'Tempine. Those are my favourites.' Mark reached for the pantry door when suddenly he collapsed to his knees with a startled cry. Clamping his hands over his ears, he shouted, 'Damnit, Gabriel, not so loud!'

The others sprang to their feet, toppling chairs and spilling wine.

'What it is?' Garec had instinctively reached for his bow. 'Mark, are you okay?'

Across the room, Lahp was awake and already crouched low to the ground, his weapons drawn. 'Sten talk Lahp!' he asked.

'I don't know yet, Lahp,' Steven said calmly, keeping his eyes fixed on Mark. His face was damp with sweat and his eyes wide. 'Mark,' Steven said, 'you have to tell us what's going on. What do you need?'

'Wraiths,' Mark whispered, and turned to Brynne. 'Hundreds of them, like Gabriel O'Reilly, only they're not on our side.' He hugged Brynne close. 'They're *really* not on our side! They're hunting us. They've already killed the trapper.'

'Sallax?' Brynne asked, afraid to hear the answer, but scared not to know the truth.

Mark closed his eyes and turned his thoughts inward again for a few moments before saying, 'Gabriel doesn't know. He came directly here after finding the trapper's body out near the river. He saw them moving through the trees and along a ridge downstream from here.'

Mark's words struck a chord with Garec. 'I've seen that too.'

'Seen what?' Brynne asked, adjusting sundry weapons at her belt.

'On Seer's Peak.' Now Garec understood why Gilmour had forced him to go over and over the details of his vision that morning. He would never forget those images. 'Lessek sent me a dream. I thought it was the forbidden forest near Riverend, and I saw hundreds of wraiths moving between the trees. But maybe I was wrong. Maybe it wasn't Estrad.'

'That can't be a coincidence.' Steven held the hickory staff, unaware that he had retrieved it from the corner near the hallway. Maybe it really did just appear in his hands when he needed it – that would be a useful attribute, if it were true. So far he couldn't feel it giving him any direction; it felt more like *he* were calling up the magic, instead of simply acting as a conduit for its power. He remembered the lodge pine in the Blackstones, the tree he had so casually brought down with one swipe, and wondered if he would be able to summon the staff's power like that again.

'Tell us about it again, quickly,' he said to Garec. 'Maybe your vision will give us inspiration on how to fight the bloody things. Do you remember how you killed them?'

'I didn't.' Garec closed his eyes in an effort to recall more clearly, but try as he might, he couldn't rid his mind of the image of Gilmour's dead body, that of an old, old man, no Larion magic left in that paper-thin, brittle bag of skin. How could they win? How could they possibly have imagined they had any chance against Nerak? He wiped a hand across his forehead and opened his eyes to find everyone staring hopefully at him.

'I can't remember anything else,' he admitted. 'The land was dying. The Estrad River ran dry and the fields were parched and cracked—' *like the skin of a dead Larion sorcerer.* 'I saw wraiths moving through the forbidden forest. I think they were hunting for something – or some*one*.'

'So that's it then,' Mark said. 'It was a look into the future. They're here now and they're hunting *us*.'

Brynne interrupted suddenly, 'Mark, ask Gabriel if they have a weakness. Can we kill them? There must be *something* we can do.'

Again Mark turned his thoughts inward, but when he spoke to the group again, his words cast a pall over the tiny cabin. 'No. Only Steven and Garec can battle them. The rest of us will be killed at first contact.'

'How can *I* fight them?' Garec demanded in desperation. 'I have no magic.'

'I don't know, Garec,' Mark replied. 'Gabriel's gone into the forest.' He reached for Brynne's hand. 'He will be back to warn us before the wraith army arrives.'

Garec paced back and forth across the cabin floor, sweating freely, until he stripped off his quivers and pulled his wool tunic over his head, tossing it into the corner. 'I won't be needing this again,' he said, a note of finality in his voice. Standing before them in his thin cotton shirt, he looked vulnerable, already lost. Mark tried to say something to build the younger man's confidence, but nothing came to mind. Garec would fight to the best of his ability, and that meant firing arrows. Sallax had nicknamed him the Bringer of Death, but now, death was coming for him. It was time to atone.

'How ironic,' Garec announced, as if reading Mark's mind, 'I will fight my last battle against an enemy who can't be turned by the one weapon I bring to the field.' He thought again of Gilmour, and how much he had admired the Larion Senator, even before he knew his true history. Garec had aspired to do great things for Rona, but would not have time; the best he could hope for would be to die well, protecting his friends from the coming evil. He expected to be joining Gilmour in the next few avens.

Lahp, still crouching near his bedroll, watched Garec with great interest, before demanding, 'Sten talk Lahp.' He pounded a hairy fist against the plank floor to encourage Steven to respond.

'Lahp, I need you to stay here with Mark and Brynne.' Steven motioned towards the centre of the room. 'I need you to stay low and keep your head down until the fight is done.'

Lahp looked at Steven as if he had just asked him to build a suspension bridge over the Danube River. 'Lahp hep Sten.' He nodded vigorously. 'Lahp na floor.'

'You can't fight these wraiths, Lahp,' Steven tried to explain. He still had no real idea how much the Seron understood. 'They are ghosts. They can pass right through you, and kill you from the inside.'

'Malagon.'

'Yes, Malagon sent them. They are here for the same talisman you were sent to find.'

'Lessek's.'

'Yes, Lessek's Key. We don't have it.'

'Ha!' Lahp laughed, and Steven did too, surprised the Seron understood the concept of irony.

'But I do need you to be here on the floor, where I may be able to keep them from getting to you.'

'Na, na.' Lahp shook his head and smiled a toothy wet grin. 'Lahp hep Sten.'

'You will *die*, Lahp, if you fight these creatures on your own.'

The Seron warrior stood slowly, crossed the floor and slapped a fist against his breast. He didn't need to say anything. They all understood that Lahp was ready to die there, on that oak and pine plank battlefield.

'Lahp hep Sten.'

Steven nodded. He had no idea what he had done to earn the Seron's loyalty. He turned the staff over, feeling its wood warm against his palms, and looked up to find Mark gazing at him.

In English, his friend said, 'This is it. This will be the test of your compassion.'

Forcing a grin, Steven replied, 'Thanks for the vote of confidence.'

'Hey, I'm not joking! I've no bloody idea how you fight these things, with compassion or with swords . . .' His voice faltered as he felt their final minutes ticking by. 'Tell me you know what you're doing.'

'I don't.' Steven reached for the wine and took a long swallow, but his mouth still felt dry. Switching back to Ronan, he urged Mark and Brynne to move to the floor at his feet. 'If I can keep them off you, I will.'

'I know,' Mark said quietly.

Steven watched as Lahp drew an array of weapons from his pack: daggers, a battle-axe, a short sword and several hunting knives, all weapons that required their wielder to look each victim in the eye. Despite the Seron's confidence, Steven knew Lahp would fall quickly to the wraiths and he couldn't risk Mark or Brynne to save Lahp. The Seron had made his choice and Steven would honour it, however much he might wish to stop him.

If he lost his concentration they might all perish. It wasn't going to be easy, watching Lahp die, but he had to remain focused on the task at hand. How brave of the warrior to share this battle, because he would not allow him and Garec to fight alone.

Then an idea began forming in Steven's mind. Sharing. They had to share the fight. Could they share the magic? The power of the staff would dispatch Malagon's wraiths, of that, Steven was confident. But could the power be shared?

'They're coming,' Mark interrupted his thoughts. He crouched on the floor at Steven's feet. 'They're just outside the cabin on the hill, but moving this way.'

'No, wait; I need more time,' Steven protested. 'I think I've got it, but I just need more time.'

'We don't have any time.' Garec was pale and his face ran with sweat, but his hands were steady as he drew two arrows from each quiver and stabbed them into the wood floor for quicker access.

'Yes we do, Garec.' Steven had put the pieces together quickly; now he had to see if it would work. 'Turn around,' he ordered, 'quickly now.' Garec gave him a curious look, but turned his back. Steven concentrated his will into the staff. He felt Garec's fear and insecurity and called upon his own determination to help the bowman succeed in the coming fight. The staff flared to life and Steven felt its familiar heat burning through his fingers.

With one end of the shaft, Steven brushed the quivers Garec wore high on his back.

'Lords,' Garec exclaimed, 'what was that?'

Steven didn't answer, but as Garec turned back towards him, it was clear he understood.

'Yes,' Garec whispered. 'I can feel it.' He hesitated, then asked, 'Should you do the bow as well?'

'I don't know, but let's be safe, anyway.' As Steven brushed the staff along the rosewood longbow the younger man's countenance slowly changed from despair to determination.

The Bringer of Death. Garec's eyes narrowed and his jaw hardened. He began drawing arrows by the score and jamming them, fletching up, in between cracks in the plank floor: ten by the window, ten in the corner, ten near the fireplace. It was close quarters, almost too close, but with a short draw he could still send shafts out quickly and accurately.

'Let them come,' he said stabbing the last of his arrows into a wide wooden plank near the hallway. 'This is going to work. This is what Lessek wanted me to know. It isn't that *I* was atop Seer's Peak; it's that *we* were there together.'

'Yes,' Steven felt his confidence rise. 'Bring 'em on.' He was surprised that he was not more afraid. He had expected to find his limbs stiff with fear and his mind unable to focus, but he had channelled that fear, sublimated it into his determination to win, to fight with grace and speed, and to kill with compassion but without hesitation. He remembered sneaking out through the back window of Owen's Pub one night to avoid a fight with a drunk, a lifetime ago. Now he was up against an army of homicidal wraiths; any one might kill him with a touch, but he was not afraid.

'I will see you again, Nerak,' he whispered. 'If you harm Hannah, Mark, Brynne, Garec or Lahp, I will make sure you pay, a thousand times over.' He caught the young bowman's eye and said more loudly, 'Good luck.'

'To you, too,' Garec replied.

Then the wraiths were upon them.

THE WRAITHS

Eldarn's twin moons rose at nearly opposite poles, north to south, and the result was a calm sea with minimal tides. A light southwesterly wind blew the Malakasian schooner, the *Falkan Dancer* north along the Ronan coast; the sheets snapped taut with each intermittent gust that bounced out-of-phase off Pragan cliffs far to the west. In the dim light of the southern moon, Carpello Jax, the corpulent merchant with the bulbous mole on his face, argued with Karn and Rala about the fate of the two captives chained securely below. Carpello had no wish to arrive in Orindale without Prince Malagon's talisman and was endeavouring to convince the Seron to kill their prisoners before reaching port. He believed the dark prince would be more forgiving if the prisoners died trying to escape. Arriving with two living captives who simply refused to disclose the whereabouts of the key would make them all look weak, and the Falkan businessman had no wish to appear weak before his prince.

Karn and Rala disagreed. If Lahp and the rest of their platoon had failed to find the key, and had killed the remaining members of Gilmour's company, these two would be their only hope. The prisoners would be kept alive until Prince Malagon decided what to do with them.

'You have an excuse,' Carpello argued coldly. 'He already possesses your souls.' The puffy-faced ship owner held an ornate silk handkerchief beneath his nose and prayed for a stronger breeze to blow the rancid stench of the Seron out to sea. 'My soul is another story, and I do not intend to forfeit it to your master.'

'Na.' Rala was firm. 'Two live Orindale.'

Karn nodded in agreement.

'Then I suggest we step up our interrogation efforts, my

disgusting friends. We have plenty of time between here and Orindale to convince them to talk.'

Karn nodded again. He was in favour of that, at least.

While the question of their continued survival was being discussed above deck, Versen and Brexan discussed their own options. Brexan guessed they were in line for a brutal interrogation. 'They can't go back to Malakasia empty-handed,' she said. 'And I'm quite sure that if your friends managed to escape from that horsecock Lahp, we've a tough time ahead of us.' They had no idea that a half aven after they had been escorted from the base of Seer's Peak, a grettan herd had torn through Lahp's platoon, scattering or killing the last of that group in a maelstrom of deadly claws and teeth.

Versen sighed. 'I'm afraid you're right. Apart from using an almor to stop us escaping, our treatment has been pretty fair, really. We're still a long way from Orindale, but sooner or later they'll decide they're bored with our silence.'

They were chained by their wrists to support beams and sat across from one another, their lower legs touching in the middle of the narrow cabin. There was no natural light and the perpetual dark weighed heavily on them. Versen had never properly appreciated the power of another's touch; now he ached for more prolonged contact with the young woman seated so near and yet so far from him. Being able to feel each other's feet was the only comfort they had, and neither commented on it. Instead, it became an understanding between them: *do not pull back. This is about us, and we will get through this together. Now, we have touch.*

They sat for days. Sometimes Brexan cried, weeping almost silently into the sleeve of her tunic. When Versen heard her trying to choke back sobs, he racked his memory for off-colour jokes in an effort to raise her spirits. When the woodsman's hope waned, Brexan regaled him with only slightly embellished tales of her training. Together, they kept each other sane.

The only light in the cabin came when one of the three Seron appeared in the doorway to hand over bowls of the oat and herb mush and to empty their shared chamber pot. With that done, the door would close again almost immediately. In those few moments, Brexan and Versen would squint across at each other, each starving for a clear glimpse, each knowing it would be avens before they saw one another again. Versen's mind raced every time light flooded the room: was she getting thinner? Did she look sick? Was her face still swollen? As the door swung closed, Versen invariably reached the same conclusion: despite the dirt and grime, she was lovely, a sight to preserve his will to live and his determination to fight back. Her image was indelibly etched in his mind's eye.

Despite the extreme discomfort, it took several days for Versen to work out that he could reposition himself. He found the chains holding him fast to the ship's hull were just long enough to allow him to turn over onto his back. Squatting low against the wall, he stepped over the length of chain holding his left wrist in place. With that accomplished, he pivoted his weight around, crossed his arms and lay backwards on the deck with his feet pressed against the bulkhead.

When his head came in contact with Brexan's feet, she yelped, 'Rutters! What *is* that?' and lashed out, catching him a glancing blow on his temple.

'Stop it, Brexan,' he pleaded quietly, 'it's just me. I've managed to turn around.' He talked her through the same steps and when her head fell gently alongside his, he took a moment to bury his face in her hair. 'Glad you could join me,' he said, trying for glib but instead sounding almost boyish in his nervousness.

'Never mind that,' she interrupted urgently, 'just get over here.'

His heart thumped beneath his ribcage as he sidled awkwardly across the floor on his back and shoulders.

Their faces met in the darkness, and when he rested his cheek against hers, Versen realised it was the greatest comfort he had ever known. Later, drifting into unconsciousness, his head tilted away from Brexan's slightly, and the Malakasian soldier commanded, 'Get back here.' Her voice breaking, she added, 'Back here with me, please.'

Versen shifted his weight, propped his head up on her shoulder and allowed his face to fall back against hers. This time Brexan turned and kissed him gently on the lips. He breathed in her aroma and fell asleep nestled against her, dreaming they were walking together among the rolling hills outside Estrad Village.

The first wraiths materialised inside the cabin like the beginnings of a dream. Falling like cascading water through the roof, emerging between loose planks, the ghostly figures began to take shape before their eyes. The hickory staff felt alive in Steven's hands, charged with the fury of powerful magic. But would it have enough strength to defeat this army? He bit on his lower lip to steady his nerves. Beside him, Garec had an arrow drawn and trained, while Lahp was crouched low to the ground, weapons in both hands, and ready to spring into the morass of spectres at any moment.

Surprising himself, Steven said loudly, 'Leave now and you may return to Malakasia.' The facial features on several of the wraiths came slowly into focus and Steven knew they understood him. 'Fight, and I will send you all back into the Fold.'

Would he? He hoped so. It sounded like an appropriate threat, given the circumstances. Seeing them hesitate, he went on, 'I have already killed the almor. You do not frighten me.'

With that, the wraiths inside the cabin charged, moving as one towards Steven, their spectral mouths agape in a silent scream, like the echo of a suicidal cry from the edge of a cliff. Steven countered. He stepped forward, imagining Hannah trapped somewhere in the bowels of Welstar Palace, calling out to him in terror. 'Come and get me,' he challenged the wraiths, and slashed at the forward-most attacker. It had once been a woman. As the staff tore through the translucent head and shoulders, he saw a look of intense pain pass over the spirit's shadowy face. This *would* work, but he had to be quick if he was going to keep them off his friends.

Steven swung the staff about his head like a broadsword, scattering scores of spirits, tearing them asunder. As before, he felt time shift slightly, and no matter where the attack originated – the walls, the ceiling, even the floor beneath his feet – he found there was enough time to ready himself and to strike. Magic burst from the staff; he could smell it in the room, the ozone aftermath of a lightning strike.

Steven breathed the whole experience in like a life-giving drug. This was repayment for all the years he had let others make his decisions – because his will was weak, *Slash!* For all the opportunities he missed, because he would not speak up for himself, *Slash!* For the lifetime he had spent hiding in the shadows, *Slash!* Life was terrifying, but this was more terrifying.

Slash! Death was in the room with him, and he screamed in its face: *Slash!*

'More!' he finally cried at the top of his lungs, 'send me more. Send them faster, Nerak, you weak-willed fucker!' He danced on his toes, leaping forward and back, spinning to strike at the strange spirit soldiers above and behind him. One spectre emerged from the floor at his feet and he stomped it out with the staff as if he were punctuating a declaration with a hickory cane.

This was what his whole life had been leading up to, and Steven realised he would not trade one day of his twenty-eight years to be anywhere else, to be any*one* else.

Periodically, one of the ghostly creatures would make an audible sound as it was ripped apart, a low-pitched groan that Mark could feel in his abdomen; he wondered whether the foundations of the cabin were about to open and drop them all into a hellish Eldarni abyss. He clutched Brynne to his chest, not just for comfort, but to ensure she stayed down, where she could be protected.

Whenever he relaxed his grip, even slightly, Brynne tried to slash at the wraiths attacking from overhead, until one passed very close to her outstretched arm and Steven barely managed to bring the staff around in time to ward the spirit off. Brynne felt the wraith's energy bridge the narrow gap separating them and pulled her arm back to her side, shaking. She sheathed her hunting knife and cowered next to Mark. 'That was too close,' she whispered, still shuddering with fear. 'You win. I'll stay down.'

Holding Brynne's hands for both their comfort, Mark peered over at Garec. Despite his fear that they would be overwhelmed at any moment, Mark watched the bowman in wonder. Garec was a thing of beauty, a true killing machine. He used his arrows sparingly at first as the wraiths focused their fury on Steven, but as more and more of the spirit intruders attacked, he intensified his retaliation. Concentrating his fire on the wraiths as they entered the cabin, Garec's arrows, imbued with the power of Steven's staff, took out scores of ghostly assailants. Howling in surprise, shocked that traditional weaponry could affect them, the ghosts flew into a rage and pressed the bowman from all sides.

Seeing them come, Garec fired twice with blinding speed then dived to the right, rolling against the wall and springing to his feet, swinging the bow like a club at his remaining attackers. He screamed thanks to Steven and the gods of the Northern Forest when he discovered he could use the bow like the determined foreigner was wielding the hickory staff, and three more wraiths fell beneath his deadly swipes.

One slow-moving spirit passed by and Garec hesitated an instant before striking it down. It looked like a man, a normal man, someone who might work for a merchant, or maybe a farmer. If Gabriel O'Reilly was right, each warrior ghost was once an Eldarni citizen, just an ordinary person who had fallen foul of Nerak, an average soul unlucky enough to join the fraternity devoured by the dark prince throughout the Twinmoons. They attacked now only because Nerak had sent them to retrieve Lessek's Key, to kill the remaining members of their company and to ensure the eventual downfall of the world.

Garec wondered how Gabriel had managed to get free of Nerak's grasp; he wished the wraith were with him now, inside *his* head as he sometimes was with Mark, to comfort him and encourage him as he dispatched these souls into the Fold.

Moving into the front corner of the room, Garec found he could protect his flank with the bow itself while firing arrows into the far corners. Twenty, thirty, forty arrows tore wraiths to gossamer shreds before they embedded themselves in the walls, and still Garec continued firing. He grinned broadly as one shaft dispatched three spirits before crashing through the hall window with a fourth in tow. *The Bringer of Death*: even to the dead, and Garec tumbled gracefully to his left, swinging the bow as he rolled to another stand of arrows.

Then it happened. Garec watched as Steven stumbled, in slow motion, his toe catching the edge of a loose floorboard. He pitched over, cursing and striking out with the staff until he managed to steady himself against the dining table – but that momentary lapse in his defences left Mark and Brynne vulnerable. Two wraiths quickly entered their bodies.

Brynne collapsed immediately, her slight frame lying deathly still on the floor a few paces away. Mark rose to his feet, raised his hands to the heavens and emitted an inhuman cry of pain and suffering.

Garec hesitated a moment, uncertain what to do. He swallowed hard, realised how thirsty he was and promised himself he would make a valiant effort to drink the river dry if he survived this hellish night. Two arrows stood, fletching up, in a wooden plank beside him. Holding his breath, he nocked one, drew and fired directly at Mark's chest. Before the shaft found its target, Garec had nocked and fired the second into Brynne's ribcage. Watching the arrows pierce his friends' bodies, Garec felt the sting, the impossibly painful burn of flint tips and wooden shafts ripping through flesh. *The Bringer of Death.* He screamed in response to Mark's cry, struck out with the bow at an attacking spirit and prayed his dangerous play had paid off.

He expected to see the wraiths burst from Mark and Brynne, like souls ascending to the Northern Forest, but nothing appeared to happen. Mark collapsed to the floor near Brynne and neither moved again. 'Rutting dogs,' Garec cursed and leaped to another stand of arrows, hoping to fire these as quickly as possible. He needed to create enough breathing space to cross the room into the circle of Steven's protection and see to his friends. Could he save them? He had no idea what to do now; he might even have killed them himself.

Garec tried not to think about that possibility and instead launched himself back against the spirit offensive with renewed hatred. Two wraiths emerged near the fireplace and Garec pinned both to the pantry door. It was only when he peered beneath their disintegrating, indistinct forms that he noticed two more arrows buried in the woodwork, arrows he didn't recall firing.

It *must* have worked: those were the shafts; they had passed right through his friends. It *had* to be magic; he had not drawn the bowstring back far enough to fully penetrate a body, let alone drive the shafts into the hard wooden walls. It *had* to have worked.

On and on the wraiths came, and the battle raged unchanging. To Steven it felt like it was half the night, but he neither slowed nor weakened, despite the near-constant actions of spinning and striking out with the staff.

Garec felt as though his arms would fall off, but still he continued to fight until his last arrow was spent. Then he backed towards Mark and Brynne, protecting them from attack along the hallway with the still-potent longbow. Standing back to back, he and Steven warded off wave after wave of ghostly assailants.

Then it ended.

The interior of the cabin bristled with arrows, each firmly embedded into the woodwork, as if the walls themselves had been the attackers. Garec dropped to his knees, rolled Brynne onto her back and began weeping when he saw she was still alive. Tearing open her tunic, he found no entry or exit wounds; he checked Mark's chest to be certain. He had not killed them.

Realising, for almost the first time, that he had gambled with his friends' lives, the Bringer of Death pitched onto his side, felt the cool floorboards against his face and sobbed aloud, unconcerned if anyone heard him break down.

Steven was not ready for the fight to end. A wild and untamed look danced in his eyes as he continued to curse Nerak. With the staff's magic still coursing through his body, he whirled about, looking for more enemies, needing someone or something to attack, thirsting for another kill, when he finally saw Lahp. The Seron lay in a heap near the front wall. His enormous hands still gripped his daggers, but Steven could see the big soldier was dead.

Not even noticing his friends, he strode to the front door, kicked it open and walked out into the cold mountain night. Darkness had fallen, but Steven found he could see where he was going. His senses were alive, acute, as he made his way through the underbrush towards the river. Reaching the banks, Steven waded in, the glacial cold unfelt as the power of the staff fortified muscle and bone with the strength of a brigade of warriors. His limp was gone, his leg healed, the bones knitted together as if they had never been broken.

'Nerak!' he screamed into the night, 'I will not hide from you, Nerak, and you will pay for Gilmour. You will pay for Lahp, and even your evil master will not be able to save you if Hannah dies!'

Steven raised the staff above his head and drove it deep into the riverbed. A wall of water leaped up before him and careened through the valley, uprooting trees and wrenching boulders from their resting places along the riverbank. He waited until it disappeared from sight then listened as it roared its way between the foothills and off into the canyon beyond. He tossed the staff to the riverbank, then leaned back until the water flowed over his head and chest.

Steven remained submerged until his lungs burned with the need for air. Pushing his wet hair back from his face and gazing down the valley towards Orindale, he knew they had won a great victory.

'Now, Hannah, I am coming for you,' he announced loudly. Eldarn's twin moons flanked either end of the valley: just over halfway to the next Twinmoon. 'Thirty days? Have we only been here thirty days?' he asked the valley as he clambered back up the bank, retrieved the hickory staff and strode back towards the cabin.

Versen squinted against the bright sunlight as Karn led them to the raised quarterdeck in the *Falkan Dancer*'s stern. The vessel moved briskly north and Versen welcomed the stiff breeze after the stale, humid air of their cell. As he breathed deeply to clear his lungs, he tried to calculate how long they had been at sea.

When his eyes adjusted he could just make out the coast in the distance, an indistinct, blurry mass that looked as though it had been sketched along the horizon. He was heartened to see land at all and for a few brief moments scanned the decks in hopes of discovering some means by which to take the ship – or at least gain control of the helm long enough to run them all aground. A cursory look was enough to dash his hopes: a tally of the crew of hardened seamen, not to mention the Seron, made it quite clear they didn't stand a chance on their own. He sighed, and quietly braced himself for whatever was going to happen next.

Karn replaced their chain manacles with heavy twine, fixed a short length of rope to the bonds, then dragged the prisoners aft. Brexan, legs cramped and aching from her tenure in the hold, tripped a number of times, which brought jeers from the crew, who hurled insults at the soldier-turned-traitor. Brexan regained her feet and sneered down her nose at the sailors with unbridled contempt. Her eyes narrowed as she wished she were armed with more than just scorn. She would have enjoyed nothing more than to summarily gut one or two of the smug-looking seamen disparaging her from the safety of the rigging.

Carpello Jax was leaning against the stern rail, uncomfortable despite the near-perfect weather. Versen decided the ship's owner could not be accustomed to long sea voyages; it was probably only his fear of Malagon's wrath that had motivated him to accompany his crew of mercenaries on this journey. At his side Rala picked absentmindedly at a discoloured fingernail and

Haden spat a mouthful of phlegm towards a scupper. The big Ronan grinned to himself as he told the nauseous merchant, 'I'll have mussel soup, mussels drenched in white wine and aromatic with savory, a venison stew thickened with a good Falkan red, with gobbets of meat spitting fat and juices, layered potatoes in double cream and cheese, and a goblet of the same— no, actually, come to think of it, I'll wash it down with beer, a bitter golden beer heady with the finest hops in Rona and with smooth, succulent barley from the lowlands—'

The thought of all that rich food turned Carpello's already unsettled stomach and Versen couldn't help his grin as the merchant retched over the gunwale, then wiped his mouth on the silk kerchief. He glared at his prisoner as he spat, 'Scum – but I am pleased to see you have not lost your sense of humour.' He gestured at the scarred Seron. 'It will bring me that much more pleasure to watch him beat it out of you.'

Versen glared back at him, all trace of humour now gone. 'How can you ally yourself with these Seron? With Malagon? Does the idea of freedom mean so little that you would allow Malagon's pets to order you around?'

The merchant came forward slowly and lashed out, slapping Versen hard across the face. 'You'll watch your mouth on my ship, traitor!' he screamed, spitting into Versen's face. 'I take orders from no one but my prince – *your* prince, you rutting son of a whore.'

Versen didn't react; his gaze was locked on Carpello's right hand.

Calmly he asked, 'That scar on your hand, have you had it long?'

Carpello Jax flexed his hand. 'Believe me, scumbag, I have had it my whole life and it will not hold me back when it comes to meting out just punishment.'

'And the mole, that mole alongside your cavernous nose? Have you had that long as well?'

With a malevolent smile, Carpello turned to Brexan, ignoring Versen's attempts to bait him. 'I must ask you some questions, my lovely.' Versen imagined he could smell days-old garlic on the man's breath. 'Depending on how you respond will determine whether the scum lives.' The merchant was clearly enjoying himself despite his discomfort. 'Since you seem so little inclined to share what you know, I doubt your woodsman will see another day. I can assure you that our little chat will not prolong your life through the end of this – I would say, under other circumstances – glorious morning.'

'A very good friend of mine looks forward to meeting you,' Versen chuckled. 'If I were you, I would take my own life rather than ever run into her again.'

'A woman? I shall be enchanted, I'm sure.'

'You'll be dead,' Versen said flatly. 'And she will make it last for Twinmoons. You will be amazed at how much pain you can feel before you lose consciousness.'

Brexan was confused by the interchange, but said nothing.

'Are you trying to frighten me, woodsman? I am not the one standing here in bonds and about to have a most unpleasant day.'

'No,' Versen replied, 'not frighten you. I just wanted to make quite sure you understand that a grisly death is on its way to Orindale right now. You should run far, run fast – maybe sail on to Gorsk and hide out in the mountains. It might take her a little longer to find you that way.'

'Well, I appreciate your concern,' the merchant said as he dismissed the warning with a wave of his oddly scarred hand, 'but I feel my own needs are the greater.'

While the two men spoke, the Seron had moved behind the prisoners; now, without warning, Haden picked up the merchant's cane and struck Versen across the back of his legs. The woodsman roared and fell to his knees. Karn wrapped his arms tightly about Brexan's torso, pinning her hands down; although she kicked and screamed curses, Karn was unmoved. She froze as Rala and Haden hefted Versen towards the stern rail and dumped him overboard. Slowly, as if he had all morning, the scarred warrior found the other end of the rope attached to the twine manacles – Versen's lifeline – and tied it to a stanchion. It pulled tight as the woodsman's body was dragged through the water behind the ship. Brexan wailed and kicked wildly at her captors. The crew cheered from the decks and up in the rigging: this was certainly better entertainment than a usual morning at sea afforded them.

Carpello watched, smiling, as Versen bobbed along in the schooner's wake, then turned to the young Malakasian. 'He does not have much time, my lovely, so I would encourage you to focus.' Brexan could see his crooked yellow teeth behind cracked and bleeding lips. 'Who has the key?'

'The what?' Brexan strained her eyes, trying to see Versen's head come above the surface of the water. There it was. He managed a breath just then; she was certain.

'Focus, my lovely,' the merchant repeated, grasping her face in his hands and forcing her to look directly at him. 'The stone. I am looking for the stone.'

Brexan's mind raced; there was no time. Versen would surely drown. She had to act swiftly if she were to save his life, and there would be only one chance for a rescue. Trusting her instincts, she cried·out, 'Yes, all right, I'll tell you.'

'That's grand, my lovely,' and then to Karn, 'Release her.'

As soon as the Seron relaxed his grip, Brexan reached back into his belt and drew his knife in a smooth gesture. She spun on her heels and brought the blade around in an arc that sliced across Carpello's stomach, opening his abdomen through his frilly silk tunic. The wound was superficial, but it was enough to make him scream in terror. Brexan would have lingered over that look for the rest of the morning aven, but there was no time. Instead, she continued her circle, next slicing through the muscles in Karn's thigh. Screaming, the Seron leader fell backwards onto the deck and the young woman saw her escape route open. Two steps to freedom. Already Rala and Haden were moving to intercept her. Using all her strength, the soldier took two running steps towards the stern rail and dived in. As she made her escape, she reached out with Karn's knife to slash the rope: one swipe, one chance from midair to sever the cord and free the woodsman.

Her heart sank as she fell headlong into the water. She had missed.

Brexan slammed awkwardly into the water and a stinging pain lanced across her neck and back. She ignored the discomfort, kicking swiftly towards the surface. She *had* to cut that line. She nearly cried out for joy when she saw the taut stretch of rope rushing by overhead, a second chance. Breaking the surface, she saw Versen's body coming up fast, not all that far from where she had emerged; she kicked hard two, three, then four times, desperate to reach the rope before he was dragged by. *Too slow!* She screamed inside her head: *Faster! Kick harder.* Swimming with her wrists bound together was nearly impossible. *Bring your hands up. Reach for the rope. Cut it. Cut it now.*

Brexan slashed at the thick hemp trailing Versen behind the *Falkan Dancer*, but the knife didn't cut through. She needed a chance to slice twice or perhaps three times in the same place, not simply to hack away at the rope as it hurtled past her at fifteen knots.

Choking back a cry, Brexan spat out a mouthful of seawater, took a deep breath and in a last-ditch effort, leaped onto Versen as he was dragged by.

The force of the schooner's progress nearly broke her grip, but she clung to his tunic belt. They were too heavy together and Versen sank beneath the waves, unable to surface, unable to get another breath. She inched her way up his body, careful not to drop the knife. Her limbs screamed with the effort and her lungs were bursting, but every time she thought she would have to give up, to let go, she remembered that Versen had been submerged far longer.

Then it was there, the knife against the rope. *Cut! Cut faster. Hold your breath. Cut!* Her eyes stung and her lungs burned for air. Gripping Versen's wrists with her fingertips, she worked the blade back and forth as quickly as she could, but it wasn't enough. She had to let go. She had to surface. She needed air. She had to leave him. Death first? No, she couldn't do it. Her will to live was too strong. She would leave him to die. Slashing one last time with the tip of the knife, Brexan let go. She released her grip and felt herself slow down almost immediately as the *Falkan Dancer* raced north.

The sea masked her tears . . .

Then Versen was there with her. It had worked – that last slice had severed the twine and Brexan, empowered by a surge of adrenalin, reached for him and hauled him to the surface.

Coughing and spitting, the Ronan patriot struggled to speak.

'Just relax,' Brexan ordered, her arms aching with the effort to keep him afloat. 'Relax and breathe. Just breathe.'

He coughed and managed, 'He—'

'Shut up, Ox. Tell me later.' Brexan heaved him as far as she could above the waterline but she got his head and shoulders clear for only a moment before Versen sank back to chin level. 'What could be so rutting important?'

Versen's body was wracked by a long, wet cough, then he managed to draw several deep breaths before shouting, 'That's the bastard whore's get who raped Brynne! That bleeding horsecock raped Brynne!'

'When? What are you talking about?'

'Seventy, maybe eighty Twinmoons ago, in Estrad.' Versen coughed again and rolled onto his back to allow Brexan to finish cutting the bonds holding his wrists. 'He raped her all night – she was young, just a kid. She's been giving that scar to every ass-grabbing drunk in Greentree Tavern ever since. She doesn't talk about it, but that's him. We have to find him again.'

They were lost at sea. The Ronan coast was at least an aven east under full sail. There was no way they were going to survive – and all Versen could think of was avenging one of his friends. She could have kissed him at that moment, but instead agreed, 'All right. We will. We'll find him again.'

Then Versen was suddenly lucid. Treading water awkwardly in his tunic and boots, his face turned the colour of parchment.

'The almor's in the water,' he said.

Carpello cursed. How was he going to tell Prince Malagon they had lost the prisoners? Please, by all the fustinating gods of the Northern Forest, let them reach Orindale first, before that black-hearted horsecock and his gargantuan floating palace. Carpello would pass the bad news on to someone else – an admiral, maybe, or one of the generals. They died at sea. It was simple. They committed suicide, jumped overboard to their deaths. That's what it was, after all, suicide: they had no hope of surviving, leaping into the ocean this far from shore. They were probably dead already.

'Come about, Captain Yarry!' he shouted urgently, 'come about! We need to find the bodies.'

Ignoring the blood running from his thigh, Karn grunted agreement.

'Sir?' the captain asked, 'come about, sir? On this tack, sir, and with this wind it will be a half-aven before we'll be back at the spot where they went in.' Captain Yarry looked around at his crew, who were all nodding. 'They're dead, sir. It's too far to swim to shore, sir, and that foul demon following us will have had them by now, even if the water hasn't killed them. They *are* dead, sir.'

'Come about, Captain, or I will have you executed for mutiny.' Carpello held a folded piece of sailcloth against his bloody midsection. 'You may be captain, but this is my ship, and we will come about this instant!'

Yarry ran one hand through his unruly hair and gave the order. The cry echoed along the deck and up into the rigging and the *Falkan Dancer* slowly lumbered to port, her bow coming around gradually until it cut through the swells, a knife's edge leading them back towards Strandson.

Three avens later, as the sun dipped below the horizon, Carpello resigned himself to the fact that he – *they* – had failed. The Seron had been particularly vigilant in their efforts, as if they knew it would be worse for them if they returned to Orindale without the prisoners or the key. Seron were assumed to be soulless and without minds of their own, but these three appeared to understand quite coherently that losing the Ronan partisans would mean death for them. Even as the sun faded in the west, they maintained their watch, squinting to improve their vision through the waning twilight.

Carpello shuddered as he imagined his own meeting with the dark prince. He had been praying for avens that Lahp and his platoon had managed to find Gilmour and retrieve the wretched stone. Although the bleeding had stopped, his abdomen burned; he spat into the waves and hoped out loud that Brexan had died slowly and unpleasantly, knowing she had failed.

'Captain Yarry,' he called softly, 'back to Orindale.'

The Seron shared a look, as if they could not believe the merchant would call off the search, then secured their weapons, pulled off their boots and dived headfirst into the sea.

'Rutting dogs,' Carpello Jax shouted: there behind the ship, the three Seron warriors bobbed in the waves for a moment before beginning to swim towards the Ronan coast. 'They'll succeed or they'll die,' the fat trader mused. 'It's that simple.' He watched them disappear into the half-light then called, 'Full sail to Orindale, Captain Yarry.'

BOOK IV

The River

MEYERS' VALE

When Mark and Brynne awakened from their coma they were both delirious. Garec was worried that the wraith intrusion had done them irreparable harm – it had affected Sallax so badly – but their bodies showed no signs of injury, either from Garec's arrows or from the spirit army attack. They were both drained, exhausted, and went without murmur when Garec suggested they lie down for a bit; when he checked on them at midday, he found them sleeping comfortably, unperturbed by nightmares or sub-conscious visions of prowling spectres.

At dawn the next day Garec and Steven gave Lahp his funeral rites, burning the body on a pyre alongside the riverbank. Watching the flames lick at the dead soldier's body, Garec knew Gilmour had been wrong about the Seron. They were not animals. Malagon had attempted to create an army of mindless killers, tearing their very souls away to leave them empty and his to command – but he had not entirely succeeded. Lahp was the proof. His kindness, and his desire to help them, even giving his life for them: this showed unquestionably that Malagon's Seron warriors were more capable of compassion than anyone had known.

Garec had drawn strength from Steven's iron-willed refusal to give up the fight during their battle with the wraiths. Their tandem engagement with the spirit attackers had been like an elaborate dance, and Garec, empowered by Steven's shared magic, had brought death to the dead with fluid grace. He doubted he would ever achieve that level of perfection again. Garec had often wondered what made a sorcerer different. The control he had whilst battling the wraith army verged on sorcery; the walls, the floorboards, even the air itself had seemed to obey his every command. He had worked magic.

The Ronan bowman wiped a smear of mud from his boots – Steven's boots – and shook his head. He wasn't that skilled; the magic had worked *him*.

Magic. Garec stared at the staff in Steven's hands. That simple stick had saved their lives several times now, and still none of them had the faintest idea where its power came from; not even Gilmour had been able to explain. Would it be enough to save Eldarn? Watching the thin, pale-skinned foreigner kick a smouldering branch back into the pyre, Garec thought their cause might not be lost, even though Gilmour was gone. Perhaps Steven wielded enough magic to protect them from Nerak, to ensure their safe passage into Welstar Palace, and to secure the far portal and retrieve Lessek's Key.

He sighed: wishful thinking. There was more to it than just bringing the stone back to Gorsk. They had no choice but to go in search of the missing Larion Senator, Kantu. They had to go to Praga.

As if reading his mind, Steven flashed the Ronan a sad smile, tossed his mysterious staff onto the ground and asked, 'Well, shall we build a boat?'

It didn't take long for their crude but sturdy vessel to take shape. Thanking God for the trapper's well-kept tools, Steven directed Garec to start hewing down a number of the huge pines that surrounded the cabin. They stripped each trunk of its branches and sawed them into sections five paces long. By evening the two men had assembled forty-five logs and started lashing the heaviest of these together to form their raft. The amateur shipwrights alternated sections, end-to-end, by thickness, to account for the gradual taper in each section's girth: the result was a relatively flat and surprisingly strong base for their journey downstream to Orindale.

By the time they got back to the cabin, they were exhausted but well satisfied with their day's work, and much of their aches and pains faded at the scent of a spicy stew: their companions had finally awakened and busied themselves at the cooking fire.

The following morning, Mark and Brynne joined them outside. Garec watched the pair closely, and after a couple of avens he decided they were back to normal. He sighed with relief: his gamble had indeed paid off. The decision to fire on his friends had been made in an instant. It had been his only moment of hesitation in that battle, but the anguished wait to ensure he'd done the right thing felt like it had lasted a lifetime. Steven hadn't seen what he'd done, and his friends didn't remember. He thanked the gods of the Northern Forest profusely, then returned to work hauling and lashing logs together.

'You and Garec were quite something against those ghosts,' Mark told Steven quietly.

'We owe our lives to Gabriel O'Reilly. Without his warning we'd have been stuffed. I had time to prepare Garec; without him we had no chance.'

'So how did that work?'

'I don't know. It just came to me, the idea that we might be able to share the staff's strength.' He looked into the forest where Garec was attaching a length of twine to a fallen pine. 'Thank God it worked. We'd be wraiths ourselves now if it hadn't. By the way, have you heard from Gabriel since?'

'No.' Mark didn't appear surprised. 'Not a word since he warned us the spirits were coming down the hill.'

'I wonder if he'll be back.'

'I hope so,' Mark replied. 'He's saved my neck twice now – and he gave us the heads-up about Sallax.' He glanced over at Brynne and asked, 'Any sign of him yesterday?'

Again Steven shook his head. 'I don't know if he made it far enough downriver to avoid the wraiths.'

'Let's hope,' Mark said. 'He's got a score to settle with Nerak, if he can just get beyond the guilt. Imagine working for your greatest enemy all that time.'

'Nerak has a lot to answer for.'

'You realise he might kill us all.'

'Maybe not. If we can get to Praga, we might be able to find Gilmour's—'

'Kantu,' Mark interrupted. 'The other Larion guy. He can help us, but how will we know who he is, or where to find him?'

'I don't have a clue.' Steven gave his friend a hopeful look. 'Let's get there first.'

By the end of the day, two more levels had been added to the base. The final step was completed standing calf-deep in the frigid water, and Mark was glad they'd had the foresight to cut enough logs to build upper levels on the raft. 'At least this way we might stay a bit drier,' he commented with a shiver. 'With only one layer of logs, we'd be soaking wet from the moment we started out.'

'And by running the inner section at right angles to the lower and upper decks, we'll hopefully cut down on water splashing up between the logs as well,' Steven explained. 'I'm not just a pretty face, you know!'

Garec and Brynne grinned at the unfamiliar expression, but Mark groaned as Steven started to explain the engineering principles he'd used. Steven was missing his weekly mathematics challenges; now he wondered what other engineering problems he might be able to solve using his maths knowledge as they navigated their way along the next leg of their journey.

With the last length of the trapper's rope, Garec tied short loops at each corner of the square-bottomed vessel and two larger loops at its centre. 'Handholds.' He smiled at Brynne as she looked at him questioningly. 'We don't want anyone falling in.'

'Make mine especially tight,' she ordered, smiling back at him.

It warmed Garec's heart to see Brynne's smile. She was desperately worried about Sallax, and it was hard to believe her brother could have survived the army of murderous wraiths scouring the foothills for them two days earlier.

Without thinking, the young man added in a whisper, 'He's tough, Brynne, the toughest person I know. He found a way to make it through alive; I know he did.' Garec's heart sank as he watched Brynne's smile fade.

'He's scared, Garec – scared, and suffering unbearable guilt. It's not his fault. We have to find him.'

'We will, I promise.'

Steven, unaware of their conversation, broke in by abruptly tossing the raft's anchor line to Garec. He was in contagiously good spirits as he looked over their collective handiwork. 'Tie this off to that tree. We don't want her floating away overnight.'

Garec moved to fasten the line to a low-hanging branch.

Steven stood beside Mark as the last of their daylight faded behind the Blackstones to the west, limning everything in dim orange. Their raft looked a little like a proper boat that had struggled for a lifetime to mask a disability, and then simply given up. But Steven loved it. It was something tangible, it represented existential evidence, proof of their lives and their continued free will, and he beamed as he wrapped an arm around Mark's shoulder and asked, 'Well, what shall we call her?'

'This crooked, not-entirely-seaworthy raft?' Mark teased.

'Nope,' Steven declared, 'that's not her. And it's too long to paint along her bow.'

'Does she have a bow?' Mark asked.

'Don't be so bloody negative; this fine vessel – this sturdy craft—' Steven emphasised the words as he gestured towards the floating wooden barge, '—this transport of delight will take us in style and safety all the way to Orindale, in a tenth of the time it would take for us to walk.'

For a moment the two men were back drinking beer and joking over fast food in the front room of 147 Tenth Street. Mark felt them fall quickly back into stride, back into the comforting, rhythmic banter that had been a staple of their lives back home.

'How about the *Capina Fair*?' Garec asked, joining the fray.

'Your girlfriend?' Mark asked.

'Former girlfriend,' Brynne answered for him. 'It ended messy.'

'Ah,' Steven said. 'So you miss her?'

'No,' Garec replied matter-of-factly, 'it's just that this vessel – this *fine* vessel,' he mocked, 'looks a bit like her. That's all.'

Brynne laughed out loud. 'It certainly has the same sturdy foundation down below.'

Even in the dying light, they all could see Garec turn a deep shade of red.

'A wide-hipped woman?' said Mark, 'nothing wrong with that, Garec. I'm sure she never blew over in a windstorm.'

Now Garec laughed as well. 'You're right, and I hope we can ask as much from this raft as we head downstream.'

Steven stood tall and dramatically placed one hand over his heart. 'The *Capina Fair* it is.'

'The *Capina Fair*,' they echoed in unison.

'Now my friends, to dinner,' Steven gestured towards the cabin, 'because apart from his skill at dispatching enraged spirits bent on our destruction, our friend Garec is a virtuoso fisherman with a longbow.'

Progress on the *Capina Fair* was slower than Steven had expected. The first day he and Mark estimated they had travelled about six miles, less than the distance they could have covered on foot. That night Garec cut and stripped three sturdy saplings, poles for them to help move the raft along more quickly; Steven would use his own hickory staff.

Although their progress improved a little, they were still not making headway towards Orindale with any alacrity. The *Capina Fair* was a clumsy vessel, clunking over rocks and getting hung up on fallen trees, and they spent an inordinately long time wrestling her free from obstacles. But Steven believed the river would widen and deepen as they moved north of the foothills; despite their daily challenge to keep moving, he was convinced easier passage lay ahead.

In an effort to keep them all lighthearted, Garec reminisced about the raft's namesake: a strong-willed, stubborn woman with whom he had fought almost daily.

'I can't imagine why you never settled down with that girl, Garec,' Brynne teased. 'She sounds perfect for you.'

'I thought about it,' he replied dryly, 'but if I'm going to spend my life with someone, I would prefer it to be someone who never makes me consider ending my life.'

They all laughed, and Brynne splashed him playfully with a handful of the icy water. The foothills were slowly flattening to meet the Falkan plains; everyone was glad to watch the Blackstone Mountains fall behind.

They fell into a rhythm, taking turns to stand on the front corners of the raft's upper level and call out obstacles and poling directions. Garec kept a ready bow and a quick eye open: he felled a large deer just after sunset on their third day out. Fresh venison was a welcome change from their steady diet of fish, and the last of the trapper's wine complemented the meat well. At night, they moored the raft to a tree trunk and slept on board.

Despite the clumsiness of their rudimentary vessel, travel along the river was easier and safer than trying to fight their way north through the forest. Steven's engineering plan had worked and water rarely splashed up between the *Capina Fair*'s floorboards. They took advantage of the long days raftbound to clean and rewrap wounds, to massage sprained muscles, organise supplies and, especially, to discuss their plans for finding Sallax and getting to Praga and tracking down Kantu. For the first time since they had arrived so precipitously in Eldarn, Mark and Steven felt properly rested.

They also used the time to mourn. Six of their colleagues had been killed or lost since the battle at Riverend Palace, but commemorating those deaths had been a luxury they could not afford. Now, as the river ran slowly towards Orindale and the sun shone down, the Ronans had the opportunity to remember the lives and loves they had left behind. The sun warmed their backs and comforted their souls as Brynne and Garec cried for Namont, Mika and Jerond, for Gilmour's passing, Versen's disappearance, and for Sallax's fall from grace. They comforted one another and renewed their vows to see the journey through to its end.

Steven was worried for Hannah, and although the journey was going well, it did little to boost his sagging spirits. Sitting alone one afternoon as the current carried the *Capina Fair* around a wide bend in the river, he looked closely at his reflection in the water. Gaunt, bearded and brooding, he almost didn't recognise himself. He was overcome by the desire to recapture some of that ignorant innocence he had enjoyed when he was nothing more than a small-town assistant bank manager. He grimaced: *that* wasn't going to happen – but at least he could do something about his appearance. He still wore his tattered tweed jacket pulled over the tunic he had stolen back in Estrad, and his jeans were filthy. His hair was long and matted, and his cheeks had sunken somewhat since food became a daily struggle.

'I am a mess,' he commented to no one.

'Well, you were never much to look at anyway,' Mark responded dryly.

Steven jumped. 'Bastard. I didn't see you there. Give me your knife, will you?'

'You have a knife.'

'Yours is sharper.'

Mark handed Steven the hunting knife. 'Careful where you point that thing. Just having it is a felony in New Jersey.'

Accepting the blade, Steven looked at it for a moment, wondering how to do this so he didn't make matters worse. He shrugged – that wouldn't be possible – and grabbed a fistful of hair, slashing it carefully in as straight a line as he could manage. 'There,' he said and tossed the stringy remains into the current, 'that's a good start.'

'Yikes,' Mark exclaimed, 'that was quick!'

'Now for a shave.'

It wasn't long before Steven was looking much more like he had on his arrival in Eldarn. Stripping to his boxers, he washed his clothes in the river and laid them out on deck to dry, then took the tweed jacket, beat it against one of the logs like a carpet and used a dampened cloth to scrub it as clean as it would get.

Seeing what a difference these ablutions were making, Mark followed Steven's lead and shaved his beard as well.

Running a hand over the smooth skin of his jaw, he admitted, 'That feels better. Of course, I prefer a bit of hot lather and some aftershave, but given the circumstances, a razor-sharp hunting knife doesn't do too badly.'

Steven considered his reflection in the water again. 'I needed that. I'm not sure why, but I needed to feel like we might some day be able to go back.'

Mark was serious. 'But you don't want to go back.'

'Not yet, no. But some day we have to. Some day we will. I need to know we can.'

'I hate to be the one to tell you this, but a shave and some clean clothes are not enough to make the transition back. This place has changed you – *us* – for ever.'

'Yes, I know, but this was something, right? This must count for *something.*'

'You need to find Hannah.'

'I do, and I need this sodding raft to move faster.' He punctuated his frustration with a hard slap on the river's surface. In response, the icy water splashed up and doused him thoroughly.

'Now you've done it! You're soaking wet, pissed off, and floating along an uncharted river in your underwear. I can't imagine any woman, never mind Hannah, ever falling for anyone else.' He turned to Brynne, who was sitting watching the exchange. 'What do you think, Brynne?'

'All women go for that pitiful, wet-puppy look. Makes me want to take him home and warm him up a bit.'

'You see?' Mark poked fun, 'my own girlfriend, and right in front of me as well. Before I know it she'll be suggesting a threesome.'

'All right, all right,' Steven smiled. 'Enough out of you.' Standing up, he stretched, then dived headfirst into the river. Surfacing nearby, he screamed, 'Mother of all things unholy!'

Garec called, 'Steven, come back aboard. You'll catch a deadly cold. Remember, if we lose you, we'll have to entrust that stick of yours to Mark or Brynne – so come out quickly, before all Eldarn is lost.'

Brynne cuffed him hard on the side of his head.

'It's fine,' Steven called, 'I'll swim along for a while. It's not so bad once you're in.'

Mark continued poling the *Capina Fair* downstream while Steven swam vigorously alongside. The exercise felt good, and he revelled in the familiarity of a hard workout. Passing the raft, he swam ahead, pushed along by the current.

He decided to wait for the others before swimming on. Treading water, Steven drew a deep breath, then submerged. Kicking towards the bottom, he could make out smooth stones, ancient, disintegrating trees, and large rocks in myriad formations dotting the sandy brown bottom. It was a new world to explore, a gloomy world half in and half out of light, a world of angry amalgams of rocks, dirt and branches, a forlorn universe trapped in silence and devoid of colour.

He swam towards an underground mass of boulders and trees, a behemoth creation, but his lungs began to burn so he resurfaced for another breath.

'There he is,' he heard Brynne say, her voice bouncing thinly along the surface. The *Capina Fair* was closer now. Steven waved at them, then dived back for another visit to the bottom.

Kneeling once again before the stone formation, Steven watched hundreds of strangely shaped fish darting back and forth between its nooks and cavities. He ran his hands along the riverbed, disturbing a cloud of mud which swirled up momentarily and blocked his view. As it cleared, he saw something, and narrowed his eyes, trying to see more clearly. Then it was there again, coming slowly into focus as the current carried the silty cloud away. Still kneeling, Steven found his hope renewed and, suddenly confident, he kicked back towards the surface and the broken beams of refracted sunlight.

Panic struck almost immediately. Something was holding him down.

'He's been under there a long time.' Garec tried not to sound nervous as he clambered to his feet for a better view. He scanned the river's surface, looking for bubbles or other disruptions that might indicate Steven's whereabouts. Leaves, several small branches and a rotten log floated by silently, en route to the Ravenian Sea. Garec noted trees growing on the far banks were reflected in hazy green, gold, and brown, a forest palette, blurry along the river's edge.

'He's a good athlete,' Mark said. 'I coach swimming, and I wish I had his lungs.'

'Still.' Garec's voice was flat as he squinted against the sun's glare. 'I don't like this. It feels wrong.'

Mark found himself poling more quickly. The bowman's anxiety was somehow contagious, and he too began scanning the river for some sign that Steven might be in trouble.

Then he spied it: a small circular area of water, bubbling up as if disturbed from below. Mark recognised in a heartbeat that his friend was in danger. 'There,' he pointed, and pushed the *Capina Fair* hard towards the centre of the current, 'out in that deeper water. Do you see it?'

Garec was already pulling off his boots. He stripped to the waist and dived into the ripples, quickly disappearing beneath the surface.

Mark reached for the hickory staff. 'Try to keep us from moving too far downstream,' he said to Brynne as he leaped in after Garec.

Steven thrashed violently against the invisible force holding him to the riverbed. It had his leg, the same leg the grettan had nearly bitten off, the one that had been healed during his encounter with Malagon's spirit army. The formless creature's grip was like iron and Steven's attempts to free himself were in vain. He grasped his ankle with both hands and tugged wildly; his lungs burned with the need for air. He exhaled hard, puffing his breath towards the surface in the hope of attracting Mark's attention. He didn't have much time.

A third hand gripped his leg. It was Garec. Steven's heart slammed away in his chest as Garec tried to extricate his foot from the river's vice-like grip. Steven thought his eyes were fooling him when he watched in horror as Garec's own hand was drawn wrist deep into the silt as well.

They were both trapped.

Garec struggled to free himself. Kicking hard and jerking his arm wildly, he inadvertently brought one leg around and struck Steven violently across the bridge of his nose. A bright light flashed before Steven's eyes, and it took the last of his strength to keep from drawing his lungs full of water. His thoughts scattered, myriad fragments: he might be fighting for his life, or he may have given up already – his sense of himself drifted away in the current. He realised, without caring, that he was about to die – *had* died – when he felt something forced into his hand.

The staff's magic flared, a wellspring of anger, determination and compassion. Steven was suddenly lucid, acutely aware, and strangely free from his mortal need for oxygen. He reached for Garec and, as he had done back at the cabin, used the staff's power for another, channelling his own magic-imbued strength to the Ronan. Moments later, Garec quieted beside him, protected from drowning by the staff's strange ability.

Steven squeezed his friend's hand and Garec returned his grip, as if to communicate that he, too, was somehow free from the need to breathe. Then Garec deliberately dropped Steven's hand and reached up to pat him forcefully on the back. *Good*, Steven thought, *he is protected. Now, to get us out of here; it's way too cold to hang about.*

Hovering above them in the current, Mark made several trips to the surface to breathe and to assure Brynne that both men were still alive. 'Something has them,' he called to her when he appeared the second time.

'What is it?'

'I don't know – I can't see anything, but they're clamped solidly to the riverbed. Steven is trying to free them now.' And Mark disappeared once again.

Brynne held the *Capina Fair* steady against the current. Having lost Sallax and Gilmour, she could not bear to lose Steven or Garec now. Hurling a string of foul curses at the river, she fought a growing desire to dive into the water with them.

Steven had no idea whether the staff's magic could continue to provide oxygen while he was focusing its power on the creature that lay hidden beneath the riverbed, but he had no choice but to try. Summoning his courage, he gripped the staff with both hands, channelled his will and drove one end deep into the silt between his feet.

At first nothing particular happened, although Steven could

feel the staff's power coursing into the earth with tremendous force. He and Garec remained firmly tethered by whatever evil lurked beneath them. Thankfully, the magic that was keeping them both alive was unaffected by Steven's attack on their captor. He glanced over at Garec: he looked calm, despite the absurdity of being trapped by the wrist twenty feet beneath the surface of the water. He was confident Steven's magic would save them.

It didn't work.

Refocusing his thoughts, Steven tried again. He envisioned the earth freeing them from its grasp and the two men floating gently along in the current like bits of flotsam. He tried to repress any anger or frustration: perhaps the force holding them prisoner might release its grip if it believed they were already dead.

Again, nothing.

Steven began to worry; sensing his concern, Garec gave him an encouraging clap on the back, intimating that he should try again.

Steven, about to try clearing his mind once more, took a moment to peer off into the gloom. An ungainly fish darted by, something caught between evolutionary endpoints, no longer what it had been but not yet what it was about to become. He watched it skim along in search of something slower and less agile to eat. Running his hands along the smooth hickory, Steven prepared for another assault on their captor when he felt they were beginning to move.

Slowly at first, and then more quickly, they were being dragged through the silt towards the gigantic moraine. His eyes widened in terror: now he could see the remains of crooked, broken trees jammed haphazardly into stone crevices: a nightmare of twisted roots and branches reaching out for them. It wasn't the current that had assembled this rock formation beneath the river's calm exterior, but rather, this beast, this invisible force that was threatening to make them both a permanent addition to its underwater construction. Steven twisted and tugged at his leg and struck repeatedly against the riverbed with the staff, but despite his efforts, he and Garec moved inexorably towards the submerged stone outcropping.

Ahead of them Steven saw a cave he had not noticed before: a dark, narrow opening between two massive boulders resting against one another. Whatever held them was dragging them slowly towards that gaping, inky hole. Above and behind, Mark appeared and grasped Steven by the hand and Garec by the ankle and pulled with all the force he could muster, but it didn't do a thing to slow them down. Garec dug the fingers of his free hand into the silt, trying to find whatever had them captive – and that was seized as well. Looking up at Steven, the fear of imminent death in his eyes, he pleaded silently with the foreigner to try *anything*, to do *something*, before it was too late.

Steven looked around, hoping for inspiration – then it occurred to him that the force holding them down might be linked with their current quest, maybe another of Prince Malagon's dark servants. He *really* needed to concentrate. He directed his thoughts to Nerak, Gilmour, Lessek, and the Larion Senate. He thought of Lessek's Key, that innocuous chunk of rock that sat waiting on his desk back home. And he envisioned himself handing over the stone to Kantu, the last of the Larion Senators, in preparation for a final war between the ancient magic of the spell table and the evil that sought to conquer it and bring about the end of all things. He focused his thoughts, his energy, his entire being on these images, forgetting himself and Garec, forgetting Brynne and Mark, even forgetting Hannah.

The staff responded to his single-minded dedication. The magic, which had thus far been a strong, warm glow as it provided oxygen for him and Garec, swelled up inside him. It sharpened Steven's consciousness and honed his perception of things around him.

This time when he raised the hickory staff to strike out at the riverbed, he knew that, if nothing else, he would be using all his heart and will. There was a shudder, a pulse that rippled out from the riverbed to resonate through the rocky hills of Meyers' Vale. Before Steven could strike out, the river released them. Jerking back reflexively, he and Garec were thrown towards the surface.

Brynne cried out when she saw the three men reappear. Forgetting her charge to keep the *Capina Fair* anchored against the current, she dropped the wooden pole and began calling frantically, 'Is everyone all right? No injuries?'

Mark shouted back, 'They're fine, a bit shaken by whatever it was, but Steven managed to free them.'

'It wasn't me,' Steven interjected.

'Well, the staff then.'

'Not the staff either.' He kicked towards the *Capina Fair*, keeping the staff's magic close within himself in case the creature emerged to drag them back beneath the surface. It wasn't difficult: the magic surged, vibrant and deadly, just behind the thin veil of his consciousness, as if it knew that danger was still imminent: it graced him with the strength – or at least the illusion of strength – to see him and his friends through to safety. He shivered at the thought of all of them being pulled back to the underwater formation – what if the magic failed again? They needed to reach the raft as quickly as possible, and then they could work out what the hell just happened, because he was damned if he knew. He was cold and frightened, but worse, he had lost confidence in the staff's power.

Meanwhile, the *Capina Fair* continued to drift downstream.

Swimming with the current, Garec realised they were failing to narrow the distance to the relative safety of the raft. 'Uh, Brynne,' he called, 'you're floating away.'

'Rutting merchant-on-a-stick! Sorry!' Brynne remembered the pole and quickly anchored the *Capina Fair*, halting its resolute flight from the haunted river bend.

They hauled themselves onto the deck, and Garec picked up a second pole. 'Let's get out of here,' he shouted, shaking a little as he pushed hard off the bottom.

Resting in the relative warmth of the sun-drenched logs that formed the *Capina Fair*'s uppermost deck, Steven felt the magic exit his body, skimming across his already damp flesh to disappear back into the staff, the earth, sky, or wherever it went when it left him alone. This time, though, it felt different, and he imagined he could still feel a bit of it there, masking itself behind his regular heartbeat and breathing. He shrugged the sensation off as vestiges of adrenalin and gazed into the low foothills that lined the river along either bank. Immediately above them was a rocky ridgeline ending with a precipitous drop into a deep valley. The cliff was capped by a small grove of pine trees that looked so out of place perched there above the river that the image stayed with Steven long after they rounded the bend and passed out of sight. The fifteen or twenty pines grew at odd angles, stabbing outwards from the bedrock, a confusing collection of natural road signs pointing everywhere and nowhere at once. Without quite knowing why, Steven made a mental note of the landmark.

Twelve days later, they reached the mouth of the canyon.

THE RAVENIAN SEA

'Get out of your boots,' Brexan directed urgently as she struggled to pull her own off, 'and your cloak, untie it. Just let it go.' They had been in the water a very short time, but already the cold was beginning to affect them. Versen didn't look well: his face was drawn and pale, his eyes red, and his skin a cadaverous white. She struggled to keep his senses sharp despite the dulling influence of the frigid seawater. Versen's fingers trembled as he endeavoured to loosen the thin wool ties holding the cloak about his neck; Brexan helped him.

'You're doing fine,' she encouraged. 'We just need to get moving again. We need to swim. It won't be so cold once we start swimming.' Brexan badly wanted to believe that, but she was dubious. She could feel the chill penetrating her bones: it would be just a matter of moments before she began to grow numb, to lose her senses and become confused. It was apparent the big Ronan wouldn't be offering much assistance.

It would be up to her to generate a way to save themselves.

As he battled to remove his clothes, Versen could feel his legs failing beneath him. In his mind, he could see himself kicking hard and paddling with cupped hands to remain above the waves, but dipping his face in the water, he could see his limbs weren't responding. His right leg turned lazy circles that did little to keep him afloat, while his left, painfully cramped in the cold autumn seas, pointed rigidly down into the depths and twitched involuntarily back and forth like a pendulum. His voice cracked as he said, 'My legs aren't working, Brexan. I can't get them to move.'

'Hang on to me,' she said. She had no idea how she would keep them both afloat, but she was determined to try. She draped Versen's arms over her shoulders. Her face resting against his, she grimaced. His skin was cold, colder than the water around them. Trying to remain positive, she said, 'There, that ought to keep you out of trouble.'

'No.' Versen struggled to pull his arms back, but he lacked the strength. 'I'll pull you under. You should try to make it on your own.'

'Ox,' Brexan said gently, 'we will either make it together, or we won't.' She knew the cold was dulling her consciousness, because the notion of failure had crept into her mind and she didn't feel terribly alarmed at it, at the prospect of giving up, of simply laying back in the water and falling asleep. Shaking her head, she forced a moment's clarity and turned her attention north. The *Falkan Dancer* was coming about in a long slow tack. It was nearly out of sight already, so there was no chance they could hail the vessel on its next pass. She cursed Carpello Jax, and wished she had driven the stolen knife blade deep into his flabby pink hide rather than just slashing him. That wound would heal; she should have killed him when she had the chance.

For a moment she thought she might have traded their current situation to be chained again to that bulkhead beneath the forecastle – being locked up in the dark, humid, stinking chamber had been difficult, but compared with their current plight, the manacles were a welcome alternative. She recalled the comforting sensation of feeling Versen's legs entwined with hers, even though she couldn't see him. But no, if they were going to die, at least they'd be free.

They were entwined again now. Versen's arms lay across her shoulders, and his long legs continued to jerk spasmodically, kicking between her ankles, interrupting her efforts to tread water, and causing both their heads to dunk periodically beneath the surface.

The Ronan coast lay far to the east, two days' swim away. Brexan nearly laughed. In another quarter-aven, both she and Versen would be a distant memory. She wondered if their bodies would sink or float in this cold water – as much as she hoped they would eventually be washed up on shore, she feared they would end up on the ocean floor. They would fall slowly, spiralling awkwardly down, and their bodies would come to rest in the deepest part of the Ravenian Sea, where the amiable reef fish feared to venture, where only the most primitive and cruel sea creatures scavenged for food. In an embarrassing fit of selfishness, she hoped the big Ronan would sink first; maybe then she wouldn't find the journey as terrifying.

Brexan's imagination frightened her awake, and with a sudden burst of adrenalin, she grabbed hold of Versen's forearms and tugged. 'C'mon, Ox,' she entreated, 'we have to swim. Kick your feet. Kick, Ox.'

'I can do it,' Versen mumbled, then choked out a mouthful of seawater. But he couldn't. As his head began to loll forward, Brexan submerged briefly to free one hand and shove against his forehead, pushing his face out of the water and away from the waves.

'Keep your head up,' she ordered, 'I'm doing everything else over here. You ought to at least hold up your own head.'

Versen didn't respond to her weak joke.

Shivering uncontrollably, Brexan felt her muscles begin to cramp. The tightness seemed to attack her all at once; it felt like her body had been seized by an invisible sea god. She howled in frustration. Her strength was failing. She couldn't support Versen's weight any longer. She had to let him go, let him sink. If she wasn't supporting him, she might stand a chance of swimming, if not all the way to shore, at least into shallower water where the waves might eventually carry her body up onto the sand. 'Please, Ox, please,' she pleaded between sharp breaths, 'I can't do it alone. At least tread water, *please*.'

Sobbing weakly, she held on until her muscles burned and then gave out. Even had she been able to summon the will to support Versen's weight any more, her limbs had already rebelled, giving up the struggle. Unable to move she watched Versen bob a few paces off before sinking beneath the waves.

Crying in earnest now, she inadvertently gulped a large mouthful of salty water and choked violently for several moments, coughing the fluid from her lungs between sobs. She struggled to fill her lungs and roll onto her back so she could float as long as possible before succumbing to the cold. She couldn't feel her extremities any more. Her time was at hand; she hoped Versen was waiting for her on the long trail to the Northern Forest.

Above, the clear blue sky was interrupted by a few thin clouds scudding north towards Orindale. Floating on her back, Brexan inhaled as if to breathe in those clouds, to draw them down with her in hopes they might bring the sun's warmth or better yet, might carry her away, carry her someplace dry. They must be warm; they are so close to the sun. Let them come. Come and take me. Just one of you, come down here.

Brexan choked as a wave passed over her face. Coughing and blinking to clear her vision, she drew a final hoarse breath, smiled up at the ghostly clouds stark against the brilliant blue sky, and gave up.

'I'm coming, Ox,' she mumbled and turned her gaze skywards. Unable to draw another breath, Brexan's vision tunnelled, and the walls of her consciousness began to close down upon her. In an ironic last vision, she was faintly amused that one of the bone-white clouds appeared to be dropping from the sky.

Karn's leg was bleeding badly from the wound the young woman had dealt him before she sprang from the quarterdeck of the Falkan schooner. Now, trailing a cloud of bloodstained water, he knew he would not survive the day. The cold had already slowed his progress, but he doggedly continued swimming, determined to get as far as he could before allowing the ocean to swallow his body. Karn understood swimming to shore was his only choice; that had become obvious the moment he realised the schooner's crew could not retrieve his prisoners from the Ravenian Sea. To return to Malakasia without their prize would mean certain death for him. Karn preferred to drown here rather than return to face Prince Malagon empty-handed.

He had hoped the cold, coupled with the healing properties of salt water, would stop the bleeding, but although the pain had lessened dramatically, blood continued to flow unchecked from the wound. He wished he had had the forethought to stitch it himself before jumping overboard, but it was too late for that. Karn swam onwards, without hesitation or regrets.

Beside him swam his fellow Seron. Rala's jaw was set, and a look of fierce determination passed across her face when she made eye contact with him. They would not wait, nor would they slow their pace to accommodate him. If he made it to shore, he would bind his injury and follow their trail until he could rejoin them.

Neither Haden nor Rala looked back as Karn began to lag

behind. Soon they were ten, then twenty paces ahead of him. At fifty paces, he periodically lost sight of them behind the waves, and by the time the pair had moved a hundred paces more, Karn was already gone.

Rala swam steadily, but not even the consistent, repetitive motion or her single-minded intention to recapture the Ronan prisoners could mask the reality: her strength was waning. Beside her Haden continued, apparently unaffected by the cold or by the impossibly long distance they had yet to cover. There was something terrible about him, something powerful and evil. Rala understood Seron were stronger and more physically resilient than most men, but he was especially strong, especially brutal and coldly cruel, even for one of their race. Lahp was smart, a heavy-handed disciplinarian and a powerful leader among the Seron; Haden was quite as strong as Lahp, his equal physically, but he was far more ruthless, content to wait in the shadows, biding his time and awaiting opportunities to kill or maim.

Rala knew when they found the Ronans, Haden would most likely kill one of them right away. She would have to protect the second if they were to retrieve the stone, even if it meant a physical confrontation. It would be her responsibility to oversee the survivor's interrogation, or they would lose critical intelligence to Haden's inexhaustible appetite for pain, torture and dismemberment.

Struggling to remain afloat, Rala considered asking him to help her, but fearing his response, she decided instead to rededicate herself to maintaining her strokes and ignoring the cold as long as possible. But it didn't work: fear began to creep into her mind, an emotion she knew little of. Slowly, she felt herself give way to panic. Her short, economic movements, designed to carry her rapidly through the water with minimal effort, became wild, jerky flailings that exhausted her physically and exacerbated her terror. Her head fell beneath the waves several times, and she cried out, choking, then hacking the briny seawater from her throat.

Finally she gave up and reached out. 'Haden, help Rala,' she pleaded in a high-pitched grunt.

'Na,' he replied, shoving her violently away, disgusted at her childish fear: she should be *proud* to die for their prince.

When she came at him again, Haden could see she had lost control. He placed the flat of one palm firmly against her chest, holding her at arm's length as she thrashed and pleaded with him to save her life. Realising he could not afford to waste his energy battling Rala, the scarred Seron gripped her by the shoulders and forced her head beneath the waves. It wouldn't take long, then he would continue swimming towards Rona. With Rala gone, he would be free to deal with the prisoners as he saw fit. Within an aven he would have the stone key, or know where it was, and the partisans would both be dead.

Rala surprised him: she was stronger than he had expected. She gripped his wrists and began pulling him down. His head submerged twice before he realised he had made a mistake. In the throes of fighting for her life, Rala discovered a store of adrenalin yet untapped, and she kicked and tugged like a wild woman until Haden released her. He decided to swim away; she was in no condition to keep up with him. He grinned as he watched her surface several paces off. He understood he might not make it to shore, but before he died, it would bring him great pleasure listening to Rala's terrified, wailing cries for help, knowing none would come.

In a final act of desperation, she plunged forward, screaming, 'Help Rala!'

Haden grimaced and spat a surprised curse as the woman managed to grab hold of his tunic. Screaming and scratching, Rala pulled wildly at his arms, his hair, and even his face as she struggled to find a solid purchase. Spinning onto his back, the scarred one raised his fists to pummel her beneath the waves, but before he had an opportunity to throw his first punch, Rala stopped struggling.

Her eyes wide in shock, the Seron woman choked out a final plea, then released her grip. Bobbing away like a tide-borne piece of driftwood, Rala's body began to shrivel, to waste away until she was little more than an empty sack of sodden skin housing a jumbled array of pale yellow bones.

'Almor,' the remaining Seron grunted approvingly and turned to continue his journey. He had not gone far before he felt the almor's touch, a faint prickling of primitive energy, as the demon creature came from below to envelop him in a warm and protective blanket that buoyed its passenger high in the water and heated his cold flesh. The milky-white fluid of the almor's insubstantial form clouded the water around him, and he felt his hands and feet pass through the gelatinous substance as he made his way steadily towards the shore.

Together they would find the Ronans, discover the hiding place of Prince Malagon's lost stone, and savour the pain and suffering of their victims through the next Twinmoon.

The rain finally stopped, and before the mud dried in the streets, heavy waves of disagreeable humidity radiated up from the sodden ground. Mornings were the worst, the sun somehow hotter than at midday: Hannah hated going about Middle Fork in the morning. Regardless of how carefully she stepped or how thoroughly she cleaned her boots each evening, by the mid-morning aven, her feet were covered with mud and she was drenched in sweat.

Cursing herself for leaving her sunglasses – she could see them now, lying where she had tossed them so carelessly, on the front seat of her car – she felt as if she had developed a permanent squint. Of course, sunglasses would destroy her efforts to blend in with the Pragan people; any passing Malakasian patrol would take her into custody in a matter of minutes – but it might have been worth it. 'At least they might take me someplace dark,' she muttered, then added with a sigh, 'No. I suppose that *would* be worse.'

This morning, she was hustling back to Alen's home near the outskirts. Over one shoulder she carried a thick hemp bag stuffed full of vegetables, fruit, fresh bread, a couple of wine flagons and the ungainly carcase of something called a gansel.

Hannah had – stupidly! – taught Churn how to play rock, paper, scissors, and now he insisted on challenging her every day, especially when it came time to help out around the house. Bring in firewood? Rock breaks scissors. Buy food for breakfast? Paper covers rock. Shovel out the ash box? Scissors cut paper. The man was a virtuoso, a rock-paper-scissors savant, and to make matters worse, Churn bellowed an inhuman laugh every time he won: it sounded like a drunken opera star practising the vowel continuum in a stairwell.

Avoiding a group of begging street children she crossed through the mud, turned down an alley, and cut back behind several large businesses before re-entering the main boulevard only a block or two from Alen's house. She promised herself she would return later with the leftovers for the hungry children, but for now, she wanted to get back to Alen Jasper. He had told her a lot about Eldarn, its people and history, but there was still a great deal to learn, especially if she were going to track down Steven and discover a way to step back into Idaho Springs.

There was something the old man was holding back, though. They had been staying with him since Churn had carried him out of the Middle Fork Tavern. Hannah shuddered as she recalled Alen's wailing plea to let him die. Hoyt had tried to make light of the situation, telling him, 'If I looked and smelled like you, old man, I would want to die, too.'

But they had realised it was more serious when Alen had replied desperately, 'No, you don't understand: *he* won't let me die.'

'Who won't?' Hoyt asked, worried now. 'You have to help me understand, Alen. Tell me what's happened.'

'Of course you don't understand. You don't have any family,' Alen growled, suddenly angry. 'But he won't let me go. He won't let me die, the mad stinking rutter. I lost my Jer. It finally happened. My baby.'

'Your son?' Hoyt asked, 'what happened?'

'My grandson. My last grandson. He died. That's the end of me, the end of my family. There may be children of cousins somewhere, but they don't count. My babies are all gone.'

'What happened? Was there a plague or something? How did they die?'

'Old age . . . but they were my *babies*.'

Hannah tugged at Hoyt's sleeve. 'What's he talking about? He's drunk as a very drunk skunk; we'll not get anything sensible out of him until he's sobered up. Let's just put him to bed – or better, burn his clothes and then put him to bed.'

Hoyt agreed, but when he tried to tell Alen what they were doing, the old man surprised him by lashing out, crying, 'Don't call me that! My name is Kantu. Call me Kantu!' He gripped Hoyt by the ankle.

'All right . . . Kantu.' Hoyt kneeled beside him and smiled in an effort to calm him down. 'Let's back up. Why do you want to die?'

'My Jer died.'
'When?'

'What Twinmoon is it?'

The old man had obviously been out of it for a while. Hoyt swore quietly. 'It's just past mid-autumn.'

'Last summer; so, twelve Twinmoons ago ... give or take.' Alen waved his hand back and forth to imply an estimation, and Hannah was momentarily comforted by something so simple and familiar. 'That's when I started drinking.'

Hoyt tried not to sound surprised. 'So you've been drinking for twelve Twinmoons?'

Again the gesture. 'Give or take.'

'A year and a half,' Hannah whispered to no one and shook her head in awe.

'*Every* day?'

'I think so.' He released Hoyt's ankle. 'It's good to see you, boy, one last time.'

'You said someone won't let you die.' Hoyt took the bony hand in his own.

'The stinking rutting horsecock,' Alen agreed.

'Who?' he tried again, '*who* won't let you die? And why?'

'Lessek.'

'Who's Lessek?' Hannah ventured softly, not wanting to interrupt the conversation, even though her hope was waning with each unintelligible remark.

Hoyt looked at Churn, who shrugged and shook his head. Without looking at her, Hoyt answered, 'A magician, a scholar, a sorcerer, a legend. Our history talks of Lessek, but that was many, many Twinmoons ago – many generations ago. I think he was supposed to be the founder of a famous research university in Gorsk, the Larion Senate.'

Alen nodded. 'He did.'

'But the Larion Senate hasn't been around for more than a thousand Twinmoons,' he continued.

'Give or take,' Alen added, and this time Churn waved his own hand back and forth, mimicking the gesture.

Alen had had enough of the conversation. Still holding Hoyt's hand, he fell backwards onto the floor, muttering, 'It *is* good to see you again, though, my boy, even in these sad circumstances. And someday, when you have your own children, you'll understand. I wasn't supposed to live this long. None of us were.

So you go now, Hoyt. Take your friends and leave me here.' His head rolled limply to one side.

Dropping the old man's hand, Hoyt moved to stand next to Hannah.

'That's him?' She failed to control the tremor in her voice. 'That's the one man who can get me back home? Him? We walked for – for I can't remember how long, to get here to meet this – this disgusting, drunken sot, because he is the best Eldarn has to offer? This wino, this stinking pile of horseshit? *He's my only hope?*' With each word her voice rose until she was shouting.

Hoyt pursed his lips and gave a half-shrug. 'He wasn't always—'

'Wasn't always *what?*' Hannah felt the tears come, tears of fury, and decided not to fight them. It was a fine time to cry, stuck here in a world that shouldn't even exist, weeks and miles away from the grove where she'd entered this dreadful place. It was a perfect time to cry. 'Wasn't always what, Hoyt? A foul-smelling, babbling idiot with fungus growing on his clothes?' She kicked at one of Alen's outstretched feet. 'Ah, shit, Hoyt . . . shit.' With that, the tears came on in earnest and she sank to the floor, sobbing unrelentingly.

'What? What did you say?' Alen sat up suddenly; he appeared determined to bring the room and its occupants into focus, if only for a moment.

Somewhat surprised, Hannah forcibly swallowed a sob and looked down on him. 'I said you were a drunk, a dirty, smelly, grumpy old drunk.'

'No, no, after that.'

Irritated, Hannah went on, 'I don't know what the f—' She stopped, bemused. 'You speak English. That was English, just now.'

'And you said "shit". I heard you.'

She looked at Hoyt and Churn. 'What is this? How does he speak English? Where did he learn English?'

Hoyt took Hannah's arm. 'Hannah, I don't understand what you're saying.'

Ignoring him, she knelt beside Alen. 'Where did you learn English?'

Obviously still quite drunk, Alen joked, 'In a place where nice young girls don't say "shit".'

Grinding her teeth together, Hannah reached out and grabbed his cloak. Pulling him up, she spat, 'Don't fuck with me, old man. I have had just about enough of this godforsaken place. Now, where did you learn my language?'

Something moist trickled between Hannah's fingers and left a trail of dull orange across her knuckles.

'In England,' Alen slurred matter-of-factly. 'And you, I suppose you learned somewhere in America, right?'

'South Denver,' Hannah whispered, and let him go. 'South Denver, Colorado, where I was born. In the United States of America. My world.'

She turned to Hoyt. 'All right. You have my attention.'

'I'm sorry, Hannah, but we don't speak this tongue.' Hoyt and Churn had not understood a word.

She switched back to Pragan. 'Sorry.'

'What is it?'

'I'm sorry for what I said. It looks like you were right.' She rubbed her hands together nervously. 'This *was* the right place to start.' Despite his pitiful appearance and his rancid smell, Alen had changed. He had moved slightly, shifting his entire being in a way Hannah couldn't even begin to describe, but whatever he had done, he was suddenly a different person, a more confident person, merely draped in the carnage of eighteen months of drunkenness.

Alen tugged at the hem of Churn's leggings and, suddenly polite, requested, 'Churn, old man. Please take me outside to the trough. Dunk my head beneath the water repeatedly for half an aven, or until I throw up and start crying for my mother. Will you do that?'

A grin split Churn's face. Hannah guessed he would set about his task with enthusiasm.

'I need to wake up a bit. We have a great deal to discuss, young lady. I will be back momentarily. Please make yourselves comfortable.'

THE CAVERN

For the next twelve days the travellers aboard the *Capina Fair* lived and ate well. Although they never spoke of the wraith attack, Mark and Brynne grew strong once again, and any sign they had ever been invaded by the spirits soon faded. Similarly, Garec and Steven quickly recovered from their ordeal at the hand of the homicidal river creature. The staff had saved them both from drowning, and there appeared to be no other lasting physical effects of the attack. Garec swore he would never venture near water again: he would find Renna, return to Estrad and remain comfortably dry among the rolling hills of the forbidden forest for the rest of his days.

Brynne reminded him he was still spending the better part of every day and most nights aboard a raft in the middle of a river, which was decidedly wet.

'Okay then, after this trip, I'm never going back in the water.'

'So, you'll never bathe?' she teased.

'Not often, no, and never in water deeper than my ankles,' Garec shot back.

'Imagine the stench.'

'That's fine,' he joked, 'I suppose I won't have many friends, but then again, I won't have strangely dressed foreigners dropping through the Fold, or thousand-Twinmoon-old sorcerers dragging me off on wild adventures in which invisible psychic creatures try to drown me before adding my body to their makeshift underwater sculptures, either.'

Steven chuckled and corrected him. 'I think you mean psychotic,' he said with a grin. The English words sounded strange, but sometimes there was no local equivalent. In spite of his smile Steven didn't feel much like laughing. As they poled the *Capina Fair* downstream, he found himself periodically struck by bouts of insecurity and depression. The others noticed the gloominess that took hold of him whenever he considered the now-familiar length of hickory. Its failure to free them from the river's grasp was the first time the magic had fallen short of Steven's needs: the Seron, the grettan, the wraiths – even the almor – they'd fallen easily beneath its apparently endless reserves of power.

Now Steven was worried: he could no longer rely on the hickory staff. The magic might fail again, and next time the dwindling company might not be so lucky. He felt responsible for the others' survival, and the magic's failure on the riverbed sent his confidence reeling: what would happen when they came up against the enormous military and magical force awaiting them on the shore of the Ravenian Sea?

Grimacing, he tried to thrust the problem from his mind, telling himself he had never understood how the staff's magic worked anyway, so he had no right to question or complain if it began to fade now. It had saved their lives several times, so he should just be grateful.

It wasn't working. He wanted to have the staff's power *with* him, to wrap himself in the sense of security it brought him. Defeating the wraith army had given him a sense of invincibility, a self-confidence he had never before experienced; at that moment he had been sure no force in Eldarn could stand against him. He supposed he was lucky that he and Garec had survived their first encounter with a power strong enough to render the staff useless.

Try as he might to push it away, there was something else troubling Steven. He had wielded a power greater than anything he could ever have imagined, and he *liked* it. He wanted it with him always – and he was certain it wanted him, that it had chosen *him* that evening in the foothills of the Blackstone Mountains. He was sure it had responded to his needs because it understood that compassion was right: terror and hatred had ruled Eldarn for generations, and the land was teetering on the brink of collapse. Compassion and caring, brotherhood and a sense of unity and understanding could save this beautiful, strange land; Steven was sure of it.

He could feel a memory of the magic, tingling through his arms and legs, as if the staff had read his mind and was responding to his reflections, encouraging him to believe that he was its rightful wielder, and that all would be well if he remained true. The desire to test it grew within him for a moment, but Steven forced the need back within the confines of his mind. It settled there, among his darkest desires, in a place he was certain everyone had but no one discussed: a cordoned-off section of himself where all his ugliest thoughts were trapped: the desire to feel the thrill of robbing a liquor store at gunpoint, to be a voyeur, to have desperate intercourse with a complete stranger, or to crash through mind-numbing rush-hour traffic and watch as rude commuters burned in a fiery conflagration – all lay sublimated in this do-not-enter region of his consciousness. They would be joined now by the desire to wield the world's most powerful force, to consume it and become indestructible, confident and powerful – and, most of all, free from fear.

Steven fought his almost overwhelming need to embrace the magic, to let it take him and make him into the instrument of Nerak's destruction. That might be his eventual end, but until he knew that for certain, he would keep it at arm's length. He didn't understand the magic, and after his failure on the river bottom he knew he couldn't always control it, but it was there, lurking patiently until it was needed.

He felt the power run along his forearms and out into his fingertips, prickly and stinging; it flickered briefly and then faded. All at once he was less-than-himself again.

The journey downstream from Meyers' Vale through the rolling hills of southern Falkan had been marked by good weather, unlimited fresh fish, wild fruits and nuts, and even a large game bird Garec had brought down, a gansel; it tasted not unlike turkey to the Coloradoans, but Garec's uncontrollable bellowing laughter when they named it in English was enough to convince them to abandon any further comparisons.

It was too late: throughout the following day, Garec continued trying out the word, as if he were going to perform for an audience. 'Turkey, tur–key, turk–ey,' he repeated over and over again, trying different inflections until Brynne was ready to throw him into the river herself. 'What a strange language you speak. I'm amazed you can understand one another at all.'

'Sometimes it's hard,' Mark said, 'and other times, we drink.'

'That always makes communication easier.'

'No, only sometimes,' Brynne chimed in.

'Yes, but those are the best times,' Garec stated firmly.

'Listen!' Steven interrupted.

'That helps too,' Garec agreed, 'but so few of us are any good at it.'

'No, no,' Steven chided, '*listen*.'

As they ceased chattering, they could hear the sound of the river had changed. Ahead in the distance, they could hear a low, grating, hollow roar, as if warning travellers to come no further. The sound, although unfamiliar, was somehow unmistakable: they all understood in a moment that they were fast approaching a stretch of white water, maybe even just beyond the next bend.

Suddenly serious, Garec regained his wits and ordered, 'Everyone tie down the packs. Use the centre loops.' He moved to secure his bow and quivers.

'I thought the centre loops were for us,' Mark asked. 'Where will we be?'

'Here.' Garec motioned towards the four outer loops, loose coils of rope forming handholds in each corner of the *Capina Fair's* upper deck. 'We'll be here, holding fast—' He paused, then continued, 'Maybe even tied fast, while we pole ourselves away from rocks or dangerous shallows along the way.'

'Out near the edge? Have you lost your mind?' Brynne scolded. 'We should stay here in the middle and hang on to these coils. We'll be safer.'

'I wish we could,' Garec answered, 'but listen, do you hear that? That roar?' Again he paused. 'That's not just a few rapids; that's powerfully rough water. There will be rocks large enough to ruin us, not just to capsize good old *Capina*, but to smash her to splinters.'

'He's right,' Mark agreed tying down his pack, 'and Steven, you shouldn't pole with that staff. If it gets torn from your hands as we go we're stuffed. We'd never find it again.'

Steven hesitated an instant before securing the length of hickory between two packs in the centre of the raft. This left him without a pole, but he gripped the fourth corner line anyway. 'So I'm just along for the ride.'

'Be grateful, lad: you're at least forty-four inches tall, otherwise, my friend, you'd have to sit this one out.' Garec and Brynne looked at Mark quizzically, but Steven laughed.

Steven felt the familiar pang of insecurity ripple through his stomach and fought the urge to hold the staff close through the coming ordeal.

As the *Capina Fair* rounded the next bend, Garec exhaled sharply, then stood upright and stared disbelievingly into the distance. 'Great demonspawn,' he cried, 'it's a rutting canyon!'

It was a canyon, a narrow gorge just a few raft-widths wide, carved deep into the bedrock over countless Ages. The deep water of the river was squeezed into the inadequate space with the force of a cavalry charge. Rocky bluffs loomed above and save for a few stunted pine trees, all they could see in either direction were the towering cliffs and the boisterously turbulent water. The bright hues of Falkan's countryside faded quickly; their world became stark black granite and foaming white water.

The *Capina Fair* slammed into the first of thousands of rocky outcroppings awaiting them and they knew they had only one choice: navigate well, or drown.

Throughout the day their sturdy craft was battered and buffeted fiercely by the brute force of the rapids. Back and forth across they jounced, over rocks, down short waterfalls, and in and out of swirling eddies, with no rest for the drenched and weary travellers.

After a while Steven motioned to Brynne and she tossed him her pole. The constant thrusting and jabbing that was necessary to keep them from being run aground or, worse, broken apart on the rocks was exhausting. Brynne collapsed on their packs, looping her arms through the coils of rope that secured their belongings to the deck. With his first few thrusts Steven realised all they had was the illusion of control over the *Capina Fair*'s trajectory downstream. At any moment the river might decide it had had enough of being poked with sharp, pointed sticks and cast them effortlessly into the granite wall of the canyon.

Still they fought on.

After a brief rest, Brynne spelled Garec, then Garec relieved Mark, and they fell into a pattern. Despite the incessant pounding, the *Capina Fair* held together well. Steven and Garec grinned at each other briefly, proud of what they'd built.

Despite the rests, it was enormously hard work. Their vigilance began to fail, and they took several blows that nearly shook them from their precarious perches on the *Capina Fair*'s upper deck.

Garec found himself doing less poling and more gripping of lifelines. Several times, lacking the strength to push them away from an underwater boulder, he simply cried out to prepare the others for impact.

By nightfall, they knew they would not survive much longer. Mark, shattered, lay with his back propped against their packs as he tied strips torn from his tunic over the huge blisters that had welled up on both palms. Brynne secured a line about her waist, but she knew if she fell overboard she would not have the strength to pull herself back up; she would most likely be dragged beneath the surface and torn apart on the rocks.

With every twist in the canyon, the group held their collective breath, some in the hope that they would spot the end of the rocky bluffs, the others in fear that a large waterfall lay in wait just out of sight. But each turn brought an audible groan from the disheartened company as nothing changed: time and again their anticipation was for naught. The river careened fiercely onwards through the curving canyon, winding its way inexorably towards the Ravenian Sea, all the while draining their spirits and slowly dismantling their craft.

Darkness came early. Deeper sections of the river that had given a scant few moments' rest were now giving way to large flat rocks that lay just beneath the surface. Anticipating a gentle touchdown from a short waterfall into the soft well of a deep hollow, Steven's teeth rattled as the *Capina Fair* came down hard on a flat boulder he had missed. Rocks and water blurred together and for a moment Steven half expected an all-black world to shroud them, just as the all-white world had blanketed him and Lahp high among the glaciers in the Blackstone Mountains. Pushing hard, he shoved them back into moving water, then suddenly angry, called to Garec.

The bowman turned. His eyes were sunk deep; in the twilight he looked like a lifeless skull; Steven jumped when the skull spoke. 'What is it?'

'Take this,' he said, passing him the pole and moving carefully across to the pile of sodden packs and the hickory staff.

'What are you going to do?' Brynne called over the water's roar.

'There's no place to go ashore, and if we're going to survive, we must have light.' His fingers, stiff and blistered, were clumsy as he untied the ropes holding the staff safe.

Mark nodded in understanding.

Holding the staff close to his face, Steven drew a deep breath and summoned the magic. *No*, he thought, *it's different this time, a release not a summons . . . like that morning in the Blackstones with the pine tree – that was a release, too.*

As it had before, the staff's power flowed through him easily; Steven felt the familiar sensation of time stretching to accommodate him – he wondered once again if time really was slowing, or if he just imagined it. Suddenly, the river seemed manageable, and Steven cursed his wretched insecurity: he should have drawn on the staff's power much earlier. A little uncertain what he should do next, he placed the end of the staff into the riverbed and envisioned the water slowing, levelling, gently moving downstream at a leisurely, navigable pace. At first nothing happened; Steven could still feel the raft being buffeted violently – then, things calmed. The river still raged, both behind and before them, but the *Capina Fair* seemed to settle, floating as if adrift on a small pond.

'Good,' Steven said, and raised the opposite end of the staff above his head. 'Now some light.'

He focused his concentration, visualising a torch he had seen hanging in a wall sconce in Estrad. Gilmour had stolen that torch, used it to light their way – and to light his pipe, of course. Almost immediately a small yellow flame burst in the air above the raft. *Bigger*, Steven commanded in his mind, and as if it had heard him speak out loud, the light grew until the walls of the canyon came into view.

With their path lighted and the *Capina Fair* floating in a gentle current, Mark commented, 'That's better. We could go on like this all night.'

'Yes, but we really ought to find some place to go ashore,' Garec said. 'We need repairs, and if we don't dry out and warm up, the cold will kill us before the river ever does.'

'We ought to rest, too,' Steven added. 'I could sleep until noon.' He used the English word.

'When?' Brynne looked at him through sodden hair, a tangled frame about her beautiful face.

'Noon,' Steven smiled. 'It means midday with some conviction.'

'I don't understand.'

'It means lunch,' Mark added dryly.

'That I understand,' Garec said, 'and if noon means sleeping until midday, with or without conviction, and then eating lunch, you have my complete support.'

'How can we get ashore, though?' Brynne asked. 'We haven't seen anyplace suitable since we entered this canyon.'

'We'll just have to keep going until we find somewhere we can tie up for the night,' Mark suggested. 'At least now the going will be easier.'

The raft, as if floating just above the surface of their tiny circle of water, floated surely over rocks, down abrupt cascades and across whirling eddies. They poled to avoid outcroppings of lethally sharp rocks and to maintain their position midstream, but those tasks were no more demanding than paddling across a windless lake. Steven's flame provided light for their passage as Steven himself continued to imagine a cushioned path for them all the way through the canyon.

The magic did nothing for their fatigue, though, and the travellers continued scanning the canyon walls, looking for someplace to put ashore for a few avens' rest. They took turns napping in pairs, but the evening chill coupled with their waterlogged clothing made proper sleep nearly impossible. Mark and Brynne huddled close together, their teeth chattering audibly. Mark brushed Brynne's hair back from her face and cupped her cheeks in his hands while he told her silly jokes and anecdotes to help them both forget their aches.

At one point, Brynne interrupted him. 'I don't want you to go back home,' she whispered.

Mark leaned forward and kissed her gently on the lips. This wasn't the place or the time he'd have chosen for this discussion.

Brynne pulled him closer and kissed him back, hard and long. He shuddered with need as her tongue moved in his mouth; just the taste of her aroused him like no woman ever had.

He pulled back slightly, and looked deep into her eyes. He put a finger on her mouth and whispered, 'You must know how I feel. But right now, it's academic, isn't it? Who knows if we'll ever find a far portal, let alone be able to use it. I do wish I could somehow let my family know where I am – no, not where I am; they'd think I was completely wacko and have me locked up, or medicated to within an inch of my life! But I want them to at least know that I'm all right, that I'm not murdered, or kidnapped or locked up. They must think we're both dead by now – people would have come to our house days and days ago: the police, Hannah, my students, the principal at my school, friends, Steven's boss from the bank . . .

'I know people have probably been in and out of the house looking for clues to what happened to us, so I can't imagine the far portal is still open. If they found it, they'd have detected its power, even if they didn't know what the hell it was.'

'You felt it?'

'It changed the air in the room. It almost shimmered.' He wagged his fingers to demonstrate for her. 'If somehow the portal closed, though, they'd think it was just an ugly old rug, or maybe a tapestry.'

'Steven is convinced that Hannah is in Eldarn.'

'I know.' Mark looked down at the log deck, and then back at her. 'Hannah would have been one of the first to come looking for us. They had plans for the following day, so it may well be true.'

'There might be others here as well?'

'I suppose,' he allowed, 'although I hope that before too long someone realised that thing was dangerous and closed it up.'

'If it's closed, you might end up falling anywhere in your land.' She tried to remember Gilmour's explanation of the far portals. 'So would Nerak.'

'That's right – listen to me go on, will you? The truth is I have no idea what happened after we got transported to Eldarn.' He ran two fingers along her face and across her chin.

She reached up to take his hand. 'Regardless, I don't want you to go back.'

Mark looked up and saw Steven illuminated in the stafflight. With his hair cropped close and his shaven face, he looked like an accountant on a weekend rafting trip, the one in the play no one gives a second thought to. 'A red top in *Star Trek*,' he muttered to himself, 'cannon fodder.' Then to Brynne, 'I don't think *he* is going back,' Mark whispered, their faces nearly touching in the darkness. 'He'll stay here until this is done, and then . . .' His voice trailed off.

'And then we'll decide what happens with us.' Brynne was back to her opening thought. The tough, knife-wielding partisan grinned, and shot him a sexy come-hither look. She ran her hand down his sodden thigh suggestively.

'What? Here?' Mark was a little taken aback.

She nodded.

'Are you crazy?' he whispered, 'it's forty degrees, and I know that doesn't mean anything to you in Ronan, but where I'm from that means it's a damn sight too cold to get naked outside on a damp raft in the middle of a bloody freezing river.'

'We really should get out of these wet clothes,' she said slyly, starting to peel her top off. 'There are a few dry blankets in these packs; we can roll one out and use some to cover us.'

Mark protested, 'But the guys are right here.'

'Then we'll have to be quiet. Maybe we can huddle down here between these satchels.' She reached under his sweater, and he jumped at her frigid touch. 'Sorry,' she said insincerely, and blew into her fingers before returning them to his chest.

'You aren't going to be denied, are you?'

'Not tonight, Mark, no.' She giggled.

Mark had resigned himself to a torrid session of covert sex with one of the sexiest women he'd ever met when Garec shouted, 'Look! What's over there?'

'Rutters,' Brynne spat, then adjusted her tunic. Mark felt the tiny circles of cold on the flat of his stomach warm slightly as her fingertips drew away.

'Where?' Steven asked, trying to follow the line of Garec's extended finger towards the canyon wall.

'It looks like a cave,' Brynne said, 'a big one, a cavern maybe.'

Mark stood beside her and peered across the water. The river crashed violently against an enormous opening that jutted upwards through the granite like a jagged flaw in the cliff. There was nothing at all comforting or inviting about the cavern's mouth. As they drew closer, he could see that the gaping crack reached nearly halfway up the canyon wall to the precipice above.

'It's huge,' Steven said.

'Yes, but we've no idea how far in it goes, or if there's a decent place for us to make camp once we get inside,' Garec said negatively.

'True,' Steven agreed, 'but if we don't take a look, we'll never know, will we?'

Garec nodded grimly, giving in, and the two of them steered the raft towards the entrance.

As they passed from the river into the cavern, the four travellers were struck by the sudden silence. The deafening roar of the rapids had provided a steady backdrop of noise all day, and the echoes rang in their ears as they passed beneath the natural archway. As the cacophony faded, they were overwhelmed by the heavy quiet. They'd been shouting at each other all day; now the travellers spoke in hushed whispers, as if they had broken into a vast stone tomb and feared waking its residents. Steven's flame pierced the darkness, illuminating a thin passageway ahead.

Mark stared up towards the cavern's ceiling, invisible beyond the stafflight, and said sarcastically, 'Oh, yes, this is much better.'

Steven chuckled. 'We do need a bit more light don't we?' He raised the staff, closed his eyes and motioned; the flame doubled then tripled in size and intensity until the cavern was dimly lit from end to end. He opened his eyes and grinned.

'Your wish is my command, amigo,' he said, clapping Mark on the shoulder. Around the *Capina Fair*, the walls of the canyon dropped straight down into the water. It looked horribly forbidding: as if no place were safe for travellers, but especially not *this* place. Far above, a crooked stone ceiling loomed over them impassively. Following the river's current to the far end of the cave, Steven could see that the ceiling dropped down towards the water's surface. There was a low, narrow passageway, through which the water disappeared into the dark reaches of the canyon wall. They would have to duck, or maybe even kneel if *Capina* was going to take them further into the cavern.

'Well, there doesn't seem to be anyplace to put ashore in here, so let's go back outside,' Mark suggested.

Brynne shook her head. 'No. Let's push ahead. The current isn't bad, and we can always pole our way out if we need to.'

Mark felt the blood drain from his face; he was glad it was too dark for Brynne to see how frightened he was. He hated enclosed spaces. 'It probably just narrows down to nothing back there. It'll be a complete waste of time.'

'So then we'll pole our way out,' she replied. 'Steven? Garec? What do you think?'

'Let's go ahead,' Garec agreed, 'what can it hurt? And if we find someplace to go ashore, we'll have shelter for the night.' His voice cracked as he spoke and he realised his trepidation was now evident. He cursed to himself and began untying the rope securing his bow and quivers.

'What's wrong?' Brynne asked. 'There's nothing here to harm us. We haven't seen a thing all day.'

'True,' Garec replied, 'but you didn't get to meet the last charming inhabitant of this miserable waterway.'

Steven laughed; it bounced from the walls in a quickly moving echo that filled the cavern from top to bottom. 'Ready?'

'Fine,' Mark agreed, drawing the battle-axe from his belt.

The current quickened as they entered the narrow passage at the rear of the cavern, and Brynne realised she had spoken too soon. There was no way they would be able to pole their way back out. Looking over at Steven, she searched his face for signs of insecurity. He looked calm and confident, and she relaxed a little. The staff-wielding foreigner would find some way to propel them back against the current if necessary.

The rock faces closed down around them until the pathway was little more than two raft-lengths across. They didn't have to kneel down, but periodically Mark and Garec were forced to duck beneath a particularly low drop in the stone ceiling. Steven's flame, now unable to float above the raft, moved out ahead to light the roughly hewn tunnel. Despite the luminance and warmth accompanying the fireball, a cold darkness settled about them and no one spoke as they wound their way deeper and deeper into the cavern.

Finally Garec broke the silence. His face was formless in the murky firelight as he said quietly, 'That's it. I can't reach the bottom any longer.'

'Neither can I.' Steven stretched low over the side of the *Capina Fair*, but he still failed to find solid ground. 'Use the poles against the walls to keep us midstream. The current here is strong but deep. We won't need to worry about unexpected rapids.'

'Where are we going?' Mark asked. 'Unless this pops out in an Orindale tavern, we're going to have to get back out to the river tomorrow. How much further should we let this carry us?'

'A bit further, that's all,' Steven suggested. 'If we can't find someplace soon to tie her off and dry things out, we'll head back.'

The tunnel wound its way in lazy curves back and forth and ever deeper into the gloom. The crisply moving current suggested their passageway stretched onwards, perhaps to the other side of the cliff, but Mark feared the ceiling would drop down suddenly, leaving this branch of the river to continue its flow underground. He wasn't looking forward to feeling the overhead stone close down upon them, or having the walls of their already cosy tunnel narrowing to trap the *Capina Fair* between ponderous granite bookends for ever. He imagined them being slowly swallowed by a great stone god so beset by the general lassitude of the ages that it would not even realise it had eaten them whole, raft and all. Garec had placed his pole beside him on the deck and now held his bow loosely in one hand. Mark wasn't sure what Garec planned to shoot, but he wouldn't deny it was comforting to know he was armed and at the ready.

Mark had never been one for nostalgia. He sometimes found it a bit worrying that important events, even entire years in his past, somehow collapsed down to just a few moments in his memory. Months of preparation had gone into the state swimming championships, which was probably the most antici-pated event in his life thus far. He swam brilliantly, winning three events and shattering two school records – but now, ten years on, the memory of that time had been reduced to just a few glimpses. He could see his coach shouting at him from above the water; he could feel the cold winter air on his still-damp hair as he waited for his ride home. And, most often, he could remember a few seconds of underwater confusion while he reached for the finish wall, looked around and felt the elation well up. Four months of work and anticipation, the greatest single moment of his youth, represented by ten or twelve seconds of colour, sound and feeling.

But thinking back over the time he and Steven had been in Eldarn, he thought that perhaps things here were different. There was almost nothing that he could not recall in vivid detail: the feel of the stones as they rubbed against his knuckles at Riverend, the smell of lodge pines burning above him as he slowly faded to sleep in the falling snow, the touch of Brynne's body against his as they lay together in the forest cabin, each having thought the other dead: these and a thousand other incidents, he could still feel them, whole, in his memory. Right now, he was dreading the recollection he would carry of this cavern: he was pretty sure he would have to swim back out of this tunnel, and he knew he no longer had the strength.

Soon they were forced to kneel. 'Turn us around, Steven,' Mark commanded. 'This is getting too tight.' The passageway closed further, and the raft bumped between stone walls as it pressed ever forward.

'All right,' Steven agreed. 'I hoped we might find something, but you're right. We should go back.' He was reaching for the staff when his eye caught the faint glimmer of something up ahead. 'What's that?'

'Where?' Garec was down onto all fours now, trying to avoid striking his head on the granite ceiling. Mark and Brynne soon joined him.

'There, out beyond the stafflight. Something flickered, like another light.'

'Steven,' Mark interrupted, 'we're running out of room here.'

Steven was about to lie flat on the *Capina Fair*'s deck when he heard Garec shout, 'Ah, demonpiss!'

'What happened?'

'The ceiling, Steven, I hit my head on the ceiling—' Garec shut up as the stafflight suddenly went out and they were plunged into a cruel and forbidding darkness, depthless, blacker than any of them could have imagined. The space ahead had grown too narrow for Steven's fireball and it had extinguished itself in the river.

Mark lay flat on his back, holding out his hands. An especially low section of ceiling scraped across his forehead and he felt a warm trickle of blood run down his temple. He tried to push against the rock, an impossible bench press, to force the raft down into the water and make room for his body to pass beneath the granite just scant inches above his face. Terrified, he held his breath and waited for Steven to summon the staff's magic and carry them back upstream.

A mantra ran through his mind: *What if it didn't work?* It had failed that day on the riverbed; what if that happened again? Why was Steven hesitating – was he trying to summon the magic now, and was it ignoring him? He had agreed to take them back to the cavern mouth, but he hadn't said a word since, and still they were inching their way forward. Where was he? Mark could hear the river rushing by beneath them; he wondered why the current was suddenly moving so quickly. 'Steven,' he cried, a muffled plea, 'are you still there?'

Get overboard. That was Mark's only option. He had to get overboard and maybe find a hand or foothold in the wall so he could stop the raft's progress long enough for the others to roll off into the water as well. *Push and slide. That's it. Push and slide. One leg down. Push and slide. Both legs.*

Mark relaxed the pressure he had been putting against the ceiling with his arms for a moment to adjust his grip, and in that instant, the *Capina Fair* buoyed upward forcing the granite down on his chest. *Get a breath in. Get a breath in, shit.* He tried to roll to one side, to inch one hand, one finger up between his chest and the rock ceiling, but he couldn't. Desperate, he tried to push with his forehead. *Not much, I don't need much, just enough to get a breath in. Breathe. Get a breath in.*

Behind him he heard Brynne scream; beside him he could feel Garec kicking violently to free himself from the bone-crushing pressure.

Suddenly everything erupted in a blinding flash. Water splashed over the sides of the *Capina Fair*, and Mark felt his lungs fill with welcome air. His hands free, he reached upwards for the granite ceiling, but found nothing there. He tried to roll, expecting the stone to hold his shoulders down, but a moment later he tumbled from the deck into the frigid water.

The cold cleared his head and as he kicked towards the surface, he saw light once again, a bright light that sliced through the darkness.

Mark broke the surface of the water in a rage. 'Steven, you stupid sonofabitch! What in the seven shades of Hell were you waiting for?' His voice echoed back in huge, swollen waves, the inane mimicry of an irritating lesser god. Stunned silent by the din, Mark took in their surroundings. The *Capina Fair*, now about twenty yards ahead of him, drifted on an underground lake. Garec and Steven stood staring into the distance while Brynne reached out to him with one of the poles. He swam towards the raft. Behind them, he could see the impossibly narrow opening through which Steven had forced the raft only seconds before.

There would be no going back that way. The river pushed through a hairline crack in the granite wall with tremendous force, and Mark marvelled at how they had managed to get through without losing their packs or supplies – or one another – in the narrow passage.

In the air above the raft hovered an enormous ball of fire – no, as Mark peered upwards at it, he realised that it was somehow more than fire. It was blinding, a brighter, more intense flame, like something that might have come from a chemistry set, or maybe a magic stick.

Around them, the lake stretched out to fill the gigantic cavern. Mark could still hear his voice, booming back from what felt like miles away: *Sonofabitch . . . Sonofabitch . . . Sonofabitch . . .*

High above, the granite ceiling had retreated to its original position. It looked different now, flecked with iridescent minerals; odd colours sparkling in the magical light. Getting chilly now the fear had worn off, Mark drew his lungs full of air and dropped beneath the surface, allowing the cold to sink in and further clear his mind.

He felt better. They were still alive. Steven's fire could ensure they were warm and dry, and after a good night's sleep, they could put their minds to finding a way out.

When Mark resurfaced, he caught sight of Brynne, who was still holding the wooden pole out to him and staring grimly.

'What's wrong?' he asked, more quietly this time.

She pointed towards the shoreline, and the grotesque discovery that had his friends silenced.

Bones. Thousands – no, *millions* of bones. Human bones: skulls, femurs, ribs, some still held together in partial cage shapes by strands of rotten cartilage, radii, jawbones, and an apparently endless array of tiny hand and foot bones scattered about: a charnel-house to rival the largest mass grave ever by ten thousand times.

'Good Christ,' he whispered.

'Mark,' Steven called, 'you'd better get up here.'

The shoreline sloped gradually down to the water; as far as Mark could see the angle and depth remained the same in any direction. The only break in the shore was the forbidding edifice that rose up behind them, a huge granite monolith. Mark wondered if that wall was devoid of a shoreline because the river that burst from it had washed the shore away eons ago. Instead of sand, the shore was made up of small round pebbles mixed with the ubiquitous bone fragments; the way the light glinted from the stones made it look as if they were diamonds. Mark dreaded the moment when he would have to step ashore, for there would be no way to avoid feeling the bones crunch and shatter underfoot.

He pulled himself up onto the deck and stood beside Steven. Clapping his friend on the back, he said, 'What a lovely place you have here. How are you getting along with the neighbours?'

'Mark, be serious,' Brynne scolded.

'Serious? I'm not the one who wanted to go into the cavern in the first place, let me remind you.'

Steven shushed him. 'Listen, I really did see something.'

'Something?'

'A light. It flickered for a moment, and then it went out. There's someone down here.'

Mark stared at him incredulously. 'Someone down here? Have you not noticed that the entire population of Uruguay appears to have their bones stacked against that wall? Of course there's someone down here, but I'm not certain he's setting out a warm welcome and a nice dinner for us right now.'

Steven ignored him. 'What do you suppose it was? A plague? A war?'

'It couldn't have been,' Garec replied.

'Why not?' Brynne asked.

'Look at the bones. They're not jumbled together like they would be in a mass grave.'

Mark exhaled. 'Holy mother, he's right.'

Garec summed up what each of them was thinking. 'Those bones were collected here, organised carefully into similar stacks, skulls here, legs there, arms across the way.'

Brynne looked like she was about to dive into the water and risk the swim back upstream. 'Who could have done this?'

'Or *what*?' Mark looked puzzled, as if trying to remember something. Grimacing, he turned to Steven. 'Can you move the stafflight nearer the ceiling?'

'Why?'

'I hope it's nothing, but send it up anyway.'

Mark's fears were confirmed: through the hazy, half-light they could see the ceiling had been decorated with bones. Some dangled downwards from the rocky roof while others lay flat, displayed against the dark surface of the stone, as if to enhance their ivory colour with a black backdrop. These bones were obviously prized. Skulls were hanging everywhere, ogling the trespassers through long-empty eye sockets.

His mouth agape, Steven stared solemnly upwards, mute with stupefaction. His mind raced, but the image of what might have committed such a gruesome act made him close his eyes; he pictured some creature, nefarious, and crafty, with an almost human capacity for understanding, but with spindly legs like a spider's, or perhaps thick membranous wings and wickedly clawed talons.

He spoke as if to himself. 'What is keeping them up there?'

Mark surprised him by answering, 'Glue, nails, John the Baptist? Who knows? It's probably some secretion that comes out of an orifice I don't like imagining in a creature I don't like imagining that hardens like epoxy and holds them fast for ever.'

'But why?'

'To comfort little baby epoxy-secreting monsters as they go to sleep in their cribs? Again, who knows? Let's focus on getting ourselves out of here before it – or they – return.' Mark swallowed hard and began poling towards shore. The *Capina Fair* had held together so far, but she was badly in need of repair, and they were all in desperate need of food and rest.

'We can use the light to explore along the shoreline. With that much water coming in here, there has to be an outlet – or maybe we can find a tunnel to the surface.' He cringed when a sickly crunch resounded from below as their raft struck the shore.

Two avens later, they had eaten, changed into dry clothing and used the stafflight to dry out the rest of their belongings. They explored a little along the shoreline; Mark and Brynne walked while Garec and Steven poled the *Capina Fair* through the shallows. It took them nearly half an aven to reach the end of the great charnel-house, and each was visibly relieved when they no longer heard the breaking of tiny hand and foot bones with every footfall.

Finally they found a recessed area in the stone wall, small but dry, and they agreed to take turns sleeping and standing guard in pairs. There was no wood to make a fire, so Steven brought the stafflight down to the ground, weakened its intensity and left it to burn like a campfire. As soon as he fell asleep, however, the flame went out.

'Well, this is a pain,' Garec grumbled. 'Steven, wake up.'

Steven sat up with a start. 'What? What is it?'

'The fire's out.'

'Oh, hell and damnation. Okay. So that's not going to work, is it? Let me think a minute.' He stared down at the space between them and moments later a pleasant campfire, devoid of fuel, was burning brightly on the pebbly shore. He lay back down and rolled over in his blanket.

'Just a moment, Steven,' Garec warned. 'It went out when you went to sleep, and since we can't have you up all night – or day, or whatever it is now, we'll need some wood.' His voiced trailed off as he searched around them. 'Mark, help me with this.'

The two men, not without difficulty, pulled a log from the *Capina Fair*'s middle deck and placed it in the fire. Garec smiled at Steven. 'Just stay awake long enough for this thing to dry out a bit on this end.'

'I'll do you one better, Garec,' Steven replied and inhaled deeply as he stared at the saturated pine log. Steam began to rise from the trunk in great clouds as Steven heated it from within.

'Hey, that's hot,' Garec yelped and dropped the log to rub his burned fingers on his tunic. Moments later the log was dry throughout, and one end was crackling sharply in the fire. Garec pondered the length of pine then shrugged. 'I guess we'll just slide more of it into the campfire as that end burns down. Thanks, Steven.'

Beside him, Mark said nothing as his exhausted friend fell back. Steven was asleep almost immediately.

Noticing Mark's stare, Garec cast him an inquisitive look. 'What is it?' he whispered.

'You didn't see that?' Mark was not confident he could believe his own eyes. He needed Garec to confirm his suspicions.

'See what?'

Mark answered, more to himself, 'A neon sign ... OIL CHANGE, twenty-six dollars and ninety-nine cents.'

'What?'

'It happened that morning when he knocked that tree down as well – the morning you two almost killed each other.'

577

Garec's face flushed. 'I don't understand. It's magic; we've seen him use it before ... many times.'

Mark didn't respond, but instead motioned towards the far wall of their recessed camp.

'So what?' Garec was still confused. Finally something clicked and he realised what the foreigner was trying to tell him.

The hickory staff leaned against the wall. In his fatigue, Steven had dried the log and ignited the fire unaided.

THE BEACH CAMP

When Brexan woke, she felt warm and rested, somehow rejuvenated, although soaking wet. She shook the hazy semi-consciousness from her head and realised she was still neck-deep in the Ravenian Sea. Oddly, it was no longer cold – in fact, it felt quite warm, as warm as bathwater. Darkness was falling, but she could make out the Ronan coast; it looked closer now. Suddenly confused, she wondered how it could be that she was still alive, and how she could have come so far. She called out for Versen half-heartedly; the last thing she remembered was crying as he slipped beneath the waves. Treading water, she turned a circle, scanning the surface for any sign of him.

She nearly sank in shock when a voice called back, 'Over here.'

Through the twilight, she saw him. His shaggy hair was matted down flat against his head, providing a frame for his bright green eyes, broad grin and chiselled features. He no longer looked pale, but robust and strong, fit enough to take up the fight against Malagon and his minions. Tears welled up in her eyes as she paddled furiously across the short distance separating them.

Throwing herself onto him, she wrapped her legs around his waist and cast her arms roughly about his neck. 'I thought for certain I had lost you,' she sobbed.

'Brexan, I—' Her weight forced his head beneath the surface and the last few words of his response were lost in an abrupt wellspring of bubbles.

'Oh, demonpiss!' Embarrassed, she let him go. 'Sorry, I'm not trying to drown you now!'

Versen floated back to the surface and playfully spat a mouthful of salt water at her. 'Good to see you again too.' He reached for her, clasping his large hands firmly on her hips, and pulled her towards him. His stomach fluttered; adrenalin pumped through his veins as she pulled him even closer. He buried his face in the crook of her neck, inhaling the scent of seawater and warm woman. He dared not speak, for fear of making a fool of himself, his emotions were running so high.

Revelling in his touch, Brexan stroked her hands down his muscular shoulders and finally gave in to the passion that had been building from the moment he woke from his coma and told her, 'I love you.' She ran her tongue over his lips, tasting the saltwater, flicking the tip of it between his teeth until he was almost dizzy with desire. He growled softly and took possession of her mouth, plundering her sweetness with his tongue. The two of them were carelessly lost in the moment and explored each other, hands stroking, pressing, teasing, while their mouths locked together. Finally Brexan pushed him slightly and he released her. As they gasped for air, she wondered, 'Are we dead?'

Brexan started to cry again. 'I saw you go under. I tried so hard to hang on, but it was so cold, and you were so heavy.'

Versen hugged her to him tightly, marvelling at her courage and strength of will. 'You did everything you could. It wasn't your job to keep me afloat.'

'But I saw you go under,' she gulped as uncontrollable sobs racked her body. Now she clung to his neck as she relived that terrifying moment when she found herself cold and alone in the middle of the Ravenian Sea, too far from land to survive. 'I gave up. I decided to die, and I was – I was afraid we'd just sink to the bottom and that it would be dark.' She felt a fool, a little girl afraid of the dark, revealing her feelings in a flood of embarrassing confessions, but Versen interrupted her.

He kissed her again, gently this time, and calmly said, 'Brexan, it's all right now. I'm fine. We're not dead.'

'But how?'

'You mean *who*.'

'Who? I don't understand.'

'I think his name is O'Reilly, Gabriel O'Reilly.' Versen groped for an explanation. 'I think he knows Steven Taylor, the foreigner I told you about. He came looking for us – well, for me – when Mark told him we'd been separated at Seer's Peak.'

'Where is he?' Brexan sounded sceptical. 'Did he swim off to find us a boat or something? And how did he know to find us out there? And how did he warm the sea up?'

'Well, those are all good questions, and I don't want you to be alarmed, but I think he's here with us now.' Versen's eyebrows climbed up his forehead in an effort to convey lightheartedness.

'What do you mean?' Brexan frowned.

'Okay, you've got to absolutely promise not to panic.' She looked at him strangely and he laughed. 'Not helpful? I can see that. Just remember: Gabriel saved us, all right?' She nodded agreement and held Versen a little bit tighter.

'Gabriel O'Reilly is a wraith, a spirit of sorts, here from Steven and Mark's Colorado. He provided a body for Nerak to travel between Colorado and Eldarn a little over nine hundred and eighty Twinmoons ago.'

'So when you say "here with us", you mean floating around here somewhere?' Brexan began searching the skies, squinting into the twilight.

'No, I mean, *here*, with us.' He placed a finger on Brexan's breastbone, just below her neck. 'Inside us, warming us from within, and lending us the physical strength we need to survive.'

Brexan looked askance at him. 'Inside us? Us both?'

'I am,' a gentle voice echoed in her mind.

Brexan cried out in surprise, 'Great gods of the Northern Forest!' and renewed her iron grip about Versen's neck. 'Was that him? Did you hear it too?'

'I did,' Versen said, stroking her arm in an effort to calm her down, 'he and I have been talking for much of the past aven. You were unconscious, but he kept you alive as he helped drag us along through the water.'

'But how is he doing that? How did he get inside us like that?'

'He did it to save our lives – without him, I would be— *we* would both be dead by now. He tracked us from the Blackstones; I don't know how, but I'm surely glad he did. And he's brought news of the others. They were attacked by an army of spirits, similar to him, but thousands of them – and definitely *not* on our side. My friends were holed up in a little cabin on the northern slope of the Blackstone Mountains, not far from the Falkan border. Steven and Garec were preparing to fight them off.' He paused.

'What happened?' Brexan asked, her mouth hanging open a

little. Versen smiled, pleased her curiosity had overcome her initial fear.

'I had to flee.' Brexan jumped a little as O'Reilly's voice spoke inside her head.

'Sorry,' she said. 'It may take me some time to get used to having you in there.'

'My apologies. I will try to surprise you less frequently as we make our way to shore.'

Brexan was so preoccupied at the thought of a thousand-Twinmoon-old spirit haunting her mind that she had briefly forgotten she and Versen were still a long distance from shore, and still in danger of drowning.

'So, what of Versen's friends?' she asked, returning to the topic at hand. 'Why did you run away?'

'The spirits who attacked the forest cabin were like me, souls summoned by Nerak to hunt down and retrieve the key to the spell table in Sandcliff Palace. There were thousands of them. I would have been tortured and cast back into the Fold had they detected my presence. If I was to be any assistance to your cause – to *our* cause – I had to get away.'

The wraith's voice was a smooth baritone; Brexan wondered if their curious saviour sounded the same to Versen.

The spirit continued, 'In the moments before the attack, I warned Mark, and then fled west to find you, Versen.'

'I am extraordinarily glad you did so,' Versen said with a chuckle.

Brexan smiled at the sight of Versen speaking aloud to no one. He was alive, so very much alive. His head was cast back slightly, and he spoke in a raised voice, as if the wraith was floating above the surface of the water rather than communicating from inside their bodies. She grimaced suddenly; she wasn't sure how keen she was on some disembodied spirit being inside her while she and Versen were kissing. She flushed bright red. If Gabriel O'Reilly had read her thoughts, he must be appalled at her forwardness . . . Brexan blushed again, and buried her face in the water for several moments. Changing the topic, she asked, 'You said "our cause" – how is this your cause?'

'I am – I *was* – a bank manager, and it was I who allowed the miner William Higgins to open the account that sealed the far portal and Lessek's Key away for almost a thousand Twinmoons.

I was the last man to carry the evil prince back to Eldarn across the Fold.' The spirit's voice hesitated, then continued softly, 'I suffered an agony unlike anything I had ever imagined when that man – that *thing* – was inside my body. I could feel parts of me dying, and yet I could do nothing to save myself. I could not cry out, could not bandage my wounds, could not share my thoughts with anyone. I was at his mercy, and in all these years, these Twinmoons, I have been able to do little more than relive that memory, again and again.'

Gabriel O'Reilly's voice seemed to crack, and Brexan found herself touched by the wraith's tragic story. 'So you have issues to settle with our sovereign lord as well,' she said, her tone icy.

'Indeed I do.'

'Then let's get moving. We need to get to Orindale and see if the others have made it into the city.' She started swimming, then stopped again and said, 'Thank you. I don't think we've actually said that, have we? You saved our lives, and for that alone we can never repay you. And thanks to you, we know the others cleared the Blackstones. That's an amazing accomplishment in itself. If they managed to escape the wraiths, they might already be in Orindale.'

O'Reilly answered for both of them to hear, 'There are several fishermen pulling nets not far from here. They will take us to shore. I will remain in you until you have slept and regained some of your own strength. Then we can travel north together.'

An elderly fisherman, shocked anyone would be swimming so far from shore, heaved the duo roughly into his small skiff. Brexan cringed as she landed in a heaping pile of enormous jemma fish. She slipped along the seaman's scaly carpet and curled up in a small space in the bow. She was asleep before her head hit the deck.

Versen spent a half-aven talking with the fisherman, attempting to explain how he and the young woman had managed to become lost, and then survived the cold autumn waters, when no vessel had been sighted since the twilight aven began. The fisherman, Caddoc Weston, continued pulling in his nets as he humoured his new passengers. He did not believe they had been on a sailing vessel that sank suddenly when some planking came loose in her hull, and a few carefully worded questions about navigation, prevailing winds and rigging confirmed the big Ronan was lying. Versen knew nothing of ships save what little he had gleaned while chained up in the *Falkan Dancer*. Realising he was caught out, he shrugged and gave a half smile. The fisherman nodded and the matter was dropped.

In an effort to redirect their conversation, Versen asked about the pile of jemma fish.

'Good night tonight,' Caddoc said laconically. 'Large schools of jemma are moving south this Twinmoon. The fishing's been good.' A series of hacking coughs racked his frame and he spat a mouthful of bloody phlegm over the side.

'Are you all right?' Versen moved to assist him.

'Fine. I'm fine.' A second coughing fit had the veins in his neck bulging. Wiping his chin on the back of his wrist, he added, 'We all die. I get to do it out here.' He gestured with a bony hand at the Ravenian Sea and Versen realised for the first time since leaving Strandson that the southern ocean was beautiful.

'You should get some sleep too,' Caddoc suggested. Versen thought, unnervingly, that he already looked like a skeleton in the waning light.

Picking his way forward to join Brexan in the bow, Versen marvelled at the irony of an alarmingly thin fisherman surrounded by such a bounteous catch. 'He must not eat any of it,' he mumbled to himself.

'I suppose not,' Gabriel surprised him by answering.

Just after dawn Caddoc carefully manoeuvred the small skiff into the shallows off a narrow strip of sand flanked by rolling dunes. Slowing to a stop, the skiff began to turn in the tide and was soon pitching lazily on the incoming waves. Brexan woke as their host began striking his sail and stowing the small mast. She started to stretch, but was alarmed to find her legs refused to move; it was only when she rubbed the sleep from her eyes that she discovered she and Versen were buried to the waist in jemma fish.

'Oh, whoring grettanlovers!' she exclaimed, recoiling from the strong-smelling cargo.

Versen woke and wrapped his arms tightly about her waist. Resting his cheek against her breasts, he yawned and grinned a greeting to the fisherman. 'You were right.'

'Yes,' Caddoc replied, rather more enthusiastic than he had been, 'I told you it would be a good night.'

'Ox!' Brexan was disgusted. 'How can you be so happy? We were nearly entombed in dead fish.'

'It appears we were.'

'Do you have any idea just how appalling you're going to smell when we get out of here?' She nudged him playfully in the ribs.

'You've been telling me that for the past Twinmoon.' He stretched and sat up. 'I suggest you learn to love me as I am.'

'Malodorous and badly in need of a shave?' She pulled a length of matted hair, thick with jemma scales, behind one ear. 'Not a chance!'

'All right,' he teased, 'but I thought we had something going here.'

'Ah, so now the truth—'

The fisherman cleared his throat and glanced down at the couple lying hip-deep in his overnight catch. Embarrassed, his face flushed red and he nodded towards shore.

Versen got it and pulled himself up, holding fast to the gunwale so he didn't slip, then he helped Brexan to her feet. They laughed at the absurdity, offered their sincere thanks, and jumped overboard into the shallows. Thigh-deep in the waves, they turned and waved again, then began walking towards the dunes.

Several paces away, Versen suddenly remembered their destination. Turning back, he shouted, 'How far to Orindale?'

'Walking? Four, maybe five days. Good luck,' he replied then reached down and hefted a large jemma fish to his chest. He tossed it to Versen and advised, 'Fillet this soon. It should be enough to get you to Orindale.'

Waving their thanks, both for the rescue and the unexpected bounty, they set off to the shore. Caddoc watched as Versen helped the young lady up the sand, then turned back to his haul. 'No accounting for the sea,' he said to himself as the strange couple disappeared behind the dunes.

It took them a quarter-aven to reach the top of the tallest dune. Versen, his bare feet buried ankle-deep in sand, held the jemma by the tail and waved out at the slowly disappearing fisherman with the other. The skiff's single sail, a tiny triangle interrupting the smooth blue backdrop, soon slipped from view. Beside him, Brexan looked around as if expecting someone to emerge and welcome them back to Rona. Or were they in Falkan now? She thought they might have been carried far enough north to have crossed the border, especially if they were only five days' travel from Orindale.

Watching the waves break across the beach, Versen said, 'We should get as far as we can today, but if you're hungry, we can eat some of this now.'

Without answering, Brexan grasped him firmly by the forearm, removed the fish from his fist, dropped it to the sand and began leading him down the dune's lee slope.

'What are you doing?' the Ronan asked.

'Hush, Ox,' she commanded, and began unfastening the leather strips holding his tunic closed at the neck.

Feeling her fingertips brush against his chest, Versen inhaled her aroma, all dead fish and tidewater. He winced: not very alluring – but his body responded to her touch regardless. As he leaned into her, his cheek brushed against the swollen purple bruise that still marked the place where Lahp had punched her. 'I thought I smelled bad,' he whispered.

'I'll breathe through my mouth,' Brexan muttered, then kissed him quickly and returned to her struggle to undress him. The Malakasian soldier finally gave up grappling with wet leather knots and turned her attention to the woollen ties holding his leggings tight around his hips.

His excitement growing, Versen slipped his hands under the edge of her tunic and pulled it up, exposing her pale skin to the cool onshore breeze. Moving to accommodate him, Brexan crossed her arms, hastily grabbed the front hem of her tunic and prepared to pull it over her head – until, without warning, Versen gripped her by the shoulders and pinned her arms down.

'Don't,' he said, despite his nearly paralysing desire to see her naked in the morning sun.

'But I want to,' she replied, with a pout that drove him mad.

'Brexan, we're not alone here.'

Pulling her tunic around her torso, the young woman exclaimed, 'Rutting gods, O'Reilly, are you still here?'

Quiet peals of laughter chimed in her head. 'Yes, I am.'

'Could you give us an aven or two of privacy?'

The ghost of the bank manager replied, 'I am concerned you may not feel very well if I depart. Without me you will find yourselves very weak.'

'We'll risk it for the moment.' Brexan did not want to seem ungrateful, but her mind was made up. She'd been waiting for this moment for a very long time.

'I will return later this morning.'

Brexan felt a wave of nausea pass through her body as the wraith departed; a thin wisp of smoky white gathered itself above their heads and drifted east into a sparsely wooded piece of ground behind the dunes. Her vision tunnelled and her head spun in a momentary attack of vertigo. Feeling an urgent need to lie down, Brexan pressed both palms against the broad expanse of Versen's chest and forced him into the sand beside her.

A while later, they both slept again.

Steven woke for his watch, rolled onto his side and stretched the stiffness from his back and legs. 'A bed. I would give just about anything for one night in a real bed. Sprung mattress. Linen sheets. Oh God—' His neck cracked as he twisted his head from side to side.

'Soon, my friend, very soon,' Garec promised. 'Orindale has wonderful taverns, with hot food, soft down pillows and warm woollen blankets.'

'I want some new clothes, too. I smell like a rotting corpse in these rags.' He tugged at the sleeve of his filthy tunic.

'Brynne and I will take you shopping.'

'I still have some of that silver we stole in Estrad.'

'Plenty to completely re-outfit both of you in the finest city fashions.' Garec's eyes danced in the flickering light. He was amused at Steven's grievances when they were buried here beneath the earth in the lair of a bone-gathering monster that might spring upon them at any moment.

'I don't need fine fashions, Garec, just clothes that are durable and comfortable.' He rubbed his eyes, then reached out, took Garec by the wrist and peered down at the watch he had given the young bowman at the start of their journey. 'Two o'clock,' he yawned. 'Of course that means nothing here. It might be the middle of the day or the middle of the night for all I know.'

'Sorry.'

'Oh, it's not your fault. Just don't let me look at that thing again. It's depressing.' He hauled himself to his feet and walked over to where Brynne lay, still fast asleep. He nudged her gently with his foot. 'Wake up, sleepyhead. We're on deck.' He was groggy himself, and not surprised that the young woman barely moved at his touch.

'On deck?' Garec asked.

'Oh, nothing,' he said and nudged her again. 'Geez, she can sleep anywhere.'

'I know,' Garec agreed. 'It is a little disconcerting sometimes. Sallax used to jokingly check her for a heartbeat.'

'Ah, forget it. Let her sleep. She needs it. I'll be all right by myself.' He tightened his belt another notch and looked about their camp. 'Where's the staff?' He didn't appear to be troubled by the fact that the hickory stick was the first thing he sought upon waking.

Swallowing dryly, Garec recalled Steven's display of magic without benefit of the staff and searched for the right words. 'Yes, well, about that—'

'Is it on the raft?' Steven wasn't paying attention. 'That's a good little fire you have going there, Garec. Ah, here it is.' He strode to the stone wall and retrieved the smooth length of wood. 'Do we have any tecan? I could use a bucket or two.'

Garec decided to drop the subject of magic for the moment. 'No, all we had was drenched as we came through the rapids. I'm sure we left a trail of brown runoff in our wake.'

'Criminal.'

'Couldn't agree more.'

Mark joined them. 'There's some food in Brynne's pack, and feel free to burn more of that log if it starts to die out.'

'I think we ought to save that,' Steven replied. 'Who knows how long we might be down here? It might come in handy later.' With that, he stamped out their campfire and allowed the absolute darkness of the underground cavern to swallow them. Garec and Mark heard him exhale deeply, then watched as a small fire burst into view where their campfire had been an instant before.

'I can keep this going while you two get some rest,' Steven said. 'When you wake we'll eat again and then continue down the shoreline.' He placed the staff on the ground near the fire and began rummaging through his pack.

Garec looked at Mark, shrugged, and folded himself within the protective layers of his blanket. He rolled over to feel the fire's warmth across his back and was asleep before Mark could spread his own blanket out on the pebbly ground.

Two avens later, Garec woke with a cry and leaped to his feet. Without really knowing why, he checked the watch, and wondered what that rune meant, the one Steven and Mark called 'Seffen'.

Brynne was already awake. She left her perch on one corner of the *Capina Fair*'s deck and asked, 'What's wrong?'

'Nothing,' he said, and peered into the darkness as if anticipating someone's arrival. 'Did you hear something?'

'Only you jumping out of bed.' She crouched beside him. 'Go back to sleep, Garec. You look tired.'

Steven observed their exchange over his shoulder, but remained where he was, standing watch out near the edge of the firelight. He *had* heard something.

'I'm all right,' Garec insisted as he continued staring at the wall of darkness shrouding their camp on all sides. 'I just thought I heard something.'

'Well, there's nothing out there,' Brynne said, comfortingly. 'We haven't heard or seen anything in the past two—'

She was cut off by a wave of shouts, commands and warnings hurled at them from the darkness. Garec dived for his bow and quivers while Brynne reached for a rapier, her dagger, and the hunting knife that was never more than an arm's length away. She scanned the darkness, half-expecting to see an army of bone-hunters skimming across the surface of the water on spiked tentacles or diving down at them from the obsidian sky – then she realised the cries were human.

Suddenly angry, Brynne prepared herself for a fight. 'Come right in,' she cried as Steven's firelight gleamed along the carefully honed edge of her knife. 'I haven't disembowelled anyone in a couple of Twinmoons and I am *ready* for you!' She felt the heat of battle rage through her body as she quickly discarded the thick woollen tunic she wore over her cotton undergarment: she needed to be agile and quick, not weighed down by heavy clothing. The number of intruders approaching their camp sounded formidable.

Then Mark was by her side, his battle-axe poised to strike. He didn't look comfortable. 'What's happening?' he shouted unnecessarily.

'We're about to come under attack.' She shot him a sexy grin and reminded, 'Remember, don't try to hack off any limbs – especially not your own.'

Mark gurgled an incoherent reply, regained his senses and yelled to Steven, 'Hey, how about some light?'

Calmly, Steven nodded, closed his eyes and held one hand out, palm-down. He made a sweeping gesture from shoreline to shoreline: this would get their attention! All at once, scores of enemy torches that had been extinguished to ensure a stealthy approach burst into flame and illuminated the cavern around their camp. The four friends gaped at the force coming towards them. Ten longboats, each loaded with twenty or more armed warriors were approaching over the lake while another crowd of assailants were creeping over the rocky shore to surround their camp: a classic pincer movement.

Mark guessed the screams were meant to intimidate and demoralise, but as all their torches sprang to light simultaneously, their shouting died out in an instant. There was an unexpected hissing as a number of the attackers, stunned by the sudden fire in their hands, dropped their torches into the water. One was so startled that his flaming branch fell into the longboat and cries of warning and anger were replaced by screams of pain and surprise as several men struggled to stamp out the strangely resilient flame dancing about inside their vessel. What had begun as a highly organised silent ambush had evolved into a confused and broken attack, all strategy forgotten, thanks to Steven's magic.

Cries of 'Evil magic! Demon fire!' and 'Retreat!' replaced the previous intimidating threats. Steven set his jaw in determination, hoping he had turned the tide before the battle began.

One voice rose above the others. 'Stand fast!' it commanded urgently, 'it's just a trick. Stand fast!'

Garec had an arrow nocked and ready to fire; two additional quivers were standing ready by his hand. He took in as many details of the enemy as possible. They did not appear to be Malakasian, or if they were, they did not wear Prince Malagon's colours. On closer examination, he wasn't even sure they were soldiers: they were a ragtag band of men and women of all ages, and in all states of dress. Even though the light was not that bright, he could see a number of bare feet. Some of the people looked fit and tough; others sported hefty paunches. They were armed with everything from bows to broadswords. Many brandished daggers and even kitchen knives; there were quite a few sturdy wooden cudgels as well. This was no organised fighting force; this was a band of thieves or pirates.

Garec thought they might stand a chance if he and Steven could kill a pile of them before they reached shore, but he had no idea how they would handle the attackers approaching along the beach, then Steven gave him the answer.

'Stay where you are!' Steven shouted above the confused din.

'Steady now,' the commanding voice called back. 'On my mark.' The voice came from a longboat off to Steven's left.

Shaking his head, Steven pointed the staff at the closest boat and watched as flames crept up its gunwales and licked along the handrail to ignite the oars. Twenty would-be assailants screamed at once and summarily leaped, fell or were pushed over the side. He repeated his directive. 'Stay where you are!'

One man, about Garec's age, had been warily creeping along. Now, hidden in the shadows with his back to the stone wall, he waited. When all eyes were on the burning longboat, he took advantage of their inattention and charged towards Mark and Brynne, weapons drawn and bellowing a battle cry. Brynne, who both felt and heard him approach, took several steps towards him, then dropped to her knees and used the young man's weight against him. Unable to slow in time, he stumbled, tripped over her and tumbled to a stop near the waterline.

Mark stared in disbelief – it had happened so quickly he hadn't even realised Brynne had moved; her skill with that blade was stunning, terrifying! The foolish man's stomach had been sliced open; Mark watched silently as the dying pirate struggled to replace several loose coils of intestine that had escaped unchecked as he rolled across the shore.

Mark shook himself and climbed over to check that Brynne was okay. She bent down to clean the knife-blade on the man's tunic, then drew herself up and glared at the group of men and women who were watching her. Although she said nothing, her expression was taunting, almost daring them to come forward and face her.

The injured man thrashed about, splashing water up as he kicked his legs and flailed his arms. He screamed for his mother, and to someone else – not a name Mark could recognise – and then, thankfully, fell silent. The ruffians on the beach moved forward slowly, waiting for the order to engage the enemy.

'This is not good,' Mark said as he shuffled nervously back and forth, his feet ankle-deep in the pebbles.

'Do not come against us,' Steven yelled towards the longboats, then, with a note of sincerity in his voice, 'I have no wish to kill you.'

'You are outnumbered, fifty to one,' their commander called back with a laugh. 'Yield now.'

'You don't understand.' As Steven raised the staff, the closest assailants cringed visibly before him. 'We will not yield. You will lay down your arms, or you will die.'

Garec searched the gloom, an arrow drawn full, hoping to pinpoint the leader's voice. He sighted down its shaft waiting for an opportunity to silence the man for ever, but he was beaten to it: off to his right, from somewhere out on the water, he heard the telltale snap of a bowstring.

There was no time to cry out a warning; he drew a quick breath and held it, waiting for the arrow to pierce him through. But he was not the target: he watched in almost stupefied amazement as Steven, with positively inhuman speed, snatched the shaft from the air and snapped it in two with one hand. Recovering quickly, the Ronan bowman found the enemy marksman crouched in the bow of a longboat and sent his own shaft hurtling across the water. With a muted thud, the arrow embedded itself in the man's neck. Several startled cries nearly drowned out the pirate's incoherent last words and Garec felt his hands shake for a moment as the dead man fell forward into the water with an insignificant splash.

The voice cried out again, this time in anger, 'Beach party, attack! Longboats forward! Take them now!'

Brynne dropped to a crouch and Mark fought the urge to run as thirty armed ruffians charged with an unholy bellow that sounded as if it would reverberate through the cavern for an eon. Behind him he heard similar cries as the group flanking them advanced as well. Oars squeaked in rusty oarlocks, groaning as the longboats made for shore.

Garec's hands were steady again. Calm and controlled, he began firing into the boats, aiming for the oarsmen, not just to slow down their approach, but to force more of the enemy to expose themselves as targets while they struggled to clear the benches of their dead. He'd made three shots for three clean kills when he caught sight of the force bearing down on Mark and Brynne. Grimacing, he changed target, but though he killed or wounded a soldier with every shaft, there were simply too many: the horde was about to overrun his friends.

Steven wished Garec would stop firing for a moment so he could try to bring a peaceful end to the confrontation. He was sorry Gilmour wasn't there; somehow the old man would have negotiated a truce by now and they'd all be sitting around the fire together, smoking pipes, chucking back the local liquor and swapping stories.

He sighed, and glanced to his right, where Brynne and Mark were about to engage a force large enough to take Denver in an afternoon. So much for peace to all humankind! Maybe he could have this deeply meaningful philosophical discussion with himself once he'd saved his friends from being chopped into the evening's main course. Steven closed his eyes and focused his thoughts.

The shoreline came to life as thousands of small, smooth, rounded stones and pebbles sprang into the air and careened through the marauding horde as if fired from an invisible catapult. With a gesture, Steven repeated the attack on the group advancing from the adjacent shore. Eyeballs were ruptured, noses broken, ribs cracked and teeth dislodged; deep welts and bruises coloured exposed flesh as the stones ripped mercilessly through the enemy ranks, denting helmets and even shattering sword blades. The raiders screamed in terror, diving into the lake or running headlong back along the beach in an effort to escape the punishing hailstorm of pebbles. A small cloud of stone projectiles pursued every one of them, punctuating the message that the small company was not about to surrender.

In spite of the blood and broken bones, no one had died in Steven's counter-attack. He wondered if they appreciated that yet.

Steven turned his attention to the longboats. His initial reaction was to sink them all, but it occurred to him that a boat or two might be useful for them, so instead, he drove the staff into the shallows at his feet and, replicating the wave he had created in Meyers' Vale, sent a wall of water forward to capsize the boats and leave their passengers adrift. 'Kill as many as you like, Garec!' he shouted loudly enough to be heard above the cries of the injured, 'but try not to hit the boats. We'll need at least one of those intact.'

Garec looked over at him, and Steven shook his head slightly. He set off to examine the pirate Brynne had so deftly gutted. For a moment he hoped the man might be saved, but he shuddered as he looked down. The massive wave had washed away the blood and if he didn't look any further than his face, the dead raider looked as though he had simply fallen asleep with his feet in the water. Steven avoided looking anywhere else; he knew that seeing entrails would make him vomit. On the beach before him lay five or six more of Garec's casualties, each with an arrow jutting awkwardly from someplace soft and vital.

He turned to Brynne. 'Did you have to—' His voice trailed off. Of course she did. The man had attacked her. He had come screaming out of the shadows, and if Brynne had not dispatched him so efficiently, she or Mark would be lying here instead.

Steven couldn't take his eyes off the corpse. He had seen the man clumsily trying to push his own organs back in, as if the act of forcing them back inside his abdomen might save his life. It was a reflex; anyone would have done the same, grasping feverishly at the slippery, blood-soaked intestines and shoving them back inside, not caring even if they were returned to their correct position. Were his hands clean? He hoped so, because forcing clumps of dirt in between the tubes might cause an infection. Looking down into the dead man's face, Steven saw that although open, his eyes were askew in their sockets, pointing in different directions. Were his hands clean? If not, it hadn't mattered for long. The body sprawled, arms and legs akimbo, somehow taking up too much space. The warden of this subterranean boneyard would not be pleased. As Steven folded the man's arms across his chest, a bemused chuckle escaped his lips. He drew back, momentarily shocked at the sound of his own voice.

'Don't get jaded, Steven,' he told himself, and ran a hand over his eyes. He wiped his hand contemplatively on his tunic. 'Don't get used to this,' he repeated.

Two large groups had formed on the beach, one behind him and one before. People were still emerging from the water, many dragging their injured with them. At a quick estimate there were nearly three hundred of the soldiers, pirates, ruffians or whatever they were still standing, but regardless of their numbers, their attitude had changed. They hovered between embarrassment and fright – embarrassed at how handily they had been put down, and frightened, because they did not expect to leave the cavern alive. Nine longboats lay capsized about fifty yards from shore. One still burned, smoke billowing up in great clouds beneath the bone-decorated stone ceiling.

Steven looked at the person emerging from the lake to address them; he assumed it was their leader, the one who'd ordered the foolish attack. He waited expectantly, silently.

Even Brynne gave a little start when the raider clasped a handful of matted hair and pulled it behind one ear. It was a woman. Steven cleared his throat, adjusted his grip on the staff, and waited.

'I have come to surrender, and to beg your mercy for my warriors.' The second surprise of the moment was the woman's voice, soft and gentle, far divorced from the commanding voice with which she had ordered the abortive attack. 'You have a power, that is obvious, and I cannot risk more of my soldiers' lives against you.'

Steven beamed. 'Well, I'm glad you came to your senses before—' Brynne pushed in front of him, her knife drawn and ready.

'Brynne, what are you doing?'

A tense murmur rippled through the ruffians assembled along the shore as they watched the interchange. Garec retreated several steps and drew his bow, ready to fire in an instant.

Brynne placed her knife at the woman's throat and with her free hand reached behind the pirate's back to withdraw an evil-looking dagger with a curved blade and a short wooden handle. 'Steven, I appreciate what you did with the rocks, and that tremendous wave, but you still have a lot to learn.' She tossed the dagger to Mark. 'One doesn't get to be the leader of a band like this by surrendering at the first sign of trouble.'

Steven paled.

'She was going to kill you, so they—' she nodded towards the pirate ranks inching slowly along the beach, '—could kill the rest of us.'

Angry and embarrassed with himself, Steven cursed aloud in English, a string of epithets that left Mark shaking his head in admiration at his friend's grasp of the vernacular. Recovering, Steven summed it all up with a rousing, 'Son of an open-sored Atlantic City whore!' and stepped forward as if to punch the woman hard across the face.

She raised her own fists, but rather than backing away, she taunted him, 'Go ahead, sorcerer, kill me. The way you pined over Rezak back there, I'm surprised you didn't kiss him good-bye.' She stared up at him, her eyes fierce. 'What's the matter, sorcerer, don't like confrontation? Afraid to kill me?'

Rezak. Steven would remember that. He looked down at the unsavoury character glaring at him. 'I'm not a sorcerer,' he said.

'Look at that,' the woman said. Steven fell back several paces as she shoved him hard and laughed, 'You *are* afraid to kill me.' Around them, members of her pirate band laughed and hooted uproariously. The woman spat at Steven's feet and, reeking confidence, stepped towards him.

In an instant Brynne was between them again, the hunting knife drawn. Steven barely had time to blink before Brynne had flicked her wrist twice and taken off both the woman's earlobes. She sounded deadly serious when she told the pirate leader, 'I, however, am *not* afraid to kill you.'

The woman recognised Brynne's unemotional savagery and lowered her fists. She drew a wet kerchief from around her neck and dabbed at the blood that dripped steadily from her ears. 'I am wondering how you managed to get in here,' she said offhand-edly, not sounding in the least bit threatened. 'You could not have come from the river with such a vessel—' she indicated the *Capina Fair*, '—and I know you didn't enter this cavern through—' She hesitated, as if discarding certain words, 'through other places. So unless you used magic to get inside, I have to assume you have lived your entire lives down here and I have simply never seen you before. It is possible. This is a large lake, and an even larger cavern. And yet, I find that unlikely, because I have met the other permanent inhabitants of this cave on several occasions, and they tend to be a good deal hairier, blinder, and—' she smiled at Steven for the first time '—less attractive than the lot of you.' She squeezed blood out of the kerchief, then bent down to rinse it in the lake before reapplying it to her ears – although they were still bleeding freely, she didn't appear to be terribly upset about it.

'So, sorcerer, how *did* you get down here?'

For the first time, Steven noticed she was using just one hand, her right hand: her left had either been hanging limply at her side or slightly behind her back since she had joined them on the beach. Looking down at it now, he noticed she was curling and straightening different fingers in a repeating pattern. Behind her, the pirates were standing perfectly still. He thought they looked to be somewhat closer than they had been when he first stood up from the dead man's body, but perhaps that was a trick of the light. He couldn't see the raiders assembled behind the first row or two, but there was some movement, as if they were shuffling nervously from side to side, or trying to move without being detected.

Then, from the corner of his eye, he saw it. A big man, older but tough-looking, with a shaved head and a long scar running across the outside of his neck, was watching the woman's fingers intently. He was bleeding from several lacerations on his face and arms, but like the woman with the now neatly clipped earlobes, he did not seem to notice his wounds. Instead he stared between Brynne and Mark, watching the curling and straightening of the woman's fingers.

She was sending messages to him. It was a code. Steven couldn't work out what the patterns meant, but there was no question the woman before him, still carrying on about him being a sorcerer, was sending orders to the ranks behind her. Steven was almost dazed: he was watching the scene unfold as if he were just a bystander. Now the big pirate began sending a message to someone flanking Steven and the others. The man's hand rested quietly on his thigh, then, slowly, his index and then ring fingers curled up beneath his palm. It was the tiniest of gestures, almost impossible to catch if you weren't looking for it. Steven assumed they had been ordered to gather their weapons and prepare an assault. The scarred man curled and waggled his fingers over and over again; Steven guessed he was communicating with the group back along the beach, behind Mark and Brynne.

His mind raced: an attack was coming, and it would come from both sides at once. He had to act fast. The woman, obviously their leader, was still taunting him, but now Steven understood why. It was a ruse: buy time. Rearm. *We have seen his magic, but we have also seen he is unwilling to kill. If he is unwilling to kill, we can take him and the others. Prepare. Prepare in silence.*

This band had not looked to be an organised fighting force, but Steven realised he had been horribly wrong: they were much more than that; this was a group of people who had been together long enough to be able to read one another's thoughts. They'd come out of the lake in certain positions not by chance, but because of what would come next. Those who could read the code were in front, because any shuffling of ranks after they had all assembled on the beach would have been suspicious.

This was no ragtag band, and now they were coming for Steven and the Ronan partisans.

Looking to Mark and Garec, Steven tried his own form of nonverbal communication to get them to move in close. Brynne was still by his side, her knife drawn and held loosely in one hand. After a moment, Mark took a few steps forward, but Garec was wary, not sure he should give up his vantage point against the cavern wall, where he was in a good position to shoot into either group. Steven cried out in his mind, and sneaked quick but piercing glances at Garec, all the while trying not to give anything away to the enemy leader before him.

Come over here, Garec. Come over here. I can't protect you if you don't get your sorry self over here now. Steven willed the bowman to understand. His grip on the staff tightened.

Garec understood that Steven was trying to tell him something, but he had no idea what. Get ready? Shoot someone? Draw more arrows? What? Confused, Garec looked left, then right, then back at Steven, trying to work out what he was supposed to do. *They had moved.* The pirates, both groups, had crept forward without anyone noticing. It was only a pace or two, and it had taken them some time, but they were inexorably closing the gap between themselves and the travellers. After what felt like an eternity to Steven, Garec seemed to get the message. The bowman started to grin, then recovered himself and wiped his face clear of all expression. He hastily took stock of what he had, and what he would need to continue this fight in close quarters.

Calmly lowering his bow, he fought to slow his heart rate and breathing. They were coming. Any moment now, they were coming. He reached slowly down to retrieve the dozen arrows he had stabbed tip-first into the beach. With those firmly in hand, he suddenly took off, running across the camp. As he leaped into place beside Brynne, he cried, 'Now, Steven, now!' and with a wave of Steven's outstretched hands, a great circle of molten fire burst from the ground to surround them. So fast did the flames appear that Garec's leggings caught fire and he spent several moments patting out the blaze before he could turn his attention back to the raiders.

The explosion of fire forced the attackers in the forward ranks to fall backwards, their faces and hands seared from the sudden blast, coughing and spluttering and trying to clear their lungs of the intense heat they had inadvertently inhaled. They gaped at the fiery wall, and at their leader, now trapped on the wrong side of the flames, in shock. The tongues of fire reached halfway up the cavern, but there was very little smoke and the heat was far less intense than Mark had expected.

Seeing Mark's inquisitive look, Steven grinned. 'Oh, don't worry. It's much hotter on their side than ours.'

'Outstanding!' Mark was impressed. 'Steven, you're getting good at this.' He gazed around their fire chamber and, almost absentmindedly, put his arm across Brynne's shoulders.

'Not really.' Steven shook his head. 'Most of the time, I imagine what I want to happen and then try to make adjustments once I get things started.'

'But still,' Mark was encouraging, 'you've come a long way since the Blackstone foothills.'

'Oh, I don't know.' Steven still wasn't so sure. 'Except for dealing with Malagon's wraiths, I'm not sure I've done much more than a bit of conjuring.' He laughed suddenly. 'What the hell am I saying? How can I be so blasé about something that shouldn't even be possible?' He turned to the pirate leader, who hadn't moved. Her jaw hung slack as she stared at the dancing flames separating her from her band of ruffians.

'However,' he said directly to her, 'I am not a sorcerer.'

'Then what are you?' she asked quietly.

'I'm a bank manager,' Steven said. 'Actually, I'm assistant manager, and if Howard ever retires, then I will become manager. I am only an assistant manager because I lack the skill to be a professional baseball player, and I lack the will and the self-confidence to risk becoming much more than I am – or than I was six weeks ago. I appear to have been chosen by this staff to wield it in compassionate defence of myself, my friends and our cause, but other than that, I have never been able to produce, let alone understand, anything magical, mystical, or supernatural.' He would have continued parodying his former life, but she interrupted.

'What are you called?'

'I am called Steven Taylor, of the Idaho Springs Taylors. You can call me Steven.' He reached out to shake her hand, but she simply stared, unsure how to proceed. Giving up after a few seconds, Steven introduced his friends: 'This is Mark Jenkins, a teacher of history, *our* history, so he finds himself with a head full of completely useless knowledge here in Eldarn.'

'An absolute pleasure to meet you,' Mark said. 'Sorry it had to be behind a wall of fire, but we're not keen on being slaughtered just at the moment.' He grinned.

'Mark Jenkins,' the woman echoed faintly.

Steven introduced Garec and then Brynne. He was about to suggest the woman reciprocate, and explain why she had ordered her crew of pirate ruffians to attack them without provocation when she interrupted him once again.

'Garec Haile, the archer. And you—' she pointed to Brynne. 'He said your name was—'

'Brynne. I am Brynne Farro of Estrad. I own the Greentree Tavern in Greentree Square, if you know the place.'

Mark added, 'We don't, Steven and me. We tried to go one night. I wanted a tuna sandwich, but a legendary, life-draining demon chased us out of town after eating a stray dog that happened by. Garec and Sallax have assured us that it's a nice place. Good food, and the kitchen's open late at weekends.' The woman wasn't paying him any attention; she didn't even query the English word *weekend*.

Instead, she stared intently at Brynne, and Steven was sure he saw a look of relief pass over her face, although it was replaced almost immediately by the grim visage he was getting familiar with.

'Sallax,' she said under her breath, 'Sallax Farro of Estrad.'

'My brother.'

'Where is he now?'

Brynne's jaw tensed. 'He is making his way to Orindale.'

'Is Gilmour Stow with him?'

Garec perked up. 'Who *are* you? How do you know Gilmour?'

The woman ignored him and continued staring at Brynne. 'You *must* tell me where Sallax Farro is right now. It is important.'

Steven broke in, 'As congenial as we are trying to make this little gathering, I think it's time to remind you that you are no longer in a position to be making demands or dealing out orders.'

Brynne ignored Steven and demanded, 'What do you know of my brother?'

The woman grimaced as she realised blood was still dripping from her mutilated earlobes. Then, grinning, as if she alone were in complete control of all their destinies, she said, 'When days in Rona grow balmy . . .' Her voice faded. She looked expectantly at them.

Steven was getting annoyed; he thought he'd behaved remarkably decently so far, given the woman had been about to kill them all without a second thought. 'Being cryptic will get not get us anywhere. Now, answer the question. What do you know of Sallax – and for that matter, what do you know of Gilmour?'

'When days in Rona grow balmy,' she repeated.

Steven grew more angry. 'We have tried to be nice about this, but I will suspend you and your entire band of bullies from the damned roof of this place for the next Twinmoon if you don't—'

Garec grabbed Steven's arm and hissed, 'Wait. Give me a moment.' He dropped his bow and began rubbing his temples, muttering to himself. The others caught bits of what he said, but with his head down and his eyes closed, he sounded more than a little crazy. 'Sallax, you rutter . . . so pissing covert – crazy old sorcerer, drunk that night . . . it's always balmy down there— I remember! I remember it now, we were drunker than demon-spawn, but I remember!' He was shouting as a thin smile broke across the woman's stony countenance.

Then, taking them all by surprise – the bleeding pirate

included – Garec threw his arm about her shoulders and drew her firmly to him in a warm embrace. Throwing his head back, he shouted, 'Drink Falkan wine after Twinmoon!'

'What the hell is happening here?' Mark was thoroughly confused.

The stranger smiled broadly at them, her arm now draped over Garec's shoulders. 'When days in Rona grow balmy—'

Garec completed the sentence, 'Drink Falkan wine after Twinmoon.' He laughed out loud, relief clear on his face.

The woman clapped Garec on the back, then reached out with her opposite hand to slap Steven firmly but good-naturedly across both cheeks. 'Welcome to Falkan, Steven Taylor, Mark Jenkins. My name is Gita Kamrec, of Orindale, and I lead the southern corps of the Falkan Resistance Movement.'

Steven looked at Gita and Garec while his firewall raged around them.

She smiled again and asked, 'Would you turn this off now, please?'

Garec nodded agreement and said, 'It's really okay.'

As Steven relaxed the wall of flame, Mark suddenly remembered the band of thugs assembled on the stony beach. His body tensed as the fiery shimmer dissipated, tiny flecks of fire dancing about them like orphan snowflakes after a blizzard. The pirates came slowly back into focus. Mark ground his teeth together and felt his stomach flop over. Warily, he reached for the battle-axe. Hearing Garec laugh and carry on with the stranger was not enough to make him entirely confident that they were out of harm's way. He held his breath, waiting for an attack and hoping Steven could retrieve their defences as quickly as he had released them.

As the flames withdrew, Gita lifted her left arm to the roof and made a fist. She then opened her fingers and rotated her hand a number of times; it looked to Steven as if she were trying to make sure every single one of her soldiers could see it. Mark tensed again; he was about to reach up and wrench Gita's hand back until her wrist snapped when he detected a sudden change come over the cavern. It felt as if the granite bedrock itself sighed with relief as the entire band of attackers breathed out – the physical exhalation was audible. The sounds of daggers being sheathed, bowstrings released and swords sliding back into scabbards echoed around the vast cavern. Intimidating grimaces were exchanged for toothy grins, some still bloody from flying stones. People started to pull out scarves and handkerchiefs and bits of rag to clean each other's wounds and a low murmur rose, sounding like the last few moments before the curtain rises on a play.

There would be no attack. The cut-throats were chatting among themselves amiably, passing the time as if some of their number were not lying dead, scattered about the beach like bloody driftwood. Mark became less anxious as men began wrapping their fallen comrades in heavy wool blankets, then arranging the bodies in a neat row alongside the back wall.

Some of them were taking longer to recover from the shock of dealing with a magician as apparently powerful as Steven. Mark laughed to himself: how embarrassed these dangerous partisans would be if they knew the most dangerous thing Steven did most days was cross Miner Street against the lights.

He could hear laughter, and teasing, and Mark wondered at the alacrity with which this band had changed from being a deadly fighting force to a group of friends joking with one another at a beach party. Some had evidently drawn the Eldarni equivalent of a short straw and had dived into the freezing lake to retrieve those longboats that remained. Garec's campfire was re-ignited and wineskins, dried meats, bread and even cheese were being produced. Mark had no idea who Gita Kamrec of Orindale was, but her command of this group was impressive. He looked nervously back at her pale hands, wondering if he would recognise the *go ahead and dismember them* sign. Catching him staring at her, Gita smiled and shoved both hands into her tunic.

She was a small, thin woman, and Mark was astonished such a tiny wisp could command an army. Her hair, although wet and matted now, was long and looked as if it were usually well cared for. Instead of the solid leather belt most soldiers used to carry their daggers, knives or rapiers, Gita wore a woven and embroidered wool belt. It may have been pretty, and colourfully decorated with beads, but it served its purpose well, holding sheaths for two short daggers, a curved, dangerous-looking blade like a fillet knife, and a long sword with a decorative pommel. Looking closer, Mark noticed Gita's skin was tanned nearly to leather, as if she had spent a lifetime outdoors. Her arms, though skinny, were muscular, and Mark guessed she would be good with a knife, quick and low to the ground.

Gita's eyes were a soft brown; they bespoke wisdom and vast experience. Mark shivered at the thought of what she must have done to earn the respect and command of the crew now making camp along the beach; he found himself unaccountably excited at the thought of watching her work.

Gita said, 'You are pretty skilled with that stick, Steven Taylor; I am surprised Gilmour didn't bring you into this undertaking fifty Twinmoons ago.'

'We were not exactly brought in,' Steven started to explain, but she had already moved on.

'And you?' she asked Mark, 'what's your skill? Good with that axe, are you?'

Mark looked down at his hands, a little surprised to see he was still holding the weapon at the ready.

She went on, 'You look a bit dark for a South Coaster, but I know many of that territory are deadly skilled with an axe.'

Mark tensed, feeling a dormant but familiar sense of rage flood his system. *They do it here, too, the racist bastards.*

When he didn't answer right away, Gita asked, 'You good with that axe, Mark? It was Mark, right?' She checked with Garec, who nodded.

He decided to let it pass. There had been nothing acrimonious in her voice.

'I am—' he shot Brynne a look and felt better, 'I'm a horseman.'

Recalling Mark's equestrian ineptitude, Brynne stifled a laugh, and added, 'He has taught us all a great deal about how to handle our mounts.'

'Good.' Gita failed to pick up the joke. 'Idaho Springs. I have never been there – wherever it is; Rona? – but Gilmour knows more than I ever will, and if he wants you two along, I am sure you must bring some powerful resources to the fight.'

'Gita,' Steven began, 'I think we need to explain—'

The Falkan leader continued to ignore everything any of them said, asking, 'Where is Gilmour, anyway? Why did he send you all down here on your own? This is a dangerous place to be if you've never been through here before.'

'He didn't send us down—' Brynne tried this time, but got no further than anyone else: this woman could apparently talk *both* hind legs off a donkey, let alone one.

'Anyway, there is plenty of time for us to catch up with your progress down there in Rona. I sent a rider out your way before the last Twinmoon. He just returned. I hope you managed to get your weapons and silver out of the old palace before it fell. Still, when that old mule Gilmour gets here, we'll have a few drinks. I'll buy – just as soon as he coughs up the five silver pieces he owes me.' She slapped her hand against Garec's chest and added, 'Garec remembers that night, don't you?'

Garec forced a smile. 'Gita, Gilmour is not—'

She waved three of her men forward, cutting Garec off in midsentence. 'This is Hall Storen, Brand Krug, and Timmon Blackrun. They each have a command within our resistance force. Hall's from Orindale, Brand hails from the Blackstone Forest, and Timmon's soldiers come to us all the way from the east, along the coast near Merchants' Highway.'

Steven nodded to the three, all of whom were eyeing him with suspicion. These were obviously battle-tested fighters; they had most likely faced Seron and an array of otherworldly creatures, compliments of Prince Malagon, over God knew how many Twinmoons. The fact that Steven had stood against them on his own, and could have readily dispatched the entire company with just his wooden stick, had obviously made them wary. He had no doubt they would have preferred a straightforward hand-to-hand brawl rather than grappling with flying stones and rogue waves. He smiled anyway. 'Nice to meet you all,' he said.

Timmon and Hall nodded, and Brand asked, 'What news of Sallax? Where is he?' Brand Krug was a small, wiry man, with narrow eyes and a pinched nose; he wore a brace of throwing knives and a short sword strapped across his back. When no one answered immediately, he repeated his question.

Brynne began, 'Sallax has—'

'Gone on ahead to Orindale,' Mark interrupted, 'he's travelling on foot, and we're not sure how far he's got.'

'Why did you not go with him?' Timmon spoke up. He was a large man, tough-looking, despite a little softness about the midsection. While Brand had long hair, drawn back tightly into a ponytail, Timmon Blackrun's short curly hair looked as if it were gripping the top of his head so it didn't blow off. Although the cavern was cool, the man was sweating profusely, and Steven started to worry that Timmon was just a few minutes away from a massive heart attack. He still carried his weapons, an enormous war cudgel – like a hammer with a nasty allergy – and a short dagger. Steven could only conclude the big Easterner wanted to be ready in case it became necessary to bludgeon someone to death at a moment's notice.

He tuned back into Mark's convoluted tale of Sallax's determination to find them a safe route into Orindale, their ensuing trip downriver, and eventually their wrong turn into the cavernous tunnel leading down to the lake.

'That was smart of him,' Gita spoke up. 'You wouldn't have made it into Orindale together, not this Twinmoon, anyway.'

'Why?' Steven was relieved they'd made it safely past the topic of Sallax's disappearance. It was obvious that he was well-respected by the band, and telling them he'd turned odd and helped slay Gilmour probably wasn't their best move right now.

'The Malakasian Army has been dispatched along the eastern border of the city. It's an enormous blockade, almost as though they were trying to find someone – or something – coming into town.' Gita beamed knowingly. 'Sallax might make it on his own, but all together, you would have been stopped, captured, and probably killed outright.'

Brynne asked the question that was on everyone's mind. 'Was it just soldiers, or were there . . . other things?'

Gita looked at the Ronans. 'So you've met the enemy along your way as well, my friends.' To Brynne, she added, 'Yes, there were more than soldiers. There were warriors, but not men or women. It was as if they had been changed—'

'Seron,' Garec said, matter-of-factly.

'Seron?' Brand asked. 'What do you know of these creatures?'

Gita interjected yet again. 'They fought like animals, biting and scratching, many without weapons, others with just a dagger or a knife, and it took three, sometimes four shafts to bring even the smaller ones down.'

'They are Prince Malagon's creation, his pets,' Garec explained. 'Their souls have been excised from their bodies and they have bred new generations of Seron. Apparently, they were employed in battle many Twinmoons ago, as was the almor, the, uh— the demon.'

Gita shook her head despondently.

Garec went on, 'We believe Malagon keeps each Seron's soul in the form of a ghost-like wraith, and these in turn are powerful creatures themselves that can kill with a touch: the wraiths are an army that battles its foe from the inside out.' Garec's voice was flat.

'Well, that explains their tenacity,' Timmon said.

'How many did you face?' Mark asked.

'Only a few hundred,' Brand said, 'but there were probably twenty thousand encamped on the eastern edge of Orindale.'

'Twenty thousand Seron?' Mark thought he might pass out.

'That's right,' Gita replied, 'and that's not counting the occupation forces already stationed at Orindale.'

'We'll never be able to fight our way through.' Garec stated the obvious.

'Fight? Ha!' Timmon's corpulent frame trembled as he laughed. 'We had three thousand, boy, and we were hacked to pieces by those beasts. We were lucky to get away with the three hundred we have here. Fighting is suicide; stealth is the only way in or out.'

Brand shuffled nervously back and forth on the balls of his feet. 'It was not just the Seron.'

'What else?' Steven asked.

'There was worse,' Gita said quietly.

'Worse?' Garec pursued.

'Demon creatures, life-draining beasts, that struck without warning, deep within our ranks. It was terrifying. Many of our men bolted and ran, fleeing into the forests, but one or two of those things followed. We found bones, weapons and maybe a few bits of tattered clothing. No bodies.'

'Jesus,' Steven whispered, 'I thought there was only one.' Mark put a comforting hand on his friend's shoulder.

'And then there is the dark mist.' As Hall Storen finally spoke, all eyes turned towards him. 'There were clouds, misty and insubstantial, but held together by some unseen force. They drifted above the battlefield aimlessly, until whomever – or whatever – controlled them sent them in to attack. They came during the day, they came at night, but it didn't matter; there was no defence.'

Hall looked to be the youngest of Gita's lieutenants. Like

Timmon and Brand, he had the stone-hard look of a seasoned warrior, but there was something else about him that piqued Steven's interest. He watched him closely as he described their encounter with the deadly mist. Even Gita remained silent while he spoke.

'We were on the far left flank, almost to the Ravenian Sea,' he started. 'We had been fighting since dawn and had taken heavy losses. We were using bowmen and foot soldiers working together to punch a hole through their forward line so we could break off the flank, encircle their men and open a passageway through to the beach, and then north into the city.'

'What would you have done in the city?' Mark interrupted. 'Attacked from the rear?'

'No, these creatures can't be routed. They can only be slaughtered, until the last one lies dead. If we had reached the city, we would have gone into hiding, regrouped, and prepared a series of guerrilla strikes against them and their supplies.'

'But you never made it.' Steven skipped ahead one chapter.

'No, we didn't. We were pushing through; all our energy focused on one slowly expanding break in their ranks, when someone started shaking me, tugging at my arm and screaming my name.' He took the wineskin Timmon offered and slugged back a mouthful. 'It's funny: you're so intent on one thing that you lose sight of everything else. I heard nothing. Everyone was screaming, the wounded and the dying were crying out for help, or water, or for their loved ones. Buildings were on fire, people running everywhere and yet I heard none of it.' Gita gave him a look of knowing compassion.

Drawing a breath, he continued, 'Then it was there, a cloud. It looked harmless enough, just a cloud, and I thought nothing of it. Half the place was on fire and it could have been smoke – but then it attacked. It hovered overhead, and I had a premonition, that it would produce not water, but stinging acidic rain. The fighting slowed almost to a stop as everyone – even those Seron creatures – looked up at it.'

'What happened?' Brynne whispered, gripping her tunic in both hands and clenching her fingers.

'I was right. It dropped down. It fell from the sky like a chest-shot gansel. I was lucky; I was out on the periphery, and I closed my eyes, held my breath and ran.' Everyone was looking at him expectantly, but Hall shook his head. 'It was worse when it came after dark,' he added.

A heavy, brooding silence fell over the small group. After a long moment, Gita broke it. 'So you see the only way into Orindale is to sneak your way in. Once Sallax sees the forces awaiting you, he'll be back.'

Steven looked at Brynne and shook his head gently, as if to say, *not yet*. He asked Gita, 'Why would they be there?'

'What do you mean?'

'Why would such an army be massed outside Orindale? What you're describing doesn't sound like an occupation force, it sounds like an army dug in and awaiting an attack. What's coming to Orindale that merits such a force? You? Your three thousand partisans?'

Gita reached out and took Steven's hand. 'You really don't know, do you?'

'Know what?'

'Several days after the army dug their trenches outside Orindale, the *Prince Marek* moored just offshore.'

Garec held his breath and tasted bitter acid in the back of his throat. Brynne groaned audibly. 'Oh, demonpiss.'

Steven was confused. 'What does that mean? What's the *Prince Marek* when it's at home?'

'It's Prince Malagon's flagship, Steven. Malagon is in Orindale. My three thousand soldiers attacked a force of twenty thousand because this was the one chance we might ever get to take the head off the snake and allow the body to die on its own. We had to attack here because bringing our force to Malakasia, where there are hundreds of thousands of soldiers massed to protect him, would be suicide. We are back in this cavern to regroup and plan our next attack.'

'But you'll just get beaten back again,' Garec muttered.

'Most likely, but if he is here, we have to keep trying, down to our very last soldier.'

A wave of nausea swept over Steven and he clung to the staff for support until his knees grew strong beneath him again. 'Okay. Fine. So, Malagon is in Orindale. Why does he care? He is a powerful monarch, and a sorcerer. Who is coming to meet him who merits such a display of military might?'

Gita grinned broadly at him. 'Gilmour, my dear. You four, Sallax Farro, and Gilmour Stow.'

Steven felt like he'd been punched in the stomach. He closed his eyes as a river of cold sweat ran across his forehead, then tensed, about to retch. Beside him, Brynne sank to her knees.

It was Garec who summoned up the courage to speak first. He leaned heavily on his longbow and announced quietly, 'Gilmour is dead, Gita.' He waited for some response from her, but she stared back at him in silent disbelief.

As if to fill the silent void, he went on, 'We were crossing the Blackstones when an assassin got him. In our camp. He's dead. We gave him a funeral pyre.' Garec said nothing about Sallax's role in the plot to kill the Larion Senator.

Slowly, Gita asked, 'What happened to the assassin?'

'He escaped.' Garec fingered the smooth rosewood of his bow. 'Whoever it was knew enough about us to cut my bowstring. He was gone from camp before we knew what happened.'

'And where were you and your magic stick?' she asked Steven coldly.

'I was badly injured at the time,' was the best he could offer. He cringed as he said it; he knew how it sounded.

Silence reclaimed the space between them. Neither Timmon nor Brand made a move to comfort Gita as her world began unravelling. Soon she began to speak again, but her comments were not directed at anyone.

'My whole life— this moment represents my whole life. We attacked them. We made time for you to get here – we sent riders to Riverend last Twinmoon, but it had fallen. We assumed you were coming, watched for you in the east along the highway, but then this— The *Prince Marek* sailed right into the harbour. We figured if Malagon's not at Riverend, he would be here. We can attack, keep them busy, because somehow Gilmour would know. He always knew.'

She wiped a sleeve across her eyes, then stood up straight and turned to Brand and Timmon. Gita was back and giving orders. 'Get your soldiers ready to travel. We'll cross in the morning and make for Orindale as soon as possible.'

'Are we going in together? Or should we plan to break up and make our way into the city incognito?' A frontal assault would doubtless mean certain death for everyone, but Brand appeared happy for either response from Gita.

Before answering, the Falkan leader turned to Steven. 'Are you heading for Orindale?'

'We were, but now that you've told us about the defences, I'm not sure. Our ultimate goal is to get to Praga and find a former Larion Senator named Kantu.'

'Larion Senator?' Gita gaped at him in disbelief. 'Young man, there have been no Larion Senators for a thousand Twinmoons.'

'It's a long story. We really need to talk before you make any decisions.'

'Fine. We can send a rider to intercept Sallax. Where had you planned to meet him?'

Steven frowned. 'No, we really *do* need to talk, before we do *anything*.' He motioned her towards the nearby campfire.

Later, while the others slept, Mark lay beside Brynne, listening for her breathing and marvelling at her ability to sleep in the wake of such momentous news. It still echoed in his mind; he didn't anticipate being able to sleep before his turn to stand watch. He stared into the darkness and imagined the stone canopy far above, blanketing them from the outside world. For once he was happy to be shrouded by such a formidable coverlet; he wondered for a moment whether it was possible to stay beneath the surface for ever.

Seron, and much worse. The Seron were terrifying enough. They'd been lucky, that night in the Blackstones, but if Steven hadn't found the staff, they all would have died, perhaps even Gilmour. And then there was Lahp. Together, Steven and Lahp had broken Malagon's hold on him, and Lahp had protected Steven, up until the moment the warrior died – and even in that moment, he had not hesitated. It had taken four wraiths to defeat the Seron. Mark swallowed hard as he imagined the ghosts tearing Lahp apart from the inside out.

If Lahp was that emotionally and physically resilient, the Seron waiting for them outside Orindale, and in Malakasia, would be impossible to defeat. On the other hand, if Lahp had withstood that brutal attack for so long because he was less than human, the Seron would be *equally* impossible to defeat. Mark sighed. This was pointless; they were in a lose/lose situation. It would take real magic to defeat the army, powerful magic.

The Falkan Resistance had been routed, and unless they adopted guerrilla tactics and stuck to them, they'd be nothing but a token force, full of determination and eloquent, rousing speeches, but devoid of any real substance. 'Like Rona's?' he wondered aloud, and then fell silent, unnerved at the sound of his voice in the vastness of the cavern. Sallax had talked of a resistance force in Estrad and southern Rona, but save for a cache of weapons lost in the cistern at Riverend Palace, they'd seen no evidence of it.

He turned his musings back to the task at hand, content to leave military engagements to those better qualified to organise them. Their path did not lie with the Falkan Resistance, anyway. If they were to find Kantu, they would need to employ stealth, cunning, timely retreats, and a healthy ration of luck.

Steven desperately needed the Larion Senator's help if he were to master the quixotic magic of the staff and bring its full potential to bear against Nerak. Mark hoped his friend was up to the task; he was worried that Steven's dogged determination to preserve life, no matter how badly they were being threatened, would cost them all dearly in the end. It had been dreadful, watching him kneel over the body of the dead soldier while an enemy force surrounded them on the beach. Mark had wanted to scream, 'Steven, pay attention, you idiot! He's dead. Leave him and see to us, before we are too.'

Mark sighed. He was pretty sure Steven had only just begun to tap the staff's inherent strength: if he'd wanted to, he could have incinerated the entire band of assailants in one sweeping gesture. Once he knew how to employ the magic properly, he might use the staff to level a mountain range, to summon fire from the sky, or to bring Welstar Palace down about Nerak's neck and bury the murdering bastard in a pile of rubble.

He'd watched Steven battle the wraith army; it had been like watching a ballet, graceful and perfectly coordinated. *That* was the magic Steven needed at his fingertips, not rock clouds and glowing balls of light.

Mark grimaced: this was pointless; he was speculating on things he knew nothing about. Steven would do his best to save them all, to save Eldarn, and to find them a way back to Colorado. He rolled onto his side and hoped once again to fall asleep.

It was a long while before he did.

THE CROSSING

In the avens before dawn, Mark dreamed of the beach in Estrad and the night he slipped and fell through the open portal stretched out across the living room floor at 147 Tenth Street. He looked to the twin moons hanging in the night sky, and the ten thousand visible stars, thick in the air like a cloud of luminous insects, illuminating a pale sandy ribbon stretching off and disappearing into the darkness in either direction. It was humid. Mark removed his sweater and boots and strode into the water, basking in the familiar caress of the waves that gently tugged about his ankles as if to drag him out to sea.

His father was there. It was Jones Beach in New York, and his father had just sat heavily on a folding aluminum lawn chair. The family's large yellow umbrella cast a circle of dim shade on the sand, and Mark heard the snap of a beer can being opened. But his father didn't face the water, nor go in swimming, nor did he stretch his bare toes towards the foam as the tide ambled in that afternoon. Rather, he faced the city, turning his chair and squinting into the distance as if to catch a glimpse of the sun flashing off the silvery jets taking off and lumbering into the sky above Jamaica Bay, huge flying fish captured for an instant in a photographer's flash. By the end of the day, his father would have finished six beers, two ham sandwiches and an ice cream cone, the latter purchased on his one trip to the public restrooms out along the boardwalk. Mark held his hand as they walked and his father regaled him with tales of Karl Yazstremski's late-inning heroics the previous night and how tiny the ball had looked as it bounced off Fenway's Green Monster for a game-winning double.

Then the almor was with them, pressing through the hot afternoon sand like an animated puddle of mucus. It came closer and closer, and Mark could smell it there, putrid and rank in the humid New York heat. He tugged his father's hand, pulling with all the strength he could muster, but for some reason the older man was oblivious to the demon lying in wait at his feet. 'Chocolate today, slugger, or vanilla?' he asked, and Mark watched in horror as his father's ankle disappeared into several inches of the almor's milky, insubstantial essence. Nothing happened. 'Or maybe we'll have a scoop of each, what do you think?' Mark could smell the faint odour of stale beer, and as his father grinned, he caught a brief glimpse of one gold filling gripping an incisor like a long-ago misplaced piece of costume jewellery.

Careful to step over the almor's puddle, Mark released his father's hand and peered down into the sand. The demon's fluid form swirled about in a tumult of anguish and loathing. Mark's heart seized and he nearly fell backwards onto the beach when he saw several forms begin to take shape within the ivory puddle. Seron. There were hundreds of Seron, twisting in and out of focus, trapped within the almor's gelatinous flesh. The Seron were crying out, trying to communicate something. To him? No. They were speaking, or screaming in anger. Some were gesturing at something Mark could not make out. Then they stopped. Staring ahead, each of the warriors began to melt away, half-human soldiers disintegrating into colourless, lifeless imperfections, stark against the almor's cadaverous, pale backdrop.

One face took their place. It was a common face, sunken-cheeked but not emaciated, with thin lips, a narrow nose, and dark eyes set close together. Mark knew instantly this was Nerak, and as quickly as the dark prince's portrait took shape, it too began to come apart. Beginning just below the eyes, Nerak's skin stretched and pulled askew in erratic, random tears, as if the sorcerer were being dismantled from within. The eyes collapsed, their fluid leaking across the taut skin of Nerak's cheeks, and his lips flattened before bursting in small explosions of sticky blood. He did not appear to be in pain, though, but revelled in the tortuous dismemberment of his human features, gaping out at Mark in a silent roar. With Nerak's ruined face peering at him, Mark stepped back from the almor and looked for his father. He stood facing westwards along Jones Beach, oblivious to the ghastly display going on just a few feet away. Peeking down at the almor one last time, Mark dashed towards the boardwalk on bare feet and into the safety of his father's protective embrace.

Mark rolled over on the rocky beach of the subterranean cavern and opened his eyes. An idea, as distant as the faint aroma of Jones Beach, began to tickle at the edges of his mind. The almor, the Seron, the wraiths, Nerak: there was something about them, something they held in common, something beyond the apparent evil in their nature. What was it? He sat up and turned the idea over, reaching into the depths of his consciousness. Careful not to wake Brynne, he got up and tiptoed towards the lake. The stones of the underground beach rubbed together roughly beneath his feet and he was glad to have his boots on – yet, in that same moment, he bent over and began to untie his laces. Methodically he worked through the dilemma again and again, each time opening his mind to different variables or possibilities. Still the answers he sought eluded him.

Mark pulled off his boots and socks and inhaled sharply as he stepped into the frigid lake water. What would his father be doing tonight – watching a basketball game? Reading the paper, or enjoying a second glass of wine before dinner? Perhaps he'd be out at Jones Beach, awaiting news of Mark's whereabouts, staring west towards the distant glow of Manhattan. No. His father would be in Colorado somewhere, clinging to the idea that his search was still a *rescue* effort and summarily ignoring news reports outlining the distinct lack of progress in the Idaho Springs Emergency Team's recovery efforts. Decatur Peak. His father would be out on Decatur Peak every day. He would need snowshoes by now, but that's where he would be.

Mark shifted his feet. He missed the gentle pull of ocean waves as they broke across his shins before retreating over his ankles. The lake didn't move. It stretched out before him, imperturbable, and unaffected by his need for clarity. The almor, the Seron, the wraiths, and Nerak. If he wanted to know how to defeat them, he had to get to know them. What weaknesses did they possess? What about them was so irritatingly familiar? An answer was out there, and Mark was determined to find it. 'Take your time,' he scolded himself, 'don't force things. Just think it through. It will come.'

He was still standing calf-deep in the water when the others woke. Brynne approached him warily. 'What is it?' She whispered, despite the background noise of three hundred people making breakfast over dozens of small campfires – the *Capina Fair*'s final contribution to the Eldarni revolution – and preparing to cross the lake.

Mark looked at her and felt his stomach flutter: she was lovely, she looked as if she had spent a few extra moments to look attractive for him, beautiful when it didn't matter, when simply waking to another day was enough. He was touched that something as superficial as her appearance still mattered to her, and he wished for a few hours of freedom, a day or two, to be in love someplace safe, someplace where one cared what one wore and whether one's hair was clean and tidy.

A desolate sadness came over him as he realised he and Brynne might never have such a time. She had pulled her hair over one shoulder, tied with a short length of rawhide, and her tunic had been belted firmly around her slim waist. Filthy, smelling foully of mud and death, she was the most beautiful woman he had ever known. He shook his head in disbelief.

'What?' she asked again, smiling sexily this time.

'Nothing,' he replied and realised his feet were nearly frozen through. He wondered if he would be able to walk.

Steven's magic dawn brightened, flaming into life above their heads, and he moved down the beach to join the couple at the water's edge. 'Going swimming?' he asked Mark.

'Just out wading.'

'Is it cold?'

'Mercilessly.' Mark gripped his friend's shoulder and stepped clumsily from the shallows to the beach. 'I've just been thinking.' He shook his feet in an effort to move blood into his toes.

'About what?' Brynne asked, still curious.

'I'm not sure,' Mark replied honestly. 'Have you ever felt as if there was something lurking on the tip of your brain, just outside your realm of understanding? Like if you could just peek around the next corner, everything would make sense?'

'Sure,' Steven answered without hesitation. 'I call it parametric statistics.'

'Seriously, think about Nerak and all the mother-uglies he's sent against us.'

Steven and Brynne were suddenly attentive.

'Wraiths, the almor, the Seron. What do they all have in common?'

They hesitated, so he went on, 'They can all be placed on a continuum from real to unreal. Actually, that's not quite right; it's more like from whole to less-than-whole.'

'What difference does that make?' Steven was interested, but still couldn't see where Mark was going.

'The almor drains the life force from its victims. The Seron have had their souls ripped from their bodies.'

'Well, we don't really know that,' Brynne said. 'Who knows what Gilmour meant when he said "soul"?'

'Right,' Mark agreed, 'but you must agree something about their individuality, their essence, has been forcibly removed.'

'Agreed.'

Mark pulled socks over his freezing feet. 'The wraiths are the imprisoned souls, if we can call that essence a soul, of Nerak's victims through time. He takes over their bodies and discards the physical being, but keeps the soul, the essence, with him. He keeps it prisoner and can control it, send it against us, and force it to kill.'

'Okay, I understand what you're saying, but I still don't know what you mean.' Steven was racking his brain, trying to get in tune with Mark's thinking.

'Neither do I, yet,' Mark answered despondently. 'It's just that if he has a weakness, I believe this is the way to determine what it is.'

'This continuum of whole to less-than-whole?' Brynne was still struggling with the concept.

'Nerak and the almor are whole, evil, and filled with the life force of thousands of dead. The Seron are still evil, but devoid of that same essence.'

'And they are alive,' Steven suggested.

'Right,' Mark nodded, 'unlike the wraiths.'

'But wait a moment,' Brynne said, 'Gabriel O'Reilly seemed alive to me. Granted, a different form to any living thing I'd encountered before, but he certainly didn't seem dead.'

'A good point,' Mark acknowledged. 'On the other hand, the wraiths, alive or not, are certainly less-than-whole, less real, less ... well, less substantial than the others.'

'So do we need to redefine what it means to be alive to defeat Nerak?'

'I don't know.' Mark was getting frustrated that his hypothesis was no more clear than it had been when he had awakened several hours earlier. 'Maybe not alive, but possessing the essence of life.'

'How is that a weapon?' Brynne fingered the hunting knife at her belt.

'It can only be a weapon for us if it works against evil,' Steven tried.

'Not against evil, but maybe against Nerak,' Mark responded. 'It may be a simple question of perception.'

'Perception?' Steven mulled the word over for a moment. 'So, the evil that possesses Nerak may only be as powerful as it is perceived to be by the people of Eldarn?'

'Or it may only be as powerful as it perceives Nerak to be – or, better yet, as powerful as it perceived Nerak to be when it took him nine hundred and eighty Twinmoons ago.' Mark was speaking quickly, trying to sneak up on his conclusion through sheer speed.

Brynne kicked pebbles into the lake. 'If Nerak has a weakness, then perhaps the evil minion that controls him has the same weakness.'

'Because it doesn't know any better.' Mark was lacing up his boots.

'But where *is* that weakness? It certainly isn't anything Nerak has acquired since he forfeited his soul to evil.' Steven groaned. They were heading around the same block once again.

'It is perception.' Mark scratched at the several days' beard growth jutting from his chin. 'What if Nerak had a weakness way back when, but he didn't believe it? He never admitted it to himself, so as far as he was concerned, there was no one more powerful in all Eldarn.'

'And the evil minion believed him?' Brynne sounded sceptical.

'Why not? In Nerak's mind it was absolute truth, regardless of how false it might actually have been. Evil arrives via the spell table in its purist form. It takes over Nerak's body, devouring his soul, the soul of the most powerful sorcerer in Eldarn. So anything Nerak believed to be fact would influence the emergence of evil in Eldarn.

'Remember what Gilmour said? That evil arrives in tiny pieces and is scattered by the sheer demand of so many people thinking ugly thoughts or committing nasty deeds. But we all know evil is nothing more than perception. One person's evil might be another's righteousness. So, Nerak, as weak as he might have been, did have an impact on the evolution of this particular minion.'

'That's fine, but I have to ask again: where is the weakness? And surely evil would have figured it out in the past nine hundred and eighty Twinmoons and dealt with it – or gone off to possess a different sorcerer?' Steven asked.

'That's where things begin to unravel in my mind,' Mark admitted. 'And I keep coming back to the victims and the creatures. How is it that Lahp and O'Reilly were both able to escape him? What about those common denominators – what can they teach us about Nerak before he was taken himself?'

'Maybe it requires those souls to continue its domination, perpetuate its power and maintain its status as the most evil thing known. Perhaps there *is* greater evil, more powerful evil, but it remains unknown, so this evil actually has limits.' Brynne was still trying to understand; she was beginning to think she would rather have been ordered to drink the lake dry.

'I'd hate to bet on that. I'd hate to bet on something unknown, never known.' Steven said.

'We may have to,' Mark said grimly. 'But that's not all of it. That's not enough.' Mark's frustration was contagious. 'Let's say the evil that possesses Nerak was misled. Nerak was never as powerful as he believed when he was taken at Sandcliff Palace. The minion that took him knows what he knows and understands what he understands—'

'That he is the most powerful and dangerous man in Eldarn,' Brynne said.

'Right,' Mark agreed. 'But he is *not*. Would the evil minion be limited to the things Nerak is able to do, to control, or to bring about as a result of his magic?'

Steven chimed in, 'That might explain why all the creatures he summons or creates seem to spring from the same origins: that might be evidence of his limitations – deadly and nearly indestructible evidence, but evidence just the same.'

'It would,' Mark agreed, 'and because the evil that controls him takes Nerak's truths at face value, it makes a mistake that costs it dearly over time.'

'How?' Brynne was lost again. 'It doesn't appear to have any weaknesses, or to care one whit if we and all the armies of Eldarn march against it together.'

'Yes, it does,' Steven said. 'If it had no weaknesses, it wouldn't have gone to the trouble of bringing Lessek's Key to the bank, and it wouldn't have worried about closing down one of the far portals for ever.'

'And it *did* know it lacked the skill to operate the spell table.' Brynne twisted a lock of hair around one finger. 'Gilmour told us it needed to create a safe environment in which to master the magic of the spell table. That's taken it nine hundred and eighty Twinmoons, and hopefully longer. So perhaps it hid the key to keep it safe.'

'And perhaps it hid the key to keep itself safe.' Mark wanted this to be true, but found himself at a loss for any evidence to prove it. He frowned and then went on, 'So, you see? It's just outside my grasp, just on the tip of my mind, but I'm convinced there is something there, some magical loophole through which we can ram that staff of yours and kick this guy's ass for good.'

Brynne reached out to wrap her arms around Mark's waist. Pulling him close, she kissed him lightly on the nose and commanded gently, 'Well, you keep working on it, Mark. I know you'll crack it. We'll need all the understanding we can get when we reach Orindale.'

The question of Nerak's possible weakness was still nagging at him as Mark packed up his things and prepared to cross the lake. Nothing seemed to help. He felt that he needed the answer, *right now*, and for some reason waiting another day, or another Twinmoon, would mean disaster for everyone.

He and Brynne ate breakfast with several of Gita's partisans; the addition of cheese, tempine and dried beef made it a feast in their eyes. The aroma of brewing tecan had Mark dashing back to the longboat to collect a mug from his pack; it wasn't coffee, but it was the best Eldarn had to offer. He smiled wryly as Brynne recounted the loss of their own supplies, and the brown ribbon of tecan mingling in the river waters on its way to the Ravenian Sea.

A ribbon. The beach had looked like a ribbon in the moonlight. Mark's thoughts spiralled; he felt trapped, as if he shouldn't take another step until he had figured it out. *Do it now; it will be too late if you wait.* This may be your purpose here, Mark. He suddenly felt very close to the Eldarni people, and began to understand more fully why Steven was determined to stay in this strange and beautiful land until Eldarn was free once again. He was struck again by the image of Steven kneeling on the beach beside Rezak. *The beach again.* It was starting, bubbling up in his mind. He replayed his dream: the beach in Estrad, the twin moons, the unfamiliar stars, feeling fear, and dreaming of his father. He had dreamed of his father that first night in Rona, long ago now, and he replayed that too, hoping something new might emerge.

Nothing. He went further back.

It had snowed. His students wanted the day off, but it was just a flurry, a brief storm that left everything dusty-white. A baseball game playing on the television at Owen's Pub; Howard carrying on about the Hall of Fame to Myrna and her friends. They were all laughing and drinking together, convivial, happy. Steven came in, carrying his briefcase: that was the moment Mark knew he had broken into the safe deposit box. He disapproved, of course, but he was just as keen to find out was hidden in the box. They stayed for a drink or two with Howard and Myrna, and Steven promised to stay late at the bank and lock up the following day. They'd called in a pizza order before leaving, and Mark pocketed a book of matches, the same matches they'd found in Gilmour's pack, weeks later in the trapper's cabin. They had walked up Miner Street, picked up the pizza, and turned right onto Tenth. Mark had accused Steven of being a felon as they approached their house.

He jumped as Brynne wrapped an arm around his shoulders and asked, 'Do you want the rest of this?' She was holding the tecan pot.

'Huh—?' He was disoriented by the interruption, still lost in his thoughts. 'Um, sure. Are we leaving?'

'Yes.' She looked pointedly around the encampment, where people were busy stamping out fires and loading bundles of food, weapons and blankets into the remaining longboats. Timmon, Hall and Brand were giving curt orders that echoed throughout the cavern as if thousands of platoon sergeants were mustering a million soldiers.

'Steven and Garec have been huddled there with Gita for the past aven,' Mark could see them sitting around a small campfire, Steven's glowing orb still hovering overhead. Even from this distance, Mark could see relief in Gita's face.

'She looks happy,' Mark commented. 'I wonder what they've decided.'

As if overhearing them, Steven searched around the camp until he spotted his friends. He picked up the hickory staff and crossed the camp, sipping at his own mug of tecan as he and Garec walked.

'What's happening?' Mark asked.

'They've got a permanent camp, a hideaway, in a series of caves up near the surface. It's where they store their weapons and silver. They claim no one's ever been followed here; they're positive the occupation forces have no idea this place even exists.'

'Let's hope,' Garec said. 'I'd hate to climb back out of here to find their secret cave overrun with Seron.'

'Is there another way out?' Brynne wondered.

'They believe so, but no one's found it yet,' Steven replied.

'Then how can they know?' Mark asked.

'Because the water is moving,' Brynne said.

'Right,' Garec confirmed. 'They know this branch of the river must continue somewhere on the opposite side of the lake, but they can't find it.'

'I wonder why,' Brynne mused.

'Because the outlet might be under water,' Steven answered. 'Where we came in was nearly under water – I'll bet when it rains south of here, or when the snow melts in the Blackstones, that tunnel is completely submerged.'

'But that's not why they've failed to find another exit,' Garec added, with a sense of foreboding.

Brynne and Marked looked curious.

Garec smiled ghoulishly and gestured back along the beach.

'Those bones—' Mark looked startled. 'You're not telling me those things are still down here?'

'Gita doesn't know,' Steven admitted. 'They think most of the bones date from long ago, Eras before King Remond, even before the Larion Senate.'

'But some of them might be fresh?' Brynne felt her skin tighten into gooseflesh.

Garec nodded. 'Gita said she's sent scouts down here before now who never returned.'

'But didn't she say she'd seen the *other* inhabitants of this cavern?' Brynne protested.

'Apparently she was bluffing.'

'She's good at that.'

'Why were all three hundred of them down here yesterday anyway?' Mark wondered aloud.

'They heard us, and they saw Steven's fire,' Garec replied, as if the answer was obvious. 'Some of Brand's men came down to get some water. They thought Malagon's forces had discovered the cavern and were flanking them.'

'So they prepared for their last frontal assault,' Steven added, 'and were mightily surprised to find our little rag-tag coterie vacationing down here.'

'Not enough sun,' Mark glanced upwards. 'And the bars close too early. Not sure I'll be coming back. Maybe the Caribbean next time?'

Brynne elbowed him in the ribs. 'Stop it! What are their plans now? Will they attack the blockade outside the city?'

'They seemed pretty determined to do that last night,' Mark said, 'but it would be suicide.'

'No,' Garec replied, 'they're listening to reason. They'll lead us to the surface, then make their way north.'

'Why north?'

Mark thought for a moment. 'To meet us.'

Steven nodded. 'Assuming we get to Lessek's Key before Nerak, we may need them to help us cross the border into Gorsk and get into Sandcliff Palace.'

'Although Gita's heard nothing from them, she thinks the northern and eastern corps of the Falkan Resistance are moving towards Orindale right now,' Garec said. 'She's going to break up the remains of her force so she can send scouts out to intercept those groups and guide them to a rendezvous somewhere south of the Remondian Mountains.'

'So, what do we do?' Mark was curious.

Steven smiled ironically. 'We move towards Orindale, make our way behind enemy lines, attack Malagon's ship, seize the far portal, retrieve Lessek's Key and escape across the Ravenian Sea, whereupon we will find Hannah and Kantu. We will then convince Kantu to help us and travel back into Falkan to meet Gita, Timmon, Hall, Brand and the others near a small town called Traver's Notch. Oh, and we have some two or three Twinmoons to achieve all this.'

Brynne feigned relief. 'Oh, well, is that all?'

Mark was stupefied. 'That's six months! Steven—'

'I know, but given what we need to accomplish, I think that's probably how long it's going to take us.'

'And what's this about attacking Malagon's ship? When did we become pirates?' Mark wished he'd had the sense to sit in on their conversation that morning. 'Why would we assume he has the far portal on his ship?'

'In case we don't have the key,' Garec said. 'He assumes we *have* got it, but none of his creatures have been able to get it back for him – and, thankfully, Sallax obviously never got around to telling Gilmour's murderer that you two underestimated the key's importance and didn't bother to bring it with you when you set off adventuring in a strange and far-off land. And thanks to a bit of magic and a bit of luck, none of his other minions have lived long enough to report back that we don't have it – not yet anyway. We still don't know what happened to Versen, of course, but since Nerak's still trying to get the key from us I think we can assume he hasn't told them anything, either willingly or not.'

'Why hasn't Nerak used the far portal to go looking for himself?' Brynne asked.

'Because he'd have to abandon Malagon's body.' Steven shuddered. 'Then he'd need another host.'

'And because he assumes we have the key,' Garec reiterated. 'Now that Gilmour is dead, Nerak isn't in any tearing hurry – he's probably quite happy to wait for us in Orindale. But he'll have the far portal with him in case he catches us, devours our minds and discovers the key is sitting on Steven's desk.' Garec began to feel queasy.

'Why not wait for us in Malakasia?'

Steven felt himself grow cold as he answered, 'Because he must be ready to operate the spell table.'

Brynne swallowed hard and Mark shifted uneasily.

'He came here to find us, kill us and to retrieve the key if necessary – but his primary reason for coming must be now that Gilmour's dead, Nerak feels he's quite safe going back to Sandcliff Palace to continue his studies, or to release his master from the Fold.' As Steven spoke, the enthusiasm drained from the small group.

Brynne put Mark's thoughts into words: 'So, he *is* ready to use the spell table.'

Garec sighed. 'He's either ready now, or he wants to continue his preparations with the table at his disposal. Perhaps he can learn faster if he has a chance to experiment, to work things out firsthand.'

'So he feared Gilmour enough to have him hunted down and killed, but he doesn't fear Kantu,' Mark mused aloud. 'I wonder why.'

'I don't know,' Steven answered. 'Maybe Gilmour knew how to kill him, or how to banish the evil possessing his soul.'

Mark looked as though he had been slapped hard across the face. *His soul, the essence of his life*. Nerak feared Gilmour, because Gilmour could kill him and banish evil's minion: that's the only thing in all Eldarn that frightened Nerak. Gilmour had it, but Kantu did not: but what was *it*? Knowledge? Magic? Power? Why had he planted such a seed in Sallax's memory, so long ago? Twenty-five Twinmoons ago – that meant Nerak had been afraid of Gilmour for a long time. Nerak might not know his own weaknesses, but maybe Gilmour had . . . but if that were the case, why had he waited so long to attack? Why was it important that Gilmour died before Nerak travelled to Sandcliff?

Mark thumped his own head, as if to shake up his thoughts: he growled with frustration as he wondered whether Nerak's weaknesses would be exposed at Sandcliff Palace – but no, he was convinced Nerak had no idea he *had* any weaknesses.

'It must have something to do with the table,' Mark said out loud. 'Maybe Nerak will be vulnerable when he operates it.'

'I hate to take that chance,' Steven commented dryly. 'I'd hate to wait until he is there, actually working the table, before we do anything.'

'But we are going to do something,' Mark retorted. 'We're going onto that ship and back to Idaho Springs for the key.'

'Assuming he doesn't kill us all and go back for it himself,' Garec said, feeling nauseous again.

'We can't think about that now.' Brynne tried to imagine what her brother would do in this situation, but drew a blank. She'd have to go with her own best guess. 'We have to get there first. Then we can work out who's going to board the ship and take those risks. It may well be pointless for all of us to go.'

'She's right,' Steven agreed. 'Without magic, you'd all be marching to your deaths.'

'You might be doing the same,' Brynne pointed out.

'That's true, but at least Garec and I have been able to use the magic. I think it should be just Garec and me going on board.'

The Ronan bowman nodded.

'I'll be coming as well,' Mark added quietly.

'Why?' Brynne asked under her breath.

'Because I'm going to figure out how to kill him.'

Mark took his place in Timmon's longboat and hefted an oak oar into the adjacent oarlock. He had insisted on rowing alongside those soldiers who had not been too badly injured in Steven's stony hailstorm. Each of the remaining longboats was outfitted with sconces running along the gunwales which Steven ignited with a quick touch of the hickory staff – after Gita had suggested, 'Let's just light them one at a time this morning, shall we?'

Steven's laugh reassured Mark: he was glad to see they were getting along. He had no idea what was waiting for them in Orindale, but it was comforting to know they had the confident support of the local Resistance forces, even if they were a little threadbare.

Brynne sat in the stern with Garec, mending arrow fletching and sharpening arrowheads; Garec would make new arrows once he found suitable trees from which to cut shafts. In the meantime he attended to those he had, fastidiously grating stone against stone to create a rough edge and then working over each tip and blade with what looked like a thick wad of chamois. He made final alterations with the tip of his knife and a small wooden brush with coarse bristles.

Mark was curious; he was sure he had seen more conventional arrowheads in Garec's quivers before and asked, 'No metal?'

Garec shrugged. 'No money.'

'Ah, I see,' Mark laughed.

'Anyway,' he said, gesturing at the array of stones and tools in his lap, 'this is a skill I like to keep up.'

'Like falling off a bike, I guess.'

Garec waved his knife. 'Some days, Mark, it's impossible to understand you.'

Steven was on board Gita's longboat so they could work out a code the Ronans could use when they got to Traver's Notch. It was obvious the entire Falkan Resistance wouldn't be barracked in town, so they needed passwords to ensure their safe passage from Traver's Notch to the Falkan encampment.

Somewhere near the bow, a rough voice began calling out a slow but steady rhythm: 'Stroke, stroke, stroke.'

Mark fell to rowing and allowed his thoughts to wander back to Idaho Springs.

He remembered smelling the pizza Steven carried as they approached their house; they had been drinking and Mark was hungry. He grinned to himself: he'd gone hungry a time or two since their arrival in Eldarn, but nothing could rival the need for food after too much beer – the kind of hunger that bore no relation to how much one had eaten or how recently. He and Steven called it foraging, because so few places were open that late at night in Idaho Springs: Owen's Pub and the diner were pretty much it. Despite his burgeoning appreciation for good tecan, Mark suddenly pined for a steaming mug of coffee, served in a white ceramic mug.

That night was typical: when they got back to 147 Tenth Street he and Steven had fallen on the pizza like starving serfs. They'd finished most of it, washed down with more beer, and finalised plans for their assault on Decatur Peak. Finally Steven had opened the briefcase. What happened next was hazy. Mark's brow furrowed as he tried to recall overlooked details. There had been a rosewood box, padded inside with something like felt; they had been amused that William Higgins had created such a beautiful box for a commonplace chunk of rock. Then Steven had opened the cylinder. It had unscrewed smoothly, as if it had been oiled once a month for the past century and a half.

'Stroke, stroke, stroke,' the voice called, muted, as if from across the lake. Slow and steady, slow and steady.

Wait. Go back again. He was missing something. The cylinder.

The cap opened smoothly, no stiffness or rust or corrosion. The rosewood box. That was it. The box. Rosewood. Where had he seen rosewood? In Rona: tight-grained rosewood grew in those forests – Garec's bow was rosewood. That wood had come from Rona. There had been hinges on the box as well. They had opened smoothly too, like the cylinder, with no rust or squeaking. The rock was the only thing inside – no, not a *rock*, Lessek's Key. That rock was Lessek's Key, the keystone to the spell table, the most powerful collection of magic imaginable, and Mark couldn't remember anything.

Go back to the box. They had opened it; the hinges had not creaked. The key had been inside, and they had thought nothing of it. They had laughed and set it aside. Mark had made a joke about mercury poisoning; he had even given the rock a name, Barry . . . Bernie . . . Betsy. Steven had set it aside, but there had been something about the key, it had made him feel something, a familiarity, as if he had suddenly happened upon someone he had known for a few moments many years before.

A shrill scream burst through the haze of Mark's recollections and he jumped suddenly, dropping his oar and disrupting the rowers' rhythm. Scrambling to retrieve it before it disappeared over the side, he cried, 'What the hell was that?'

The scream came again, a piercing wail that retained its intensity without fading or tailing off. Mark wondered if whatever was emitting the horrible shriek had just found the remains of their camp on the pebbly beach. He froze, waiting for something to happen, or someone to tell him what to do.

Everyone had stopped rowing and two of the tallest men stood on their benches, craning their necks in an attempt to spot the shrieking creature. No one spoke, or even moved, as a feeling of foreboding blanketed the longboats.

Far in the distance, Mark heard a heavy splash. He looked up: he couldn't see the stone ceiling above them, but the image of the bone ornamentation was etched in his memory. He tried not to think about the possibility that whatever had entered the water had dropped from the ceiling.

The sound of the splash broke the spell and people around him began simultaneously shouting questions and orders. The cox-swain took up his charge again; his, 'Stroke, stroke, stroke' was a little shaky, but the rhythm helped. Mark realised this was why soldiers marched into battle, all together in step. He fell back into pace with the others and they made their way quickly towards the far shore.

Mark had no idea how long he'd been lost in his reverie. He nudged the man beside him and asked, 'How far is it to the opposite shore?'

'Half-aven, last time across,' he said helpfully, but Mark was still lost. What had Steven said? An aven was about two and a half hours. So seventy-five minutes to cross – but he had no idea how long they'd been rowing. He wondered how fast the shrieking thing could swim, and whether it was chasing them. Maybe there was more than one . . .

The soldier interrupted Mark's panicked calculations, adding, 'But we were coming very slowly, trying not to make a sound, and without torches. It shouldn't take much more than a third-aven or so to make it back at this rate.'

Great, Mark thought, *what's one-third of two-and-a-half?* Steven would laugh if he were here – the maths genius had probably already figured it out. Mark set to the task and, grimacing fiercely, came up with five-sixths of an hour.

'Well, shit! That's no damned help,' he barked in English, making his companion jump. 'Bugger – no, wait—' He grinned at the man beside him. 'Fifty minutes. That's just fifty minutes. We've been out here nearly that long already, I'm sure.' He had started to feel better when he saw Garec spring to his feet in the stern. 'Oh no,' he groaned. 'That looks like trouble.'

Garec steadied himself and nocked an arrow while peering up at the ceiling. Then Mark heard them too.

It began as a distant clatter, sounding as if someone had dropped a handful of marbles down a wooden staircase, then the flurry was replaced by a steady tapping: something solid against stone. Three or four taps marked time for a few moments before the rattling clatter began again. It sent chills through Mark's already cold body. When the noise reached their longboats the second time, he realised it was coming closer. It was running across the ceiling. Mark imagined clawed toes clicking off stone. 'It must have multiple legs,' he said aloud, 'or hundreds of toes, to be making that racket.'

He leaned forward and pulled with all his might. Where was the opposite shore? Fifty minutes: that wasn't very long. One class period. Not long at all. Mark realised he lived most of his life in fifty-minute increments: open with a warm-up question, five minutes, move into a reading or a few minutes of lecture or discussion, give them some guided practice, or extend the discussion, circulate while they work independently, answer questions or clear up problems and close with a reminder of the day's objectives. Fifty minutes. There was nothing to it. He did it five times a day. Fifty-minute increments were in his blood. Where in all the circles of Hell was the opposite shore?

The unholy scream came again, much closer this time, and Mark was not the only one to cry out in response. He felt his skin crawl, as if the yelp had pierced his flesh and buried itself in his bones like a tiny burrowing parasite. They were being hunted. The clattering came from somewhere up above, like clamorous rain, and Mark hunched down, an involuntary response. 'Please don't let it drop down on us,' he whispered, but somehow he knew that was inevitable. It was dark, so dark . . . his throat tried to close and he struggled to swallow. 'Surely it's too dark for anything to live down here,' he muttered, knowing he was kidding himself.

By now they were all rowing madly, pulling with all their might. As the strangely terrifying tapping drew ever closer, the coxswain's rhythm began to speed up. '*Stroke, stroke, stroke.*' Mark could see Steven standing in the stern of Gita's longboat; his friend raised one hand and sent a glowing fireball up towards the ceiling. All eyes were on the hazy light of the magic orb as it wafted ever closer to the distant stone ceiling and the boats slowed to a drift. There was a short cry, and a quick bustle of inhuman footsteps as the creature retreated from the light. Mark thought he had seen something, a shadow, maybe the irregular outline of a misshapen form. He coughed, and tried to mute the sound. Above, Steven's fireball moved slowly back and forth, and each time it came near the creature, there was a brief shriek and a commotion as the monster hustled off.

The light. That was it! Mark craned his neck over the side and called to Steven, a hoarse whisper that emerged much louder than he had intended, 'The light, Steven, intensify the light.' Steven shot him an understanding look and almost immediately the light grew brighter, changing from a warm yellow to an intense white. As it did, a hulking dark mass dropped from the ceiling a hundred yards away and crashed into the water with a resounding splash. So he was right: despite the weirdness of any living creature calling such a place home – this monster obviously did – living in constant darkness meant it couldn't stand light. And if it *was* the bone-collector, then judging by the size of its charnel-house, it had been down here for some time. Mark imagined it with great round eyes, with pupils as large as his fist; even the smallest pinprick of light would be blinding.

He took advantage of the additional light to turn around and search for the opposite shore. It was there, some two hundred paces out: a gently sloping beach that led up to a series of caves. There was a big opening off to the left, with footprints and tracks leading in and out: that would take them back to the surface and safety – well, of a sort, as long as the Malakasians hadn't found the entrance yet.

Their coxswain sounded comforted by the bright light; his chant was stronger now: 'Stroke, *stroke, stroke.*'

Mark turned back to his oar and was about to take up the rhythm again when he saw the longboat beside them start to turn slowly about. The two vessels had been moving alongside each other, but now their stern bumped gently into his oar.

'What's happening over there?' he asked his companion. 'There's no current here, is there? It can't be that creature; I can still hear it splashing around back there.'

His companion stopped rowing and looked at him for a moment, but just as he opened his mouth, Marked interjected, 'Oh, shit! There are *two* of them!' He started to shout a warning, but it was an instant too late. The longboat beside them exploded in foam and water. A profusion of long, muscular legs gripped the vessel from below, crushing it to splinters and trapping its inhabitants between the broken planks.

The attack lasted only a few moments, but it was long enough for Mark to see what had been making the tapping sound against the cavern ceiling: each leg was encased in armour plating, a protective exoskeleton of some thick chitin-like substance. At the end of each leg, there was a solid mass of dark, muscular flesh, with six or eight long, thin appendages attached, like elongated toes, each tipped with fierce-looking clawed nails. It must have been those nails tapping across the ceiling.

Garec had reacted at Mark's first cry and was already firing arrows rapidly into the creature's hidden bulk, but though he was doubtless hitting his target, his strikes appeared to have little effect.

The victims, held fast by the creature's legs, started screaming for help and mercy, and Mark stared in horror as the elaborate, clawed toes began tearing the Falkans apart, shredding flesh and plucking off limbs. 'Good God,' he whispered, frozen in place by the macabre scene.

There was a cry, and a large splash beside him. The feel of cold water on his face startled him enough to tear his eyes away from the carnage. Timmon Blackrun had drawn a short dagger and dived over the side. Mark was incredulous as he watched the corpulent Falkan leader swim the few strokes that separated the two boats. 'Does he think he can fight that thing?' he asked out loud.

No one answered.

'He must think he can.' Mark answered his own question and looked over at Brynne, but she wasn't listening; she had her own knife in her hand and had stripped off her tunic. 'Brynne, no!' he shouted, but she ignored him and dived in after Timmon, closely followed by Mark's rowing companion.

Mark could see Garec was almost out of arrows. Before he could talk himself out of it, he stripped to the waist, grabbed his axe and leaped in behind the others.

The water was cold and the chill swept over his body like a sudden Arctic wind. He dived beneath the surface into a cloudy green glow and watched as the creature began to take shape through the gloom. What was it? It was huge, much larger than the boat. It obviously ate people – there wouldn't be enough fish in this entire lake to keep something this big alive, even for a Twinmoon. He wondered for an instant how it managed to feed. Did it go to the surface or lurk about in the caves? Did it sneak out at night and steal animals from nearby farms? He shook his head to banish his unanswered questions: this was *not* the time for Show and Tell . . .

Don't try to hack off any limbs! He could hear Sallax's words – the big Ronan had never seen *these* limbs, but he was right: it wasn't the monster's legs Mark needed to attack. Christ, he'd be at it until spring. Instead, he had to find those big bulbous eyes he was certain it possessed and hack them out with the axe. There was no way they were going to be able to kill this thing, not with such rudimentary weapons; the most they could hope for was to drive it off before it killed even more of Gita's already weakened force – or any of *them*: Steven, Garec or Brynne. Blinding the monster would cripple it; if it couldn't see, surely it would have to give up the offensive.

Mark swam beneath the creature and reached out with his free hand to anchor himself. In the half-light he could see thick hair growing across a nearly flat area – maybe its back, or its underbelly, he wasn't sure which – but as his hand drew near he realised that what he had taken to be thick fur was actually an expanse of clawed toes similar to those that spiked the ends of each armour-plated leg. The spindly tentacles had already gripped him by the wrist; now they began to pull.

He brought the battle-axe around and lopped off the spindles holding him fast, then surfaced quickly to draw a much-needed breath and to survey the battle going on above. He felt something moving fast, brushing against the bottoms of his feet and realised the second creature was closing in on them. He caught a glimpse of Steven, standing in the stern of Gita's longboat and looking indecisive. If Steven joined them in the water, he might not be able to control the magic fuelling the now-powerful fireball. They would be plunged into darkness – and that would be the end of them all. These bone-collectors ruled the dark. The water's chill sent an icy finger along his spine as he kicked back beneath the grim assailant. He hadn't spotted Brynne but couldn't think about that now.

Mark came up beneath the monster once again, careful not to get too close, and swam towards one end, searching for an eye, or anything that looked vulnerable, but he found nothing except a narrow, tapered end of the tentacled expanse: wrong end. He was about to swim back when the monster began to sink, dragging the remains of the longboat and its crew with it. Mark could see that many of the crew, although injured, were still alive: it looked like the beast was going to drown the remaining survivors, then drag the whole lot off to a quiet beach to feed.

Something went by him in a rush: the other creature? It had circled around and now came at full speed to attack another of the boats. *Please don't let it be Steven's boat, or Garec's.* Cold comfort that Brynne was already in the water, but maybe while she was trying to kill the first monster she'd be overlooked by the second.

'Stay there, Steven,' he prayed, 'keep the light burning. Hit it if you can, but keep the light burning.'

He turned his attention back to the bone-collector: its surviving victims didn't have much time. Dodging an armour-plated leg and lashing claws, he kicked down. Maybe he could tug free some of the struggling soldiers.

Then he saw it: glinting in the light, reflecting Steven's fire like a pane of glass. It shut off suddenly, but that one quick glimpse was long enough: Mark had found the creature's eyes. So the tapered end *was* the creature's head. Perhaps, in battle, it folded its head beneath itself for protection while it gripped its victims with its mighty arms and legs. Arching its protective back and tucking in its head and underbelly would leave no part vulnerable – but Mark had seen the light reflected briefly off its wide black corneas. He knew what to do.

Mark swam to the surface and filled his lungs then, exhaling slowly, he descended back to the monster's face. As he passed through a thermocline he realised it was getting too deep: he had just this one chance. The creature, as if sensing his approach, swiped a massive forearm, trying to crush the annoyance, but Mark saw it coming and just managed to spin out of the way. He could see, even in the murk, a number of Garec's arrows *had* pierced the creature's armour after all.

Suddenly he spotted an opening. The beast, a hideously mutated child of the gorgon, lashed out at him with the spiked appendages that dotted its face and neck. Mark chopped away half a dozen of them, but had to dodge and dive to avoid the one free limb still groping for him.

There it was! The creature's eye opened again, and without even pausing to think, Mark took his best shot, plunging the blade of the battle-axe deep into the iris. The monster screamed, a shriek that resonated throughout Mark's body and echoed around the vast cavern like a crowd of banshees heralding the death of deaths; it so unnerved him that he inadvertently drew a breath, stopping just in time as the lake water filled his mouth. As he stretched for the surface the monster released its grip on the longboat and its crew. The creature rolled its head, presenting the other eye, and even though he was in danger of choking, Mark could not resist the chance to repeat his success and swiped with his axe as he swam past. This time he wasn't so lucky: a flailing tentacle sliced a gash across Mark's stomach, and he clutched the wound as he broke the surface of the lake. He trod water for a few seconds, gasping and coughing out the last of the water. His stomach hurt, but he wasn't dead.

He looked around. No sign of the monster, and Mark had no idea if any of the victims had survived. Flotsam from the wrecked longboat bobbed on the water around him. He started to push his way past the bloating corpses, feeling weak, exhausted and in pain.

Then Steven's light went out.

Steven had watched, terrified, as the first longboat was dragged beneath the surface. Standing in the stern, he had hesitated, not out of fear, but to consider his options. Mark and Brynne were already in the water, following Timmon; he saw Brynne fighting bravely, ramming her hunting knife into one of the creature's forelegs and pulling its victims to safety. Should he dive in and try to blast the creature from below? He could do it, he was sure, but it was already hard work keeping the intensely bright light glowing; he didn't want to lose his concentration and leave them all in total darkness. There were at least two of these monsters, and it seemed like the light was keeping the second away – but what if there were three, or thirty? He had no choice: right now his magical light was their best defence.

He wondered if he could strike out at the monster without injuring any of Gita's men, but he was already too late: the longboat was gone. Brynne and Timmon's crewmen had collected the few survivors and were swimming back to their own boat. There was no sign of Timmon himself. Garec was still standing in the stern, waiting for another opportunity to fire on the beast. Steven could see his quivers were nearly empty.

Where was Mark? Steven shouted ineffectually at the water, 'Mark, where the hell are you?'

Hearing him, Brynne turned around and began searching frantically, but he was nowhere to be seen. He was a strong swimmer, they knew that, but no one had seen him since Brynne jumped to Timmon's aid. How long ago had that been? Could he remain submerged that long? She looked up at Steven; they didn't need to speak. Brynne drew a deep breath and disappeared beneath the surface of the lake.

Steven tore off his jacket and tunic, gripped the staff in one hand and dived in. He swam vigorously and, realising the creature was dragging the longboat to the bottom, followed it. Judging by the number of bodies, it didn't look as if any of the longboat crew had survived; several of the dead had already been dismembered and large bites had been taken out of limbs and torsos. Timmon's huge frame floated by. Steven marvelled at the peaceful look on the soldier's face. He had died in battle – perhaps that was enough for him. Steven was praying that his friend had survived, but doubt began to elbow its way past the chill and settle in his bones.

Something rushed by him with a whoosh and Steven was turned over in the strong current that followed in its wake. A second beast was attacking.

Mark? Where the hell are you? Steven struggled with his conscience: if he didn't return to the surface, another boat might be taken – no, never mind. It was too late: at that speed, the monster would have reached the little flotilla: it probably had a vessel in its grasp already. He needed to find Mark. He needed to keep the light burning.

Keep the light burning, Steven thought, but his lungs ached and the hand clenching the staff was cramping. *Mark! Keep the light burning, Steven. Where are you, Mark?* It was taking too long. He wasn't as strong a swimmer; he couldn't stay submerged much longer. He was torn by the need to find his best friend and the need to keep the orb at its current brilliant intensity, but he had little choice now. He would deal with the consequences if they lived through the next five minutes. As he had beneath the river in Meyers' Vale, Steven summoned the staff's magic to fill his lungs with air. The magic came quickly, but his fears were confirmed, for as his breathing eased, the cavern above was plunged into complete darkness.

Steven had to search by hand now, putting aside his squeamishness to grope over the bodies trying to identify Mark, but so far all he had found were dead Falkans. Finally he decided his search was pointless. If Mark was still submerged, he was dead. He summoned the staff's magic to his fingertips and swam towards the longboats.

As soon as he emerged, the brilliant light returned. He cast it high into the air above the carnage and shuddered as it illuminated the second beast: the bone-collector looked like an offspring of Cthulhu, and it was lying astride the remains of a crushed longboat, using its hideous tentacles to shred its victims. In the stafflight Steven could see blood gushing and splattering into the water as heads were torn from torsos and legs and arms ripped apart. The crack of splintering bones punctuated the air, as did the screams of pain, horror and despair, a veritable wall of sound that echoed about the cavern. Steven shuddered: he would hear these sounds for ever in his nightmares.

In a white-hot rage, he cast the staff's magic into the beast's body, with devastating effect, as the inhuman howl of the monster mingled with the sobbing screams of the dying. Steven, caught up in almost physical fury, imagined breaking the creature's legs as it had pulled apart the Falkan partisans. As if in response to his thoughts, the beast's chitinous exoskeleton snapped with an audible crack. Two of its forelegs were torn off and left to sink into the lake.

Steven thought he heard someone calling his name; was that Mark gripping the gunwale of Garec's longboat? But he ignored his friend and turned his attention back to the Cthulhoid monster.

'Get off them, you bastard sonofabitch!' he raved, and released another burst of magic. 'Come over here, come over here to me,' he crooned. He could feel nothing, not the cold water nor the heat from the gigantic fireball suspended above. For a moment he became faintly aware that people were swimming towards him and he roared, 'Get back! Back away! It's coming!'

With a mighty cry, the black-tentacled bone-collector found purchase on the surface of the water and leaped into the air. What was this wretched creature that dared to challenge it? Humans did not dare; they squealed and ran and suffered. It would kill him, dine on his flesh, suck out his brains and polish his bones. It would kill this interloper, and then slowly feast on the others as it healed over the next generation. But blinding pain started to crest through its body as Steven's magic tore it apart.

The monster screamed, an ancient curse that only a god could now decipher, and sprang full-bodied into the air, its deadly legs

637

and writhing tentacles poised to grasp and disembowel the annoying staff-wielder.

Time slowed. Steven knew the creature would come for him; it would come from the air, as it had attacked the longboat. But he made no move to escape; instead, he remained with his head and shoulders above the water, peering up at the bone-collector as it hung in the air for a moment, then came crashing down upon him.

Mark, watching in awe and horror from the longboat, saw Steven finally move, reaching up at the last possible moment, just as the monster's legs were closing down on him and the huge body was about to push him down into the very depths of the lake. 'No!' Mark yelled, but his cry was cut off by a deafening explosion that echoed and re-echoed through the cavern. A shockwave of water threw him backwards and capsized the remaining longboats.

Mark endeavoured to get his wits about him again. Save for the light from two torches that had miraculously survived, the cavern was dark. Steven's fireball had been extinguished when he called upon his magic to destroy the subterranean creature. The Falkans, many stunned to find they were still alive, swam around trying to right their boats. Mark was surprised at the silence – until he realised he couldn't hear anything except for the dull ringing that clamoured in his head. He dreaded the headache that would follow, but at least his ears weren't bleeding. He looked around for Brynne: she was clinging to the side of a longboat with Garec. They both appeared unharmed.

Then he looked around for the monster, but all he could find were pieces of black chitinous carapace floating on the surface: it looked as if the creature had been blown to pieces by the force of Steven's explosion. Mark called out to his friend before he realised Steven was missing.

'Fuck!' Mark swore, as loudly as he could manage, but he heard nothing. He took a deep breath and dropped beneath the surface. It was dark, too dark to see anything, so he had to trust his instincts. He felt the thermocline again, so he was at least twenty feet down, and dropping deeper with each moment. He equalised the pressure in his ears and continued kicking towards the lake bed. He'd be enormously lucky to find *anything* – if he were off, even by a few feet in either direction, he might swim right by Steven's body.

Thirty feet: it would have to happen in the next few seconds. Thirty-five. His lungs ached, but he was determined to last at least another thirty seconds. He allowed his breath to begin escaping his lungs, slowly, so slowly; the simple act of exhalation helped him to hang on.

Forty feet. He could see nothing, sense nothing. It was cold and dark. Then he felt them. Tentacles.

At first Mark was frightened he had come upon the blinded creature, lurking below and entirely capable of ripping him to pieces, but he quickly realised these tentacles were not moving, not reaching for him. They swayed gently in the current, but they were lifeless. This was it. This chunk of the creature's broken body was huge, and somehow he knew Steven lay trapped beneath it.

Twenty seconds more. He began to count: *twenty. Nineteen. Eighteen* ... He ran his hands through the forest of tentacles, trying not to focus on the pain when the evilly serrated claws sliced through his flesh. He found the ragged edge where the monster had broken apart in the explosion and gripping hard, Mark pulled with all his might.

Fourteen. Thirteen. Twelve. Eleven. He started as the body shifted, then stretched out on the sandy lake bottom, reaching beneath the carcass for any sign of Steven. *Nothing.* He exhaled more bubbles, trying to fool his body into staying down for a few additional moments.

He tugged again, moving the corpse further away. *Nine. Eight. Seven. Six.* He stretched as far as he could beneath the monster—

Finally! Mark's fingers closed around a leather boot. He pulled, and felt something give. *Four. Three.* He shifted his weight and pulled again. *Two.* Finally, Steven's body came free. *One.*

Mark kicked off the bottom, dragging Steven's inanimate form behind him. Forty feet. That would take fifteen seconds, twelve if he were lucky. Steven had been under water far too long; Mark's worry overcame his own need for air. At about twenty feet, his temple struck something hard, but as he raised an arm to brush it away he realised it was the staff. He shoved it towards the surface like a javelin, following as fast as he could. When he broke through the surface he was screaming, 'Someone help me!'

THE MEADOW

Versen and Brexan were moving north along the coast. They had no waterskins, so they drank from every stream they passed. The jemma fish was finished, leaving nothing but the smell – they'd stuffed their pockets full of the cooked flesh and the fisherman's generous gift had seen them through to the second day. They were happy to be alive and their spirits were high: they held hands while they walked, and chatted amiably. Brexan talked about Malakasia; she was pleased to dispel the myths that the entire nation was shrouded in ghostly fog, and that strange and horrible creatures wandered freely committing gruesome acts of dismemberment or murder.

'Except around Welstar Palace,' she added as a caveat. 'No one goes there by choice – unless they're stationed there, of course. And Prince Malagon's generals are very selective about that: only the Home Guard, his own personal security force, are permitted in the palace, or even on palace grounds. I understand it's very dangerous.'

'Outstanding,' Versen said sarcastically. 'That's where our group is heading.'

Brexan frowned. 'You'll never make it inside. You might not make it through the forest surrounding the keep. I was only there once, for a short time before we were deployed to Rona, but Ox, there must have been a hundred thousand soldiers massed around the palace.'

'Why?' He was dumbstruck. 'What does he have to fear?'

'Fear? Prince Malagon? Nothing.'

'Then what's he planning to conquer?' Versen tugged at his whiskers. 'You don't have an army that size unless you're about to defend or attack something. It's too expensive to keep them all fed, and an idle army is a terrible thing.'

'I don't know,' she admitted, 'but it was a sea of warriors, stretching across the valley and blanketing the hillsides leading up to the palace.'

Walking through a grove of scrub cedar in bare feet, stinking of fish, nothing to eat other than a few bits of jemma stashed in his tunic pocket, Versen really didn't feel up to the task of invading Malakasia and storming Welstar Palace. He sighed. 'This may be hopeless. We're a lifetime – ten lifetimes – away from being ready to battle that army.' Suddenly tired, he sighed and said, 'I don't even have a pair of boots.'

Flashing a sexy grin, she pulled him towards a sandy patch of sunlit ground just off the narrow trail. 'All the easier for me to get you out of your clothes,' she laughed.

'Incorrigible hussy,' Versen cried with feigned disgust.

'Trying to get me excited, Ox?'

Resisting for a moment, Versen asked, 'What about O'Reilly?'

'I haven't heard from him all day, have you?' She continued dragging him towards her chosen spot. 'And if he is around, let him watch. He's been dead for more than nine hundred Twinmoons, after all.'

Versen gave up trying to be sensible and grasped Brexan around the waist, pulling her to the ground. His tongue flicked over her full lips and she responded with a low growl as she slid her own tongue playfully into his mouth. As they sank into a tangle of arms and legs and sighing and moaning and deep breathing, a ghostly figure took position on the trail ahead. Gabriel O'Reilly was on sentry duty.

Had anyone observed the translucent figure standing vigil, they might have noticed that the spirit's attention was focused on a small hillock behind a meadow that stretched outward from the cedar grove's edge. The almor was waiting. The spirit could detect its putrid stench defiling the air, overlaying the crisp scents of autumn with the dank smell of death, rotting flesh and disease.

At least one Seron waited as well, but the wraith did not think twice about him. The lovers would have to deal with that one – he would be too occupied with the demon. Waiting patiently for the sun to come up, he reflected on what he could recall of his life. A lot had faded since his death, but he could still remember sensations, often more distinctly than events or people: the heat and humidity along the Warrenton Parkway at Bull Run, the pain of the rifle slug in his leg and the worry that it would have to be amputated; the excitement at beginning life again in Colorado. These memories wandered through his mind as he stood at his self-appointed post. He remembered what it had felt like to be loved; that was the recollection he wished to immerse himself in for the few moments he had before battling the demon. He could not now recall any specific scripture, but he had believed most faithfully that Jesus Christ would ensure that his soul ascended to heaven. But He had not.

Just after dawn, O'Reilly detected the almor moving closer and wafted over to where Brexan and Versen lay sleeping beside the trail.

'You must wake up now,' the wraith urged.

Versen stirred. 'What? What is it?' He sat up and pulled his wrinkled tunic on.

'A Seron,' O'Reilly said. 'Be ready.'

'Oh, demonpissing rutters,' Versen spat, suddenly lucid, and shook Brexan hard. 'Up, quick,' he ordered, scanning the copse for anything he might use as a weapon. Brexan still had the knife she had managed to swipe before leaping into the ocean, but he had nothing. 'No boots. I can't believe I don't even have a pair of boots,' he muttered to himself as he picked up a short but sturdy length of cedar.

Versen turned back to Brexan, who, ever the soldier, stood silently beside their sandy bed, her tunic adjusted and trim, her hair pulled back neatly with a leather thong and her knife held loosely in one hand. 'Ready?' he asked.

Brexan nodded. 'It's worse.'

'What could be worse?'

'He has the almor with him.'

Versen held his breath. 'Can O'Reilly—'

'He says he'll try.'

'Right.' Versen swallowed, fighting the dryness in his throat. He hugged Brexan hard, then pointed through the trees. 'Let's go.'

Neither was surprised to see the Seron was Haden. 'I knew that horsecock would never give up,' Versen muttered. The Seron was standing alone in the centre of the meadow. He didn't move as they left the woods and came towards him: his ruined face grim, he seemed to stand even more rigidly, as if preparing himself for the coming battle.

'Him again,' Brexan groaned. 'I was hoping it was Karn or Rala. Where do you suppose the almor is waiting?'

'We've got enough on our plate; let's leave the almor to O'Reilly and hope to all the gods of the Northern Forest he's powerful enough to keep it off us while we deal with this one.'

'He's got no weapons,' Brexan observed as they emerged onto the meadow. Thick morning dew coated the knee-deep brush and her feet were quickly soaked wet and growing cold.

'Gilmour said they sometimes like to attack with their hands, feet and teeth. The ones who attacked us in the foothills didn't have weapons.'

'So you had the advantage?' Brexan asked hopefully.

'Not exactly. Sallax and I managed to kill one each, but he had a rapier and I had an axe. Steven Taylor dealt with the rest. A friend of ours was killed, beaten to death, before Steven could save him.'

Despite her cold feet, Brexan felt herself begin to sweat. Suddenly, she wanted to let the battle begin. 'C'mon Ox, let's go. It's two of us against him, and I have a knife. Let's get started.'

'I hope O'Reilly's dealing with the demon, otherwise this might end up being a very short engagement.'

Brexan blanched as her feet slipped on the wet grass. 'It could be anywhere out here.'

Gabriel O'Reilly moved like autumn wind. He could sense the almor's presence everywhere: it felt as if it had blanketed the entire meadow. The wraith couldn't decide where to engage – he wasn't even sure the monster would be vulnerable to his assault – but he knew he would have to act quickly, if only to distract the demon while his friends battled the Seron. *His friends.* Were they his friends? He had almost forgotten what it meant to have friends, but a recollection of Milly and Jake Harmon, and Lawrence Chapman, and his friends from Idaho Springs brought him up short. Versen and Brexan were weak and essentially unarmed, ill-equipped to survive the season, never mind an attack on Welstar Palace. Yes, they were friends, like Mark, and there wasn't much he could do to help them in their mission, but he was determined to see them safely past the Seron. That's what *friends* did. He spiralled up into the morning sky. As he cleared the tops of the tallest trees he caught a glimpse of the Ravenian Sea and the Falkan countryside. It was beautiful in the bright gold of the rising sun, though not nearly as breathtaking as Clear Creek Canyon. The former bank manager readied himself for battle and plunged headlong into the meadow.

Versen stumbled as the ground beneath his feet seemed to shift suddenly. 'That was O'Reilly,' he said with a burgeoning sense of confidence. 'He has the almor.'

'How can—?' Brexan's question was interrupted by a desperate wail that shattered the morning; she could feel its resonant vibration underneath her bare toes. If they survived to reach the opposite side of this meadow, they would owe their lives to the wraith once again.

She looked up to see the Seron had lost his balance as well. As a look of surprise passed over his face, Brexan seized the moment and rushed forward, crying, 'C'mon Ox, he wasn't expecting that!'

'I'll go low,' he whispered, hoping she'd heard him.

Ahead, the Seron stripped off his tunic and threw it to one side. 'Smart,' Brexan mumbled: less for his assailants to grip. Haden's upper body was a mass of lean muscle tissue crisscrossed with thin, pink scars.

Brexan felt adrenalin warring with terror inside her and she forced herself to continue running. She was a soldier. It wasn't right to let Versen lead the way. She was still embarrassed that she had hoped he would be first to drown so he could be a comfort for her in death. Now they'd face the Seron together. As she and Versen pounded along, side by side, a coldness filled her mind and washed over her body. Her vision narrowed down to encompass the Seron alone as Versen dropped from her peripheral sight.

Haden crouched, awaiting them stoically, a low growl in his throat and rage on his face. Versen had a plan; it was too late to discuss it with Brexan so he'd just have to hope she would pick it up as he went along. This was it: he'd have just one chance to disable the giant Malakasian. Using the wet grass as an impromptu slide, he threw himself feet-first towards Haden, slipping beneath the Seron's outstretched arms, and swung his cedar staff in a vicious blow that shattered one kneecap.

The Seron bellowed in rage as he felt his leg buckle beneath him and lashed out as he fell, catching Brexan solidly in the ribs.

As Haden collapsed under Versen's bone-crushing swing, Brexan went into action, but she misjudged how quickly Haden was toppling over and instead of driving Karn's knife deep in the Seron's neck, her thrust ran into his shoulder. It was a painful cut, but Brexan had over-extended her arm, which allowed Haden the opportunity to land a vicious punch that sent her tumbling.

Rolling to a stop, Brexan winced as she struggled to draw breath. She pulled herself onto her hands and knees, then collapsed face-first into the grass as agonising pain gripped her side: she recognised broken ribs. *Get up*, her voice commanded from somewhere deep inside, *there's no time for this*. She stumbled to her feet and turned back to the fray, the bloodied knife clenched in her hand.

Versen had suffered badly in those few moments she was down. Haden rained blows down on him, but the woodsman was fighting back, repeatedly punching the Seron's fractured knee. Haden cried out, an unnerving mixture of agony and rage, but still the scarred warrior continued to pummel the Ronan.

Now Versen was hanging onto the Seron's leg with one arm and punching with the other; though he was causing the enemy soldier almost unendurable pain, his own face and neck were receiving vicious blows from the Seron's massive fists. Versen was clinging on in pure desperation, praying he could last long enough for Brexan to come back and finish off the Seron with her knife. As he watched her rise awkwardly from the grass he realised she had been injured herself; for a moment he forgot his own pain and worried about the young woman instead, until a solid kick to his chin brought him back to the present.

A primitive survival instinct was all that was keeping Versen going, but he was exhausted, and fading fast. In a final burst of energy he violently twisted Haden's broken leg, causing the Seron to throw his head back and bellow in agony.

The Seron, momentarily paralysed, had just realised that irreparable damage had been done to his knee by the irksome Ronan when the equally aggravating woman came at him from above, landing hard on his chest and driving her blade deep into his left lung. The meadow began to tilt back on itself, leaning as if to discard the three combatants into the Ravenian Sea. Haden knew he was about to lose consciousness, and in a final act of vicious rage, he raised one arm above his head and brought his elbow down against the woman's already damaged cheek. The blow tapped nearly all his strength, but it was worth it as he felt the woman go limp and slide off his chest onto the ground.

Versen nearly released the Seron's mangled leg to applaud as Brexan drove the knife into Haden's chest. He grinned despite a crack in his jaw, a broken nose and a swollen, maybe even ruptured eye socket: they were going to win. They were bloody and battered, and they might not survive the journey to Welstar Palace, but at least there would be one less Seron to terrorise Eldarn.

We'll thin the rutting herd by one, Versen thought, but that image wavered as he fought to maintain consciousness. 'Finish him,' he tried to shout, but only a wet gurgle escaped his throat.

As the Seron smashed his elbow into Brexan's poor damaged face, Versen's rage erupted anew. 'I'll finish you myself, you dog-rutting half-human piece of ganselshit,' he screamed, reaching towards the knife, but with one arm wrapped around the Malakasian's injured leg and the other stretched out, Versen realised he had made a fatal error.

You're exposed! The warning blared in his mind, but it was already too late. The Seron was too strong and too malicious: not even fatal injuries would get in the way of this victory. Versen's eyes bulged as he saw the Seron's boot coming towards him. As it struck, consciousness faded. He and Brexan were at the mercy of the scarred warrior.

Brexan awakened to the sun high in the sky; she watched as a pair of greyish-white birds winged lazily towards the ocean. Thick grass had provided a soft bed and she was sheltered enough to enjoy the sun's warmth without being chilled by the autumn breeze. She had no idea how long she'd been unconscious; for a moment she contemplated going back to sleep – then she remembered Versen and the Seron.

She sat up too quickly and nearly passed out from the pain in her face and ribs. With her vision tunnelling, she was forced to slow her breathing and to close her eyes while she fought the nausea and marshalled her strength. Rolling to all fours, she crawled the few paces to where Versen lay beside the body of the Seron. There was no doubt the Ronan was dead. His face was bloody, and brutally beaten, and his throat had been torn out by the Seron's bare hands.

Tears welled up at the thought of how much pain he must have suffered. Brexan ran one hand through his shaggy brown hair and her fingers came away dripping with his blood. It had pooled around his battered body before being absorbed into the Falkan ground.

She turned away from her lover and vomited repeatedly until the pain in her ribs and face caused her to pass out once again.

Later that aven, Brexan sat by Versen's body. She was too weak, too damaged and too tired to find enough wood for a pyre so she turned him onto his back and folded his arms across his chest. Using her tunic as a cloth, she cleaned the blood from his face and closed his eyes. It was at that moment she finally lost hope. She no longer cared what was to come.

She curled up on the ground beside Versen's cruelly desecrated body and sobbed uncontrollably. As she wrapped herself in her grief and despair she nearly missed the guttural moan that came from the Seron lying behind her. Convinced he was dead, she hadn't given Haden a second glance when she woke earlier. Now her sobs waned immediately. She pulled herself to her knees, ignoring the arcing pain in her ribs, crawled over to the Seron and slowly withdrew the knife from his chest. A trickle of blood ran from the wound. He was still alive.

Brexan's eyes narrowed. 'I cannot tell you how pleased I am to see you again,' she said in a flat monotone, then shouted, 'Wake up! I'm talking to you!' She punctuated her commands with kicks – she hoped each one would break a few more ribs.

'Come on now, my friend – I want to know that you are aware of what's happening to you.' She grinned devilishly when she saw his eyes slit open slightly, then gulped as she realised this evil, murdering, inhuman beast had eyes the same colour as Versen's. She flinched as she recalled Versen's light-green eyes gazing at her face while they made love hungrily in the sand.

The cold wave washed over her again and this time Brexan allowed the unbridled homicidal hunger to take her.

'Can you see me? I want you to remember me. I want you to know who is doing this to you.' She leaned in close.

A threatening murmur emanated weakly from the Seron: he was lucid, perhaps not ready to ponder life's ironies – pale green eyes, for example – but certainly aware of his condition. 'You are in hideous shape, my friend,' she observed. 'You may not live through the day—' she began rolling up her tunic sleeves, '—but then again, you just might.' She wiped the knife blade clean on her leggings, pushed her hair behind her ears and began cutting.

BOOK V

Orindale

THE HOUSE OF ALEN JASPER

Alen Jasper's house was deceptively small from the outside. As Hannah walked from room to room she thought that the strange mystic had somehow forced a much larger dwelling under the nondescript shingle roof. There was a veritable maze of narrow halls, twisting stairs and curiously placed chambers, several of which had stone fireplaces, although she could only see one chimney outside. The four companions spent most of their time in these rooms as the nights were cool no matter how hot Middle Fork got during the day. It reminded Hannah of early autumn in Colorado, when beautifully warm days were followed by cold nights heralding the coming winter.

Then there were Alen's books, printed in secret or preserved since Prince Marek first took the Eldarni throne more than nine hundred Twinmoons earlier. The illegal collection, thousands of volumes, was the size of a small town library, but the books were arranged in no order Hannah could discern. Gardening books were stacked near physiology treatises; stories of great Eldarni athletes were thrown in a wooden crate with studies on nutrition; legends of man-eating fish and sea creatures were lost among a treasury of books on Eldarn's stained-glass windows. But no matter the peculiar filing system, Alen, the suicidal drunkard, appeared to be able to find any volume he wanted, regardless of whether he was searching for an obscure reference to cheese or a mathematical algorithm governing motion in Twinmoon tides, within a few minutes.

He had not spoken again of suicide, but Hannah knew he was still drinking heavily in secret. She often heard him in the hallway maze at night, and in the morning she would find the empty bottles or flagons. One night she heard him stumble past her chamber door, then pause and retrace his steps. As he stood outside her room, Hannah fought the desire to throw open the door and ask what he wanted. He didn't knock, or try to force his way in, but after a long while, he whispered, 'We shall both get what we want, Hannah Sorenson.'

She heard him later that night as he rounded a corner somewhere near the front of the house and cried out, 'Jer.' The muffled cry was filled with such pain it almost broke her heart. It reminded her of Branag and his lonely vigil at the leather shop: *Children are as close as we are allowed to come to feeling as though we have, for just a moment, been singled out by the gods.* That was what Branag had told her. Hannah realised suddenly this struggle was *real*, this strange land, with all its peculiarities, was made up of ordinary people who were wrapped up in their desperate fight for freedom from an all-powerful dictator with legions of soldiers to deploy at his whim. They did commonplace things, like caring for their families, and adoring their children above everything.

Commonplace normal things, she thought. *Things I would expect* from— Hannah paused before admitting — *from people back home, from people like me.* The walls of her bedchamber seemed to close in on her. *Nothing was different.* 'Children are as close as we are allowed to come to feeling as though we have, for just a moment, been singled out by the gods,' she whispered to herself. It was love, compassion, and a genuine desire for all the things Hannah had once believed unique to the narrow world from which she came that fuelled this revolution.

Before drifting off, she heard Alen again. 'We shall both get what we want, Hannah Sorenson.'

THE PICKET LINE

Mark watched the sun come up. Its glow shone through the branches with a comforting predictability. He stoked their campfire, drew a large packet of tecan leaves from his sack and began brewing a pot as the grey colours of pre-dawn magically gave way to the myriad hues of autumn. Red maple, yellow oak and fiery aspen mixed with the stolid evergreens to create a morning palate so picturesque he could almost taste it. Far behind him winter raged about the Blackstones: he could just make out the craggy white, grey and black peaks jutting above the horizon like the spiked backbone of an ancient dragon. Mark inhaled the essence of a Falkan autumn, chill despite the sun.

He hummed quietly to himself, pleased he could hear again. Two days after the battle on the underground lake Steven remained unconscious – he had taken a tremendous blow to the head, and then nearly drowned beneath the weight of the dead bone-collector – but Mark thought he might wake soon. After hauling Steven into the longboat, Mark had cleared his friend's lungs and restarted his heart with a flurry of blows. Steven's nose had bled for a while, and he'd coughed up a few mouthfuls of blood, but by the end of the first night, his condition had improved markedly. Fearing concussion, they had taken turns waking him periodically to answer simple questions, and he had given groggy but accurate answers each time.

Mark wondered if the staff's magic had been helping Steven's recovery: it seemed to him that the magic had somehow permeated Steven's body and now refused to allow him to die. There was no other way Steven could have survived the bone-collector's attack. Mark worried for a moment about how he would manage the transition to life in back in Colorado then, catching himself, he stifled a laugh. 'Too far ahead, dummy. First things first.'

He poured himself a mug and winced as he took a seat beside a maple tree. Gita had applied querlis to his injured stomach before Hall had neatly stitched the loose flaps of skin back together – he was a cobbler, and skilled with a needle and thread. Mark ran the flat of his palm across the scar: very neat. Breathing the fresh sea air, he let his thoughts wander back to his dream. With everything that had happened, he'd had no time to think about Nerak's possible weakness.

He let his mind drift back in time.

The rosewood box lay on Steven's desk in the corner of their living room. The tapestry was stretched out on the floor in front of the fireplace – they'd pushed the coffee table back against the couch to make room for it. Mark would never forget the shimmer that played in the air, or the tiny flecks of coloured light that danced about like a wellspring of magic and energy emanating from the far portal.

Afraid that the tapestry was radioactive, they'd planned to hurry back to Owen's Pub and call the police – or perhaps a geologist, or a radiation expert. But they never made it: as Steven rushed down the hallway to grab Mark's coat from the kitchen, Mark stood up and tripped on the hearth. As he stumbled, he planted one foot firmly on the tapestry – and an instant later it had come down in a shallow stream running into the ocean south of Rona's forbidden forest.

Beside the fire, Brynne stirred, roused by the aroma of tecan. She lifted her head and sniffed, and looked around for Mark; he gave her a quick, reassuring wave and was pleased when she smiled and rolled back over. She was obviously still as tired as she looked: she was asleep again almost immediately.

The beach in Estrad had been hot and humid: Mark had pulled off his sweater and boots. He had spent much of that night mapping the unfamiliar constellations in the sand, poking holes to mirror the heavens. None of the patterns were even remotely familiar, even after racking his brain to recall any obscure Scandinavian, African, or South American star shapes. And there were two moons. Nothing could explain that away. Mark remembered leaving his star map to wade through the cool ocean water as it pushed and pulled at his legs.

With every group of stars he drew on Rona's sedimentary canvas, his hopes for a sensible explanation had waned. By the time he fell asleep, he had accepted that either he was dead, or something impossible had happened.

But had he dreamed that night? He turned the question over and over in his mind, but had to give up. He had no idea. But something about that night continued to play about in his memory. He'd been half drunk. He remembered looking around for cigarette butts, cans or wrappers and finding nothing, and he remembered sitting down heavily in the sand and digging parallel ruts in the ground with his heels, something he always did when he sat in sand. He had done it that night.

That was it. Not a dream, but a memory. What had he been thinking about while he sat there digging his heels into the sand? What had he remembered – and why was it important? It *was* important: it was the only time in those early days in Eldarn when he was not frightened, when he had not cared that he had gone from Idaho Springs, Colorado, to Estrad Beach in Who-the-Hell-Knew-Where? For those few moments, he was back on Jones Beach with his family and things were fine. He was safe.

A flood of memories washed over him: he was staring out at the twin moons hovering overhead, recalling his father, the large yellow beach umbrella and the summer days on Jones Beach. His father would sit in a folding lawn chair drinking beer. Mark had been drunk when he arrived in Eldarn, drunk on beer he and Steven had consumed over a pizza – so why was that important? And why had he felt completely at home on that beach, not ten minutes after the most profound and unusual experience of his entire life? He had fallen through a crack in the universe, had found himself in another world – maybe even another time – and an errant memory had brought him peace.

It meant something, but he was missing the point. His father sitting on Jones Beach, drinking beer and eating ham sandwiches: that was the dream and the recollection. Mark sat on a beach in Estrad digging ruts in the sand with his heels. He had dug ruts in the sand as a child. The beach? The beer? His father.

'Sonofabitch,' Mark cried and leaped to his feet, spilling his tecan over his sweater. '*Lessek!*' He was not missing an important lesson, he was missing a message: Lessek was trying to tell him something. Mark sat down and ordered himself to start again at the beginning.

It took two days for the small company to reach the outskirts of Orindale. They had been forced to take cover a number of times to avoid occupation forces patrolling the roads; thankfully, the horses could be heard thundering towards them from a great distance. Garec finally suggested they leave the road and use a parallel path through the forest, slower, but with less risk of being spotted. That night they huddled in a thick clump of trees. The Twinmoon was nearly complete and in the northern sky the two glowing bodies appeared to merge into one. The winds began to blow off the ocean with a fury: the tides would be high.

North lay the Malakasian army lines, their fortifications and trenches circling the city. Gita had not exaggerated: there were tens of thousands of soldiers. The light from their fires lit the horizon, like a great swathe of stars fallen to the ground. The random flickering gave the city the illusion of motion. The ocean breeze blew the smells of the army – smoke, grilled meat and open latrines – into the thicket where the friends were hiding. From this distance it was impossible to determine which platoons were Seron and which were traditional soldiers, but it made no real difference: one look was enough to tell them their tiny band of ragged freedom fighters would need an Abrams tank to break through those lines. Steven rubbed his temples. He was still getting headaches after his confrontation with the bone-collector, but this one was noticeably weaker: he hoped that was a good sign.

He remembered virtually nothing after the moment the Cthulhoid cavern dweller attacked him. He had a hazy recollection of Gita's hideout, a large granite cave located somewhere near the surface, but he had no memory of either the fight or the journey through the upper caves to the Falkan forest beyond.

He was back in his tweed jacket. It had been washed, and covered a trimly cut tunic he assumed had come from the partisans. He felt clean and presentable for the first time in months. Garec's quivers were filled and even Mark's red sweater had scrubbed up nicely. Their packs were stuffed with dried fruit, smoked meat, bread and cheese and each skin was filled to bursting with a sweet Falkan wine that reminded Steven of a vintage Tokaji. Mark had a pouch of tecan leaves. Steven smiled: were it not for the thousands of enemy warriors encamped several hundred paces away, they might have been on an autumn camping trip.

They had approached the shore carefully: Garec and Mark had been wary of mounted patrols, while Steven could not help scanning the skies for the clouds of deadly mist Hall had described so vividly. Just before sundown they had spotted several of the deadly clouds massed over the Malakasian fortifications, quiet sentries hovering threateningly overhead like an Old Testament nightmare. Steven shuddered at the thought of battling the nebulous enemy.

There were two major roads running into the city from the east, both heavily guarded, with regular checkpoints. They had no chance of getting into Orindale that way.

Gita had told them about the large park in the centre of the city, once the private garden of the Falkan royal family, with the imperial palace, now a Malakasian military outpost, on the eastern edge. The former palace was a grand edifice, a three-storey building flanked by servants' quarters, stables, gardeners' sheds and livery, each painted the same pale beige. The doors were made of mahogany and opulently gilded bas-reliefs marked the keystones and window lintels. Since the collapse of Falkan's government beneath the heel of Prince Marek's dictatorial boot, the imperial complex had been allowed to fall into disrepair and now, like Riverend Palace in Estrad, there was only the vaguest resemblance to the majestic compound it had once been.

The river that had been both their lifeline and nearly their death disappeared between two enormous sentry fires some thousand paces north of their hiding place, cutting a watery path through the imperial garden and on into the Ravenian Sea. It was much wider and deeper here than in Meyers' Vale, when it had so thoroughly battered the *Capina Fair* and her unhappy passengers.

As tempted as Steven had been to risk a night-time approach along the river, he realised that was too foolhardy. He was quite sure the Malakasians had been as thorough in closing down the river as they had been with the roads: they might not be able to see from here, but there would be barges lined with archers, and a series of sunken obstacles to inhibit the progress of enemy ships.

And apart from staying very low in the water and hoping they would not be seen, Steven was not plagued by creative ideas as to how they would use the river for safe passage, anyway.

Mark's suggestion, to stow away on one of the merchant vessels that appeared to move largely unaccosted through the checkpoints, was shouted down too: if their vessel were searched, they'd be cornered. In the end, with the surf pounding away endlessly, a cacophonous backdrop to their plotting, they agreed the beach would have to be their way in.

With this decision made, Garec insisted everyone study the roads and the river, in case they had to make a hasty retreat out of the city.

'Good point, Garec,' Steven agreed, 'but we need somewhere to meet up if we get separated.'

'Get back to the partisan cave and wait there,' the bowman replied.

'That won't work for me.' Steven shook his head. 'I didn't see enough of it to know where it is.'

'But you remember our camp,' Mark suggested. 'Let's at least get back there.'

Brynne pulled a wool blanket about her shoulders. 'We should try to find a safe place in the city.' Her breath formed small clouds that faded quickly on the breeze. 'It's a long way back to our camp.'

'She's right,' Steven agreed. 'Let's hope Gita's safe havens are still safe. She was pretty convinced those that had escaped the gaze of the Malakasian occupation were foolproof. "Hide in plain view", she said.'

'Her hideouts make me nervous,' Mark admitted. 'I'm not convinced that woman is entirely committed to her own self-preservation.'

'Chicken,' Steven teased.

'Well, think about it,' Mark argued, 'a Malakasian warehouse?'

'She said the merchant was at sea,' Garec replied, 'which is why the place is empty.'

Brynne joined in. 'And he moors his ship right offshore, so we'd have a good three avens' warning if he came back.'

Mark suggested Hall's cobbler's shop. 'We could hole up there, be warm, eat real food and sleep someplace dry.'

'That's the one that makes me nervous,' Brynne said. 'A

Malakasian sympathiser as a landlord? At least we know the merchant is gone until the ship appears on the horizon. Hall's landlord would be right next door, underfoot all day. I don't know.'

Mark shrugged. 'It's certainly hiding in plain view.'

'And it appears to have worked just fine for Hall,' Garec agreed.

Brynne was unimpressed. 'I still think the warehouse is our best bet.' She looked pleadingly at the others. 'And who knows what supplies or weapons might be there for the taking.'

'True enough,' said Steven.

'We'd have to keep watch round the clock,' Mark said, working through his strategy. 'That way we'd be sure to see them if they come into harbour.'

'And we'd hear anyone coming into the warehouse from the city.' Garec added.

'All right then.' Brynne finally smiled. 'That's where we'll go.'

'And assuming it's not breached, that's where we'll rendezvous if we get separated.'

'Done.' Garec adjusted his quivers with a sense of finality. 'It's dark enough now. Let's go.'

The dunes rolled away, ranks of rogue waves frozen in place. The two moons illuminated the ghostly no-man's land through which the killer moved stealthily, inching his way north on his stomach towards the distant city. It was difficult to discern where the stalker ended and the surrounding darkness began. Patience was one of his weapons. The Falkan partisans had come against these Malakasian lines with a force of thousands and had been routed easily, but could they do so with just one man? The few sentries standing guard this far west had no idea he was there; he would make that their fatal mistake.

Garec slid another few paces forward through the sand.

Gilmour had been positive that Nerak couldn't detect the magic of Steven's hickory staff, but this close, no one was willing to take that risk. Steven would refrain from using magic until it became absolutely necessary – hopefully, not before they were aboard the *Prince Marek*. Garec wasn't sure how far behind him they were now; he tried not to worry. He had told them to wait two full avens before following.

'Besides, we won't need magic tonight,' Garec whispered silently to himself. He slithered to the top of a shallow gully between two dunes and stopped to check the wind's direction. Approaching from downwind had saved his life that morning in the forbidden forest so long ago, when he and Renna had fled from the grettan pack. He smiled at the thought of Renna; he hoped she had survived the attack on Seer's Peak.

Around him the misty ocean spray blanketed him in a damp shroud. The length and breadth of his world fell in about him and shrank to the few paces separating him from the Malakasian soldiers guarding the beach behind three large picket fires. The Bringer of Death felt neither hunger, nor thirst, nor fatigue as he crawled forward, unseen. His senses were sharp, his heart rate quick but strong. His hands were steady. From where he lay, he could see six or seven Malakasian guards idling about the fires, drinking wine, while what smelled like steaks were cooking over the coals.

They would all be dead in a few moments. Garec knew he would regret killing them later, but he had to see his friends safely into Orindale, and this was the only way to do that. He must be quick: he had just a breath or two to silence every soldier on the beach. Arrows through the neck would be the only way to keep them from raising the alarm, but six of them? Seven? He had never attempted anything that difficult. As he lay there, feeling the salty spray of the ocean on his face, he considered summoning Steven forward to wipe them all out with one sweep of the staff – but no. He could do it. He could make the shots.

He would wait another half an aven: they were drinking and eating and would grow sleepy soon. A couple might even return to their encampment further east in the dunes; that would even the odds a little. It was a good two hundred paces to their tents: Garec was sure the pounding waves would mask any sound of trouble.

'Go on,' he encouraged, 'go on back to camp. Get some sleep.' He licked his lips, surprised at how dry they were in the mist, pulled the hood of his cloak up over his head, and settled in to wait.

Private Fallon trundled slowly up the beach, grabbed a chunk of driftwood from the dwindling stack thrown carelessly in a pile and turned back to join the others. He had been with this platoon for a Moon now and had hustled about his duties in hopes of earning the respect of his fellow soldiers. It had not worked. Instead, the sergeants simply had given him more to do, more menial tasks, more late-night duties, while the other soldiers had ridiculed him mercilessly. 'Fallon, you rutting fool,' they chided, 'why such a hurry? Is there a war going on somewhere you're missing?' They had all laughed at his expense; when he had tried to join in, hoping his ability to laugh at himself might make them like him, they had bullied him mercilessly. Now here he was, posted two avens' march from the closest action – not that that had been much, just a skirmish against a band of local ruffians. Prince Malagon's Special Forces had taken care of that by themselves.

The officers told them little. Dig in. Stand your post. That was it. They had no idea what was happening. There were rumours of a huge Falkan and Ronan resistance force crossing the Blackstones in the east, but Private Fallon believed the Malakasian Army was stretched out around the city for no other reason than to feed Prince Malagon's ego. He snorted: some prince! Travelling in that huge, cumbersome ship, the *Prince Marek* – and it was all black, black rigging, black sails, black flags. What message was he trying to send anyway? Was he planning to outlaw colours next? He never gave the troops anything, not even a wave: his own army and he never acknowledged them, never lowered the curtains of that black carriage for one moment to smile or salute. He just climbed in, all robes and secrets, ordered the driver east to that broken-down Falkan family palace and sequestered himself there with his generals and admirals.

Private Fallon spat in the sand and imagined the prince warm beside a fireplace, sipping vintage wine from a fine crystal glass while he was out here, the least popular soldier in the entire battalion, forced to haul firewood all night along a flank that couldn't be reached by all the combined military forces ever assembled in the Eastlands.

Tonight he had cleaned the pots, cut stakes and polished the lieutenant's boots. Now he was on firewood duty. He was sick of being the platoon's lackey and he deliberately picked up just one log from the stack at his feet then sauntered back towards the pickets.

Sergeant Tereno called out, 'Fallon, you dog-dumb mud-rutter!' The others chuckled. 'Don't you dare come back down here with only one log, laddie, or I'll beat your frame to grettan dung. Get back up there and haul an armload. We have to keep this thing burning until dawn.'

Fallon stopped and spat down the beach at his platoon mates, but Sergeant Tereno was unimpressed. 'I'll deal with your attitude problem when you get back, laddie. Now, at the double!'

Fallon turned on his heel and stomped quickly back up the beach, taking his frustration and fear out on the forgiving sand. 'Mud-whoring rutters,' he muttered, 'this is it. They're going to kill me.' And for the ten thousandth time in the last thirty days he wished he were someplace else, someplace warm and dry.

He pulled a large log from the stack. 'Fat, slovenly, drunken tyrant,' he grumbled to himself as he bundled a collection of thinner branches and logs around the first and bent over to heft the entire load. 'I ought to whip him hard across that puffy gut of his with one of these branches. That'd show him.' Fallon knew he would keep his head down and his face expressionless in the vain hope of avoiding a terrific thrashing at the hands of Sergeant Tereno and his bullyboys. He sighed heavily.

Private Fallon had taken several steps before he noticed something odd – not a stupid joke, as he first thought, but something else. Something was wrong. Three of his platoon mates lay still, one with an arrow protruding from his chest. Two were kneeling, their foreheads resting on the sand as they groped awkwardly at the cruel shafts impaling their throats. Thick black blood ran down each to soak the dusty brown sand. Sergeant Tereno had an arrow through his abdomen. He looked up and saw Fallon, and reached for him imploringly as he gurgled a plea for help. Blood dripped from his wound. Fallon froze for a moment, then, still gripping the wood firmly against his chest, turned down the beach and waited to see or hear the forward ranks of an approaching Resistance army.

Materialising out of the gloom like a wraith, the killer slowly took shape. He came alone, cowled in black, on softly padding feet that left barely a trace, while the booming crash of the surf drowned out all sound, as if the land itself were muting the man's advance. Fallon wondered whether the mysterious assassin were

662

truly there: he could have sworn that he had seen the surf breaking white through the midnight folds of the bowman's robe.

Private Fallon was still holding the driftwood when Garec clubbed him hard across the temple. His vision faded to black.

Garec kicked the driftwood aside and began dragging the fallen soldier's body north towards Orindale.

When Private Fallon woke, it was still dark and he could feel sand moving beneath his body. Despite a ponderous headache and what felt like a splash of blood across his cheek, he didn't think he was seriously injured. He had not been unconscious for very long. He struggled to catch a glimpse of his captor, then he remembered the mysterious bowman and he closed his eyes tightly, hoping against hope that it was his fellow soldiers who were dragging him, and they were heading back to camp. Then they stopped and Fallon was dropped onto the beach. His worst fears were realised: he was the archer's prisoner.

A gloved hand closed over his mouth and a voice whispered harshly in his ear, 'Where is Malagon?'

The hand relaxed slightly as Fallon choked back an incoherent sob.

The hand closed over his mouth again and the voice repeated, 'Is he on board the ship? Where is Malagon?'

Answer the questions. Answer and live. Blinking to clear his vision, Fallon nodded clumsily.

The gloved hand pulled slowly away and Fallon swallowed hard before croaking out, 'He is at the old palace. He made a big show of going there in his carriage and hasn't come out since.'

'Good.' The voice was hollow. 'What about the ship? Where is it moored?'

Fallon's mind raced, searching for anything he could recall that would help save his life. His stomach turned and he felt his vision begin to fade again. He had never imagined fear like this.

'The ship? Where is it?' The bowman was unaffected by the Malakasian's terror.

Fallon forced himself to focus. 'Orindale. The wharf.'

'The town wharf? Which one?'

'Ah— ah . . . north. The north wharf, that's it. About a thousand paces out. You can't miss it, all black, big as a city.'

Fallon thought he detected the presence of other people coming up the beach behind them.

'Very good.' The gloved hand once again closed over his mouth and he felt the stranger's knee lean heavily on his chest. 'And now, my friend . . . I have to kill you.'

Fallon thrashed wildly beneath the bowman's grasp, but it was no use. His chest. He could not raise his chest. His breath came faster and faster, but it was not enough. His eyes filled with tears and a sharp pain lanced across his torso. He gripped handfuls of sand, dropping them and picking them up again, and all the while a voice in his mind was asking, 'What good is that doing? Think of something! Think of something!' Panic overtook him completely and Fallon lost control of his bowels. He tried to scream, but couldn't draw breath. His vision narrowed to a point and Fallon stopped struggling.

Garec stumbled to his feet and staggered for a moment like a drunk, no longer the cool assassin. Brynne gripped him in a bear hug and whispered, 'He'll live, Garec. He'll live.'

Steven, kneeling beside the young soldier, reported, 'He has a couple of cracked ribs, but he'll be fine in a few days.'

'Sore, but fine,' Mark added.

'The others won't,' Garec choked and collapsed to the sand beside his victim.

Brynne started to cry softly as she watched her lifelong friend struggle with what he had done. She wished it could have been her responsibility; she would not have wrestled with her conscience as Garec always did. Garec had the most skill, but he also fell furthest after each battle. He could never stand himself after using his skills to their full grim potential. Brynne's heart wrenched as she watched him curled up in the sand, so unlike the entirely professional soldier who had started stalking the enemy such a short time ago.

'Just give him a moment,' Brynne said as Steven moved to help him up. 'He'll be all right.'

THE SOUTHERN WHARF

Morning found the four of them hiding in an abandoned shanty on the edge of the city, part of a small community of fisherman's shacks, smokehouses and boathouses assembled randomly beneath the overhanging branches of the coastal forest just south of an enormous wooden pier. The pier was flanked by a number of huge warehouses: Mark guessed that they had found Orindale's southern wharf. A few stevedores hauled crates from a nearby warehouse to a waiting single-masted sloop; it looked like the tide was turning and judging by the string of orders and obscenities, the captain was eager to set sail.

Finally a small group of Malakasian soldiers emerged from one of the warehouses and boarded the ship. From where Mark was hidden he could see them searching the vessel and interrogating the officers. There was endless paper-shuffling before they granted the captain permission to shove off.

'Just when we thought it was going to get easier,' he grumbled, checking the pot of tecan brewing over a tiny fire out behind the shanty. 'That rules out the warehouse, I suppose.' He blew gently across the top of his cup, the steam dissipating quickly in the swirling Twinmoon winds.

Garec, Steven and Brynne were sleeping while Mark stood the dawn watch. The sea was wider here than he had imagined after hearing all the tales of trade ships and merchant vessels crossing so frequently between Falkan or Rona and Praga in the Westlands. Squinting in the pale orange glow, Mark could not make out the Pragan coastline in the distance. A collection of ramshackle boats, skiffs and sailing vessels were tied to mooring pylons and rocks in the shallows. Mark made a mental note of one craft hauled up above the high-tide mark; it looked as if it was stowed for winter: a lucky break for them if that were the case. The sailboat was about twenty-two feet in length and had a single mast. He couldn't see the tiller, rigging, or even sails, but hoped they might be stored beneath the gunwales, packed away until spring. If not, he'd done enough sailing to know what was needed – steal or buy, he didn't care, he was happy just to know they would be able to get the vessel rigged and ready to flee should the need arise for a seaward retreat. 'It might even take us to Praga,' he considered aloud, and mentally checked off one of three hundred things that needed to go according to their plan in the coming days.

He sipped his drink and gazed down at his friends sleeping soundly on the hard wooden floor of the fisherman's shanty. They would remain here all day, maybe longer, if Garec needed it. He'd not yet recovered from his ordeal.

By now, their attack must have been reported, maybe by the one soldier Garec didn't kill. With so many footprints scattered about the Malakasian picket line, he hoped they would assume it was a partisan strike, that they had killed the sentries, then fled south. Allowing that young man to live caused a problem: he knew they were looking for Malagon, or at least for the *Prince Marek*. Garec had released his grip at the last minute, and that made their current predicament far more dangerous.

Although he was angry with himself for thinking maybe Garec should have dispatched that soldier too, Mark couldn't banish the thought. He kept a wary eye out for the patrols that must be coming for them.

They had done what they could to disguise their trail, moving all the way to the warehouse, then doubling back through the forest. The Twinmoon tide had roared all the way in and wiped clean most of the footprints along the beach. Mark hoped a few out-of-season fishermen might show up and begin working in the nearby smokehouses as soon as the sun rose. *Hide in plain view*: Gita's words echoed back at him. This was about as plain view as Mark could stand.

With any luck, the Malakasian force would come through the shanty village, detect nothing out of the ordinary and continue along the waterfront towards the north wharf and the *Prince Marek*. He finished his first cup and poured a second. *That might be hoping for too much*, he thought. He stared down at the bowman asleep at his feet. Garec needed time to recover from the horrors of the previous night, but if they were overrun by a Malakasian patrol, he might be called upon once again to use his gruesome skill and help them escape.

As if thinking about them had made his fears concrete, Mark heard the telltale sound of horses' hooves, pounding along the sand. Five riders approached at a gallop and Mark quickly doused the small fire with the remains of his tecan, scolding himself as he did so. 'Stupid bastard,' he muttered, 'what the hell do you think you're doing making a fire?' Mark tossed his blanket over the coals as a great cloud of smoke and steam rose from the soggy embers: not a perfect solution, but the cloud dissipated somewhat. He heard terse commands as the riders reined in out near the water's edge, but huddled beneath the front wall of the shanty, he couldn't make out what was being said. He longed to peer through the window to see if anyone was coming through the trees.

He looked around at a slight sound. Garec was awake and on his feet, an arrow nocked and ready to fire. Mark shook his head and held his breath. *Please, God, don't let it happen again*, he prayed, over and over, *please God, let them ride on*.

A great weight fell over the shanty, as if a waterlogged cloud had blown in off the ocean and settled above their hiding place. Despite the morning chill, Mark felt sweat bead on his forehead. The stitches in his abdomen began to sting; it was hard to breathe. Beside him Garec was a rock, stern-faced and impassive: he would do whatever was necessary to protect himself and his friends.

Mark suddenly realised that it wasn't just the deaths of the soldiers that were weighing so heavily on Garec's heart; it was Gilmour – he blamed himself for Gilmour's death. He needed to make peace with himself and forgive himself for allowing Gilmour's killer to escape.

Now Garec stood stock-still by the crooked door of the shanty, poised and ready for the mounted patrol to find them. It would be a costly discovery.

But they never did. After a few minutes' tense wait, they heard the clopping of the horses fading as they trotted off along the wharf.

Garec lowered his bow and folded like a discarded rag. Mark finally exhaled and returned to his watch at the shanty window as

Garec wrapped himself back in his blanket and curled up on the floor.

For the moment at least, they were safe again.

Hannah was up early, before dawn, brewing tecan and warming two loaves of day-old bread in one of Alen's fireplaces. She was kneeling on the hearth and didn't hear him enter the room. When Alen spoke, she jumped, inadvertently spilling several burning logs onto the floor.

'Jesus, you scared me,' she exclaimed in surprised English, then smiled disarmingly and switched back to Pragan. 'Good morning to you too; sorry, you startled me.' Hannah used the poker to shovel the smouldering logs back onto the flames.

'Sorry I frightened you.' Alen moved to the big old chair beside her. 'The nights are cold this late in the season. Thank you for building up the fire.'

'I was up early.' She moved a large stew cauldron from the hinged iron rod suspended above the coals then poured two mugs of tecan. Handing one over, she said. 'Here you go. I'm afraid it isn't too strong yet. I never know how long to leave it on.'

Alen watched her with a sense of detachment. 'You know, you remind me of someone I knew a long time ago.'

'I do?'

'The resemblance is uncanny.'

'Really? Who was she?' Hannah burned her tongue and blew gently on it to calm the sensation. 'I assume it was a *she*, or else our friendship is going to have a difficult morning.' She laughed.

'Her name was Pikan Tettarak,' Alen said, warming his hands on the full mug. 'She was a member of the Larion Senate.'

Hannah looked nervously about the room and fought off a sudden chill. Alen had spoken several times about the fabled band of sorcerers, but Hannah had summarily dismissed the notion as the ravings of a suicidal alcoholic. Yet, here he was, sober and clear-eyed, his first drink of the day still ten hours off. Hoyt and Churn were asleep in a chamber at the back of the house. If she cried out, they would be in the room in seconds – or whatever passed for seconds in this strange place.

Maybe now was the time to straighten out a few things. She looked Alen squarely in the face and said, 'You must understand how difficult it is for me to believe you when you talk about this

668

sort of thing. It's completely outside the sphere of my experience: how on earth do you expect me to just accept that some people can do magic, or live for as long as you claim you have?'

'For an intelligent woman you're very shortsighted, Hannah. Until this past Twinmoon it was probably "outside the sphere of your experience" to fall through a Larion portal into another world.'

Hannah smiled in reluctant agreement.

'So you ought to try to be a bit more openminded.'

'Fair enough,' she agreed. 'So who was Pikan Tettarak?'

Alen's gaze grew distant and he stared into the crackling flames. When he spoke, it was as much to the fire as to Hannah. 'She was my wife.'

'Hoyt never said you were married.'

'He doesn't know – no one knew. We were married in your England, in a small chapel near Durham Castle. It works slightly differently in Eldarn, but we loved the idea of making a lifelong commitment to one another, and your marriage vows captured the essence of our passion better than anything here. It was spring, and Pikan carried wildflowers, a handful of colour, like a rainbow. She loved the wildflowers there – we lived in Gorsk, and except for a few resilient shrubs, it had been a long time since either of us had seen anything like the flowers that grow all over England.'

Still fighting to maintain an open mind, Hannah asked, 'What were you doing there?'

'We were working. Actually, I should say *I* was working. I was conducting research into health, some projects I was planning to start up in different Eldarni cities. I was especially interested in how the English handled their sewage, rubbish and fresh water.'

'And Pikan?'

'She was a magician, very skilled, one of the strongest.'

'Was she there to research magic? Magic in England?' Hannah was horribly afraid he might say yes and cast another depth charge into everything she held as truth.

'No. Her own magic was far greater than anything she might have found in England at the time. Pikan was along with me for other reasons.'

'How did you meet?'

'I was a director of the Larion Senate. Pikan joined us much later, after the Senate's reputation as a congress of scholars had spread to the furthest corners of Eldarn. Nerak, Fantus and I had already been Larion Senators for a very long time when Pikan joined us.' He noticed her confusion, and clarified, 'Nerak and Fantus were the other division leaders, Nerak for magic and medicine and Fantus for research and scholarship. They were friends of mine as well as colleagues. Pikan was two hundred Twinmoons old when she arrived – old for a novice – but it was blindingly obvious from the day she took the vows that she possessed a strength of character and power unusual for an untrained sorcerer.' He shifted in his chair, then continued, 'I was in love with her from the beginning. I know people say *that* is impossible, but it is true. I have lived now for nearly two thousand Twinmoons and I have never felt about anyone, except my children and even that is a different love, as deeply as I felt for Pikan – and that after knowing her for three days. Can you believe that? Educated people, scholars, magicians: we are not prone to such silly, infantile attractions. We knew after three days we were meant to be together for all time.'

'What happened to her?'

Alen ignored the question, but continued with his story. 'Pikan went to work on research with Nerak.'

'The director of magic and medicine?'

'Right, and the most powerful of all Larion magicians since Lessek himself. Nerak was driven, a veritable machine; he worked constantly, pushing himself further and further, always working to unlock magic's secrets. Under his guidance, the Larion Senate experienced an era of growth and maturity unlike any in our history. He established standards by which our research was judged, by which our interventions and contributions to Eldarni culture could be measured.'

'He sounds impressive.'

'He was. And Pikan was his assistant. She thirsted for the knowledge he had at his fingertips. Together, they made a powerful team.'

'But something went wrong?'

'Not at first, no. Their efforts were a model for all our teams for many Twinmoons . . .' He drifted off and stared into the fire.

'But then?' Hannah prodded, expecting the worst.

'Then? Then Nerak began to grow distant. He allowed Pikan

to recruit young sorcerers. Together we travelled throughout Eldarn, looking for children and young adults who showed promise, like Pikan had when she joined the Senate already grown. We figured if we could detect that level of potential early in life, we could foster a generation of sorcerers nearly as powerful as Nerak himself. Pikan was entrusted with their initial training. Nerak only took over when an especially promising magician came to Sandcliff.'

'What was he doing instead?'

'He was studying, experimenting, pushing ever deeper into the hazy morass of power and knowledge buried in the Larion spell table – that was the vehicle through which Larion magicians were able to tap power and in turn introduce certain magics to our world.' Alen thought this over for a moment, then added, 'To your world, too, I suppose.'

'Really?' Hannah tried to control the scepticism in her voice. 'Sorry. It's a little hard to believe we have *any* magic in my world.'

'You have plenty, trust me – you need to learn how and where to look. Anyway, Fantus, the third director, and I decided it was time to intervene. Nerak was becoming too removed from his responsibilities, from our values. The Larion Senate was there as a service to Eldarn.'

'He was greedy?'

'He was. He had the potential to bring great things to our land, but after a while, he decided to keep it all for himself.'

'And Pikan?'

Alen pursed his lips. 'I blame myself for that. I should have paid attention. I never noticed how he looked at her. More than anything, that should have tipped me off – you know? When you cannot allow a person to leave the room without that last look, that final glimpse that says *I will imprint this image on my mind until she comes back*. That's what he was doing. The line of her face or the taper of her legs, he needed those things to bring him back from the brink of whatever nightmares he explored while immersed in the spell table. Yes, I think he loved her very much.'

'What happened?' Hannah's curiosity was aroused. 'I mean, the way you are describing this – this triangle – it doesn't sound like it had a good ending.'

'It didn't.' Alen poured himself another mug of tecan. He

offered Hannah the pot, but she shook her head. She was eager to hear the rest of the drama. 'Nerak said something about her once; it was a shock and I wasn't ready for it. I got angry and attacked him, but he was much more powerful than me, even then. I think he might have killed me if he'd had any idea of what the future held.'

'I don't understand.'

'He lashed out with a spell. Oh, it wasn't much, but it hit me hard and I fell and sprained my ankle. We were on a ship at the time, rounding the Northern Archipelago towards Larion Isle. It was a trip we made every ten Twinmoons or so – to do research and try out new magic.' He chuckled; Hannah smiled at the rare sound. 'Like checking out recipes, I suppose. Anyway, I spent the entire journey hobbling about in agony. We told everyone I'd tripped and twisted my ankle. They never knew we'd had a spat. Nerak and I never physically fought again, but we were never as close as we had been either.'

'What did you mean when you said he would have killed you if he had known—'

'Known what the future held.' The old Larion Senator paused, still staring into the fireplace. 'Pikan was pregnant; I think if Nerak had known that, he would have killed me that day and tossed my body overboard.'

'Your baby?'

'Our baby— Yes. That's why she came with me to England.'

Hannah looked confused, so he elaborated, 'I knew it was going to be a long trip. Pikan wasn't showing yet and she hid the early sickness, so no one knew. I only needed Fantus's approval for going to England, and we stayed until the baby was born and then—' Alen stopped to wipe his eyes on his sleeve.

'You left the baby there.'

'We did.' He choked back a sob, a disconcerting sound. 'We left her there because we knew Nerak would kill her if he found out about her. We were married, Pikan had the baby and we found a family, a good family, there in Durham. We promised we would always come back to visit, and when she was old enough we would bring her home with us. I even made plans to construct a third portal without anyone knowing. I could have done it. I would have done it . . . but I never had the chance.'

Hannah was on tenterhooks now; her arms and legs were

numb from sitting so long on the floor, but she dared not move and break the spell. 'So what became of the baby? Did you visit? Did you bring her back?'

'Reia.'

'I'm sorry?'

'Reia. That was her name, Reia. And no, we never made it back. She was very young, just a few Twinmoons old, when we returned to Eldarn, but we had to – there was no way I could justify our absence any longer.' Alen cleared his throat, though his voice still shook as he spoke. 'We had to keep up appearances while we planned some way to bring Reia home and find somewhere where she would be safe and where we could be together as a family. But I had to come to Praga, to Middle Fork. Pikan was so distraught she nearly collapsed the day I left, but I promised her – just as I promised Reia – anyway, I swore to Pikan we would figure out a way, even if it meant challenging Nerak, killing Nerak. I didn't care at that point, but Pikan didn't want it to come to that. At least we knew Reia was in good hands.'

'So you came to Praga.'

'To Middle Fork, and while I was gone, Nerak finally lost his battle for sanity. He destroyed the Larion Senate.' Alen's voice was calm now; he spoke in dead, flat tones. 'He killed Pikan, his team, everyone.'

'Why?'

'My guess is that the magic he sought to control finally took control of him and in doing so, he lost what was left of his already tenuous grip on reality. He killed them all.'

'What happened to Reia?' Hannah whispered, almost hoping Alen might not hear.

But he did, and he broke down again, weeping into his hands. 'The far portals were lost, Sandcliff was all but destroyed and any means I had to get back to Durham was gone for ever.'

'The far portal Steven found in Colorado—'

'Was one of two we used to travel back and forth.'

'Where was the other?'

'In Prince Marek's royal chambers at Welstar Palace in Malakasia – the lion's den. I think Nerak placed it there. And I know in my heart that he remains involved to this day. He protects it. He is there. I can feel him, even from here, I can feel him there, laughing at me.'

'Why not confront him? It's been so long. Why not go and tell him of the baby, and ask for – demand, or, hell, *steal* the far portal if you have to?'

'I was not permitted to go. It would have been suicide.'

'Not permitted? What do you mean?'

'Lessek.' Contempt filled his voice.

'You mentioned that name before.' Hannah searched her memory for a moment before finding it. 'That night – that first night when Churn carried you in. You said Lessek wouldn't let you die? Why? First he wouldn't let you confront Prince Marek, or Nerak, and now he won't let you commit suicide. Why? What does he care?'

Alen shook his head grimly. 'There must be something left for me to do.'

'But it's been so long – what could come up now?'

'You, Hannah Sorenson. You and these men you talk about, Steven Taylor and Mark Jenkins. Obviously you have discovered the far portal; I imagine I am still here, in Middle Fork, after all these Twinmoons, because you were coming.'

Hannah shuddered. That could not be. It was too much for her deal with right now. A little frightened, she changed the subject. 'You must have remarried.'

'I did. I missed Pikan and Reia so badly that I felt as if I would turn to dust, but I had been touched by the gods once and I wanted it again.'

'Love like Pikan's?'

'Oh no, I knew I would never find that again. No, I wanted children, lots of children.' He managed a chuckle and his voice rose, lilting, as he said, 'And I did have children, and they were wonderful.'

'Jer?'

'Jer was the last of my grandchildren, the last of eleven grandchildren.'

'I don't see how that's possible.' Hannah felt her scepticism rise once again.

'I don't care what you believe is possible or impossible, Hannah Sorenson. It has happened, and I am alone, and I will go with all haste to whatever end Lessek has chosen for me.' He placed the empty mug on the floor at his feet. 'I can only hope this is my chance to destroy Nerak, to look into his eyes as his life ebbs and remind him, one last time to echo through all eternity, that she loved me. She loved only me, never him.'

'And then you can die?'

'Killing Nerak will mean my death as well, but that's fine.' As an afterthought, he added, 'If at all possible, I will try to send you home first.'

With that, Alen Jasper of Middle Fork rose, nodded pleasantly and strode from the room.

It took five days to work out how they would move against Malagon, and it was a stroke of exceedingly ironic good luck that brought them the answers they needed to the final nagging questions.

Before nightfall that first day, an elderly fisherman appeared at the next-door shack with a pile of nets. He sat outside on the beach, examining them closely, tugging at tiny knots and deftly stitching torn sections together with a length of thin twine and a wooden needle. After a while, Garec took a chance and went over to ask about the shanty they were using. Coins changed hands. The shack was used by a group of brothers who worked a tempine farm in Rona during the winter; they generally returned when the great schools of migrating fish moved north in the spring. A second coin ensured the fisherman's silence about their presence – he appeared happy, almost amused, to keep silent. As night fell, he loaded and paddled a dilapidated rowboat out beyond the relative protection of the pier. He soon shrank to a point on the slate-grey horizon.

'Well, that's a stroke of luck,' Steven said, 'unless of course he tells the Malakasians we're here.'

'I don't think he will,' Mark said. 'Did you get a look at him? He doesn't look like he's doing especially well under Malakasian rule. He probably fishes at night to keep from handing over half his catch to the customs officers.'

'There are people like him throughout the Eastlands,' Garec said. 'The silver I gave him is probably more money than he makes in a Twinmoon. If we have anything to fear, it's that he comes back with a small army of his own to rob and murder us in our sleep.'

'Grand,' Brynne commented dryly. 'So now we have to keep

watch for the Malakasian soldiers *and* the Falkan fishermen as well.'

Garec laughed for the first time in two days.

At dawn the following morning, Steven watched the old man return, pulling hard on the oars against the outgoing tide. He moored his skiff in shallow water and began lugging boxes of fish up the beach to one of the smokehouses. Steven left the staff leaning against the wall and went down to help; he was rewarded with a huge fish, large enough to feed the four of them for a couple of days.

'Thank you,' Steven said graciously, wrestling with the slippery corpse. 'What kind of fish is it?' He thought it looked something like a yellowfin tuna.

'Jemma,' the old man answered, 'best you can get. It's good smoked, or you can cut it into steaks and cook it over your fire.'

'Jemma,' Steven echoed. 'Thank you again.'

'You are here to kill the prince, right?' The tanned leathery face looked inquisitively up at Steven. 'You killed those soldiers on the beach, too, right?'

Steven was speechless.

'It's all right,' he waved a wet hand in a gesture of reassurance, 'I'll keep quiet, but you must know the prince cannot be killed here.'

Steven still didn't know how to react, so he just thanked the man again for the fish. 'We are grateful,' he said quietly.

The old man spent most of the day in the smokehouse; the scent filled the air and made Steven nearly insane with hunger. He cut hearty steaks from the thick jemma and cooked them on a flat rock in the fire, the same way Lahp had cooked grettan steaks in the Blackstones.

They revelled in the succulent flavour. 'We need wine and potatoes with this,' Mark said through a mouthful of flaky fish.

'We've got some of Gita's wine left, but I'm afraid we're fresh out of potatoes.'

'We'll have to go into town for those,' Mark said. 'And if we went, we could get some tomatoes, maybe some bananas and a whole gallon of chocolate-chip ice cream.' He lapsed into English for the dessert course.

'Ice cream?' Brynne asked.

'One of the world's most perfect foods,' Mark replied, licking his lips at the memory.

'Let's go then.' Garec stood suddenly.

'What?' the others echoed in unison.

'We can't just walk into town!'

'Actually, we can,' Garec assured them. 'Mark, come on, lose that dreadful red tunic you wear and borrow Brynne's cloak. We've been here too long. We need to get our bearings and move on. Hiding's doing us no good and eventually someone will come along who can't be bought.' He leaned his longbow against the shanty wall. 'I can't take that, and you need to leave your weapons. We're a long way from Estrad Village.'

Mark looked dumbstruck for a moment, then he started pulling his red sweater off. 'Right, let's go. Steven, I need some money. I want to get some more of that fennaroot, if I can find any. That's powerful stuff; it makes caffeine look like baby formula.'

Steven flipped him the pouch of silver pieces they had stolen in Rona.

'Take just one,' Brynne suggested, 'you've enough silver there to buy a corner of the city. Carrying too much will make you a target.'

'Or worse,' Garec agreed, 'it'll bring unwanted company back here.'

Mark donned Brynne's cloak. 'Any special requests?'

'Bread and cheese,' Steven replied. 'And maybe some fresh vegetables, something green. We have been pretty bad about our diet recently, my friend.'

'And bring some— some ice cream,' Brynne added excitedly. 'It is not often one gets to try the world's most perfect food.'

'If they make it in the city and we can find some, I promise we will.' Mark kissed her lightly.

'And see what you can find out,' Steven ordered. 'See if that soldier was telling the truth about Malagon and the old Falkan palace. And be careful!'

'Will do. We'll be back.' Mark followed Garec out into the forest behind the southernmost warehouse.

Over the next few days, they each visited the city, although never all together. Steven finally abandoned his tweed jacket and Mark gave up his red sweater. Sharing the two woollen cloaks, they travelled in pairs, shopping for supplies, eating hot food in warm taverns and even bringing back bottles of wine, freshly baked bread and blocks of cheese. Although there was no sign of Sallax, and Brynne remained concerned for her brother, Mark and Steven revelled in the novelty of an Eldarni city.

Their experience in Estrad had been so limited that they'd had no idea such an array of goods and services would be available: tailors and cobblers, breweries and bakeries, butchers and pastry shops lined the narrow streets and the wider, tree-lined avenues. There were tobacconists, craftspeople, leather-workers . . . whatever they had been expecting, it wasn't this.

They made dozens of purchases, mostly food and supplies, paraffin candles and wine. Steven enjoyed walking along the wide plank sidewalks that flanked the broad muddy avenues and narrow side streets. He chatted with artisans and merchants, sampled stews and sweets and even tried his hand at a popular gambling game that involved several smooth stones, a scarf and an empty goblet. He tossed the stones onto the multi-coloured kerchief stretched across a flat tabletop and depending on where they fell, his bet was doubled, tripled or forfeited to a gaunt but friendly old woman with a pockmarked face. Having lost three tosses in rapid succession, Steven moved away, despite the encouragement of the elderly woman and the small crowd that had gathered to watch the game.

Mark handed him a piece of wheat bread. 'How much did you lose?'

'I don't know – twenty-five bucks? Twenty-five thousand? I haven't been able to figure out this system of currency yet. All the coins have Malagon's ugly pinched snout on them and I can't tell the difference.'

'Well, from the crowd you drew, I'm guessing you're a high roller.' Mark paused to tear a fruit pastry in half, then said, 'Maybe you can get us a comp room at the Stardust.'

'Monopoly money,' Steven shrugged. 'You know, I thought it would have been more—'

'Depressed?'

'Right.' He gestured along the busy street. 'I mean, these people don't act as though they're living in the shadow of an occupation army.'

'Look closer.' Mark pointed to a group of men unloading

lumber from a cart. 'Look at their shoes, their clothing. Notice how few of them are overweight. They don't look terrified because they've been occupied for five generations; they're used to it. But these people are not prospering, despite the diversity of shops, goods and services.' He gnawed thoughtfully on a corner of the pastry. 'I can't imagine what the tax rates are. Seventy, maybe eighty per cent? We rarely see this at home because we live in a place where – generally – people help the oppressed, and it doesn't take five generations for that help to come. So we never see this.'

'The long-term look of a beaten people?'

'Exactly. And in those cases where it has occurred, the end result has been tragic.'

Orindale's architecture reflected the region's resources: there were a great many wood and stone buildings with wood-shingle roofs and rock and mortar foundations. Steven guessed the stones were quarried somewhere nearby, or perhaps shipped in by the many great merchant vessels moored in the bustling harbour. The waterfront hummed with activity from dawn until well after dark. Although they saw plenty of soldiers, they were never stopped for more than routine questioning. Life in the Falkan capital went on as if no one had noticed – or minded – that they were encircled by an entire army.

One afternoon Garec brought back a crate of Falkan beer and they sat around their small fire eating from the old man's daily catch and drinking heartily from ceramic bottles.

Swallowing a mouthful of sudsy brew, Mark commented, 'The one thing I have yet to see is a bookshop. I would love to read some Eldarni history.'

Garec and Brynne both quieted at that.

'What did I say?'

Steven got it. 'No books?'

'Only outlaw copies,' Garec replied. 'Ancient books, those that survived the initial razing of all libraries and bookshops nearly a thousand Twinmoons ago.'

'When Prince Marek took the throne.'

'That's right,' Brynne answered, 'and closed the universities.'

'There's no school?' Mark was stunned.

'We all attend school until we're one hundred Twinmoons old.'

'Do they have books there?' Steven asked.

'Yes, but our history books only cover the period since the five lands of Eldarn were seized and ruled by Prince Marek's descendants. Even in school we don't have many books, so many people are illiterate.'

Mark looked glumly out the window and placed his bottle gently on the plank floor. 'No school. That's not right.'

'No, it isn't,' Brynne agreed. 'And it's one of the first things we would change should we win back Rona's freedom.' She stopped herself. 'I suppose now I should say Praga's freedom too – Eldarn's freedom.'

'What about religious leaders?' Mark asked. 'Don't they act as teachers? Do they instruct in reading, writing and basic skills?'

Garec and Brynne exchanged glances before Brynne said, 'Our temples and sects were all destroyed by Prince Marek. For five generations we have had no organised religion.'

Garec added, 'We're told some religion survives in the north; many people worship the gods they believe inhabit the Northern Forest. But our religion is an oral tradition; it always has been. Now most Eldarni people grow up, raise families, grow old and die and never know – or discuss – religion in any way. It's safer.'

'Where do your core values develop?' Steven asked. 'Are there no institutions that help preserve a system of beliefs or traditions to define them over time?'

'Some are dictated by the Malakasian prince or princess.'

'Values can't be dictated,' Steven growled. 'They have to be fostered by – well, by family, the local community, the faith-based organisations, even the government, I suppose.'

'I don't know that this is a function of any institution in Eldarn,' Garec tried to explain, 'as much as it is the evolution of ideals passed down from the days of the Larion Senate. Our values, traditions and beliefs may change according to the evolving make-up of any group, so one city's values may change as its populace ages. We've grown used to living this way because no one alive now has ever known anything different.'

'Most people wouldn't know the benefits of an organised religion,' Brynne said, 'because none of us can remember what it was like. That's why so few religious traditions have survived the occupation.'

'And as you've seen over the Twinmoon you've spent with us, war, death, violence, closed-mindedness, hatred and an assortment of other nasty behaviours have permeated our culture and been allowed to flourish here,' Garec continued on, 'and I'm a microcosm of that reality. I'm a skilled killer; it's one of my greatest strengths – and it is the one thing about myself that I deplore, more than anything else.'

'So why continue to do it?' Steven tried to work his friend into a corner.

'Because I must. I am a member of the Resistance – by choice – and however hideous, it's a necessity.' He upended the beer bottle and drank deeply. 'I just hope the right leadership will emerge to help us all heal when this business is through.'

'I hope so, too,' Mark added, trying not to sound condescending.

'I know it must happen all the time, but it seems strange that a world so diverse as Eldarn would have gone so long without a faith – or faiths – impacting and shaping your culture.' The lack of religious beliefs and values still left Steven a little incredulous.

'When you don't know what you're missing, I suppose you don't miss anything,' Brynne said.

Mark's eyes grew wide and he stood suddenly, spilling his beer in a foamy puddle. 'Say that again.'

'What part?' Brynne asked.

'What you just said to Steven.'

She thought for a moment. 'When you don't know what you're missing, you don't miss anything?'

'Sonofabitch.' Mark turned to look out the window.

'I don't suppose that word translates into Ronan,' Garec grinned.

Mark ignored him. 'Nerak. That's it.'

'What's it?' Steven stood as well.

'It is not what Nerak *knows* that is his weakness; it is what he *doesn't* know.'

Brynne took him by the arm. 'What doesn't Nerak know?'

Mark pointed towards the hickory staff leaning against the far wall of the shack they had been calling home. 'He doesn't know what's in there, for a start.'

THE NORTHERN WHARF

On the morning of their fifth day in the shanty, Garec and Steven journeyed into town together. By now they had determined that Prince Malagon was indeed holed up in the old Falkan palace, although Steven had not yet summoned the courage to move far enough into the city to actually see the grounds. Somehow he knew Nerak would recognise him if he got within ten yards of the estate.

This morning, he and Garec were determined to get a better look at the *Prince Marek*. They didn't want to draw any attention to themselves, so they left their weapons in the shanty. Garbed in dark woollen cloaks, they looked like brothers striding together along the waterfront, heads down, deep in conversation.

Crossing the wide inlet via the stone bridge separating the northern and southern districts, Steven inhaled the ubiquitous aromas: woodsmoke, sewage, the harbour and the ocean. A fierce wind assailed them off the water. To their right, the river wound its circuitous path back through Orindale and south to the forests, Meyers' Vale and the Blackstone Mountains. To their left, it widened as the river coursed through the final leg of its interminable journey to the Ravenian Sea.

Steven remembered dreaming about this place, this very spot, and he turned his face towards the sun to bask for just a moment in the success of having made it this far.

Garec looked at him quizzically and asked, 'Anything wrong?'

Steven reached over and removed Garec's saddlebag from where it rested on his friend's shoulder. He unfastened the clasp and allowed the soft leather flap to fall open across his forearm, displaying the rudimentary map of the peaks they had made at the top of the first pass they had traversed. Running his thumb over the drawing scratched into the leather, he said, 'We've come a long way, Garec.'

The bowman pointed to a narrow groove running northwest across the cowhide atlas. 'That's the valley, the headwaters of this river.'

'We made it this far.'

Thinking of Versen, Gilmour, Sallax and others, Garec added grimly, 'Some of us did, anyway.'

Steven put a hand on Garec's forearm. 'Making it this far means we have a chance to set things right, to avenge our friends, maybe even to bring an end to Eldarn's nightmares. Mark's pretty convinced that Malagon will find the staff's magic a surprisingly adequate foe. I may not be as confident, but I'll do my damnedest. I have to. Getting Lessek's Key to Kantu is our only hope.'

'Let's hope that boat Mark's rigging will get us across then.'

Steven thought of the preparations Mark had been making to the small sailboat. 'It will. Mark's got sails, extra line and plenty of tar. Brynne is organising our supplies. All we need to do is figure out a way to get aboard the *Prince Marek*.'

Garec laughed. 'I forgot. We have the easy job.'

'Right,' Steven agreed half-heartedly. His attention was diverted by a small skiff making its way downriver and out of the inlet. He gestured across the bridge. 'Isn't that our friend the fisherman?'

Garec squinted, one hand above his eyes to block the bright morning sunlight. 'I think it is. Do we know his name yet?'

'I guess he doesn't want us to know it,' Steven replied.

'So if we're captured, we won't be able to turn him in.'

Steven watched as the small boat followed the shoreline south towards the southern piers and the shanty village beyond. 'For an old guy, he certainly can row: he moves that thing like a champion.'

'Nothing like a lifetime of practice, I suppose.'

Steven watched the fisherman another moment then suddenly stood up straight, using both hands to block the sun as he leaned across the bridge rail to watch the skiff disappear.

'What is it?' Garec asked.

'Nothing. I just thought I saw him wave.'

With their attention on the little boat, neither Garec nor Steven saw the tall figure wrapped in a dark robe and shouldering a walnut longbow as he strode silently past and headed towards the row of warehouses along the southern wharf.

A quarter-aven later, the two men took their first look at the *Prince Marek*, Malagon's personal sailing vessel, moored in the harbour off the northern wharf.

Steven voiced his first impression aloud. 'We'll never make it. We'd have to be on board for three days just to find his cabin.'

The ship was a behemoth. As Steven studied it from their vantage point on the pier, he felt his hopes sinking with each passing moment. 'The far portal could be anywhere. There are – what? Six decks? Two hundred chambers? It's bloody gigantic.'

'And black.'

Black it was: the gigantic vessel floated silently in the harbour, dwarfing even the largest Pragan galleons several times over. Steven estimated her length at nearly four hundred feet, with a beam of well over one hundred and a draught of at least thirty-five running empty. Seven masts jutted proudly from her decks – three mains, a foremast, a mizzen, a jib from the bow and a spanker flanking the quarterdeck – and she was outfitted with enough rigging to tie down a rogue hurricane. The main mast sported five levels of sail, all reefed, as she rode at anchor. Two sets of topgallants towered over two sets of topsails hanging above a mainsail that would have easily blanketed the entire lot at 147 Tenth Street. The raised quarterdeck was as broad and as long as a basketball court and Steven marvelled at the size of the helm standing alone in its centre. 'He must have a giant in his crew just to move the tiller. I couldn't reach high enough to turn the wheel.

'Garec, where do ships like this come from? Jesus Highdiving Christ, how is it possible that there are farmers tilling the Ronan soil with wooden plough blades, and this behemoth can roll in here looking like Nelson's *Victory* with a glandular problem?'

Garec had been silent since they'd caught their first glimpse of the tremendous floating palace. 'That is the great irony of Eldarn, Steven. It illustrates how and where Prince Malagon – Nerak, I suppose – has focused the emphasis of his economic resources. We have no higher education, no research institutions and no hospitals worth a pinch of grettan shit, but that rutting horsecock sails around in that thing.' He gestured toward the remaining boats in the harbour. 'Look at the others. Naval vessels, merchant ships ... all of them state-of-the-art in their design. Nerak had Twinmoons and Twinmoons of Larion research and knowledge in his head when he left Sandcliff Palace, Steven, but he was very careful about which Eldarni institutions benefited from that knowledge over time.'

Steven shook his head. 'Well, no point in dwelling on it now. What do we do?'

'We'll have to enter along the stern line, there, aft beneath the quarterdeck.' Garec pointed to a thin black line that ran from the stern rail down into the water, barely visible against the hull.

'Why there?'

'She's too long for us to come up the anchor line in the bow and make it safely aft to the stern cabins. That's where Malagon's private cabin will be. He'll have the ship outfitted for his comfort. The raised quarterdeck provides enough room for a spacious apartment. I can't imagine Nerak would give up that level of comfort to the captain or his officers.'

'I bet you're right,' Steven answered. 'I can't see that many men above decks either.'

Garec nodded. 'Skeleton crew, maybe.'

'Why not? No one in the five lands of Eldarn would be crazy enough to attempt to board the prince's private yacht.'

'Or powerful enough to break through the army around the city. Malagon knows what resistance there is on land; here in the harbour, it would take the combined merchant and Resistance forces of the Eastlands and Praga just to take that ship. Most merchant vessels don't ride high enough in the water to get a grappling hook over her gunwales. They would need ten thousand fire-arrows to get her kindled, and I bet you a beer that whatever that black substance is that she's coated in doesn't burn too easily, either.'

'No thanks.' Steven frowned. 'I already lost my shirt to that old lady with the stones.'

Garec chortled and turned his gaze back towards the *Prince Marek*. 'So that's it, then. We'll sail Mark's boat out beyond her stern, towing something small we can paddle in, anchor, tie off to the stern line and board her from the quarterdeck.'

'Mark and I will climb aboard if you'll—'

685

Garec finished his thought. 'I'll stay in the skiff and take out anyone who approaches the stern rail.'

'Garec,' Steven offered, 'maybe I can come up with some spell to put them all to sleep for a few moments. I know the only effective magic I've been able to muster so far has been fireballs, tricky campfires or massive blasts, but maybe I can work something in between.'

'It's all right, Steven,' Garec assured him. 'We're close to the end. I can do it.' The Ronan ran one hand through the wavy brown hair that hung about his forehead. His eyes danced and he added, 'Perhaps I'll get lucky and they'll be firing back at us this time.'

Steven tried to swallow. 'Sure, lucky. Anyway, Mark and I will find Malagon's cabin, open the far portal and I'll leap back to Idaho Springs for Lessek's Key. Mark will steal the portal, rejoin you in the skiff and sail south along the coast.' Steven's heart raced at the thought of being home: he'd have a chance to confirm whether Hannah was still there, or had managed somehow to get home. He just needed a few hours to try to explain what had happened, or to confirm that she, too, had come through the portal to Eldarn.

'And I finally get to use this.' Garec held his wrist aloft, exposing Steven's watch.

'Exactly. You open the portal on this side every twelve hours at five o'clock.' Steven was using the English words so Garec got used to them. 'Leave it open until five-fifteen and if I don't appear, close it up and keep going.'

'And you have another watch somewhere in Colorado to know when it gets to be five clocks.'

'Oh yes,' Steven chuckled, 'no shortage of watches there.'

Garec stood tall and gazed across the harbour at the ominous black vessel, bobbing gently in the sheltered harbour. 'Very well, then. If the boat is ready, we should go tonight.'

Steven felt his stomach roil. 'Yes. Tonight.'

The two men returned south through the waterfront. Steven was hungry, anticipating a hearty last meal before setting out to board the great black ship. The trip seemed to take longer than it had coming into the city and by the time the two friends crossed the stone bridge over the inlet, the deep reddish-orange sun was setting across the Ravenian Sea. Above, dark clouds massed, heralding a coming storm. Garec and Steven pulled their hoods around their heads and held the folds tightly.

The normally bustling wharf was nearly abandoned and Steven mentally ticked off the final six warehouses as he and Garec passed them en route to a warm fire and a thick jemma steak.

Huddled in the shadows between the southernmost warehouses, the dark figure readied the walnut longbow, then withdrew a long black arrow and nocked it carefully. Chilled to the bone from his vigil, the archer breathed through his mouth to avoid smelling a forgotten crate of rotting fish. Rats scratched and clawed hungrily at the wooden slats lining the crate and he kicked them aside with the toe of his boot as he inched his way forward towards the warped plank walkway. His prey was approaching slowly; the bowman felt his heart thud in anticipation. Risking a glance around the corner, the hunter cursed in a hoarse whisper and retreated quickly into the shadows. The two men walking towards him had enveloped themselves within the folds of their cloaks and with the hoods drawn up, there was no way the archer could tell one from the other. Pulling his own hood back slightly, he glanced around the corner once again. They were much closer this time. *Think!* he commanded himself. *I'll never get off a second shot; the customs men will be mustered and out here in a whore's breath.*

Grimacing, he spat another curse at the rats beside his feet and then, watching as they scurried away, his mouth curled into a sly, tight-lipped grin.

Steven tallied warehouse number three before pulling his cloak tighter about him. 'I hope it doesn't rain tonight.'

'I don't think it will, but it's going to be cold.' Garec shrugged his own cloak closer. 'We'll need to stay dry if we hope to—'

A dull thud emanated from the insignificant space between the two men and Steven stopped, thinking Garec had accidentally dropped his saddlebag. In a heartbeat he knew what the sound had been. Garec was on his knees, an arrow protruding from his ribcage.

'Garec! Oh Christ, Garec—!' Steven dropped beside his friend, who exhaled a great sigh and fell over onto his side.

'Steven, bloody demonpiss, Steven, I'm shot! Someone shot me!' His voice trailed off as he struggled to draw breath. With each raspy inhalation, Garec emitted a thin wail of pain. 'It hurts, Steven—'

'I know. I know.' For a moment Steven had no idea what to do. 'Try to relax. I'll get some help.' He stood up and roared out, 'Who did it? Where are they?' He felt as though he had been sprinting. Strangely, he thought he could sense the staff's magic swirling through his body, encouraging him to find Garec's assailant and rip the man's arm off. 'Who did this?' Steven cried again, throwing his head back and allowing his hood to fall across his shoulders.

His shouts brought help as people came quickly to offer assistance, a small group of Malakasian soldiers included. Once he could see the injured man was being looked after, a portly Malakasian soldier, a sergeant, Steven guessed from the uniform, demanded Steven tell him what he had seen.

'What?' Steven replied brusquely, then more calmly, added, 'Nothing – no one. The shot came from over there.' He gestured between the last two warehouses on the wharf. 'But you won't find anyone.'

'How do you know?' the sergeant asked.

The question gave Steven a moment's pause. Somehow he was certain their attacker had fled south through the forest behind the shanty village. In his mind's eye, he could almost see the man, tall, wearing a dark robe and carrying a longbow, sprinting through a tangle of brambles. But there was a problem with the image. It was more than the forest or the warehouses. His mind's eye filled in the missing spaces: dark areas where he assumed shadows fell between trees or at the base of the great warehouse. Steven saw things, bright things, he finally recognised as neon illuminated signs, *COLD BEER*. That was across Tenth Street in the front window of Abe's Liquor Store, and *OIL CHANGE* $26.99, the ten-minute oil place on the corner. The yellow, green and orange letters were a shock of colour against the fading hues of the Orindale forest at twilight and Steven watched as the tall man who had just shot Garec fled between the trees. The neon blinked another time or two then faded.

Steven shook his head to clear the images and looked back at the soldier. 'I'm sorry, sergeant, I don't know what I was thinking – of course I can't be sure. He was tall, I think, and cloaked, of course. Not much help, I guess.'

The soldiers hustled off to search for the attacker and Steven walked slowly back to where Garec lay, a bundle of black robes in a growing pool of black blood.

'Excuse me,' he said calmly to the crowd gathered about. 'We live quite close by and our brother knows something of medicine. Please, excuse me, I need to get him home.' Steven knelt beside his friend. Garec's eyes had glazed over and his breathing was shallow and wet. It sounded to Steven as if his lung was filling with fluid and had most likely collapsed. There wasn't much time.

'I had this coming, Steven,' Garec managed in a strangled whisper.

'Bullshit, Garec.' Steven tried hard to sound assuring. The English obscenity sounded harsh.

Garec laughed weakly, then winced. 'Bullshit – turkey – what a strange—' His head rolled lazily to one side.

As soon as he touched the injured man, Steven knew the staff's magic was alive inside him, even at this distance. With the strength of twenty, Steven lifted Garec as easily as he might have carried a bag of flour. The magic crackled sharply along his muscles and danced about across his back. Running one hand over the Ronan's chest, he read his friend's condition: he was right, one lung punctured and collapsed, heart rate weak and slowing, breathing shallow and difficult. If he were to save his friend's life, he had to get him back to their shack immediately. Calling out thanks, Steven ran as carefully as he could down the wharf, then leaped from the plank walkway into the sand and along the beach towards the fishermen's village.

'Curse, that wretched, rutting horsecock!' Jacrys cried as he ran through the coastal forest. 'They traded boots! Why in the name of all things would they trade boots?' Even at this distance, he knew he was at risk if Steven chose to unleash his magic. He could not turn back. Lessek's Key had been in his grasp and he missed the opportunity to retrieve it. His most powerful bargaining chip, the one thing that would save his life – and he had lost it because two fools had traded boots. 'Aaargh!' he screamed in a wild rage before disappearing south towards the Malakasian army pickets.

*

Garec was nearly dead by the time they reached the shanty. Brynne and Mark had been working on the sailboat, packing supplies, an extra sheet, ropes and several balls of sturdy twine beneath its gunwales when Steven sprinted into view. 'Come quickly, Garec's been shot!' Steven cried.

They jumped into the frigid shallows and hurried up the beach, calling questions as they ran.

'Great northern gods, this is bad,' Brynne said as she gingerly opened Garec's cloak.

Tears welled up in Mark's eyes. 'Who the hell did this? Who in God's good name even knows we're here?'

'I'm not sure,' Steven replied tersely, 'although somehow I saw a man, a man in a long cloak, he had a bow and was running through the woods back there.' Steven gestured behind the warehouses and into the dense brush flanking the dunes.

Mark was kneeling as well. 'Jesus, he's dying. What can we do? He's dying.'

Steven had already left.

He burst into the broken-down hovel and grabbed the hickory staff, cursing himself for ever going anywhere without it, then pounded back to where Mark and Brynne were trying to make Garec comfortable.

Several steps out, the old fisherman stepped in front of him, a shadow in the darkness. Steven nearly ran the gaunt figure down. 'Sorry, not now. My friend has been shot. He may not live.' He was frantic, trapped in the throes of a full panic attack, his thoughts coming too quickly – every idea on how he might save Garec was dulled by the reality: his friend's life was ebbing away. His hands shook as he struggled to focus on anything, sand, water, the wharf, the old fisherman – nothing registered, and to make matters worse, the magic was flaring up in great bursts that raced through his body like an electrical storm, enough to level a mountain. Steven worried that if he unleashed it, there would be nothing left of Garec to revive.

'You must save him.' The fisherman spoke calmly, and grasped Steven's upper arm with a vice-like grip that hurt enough to slow him down for a moment. 'Use the magic, Steven Taylor.'

'What—?' Steven cared only that the old man was keeping him from Garec. 'I must go.'

'Save him, Steven,' the old man repeated.

Steven shook his arm free and hurried down the beach. Brynne was sitting quietly on the sand, her knees drawn up to her chin. Mark was pushing down on Garec's chest in a rhythmic motion. Yes, CPR. That's right. That's good. Steven was glad to see some evidence of home, of something sane and sensible working to save Garec's life.

'He's dying, Steven,' Mark whispered. 'Can you do anything?'

Mark's plea was another slap in Steven's face. They were not in Idaho Springs. CPR was not enough. Garec needed him to work magic, to summon the strange, unimaginable force he had at his command, to heal the damaged tissues in the Ronan's lung and to drain the blood from the wound so Garec might start breathing on his own.

'And restart his heart, Steven.' Mark had read his mind. 'You'll have to restart his heart.'

Tentatively, Steven reached out to touch Garec's chest. Nothing. No signs of life. *How did the old man know my name?* He called me Steven Taylor. How did he know that? Concentrate. *He knew my name.* He knew I had magic at my disposal. Focus. Focus on the problem at hand. Steven drew a blank. Take your time. Slowly. Take your time. He is already dead. Catch your breath.

Steven felt the magic that had been raging inside him inch its way slowly through his wrists and out into his fingertips. Dr Smithson. Dr Smithson taught Anatomy and Physiology. Classes on Monday, Wednesday and Friday, with a Tuesday afternoon lab. Steven had hated that lab. One o'clock to four o'clock every week, every Tuesday. He was a business major. What in all hell was he doing in a lab class? The heart, the lungs. Get them started. They would know what to do. Garec's lung had an arrow piercing it. That was where to start. Gentle bursts of magic sprang from Steven's fingertips, lancing their way through the dead man's tunic and into his flesh. Remove the arrow. His heart has stopped; his lung will not flood with any more blood than is there already. So remove the arrow.

Steven started to pull the black shaft gently from Garec's chest, but it was embedded firmly, several inches deep. 'Mark, you'll have to help me,' he whispered.

As gently as they could manage, they tugged the arrow from Garec's ribcage. Mark winced as it scraped bone, but with a final hard pull it was out, and Steven tossed it down the beach and turned his attention back to the injury.

Garec's heart had not started beating. How long had it been? *How did that old man know me?* Damnit. Focus on the task at hand. How long could he go without brain damage? Three minutes? There is no word for minutes in Ronan. He savoured the English: minutes, seconds. One Mississippi, two Mississippi, three Mississippi. Three minutes was a long time. You'll be fine, Garec. I just have to figure this out.

Steven sent the staff's magic into the injury. The power leaped from his fingers and he and Mark felt the Ronan's inanimate form twitch in response.

'Sorry,' he spat, 'sorry, Garec, sorry.'

Steven pulled the magic back and focused his thoughts. How far were they now? Maybe thirty-five Mississippi? He had until one hundred and eighty Mississippi. There was still plenty of time.

'Plenty of time,' he whispered aloud. From somewhere far, far away he heard Brynne pleading with him to do something. *Plenty of time.* Steven closed his eyes and remembered Dr Smithson's class. The heart and the lungs. Involuntary tissue. Get them started and they would work day and night for a hundred years. Get them started. Steven imagined Garec's lung, the torn tissue free from injury, empty of the pool of blood that saturated it now. He kept the image alive in his mind as he allowed the magic to gently enter his friend's body, a soft caress like a trickle of warm water rather than a burst of ancient power.

It was working. Slowly, he felt Garec's lung tissue begin to heal. He felt the blood drain out through the wound and seep into the cloak beneath him. Garec's diaphragm was alive now, and willing to expand and contract. He must get some blood to the brain. Where were they? One hundred and thirty Mississippi? No. It had been too long; he couldn't guess. Any guesses now would be feeble attempts to make himself feel better. Blood to the brain, that was his next chore.

Employing the same strategy, Steven placed his hand over Garec's heart and, breathing deeply, he imagined the heart of a young man, a vibrant and powerful muscle imbued with compassion and love and a sturdy constitution that would keep it beating for many years – Twinmoons – whatever. Again, he released the staff's power.

Mark had two fingers pressed along Garec's carotid artery. When he felt the first thump, he bellowed wildly, 'You did it, Steven! He's alive!'

Brynne jumped to her feet and threw her arms around Steven's neck. Weeping openly, a breathless Steven returned her embrace. He had done it.

Steven fell back into the sand, exhausted, overwhelmed. He lay for a moment catching his breath and gazing up at the Eldarni stars: a jumble of incoherent constellations. He had done it. He had saved Garec's life. The power was exhilarating and Steven had to fight the urge to spring to his feet and send a forty-foot tidal wave raging across the sea to crash against the Pragan coast.

Then abruptly he stopped. 'How did he know my name?' Rolling onto his side, Steven gazed up the beach to where the grizzled fisherman sat comfortably in the sand, smoking a pipe and watching the scene unfold.

'No,' Steven mouthed the word more than articulated it. A moment later he was on his feet and striding quickly towards the weather-beaten old seaman.

'Well done, young man,' the fisherman said. 'It appears you have learned a great deal.'

'I thought you were dead—' Steven hovered over him, mouth agape.

The seaman placed one finger over his lips in an effort to silence Steven's forthcoming accusation. 'Don't say that name; don't even think it here. Simply uttering it could bring Nerak's full wrath down on you. He may be at the far end of the city, but he could be here in a matter of moments.'

Steven was not sure he could withstand another emotional blow. His vision blurred and for a moment he felt as though he might faint. 'You don't— you don't look like yourself.'

'Well of course not!' The old man was suddenly indignant. 'Garec, the bloody fool, burned my body to ash there in the Blackstones. I liked that body. That one suited me well.' He grimaced. 'I am glad he's going to be all right, but did he have to burn me on a bloody pyre?'

Steven was speechless.

'And what a fire. You missed it. He nearly took down the

whole side of the mountain. Flames were leaping from treetop to treetop—' He took a long draw on his pipe and the ashes glowed a warm red, like an old man's last memory.

'So you're like him?' Steven gestured over his shoulder in the general direction of the former royal residence.

'There are aspects of my skills that are similar to Nerak's, but he can live without a physical form, a host, if you will. I cannot.'

'This body? Did you—?'

'Absolutely not.' He looked stern. 'Never do that. Natural causes. I was on hand when this gentleman died. That's why there's no wound on my . . . his wrist, no forced entry.'

'Has this happened before?'

He lowered his voice to a barely audible whisper. 'Just once, long ago when I became—' He paused. 'When I became the man you met in Rona and abandoned my old body. Lessek helped me then, and thankfully, he made the decision to assist me in the Blackstones. One of these days, he won't be there to patch me back together.'

'What will happen then?'

'Then I imagine my work here will be finished.' He smirked.

'So Lessek keeps you alive?'

'Lessek – with some help from the spell table, I suppose.'

'But I thought the table wouldn't work without the key.'

'It won't, but that doesn't preclude its power from continuing to affect us.' He tapped his pipe ashes into the sand. 'The spells keeping me alive – me and Kantu – were cast so long ago, I don't even remember who chanted them. He chortled ironically. 'It was probably Nerak.'

Steven forced a smirk himself, but he still felt as though he might be sick.

'Anyway, I'm glad you've been working so diligently with the staff's magic. When you return from Idaho Springs, I would be happy to help you hone your skills.'

'You know I plan to come back?'

'I know many things.'

'I have to sit down.' Steven slumped heavily in the sand beside the old sorcerer. 'Well, it is good to see you.'

'It's good to be here – but come now, we have a great deal to do tonight.'

THE *PRINCE MAREK*

Brynne reached out to take hold of the stern line hooked fast to a deepwater mooring; it kept the great ship from turning with the tides and crushing unsuspecting smaller vessels in the harbour.

'Tie it to this,' Steven whispered, handing her a length of rope affixed to their bow, short enough to keep them in place; they just had to hope the gentle rise and fall of the waves would not run the skiff into the *Prince Marek*.

Steven, Brynne and the old fisherman prepared to climb up the line and ease themselves over the stern rail and onto the quarterdeck. Mark positioned himself against the narrow transom, a borrowed longbow and full quiver at his feet.

The trip through the harbour had been marked by several disagreements, the worst of which was between Mark and Brynne.

'I don't want you going aboard,' he said firmly.

'Garec can't make it. I have to go.' Brynne was equally adamant. 'I'm much better at hand-to-hand fighting than you, Mark. Steven might need my help.'

Brynne bristled with knives, daggers, even Mark's battle-axe. The light of the Twinmoon glinted on the arsenal of razor-sharp edges. Mark, still unhappy about her decision, insisted he accompany them in the skiff to offer covering fire should a Malakasian sentry approach while they were boarding.

Brynne stifled a laugh. 'I've seen you shoot, Mark, remember? Trying to kill fish, you missed the river three times.'

Mark was not amused. 'Funny haha. And you're right; maybe I'm not a great shot, but their soldiers don't know that.' He wished he'd paid more attention to Versen's lessons, but it was too late now.

The old fisherman came along as well – neither Mark nor

Brynne knew why, but Steven insisted, and when the seaman offered the use of his skiff, they were happy to accept.

They couldn't bear to leave Garec alone on the beach, in case whoever had shot him came back to finish the job, so he slept in the bow of the sailboat, wrapped comfortably in their collective blankets. He was definitely alive: his heart thumped, strong and steady, and his breathing, though slow, was deep.

Mark's stolen vessel made the trip without incident, coursing across the harbour on a swirling southern breeze, the skiff skipping along in their wake. The raiders dropped anchor and reefed sail some thousand paces west of the sleeping giant. Darkness surrounded them, and with the old fisherman at the oars, their approach to the *Prince Marek* was as silent as a piece of buoyant flotsam on an incoming tide.

'So far, so good,' Mark whispered as he watched Brynne reach for the stern rail. She had gone up first, insisting – and even he had to agree – that if anyone saw her come over the transom, no one would be able to silence them as quickly and efficiently as she. Mark held his breath. It was a long climb, thirty feet of hand-over-hand ascent, but it was just a few moments later that she was there, draping one arm over the rail and drawing a slender hunting knife from her tunic belt with the other.

'Damn, damn, damn,' Mark cursed: in his concern for Brynne he had forgotten the bow. He quickly nocked an arrow and pointed it aloft, waiting for someone to appear. 'Please God, don't let me pierce one of my friends,' he prayed quietly, but thankfully, none of the *Prince Marek*'s crew seemed to have heard them. Brynne motioned for Steven and the fisherman to join her. Mark watched intently as she peered around, then hefted her lithe form over the aft rail and disappeared from sight.

Steven went up next, with the staff tied in a makeshift harness, nimbly pulling himself hand-over-hand until he reached the stern cabin. Mark and the fisherman exchanged a worried glance as Steven slowed his climb to a stop, dangling precariously above the water.

He had paused to look through the cabin window, into an enormous chamber, so opulently decorated that it must be Prince Malagon's. Tapers burned around the main room, and through the dim, shimmering light he could see gilded artwork on the bulkheads, delicately woven rugs in a thousand hues on the floor, ornate tapestries hanging above a huge bed draped in rich brocaded silk and velvet, and a bookshelf lined with several hundred silver-embossed books – the first books he'd seen in Eldarn.

'Silver,' Steven muttered, 'you bastard. I wonder where you developed a love for silver.' The staff responded to his anger and flickered to life, its energy lancing though Steven's jacket. He forced himself to continue climbing.

On the water, the fisherman grabbed the rope and prepared to follow.

'You need a hand, my friend?' Mark asked, dubious that the old man would make it all the way up.

'No, thank you,' he replied. 'I learned to climb long ago, in another life. My history teacher was quite a mountaineer.' He flashed Mark a boyish smile and scrambled up the stern line with the agility of someone less than half his age.

Mark allowed the bowstring to relax slowly and stared after the old man in wonder. 'It can't be,' he whispered, and sat down clumsily on one of the skiff's wooden benches.

Brynne couldn't see any crew from where she crouched behind a stack of tarpaulin-covered crates. As Steven and the fisherman joined her, she motioned for them to get down. The raised deck stretched out in front of them: a barren expanse of oak planking. Several watch fires burned in large sconces mounted above the gunwales and a warm golden light cast dull, flickering shadows across the ship's broad beam. Their most difficult move would be from their current position down the starboard stairs to the main deck, and then through the cabin door to get to Prince Malagon's chambers below. Wisps of Brynne's flaxen hair blew lazily in the cold evening wind. Thankfully, it had not yet begun to rain.

She drew a second blade from her belt. 'I will go first—' it was not a request, 'and you two come on quickly behind me. I'll position myself behind the aft mast there on the main deck while Steven makes his way inside. You—' she gestured towards the fisherman, 'stay with me.' She sounded fiercely determined. Reaching into her belt, she withdrew a thin-bladed knife and a small axe. 'Do you know how to use these?'

The seaman shook his head. 'I never use such weapons, my dear.'

Angry, she snapped, 'Well, what in all Eldarn did you come—' She paused and pushed the unruly strands from her face. Hidden behind the relative protection of the crates, her stoicism suddenly vanished. 'Is it you?' Her voice broke. 'Is it?'

He grinned and kissed her on the temple. 'It is. No names, mind.'

Unable to contain herself, Brynne dropped the weapons and threw her arms around the old man's neck, squeezing him to her as if to never lose him again. 'You don't— you don't look like—'

'No names,' the old sorcerer repeated. 'Our plan, my dear?'

Brynne was suddenly serious. 'Right,' she said as she wiped away an errant tear with a tunic sleeve. 'No one's appeared yet, but this ship is huge and the watch might take their time getting from one end to the other.'

'Should we wait one cycle to see?' Steven whispered.

'No,' the fisherman answered, 'if there is a watch, and on a ship this size there must be, even if just to remain vigilant for other vessels, he probably isn't patrolling.' He retrieved Brynne's weapons and handed them back to her. 'If he does come aft, Brynne can take care of him.'

'You sound confident.'

'Only because I'm certain the critical chambers of this vessel are magically warded. No ship is going to run into this one, so there is no real need for an attentive watch.'

'Magically warded?' Steven felt a lump develop in his throat.

'Of course,' the fisherman said, as if magical traps were commonplace, 'if you were he, would you leave the far portal in your cabin unprotected?'

'I suppose not.'

'Certainly not.'

'Then how do I get in?'

'Delicately, if you don't wish to be detected.'

'Or?' Brynne said.

'Or crudely, if you don't care about Nerak hurrying back to destroy us.'

For the first time all evening, Steven laughed. 'Okay. I opt for delicately.'

Overcome once again, Brynne reached over and squeezed the old man affectionately. 'It is nice to have you back, even if you are a bit thin. I've missed your skill at pinpointing situational danger!'

The old man smiled back at her and went on, 'So if Brynne is on hand to dispatch any wandering sentries, and you can use the staff to open the door to Nerak's cabin, we ought to be able to get in and get out before he arrives.'

'I thought you said if I were delicate, he wouldn't know.'

'Perhaps – that's the one real risk we have to take. I *am* confident that he has no notion of the true power in that staff.'

'So how will he know I'm here? As long as you don't employ any magic, he'll have no idea we've broken in, right? That's why I had to be the one to save Garec and not you?' Steven's voice started to rise in anxiety, and he forced himself to speak softly.

'True to a point, Steven. He cannot detect the staff's magic, but I worry he will know when his safeguards have been breached.'

'Well, hell, why should I be delicate if he's coming regardless?'

'That's a great question, my boy.' The old man pondered the idea for a moment, then shook his head. 'You're right. Let's go for crude and fast.'

'So there really is no way we'll get out of here without a fight?' Brynne was afraid she knew the answer to that one.

'We – Steven and I – will probably find ourselves in a fight to the death with Nerak tonight.' The old man rubbed a finger beneath his crooked nose.

Brynne tossed her head. 'Then why didn't you say so in the first place?'

His voice darkened and his face lost any hint of boyish charm as he said slowly, 'If Steven can get through the portal quickly, I will face the dark prince alone.'

No one spoke. Brynne set her jaw and moved silently along the quarterdeck towards the starboard steps. A moment later, she disappeared.

Steven took a deep breath, gripped the staff like a lifeline and followed Brynne's lead.

Nerak's cabin was locked, but Steven could see and smell the wax tapers burning through the louvred doors. 'This is it,' he whispered. 'I saw inside while climbing up the stern line.'

The old man gently placed the flat of his palm against the door and nodded. 'I was right. It *is* locked with a spell.'

'How do I open it?'

'You follow the magical threads and untangle them, one by one.'

'I'm not that good. I still don't know how I saved Garec.' Steven felt his chest tighten and a thin line of sweat ran down his spine. 'You do it.'

'The moment I employ my magic on this door, he will know.'

'But if I try—'

'He might not detect it.' The old sorcerer shot Steven a dubious look. 'It's our only chance to gain time.'

'Right.' Steven felt the magic burst from his body like a thunderclap as he released it on the doorframe. The door exploded from its hinges and fell to the floor in a shower of oak splinters. 'How was that?' He smiled proudly.

The old man was dazed. 'A bit noisy, but not to worry: it's done. You find the portal. I'll help Brynne.'

'Brynne?' Steven was a bit slow. 'Does she need our help already?'

'After your little demonstration here, my boy, she'll probably need considerably more than just me.'

'Damnit,' Steven spat, and cursed his haste. He'd been so focused on Nerak that he'd been oblivious to the obvious: blowing up the door would bring everyone on board the *Prince Marek* rushing to see what the noise was. 'Go! Help her!'

The old man took Steven by the shoulders. 'Find the portal, Steven. That's all you need worry about now. Just find the portal.' Then he was gone.

Steven hefted the staff and collected his thoughts. 'Find the portal. That's all *I* have to worry about.' But as he crossed the threshold, he heard a low roar, a distant explosion that careened across time and distance to reach him, rolling through his chest and leaving him reeling. He braced himself against the bulkhead.

'Shit,' Steven said. 'He's coming.'

Hidden behind the aft mast on the main deck, Brynne watched and waited, but there was absolutely no activity of any sort. Although she was beginning to wonder if there was anyone on board, she kept her eyes focused through the torchlight. Suddenly a loud explosion reached her ears: this was it: they'd done it! Her body tensed and she gripped her knives with renewed determination. Waiting for the enemy to arrive, she wondered what she would do if Nerak were to appear on deck, materialising before her in a brilliant flash. Would she run, dive over the side? Or would she attack him, slashing and cutting her way through his robes to the vulnerable flesh beneath? *Was* there vulnerable flesh beneath?

There was no time to answer her rhetorical questions: there *was* someone on board after all. Below decks she could feel the resonant thumping of people running: enemy sailors making for an open hatch twenty or thirty paces in front of her. She cursed herself for being such an idiot: any moment now a great crowd of sailors would spill from that hatch onto the deck and she would be overrun. *Close the hatch, lock it down, then find and secure the others – that would buy some time.*

Now she could hear voices, crying out in warning, or shouting orders. She was right on top of them. An arm reached out – too late. She slashed with her hunting knife, slicing the man's arm across the wrist in her trademark half moon. A muffled cry echoed out of the small rectangular opening as she slammed the hatch closed and set its bolt.

She sprang to her feet and assessed the main deck as the men below pounded on the locked hatch. She could see six more open, and she was pretty sure there'd be others further forward. There was no hope. She'd never get to all of them in time.

'But I might get to some. I might delay them for a moment or two,' she cried and sprinted towards the next hatch, trying not to think that this might be the last thing she would ever do.

Mark was so startled by the prolonged rumble of distant thunder that he nearly fell overboard. He nocked his arrow again and braced himself against the transom. It would be a pretty onesided fight, but he would make a memorable stand.

A cacophonous roar bellowed out from the city. 'That has to be Nerak,' he groaned. 'Okay, I'll stand my post. I am not leaving without them,' he said aloud, as if to convince himself.

Brynne got four more hatches closed before the first sailors emerged from below, spilling out of the narrow opening like a roiling mass of insects. She was greatly outnumbered, but they hadn't spotted her yet: if she took up a defensive position outside Malagon's cabin she'd have a better chance. And if they hadn't seen her, they might not come all at once; for all they knew, the *Prince Marek* was being attacked by a large force of Falkans, not just one woman with a few knives. She waited for them to come.

As she reached her chosen position she was about to huddle down, to hide for as long as possible, when she spotted the lone sailor above on the quarterdeck, armed with a bow: the sentry. How had they missed him? Where had he been – and how had had he managed to get behind her? He was working his way towards the stern rail; she guessed he had no idea they were on board. He probably thought the muffled explosion was enemies trying to break through the stern bulkhead. She had surprise on her side, but he had a bow. Then she remembered Mark.

Ignoring the potential threat behind her, Brynne hurried back to the quarterdeck: *get to the guard before he fires at Mark*. She did not muffle her steps, nor disguise her approach. Her lips were pressed together in a grim half-smile, her eyes fixed straight ahead. Her hair was tucked beneath the collar of her tunic. She held a knife loosely in each hand and rolled her fingers along the hilts, as if searching for the perfect grip. She watched as the sailor reached the stern rail, saw the look of surprise as he saw the skiff tied to the stern line, and inhaled sharply as he drew an arrow from his quiver, nocked it and took aim.

Brynne, unconcerned for her own wellbeing, cried out to the Malakasian bowman, but he didn't appear to hear. He was focused on his target. He drew the bowstring taut and sighted along the shaft.

Mark saw the Malakasian appear above the stern rail: he'd been spotted. For an instant his thoughts flashed to Brynne. Was she hurt? Had this man killed her? He felt anger burgeon inside himself and suddenly he wanted very badly to deal with this man, this enemy, one-on-one. He drew an arrow from the quiver, nocked it, took aim and fired.

A startled look of surprise passed across the Malakasian's face as Mark's arrow flew wide over his shoulder and into the night. Mark drew again. This time he closed one eye, placed the arrowhead in the centre of the man's chest and fired. The arrow leaped from Garec's bow, sped towards the sentry and embedded itself in the wood of the stern rail.

'Come on!' Mark shouted up in English, 'take your best shot. Go ahead and kill me, you chickenshit asshole!'

Too angry to feel afraid, he drew another shaft as the sailor nocked his own arrow and prepared to fire. Mark turned his attention skywards for his final attempt.

The sentry peered down at him along the thin black arrow as Mark, crying out, loosed his third shot and watched his arrow sail up and out of sight. It missed the man by a good fifteen feet.

'Here it comes,' Mark whispered, and braced himself. He started shuddering as he imagined the burning sensation of the thin obsidian arrowhead ripping through his muscles and maybe piercing a bone. For a fraction of a second he thought of Garec lying immobile and glassy-eyed on the ground in front of the fisherman's shanty.

The Malakasian drew a breath, held it and fired.

Mark didn't see the arrow rocketing towards, him nor did he see Brynne as she reached the man an instant later. A dull wooden thud resounded as the Malakasian arrow sank deep into the bench not six inches away.

'He missed,' Mark cried in disbelief. 'You missed, you blind bastard!' He started laughing maniacally in relief until a splash of cold water snapped him out of it. 'What the hell?' He stared into the dark water. His first thought was that the man had leaped over the side to engage him in close combat. Brynne had his axe; now he searched fruitlessly for a weapon until his hand fell on the arrow embedded in the seat beside him. He tugged it free and brandished it menacingly above his head.

The corpse bobbed to the surface; the dead man's face bore a look of surprise. Almost placidly the body rolled over and sank beneath the waves.

Mark looked up at the stern rail. Brynne looked down at him, brandishing her bloodstained hunting knife.

'I love you,' he called out in English.

'Speak Common, vile foreigner,' she teased and disappeared.

The old sorcerer met her halfway back to the starboard stairs. 'Watch your back,' she whispered, 'half the crew is coming out of a forward hatch.' She moved past him, knives at the ready, preparing to leap into the fray.

'I know,' he said, grabbing her arm. 'I met them as I came out of the main cabin.'

'Where are they now?'

'They are ... resting.' He seemed to be enjoying himself immensely. 'I'm afraid they'll all have terrible headaches in the morning. At least they'll be alive, though.'

'You'll give us revolutionaries a bad name,' she teased as she climbed back to the deck.

'Nonsense, my dear. I did not come here to kill sailors.'

'That loud rumble?'

'The old royal residence is probably going to need a few new windows.' He looked towards the flickering lights that marked the docks and the city beyond. 'Nerak knows we're here.'

She couldn't repress the look of fear that passed over her face, but she braced herself and banished the feeling of terror. 'All right then. Bring him on.'

'Absolutely,' he said as he checked the knot holding the stern line in place, 'but your part is done.' He gestured her over the side.

'No, I'm staying.'

'My dear child, you have no weapons to fight him. He is dead already. And I need not to be worried about you.' He looked back at the dock and, a little impatiently, ordered her, 'Quickly now, over you go.'

Brynne knew when she was beaten. She sheathed her knives, wrapped her arms tightly about the old man's neck and whispered, 'Please be safe. I don't want to have to go through the rites again.'

He hugged her, and said comfortingly, 'I have spent half my life preparing for this. I'll be fine. But please, Brynne, you must go now.'

Brynne nodded, and slipped over the rail.

Steven ignited a small fireball to bring some light to the dark prince's private chambers, but as its soft glow banished the shadows, it also banished the opulence: the lush décor, the rich tapestries, the brocaded silks and velvets were all an illusion. When the hickory staff had breached Nerak's magical defences, it had also shattered that spell. The thunderous eruption from across the harbour confirmed that Nerak was coming – how long did he have? A minute? Two? Twenty? Steven tried not to think about it and instead set his mind to finding the far portal.

Contrary to what he had seen through the porthole, Nerak's cabin was sparsely decorated: no comforts, no bed, no books, no fireplace. There were no clothes in the closet, no tapestries on the walls and no carpets covering the floorboards. The wooden walls, floors and ceilings of the large square room were dark, almost black with age, and dust covered the floor: Steven was leaving boot prints in the grey blanket like tracks in city snow, as he made his way towards the centre of the room. Nerak – and the evil minion that possessed him – did not appear to sleep. He did not eat, read, or entertain guests. It looked like no one had entered this cabin in years, and Steven guessed the dark prince was more a spirit than a man, more *the idea* of evil than an actual person.

Against the far wall a rectangular wooden table had been pushed back into the shadows. There were two things on it: a leatherbound book and a black metal box with curious raised markings. Nervous that the Larion monster would arrive before he'd found the far portal, Steven moved hastily, kicking up a cloud of dust in the process. He brightened his fireball with a glance and reached out to open the book – then thought better of it.

'How did he do that?' he asked aloud, feeling unsuccessfully for any evidence of magic imbued in the table, or within the items upon it. *Nothing.* He closed his eyes and concentrated, hoping something would happen.

'Why would I pick them up?' he asked, his hands stuffed protectively in his jacket. 'I'll be eviscerated or some damned thing.' Too much time had passed: he felt an overwhelming need to hurry. 'Just do it,' he told himself, 'pick them up.' He reached for the box, then pushed his hands back into his pockets.

'Right,' he said forcefully. 'The *room* was rigged, so there is no need to rig these two.' Slowly he took out one hand and reached forward for the book. 'Right?' he asked hesitantly of the empty chamber.

As soon as his fingers touched the book he could feel magic surge through him – like the feeling when he and Mark first opened William Higgins's cylinder back home at 147 Tenth Street. But this time Steven savoured the sensation. He laid his palm against the book's cover and allowed it to rest there for a few stolen moments, basking in the now-familiar sensation of an untapped, unbridled magical force.

Unfamiliar colours and irregular shapes moved across his field of vision, followed by images and ideas, both evil and benevolent. Some were ancient, others not even imagined: promises of futures filled with growth and with ruin, with pestilence and with prosperity. Steven could feel these possibilities move through his body, slipping through his veins, diffusing through his muscles: a patternless cascade that drowned out his thoughts and filled his mind with the atonal polyphony of imperfection and scattered logic.

Steven lost track of time, revelling in the myriad hues of unknown colours, unfamiliar aromas, untasted flavours and memories both real and imagined. This was a power greater than anything he had ever known and he felt himself draining, spiralling away, losing himself inside the mysterious tome.

He began to sway on his feet until, his hand still resting on the book's smooth cover, he heard someone calling to him faintly. 'Hurry, Steven. You must hurry.' It was his own voice.

He jerked his hand back in a protective reflex and swore vehemently. He shook his head to clear the remnants of the seething thoughts and muttered, 'Goddamnit. What is that thing?' He blinked his eyes and leaned forward for a closer look at the book's spine, frowning when he saw it was blank. 'Well, what the hell did you expect?' he asked out loud, 'an ISBN number?'

He reached for the box, careful not to touch the book again. The box was cold, and he could detect no magic or mysterious energy emanating from within. He ran his hand curiously over the smooth metal container. There did not appear to be a latch and he could find no hinge or crack along which it might open.

The top and sides were adorned with raised silver ornamentations that looked like a child's drawing of a perfectly formed Christmas tree, smooth on each side and rising to a point in an exact isosceles triangle. On the upper corners of each side were two cones, separated by four more along the centre edge. On the lower corners of each side were single ornaments separated by two more along the centre edge. Steven pushed and pulled against the tiny silver sculptures, trying to find a catch: they could be moved back and forth slightly, or depressed until they flattened flush against the metal. But still the box remained determinedly shut.

He turned it over: the bottom surface was flat and featureless. 'Okay,' he said, fingering one of the single cones, 'so this is the top. Now to open it.'

He considered the box: 'Two, four, two and one, two, one repeated on five sides . . . no, four sides and a top.' He pushed each one, felt them depress until flat, then bounce back against his fingertips. He tried them in combinations: side-to-side and up-and-down, then the single cones, double cones and quadruple cones in order. Nothing happened.

'Four sides and a top,' he said, pushing and sliding cones as he spoke. 'Top first—' push and slide, '—sides first—' push and slide, '—top, sides and top again—' push and slide, '—sides, top and sides again—' push and slide.

Push-and-slide combinations were followed by slide-and-push, but nothing changed: each time the silver ornaments simply returned to their original positions.

'Two, four, two and one, two, one . . . four sides and a top—' Steven said the numbers slowly again, trying them out in different patterns and arrangements—

Until a second thunderous rumble roared through the cabin, nearly knocking him off his feet. This one felt much closer.

'Oh, screw it,' Steven cried and slammed the staff down on the box, a massive blow that shook the *Prince Marek* as much as her master's fury had. Box, book and table were unaffected.

'Well, shit,' Steven spat. He'd run out of ideas.

Suddenly the old fisherman was by his side. 'That was you, was it?'

'Yep.'

He nodded approvingly. 'Well, you've certainly learned how to produce a fine blast.' He dragged a boot heel through the dust, drawing an arc. 'Might I ask why?'

'This box.' Steven shook it. 'I think the far portal may be inside this box, but I can't get it open.'

'Did you push these buttons?' He played with a few of the raised carvings. 'That's probably how it works. Maybe one of them opens it.'

'I tried forty-six different ways, using every combination I can imagine.' He shook his head dejectedly. 'There are too many possibilities and I've run out of ideas.'

'Maybe it's in another cabin – this is a huge ship.' The old man looked about the sparse chamber. 'We don't have much time before Nerak gets here; I want you long gone before that happens.'

'I know it's in here: I can feel it.' He didn't take his eyes off the curious box. 'Look: Mark pointed this shape out to me the night we opened the portal in our house. It was there, stitched into the fabric. We thought it looked like a tree.'

Gilmour squinted and rubbed his eyes. 'I'm afraid this fisherman didn't have very good eyesight; I may have to work on that a bit when we get out of here. But you're right.'

Steven tried not to think about how little time they had. 'Maybe we should just take it and run, get back to the boat and try to escape.'

'No, either we figure it out here, or we use our combined forces to delay Nerak long enough to get it open and then escape. There's no point running away at this juncture: no matter how quickly we paddle away in that little boat he'll find us, and we'll have no chance.'

Steven's heart raced. This really was it. He struggled to open his mind as he examined the box from every angle. While he paced, the old sorcerer tried using his own magic, but it too had no effect. He scratched at the stubble on his chin and announced, 'I don't think it's magic.'

'What?' Steven had not been paying attention. 'Say that again.'

'The door, this room, that book there on the table, even the table itself: I can feel the magic in the fundamental fabric of each. Although there's a spell protecting this box from being destroyed or blown apart by our power, I don't believe it's a spell keeping it locked – I would be able to detect it. It's just a confounding, tricky box.'

Suddenly Steven's thoughts shifted. This wasn't a problem he had to address with his limited understanding of the staff or its magic. This was far simpler, like a problem he might have tackled in school, or while working out a loan at the bank, or even— Steven paused. 'Jeffrey Simmons.'

'Who?'

'Jeffrey Simmons,' Steven grinned. 'He's a doctoral student in mathematics at the University of Denver in Colorado.' His face had changed. This was what he was good at: the abstractions that made sense in layers of cognitive twists and turns; it frustrated and confused most students, but not him. Steven worked the problem.

'How can Jeffrey Simmons help us? I remind you, our time is alarmingly short.'

'Two, four, two, one, two, one on four sides and a top,' Steven muttered to himself, and began pacing more quickly.

'Steven?'

'Two, four, two, one, two, one on four sides and a top. Think it through: what makes sense?'

'To me or to Nerak?'

'Neither. What makes sense mathematically?' Steven smiled and continued, 'You said yourself there was magic protecting the box, but no magic keeping it locked. So it has to be a mathematical riddle. Watch—' He began moving the silver ornaments. 'If two from the right and two from the left slide to match the four in the middle—' He slid the ornaments simultaneously and for the first time both double cones remained in place. Steven repeated the process on each side. 'And one cone from the left and one cone from the right slide to match two cones in the middle— ' He slid the single cones towards their matching twins on the top.

'Now we should be able to open the box.' He released the cones. Both slid back into place.

'Bloody demonpiss,' the old man grumbled. 'I thought you had it.'

'Don't get discouraged. That was only the first side.' Steven repeated the process with one of the remaining four sides, but the cones slid back to their original position. 'Shit.'

'This isn't working,' the fisherman entreated. 'Steven, we're almost out of time. We have to think of something else.'

'No,' Steven said brusquely, 'there are three more sides. Maths makes sense.'

'It never did for me.'

'It does. Trust me. This will work.' He tried sliding the single cones to match the double cones on each of the final three sides, but each time the raised silver knobs slid silently back home.

Steven's resolve began to flag, but he gritted his teeth and muttered, 'No, this *has* to be the answer.' He ran through the entire process a second time – but still again the uncooperative cones failed to align with Steven's geometric logic.

His mind raced. This was not right. Curse this miserable land. Nothing made sense here, not even maths. And yet mathematics went unperturbed by the soft philosophies and gummy epistemologies that trapped so many thinkers by the ankles: it was almost truculent in its determination to make sense. That's why he adored it, because with enough time and intellectual determination, it all added up.

But not in Eldarn. Not in this inane land of horse-lion creatures, subterranean demons, dictators evil beyond the ken of mortal man, Cthulhoid cavern-dwellers with a penchant for bone-collecting, murderous spirit wraiths and long-dead sorcerers giving orders on barren mountaintops. What kind of place was this? Damn, damn and curse this hellish land.

Why was he here – and who or what had gifted him the hickory staff? More importantly yet, why couldn't he stomach the thought of just going home and leaving Eldarn to the natives? Let Gilmour and Kantu – or even Lessek – sort out the problems.

Sweat poured off him as Steven struggled to understand. *What am I doing here?* Nerak is coming to kill me and I don't know what I'm doing here. What do I care if Sandcliff Palace crumbles, if the spell table is opened again, if Lessek's Key is ever found?

Steven stopped abruptly. Lessek's Key. Lessek. 'Holy shit,' he shouted, '*Lessek!*'

'What of Lessek?'

'My dream – that night on Seer's Peak, I had a dream. I remember it as if it were last night; you made us go over it, again and again.'

The old man was looking over his shoulder now, as if he expected Nerak to stride into the room at any moment. 'Yes, yes, your dream. Lessek. Please Steven, *focus*! What of your dream?'

'I was at the bank with Howard and Myrna, the day I met Hannah. I thought it was supposed to show me that Nerak was telling the truth, that Hannah was here in Eldarn – but that wasn't it.'

'So what was it?'

'It was the maths.'

'Yes, yes, I remember, the maths. You said something about pyramids, or Egyptians. I never saw the pyramids, myself – well, once, in a book—'

'No, it's not the pyramids, nor the Egyptians – I thought that too, because when I came out of my office to leave for Denver, I caught Myrna Kessler working on a problem, a circle drawn on a notepad, but that wasn't it.'

'I don't want to rush you, my boy, but if you would get to the point, I would appreciate it.'

'Telephones and calculators.'

'Now you've lost me. And if you don't get a move on, you'll have lost us all.'

'They're simple electronic devices, each with a series of numbers, zero to nine. The telephone is organised top-to-bottom, one through nine with a zero at the bottom; the calculator is organised from bottom-to-top, zero through nine.' He laughed.

'I don't understand. What is funny? We're about to lose everything!'

'It's a trick question: why are the numbers on a telephone and a calculator organised that way?'

'Steven, just open the box.'

'When we use a telephone, we dial a telephone number, but it's not a number at all: it's a series of digits.' Steven did a little jig. 'On a calculator we use actual numbers, quantities that compare to one another against a common standard ... the number one.'

'So the telething and the calculus machine—'

'Calculator.'

'They both contain the same series of numbers. They look similar, but they mean different things.'

'Exactly. A similar design – with a few key differences – but an entirely different purpose.'

The old man studied the box. 'So with this box, the two double cones slid to match the four cones together.'

'Right. Two and two equals four. Couldn't be simpler.'

'However, the single cones do not slide to match the twins—'

'Because they're not numbers, they're digits denoting something else.'

'What?'

Steven's heart sank. 'I don't know. My guess is they denote a progression of sides.'

'One, two, one. Same on every side.'

Steven was already at work: 'If we start here on the front side and we call that side number one, then any of the adjacent sides might be side number two.'

'Don't wait for me. Just figure it out.'

Steven carried on thinking aloud, in case the Larion Senator picked up something he'd overlooked in the process. 'If this is side one and either of these are side two, we can depress the first cone on side one.' He did so and the cone remained in place. 'Now the twin cones on side two.' The conical carving remained flush against the smooth metal long enough for Steven to draw half an excited breath, then it popped back to its original position.

'Damnit. Wrong.'

'But look—' The old man's voice jumped an octave. 'The first carving's stayed in place.'

'Excellent – so that must be side number one.' He turned it round. 'The other adjacent side must be number two. Let's try it.' He'd just spun the box on the table and was reaching for the twin silver cones when Nerak arrived.

THE QUARTERDECK

Malakasian Home Guardsman Private Kaylo Partifan struggled to push the clumsy wooden hatch open above his head. He had been sleeping in a tiny berth beneath the foredeck when a muffled explosion awakened him. His first thought had been to ignore it and go back to sleep; there were a number of members of the Home Guard on board, as well as a skeleton crew of some twenty-five seamen, at least six of whom would be standing watch. But lying there in his cramped, uncomfortable bunk, his thoughts returned to Devar Wentra, his former platoon leader – *his former friend* – killed by a glance from the dark prince. As Kaylo lost the wrestling match with his wool blanket, he could not tear his memory away from the sight of the lieutenant collapsing beneath Prince Malagon's gaze.

He decided to grab some fresh air while investigating what would no doubt turn out to be nothing.

Most of his platoon had been ordered to the Falkan Occupation Headquarters. They very rarely travelled, so they'd had no idea what to expect. They had boarded the *Prince Marek* in Pellia, set sail for the Northern Archipelago and had not seen Prince Malagon again until they moored in Orindale Harbour. Kaylo had been a little surprised that the Home Guard escort was so small, although rumour had reached the *Prince Marek* that the combined occupation forces of southern Falkan were entrenched along the outskirts of the city. Prince Malagon might have feared an attack on Orindale, or perhaps even an attempt on his life, but he seemed confident that a single platoon of his Home Guard would be ample protection at Occupation Headquarters.

Apart from wishing he could see the old Falkan royal residence, Kaylo was happy to be one of the detachment overseeing security on board the *Prince Marek*. Being at Occupation Headquarters meant greater risk of ending up like Devar.

The city of Orindale was so close: Kaylo yearned for shore leave, but he knew his chances were slim. Still, the journey itself had been an adventure – he was only a hundred and fifty Twinmoons old, and he still was excited at the prospect of seeing new places and doing new things. He had wondered if sunsets looked different in other parts of Eldarn, if the fruit tasted sharper, or the wine sweeter. But thus far, he had seen and done nothing new except learn to stand watch on a rolling sea and to keep a trencher and goblet from falling off a listing tabletop.

Pausing on the narrow wooden ladder leading above decks, he stretched the stiffness from his back and legs and cursed his unyielding wooden berth. Sleeping on board had been the worst part of this trip; how he envied his colleagues who were resting ashore tonight, sleeping in comfortable – unmoving – beds. Then he thought of Devar and sighed, 'No, I'm better off here.' He stifled a yawn and pushed his way onto the deck above.

He found himself suddenly awake and quite lucid in the cool night air. He drew a deep breath of the sea-scented breeze and moved rapidly along the main deck. He could see no sign of the overnight sentry, but he wasn't much surprised. The sailors were rubbish compared with Prince Malagon's Home Guard, who were famous for being the best-trained and most efficient soldiers in Malakasia. Kaylo, despite his youth, was deadly with a bow, a short sword, a broadsword, a rapier, and an assortment of knives and daggers, and he was trained not to hesitate to engage an enemy of any size or strength in the prince's defence. He was young to be a member of the élite force, and good as he was, Kaylo knew he still had a great deal to learn – 'Like how to be as stealthy and near-invisible as whoever has watch tonight,' he whispered, and searched for any sign of another Home Guardsman.

No one else was about. He needed to find someone who could tell him what had happened so he could go back to sleep. He wasn't worried: there was little to threaten a ship of this size, especially as the Malakasian Navy controlled all shipping in the Ravenian Sea.

He was getting cold now. Kaylo squinted into the dim light provided by the sconces and marvelled at how far he had come without finding anything out of the ordinary. That began to alarm him somewhat. He considered how far he had already walked along the main deck and the distance the sound of the explosion had travelled to reach and wake him. He quickened his pace. 'Destroying the ship ourselves,' Kaylo grumbled, 'I'd hate to have to explain that one to Prince Malagon.'

Mark sighed with relief as Brynne slipped over the stern rail and began climbing nimbly down to the skiff. He had no idea how many men she had been forced to deal with, but at least now she was back in the relative safety of their rowboat – not that there were any guarantees they'd be able to escape to their little yacht and sail away. But he felt better just knowing Brynne was off that ship.

He watched carefully, counting the seconds and hoping she wasn't going to fall when Brynne surprised him by hefting herself back up the rope and over the side. 'What the hell are you doing?' he whispered as loudly as he dared. 'Come back!'

'I'll be just a moment,' she said, her voice low. 'I heard something.'

'*He* wants you off that ship!' Mark tried to avoid yelling.

'Yes,' she agreed, 'and *he* was a little too quick to want me away. I'm worried something isn't going well in there.'

'Brynne,' Mark pleaded.

'I love you,' she mimicked in broken English before slipping silently from view.

Kaylo stumbled across the first body. He crouched low and drew two knives from his tunic, cursing himself for leaving his sword and longbow stowed beneath his bunk. Creeping quietly, avoiding the pools of firelight beneath the sconces, he strained his ears to detect anything out of the ordinary. He laid his palms against the main deck to feel for vibrations of anyone moving through cabins or along companionways below, but save for the distant rumble of a prolonged thunderclap somewhere east of the city, he heard and saw nothing.

Twenty sailors and one Home Guardsman lay strewn about the main deck like forgotten marionettes waiting for the curtain to come up. No one moved. Kaylo checked carefully, but except for one burly seaman who had a gash like a half-moon across his forearm, no one showed any sign of injury. He moved further into the shadows and made his way towards the stern cabins. He fought to keep his head clear, but an uneasy thought kept recurring: the dark prince returning, finding something that displeased him, and wiping out every member of the skeleton crew left aboard.

He had nearly reached the aft end of the *Prince Marek* when he saw a solitary figure climb down the starboard stairs. Even from a distance, the Malakasian could see the man was scrawny, and unarmed – and something in the region of five hundred and fifty Twinmoons old. He watched, a little incredulously, as the unknown visitor walked – with no apparent concern or stealth – into Prince Malagon's private chambers. As he recalled the bodies scattered across the main deck, an alarm went off in his mind.

'Be careful,' Kaylo warned himself. 'Don't be fooled by appearances. Those are strong, battle-hardened men unconscious on the deck.'

He kept his guard up, watching and listening for any sign of other boarders as he moved warily towards the narrow door that led into the aft companionway, but there was still no sight or sound of any other crewman or Home Guardsman. Kaylo had to assume they had all been taken – maybe even killed – by whomever had overpowered the men on deck. Moving almost silently, he covered the final few steps to the aft cabins. He listened for what felt like a long time but might only have been a few breaths, then reached for the thin leather latch holding the companionway door closed. *Oh gods*, he thought suddenly, *what if that old man is the prince?* He'd never seen Prince Malagon disrobed. Kaylo feared he was about to enter the prince's private chambers unannounced and uninvited, and the image of Devar's lifeless body came back to him in a rush. He looked back at the score of sailors and crewmen slumped and crumpled in awkward positions about the main deck and dropped the leather thong. He stepped hesitantly back from the door.

Someone called from above, 'I was hoping you wouldn't leave me out here in the moonlight alone.'

Shocked by the sound of an unfamiliar voice, Kaylo leaped back into the shadows, his knives at the ready. 'Who's there?' he rasped, trying to control his breathing.

'It's just me.' Brynne stepped towards the rail that lined the forward rim of the quarterdeck.

Kaylo was taken aback. It was a woman, and except for a selection of knives and a small axe, she appeared to be unarmed. Was she alone? He couldn't see any grappling hooks, so how did she get up there? Panting slightly in surprise, he looked around, trying to locate the other members of her raiding party. He had to assume he was now acting alone in defence of the ship.

'What are you doing here?' He was almost embarrassed by the absurdity of his question.

'Just enjoying a night out.' The woman was backlit by torches; he could hear her smile, even though he couldn't see it. 'You?'

He did not answer. He was in an untenable position. He backed away slowly, trying to improve his view, but he had to stop when he bumped into the thick oak trunk of the aft mast.

'Where are you going?' Brynne began to move towards the starboard stairwell. 'We were getting on so well.'

Kaylo decided the old man was not Prince Malagon but an intruder, working with the young woman – but how exactly could one woman and one bandy-legged old seaman take the *Prince Marek*'s crew? Sweat ran freely across his face and neck and he tried, too late, to lie. 'I should warn you: there's a crew of a hundred and fifty below decks. They'll be on hand in a moment.'

'Sorry,' Brynne said, 'if you'd opened with that one I might have believed you, but you spent too long trying to find an escape. Just like a man! You squirm around and then try to lie your way out of trouble.' She took several steps towards the stairs. She had to keep him talking until she could get close enough to engage him hand-to-hand.

As Kaylo watched her approach the starboard stairs, he spied the answer to his dilemma from the corner of his eye – it was a risk, especially if she had archers with her, but it was the only way to assess the quarterdeck. He sheathed his knives and leaped into the ship's rigging, climbing the stiff but awkward rope ladders as rapidly as possible until he had climbed high enough to see clearly. The quarterdeck was empty. There was no one with her. She was alone. Who was this woman who thought she could just wander about the decks of Prince Malagon's ship?

A wry smile played across Kaylo's lips as he dropped to the main deck with the agility of a cat. 'You're by yourself.' He had no idea how many intruders had already entered the aft companionway, but he was confident that if he killed this woman, he would have the advantage of higher ground whenever her accomplices emerged from the prince's quarters.

'Of course I'm by myself.' Brynne paused. *Good. Let him come to me. Get him away from them.*

Kaylo drew his knives with a flourish and strode confidently towards this curious girl. 'Might I ask who you are?'

Staring down at him from above, Brynne's voice was icy as she replied, 'I am the one who is going to cut your throat if you go anywhere near those chambers.' She gestured towards the companionway with the toe of her boot. Her response had the desired effect.

Kaylo saw the strange woman draw twin blades with a practised, graceful motion and mounted the starboard stairs. 'Well met, then, my staggeringly attractive adversary.'

Brynne bowed slightly to acknowledge his flattery, covertly examining his movements, his grip, even the style and length of the blades themselves. 'I thank you for the compliment, but I am afraid I am spoken for, and I also have a prior engagement, so might I suggest we just get this over with.' She considered him for a moment before adding, 'The quicker the better, my pock-marked, homely and unfortunately malodorous adversary.'

Kaylo recognised that she was sizing him up and he dropped to a crouch to reduce the exposed surface area of his torso and neck to a minimum. Seeing how she maintained her composure, he thought she might prove skilled. He swallowed hard and attempted to remain calm.

'Now that's unfair,' he whispered, 'I am too far away for you to know I smell bad.'

'Well, come closer then, and we can discuss it.' She grinned fiercely.

It had taken Twinmoons for Brynne to recover from being raped and beaten in that corner room at Greentree Tavern. Sallax had wanted desperately to help, but he was young too, and had no idea how badly such an attack could emotionally scar a woman, marking her as damaged goods in her own mind for all time. What he *could* do was teach her to defend herself. Nothing brought Brynne the sense of grim satisfaction she required except for the knife. She had told her brother, 'I have to be in close . . . Sallax, I *want* to be in close. I want to see them suffer.'

The first time Sallax saw Brynne use her newly developed skill had been devastating. The tavern had been bustling with out-of-town travellers and locals and Brynne scurried about the front room serving wine and beer and food while her brother manned both bar and kitchen.

Returning from his cooking range he detected a change in the atmosphere: the fire crackled contentedly on the far wall, but across the room, something was different. Then he saw his sister. Brynne was struggling to make her way past three brothers who had positioned their chairs to block her into a corner. The men had been drinking heavily and what might have been a moment of sexual banter had elevated quickly to a potentially violent incident. Dropping a stew-stained towel, Sallax called for Garec and Versen, but they had not gone three steps when one of the men reached out to Brynne.

'Don't!' Sallax cried, but he was too late.

Brynne dropped the tray, and her knives appeared as if by magic. She delivered a deft slash to the first brother's wrist, a half-moon across the back of his hand that mirrored the scarred merchant who had raped her only five Twinmoons earlier. Bellowing in pain and surprise, the young man stood, toppling his chair and reaching for a dagger at his belt, but Brynne was there first, slashing her blade across the man's chest: a wide backhand that opened his tunic and left a deep wound.

His brothers were moving now as well, drawing short swords as Brynne dropped to a crouch, lunged across the small round table and buried one knife to the hilt in the fleshy part of the second brother's abdomen, then pulled it out and, spinning gracefully, brought both knives around in a sharp arc that left twin parallel slashes across the third brother's stomach. She completed her movement by burying one blade hilt-deep in the first brother's thigh.

The entire engagement had lasted less than two breaths. A moment later, the entire front room at Greentree Tavern erupted with shouts; patrons sprang to their feet, some to help and others to escape. Sallax was forced to leap onto the bar to see what was happening; he saw Versen and Garec dragging the three men out and dumping them into the muddy street. None of them would die, but each would think twice before trying to have his way with an unwilling woman again.

Brynne was smiling, but there was no joy in her face. There was a fierce pride, and triumph, and bitterness. And there was an unremitting hatred. Sallax shuddered. The merchant had created a monster of his beloved sister.

Now Kaylo saw that smile. Despite himself, he shivered.

Brynne did what she always did when called upon to fight. She superimposed the shadowy image of the Falkan merchant who had stolen her life over the Malakasian's face. Now she could kill with impunity. She couldn't remember a hand-to-hand struggle that had lasted more than a breath or two. Someone always lunged a bit too deeply, exposing too much flank, or extended an arm too far forward, and that was when she moved. Would it be the same with this fellow? He seemed well trained.

Brynne looked into Kaylo's eyes and saw the Falkan rapist. 'I will kill you again tonight,' she said, her voice low as her body fell into a practised stance.

'Kill me again?' Kaylo twisted one knife back in his hand, perhaps an involuntary response to the stress of the upcoming fight, but Brynne watched as the sharpened edge of the blade turned back towards its wielder. She saw her opportunity and lunged.

Steven and the old man were so engrossed that neither detected the charge in the air, a shimmering wave that passed across the harbour like a rogue gust of winter wind, nor did they hear the foreboding silence that fell over the waterfront.

The dark prince came out of the night sky, cowled in black and nearly invisible, the folds of his robe an inky darkness that extinguished the dim twinkle of distant stars. He came to rest gently on the deck and raised his arms ceremoniously, blasting away the *Prince Marek*'s quarterdeck. If he noticed two bodies resting silently on the smooth planks of the raised deck, he made no sign. One was already dead, a long knife wound stretching across his face and another laying open his stomach. The smooth wooden hilt of a thin hunting knife still protruded from his thigh. Nearby, a young woman lay with a knife protruding from one shoulder. Blood soaked her tunic. Her legs were curled up to her chest and her breathing rattled, marking out a moist and ragged rhythm as her eyes fluttered in an effort to remain conscious. A small puncture in her abdomen leaked dark blood, indicating a deep wound; she groaned in dismay as she examined her stained fingers.

As Nerak's rage destroyed part of his great ship, Brynne felt herself cast away. Terror gripped her for a moment, because she knew she was about to strike the water. It would be cold and dark, and she didn't have the strength to swim. But she was unconscious before she hit the surface, falling amidst a hail of broken planks.

Steven and the old sorcerer were thrown across the floor as the aft end of the *Prince Marek* exploded from the main deck, but the table, and the leatherbound book upon it, remained untouched. As he clambered to his feet, the metal box still clutched firmly in one hand, Steven realised the hickory staff had rolled away to the other side of what was left of the cabin and was now balanced precariously on the edge of the deck, some thirty feet above the water – and Nerak was standing in front of the old fisherman.

Steven did a quick check of himself: except for a nasty bulge above his left eye, he did not appear to have been injured. Now to retrieve the hickory staff. He tried to ignore the fact that the two master sorcerers were glaring at each other across the battered plank deck and started inching his way nearer to the staff.

'Fantus!' Nerak's voice was overwhelming, and Steven felt its resonance shiver along his bones in jagged waves. 'Fantus!' His voice held a mixture of hatred and joy. 'We meet again, my dearest, *dearest* friend – and how glad I am you managed to not stay dead. You have grown more skilled since our last meeting.' As he spoke, the dark prince threw something at his former colleague; though his hand was empty, Steven watched in terror as the blow hit the old man directly in his chest. A spell. He expected his frail companion to fly back through the air, broken and bloody, or maybe even to disintegrate on the spot, but instead, he crumpled to the deck, folding like a dropped handkerchief.

Steven, struck motionless, watched for interminable moments until Nerak began chuckling.

'Too easy, Fantus,' he crowed. 'You have had nearly a thousand

Twinmoons – and still you made it too easy. You should have let me kill you that night at Sandcliff. It would have saved you all that unnecessary worry and work.'

The dark prince didn't appear to notice Steven at all. His attention remained focused on his lifelong enemy, now lying prostrate at his feet. 'And there goes your revolution, you hapless fool. You might have done better with that broadsword.'

Steven was unable to move: Nerak must have cast a spell to keep him still. Was the old man – was *Gilmour* – really dead? It didn't matter if he thought the name now, or even said it out loud; it was too late. Could it really have been that simple? All those years, and all that power, and raising himself from the dead – and all it took was one spell . . . surely Gilmour would have been better prepared than that?

So what do I now, Steven thought, *faced with a pantomime villain from the blackest of fantasy stories?* Should he have tried to share the power of the hickory staff with Gilmour as he faced this most dire of enemies? Well, it was too late – and in any case, he was still fifty feet away from the staff. Nerak would crush him to dust before he took three steps towards it.

But Gilmour was not done yet. As the emaciated frame began to move, he whispered, 'That was well done, Nerak, very well done.' His voice started soft and grew to an amused howl, mocking the black magician. The old man sat up and smiled. 'Did it weaken you? And do you have more of those little spells at the ready, hidden in those absurd pyjamas you insist on wearing?'

Nerak's cloak flapped in the wind from the harbour, but the dark prince remained silent.

Gilmour prodded him again. 'That was your best, wasn't it? Was that the same spell you used to wipe out Port Denis? It would have worked just fine – more than enough to do the job, I would think.'

The former Larion Senator regained his feet. 'You never were a very good student, Nerak.' He gestured towards the small wooden table and the leatherbound book. 'What are those? Lessek's spells? One thousand Twinmoons and you *still* don't have it figured out?' He shook his head, the teacher disappointed.

Steven started to worry again: the old man's words were having an effect now and Nerak looked as if he were about to explode with rage.

'That was naught but the tiniest of tastes, Fantus, a minuscule sample drawn from the very furthest reaches of my power.' With each breath Nerak seemed to grow in size. 'I toy with you, to enjoy seeing how little I need to do to crush you beneath my boots.

'I will dine on your flesh, Fantus, and suck the very marrow from your bones as I replace Lessek's Key and open the spell table for my master's arrival.'

For the first time, Nerak acknowledged Steven's presence. 'And you,' he said, looking down at him. 'Steven Taylor, my little Coloradoan. You have done well, found reserves of resourcefulness you never knew you had. Hurrah for you!' His voice grew harder as he continued, 'You have used Gilmour's little wooden toy well in your own defence, Steven Taylor, but it's a stick, and no stick is a match for me. And I'm getting bored with this little charade. You will turn Lessek's Key over to me now, or—'

As the dark prince started his threat, Gilmour struck without warning, throwing open both arms and propelling himself forward suddenly as he cried out a strange, multi-syllabled word that twisted and turned in Steven's mind. Nerak tumbled backwards with an ear-splitting shriek that cracked the thick oaken mainmast and sent it crashing into the deck in a ponderous tumble of rigging and sails. Several of Nerak's still-unconscious sailors were crushed before it rolled to a stop. The Malakasian prince lay stunned himself, overwhelmed for a moment.

'Now, Steven!' Gilmour cried, 'open it now!'

Steven snapped out of his reverie and returned his attention to the metal box. 'One, two, one,' he whispered, trying to ignore the black sorcerer and focus on his task. The first cone on the front face was still depressed, flush against the smooth metal. 'Damnit. Which side was next?' Steven's hands began to shake. 'Did we try right or left?'

Nerak drew his legs up beneath him, preparing to stand.

'Right or left?' Steven's mind went blank and in desperation he depressed the twin cones on the adjacent side to the right of the front face of the locked box.

Nerak sat up and looked at him. A low rumble vibrated through Steven's body and he realised Nerak was laughing.

The twin cones in the centre of the lower edge of the adjacent side refused to stay in place. Steven turned the box over and depressed the centre carving on its opposite side. The silver ornament snapped flat and remained flush. 'Two,' he shouted gleefully to Gilmour, then silently berated himself for attracting Nerak's attention.

'What *is* he doing, Fantus?' Nerak said, and Steven wondered if he had imagined the dark prince's look of confused hesitation.

Gilmour didn't reply.

'You're not here for the far portal, are you? I would have thought you wanted the spell book; you cannot have any hope of defeating me without it.' Nerak was standing now and his voice reverberated in Steven's mind, a great tidal wave of sound crashing in on him from everywhere at once. 'What good will the far portal do you? Are you hoping to run from me? That's absurd, little Coloradoan. You should know there is no place you can hide from me.'

Gilmour remained silent, summoning the power to beat the dark prince into submission long enough for Steven to escape. Flecks of coloured light danced from the older man's fingertips and veins bulged along his anorexically thin forearms.

'One, two, one,' Steven whispered and depressed the second single cone on the front face of the metal lock box. Now he was able to ignore Nerak as the silver ornament clicked into place; he rushed to press the quadruple cone carving left protruding from the upper edge of the box's top. 'Four!' he shouted triumphantly as the four sides, top and bottom of the metal box fell open and clattered to the wooden deck with a series of resounding clangs. He shuddered as he looked down at the length of folded cloth in his hand: the sensation was just the same as when he and Mark first unrolled the stolen tapestry across the floor all those months ago at 147 Tenth Street, Idaho Springs, lifetimes and worlds away from here. He looked quickly at the hickory staff, wishing he had it to take with him, but it was too late for that – he would be lucky enough if he managed to get the far portal unfurled before Nerak battered through Gilmour's defences and killed them both.

Nerak almost hovered in the air as he advanced on the infuriatingly resilient old man. His head tilted slightly to one side, he considered Steven's hasty attempt to escape.

'Really, Fantus, what is your little protégé doing now?' He looked down at the novice sorcerer. 'You have impressed me, boy, opening my box, but now you have a choice. I will not just kill you, but I will make your death last days, or weeks, or millennia of your time, if you do not hand over the key. But should you come to your senses, I will allow you to depart my ship alive. Choose now, choose quickly and choose well. My generosity will not be repeated.'

Steven clapped both hands over his ears and dropped the far portal for a moment as Nerak's voice nearly tipped him into unconsciousness. He shook his head violently to dispel the echoes, then reached down and gripped the portal by a corner and cast it out before him. In a stroke of good luck, most of the tapestry fell flat on the deck of the great black ship; just one corner remained folded back over itself and Steven cursed as he crawled bodily across the cloth in an effort to smooth out that final fold and fall into his living room at 147 Tenth Street. Unnervingly, even that familiar address sounded strange to him.

As Nerak saw Steven crawling on all fours across the tapestry, he finally realised his mistake. He turned to Gilmour and spat, 'You don't have it! *Where is my key?*'

With studied satisfaction, Gilmour ran one hand across his nearly bald head and grinned. 'Lessek's Key, I think you mean – no, we don't. And we never did.'

'Jacrys!' Nerak's scream rent the night in two and Steven collapsed to the deck, unable to move until the echoes of the dark prince's anguish had faded over Orindale Harbour. The staff may have been several yards away from him, but once again its magic reached out to envelope him. It thrummed beneath his skin, a protective layer of mystical power without which he would surely have been killed, crushed to a pulp by the force of Nerak's cry.

The dark prince dived for Steven, bearing down on him like a terrible vision of evil, anguish and death, and Steven cried out as he flicked two fingertips out to flatten the last corner of the far portal. It was not enough. Nerak moved so quickly, faster even than the nimblest of nocturnal hunters—

As Nerak flew through the air, his cowled face turned towards Steven, he cast a deadly spell out before him in an effort to slay the foreign intruder before he could open the portal entirely, but his spell was an instant too late. Gilmour unleashed his own magic once again, and his power lanced through the night, striking the evil sorcerer a vicious broadside, which sent him reeling across the deck.

And Steven Taylor disappeared.

Mark nearly lost consciousness when the *Prince Marek*'s quarter-deck exploded over his head in a thousand splintered planks. His eyeballs throbbed with every heartbeat and his ears felt as though they had been clapped between a pair of cymbals. He sat dazed for a time in the wildly rocking skiff before he was able to collect his thoughts.

'Nerak's here, then,' he whispered.

The stillness that followed on the heels of the blast was unnerving, and for a moment Mark worried that his hearing had been damaged. 'Sonofabitch,' he shouted out, and then, encouraged by the sound of his own voice, 'Brynne! Where are you?'

The rope they'd been using to climb onto the ship had been blown away: Mark was trapped on his little boat, unable to help his friends. He had to have faith that Steven would find the far portal and Brynne would return safely to him. All he could do was what he'd been ordered: sit and wait. He picked up Garec's bow and the quiver full of arrows and resigned himself to his silent vigil.

As he scanned the night sky, he noticed a peculiar cloudbank, dark, running low to the ground, moving like a fogbank, but backwards, from land to sea. It looked more mist than cloud – and Mark blanched as his mind flipped back to a conversation with Gita Kamrec's men. He dropped his bow and stood up in the little boat facing east towards the distant lights of the city, remembering the dark river cavern, and the Falkans' tales of unimaginable nightmares hidden in these clouds.

Hall Storen had told them how they'd tried to keep an eye on the clouds after sunrise, in case they had to avoid an attack from above. 'It was worse when it came after dark,' Mark repeated to himself, shuddering. And here they came, Nerak's own little weather army.

Fear roiled through Mark's stomach. His thoughts faltered: what could he do? He was defenceless and time was running out. The obsidian fogbank appeared unaffected by the stiff sea breeze as it moved inexorably towards the *Prince Marek*. Mark, in a desperate effort to warn the others, began to scream.

Nerak raised his arms as if in supplication and whispered, 'Oh, well done, Fantus.' He exhaled and, voicing a gruesome curse, brought his arms down violently to his sides, sending a destructive spell deep into the bowels of the *Prince Marek*. The great black ship shivered and creaked as she began to come apart at the seams.

Nerak's decision to destroy his own ship took Gilmour by surprise. That few moments' inattention was all the dark prince needed; before Gilmour could strike again he had leaped into the far portal and vanished from view.

For an instant, Nerak's pursuit of Steven came as such a shock that Gilmour nearly stepped into the portal himself, but rational thought intervened. Even that brief span of time before Nerak followed him gave Steven ample opportunity to close the portal at his home in Idaho Springs. Nerak would be elsewhere, cast somewhere at the whim of the portal, maybe whole worlds away from 147 Tenth Street in Idaho Springs.

As Gilmour smiled to himself, the *Prince Marek* came apart beneath him. The remaining masts cracked and collapsed, smashing through the upper decks. The forecastle snapped off; thick beams burst asunder and heavy planks warped and splintered, a barrage of cracks that reminded the old sorcerer of rifle-fire at Gettysburg. The dark waters of the Ravenian Sea started to rush into what was left of the *Prince Marek*'s hull and the great ship began to list heavily.

Taking a final look around the wreckage, Gilmour breathed, 'Good luck, Steven Taylor.' Moving with a speed and grace that belied the old fisherman's age he crossed the deck and collected the tapestry then dived for Steven's hickory staff, which was rolling dangerously close to the broken edge. Finally he removed his cloak and wrapped the tapestry and the leatherbound book of Lessek's spells in its protective folds.

Gilmour took one swift look around what was left of Nerak's cabin and hustled up the now steeply sloping deck until he was perched on an uneven ledge. The former Larion Senator held fast to the cloak-wrapped bundle and the hickory staff and leaped into the chilly water below.

EPILOGUE

Charleston International Airport

CHARLESTON, SOUTH CAROLINA

David Mantegna ran an index finger up the smooth leather of the holster. It still felt strange – he and his partner, Sandra Echols, had been wearing their 9mm sidearms for just a week and were still getting used to the idea of carrying guns in the airport. In the wake of the ongoing threats to commercial airliners, the Charleston City Police now had officers stationed at the security gates to provide support for those airport staff operating the detectors and checking for weapons or incendiary devices stashed in passengers' carry-on baggage.

Funding cuts meant no extra police officers, so the airport's security detail had been put through exhaustive – and embarrassing – background checks, followed by eight weeks of surprise urine tests, then two months' intensive training at the State Police Academy. Thanks to a creatively inexpensive political manoeuvre on the part of the Charleston City Council and the Mayor's Office, he and Sandra were now licensed deputies of the city police force, and could be called upon as law enforcement officers in crimes ranging from breaching airport security, to drug trafficking, to terrorism.

Of course, they still had to do their fair share of gate security, checking bags, examining X-rays and basically ensuring nothing threatened the passengers and planes scheduled through Concourse B, gates 1 through 5. Thousands of bags passed through the X-ray machine every day and Mantegna was desperately hoping the city economy would improve enough so he could complete his studies and join the force as a fully fledged city officer.

'I'm bored,' he sighed, reviewing the black-and-white image of an elderly woman's cosmetics case. Sandra smiled at him briefly. He liked her smile. She had one tooth that lay just slightly over another, giving her a bright but crooked grin that he found endearing. He teased her mercilessly about her uniform. Sandra's blues had been well tailored and fitted her contours closely: she was fit and athletic, and obviously aware of her body and how attractive she looked in the wide leather belt and Kevlar vest. He openly ogled the curves of her lithe form as he remarked that she should stop showing up for work in her younger sister's clothing. Sandra could give as good as she got, judging by the off-colour comments about the calibre of Mantegna's weapon. 'Only nine millimetres, David?' she'd respond. 'That'll simply never do!'

'I said, I'm bored,' Mantegna repeated. There were only two flights scheduled out in the next hour and most passengers had already come through the security checkpoint.

'Well, stop whining and go help that woman,' his partner suggested. 'Might as well earn your pay today.'

He looked beyond the upright rectangle of the metal detector to the near-empty terminal. A young woman was approaching, pushing a baby stroller and carrying the sort of bag common among new mothers. This one was lime-green, adorned with small pictures of Peter Rabbit, and jammed full of baby kit: bottles, plastic toys, clothes, Pampers, and a dog-eared novel. It started to slip off her shoulder as she reached in to remove the sleeping infant.

Hoping a show of gallantry might impress his partner, David Mantegna hurried to assist the young mother. 'Let me help you, ma'am,' he said, picking up a couple of toys that had fallen from the bag.

'Oh, please don't call me "ma'am". I can't possibly be a "ma'am", I'm only twenty-seven,' she laughed before adding, 'but thanks, I could do with a hand.' He pushed the stroller through his security checkpoint, then looked into the empty storage area under the seat and felt the cushions for any hidden items. As he'd anticipated, he found nothing.

While the Peter Rabbit bag rolled through the X-ray machine, Mantegna saw what he expected to see: bottles, clothes, toys and a book. He returned the stroller and watched as the young woman walked down the concourse towards her gate, B4, and the morning flight to Washington, DC.

An alarm went off in Mantegna's head as he turned to see a young man walk through the metal detector. He seemed nervous and uncomfortable, and his clothes were badly wrinkled, as though he had slept in them – or worse, showered in them. He had several days' beard growth and carried no bags, just a ticket. Mantegna squared his shoulders and unconsciously patted his 9mm pistol. This was it. This was what all the training was about. He hustled back towards the security station, expecting the metal detector to sound any minute, but nothing happened. The dishevelled passenger simply walked through and hurried down the concourse towards Gate B4. Mantegna let his shoulders relax, almost disappointed. Just a bum with money then.

'Did you catch a whiff of him?' Sandra asked as she absentmindedly adjusted a focus knob on the X-ray machine.

'No, I try to avoid smelling the passengers as they come through,' he joked and was rewarded with a short laugh and a flash of her sexy crooked tooth.

Steven Taylor boarded Express Airlines Flight 182 to Washington, DC at 10.25 a.m. He had a connection to Denver International Airport scheduled to depart Reagan National at 1.20 p.m. He'd gain two hours on the flight west and be in Idaho Springs by early evening. His ticket had been expensive – $1200 – because he was flying at the last minute, and he silently thanked God he had remembered to pay his Visa bill that night outside Owen's Pub, so long ago. And at least he still had his wallet, even if it had been soaked and dried out so many times since his arrival in Eldarn that he had been forced to covertly re-sign the signature block on the back. With his Colorado driver's licence in hand, he purchased the ticket, checked in and waited for the gate attendant to call his row number for boarding.

Thanks to the careless behaviour of Arthur Mikelson, a banker from Charleston currently suffering from a nasty hangover – and probably sunburn by now – Steven was dressed in an unprepossessing pair of sweatpants and a decade-old T-shirt from Gold's Gym in Hilton Head. He had also had a ride to the airport courtesy of Arthur's very comfortable Lexus sedan. Mikelson's gym bag had a pair of Nike trainers inside, near enough Steven's size, but he had turned them down in favour of Garec's boots, which he was still wearing. Steven had every intention of returning them.

Arthur had also been kind enough to leave his wallet stuffed under the front seat before heading onto Folly Beach to drink himself blind. With cash in hand, Steven had taken a few minutes out for eggs, pancakes, bacon, buttered toast, hash browns and six mugs of steaming black coffee. He thought of Mark as he breathed in the aroma: whatever else he did, he *had* to introduce the coffee bean to Eldarn.

Now he was beginning to seriously regret not taking the time to find a shower: as he took his seat and awaited lift-off he was conscious he looked and smelled out of place. He was covered in dry, briny salt and he stank of sweat and low tide. Being this filthy made him feel uncomfortable and conspicuous.

His self-conscious musings were interrupted as he watched a woman coming down the aisle. He had seen her at the gate, quietly rocking an infant, and he thought it a little odd that she hadn't taken the opportunity to pre-board and get settled. But here she came, carrying the child in the crook of one arm, rather strangely, like a halfback might hold a football. Her other hand was tucked into the front pocket of her khakis and a small green bag bursting with essential-looking baby items hung from her shoulder and bounced uncomfortably off her hip and across the small of her back.

He blushed, realising he'd been staring, and looked away as she took her seat several rows behind him. He lay back and closed his eyes, trying not to think about everything that had happened over the past months. He hoped sleep would take him for the flight home.

Steven opened his eyes with a start. Something was wrong. He heard Gilmour in his head: *If it looks strange, it's probably strange.* Something wasn't right about this flight. Had he been followed? He couldn't put his finger on it, but there was something wrong. He hadn't seen anyone since his arrival, apart from the generous Mr Mikelson on the beach and the woman at the truck stop who had served him breakfast just after dawn. Had Arthur Mikelson actually followed him through the portal – was he a member of Malagon's army? No, surely not: he hadn't heard other splashes, or seen other swimmers – and how the hell could Arthur Mikelson have found a Brooks Brothers' suit, a Lexus, nine beers, a pack of cigarettes and the time to get drunk, throw up and fall asleep, all while Steven was swimming ashore? It couldn't possibly be him.

The airplane window was a small porthole onto a new world, and the airport tarmac stretched out to the horizon. *If it looks strange, it's probably strange.* But *what* was strange? The swim, breakfast, the drive to Charleston, the flight, the plane, the woman with the baby, her hand in her pocket ... that was it. Where was she? Slowly he lifted his head and turned around to peer behind him. She was there. Young and pretty, maybe twenty-five, *and she was looking right at him.* Strange. The baby was crying loudly, and yet she still looked straight ahead. Really strange. Her face was impassive, emotionless, and now Steven knew who had followed him through the far portal. Her hand had been in her pocket to hide the unsightly wound Gilmour had described, the festering sore that had marked all of Nerak's victims.

But Gilmour had told them the far portal on the *Prince Marek* was the weaker one, and his arrival off the coast of South Carolina confirmed that the portal in Idaho Springs had been closed somehow. If Nerak had followed him through, why hadn't the evil bastard been deposited in Alaska, or over in Nepal somewhere? *Shit, Gilmour, you were wrong. Nerak is able to come across the Fold. How did he do it – did he track me? Or track the magic – no, impossible. The staff is still on the ship. But however he did it, he followed me here.*

Steven felt his stomach turn over. The pressure in his forehead felt like it might crack his skull. *Get away*, he thought finally, *just get away.*

Steven excused himself to his seat mates and made his way towards the airplane lavatory as a flight attendant was asking the young mother, 'Is everything okay here, ma'am?'

Tonelessly, the woman answered, 'Oh, things are fine. He just needs his formula.' She pulled two half-filled bottles from the green bag and slowly, in a well-practised motion, opened both, poured the contents of one into the other, screwed down the nipple cap and gave the now full bottle a gentle shake. Bubbles escaped from the nipple as she stood the bottle on her tray table. All the while she prepared the formula the young mother looked ahead, her eyes fixed on the forward lavatory.

David Mantegna was standing near the stainless-steel table used for baggage inspections at the security gate. A passenger had come through carrying a laptop computer and, as federal regulations permitted, he asked the man to switch it on to prove it hadn't been tampered with.

When the explosion came, it was the stainless-steel table that saved David's life. As the force of the blast threw him backwards into the wall, the table was thrown in front of him and acted as a makeshift shield against the shards of flying glass and metal that tore through the terminal building an instant later. While still at Gate B4, Express Airlines Flight 182 to Washington, DC exploded with such force that an enormous fireball raced up the jetway and into the terminal building, incinerating a dozen passengers on their way through the concourse.

The fuel truck filling a plane standing near Gate B3 lifted off its wheels for a moment before exploding in a devastating blast that quickly ignited the fuel in the wing reservoirs. Express Airlines Flight 64 didn't explode, but the fire that started when the wing tip was blown away spread almost immediately and the one hundred and sixty-four passengers bound for Atlanta were being burned alive, clawing and fighting one another in their desperation to reach an exit.

David Mantegna looked down. On the floor next to him was the passenger's laptop computer, still beeping away – that hadn't been the bomb. *So what had caused the explosion?* He couldn't quite keep his thoughts together. He felt oddly unbalanced as he stood up, and soon discovered blood running from his right ear and down his shoulder. The owner of the laptop was on the floor, screaming, over and over. The man's arm had been torn off above the elbow and blood ran steadily from the stump. Mantegna was strangely surprised that the wound was not pumping blood out in spurts, like it did in war movies. He stumbled back to the security check station to see what had happened to his partner.

Sandra Echols was dead, her eyes staring out at nothing. Her mouth had fallen halfway open and a shard of glass had torn through her upper lip and across her left cheek. Her left arm was broken and twisted at an impossible angle. Her uniform shirt and vest had been ripped open, revealing a deep wound under her left breast where a large piece of metal remained lodged, one jagged and bloodstained edge still protruding outward. With her arm twisted behind her back and her breasts revealed so prominently, the security guard thought she looked beautiful, like a sculpture he had once seen in an art-history book. His vision faded, then returned.

Mantegna made his way back to the exits airside to find mayhem surrounding the Atlanta-bound plane. Someone had managed to get an emergency exit door opened and badly burned people lay screaming on the concrete beneath the aircraft. He watched as a flight attendant crawled to assist a frightened child and wished he knew what to do. He sat down heavily and looked beyond the carnage at Gate B3 to gate B4, where a smoking pile of torn metal and melted plastic was all that remained of Express Airlines Flight 182 to Washington, DC.

Follow the next exciting instalment in
Eldarn's fight for freedom

LESSEK'S KEY

the second volume in
The Eldarn Sequence

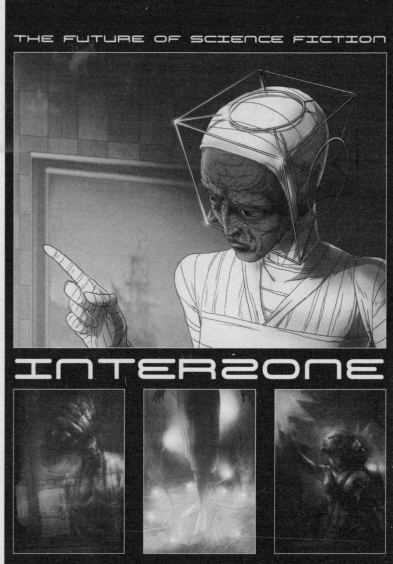